Day
Reckoning

Stephen England

Also by Stephen England

Sword of Neamha

<u>Shadow Warriors Series</u>

NIGHTSHADE
Pandora's Grave
Day of Reckoning

ISBN-13: 978-1491259047
ISBN-10: 1491259043

Cover design by Louis Vaney
Author photo by Rachel Cox
Formatting by Polgarus Studio

To every man, and to every woman who came home from the war with wounds impossible to see and harder to understand. To those who live with the daily reality that "only the dead have seen the end of war." It is to you that this book is dedicated. May God watch over you and protect you even as you have stood watch over this nation.

"For what is a man profited, if he shall gain the whole world, and lose his own soul? Or what shall a man give in exchange for his soul?"—Matthew 16:26

"Whoever fights with monsters should see to it that in the process he does not become a monster. And when you gaze long into an abyss, the abyss also gazes into you."—Friedrich Nietzsche, *Beyond Good and Evil*

Glossary

APB—All Points Bulletin
BOLO—Be On Look Out
CAIR—Council on American Islamic Relations
CI—Confidential Informant
CINCLANTFLT—Commander-in-Chief Atlantic Fleet
CLANDOPS—Clandestine Operations
CO—Commanding Officer
DCIA—Director of the CIA
DCS—Director of the Clandestine Service
DD(I)—Deputy Director(Intelligence)
DEA—Drug Enforcement Agency
DOA—Dead On Arrival
DoD—Department of Defense
DHS—Department of Homeland Security
ECHELON—NSA surveillance program
E&E—Escape and Evade
FISA—Foreign Intelligence Surveillance Act
FLIR—Forward Looking InfraRed
FSB—Federal Security Service of the Russian Federation
HHS—Health and Human Services
HRT—Hostage Rescue Team
IED—Improvised Explosive Device
JSOC—Joint Special Operations Command
JTTF—Joint Terrorism Task Force
LEO—Law Enforcement Officer
LVMPD—Las Vegas Metropolitan Police Department
NCS—National Clandestine Service
NRO—National Reconnaissance Office
NSA—National Security Agency
PAC—Political Action Committee
PD—Police Department
PDA—Personal Digital Assistant
PHOTINT—Photographic Intelligence
POTUS—President of the United States
PTSD—Post-Traumatic Stress Disorder
ROE—Rules of Engagement
SAC—Special Agent-in-Charge
SAD—Special Activities Division

SDR—Surveillance Detection Route
SIGINT—Signals Intelligence
Sitrep—Situation Report
SOP—Standard Operating Procedure
SVR—Foreign Intelligence Service of the Russian Federation
TACSAT—Tactical Satellite Phone
TOC—Tactical Operations Center

Prologue

11:23 P.M. Local Time, November 23rd
Big Bend National Park,
Texas

No one came to Big Bend. At least that was the joke. The national park had never been a favorite with vacationing baby boomers, and with the recession...even that trickle of visitors had dried up.

That left the *coyotes*, Emmanuel Gutierrez thought, clucking gently to his mare as she picked her way over the rocks, edging around a cluster of prickly pear. Coyotes...not the four-legged kind, but the smugglers, guides for illegal immigrants crossing the Rio Grande a few miles to his south.

He'd spotted the fire nearly an hour before, an uncautious flame flickering into the night sky—no doubt a *coyote* and a group of migrants heating up a meal before traveling on. It was a cold, cloudless night, the moon shining down on the rocky terrain, the temperature hovering just a few degrees above freezing. His Remington 870 shotgun hung in a loose scabbard from his saddle, within easy reach of his hand—a non-lethal "beanbag" round in the chamber, five rounds of 00 buckshot behind it.

The thirty-five-year-old Border Patrol agent had seen it all. Four years on the U.S.-Mexico border, two deployments to Afghanistan in the years before that. He'd left friends in the Helmand.

"You in position, Zac?" he asked, toggling the switch of his radio as he moved into the sagebrush. He and his partner had separated, moving in on the encampment from both sides.

"Almost, Manny. Looks like we've got nine, maybe ten males. I'll move in on foot and challenge them. You back me up and stay mounted if anyone does a runner."

"Roger that," Gutierrez replied, a brief smile touching his lips. Someone always thought they were smart. *Always.*

He could hear the low hum of voices as he crested the ridge, looking down the slope into what amounted to a boulder-filled gulch.

Come on, Zac, he thought, drawing his Remington from its scabbard and laying it across his lap. Silhouetted against the night sky, there was every chance that the migrants would spot him.

And then he heard his partner's voice from down the gulch, raised in a brusque command. Saw men scramble, throwing water over the fire.

The metal glint of a gunbarrel in the moonlight, materializing from under a coat. "Keep your hands where I can see them," he called out, kicking his mare into a trot as he rode down the ridge, the Remington in his hands now, leveled. He saw the man look up, seeing the rider for the first time.

Saw him hesitate, his face visible through the rear "ghost-ring" tactical sight of the Remington. A split-second of indecision, hanging between them in the night. Not long enough.

The gun came all the way out, a long gun. *Warning over.* Gutierrez flicked off the button safety of his shotgun, the twelve-gauge recoiling into his shoulder as he squeezed the trigger.

It was too dark to see whether he had hit the man, but nothing could have stopped what happened next. A sound like a string of firecrackers exploding, the migrant's rifle erupting in flame. *Fully-automatic,* the agent's mind registered, even as a hail of bullets began to tear up the ground around his rearing horse. He knew a Kalashnikov when he heard one.

Something struck Gutierrez in the leg, white hot pain shooting through him as he toppled backward off the horse, landing in the dust, his leg bending beneath him. He screamed a curse, fighting against the panic that threatened to overcome him.

It was Afghanistan. Had to be. Their convoy under attack, the sound of the Browning on the roof ripping through the air. Mujahideen *moving in—air support twenty minutes out.*

But it wasn't the Helmand—there was no air support on the way, no Ma Deuce on the roof of the Humvee providing suppressive fire. They were alone.

He could hear automatic weapons fire from down the gulch—coupled with the lighter crack of Zac's M-4. The sounds of war. Ignoring the pain shooting through his bleeding leg, he raised himself up, reaching for his shotgun.

Another burst of fire spattered against the rocks around him and he collapsed back into the shelter of a boulder, pressing his radio to his lips.

"This is Charlie Patrol, we are taking fire. I repeat, we are taking fire. Need help."

Static. Reception could never be counted on out here on the border. Not when you needed it.

He raised himself up, jerking his Heckler & Koch .40 semiautomatic from its holster on his hip. He leaned forward on the boulder, firing downrange at the shadowy figures moving in the gulch below him.

Another ragged burst and Zac's carbine fell silent. *The silence of death.* Gutierrez fired until his H&K's slide locked back on an empty magazine, bullets whistling through the air around his head.

He thumbed the magazine release, metal clattering against stone as it fell free, his fingers fumbling with the pouch on his belt.

A slug tore through the flesh of his arm, half-turning him around as another round smashed into his chest. The Border Patrol agent crumpled backward, his sidearm falling from his fingers.

Darkness. The stars seemed to swirl over his head as he lay there. It didn't seem real, none of it. How long had the firefight lasted? Two minutes? Three? Not long, not long at all compared to the years of war he'd survived.

And yet he was dying.

Gutierrez coughed, blood flecking his lips. Voices, footsteps moving closer in the rocks.

Searching. For him.

The voices were closer now, talking in their native language. *It wasn't Spanish*, he realized in a moment of sudden clarity. But he had heard it before…somewhere.

He closed his eyes, straining to remember, a nagging doubt probing at his brain.

And he was in Afghanistan again, ferrying supplies up into the north. Along the Pakistani border. Listening to their 'terp talk with the villagers. He had even learned a few words over the months. Words of…Pashto.

But this wasn't Afghanistan. He was *home*. In the United States.

His eyes flickered open and Gutierrez found himself looking up into the swarthy, bearded face of a young man. Into the muzzle of the pistol in the man's hand.

Another voice in the distance, speaking in Pashto. It took a moment for the question to filter through his darkening mind, then the translation came to him. *"Is he dead?"*

Above him, the Pakistani shook his head, drawing back the hammer of his pistol. "No."

Chapter 1

5:25 A.M. Eastern Time, December 13th
CIA Headquarters
Langley, Virginia

The room was spartan in its furnishings, white walls on three sides and a pane of one-way glass beginning waist-high on the remaining wall. A folding table sat in the exact middle of the room, a chair on each side, beneath the panel of bright fluorescent bulbs in the ceiling.

Three men were the sole occupants of the room, the one a young Asian technician working over a polygraph machine mounted on the table. The second man was in his mid-fifties, heavy-set, dressed in a dark suit that had seen better days, the permanently bored expression of a bureaucrat plastered on his face. His name was Lucas Henderson Ellsworth IV, and he was proud of it, along with a pedigree that stretched back to Jamestown. What those illustrious ancestors would have thought of his position as CIA inspector general was unknown.

The man that sat across from him was thirty-eight years of age, tall— six-foot-three according to his personnel records—a lean, wiry frame concealing its potential for power, its capacity for violence. Eyes the color of blued steel shone from a smooth-shaven, rugged face. A smile might even have made him somewhat handsome, but the man beneath those lights was not smiling. Wires ran from the polygraph machine to electrodes attached to his arms and a strap encircling his bare chest.

The technician and the bureaucrat exchanged a few words and then the tech left, the door closing with the finality of a cell door.

Ellsworth smiled, opening the folder on the table before him. "You have an impressive history, Mr. Nichols. Fifteen years in the Clandestine Service—actually several in the former Directorate of Operations before the formation of the NCS. Awarded the Intelligence Star five years ago for an operation...the details of which have been redacted. Most regrettable. I'm sure it would have made for an interesting read. But that's not why we're here this morning."

The man shifted restlessly, clearly annoyed at the small talk. "I was waiting for you to come to the point."

"Very well. Let me ask a few preliminary questions to establish a baseline for the machine. Your full name?"

"Harold Nichols. I was given no middle name."

"In early October of this year, you and Alpha Team of the Special Activities Division were involved in an operation in the Middle East. You're the leader of Alpha Team, are you not?"

"That is correct."

"Very good. May I call you Harry?"

"My friends call me Harry," the man replied, his voice perfectly level, without a trace of inflection.

A moment of embarrassed silence followed, then the bureaucrat cleared his throat. "Good. We'll begin, Mr. Nichols."

The man lifted a hand from the table, gesturing around at the wires, the equipment. "What do you hope to accomplish with all this?"

Ellsworth seemed to consider the question, then he replied, "The truth, Mr. Nichols. I hope to get at the truth."

A smile crossed the man's face, an ironic, cynical parody of a smile. "Let me tell you something. I lie for a living. In 2008 I was captured by a Taliban splinter group in the passes of the Hindu Kush. I spent three months in captivity before a team was able to extract me. I was tortured on a daily basis for information. It was five months before I could run the mile again. My body still bears the scars of those days. In all those months, all they learned was what I wanted them to know. Disinformation, and they never knew the difference. Now, if you think this machine of yours can accomplish something they couldn't, you're wasting your time..."

5:42 A.M. Eastern Time
A brownstone residence
Fairfax, Virginia

Anymore, the alarm always seemed to come too early. David Lay opened his eyes and stared up through the darkness at the ceiling as the alarm continued its discordant clangor.

With a groan, he swung his legs out of bed and fumbled for the luminous display. At the age of sixty-two, he wasn't as young as he'd once been, which had to be a contributing factor. But hitting the snooze button wasn't an option for the Director of the Central Intelligence Agency.

Wrapping a robe around his body against the morning cool, Lay pushed open the door that led into the hallway. The temperature had dropped below twenty degrees Fahrenheit the night before, a snow squall blowing in from the west, forecasted to leave a dusting to two inches on the ground. The faint odor of smoke struck his nostrils and his steps quickened as he made his way toward the kitchen.

"Good morning, boss," was the nearly clairvoyant greeting as a short, stocky man emerged from the smoke shrouding the stove.

"Well, Pete, I see you're giving them the old college try," Lay observed, casting a critical eye at the stack of pancakes that surmounted the island.

Peter Ramirez laughed, waving his spatula in the DCIA's direction. "They taste better than they look, *comprende?*"

"Don't see how they could help it," was Lay's reply. "What's the latest from Langley?"

"The hourlies are on the table," Ramirez responded, turning back to the stove. Lay took in the incongruous bulge of a holstered Glock 21 beneath the bodyguard's apron and shook his head.

At thirty-two, Pete Ramirez was a retired Navy SEAL, sidelined from active duty after suffering a back injury during a mission on Mindanao. A solid, five foot-six battleship of a man, he had joined the Secret Service upon recovery. A year and a half had now passed since he had been assigned as Lay's personal bodyguard and the two men had bonded well. Protector and principal.

"Any progress with Sergei Ivanovich?"

Ramirez shook his head. "Carter's team is on it, but so far nothing. If his face hadn't been caught on those surveillance cameras…"

"Tell me it shouldn't bother us that a former *Spetsnaz* commando with mob ties could wind up in Philly without us knowing he was in the country." Lay sighed. "Reading in the Bureau without explaining exactly how we obtained that footage will be one of this morning's joys."

There was nothing else notable in the stack of hourly reports, and the DCIA set them aside wearily, reaching for the TV remote.

"...and the election battle continues, now a month after the election, with continued reports of voter fraud in New Mexico. It is believed that the Supreme Court will take up the case next week, making it the first time the high court has intervened in a presidential election since the 2000 Florida recount between former President George W. Bush and former Vice President Albert Gore. With President Hancock's lead dwindling to a mere fifty thousand votes over Senator Richard Norton, the allegations of thousands of votes having been cast by illegal immigrants in the border state could have a profound impact on the outcome of the election. Here to discuss the allegations and the possible impact of a Supreme Court decision on the legitimacy of a Norton administration, is the Senate minority leader, Senator Scott Ellis, of Utah. Senator, you've long spoken out—"

With a snort, Lay turned off the TV. There wasn't anything about the election he cared to hear, unless perhaps it was a concession speech from President Roger Hancock. And even that would be marred by some stupid talking head who wouldn't have a clue. Wouldn't understand the darkness beneath.

Perhaps that was for the best. The country had been through enough...

6:01 A.M.
CIA Headquarters
Langley, Virginia

It was fated to end like this, Harry. There is no escaping the will of Allah...

He hadn't slept in three days. It was the classic sleep deprivation before an interrogation, standard Agency protocol. He was trained for it.

And that's what this was...an interrogation. The polygraph was there, but Ellsworth wasn't following the protocols by which those were conducted. The familiar routines, the standard format of *yes/no* answers.

He was going for blood.

That voice. Haunting his dreams. Truth be known, he hadn't slept for a long time. He closed his eyes momentarily, willing it away.

Ellsworth was speaking again and Harry raised his head to face the inspector general.

"Following the defection of Hamid Zakiri from Alpha Team, you were ordered to bring him in for interrogation. Is that correct?"

"You were ordered to take me alive, weren't you?"

The voice of a dead man, reaching back from beyond the grave. He could still see the face, there in the darkness of the Masjid al-Marwani, beneath the Temple Mount. The face of a dying friend. The face of a traitor...

"Did you receive such an order?" Ellsworth repeated, testy at the delay. It wasn't typically the responsibility of the inspector general to perform an interrogation like this himself, but he had an ax to grind.

"Yes," Harry replied, his eyes locking with Ellsworth's in a cold, icy stare.

A nod. "And you chose to disregard that order. Following his murder of your fellow team member, Davood Sarami, you wanted to take upon yourself the role of executioner, didn't you?"

"He screamed when I shot him, Harry. I enjoyed myself..."

A involuntary shudder rippled through Harry's body and he looked away. Even now, two months later, he could still feel the anger, the rage burning through him. Executioner...

Yes, that much was true. He could still remember the sneer in Hamid's eyes as he lay there helpless, awaiting the final bullet. The big Colt recoiling into his hand. Every moment, playing endlessly through his mind.

"No," he replied, mastering his emotions with an effort. "Zakiri's death was unavoidable, the inevitable consequence of close quarters combat. If I could have aimed to wound, I would have. He died with a loaded weapon in his hand."

Darkness. Standing over his friend there in the darkened prayer hall of the masjid. No, not his friend—the *traitor*, he reminded himself, his mind still struggling with the realization.

A burst of submachine gun fire had broken Hamid's pelvis and he'd been lying there helpless when Harry had reached him. A weapon in his hand?

He'd been struggling to reach his Glock. Harry had kicked it away from him. Disarmed...

"Is that the way it happened?" Ellsworth asked, skepticism clearly visible in his eyes. Harry sensed the warning bells—emotion was filtering through into the machine results. His emotion. Control. "Let me tell you what I think, Mr. Nichols. I think it was deliberate—I think you wanted to kill him."

Harry's head came up with a jerk, his eyes flashing daggers at the bureaucrat. "Wanted to? *Wanted* to?" he demanded, his voice barely above the level of a hiss. "He was my friend."

Even as the words left his mouth, he saw his mistake. A neatly-laid trap, he realized with a detached sense of emotion. Or the lack thereof. Ellsworth was smarter than he looked.

9

"That's right," Ellsworth responded, "he was your friend, wasn't he? Your recruit, too, if my memory serves me. You brought him into the Agency, vouched for him. Is that correct?"

"Yes."

"Tell me, Nichols, perhaps there is another reason you killed him?"

6:18 A.M.
Lay's residence
Fairfax, Virginia

The sound of the SUV engine starting struck David Lay's ears just as he finished tying his necktie. Undoubtedly Ramirez had finished his search for explosives. That was part of the morning routine, along with the continually-varied route to work.

Lay grimaced, adjusting his collar. It was probably paranoia. No CIA director had ever been assassinated. No one had ever even bothered to try. No matter, he didn't plan to be the first. And with the enemies he had made in this past month...

His gaze fell to the framed photograph on his nightstand. The face of a young woman in her late twenties stared back at him, a smile dancing in those azure-blue eyes. She had her mother's smile.

To have his daughter Carol back in his life—after well over twenty years of separation. It was a blessing beyond anything that he deserved. His wife had left him just weeks after Carol's fourth birthday, tired of the long absences and lonely nights. He still couldn't find it in himself to blame her.

He'd been an up-and-coming young CIA field officer in those days, the waning years of the Cold War. Young and brash. Patriotic. Or maybe just ambitious. He still didn't know. All he knew was that it had left his family in ruins.

Even his daughter no longer carried his name, despite their recent reconciliation. And his wife was dead, stolen away by breast cancer. There were times that forgiveness was unobtainable.

A knock on the door disturbed his thoughts. Ramirez's voice. "Think it's time to roll, sir. Looks like the traffic could be interesting this morning..."

6:27 A.M.
National Clandestine Service(NCS) Operations Center
Langley, Virginia

Sometimes the most frustrating thing about betrayal was that you never knew the *why* of it. Or at least it made no sense. Carol Chambers brushed her blonde hair out of her eyes and clicked once more through the open windows on her workstation monitor. Nothing.

That's the way she had always felt about her father. Perhaps finding the answer to the *why* was the reason she had joined the Agency.

It couldn't have been anything else. Her degree from the Massachusetts Institute of Technology notwithstanding, she was a hacker pure and simple, and while the CIA was at least a semi-legal use for her talents, she knew corporations that would have paid better.

"Still no money trail?"

Carol Chambers looked up from her workstation in the operations center. "Still nothing, Ron. There's no evidence that Tehran ever paid him a dime."

Ron Carter nodded, a sober look on his dark face. The African-American was in charge of NCS Field Support and Analysis, and one of the best photo-analysts Langley had ever seen.

"I think we had a true believer there."

"And to think we thought he was one of us." Carol let out a long sigh. The story of Hamid Zakiri was quite possibly the biggest intelligence fiasco in CIA history.

Born in Iraq, or so they'd been led to believe, he had come to the US as a child following Operation Desert Storm. Joining the US Army at the age of nineteen, he'd made it into the Special Forces, the legendary "Green Berets".

Zakiri had been awarded the Bronze Star for gallantry in Afghanistan, along with a Purple Heart for a leg wound received in Tikrit, Iraq. And that was where he had come to the attention of the CIA.

Six years in the Army, nearly another ten in the Clandestine Service. They'd trusted him. Even now, over two months following his betrayal, it was hard to believe that he had been an Iranian sleeper agent.

The files on the operation were sealed. Only those who had been a part of it knew the full truth. Those he had betrayed.

The world had been on the brink of war. A biological attack on the al-Aqsa Mosque in Jerusalem, engineered by the regime of Iranian president Mahmoud F'Azel Shirazi and carried out by elements of Hezbollah. A well-coordinated plan to implicate the state of Israel in the attack, and bring about her destruction.

The CIA had positioned a strike team to stop the release of the plague bacteria, but they hadn't had any way of knowing that they were about to be stabbed in the back by one of their own.

And in the end, the attack had been foiled, but at a terrible cost. Another star placed on the wall, for fallen officer Davood Sarami. Killed by a fellow Muslim.

Carter was speaking again. "We're re-tasking," he said, placing a thumb drive on her desk. "Sergei Ivanovich Korsakov."

"Former *Spetsnaz*, right?" Carol asked, refocusing her thoughts. "Seems like he's been on our radar before."

"Go to the head of the class. He has. Following his discharge from the Russian military in 2000, he's become a bit of a gun-for-hire, with close ties to the Russian mob and a half dozen other equally unsavory entities in Eastern Europe. Implicated in the assassination of the finance minister of Ukraine three years ago, he's been out of sight since."

"Until he showed up in Philly two days ago."

The analyst nodded. "I'm putting you and Danny in charge of running this. The DCIA has set up a teleconference at 0800, at which we'll brief Haskel and the G-men on what we know. Make sure it's something."

"Isn't it the FBI's area of responsibility anyway?" Carol asked, allowing herself a smile of amusement at Carter's reference. Bureau director Eric Haskel was far from popular at Langley.

"That's right. We wrap it up like a big fat Christmas present and hand it to them. Just make sure it's nice and maybe the gods of bureaucracy future will smile upon us."

6:31 A.M.

"When did you first meet Hamid Zakiri?"

"In 2004," Harry replied, his tone curt. "In Tikrit."

Ellsworth shook his head. "I mean the *first* time, when he recruited you. Or was it the other way around? You were responsible for his infiltration of the Clandestine Service—what did you get in return? Money?"

Anger flashed in Harry's eyes, simmering there below the surface. Another outburst wasn't going to get him anywhere. "He saved my life in Iraq. I believed he was a patriot—I believed he was one of us."

The inspector general continued as though he hadn't even spoken. "Isn't that why you killed him? Better that one should die than both of you spend the rest of your days behind bars?"

"*Enough!*" Harry rose to his feet, slamming both hands down on the table and leaning in toward Ellsworth. The world seemed to close in on the two of them and he could almost smell the fear like liquor on the bureaucrat's breath. The sensation was heady, almost intoxicating. He could have snapped the man's neck in a trice, and they both knew it. Nothing could have saved him.

"You don't know what it's like out there, out beyond these walls," he whispered, a menacing edge to his voice. "Out where a mistake means death, not a bureaucratic slap on the wrist. There is nothing and no one out there you can trust. No one except your team. And then you can't always trust them."

Hands on his arms, guiding him firmly back into his seat. Security guards, he realized gradually, gazing across at a shaken Ellsworth. It might have been enough, but it wasn't going to stop here. Maybe it never would…

6:35 A.M.
Virginia

The man rubbed his hands together, the heater of the aging Toyota Corolla barely keeping away the chill. It was almost time, he thought, glancing down at the Glock in the pocket of the door. They had assured him that it was clean, that there was no way the gun could be traced back to him.

He glanced across the parking lot, watching as a Virginia state trooper walked out of the convenience store, a steaming cup of coffee in his hand as he headed back to his patrol car.

Jack-booted thug, the man thought, watching the gun on the trooper's hip. Their time would come soon enough…when America would rise.

"He's on the road," a voice in his ear informed him, and he reached nervously up to turn down the volume of his Bluetooth. As if the police would be able to hear him.

Meeting this man…had given him purpose. Direction. For years, he had watched in helpless frustration as the globalists met, planned, stealing his newfound country away from him. Bold in the certainty of their victory, the corporations—the banksters. Jews scheming in the dark corners of world.

And then he had come into his life…a man like none he had ever known. And all he needed was *his* help.

If you want to fight with a serpent, you put out its eyes, the man had said, his voice full of knowledge. Confidence.

And who serves as the eyes of the New World Order? The NSA, the CIA—the men who run them. Men like David Lay.

"I'm moving," he whispered into his earpiece, his mouth suddenly dry as he put the sedan into drive. "*Sic semper tyrannus.*"

So always to tyrants.

There was a moment's pause before his friend's voice came over the line—the voice of reassurance that had guided him down this path. "In liberty, my brother."

6:38 A.M.
Along I-495
Near Tyson's Corner, Virginia

"What is *that* supposed to mean?"

The driver allowed himself a smile, glancing out the tinted windows of the Dodge Durango at the passing traffic. The vehicle was pulled over on the shoulder of the interstate—a worn t-shirt flapping in the cold winter wind between the window and the door signaling that the vehicle was abandoned—perhaps out of gas or suffering mechanical problems.

Or, just waiting... which was more to the point of it.

"Just something they say, Pavel," the driver replied, catching his partner's eye in the rear-view mirror. Seven weeks of planning, all of it leading up to this day. Less time than he would have liked...but recruiting the American had turned out to be the easy part of it. *Useful idiot.*

Consumed by his fantasies of a coming New World Order, of being liberty's hero, he had never guessed how he was being played. That he was, in fact, nothing more than a pawn in a much larger game.

Or that he would be dead within the next twenty minutes.

6:39 A.M.
Virginia

"They're reporting a two-vehicle accident on the primary route," Ramirez remarked. "Apparently somebody was tail-gating and skid on the ice. Idiot commuters."

A smile crossed Lay's face. The snow wasn't bad, but folks in Virginia weren't used to it. He had spent his childhood in Vermont, and learned to drive up there. Now *that* was snow. "We're taking the alternate, then?"

The SEAL nodded. "It's a bit longer, but they're liable to be backed up with the accident. And we've not used it for two days, so we should be good."

Always security-conscious, the DCIA mused. That was Ramirez. There had been a time he would have dismissed it. Not now.

Behind them, the Toyota merged with traffic two cars back. "I have them," the man announced, speaking into the wireless headset of his cellphone. He pulled the Glock out of the pocket of the door, laying the polymer handgun across his lap with sweaty fingers. Cursing his fear. "They are proceeding along Route Three, the same one they used two days ago. What do you want me to do?"

"Just maintain a following position," came the calm voice. "I'll talk you through this. You're going to be fine."

6:43 A.M.
An apartment
Manassas, Virginia

A blurred image of himself in the mirror was the first thing Thomas Parker saw of the morning. He felt suddenly dizzy and threw out a hand, steadying himself against the edge of the sink.

A wave of nausea nearly overcame him and he coughed, feeling sick. Very sick. He reached for the faucet, turning on the cold water, splashing it over his hands and face. His aching head.

It might have been easier if he'd actually been sick. Knowing the headache and nausea were a direct result of too much alcohol the previous evening didn't help his mood any.

One way or the other, he was going to have to sober up or he was going to be late. The CIA didn't know about the drinking problem he'd developed, and he planned to keep it that way. He was on a strike team, after all. Mistakes weren't tolerated. Mistakes killed.

His gaze drifted toward the sticky note on the mirror, the phone number written there. The number of Harry's pastor. Nichols, his team lead, knew about the problem, and *that* was his solution.

Thomas snorted. Yeah, some solution. An avowed agnostic for all of his adult life, he saw no reason to change his mind now. Certainly the betrayal of Hamid Zakiri had done nothing but deepen his cynicism. And his drinking.

They'd shared this apartment, he and Hamid, a way to keep down the cost of living in suburban Virginia. It had been for Hamid's benefit, not his own. He'd been the manager of a Fortune 500 tech company in the years before 9/11, and his money was invested wisely.

About the only thing he'd done wisely.

"Thomas?" Her voice sounded shriller this morning. He looked into the mirror to see a brunette standing in the bathroom door, her hair a mess and wearing one of his shirts.

She'd looked better when he was drunk too, he realized sourly. He couldn't remember her name, nor much of anything else from the previous evening, in fact. The Agency would have a cow if they knew.

With their jealous watch over security clearances, the CIA took a dimmer view of one-night stands than most parents. Make that parents with a multi-million-dollar surveillance budget and you have the picture.

He turned back to the sink, trying to block her voice from his head. He was going to be late for work...

6:51 A.M.
Virginia

"Target is closing, approximately five hundred meters now. Are you ready?"

They spy on us, we spy on them, the man had said. *They target us...we target them.* It was true, what Jones had always warned about the shadow government. The tyrants in Washington had been killing people for years...now was *their* time. The driver of the Toyota nodded nervously, covering his fear with a laugh. "Yeah. Yeah—I can do this."

"Then be quiet and focus," came the calm reply. " I'll guide you in. Three hundred meters."

For a moment, the driver took his eyes off the target SUV two cars ahead, glancing nervously once more at the Glock. He'd never killed a man, but *this*—this was justice...

"Two hundred meters," the voice in his ear intoned. The driver hit his turn signal and accelerated hard into the fast lane...

Defensive driving hadn't been a part of Hell Week, but the Secret Service had taught Ramirez everything he needed to know on the subject.

A curse escaped his lips as he saw the Toyota in his driver's side mirror, accelerating fast. A threat.

Alerted by his bodyguard's outburst, Lay looked up into the mirror. The small sedan filled his field of view, and in that moment he knew. It was them...

There was no time to react, no time for self-recriminations or doubt. It all happened too fast.

Ramirez put the wheel over, hard to the right, flooring the accelerator in an attempt to thread the needle up the shoulder of the road.

Too late.

The sedan impacted hard against the front driver's side of the SUV, sending it skidding toward the guardrail on the right shoulder.

Impact.

It struck David Lay with the force of a punch as the airbags inflated, slamming him back against the seat. Dazed, he reached for the clasp of his seatbelt. There was little time. He had no idea how little.

The men inside the "stranded" Durango watched the collision unfold from several hundred meters back along the interstate. The driver lowered his high-powered binoculars from his eyes, glancing down at the phone which lay open on the seat beside him. A simple, pre-paid flipphone, a number already dialed on the small screen.

A grim smile crossing his face, he reached down with a single finger...pressing SEND.

No. It wasn't supposed to be this way, the man thought, flailing against the airbags that pinned him against the seat of the Toyota. *The Glock.* Where was it—where had it gone?

Outside the passenger's side window, over the billowing airbag, he could see the guardrail he had slammed into, coming to rest direct in front of the SUV. He swore, knowing that every second he struggled decreased his chances of success. That *they* would win once more.

The next moment, his world erupted in a blinding flash of white. Flames and fire...

The driver of the Durango watched in silence as the explosives layered into the frame of the Toyota detonated, sending both vehicles careening through a wall of traffic toward the median.

People...were so easy to deceive, he thought—perhaps because it was easier for them to believe a lie that confirmed their beliefs than a truth that contradicted them.

Tell them what they want *to hear.*

It was the secret of any good recruitment. He looked over at his partner. "Good enough, don't you think, *tovarisch*?" Comrade.

A nod, and he reached forward, a gloved hand closing around the ignition key. One target down.

One to go.

Chapter 2

The interrogation had been going on for just under an hour and a half when Harry's tactical satellite phone went off, buzzing loudly against the table inches from his hand.

"Ignore it," came Ellsworth's peremptory command, annoyance at the interruption in his voice.

Harry ignored him with a smile, palming the TACSAT and flipping it open. "Nichols here."

It wasn't a social call and the smile faded from Harry's face as he listened. Finally, "All right, boss. I'll be with you in five."

Returning the phone to the pocket of his jeans, he rose, roughly tearing off the electrodes taped to his arms, while the inspector general watched, speechless.

"We're done here."

At that, Ellsworth seemed to find his voice, springing up from his seat like a jack-in-the-box. "I should say we are *not*! Sit down, Nichols."

Harry turned, coolly looking the bureaucrat in the eye. "We're declaring Code MAGI—there's been an attempt on the life of the DCIA. I'll have security escort you back to your office, *sir*."

"Wait—*what's* going on?" Ellsworth demanded, but Harry didn't answer. Grabbing his shirt from the rack by the door, he moved to the security panel and tapped in the code he had watched Ellsworth enter earlier in the morning.

And then he was out, in the corridor, buttoning his shirt as he headed for the stairs. Crisis mode...

5:07 A.M. Mountain Time
Apache Reservation
New Mexico

The morning was cool, a chill breeze blowing as he walked out into the desert, stealing glances at the horizon as if he awaited the coming of the sun.

Jack Richards pulled his Stetson down over his forehead, his hands jammed deep into the pockets of his overcoat. He'd been colder. The big man could still remember the mountains of Afghanistan, the intense cold. The snow. He'd been in the Corps then, Marine Force Recon. A demolitions specialist.

"Thanks for coming," the man at his side remarked, and he turned to look down into the face of his half-brother. "I wasn't sure you were going to."

Jack, or "Tex" as most of his friends called him, acknowledged the comment with a silent nod. He wasn't given to talking any more than necessary.

And he nearly hadn't come, but there were ties that were stronger than blood. "How did Manny die?" he asked, looking down at the fresh-dug grave, the small veterans marker bearing the name *Emmanuel Gutierrez* stabbed into the earth just above the mound marking the grave of a lifelong friend, a man who had once been closer to Richards than most of his own family.

"His patrol went missing in Big Bend three weeks ago. He and one other agent—their bodies were finally found on the 8th. Shot dead. They're investigating...but everyone's money is on the cartels."

Summers on the reservation...Richards thought, his coal-black eyes gazing out across the desert. Remembering the long days, the games of football, Manny's face shining bright as he reached into the air for a pass.

Golden days. Before he had moved to Texas in his mid-teens. Long before they both went off to war.

"I'm sorry," he whispered, kicking at the loose dirt with a booted foot. The funeral had been the day before, a gathering of family and friends, but he had been unavoidably detained. *Business.*

Richards was Mescalero only through his maternal grandfather, his half-brother the son of his mother and the full-blooded Apache she had married after his father's death. Still, he had spent the best part of his teens on this very reservation. The *best* part...

"How much time do you have off?" came his half-brother's voice, his eyes searching Tex's face.

So many unspoken questions there…so much unsaid.

"Two days," he replied, lifting his eyes from Manny's grave to look out over the desert. Remembering a similar morning, from so long ago—his coming-of-age, a journey out into the desert to meet the spirit which would guide his life. What exactly he had encountered out there he would never know. What he did know is that he hadn't found God until years later.

The distracting buzz of his satellite phone erupted from his pocket and he pulled the TACSAT out, glancing idly at the screen.

"I have to take this," he whispered, placing a hand on his half-brother's shoulder. The Texan stepped a few feet away and flipped it open. "Richards."

From the first words, he knew. His vacation was over…

7:13 A.M. Eastern Time
NCS Operations Center
Langley, Virginia

"What do you mean we don't know?" Bernard Kranemeyer demanded, glaring across the conference table in Ron Carter's direction.

Now in his early fifties, the Director of the Clandestine Service still had the commanding presence of the Delta Force sergeant major he had once been. Along with the voice. And the acerbic temperament. It was no accident that members of the clandestine community called him the "Dark Lord".

Carter shook his head. "Highway Patrol was on the scene five minutes after the bomb went off. They found two bodies. The body of an unidentified Caucasian male in the sedan, and the body of Lay's bodyguard, Peter Ramirez, in the driver's seat of the SUV. The DCIA was nowhere to be found."

"Any ID on the driver of the sedan?" Kranemeyer asked, a grimace of pain crossing his face as he reached beneath the table to rub a leg that was no longer there.

An improvised explosive device, or IED, had put an end to his military career one sunny day in Fallujah, Iraq, 2003. He'd been an old man by spec-ops standards even then, fighting off forcible retirement.

The explosion had killed the man beside him, his fellow sergeant, the genial Stan Sniadowski. Left Kranemeyer's right leg a bloody, mangled mess below the knee. All the reconstructive surgery in the world couldn't have saved it.

So, now he had a prosthesis and phantom pain. Occupational hazards. And he knew what bombs could do.

"Not yet," Carter replied. "The Bureau has promised they'll share everything with us."

"They'd better," Kranemeyer replied, a dangerous glint in his eyes. On the surface, he and the DCIA had shared little in common.

Lay was the politician, he the soldier. But over the years, the two men had developed a close friendship. And now he was gone. Or dead...

7:21 A.M.
CIA Headquarters
Langley, Virginia

A metallic beep sounded and the door of the conference room opened to admit the figure of Harry Nichols.

"You're late," was Kranemeyer's quiet comment. "What's your status?"

"I've diverted a Gulfstream from Monterrey to New Mexico to pick Richards up," Harry responded, making a reference to the CIA language school in California. He chose to ignore the sharp edge in the voice of the DCS. "Thomas is on his way in. Should be here in fifteen minutes."

Kranemeyer absorbed the information without comment, turning back to Carter. "Where's Shapiro?"

"We've sent a helo for him. The White House has authorized a pair of Apache gunships as escort."

The DCS nodded. The AH-64 Apaches typically provided overflight for the presidential motorcade, and their release for the protection of Deputy Director (Intelligence) Michael Shapiro was an indication of just how seriously the administration was taking this. As well they should.

"Where was Shapiro, anyway?"

"Hadn't left home."

"That's the Banker for you," the DCS acknowledged with a derisive snort. Shapiro was the only one of the deputy directors with no background in the intelligence community, and it showed. Now, he was in charge and they were going to have to live with it. And his penchant for what Carter had once called a "negotiable nine and a punctual five."

Kranemeyer took a deep breath, turning to look Harry in the eye. "I want your team in readiness. When we find the people that did this, we're going to strike back. Send a message, loud and clear. Don't mess with us."

"My team is two men down," Harry replied, clearing his throat. "Until we can find replacements for Sarami and Zakiri, I can hardly describe Alpha Team as mission-ready."

"Are you saying you can't do it?" the DCS demanded, a challenge in his eyes.

Harry stared the DCS in the face, his gaze unwavering. "That was an objective assessment of our readiness. You want heroics, you'd better find another guy."

A moment passed, then a grim smile spread across Kranemeyer's face. "Assessment accepted, Nichols. Thing is, we're stretched thin at the moment. As you know, Nakamura and Bravo Team deployed to Tajikistan last week. So, you're the designated hitter. Carter will coordinate with the Joint Terrorism Task Force on your behalf."

Harry and Ron exchanged glances. They'd worked together many times through the years. But never under these circumstances. There had never been an attempt on the life of the DCIA.

Kranemeyer put both hands down on the table and levered himself to his feet. "Let's roll, gentlemen."

7:22 A.M.

"Got any working theories?" Harry asked as the two men left the conference room and headed back toward the op center.

Carter glanced up as though startled from thought. "Yeah. I do."

A moment of silence followed as they continued down the corridor. Harry cleared his throat. "Mind reading me in, or are we going to start this day off playing 'Twenty Questions'?"

"Oh. Sorry," Carter returned absently. "I've asked Michelle to pull footage from the VDOT cameras. I want to know who was in the area."

The Virginia Department of Transportation had a lot of cameras, particularly in the sprawling suburbia immediately south of the Potomac, but their coverage couldn't be described as comprehensive. "Looking for a face?"

"Sergei Korsakov."

Harry stopped short, turning to face the analyst. "The ex-*Spetsnaz* hit man? Why?"

"He's in the States," Ron replied. He took a deep breath and continued, "You've not been cleared for this, Harry—you didn't hear it from me—but Korsakov was picked up on surveillance footage in Philly two days ago. We've been on a frantic scramble ever since, trying to figure out how he got in and why he was here. This morning, I'm afraid we got the answer to the last half of that. The hit this morning is almost a mirror image of his assassination of the mayor of Chelyabinsk in 2002. It was one of Korsakov's first mob hits."

"Then you believe he's dead." It was more of a statement than a question.

"That or taken hostage. In which case we'll start receiving fingers in the mail," Carter retorted with characteristic bluntness. "That's another Korsakov trademark. There's just one thing I don't understand."

"And that would be?"

"What does the Russian mob here in this country have to gain by taking us on? They've always been about money, pure and simple."

"Then somebody made it worth their while," Harry observed. "Who did you have working on Korsakov? I'll need to talk with them, see if they can make any connections we're missing."

Carter snorted. "Pretty near my whole team, the last couple days. Carol was heading it up, but they have her under lockdown security now, a protective detail down in one of the interrogation rooms. Pretty shook up, the way I heard it. I'll have Lasker give you the codes to access her files."

"Sounds like a plan."

7:31 A.M.
Northbound I-495
Virginia

A car horn sounded somewhere to his rear and Thomas rubbed his forehead, the noise only adding to his headache. Traffic was snarling in the wake of the assassination attempt, as whole lanes of the interstate were shut down for emergency use.

He looked ahead at the long line of backed-up traffic and popped another Altoids mint into his mouth. With any luck, the smell of liquor would be gone from his breath by the time he got to Langley.

A moment later, he felt the buzz of the satphone in his pocket. For the second time in ten minutes. A glance at the screen of the TACSAT confirmed his suspicion.

"Thomas here," he announced, flipping it open.

"Where are you?" a voice demanded. Nichols

He shook his head wearily, staring out the window. "I've made three miles in the last ten minutes, Harry. I'll be there when I get there."

"You got a late start this morning, didn't you?"

He didn't respond for a long moment, gazing out the window. His team leader went on without waiting for an answer. "The AA meeting was last night at church, Thomas. Did you go?"

"No."

A long sigh came from the other end of the phone. "I've been covering for you, Thomas. But this has gotta be a two-way street. If you're not willing to get your act together, I'll have to talk with Kranemeyer."

Not that. "No," Thomas managed, fighting against the flash of anger that surged to the fore at his friend's words. "Don't do that. I've told you, Harry, I just need a little more time. You understand that, don't you?"

"What I understand right now is we have a crisis on our hands and one of my best men is stewed. Now, I'll see you here inside of thirty minutes, and you *will* be sober. Tex is flying in from New Mexico and I want us fully operational by the time he gets here. Am I coming through?"

"Loud and clear, boss."

7:33 A.M.
NCS Operations Center
Langley, Virginia

Harry put the phone back in his pocket and sighed wearily, glaring across the op-center at the blank wall.

He had never attempted to impose his own Christian faith on the members of his team. It just wasn't him. The way he looked at it, what they did in their private lives was their own business, just so long as it didn't affect the job. And now it was.

And he didn't have time to deal with it. Not today. Not with all hell breaking loose. Reaching down, he pressed the button on the side of his workstation terminal, listening as the computer booted up.

It had been a few weeks since he had logged into the Agency system, what with Ellsworth's investigation breaking into everyone's work routine. It would take some time to get up to speed.

Unfortunately, that was time he no longer had. Because Lay was gone.

The screen came on, and Harry typed in his access codes, watching impatiently as the terminal sped through the authentication process. He and Lay had a long history, a working relationship that went back to Harry's first days as an operator.

Back then, Lay had been in his closing days as Station Chief Tel Aviv, and Harry entered his territory running an op for what was then called the Directorate of Operations.

He'd struck Harry as a man of principle back then, a hard man—but fair. Unafraid.

Their relationship had grown distant over the years, as Lay climbed the ladder and won the political appointment of DCIA.

How he had done that, Harry had no idea, but to all appearances, he had kept his integrity. Maybe that was what had gotten him killed.

7:35 A.M.
The roof of the CIA HQ Building

He heard them well before he saw them, three helicopters swirling in from the south. Anyone laying in ambush would have as well.

Kranemeyer zipped up his jacket and shoved his hands into his pockets, sheltering them from the raw December wind.

Snipers from the Special Activities Division were posted across the roof, their slate-gray ghillie suits melding into the concrete. For most of them, it was the first time they'd ever unslung their weapons on American soil.

The H-76 Sikorsky pulled into a hover and settled down toward the helipad, the twin Apache gunships remaining above, providing cover.

He cast a critical glance in their direction, taking in the pintle-mounted 30mm chain gun under the chin of each helicopter. God help the man who got caught in their crossfire.

The Sikorsky came to rest on the roof, and Kranemeyer strode forward before the rotors had even stopped turning.

A short man in a business suit emerged from the side door of the helicopter, his jacket flapping wildly in the downwash of the rotor blades. A pair of bodyguards with drawn weapons flanked him as he moved to meet the DCS.

Michael Shapiro.

"Any problems on the way in, sir?" Kranemeyer asked as he moved in close, yelling to make himself heard over the noise of helicopter engines. Despite his personal dislike for Shapiro, the man was in command now, and they had a crisis to deal with.

"No, no," the Deputy Director responded with an effort. His face had taken on a slightly greenish cast. "I hate flying. All those evasive maneuvers…"

Kranemeyer ignored the comment as the men moved toward the utility door. "My team has contingency plans drawn up and on your desk. They will need your approval for implementation."

"Contingency plans?" Shapiro wheezed, still getting his breath.

"A list of operations that need to be shut down ASAP. Assets in need of extraction. It'll take a lot of resources to get them all out, but we owe these people."

Shapiro stopped short and stared at the DCS with a look of bewilderment. "Whatever are you talking about?"

25

"As calloused as it sounds," Kranemeyer responded, a hard look in his eyes as he returned the stare, "it would be a lot better for all of us if we knew that Lay was dead."

"*What?*"

The DCS held up a hand. "As long as he's alive out there, potentially in the hands of terrorists, we have to assume that every operation, every asset of which he had detailed knowledge, is compromised. For sale to the highest bidder. It's a list longer than my arm."

"My God, you don't think he would betray us, do you? You don't know David…"

"All due respect, sir," Kranemeyer growled, moving in close enough to Shapiro that his bodyguards reacted, "but you've never been in the field. Any man can be broken, given enough time and resources. And that's the assumption we have to act on."

7:41 A.M.
NCS Operations Center

To say that the CIA dossier on Korsakov was incomplete would have been an understatement of epic proportions. There were massive holes in their knowledge, gaps in the file. No one seemed to know what he had been doing in the interval between his discharge from the Russian army in 2000 and the assassination of Mayor Anton Suvorov in 2002.

One thing seemed certain. During those two years, Korsakov had become a trusted member of the *mafiya*.

An annoying *beep* alerted Harry to an incoming e-mail and he scrolled through the windows, expecting to see an update from Tex or Carter. Unfortunately, ignoring messages wasn't an option on this morning.

It was his private e-mail, he noted with a growing sense of disquiet. Not too many people had that one, and still fewer used it.

The subject line read, "CRITIC". . .and the sender's address, well, it was a jumble of letters—the provider itself a free e-mail service originating from somewhere in the Czech Republic.

The body of the e-mail was as terse as the header, his eyes narrowing as he scanned over the text. *Parking garage, sub-level. Fifth column. Freefall.*

It was the last word that caught his attention. *Freefall.* Not one word, not really. Two. A codephrase from long ago.

And he knew in that moment who the sender was, knew all that the message portended.

They had been betrayed—again…

26

7:49 A.M.
CIA Headquarters Complex

The name on his identification badge read *Alex Hall.* The employee of one of the dozens of private contractors brought in by the CIA to perform maintenance, he had spent the last five days re-wiring lights in the parking garage beneath the headquarters building.

He allowed a tight smile to creep onto his face as he neared the final checkpoint. Like so much of security all over the world, they weren't nearly as concerned with the people leaving as the people trying to get *in.* Beyond a physical search of his person and vehicle—as of all the outside contractors—he had experienced no trouble.

"Leaving early?" the guard asked as he handed over his identification. No personal interest there, no smile. Just a cold, searching question.

Hall nodded, taking a hand off the steering wheel to cover a weary yawn. "Spent a long night replacing circuitry. Soon the lights in the underground garage will actually come on when you want them to."

The guard nodded and handed back his badge, motioning for the gate to be raised.

He tapped the gas and the car accelerated gently down the access road, heading out toward the main highway. Home free.

The cell phone in his pocket buzzed and he reached for it with one hand. "Hello."

"Aleksandr," a familiar voice began, "is the package in place in the garage?"

"Yes."

"*Spasiba bolshoi,*" the voice responded. Thank you very much. "I will see you shortly, *tovarisch.*"

The call ended as Aleksandr turned out onto the main highway and he rolled down the driver's side window, carefully throwing the prepaid cellphone out onto the asphalt.

Within seconds, it was crushed by the wheel of a passing car.

7:53 A.M.
The underground parking garage
CIA Headquarters

Betrayed. And once more, it had claimed the life of a friend. Harry glanced up into the ever-watchful eye of the security camera as the elevator doors opened, revealing darkness beyond. Contractors, all of them carefully vetted by

27

the FBI, had been at work rewiring the lights for weeks. Apparently their work wasn't done, just yet. At least not on this level.

The underground parking garage was one of the Agency's better-kept secrets, constructed under the New Headquarters Building in the years following 9/11. They weren't the only ones with spy sats—not anymore.

Fifth column. A pair of words loaded with double entendre. Moving among the cars, he made his way forward…silently counting off the concrete support columns as he moved.

Three…four. And then column five—a dark corner maybe ten feet from the nearest light—well away from the closest security camera, the concrete damp with moisture beneath his fingers as he dropped down on one knee.

Nothing. For a moment, he thought he had misinterpreted the message—that perhaps it was another column, another level of the garage. Or perhaps not a real column at all. If he had been wrong…they were running out of time.

Free Fall.

And then his groping fingers closed around a small waterproof pouch, pulling it toward him. The pouch contained a small cellphone, prepaid, most likely—and he leaned back against the wheel of the nearest car as he held it up, powering it on. It was his means of contact. Had to be.

Nothing was saved in the contacts. No numbers to be redialed under "missed calls", no way to get a signal underground if there had been. The phone seemed to be perfectly clean—a burner, clearly. But for *what?* Lay had been dead for almost an hour. If he didn't move quickly.

And there it was, under a data folder…a small .mp3 file of recorded audio. Selecting the file brought up a password screen and he tapped *Free Fall* into the box, watching as it opened. He glanced around the garage once more, marking the position of the nearest camera as he raised the phone to his ear.

"Harry," a man's voice began. *So familiar.* David Lay. "If you're listening to this, I'm most likely dead—my enemies have made their move. And I've lost the battle. I've known it was coming, just always thought I could stay ahead. Foolish, maybe, but I have no regrets. It was the only way—for the sake of the country. A couple years back, none of this would have mattered, and I never would've dreamed of bringing you into this. That was before Carol walked back into my life."

A pause and the iron voice faltered, trembling ever so slightly. "She's all I have left, and I swore to never fail her again. They will try to reach her as well—there is no way for them to be sure of what she knows. The Agency will move to protect her after I'm gone, but none of that will matter. There's evil in high places at Langley, and no one is safe. Take her, Harry, take her and run—

far and fast. Go dark. Trust no one. Remember the Moscow Rules, Harry. Anyone could be under the control of the enemy."

Anyone. Elevator doors began to open in the distance, back from where he had come. A threat?

"As for what has brought me to this place…that needs to end here. With me. With knowledge comes dangers."

It was a bureaucrat, one of the hundreds of drones that populated the headquarters building—a briefcase in his hand as he moved toward his car. Harry held his breath, sheltering the phone's speaker with his hand as the man passed. "I can trust you to do this, Harry. I know you. I know what you'll do. *Vaya con Dios.*"

Go with God.

And then there was silence. Harry closed the phone, cold, hard resolution coming over his face.

He had his orders. That they came from a dead man made not one wit of difference.

It was time to carry them out…

7:55 A.M.

"I know, I know—put Michelle on it," Carter instructed, slipping a thumb drive into the side of Daniel Lasker's terminal. "I need you running comm for the extraction."

At twenty-eight, the short, fair-haired Lasker looked more like an office temp than the head of CLANDOPS communications, but such was his title at Langley. And he was one of the best. "We ever tried to pull off an operation on this scale, Ron?"

Carter responded with a shake of the head. "Twelve assets. Nine countries. And it's only the beginning."

He felt a presence at his elbow and turned to find Harry standing there. "How are things coming along?"

"We're positioning teams across the Middle East," Carter responded. "Try to pull our people out before they can be snapped up."

"You could drive a car through the hole that's gonna leave in our HUMINT network," Harry observed, a grim edge to his voice. Human intelligence, the community's ace of spades.

"I know. But until we find the Director…we have no other choice." The analyst shrugged. "Was there something you needed?"

"Matter of fact, yes. I need to speak with Carol."

Ron frowned. "I'm not sure that's the best idea. Why?"

"She didn't finish running the profiles on Korsakov. I just need to talk with her a couple minutes, figure out where she was headed, particularly on any possible U.S. connections. Where is she?"

"Down in Interrogation Room A-13," Carter responded after a long pause. He reached for the phone on Lasker's desk. "I'll tell them you're coming."

6:03 A.M. Mountain Time
Airport
Albuquerque, New Mexico

Parting with his brother had not been one of the highlights of the trip for Richards, but that was nothing new. Relations had been strained ever since he had left the family ranch in Texas to join the Marine Corps at the age of nineteen.

They had been a man short that summer with him gone, a bad summer of drought—disease among the cattle. Not much he could have done to stop it, even if he had stayed, but there were elements of his family that viewed his departure as something akin to desertion.

Five years later, the ranch had gone under and his family had moved back to the Mescalero reservation in New Mexico. End of story.

He sighed, watching as the Gulfstream IV taxied in from the west, an unusual sight on the small runway. He only had one bag, traveling light as he had for the past fifteen years of his life.

A chill December breeze rippled across the small airfield, his jacket flapping back to expose the holstered Glock on his hip. He was ready. It was time to go…

8:05 A.M. Eastern Time
CIA Headquarters
Langley, Virginia

The NCS ready room was deserted, just as Harry had expected it to be. He left the lights off and moved quickly to his equipment locker, on the far side of the room.

Swiping his CIA identification badge unlocked the door and he reached inside, withdrawing his Colt 1911 and another pistol-sized weapon.

The Colt was loaded, as it always was. He racked the slide and chambered a round, carefully putting the safety on before slipping the big pistol into the paddle holster on his hip. Cocked and locked.

Moving across the room, he laid the second weapon, a Taser X3, on the table. The stun gun, which looked for all the world like an artist's conception of a laser pistol gone bad, had been developed in 2009 as a response to the law enforcement community's main critique of the original X26: its limited, single-shot capability.

The new and improved Taser aimed to address that problem, utilizing a neuro-muscular impulse rotating across the firing bays to engage multiple targets. It was capable of three shots, one right after the other. And then it was empty, but that didn't bother Harry in the least. From the surveillance footage of the interrogation room, he only had three targets.

Finishing the weapons check, he slipped the Taser into an inner pocket of his leather jacket, in a cross-draw position. Eight minutes past eight o'clock. He had fifteen, maybe twenty minutes before someone realized he had looped the security footage down in the interrogation rooms.

It would be time enough...

7:12 A.M. Central Time
An apartment
Dearborn, Michigan

"How many died?"

Nasir al-Khalidi looked up from the breakfast dishes to see his brother Jamal standing in the kitchen doorway of the small apartment they shared.

"The Americans aren't saying," he responded, gesturing with his head toward the TV in the corner. "Looks like a car bomb to me."

He would have known. Both young men had spent their childhood in Lebanon, dodging the bullets and car bombs of a bloody civil war.

"Maybe it was one of ours. *Insh'allah.*"

If God wills it.

"You shouldn't talk like that," Nasir began, glancing back at his brother. "If the wrong people heard you..."

His older brother snorted, picking up his jacket. "Pick up a case of Mountain Dew at the store when you go, will you? We're almost out."

Ignored. At the very least, it was better than one of Jamal's typical rants.

"What time should I expect you home?"

"Classes until mid-afternoon, then I'll be at the mosque. I don't know, really."

"I should be off the garbage run by five," Nasir nodded, pulling the last saucer from the water and placing it on the rack to dry. He spent his days riding on the back of a garbage truck, a constant reminder that he, unlike his brother, wasn't in the U.S. legally.

If he'd been able to get a student visa…things would have been much different. A lot of things.

He heard the outer door close behind Jamal and sighed. Something was going on at the mosque—had been the last couple months. And his brother was changing, this country had done something to him.

These United States.

Nasir snarled something profane under his breath and washed his hands, grabbing his jacket as he headed for the door himself. It was turning into a cold December in Michigan.

8:13 A.M. Eastern Time
CIA Headquarters
Langley, Virginia

As he passed from one section of the building to the other, Harry displayed his security pass to the guard at the entrance and was waved through without so much as a second glance. Even on this day.

It wasn't to be wondered at. He had spent the last fifteen years of his life working from the building.

Turning the corner, he quickened his pace, footsteps like handclaps against the tile as he hurried down the whitewashed corridors. A death march.

Just another few yards. Despite the slight chill in the building, his hands were damp with perspiration. In all those years, he had never attempted anything like this.

No illusions. He knew how his actions would be perceived. At the door of A-13 he spoke to the security guard standing watch, a man named Kauffman.

"Everything clear?"

Just a nod by way of reply. "Ron told me you were on the way." A tall, muscular man in his late forties, his blond hair now streaked with gray, he'd been a part of Langley's security force for as long as Harry could remember. Ex-military, and no one to be trifled with.

The guard's face softened as he turned to swipe his passcard at the door. "Don't take too long, Harry. She's been through hell this morning."

"I understand," Harry replied with a grim smile of acknowledgement, reaching for the handle of the door.

One thing was certain. When he reemerged, he would be a fugitive…

Gone. It seemed almost impossible to comprehend. That after so long, he could be lost to her once more. A childhood spent longing for his presence, an adolescence feeling the pull of an absent parent. The bittersweet pain of their reunion.

All gone now. All for nothing.

An electronic beep signaled the opening of the door and Carol passed a hand over her eyes, angrily wiping away the tears. Her hand came away streaked with mascara, dissolving in the evidence of her grief.

She no longer cared.

The soundproofed door closed behind Harry with an ominous *click*. He turned, forcing all emotion aside. *Calm.* Become the eye of the storm.

His gaze swept the room, a threat assessment. Two guards were with Carol, both of them armed. Lopez and Hendricks, he realized, recognizing them both.

"Morning," he greeted, a nod to the guards as he crossed the room, moving past them.

Hendricks gave him a tight smile. "Morning, Harry."

"Ron says you need intel on Korsakov," Carol managed, looking up as the NCS team leader moved toward the table where she sat, reaching inside his jacket. "Is he responsible?"

He seemed to hesitate, something unusual there in his eyes. He glanced from her to Lopez, the ranking security officer. "This discussion is well above your clearance, I'm afraid. Can we have the room?"

Lopez inclined his head toward the window covering one wall of the interrogation room. "We'll be on the other side of the glass."

It wasn't the way he had planned it—but plans had to adjust to compensate for a situation that might best be described as "fluid".

"Make sure the mikes are off."

"Roger that." He waited until the door had closed behind them before leaning toward her, his hands on the table. "This isn't about Korsakov—this is about your father. He sent me."

She flinched as if he had struck her, pain glistening in those eyes. "My *father* is dead."

And my friend, he thought...but now wasn't the time. Or the place. "I know," he responded, glancing toward the window, the one-way glass reflecting his own image back at him. "And he believes that you're next. I have to get you out of here."

He had her attention now, a look of disbelief. "We're underneath the CIA Headquarters Building, Harry. Shapiro has given me a protective detail. It doesn't get more secure than this."

"Your father was given the Agency's protection as well." It was a statement as brutal as it was necessary. " 'Evil in high places at Langley', those were his words. We have to run."

She lifted her head to look him in the face, some of her father's defiance glittering in her blue eyes. "No, I don't. The men who killed him are still out there. Finding them…that's what I *have* to do. And that's what I will do."

"Not if they find you first."

8:16 A.M.
NCS Op-Center

The trick to appearing stone-cold sober was not to spend too long in the presence of any one person. Thomas swiped his card at the door, straightening his jacket as he entered the op-center. Time to make this look good.

Harry's workstation was unexpectedly deserted and Thomas hailed a passing Daniel Lasker.

"Harry's down in Interrogation," was the reply. "There's a print-out of possible targets on his desk—said he wanted you to work up mission protocols."

Busy work, Thomas thought, staring at Lasker's retreating back. Working up mission protocols wasn't his job. His job was to execute them.

A chill danced up and down his spine. Was he being sidelined already?

8:18 A.M.
A-13

"So we're done here?" Hendricks asked, re-entering the interrogation room with Lopez right behind him.

Done? Not so you'd notice it—only one thing seemed to matter to her, and it wasn't her own life.

She was her father's daughter, no question of that.

Harry nodded, reaching for the door—his face well-nigh expressionless as he slipped a hand into his jacket. "I believe so, thank you."

And he saw it in her eyes, the sudden knowledge of what he was about to do. Her lips parted, as if to issue a warning.

His hand came back out, the Taser a blur as it swung up to eye level, aimed directly at Hendricks' chest.

Shock and alarm on the face of his target and he squeezed the trigger, sending a pair of electrodes lancing in slow-motion through the air.

The guard cried out and fell back, his body twitching as he slid to the floor.

Distantly, as if in a nightmare, he heard a woman scream. Recognized Carol's voice. Pushed it aside.

Lopez already had a hand on his weapon, his Beretta half-way out of its holster as he reacted, surprise filling his features.

The electrodes bit into his chest in mid-draw, stopping him cold. His body shook as though in the grip of a seizure and he crumpled to the floor, his head striking the edge of the table as he fell.

He turned to face her, the Taser leveled in his outstretched hand. She was staring at him in disbelief, her mouth open in shock. "Your father and I...saw a lot of hard times over the years, and I have no intention of failing him now. I owe him that much. Now how hard do you want to make this?"

The implication of his words was clear. Time was running out—no more games.

Without a word, she reached for the handbag on the table and slung it over her shoulder, her decision apparently made. A defiant tear trickled down across her cheek as she reached up, brushing back a strand of hair. "Then...we run."

That would work.

"Follow my lead," Harry admonished, moving quickly toward the soundproofed door. He could hear her footsteps behind him.

It swung open under his hand and he glimpsed Kauffman in the corridor outside. The older man started to turn, eyes widening as he saw the stun gun in Harry's hand.

There was no time to react, no time to shout a warning up the corridor, as Harry jammed the Taser into the man's ribs. Pulled the trigger.

Kauffman went limp and Harry wrapped an arm around his waist, lowering him gently to the floor. They'd gone back a long way.

But all that...was past now. The die had been cast and he was a fugitive. A *traitor.*

No time to think about that. He threw the empty Taser back into the interrogation room and motioned for Carol to grasp one of Kauffman's arms as he lifted the man's body. "Come on, come on. We've got to hurry."

8:22 A.M.
The scene of the bombing

The smell of burning flesh. It was the kind of smell one never quite got used to, the way it lingered in the air even after the bodies had been removed. A smell you could never forget.

It had been years, Vic Caruso thought, kneeling by the twisted scrap metal that had once been part of the Toyota's doorframe. Years, and yet it all came pouring back, like flood waters through a broken dam.

The FBI special agent closed his eyes, as though that alone would force the memories away.

The deserts of Iraq. Convoys running north to Mosul. Homemade IEDs, just like this one. Explosions.

He'd been a younger man then, a freshly-minted Army lieutenant. Learning a hard lesson. In the end, all the money in the world didn't matter. A million-dollar Tomahawk missile or a grenade tucked inside an empty can of Campbell's soup, you were just as dead.

His fingers were trembling when he rose and he thrust both hands into the pockets of his overcoat. A Sicilian by ancestry, Caruso had never been given to public displays of nerves.

Flashbacks. "Any thoughts on the driver?" he asked, turning to the tall female agent at his side.

"A Russian," Marika Altmann responded without a trace of hesitation in her voice.

"You're sure?" Due to the placement of the explosives, the driver of the sedan had ended up taking more of the blast than even his intended targets. The condition of his corpse had suffered as a result.

"Of course," she replied casting an irritated glance in his direction. "I grew up in the *Deutsche Demokratische Republik*, remember? I know a Russian when I see one."

She fell silent again, brushing a strand of hair away from her eyes. Hair once golden, now tinged with silver.

Caruso pushed at a mound of the dirty snow with the tip of his wing-tipped shoes. She would know.

Altmann had been seventeen when her family had fled East Germany at the height of the Cold War. Nine years later, she had made her way to the States.

And the rest, as they liked to say, was history. Known in the Bureau for keen insight and an explosive temper, she was a legend among the field agents. A legend, and a terror. Caruso still wasn't sure whether being assigned with her was a compliment...or punishment for botching up his investigation of that CIA field team in September.

It was at that moment that the cellphone in Caruso's pocket began to ring. He answered, listened for a moment, and then turned to his fellow agent. "They want us back at the Hoover Building."

For a moment, he thought the older woman hadn't heard him. She inhaled sharply, as if sniffing the air, and glanced toward the crew of agents sifting through what was left of the interior of the sedan.

"It wasn't just him."

"Excuse me?" Vic demanded.

"It wasn't just the driver. That's not the way they work. There's a team of the Russians. Here in this country..."

Chapter 3

8:26 A.M.
CIA Headquarters
Langley, Virginia

There were five minutes remaining by Harry's watch when they reached the underground parking garage.

Five minutes before the Agency realized something had gone wrong. Five minutes before the lockdown began.

Knowing the caliber of people he worked with, he was surprised it hadn't begun sooner. The caliber of people he *had* worked with, he reminded himself, pushing open the door to the garage.

He heard Carol behind him, fumbling in her purse for her keys.

"We can take my car," she announced, following him out into the open. Her voice held a tense edge, but she had pulled herself together surprisingly well.

He cast a glance back over his shoulder. "Your car has built-in GPS?"

"Yeah, it does…" He heard her voice trail off as the hacker within her recognized the implications.

"We'll take mine," he responded quietly. Hand tucked inside his jacket, grasping his pistol, Harry led the way across the parking garage, stopping beside a nondescript black 1993 Oldsmobile Cutlass Ciera.

"Your car?" Carol asked, going to the passenger side of the vehicle.

Harry nodded, holding up a hand for her to stop. The parking garage was supposed to be secure, *supposed* being the operative word. He never entered the car without doing a check for explosives, and now was no different, despite the need for haste.

All the hurry in the world wouldn't help them if there was a bomb in the undercarriage of the Cutlass...

8:35 A.M.
NCS Operations Center

"Right, Ethan, I'll get right on it." Daniel Lasker replaced the phone on his desk and shot a glance of exasperation over at Carter.

"Not sure when I became part of the Security Directorate."

"What's going on?"

"Surveillance cameras have gone on the fritz down in Interrogation and they want to know if I can straighten it out from here," Lasker sighed. "Like they can't send a man down themselves."

Ron looked up from his workstation, a weary grin crossing his face. "That's what comes from getting a reputation as a techhead around this place."

"No," Lasker replied, typing a command into his terminal. "That's what comes from dating his sister. Ethan's been asking favors ever since he introduced me."

"She worth it?"

A sly grin played at the corners of Lasker's mouth. "Gentlemen don't kiss and tell, Ron."

"Gentlemen...what does that have to do with you?"

The younger man started to laugh, a retort on his lips. Then the screens came flashing across his terminal and the laughter died. "What on earth?"

Hearing the change in the comm chief's voice, Carter gave himself a push, sending his office chair gliding over the smooth tile of the op-center to Lasker's side.

It wasn't so much what the camera was showing, but what it wasn't. There was no guard in the corridor outside A-13. Deserted.

Switching to the camera inside the interrogation room revealed nothing, just the weave of a jacket that had been hung over the lens.

Carter reached for the phone without hesitation. "I need Security to Interrogation A-13 ASAP. Lock down the building."

8:36 A.M.

It was standard protocol. He knew that. Still, it seemed as though the guard took an unnaturally long time looking over their identification.

The pistol seemed to tremble under Harry's jacket. He didn't want to fire on a fellow agent, but his *wishes* were secondary. The mission came first.

"Everything seems to be in order, sir," the guard announced finally, reaching for a lever beside him to open the barrier.

Harry shot Carol a tight-lipped smile as he accelerated gently forward

"How long do you give them?" she asked, looking out the window.

"Not long. The alert's probably going out as we speak. Once we get off-campus, we're out of their jurisdiction, so they'll have to mobilize local law enforcement. Another delay. Maybe ten, fifteen minutes."

Carol turned to look at him, and he saw her father's determination written there in her eyes. "Are you sure that will stop them?"

"It wouldn't have stopped your father," he replied quietly. "But Shapiro's in charge now. And Shapiro does things by the book. He'll send out an APB and shift the responsibility."

Carol went silent for a long moment. "Do you have a plan?"

"The germ of one. Open the glove compartment and take out what you find."

She hesitated, and he could feel her eyes on him. He tapped the brakes, flicking on the turn signal as they neared the highway. Their greatest safety lay in blending in with the westbound traffic. You never win a car chase except in the movies. And this wasn't Hollywood.

He heard the glove compartment open and glanced over to see Carol withdraw a holstered semiautomatic.

"It's a Kahr PM-45," he announced without preamble. "Subcompact semiautomatic, striker-fired. Chambered in .45 ACP, you've got five shots. You know how to use one?"

"Yes," she replied, a trace of irritation creeping into her voice. "I spent five months at Thunder Ranch when I was twenty."

That was the good news, he thought, processing the information as he checked the rear-view mirror.

Thunder Ranch had always been among the top firearms training schools in the country, and Clint Smith's instructors weren't paper punchers. They were focused on the real-world. Still...

Their tail was still clean, so far as he could see. He spotted an opening and changed lanes, speeding up until they were nestled in the shadow of a tractor-trailer. "Ever killed a man?" he asked bluntly, glancing over to catch her reaction.

There wasn't one. Carol looked down at the pistol in her hands and shook her head.

"Then pray to God you never have to..."

8:43 A.M.
Annapolis, Maryland

One hundred meters from the marina in Annapolis, the sea breeze suddenly seemed twenty degrees cooler, a chill rippling through Sergei Korsakov's body. It couldn't be.

"No," he responded bluntly, speaking into the encrypted satellite phone pressed against his ear. "That's impossible."

"I tell you, that is the report on my desk. You missed him."

"They're lying," Korsakov spat, adding several Russian curses for emphasis. He closed his eyes once again, envisioning the scene the way it had looked through the windshield of the Durango. The fiery explosion, metal flying like shrapnel through the cold winter air. This operation had been planned for weeks, everything laid out to the last detail. And he had watched…

"They wouldn't, Sergei," the voice replied, smooth and certain. "Not to me. You know that."

He was right. The former *Spetsnaz* commando swore under his breath, looking left and right down the street. "Why are you calling me?"

"I think you know."

And he did. Korsakov cleared his throat. "I'm not sure you're grasping the scope of the problem. If what you are telling me is true—our friend has gone black. And I'm not going to be able to get another chance at him. Not with the Bureau looking for me. My men and I need to leave the country immediately."

"They're not looking for you, Sergei," the voice replied once more, "and if you'd like it to remain that way, you need to listen very carefully…"

Anger flashed in the Russian's dark eyes. For a long moment he waited, feeling the breeze play with the hem of his coat. Then he licked dry lips and spoke. "Go ahead."

8:50 A.M.
NCS Operations Center
Langley, Virginia

"Would someone mind telling me what exactly is going on?" Kranemeyer bellowed, arriving on the op-center floor like a gust of wind. For a man with one leg, he could still make quite an entrance.

"We got the alert out to Metro PD five minutes ago," Carter responded, looking up from his terminal. "Perimeter security reports that Nichols passed through the outer checkpoint thirteen minutes ago."

"Carol was with him?" Kranemeyer asked, his face darkening.

STEPHEN ENGLAND

"Yes."

The DCS swore under his breath. "What are we supposed to believe—he took her hostage?"

"We've got three security guards in Medical right now. They were tazed and handcuffed. Camera footage in the parking garage shows her getting into the car with him, but God knows. He probably had a gun on her."

"What about her cellphone?" Kranemeyer asked. "There has got to be a way to trace them."

"Her phone went off-line just after they left the campus," Daniel Lasker responded, still focused on his screens. "I have a fix on their last known location. Five hundred meters outside the perimeter. Our only lead is the car. Nichols was driving his Cutlass when he left."

The DCS responded with an oath and a shake of the head. "No good, he'll ditch the car the first chance he gets. That's SOP."

At that moment, the phone in Kranemeyer's pocket began to ring. Lasker's brain registered the ringtone as Jon Bon Jovi's "Wanted Dead or Alive" in the moment before a strange flush spread over the face of the DCS.

"It's him," Kranemeyer hissed in what passed for a stage whisper, pointing a long, thick finger in Carter's direction. "Get on it."

Four rings, and then he answered. "Kranemeyer here."

"Free fall," a familiar voice responded, followed immediately by a sharp *click*, leaving the DCS staring at a dead phone.

"Anything?" he asked, shooting a sharp glance over at Carter.

"No," the analyst responded. "Didn't have enough time. What does 'free fall' mean?"

"It's an Agency distress code," Kranemeyer responded, his face strangely pale.

Danny Lasker typed something into his workstation, then looked up at his boss. "Why haven't I ever heard of it?" he asked, the bewilderment clear in his voice.

"Before your time," Kranemeyer responded, managing what passed for a grim smile. "It dates back to the old Directorate of Operations. I was in Delta back then, tasked out to the Agency for a black op in the West Bank. David Lay was running the op as Station Chief Tel Aviv and Nichols was the Agency's version of boots on the ground. He was little more than a kid then, his second year in the field."

"Then what does he mean by using it now?" This from a baffled Ron Carter.

The DCS shook his head. "No idea."

8:57 A.M.
The highway

"What did you mean?" Carol asked as Harry handed her the TACSAT.

"Take the back off and remove the SIM card," he instructed, ignoring her question. "We'll ditch it and the car."

"How?"

He gestured ahead toward a Wawa's service station and put on his turn signal. "Be ready."

Commuter traffic. The service station was doing a bustling business in the early morning commute, and Harry pulled the Cutlass into one of the few empty parking spaces. "Put that pistol under your jacket," he instructed, shooting a glance in her direction. "And stay close."

The icy morning air nearly took Harry's breath away as he swung his legs out of the car. Motioning for Carol to follow, he strode across the lot toward the cars parked directly in front of the Wawa's.

His gaze swept the eaves of the building as he moved in, checking for security cameras. At a glance it appeared as though the service station had none. Probably just one inside to film any possible robberies.

That made life easier. Three cars from the door he spotted a late-model Chevy Impala, exhaust spewing from the tailpipe as it sat there, idling.

A grim smile crossed Harry's face. He'd never understand people who left their car running while they went in to get coffee. "We'll take this one," he announced, reaching out and pulling the door open.

"You're going to steal a car?"

He turned to see a look of disbelief on Carol's face. The look of someone who had never been in the field.

"Yes," he replied, taking her by the arm and steering her through the open door of the Impala. "Of course."

8:18 A.M. Central Time
The Gulfstream IV
Over Louisiana

"A phone call for you, Mr. Richards." The Texan looked up from his sudoku to see the CIA's version of a flight attendant standing in front of him: 40-ish, overweight, and balding.

Tex took the phone without a word. "Richards here."

"This is Thomas. Listen, we've got a problem." That much was obvious from the voice, Tex thought. It wasn't vintage Parker at all, the calm steady equilibrium that had made him one of the Service's best snipers. This Thomas was distracted, nervous. Agitated.

"I'm listening."

"EAGLE SIX has gone rogue."

"What can you tell me?" Tex asked, glancing forward at the closed cockpit door. "Bear in mind, this isn't a secure line."

"I know, I know. He kidnapped Carol Chambers from Interrogation and made it off-campus before the alarm was sounded."

"That doesn't make any sense," the Texan replied, his mind turning over the possibilities. "Where is he now?"

"We don't know. Metro PD found his car abandoned at a service station about ten miles west of Langley—along with a rather distraught single mother who was trying to report a car theft."

"Standard operating procedure, Thomas," Tex observed. The only question was *why*? "You said ten miles west?"

"Yes," Thomas replied. "You thinking what I'm thinking?"

"Probably. Don't do anything until I get back. See if Kranemeyer will let you pick me up at Dulles. That way we can keep things off the official manifest."

"Right. Goodbye."

Seemingly exhausted by the flow of words, Tex simply clicked the "kill" button on the phone and laid it beside his seat. Outside the window, clouds drifted past the swift business jet, dulcet and white. Peaceful. *What are you doing, Harry?*

9:22 A.M. Eastern Time
A Wal-Mart
Manassas, Virginia

For a man who had grown up in '80s Russia, Wal-Mart was still a vision of almost unimaginable wealth.

And yet no one seemed to appreciate it. That was America for you. Pavel Nevaschkin sighed heavily as he reached down, picking up the motorcycle helmet that hung on the handlebars of the Honda cycle. The December breeze was cold, even through the thick wool lining of his leather jacket. Not as cold as Chechnya, though. Nothing could be that cold.

He'd been in Alfa Group back then, as the new millennium came around, bringing with it nothing but the promise of more violent death. Bad days. Even the *Spetsnaz* weren't paid enough to take those risks.

Pavel checked his saddlebags one last time, making sure the Glock 21 would be ready. Round in the chamber, another pair of full magazines in the pouch clipped beside it.

Everything was in readiness. He cast a glance over at his partner, the shooter, a Muscovite he knew only as Grigori. "Remember the plan?"

The man smiled, displaying teeth that bore testament to the finest of East European dental work—cracked and chipped. "Of course—kill the man, snatch the girl. Should be simple, *da?*"

Pavel shrugged. "*Da.* Just stick to the plan. Sergei said they're about sixteen kilometers ahead, so we should be able to catch up with them readily enough."

The next moment, the engine of his motorcycle sputtered into a full-throated roar, drowning out any further conversation. Pavel threw a leg over the throbbing saddle of the cycle and waved at Grigori to climb on behind him. The job would be done within the hour...

8:31 A.M. Central Time
Dearborn, Michigan

The house was the thirteenth on Nasir Khalidi's route. Certainly his unlucky number. As the garbage truck slowed to a stop, he jumped off, hurrying across packed snow toward the trash cans.

It was the third can. Always the third can. He blew on cold hands as he watched a mechanical arm dump the can into the compactor in the back of the truck. As bad as the cold was, heat in the summer made the job even worse. Then the garbage reeked.

As the can came back down, Nasir unzipped his jacket, shivering as a cold blast of wind came swirling down the street, the multi-story projects on either side forming what amounted to a wind tunnel.

So different from his native Lebanon. Looking both ways down the street to ensure he was not being watched, Nasir reached into the inside pocket of his jacket and pulled out an eight-inch manila envelope. With another furtive glance at the surrounding buildings, he dropped it into the can, wheeling it back toward the sidewalk.

Yes, there were worse jobs than garbage disposal. He should know. He had one of them.

Inside one room of the decrepit tenement, a man looked up from the bank of screens mounted into one side of the wall, watching Nasir Khalidi on the discreetly-placed cameras. He played back the footage in slow-motion, watching as the yellow envelope tumbled into the gray plastic depths of the trash bin. A slow smile crossed his face and he reached for the phone that lay on the console before him, right beside a Beretta. "Status confirmed," he announced when the call was answered. "He's made the drop."

9:47 A.M. Eastern Time
The Impala
Virginia

Silence. Harry stole a glance in Carol's direction as the car sped south. She hadn't spoken a word since they'd "switched" cars at the service station. Just sat there, staring away from him, out the window. A cold blonde statue.

He sighed, watching the needle on the gas gauge waver with every dip in the road. They had a quarter-tank, enough to get them where they were going.

"You don't approve of my methods, do you?" he asked finally, breaking the silence between them.

A long pause, and then she looked across at him. The emotion of loss was still there in her eyes, but so was an unexpected resilience. "Theft? No."

"What do you think I do for a living?" Harry asked. "I break the law. It's what I'm trained to do."

"Not *our* country's law," she replied, an edge creeping into her voice. "We all know that's where that line is drawn—it's the first thing they teach at the Farm."

"And like a lot of things they teach in a classroom, it becomes irrelevant once you leave those walls." Harry's eyes narrowed as he glanced in the rear-view mirror. The CIA's training facility at Camp Peary—the Farm, as it was called—was good, but there were so many things you just couldn't teach.

There was a motorcycle in back of them, two vehicles back as they moved through the small township. "The first time you go out on protective detail, you realize life's a lot simpler. And there's only one law that really matters: protect your principal. Do whatever it takes to keep them alive."

Carol looked over at him. "It didn't even do us any good. Just exchanged one hot car for another."

"Not quite," Harry observed, taking another look into his rear-view. "It bought us some time and a car we could be sure wasn't bugged. Couldn't say that about mine. Not in the time I had."

"How long has that motorcycle been following us?" she asked, abruptly changing the subject.

Well done. She hadn't forgotten *all* her fieldcraft from the Farm, Harry thought, accelerating to pass a slow-moving truck. Desk types often did. "Too long," was his only reply.

There were two men on the cycle. Unbidden, his mind flickered back to an operation in Italy, just a few years before. Different climate, different time. The same sight. Following years of political assassinations, the Italian government had banned motorcycles from carrying a passenger.

Not that the law had mattered to the Tunisian assassins that had attacked the motorcade of the American ambassador—with the CIA's chief of station, James Holbrook, caught in the cross-fire. Not that it mattered now. This wasn't Italy.

The distance had closed now. "The police?" Carol asked, her voice striking his ears as though from afar.

He shook his head, focusing on the threat at hand. "No, it's not the cops. And they're way too aggressive for a tail."

"Then why are they following us?" The tone of her voice told him she already knew.

"Ever been shot at?" he asked, cutting in front of a tractor-trailer. The urge to floor the accelerator nagged at him, but he fought the impulse. *Not yet.*

"No." Harry looked over to see her reach inside her purse for the Kahr. Her face was pale, but he glimpsed a flash of determination in her eyes as her hand closed around the semiautomatic. Her father's daughter.

The cold air flowed fast around Pavel Nevaschkin's body as he bent low over the motorcycle, accelerating rapidly down the highway. Their target was in full evasion mode now. They had been spotted. All that remained now was to go in for the kill.

He heard the squeal of airbrakes as they swung in front of a tractor-trailer, chasing down their prey. In so many ways, their task was made easier by the fact that their target was driving a stolen car. With his own vehicle, they would have had to factor in the possibility of armor. That was no longer in the equation.

Taking one hand off the handlebar, Pavel reached back and tapped his partner on the knee. *Be ready.*

Harry stole another glance in the mirror. The motorcycle was closing fast now. No question about it. They weren't the cops. And they hadn't been sent to tail Carol. They were a kill squad. "Put it away," he instructed, motioning toward the Kahr in her hand.

No matter how the movies portrayed it, shooting at a combat-trained biker was more a matter of luck than skill.

And they had no time for luck. Not now.

The motorcycle appeared in his driver's side mirror now, angling for a side shot. At him.

He was the target? He pondered the question for a moment, then dismissed it out of hand. It didn't matter. Not now.

The assassins hadn't opened fire yet. That alone bothered him more. These guys were pros.

He swung the car toward the median, crossing two lanes of traffic in the space of a heartbeat. Harry winced as a car slammed on its brakes behind him, only to immediately be rear-ended by an SUV.

Nothing matters. Nothing except the life of the principal.

The motorcycle was still coming, faster now as it wound its way through the chaos behind them, but now he was tight against the median and his left flank was secure. The Suzuki was designed for speed, not off-road traction.

"Get down," he ordered, never taking his eyes off the road, "and get ready."

With the Impala speeding tight up the side of the median, the only side the kill team could approach from was Carol's. Hollowpoint slugs could punch straight through the plastic body of the car, but if they were going to fire blindly, he reasoned, they would have already started.

At times you could even use people's very professionalism against them.

"They're going to come up on your side," he declared, speaking slowly, calmly. Nothing was so serious that it couldn't be made worse by miscommunication. "And they're going to come up shooting."

From her position on the floorboards, Carol nodded, her lips pressed into a thin, bloodless line. "At my signal, I need you to push your door open, as hard and fast as you can. Can you do it?"

Another nod. To her credit, she didn't ask for an explanation. They were running out of time…

A curse exploded from Pavel's lips as the car slid back tight to the median, forcing him to throttle back or risk a collision. He didn't dare lose time taking the Suzuki onto the turf.

There was only one option left to them. Go up the passenger side. He tapped Grigori's knee twice. *Going in.*

He couldn't hear the Glock slide out of the saddlebags behind him, but he knew it was there, in his partner's hand.

There: the man they had been sent to kill was behind the wheel, still relatively upright in his seat. The girl was nowhere to be seen, but undoubtedly she had taken cover. No matter.

Pavel gunned the cycle, coming directly alongside the Impala. Time to end this.

The roar of the Glock struck Harry's ears almost simultaneously with the sound of shattering glass. He heard the bullet whine past his ear, exiting through the driver's side window by his head.

Time itself seemed to slow down as he glanced right, assuring himself one more time. All he saw was the cold black muzzle of the Glock staring back at him.

"*Now!*"

Pavel was steadying the bike, moving in closer so that his partner could get a better shot, when suddenly the door of the sedan flew outward, slamming against his left knee.

The handlebars of the cycle twisted in his grip as the bike flew off course and off balance. Nearly blinded by pain, the ex-*Spetsnaz* paramilitary fought to regain control of the bike as it slid across two lanes of traffic. He saw the SUV in just enough time to scream…

"You all right?" Harry asked, looking down to where Carol sat on the floorboards, the doorhandle still in her hand. He'd brought the Impala to a stop, pulled off to the side of the median.

She nodded, seeming dazed by what had just occurred. He unbuckled his seatbelt and reached out a hand. "Come on, come on. We have to go."

The Chevy Tahoe that had struck the assassins' motorcycle had stopped by the side of the road. Traffic was starting to back up. With a backward glance to make sure Carol was following, Harry strode purposefully across the highway, alert for further danger. The Colt was in his right hand, ready for use.

The driver of the Tahoe, a heavy-set, middle-aged woman, was already out of the vehicle, sobbing hysterically into her cellphone.

"…they just came out of nowhere. I didn't have time to—dear God, they may be dead."

"Ma'am," Harry began, coming 'round the front of the Tahoe, "I need you to shut off the phone."

Her eyes widened at the sight of the pistol gripped firmly in his hand and she started to speak to the 911 dispatcher on the other end of the line. With one smooth motion, Harry snatched the phone from her and flung it across the road.

"What are you doing?" he heard Carol ask, but he ignored her, focusing in on the terrified woman before him. She was alone, he realized, scanning the seats of the SUV.

"Ma'am, I'm a federal officer," Harry continued, flipping open his wallet. The CIA identification card wasn't as flashy as an FBI badge, but most people never noticed. "I need your vehicle."

"What's going on?" she asked, her hand over her mouth. She kept backing away from him, fear clearly written in her eyes. "Who were those people?"

"Trust me when I say you don't want to know. Keys?"

She shot a frightened look from his face to Carol's and back again. "They're in the ignition."

"Good. Now, you can go with emergency services when they arrive. In the mean time, please stand back." He gestured to Carol. "Go ahead and get in."

"Where are you going?" he heard Carol's voice ask. Harry pulled a thin metal cylinder from the pocket of his jacket and screwed it into the threaded muzzle of the Colt. "Unfinished business."

9:02 A.M. Central Time
Dan Ryan Expressway
Chicago, Illinois

Sometimes the hardest thing to remember about America was that the police actually needed a *reason* to stop you.

Tarik Abdul Muhammad folded his hands, staring intently out the backseat window of the SUV at the flowing mass of traffic. It was in the interests of not giving them such a reason that he had requested a local driver.

Even a black man was better for this task than the men he had brought with him across the U.S.-Mexico border. His own Pakistanis, though they were fierce fighters and willing to die for the cause of God, viewed driving as the ultimate test of their virility. A no-holds barred competition.

It might have served them well in Peshawar, but in the more "civilized" driving environment of the United States, they wouldn't have lasted five minutes.

America. He leaned back in his seat, the memories flooding through his mind. The closest he had ever come to this country was Cuba. The imperialist military base overlooking the Bay of Guantanamo. Gazing out from behind the wire.

He reached forward and tapped the negro on the shoulder. "How long before we reach Dearborn?"

He had learned his English there on that desolate rock in Cuba. It was good but not fluent.

"Hey, man, it all depends on the traffic," the black man responded. "You want to be at the mosque by afternoon, right?"

Tarik nodded. "That would be best."

"Then I'll get you there, brother."

Brother. Tarik returned his focus to the traffic outside the window. Perhaps...

10:03 A.M.
The highway
Virginia

The shooter was dead, his neck snapped by the force of the impact. He'd probably never seen it coming.

Harry rose from where the assassin lay like a broken doll on the asphalt and turned toward his partner.

The driver had been thrown clear of the Suzuki and lay roughly fifteen feet away. He was moaning, his helmet ripped half off to reveal a distinctly Slavic face. His right leg was twisted below the knee, sticking out at right angles from his body.

"Who sent you?" Harry asked in Russian, dropping to one knee beside the driver.

The man's cough was the only response, blood flecking the pavement. Defiance glinted in his eyes. Harry sighed, looking around him. Traffic was stopping. The police would arrive within minutes.

And he was a wanted man himself. After a moment's pause he reached down, applying pressure to the Russian's injured leg and twisting it sideways.

"I want a name," Harry whispered, his lips only inches away from the prostrate man's ear. "Just a name and the pain will stop."

Sweat streamed down the Russian's face, drops of perspiration crystallizing in the cold winter's air. His face was twisted in agony, but his mouth never opened, teeth grinding together.

"A name, that's all. Who sent you to kill me?"

Still silence, not even a moan escaping the driver's lips. Another moment passed, then Harry released his pressure on the leg and stood.

"Have it your way," Harry announced, checking the chamber of his 1911 as if to make sure it was loaded. "I'll have you deliver a message to Sergei Ivanovich."

And he saw it, there in the final moment just before he put the suppressor of the Colt between the Russian's eyes and squeezed the trigger. The recognition. The realization of having died for nothing.

Korsakov was behind the hits.

10:06 A.M.
CIA Headquarters
Langley, Virginia

"We're moving strike teams into place—all we need is your signature on the authorization," Kranemeyer announced, laying a folder on Shapiro's desk.

The DD(I) put on his glasses and opened the dossier, scrutinizing the files. "This doesn't just need my signature, Barney. An operation of this nature needs the President to issue cross-border authority."

"I'm aware of standard protocols, director," Kranemeyer replied, leaning forward until his palms rested on the smooth glass of Shapiro's desktop. "The fact remains that the President is in Paris for the G-8 summit. His attention is currently divided between the precarious financial state of the EU and the latest argument made on the behalf of his campaign before the Supreme Court."

"Your point, Barney?"

Kranemeyer let out a long sigh. "My point is that if the DCIA has been compromised, we have only hours to act. The President isn't going to make the decision fast enough, not with everything else he's got on his plate."

Shapiro seemed to consider the argument for a long moment, then he closed the dossier. "I'll consider it, Barney. I've got a teleconference with Director Haskel and the Bureau in five. Would you care to join me?"

10:07 A.M.
The highway
Virginia

"You killed him." It was more of a statement than a question, but there was doubt in the voice.

Harry looked over, his eyes meeting with Carol's. Her face was ashen pale, her eyes regarding him as though she was seeing him for the first time.

"You shouldn't have watched," he responded, turning his attention back to the road as the Tahoe continued to speed toward Culpeper. "It's never pretty."

"*Pretty?*" she asked in disbelief, her voice trembling. "How did you get to be so cold? For God's sake, Harry…you blew his brains out."

"That's not important right now," he retorted, his words clipped. He couldn't allow himself to think about it. Too many variables still in play.

"What's important is how they found us," Harry continued without giving her time to think about it. "They were on top of us way too fast. Is there anything you have on you frequently?"

His question seemed to jar Carol from her thoughts. "What?"

"Shoes, a purse, anything—something they could roll the dice on you wearing."

The light of realization spread across her face. "I don't know—not really."

"Think," Harry urged. "Ten to one you're wearing a tracker."

He glanced over, his gaze sweeping her body from the tip of her shoes to her head. "Those earrings look familiar."

"They were my mother's," she responded, her tone defensive.

"And you wear them nearly every day, don't you?"

10:12 A.M.
CIA Headquarters
Langley, Virginia

The teleconference room was not overly warm, Kranemeyer realized as he took his seat to one side of the table. President Hancock may not have yet responded to the economic situation by wearing a sweater in the grand tradition of Jimmy Carter, but it seemed that other governmental employees were expected to.

"Director Haskel," Michael Shapiro began, initiating the conference, "I'm here with the Director of the Clandestine Service, Bernard Kranemeyer, along with his head analyst, Ron Carter. Go ahead."

"Thanks, Mike," Eric Haskel responded over the video uplink, "I'm sure you gentlemen are very busy, so I'll keep this brief. In short, we have identified the driver of the sedan that crashed into Director Lay's SUV this morning, and our findings seem to rule out the Russian Mafia connection which was initially suggested by your people."

A file photo came flashing up on screen as the FBI director continued to narrate. "Michael Fedorenko, a naturalized US citizen, formerly Mikhail Fedorenko of the USSR. Forty-five years of age, he came to this country following the fall of the Soviet Union. A former demolitions specialist in the Red Army, Fedorenko made considerable money in construction through the late '90s, most of it coming from private development in northern Virginia."

More files came across the screen, mostly financial reports. "Then the economic crisis struck in 2008 and his construction company went down the tubes. Out of work and running low on funds, Fedorenko seems to have become increasingly disenchanted with his lot in this country. In the spring of 2009 he became affiliated with a TEA Party group in the Alexandria area, and launched an unsuccessful bid for county supervisor."

Shapiro nodded. "And how did this man go from TEA Party candidate to bomber?"

"We're investigating the connection," Haskel replied, his voice tight. "We're also investigating any possible connection between Fedorenko and your rogue agent. This is what is clear."

More images on the screen, this time showing a SWAT team executing an assault. "Thirty minutes ago, I authorized a SWAT team to search Fedorenko's farm outside Manassas. The farm was deserted, but in the barn they found blasting caps, dynamite and three hundred pounds of ammonium nitrate."

Shapiro blinked, adjusting his glasses as he refocused on the screen. "Any electronic records?"

At that moment, Ron Carter's phone went off with the annoying jangle of an incoming text.

Kranemeyer shot him a dark look of disapproval.

"That's a negative," Haskel replied, not seeming to notice the disruption. "Following his connection with the TEA Party, Fedorenko seemed to have become obsessed with the notion of going 'off-grid'. It appears that he didn't own so much as a cellphone."

"Except for the one that was used to detonate the bomb," Kranemeyer interjected.

"That's correct, probably one purchased for the purpose. It seems to have been a small operation—I am optimistic that, providing he is still alive, we'll find both Lay and his daughter very shortly."

Carter looked up from his phone. "I don't know if I share your optimism, director. I was just notified by a source that Virginia state troopers responded in the last ten minutes to a double homicide on Route 211 near Warrenton. Both victims appear to be Russian. Perhaps we should reexamine that *mafiya* connection."

10:31 A.M.
Culpeper, Virginia

Harry had always liked farms. Rural, out of the way places. Minimum people, maximum line of sight. Fewer people to ask questions, less collateral damage if things went south.

The only downside was, what people there were all knew each other.

Which was why the safehouse was located well off the road, a long driveway shielded by eighty-year-old pines.

Harry pushed open his door and stepped out of the idling Tahoe, his eyes scanning the surrounding territory as he moved to the newspaper tube that stood there by the entrance to the drive.

There was nothing in the tube. That was to be expected—they had never subscribed to a paper. He allowed his hand to drag across the side of the tube and then climbed back into the SUV.

"What's with the chalk?" he heard Carol ask. He allowed himself a grim smile, glancing back at the thin line of yellow chalk across the side of the newspaper tube. She may never have been in the field, but she didn't miss much.

"It's for the caretaker," he explained, putting the Tahoe in drive. "So he knows not to come home."

The pearl earrings lay on the dashboard, smashed into a thousand pieces by the butt of Harry's Colt. The GPS tracker that had been embedded in the left earring was still headed south, in the saddlebags of a Harley Davidson where Harry had dumped it when they had stopped at a gas station.

The biker had looked capable of taking care of himself.

"I'm sorry they had to be destroyed," Harry said gently as the SUV continued down the drive.

She didn't look at him. "Don't be," she responded, her voice infused with an artificial calm. "There wasn't any other way. Sometimes even memories have to die…"

10:39 A.M.
CIA Headquarters
Langley, Virginia

Free Fall. The DCS closed the door to his office, reflecting once more upon Nichols' final words.

There was a message there, of that he was certain. Despite his statement to Carter and Lasker, *Free Fall* was more than just a distress code. *That* code had been used.

Phantom pain shot through Kranemeyer's nonexistent right leg as he limped to his desk.

There was a photo on the desk, of him in the Chesapeake 5K. Running for charity just nine months ago. Oh, well…that was nine months ago. Before his own world had been turned upside down by the defection of an agent.

The DCS gritted his teeth against pain as he lowered himself into the desk chair. On this day, he couldn't have run a 5K to save his own life.

Quite possibly the worse thing about a traitor like Hamid Zakiri was that their defection caused you to start seeing traitors in every shadow. Paranoia was an important skillset for any spook—the trick was to keep it from pulling you over the edge. Devilishly hard.

Kranemeyer buried his head in his hands, striving to remember. There was something there, an elusive memory from the past. But Nichols wasn't a traitor.

He pulled his cellphone from his pocket and gazed at it a moment in contemplation before dialing in a number.

"Marcia," he began when the line was picked up, "I need you to retrieve a dossier from Archives. I want everything we have on a CIA black-op run in the West Bank in 2000. Operation RUMBLEWAY, to be exact. Yes, Marcia, I know it's eyes-only access. That's why I'm asking…"

10:41 A.M.
The safehouse
Culpeper, Virginia

"You'll have to forgive the interior decorator." Standing in the entrance hall of the safehouse, Harry motioned toward the faded wallpaper and chipped paint. "We don't do a lot of entertaining."

Carol shook her head. The safehouse was a small rancher, built in a style dating back to the '50s. Which was probably the last time it had been decorated.

"Who owns this place?" she asked, looking around. "Langley?"

Harry cleared his throat. "Not exactly. We do, actually."

"Your strike team?"

"Yeah,," he replied, unzipping his jacket as he moved into the next room. The Colt remained holstered, only inches away from his fingers. "We just moved in, actually…had to move the safehouse after—well, after Zakiri."

Even now, he felt his chest tighten painfully at the mention of the name, anger and hatred boiling deep inside him. At the betrayal.

At a dead man.

"Why run your own safehouse?"

"Because of days like today," he replied, grateful for her question. The distraction. "Have a plan for every contingency—isn't that what they tell you in training?"

A nod.

"This was our plan for the contingency of our own government being unable to protect us—or coming after us itself," Harry continued, checking his watch. "We'll be here two hours, no longer."

She turned to face him, surprise written in her eyes. "We're not staying?"

"No. This was never designed as a permanent refuge, just a place to store supplies. I'm headed out to the barn to fuel up our new vehicle," he said, his hand on the door. "Get a shower."

"Why?"

"Might be your last chance in awhile. And I'm going to need to search your clothes for any more trackers. You'd probably find it more comfortable if you weren't in them."

10:52 A.M.
U.S. Route 211
Virginia

The bodies had been taken away, but the police remained, flashing lights filling the highway as far as the eye could see, the wail of sirens piercing the chill morning air. Chalk outlines marked the positions of the bodies on the freezing asphalt, the agents in FBI overcoats standing over them caught up in a futile endeavor to stay warm.

Sergei Korsakov stayed at a distance, losing himself in the crowd that had gathered despite the attempts of the Virginia State Police to keep them back. It wasn't every day that a double homicide happened in this part of Virginia.

The CIA officer hadn't been part of the plan—their intel had been flawed. Fatally so. Everything had pointed toward the man accompanying Carol Chambers having just been a friend. Another analyst. A desk jockey.

Korsakov looked down at the CIA dossier, scrolling across the screen of his PDA. *Harold Nichols.*

Desk jockey? Right.

The former *Spetsnaz* sergeant rubbed a hand through his two-day-old beard. *Know thine enemy.*

If he had known, he would have never sent a two-man team after Chambers, not even with a man as good as Pavel Nevaschkin heading it.

Korsakov turned away, sighing heavily as he made his way toward his SUV. It had been the early winter of 1997, a dark night in Dagestan when he and Pavel had met, both of them part of a *Spetsnaz* team assigned to a tank base at Buinask.

Led by foreign *mujahideen,* the Chechens had struck without warning, small-arms fire and RPGs coming through the wire.

He'd lost friends that night—would have died himself, if not for Pavel coming to his aid when his AK-74 jammed.

He closed his eyes for a brief moment, feeling once again the ice-cold fear of those hours. And now Pavel was dead.

Korsakov put out a hand and pulled open the door of the rented SUV. The hit on David Lay had started out as business, pure and simple, but he had read Nichols' message clear in the bullet hole between his friend's eyes.

Now this was personal. It was war. And it would only end in death.

11:03 A.M.
CIA Headquarters
Langley, Virginia

"The Bureau just sent over the pictures of the two dead men found on Route 211," Daniel Lasker announced as Ron Carter walked by his workstation.

"Just in time for lunch," was Carter's sardonic response. "Run them through the database and send the results to my terminal. There you are, Ames, just looking for you."

A young man at the espresso machine looked up at Carter's hail. At twenty-two, Luke Ames was one of the youngest analysts on the NCS staff, and arguably one of the best-looking—at least among the men. He was also new, having been brought into the fold only days before the Iranian crisis of September.

"Catch," Ron warned, tossing a set of keys underhand across the op-center.

Luke smiled easily, holding his espresso in one hand while plucking the keys out of mid-air with the other.

"Real simple job, Ames," Carter continued, forcing a tone of light banter into his voice. Anything to distract himself from what the morning had become. "I need you to go down to the parking garage and open up Chambers' car so that the boys from the Security Directorate can work their magic. A job even a batboy can handle."

"Right." He'd been in the NCS long enough to know that being the new guy meant being the go-fer. As he swiped his access card to leave the op-center, he tossed one back over his shoulder, "Just for the record, Ron, I was an outfielder, not a batboy. Not that you'd know the difference."

Lasker watched him go. "Gotta say, the kid's got potential."

Ron looked over at his comm chief and couldn't suppress a smile. Coming from the cherub-faced Lasker, that was quite a statement. "Yeah, you're right. Now where were we?"

"Dead Russians."

"I knew it was somewhere pleasant."

11:16 A.M.
The safehouse
Culpeper, Virginia

The shower was probably as old as the house itself, a shade of avocado green roughly the color of vomit. He hadn't been kidding about the decorator.

But the water was hot. Carol leaned back against the tiles and closed her eyes, letting the water wash over her body, steam billowing from the shower stall to fill the bathroom.

Four hours.

It seemed impossible that one's world could change so drastically in such a short time. Yet it had.

She turned off the water and stumbled out of the shower, brushing wet strands of golden hair away from her eyes. A man's housecoat hung from the peg on the back of the door and Carol wrapped it about her body, noticing absently that it came to her ankles.

A man's housecoat. A tall man. Like her father. She glanced into the foggy mirror, barely recognizing the shadowy silhouette as her own.

Four hours.

She could still remember the sound of his voice when he had called the previous night. He'd just called to check on her, so he said. He'd been doing that a lot lately, ever since shortly after the Jerusalem op.

He had known. The realization came washing back over her with the strength of a flood tide. He had known.

And now he was dead. Or, perhaps worse, taken hostage. She'd worked at Langley long enough to understand the ramifications of that.

Gone, either way. She caught herself with a start, realizing that the tears would not come, the sorrow of those first few hours having been replaced by a brittle, equally terrifying calm.

Carol took a deep breath and turned the doorknob, letting herself and a blast of hot, moist air into the adjoining bedroom.

If she'd expected to be alone...Nichols stood by the side of the bed, busy loading ammunition into the rifle magazines strewn over the sheets. Her clothes were neatly folded and laid across from him, her top and skirt in one pile, her underwear in another.

She felt a hot flush creep across her face and almost reflexively tightened the sash of the housecoat. Couldn't he have gone elsewhere?

"I'll be out of here momentarily," he announced, as though reading her mind. "You're clean."

"Oh," Carol responded, realizing a moment later that he was referring to GPS trackers. Of course.

He looked up. "I'd wait to get dressed. At least until I cut your hair."

"Give me a moment," she responded, still unsure of herself. It all felt so strange.

"Of course." Harry laid the AK-47 back in its polymer carrying case, along with five fully loaded magazines. One hundred and fifty rounds of brass-jacketed 7.62mm—enough to start a small war.

Or end one.

He closed the case and hefted it on his back, closing the door behind him as he made his way out to the waiting SUV. There was no way of knowing how much time they actually had.

11:18 A.M.
CIA Headquarters
Langley, Virginia

There were already five officers from the Security Directorate surrounding the car when Luke Ames arrived, accompanied by a German Shepherd dispatched by their K-9 unit.

Chamber's car was a light-blue Toyota Camry, a four-door sedan.

The agent in charge of the security detail glanced over Ames' credentials as he advanced toward the vehicle. "Everything's in order, sir. Our preliminary scan isn't picking up any explosives."

The young analyst just nodded, his mind elsewhere. That Carol could be gone—it seemed unimaginable. She'd been the one that had shown him around the headquarters building his first day on the job, and they'd developed a close friendship over the last couple months. Never had gotten quite to the point of asking her out, but...

And now the DCIA was dead. And she'd been kidnapped. By one of their own.

Ames punched the Unlock button on the remote as he moved toward the car. Nothing.

Well, hey, batteries died all the time. Without a second thought, he slid the key into the lock and turned it.

As the key turned, it activated the triggering mechanism that had been built into the car's door earlier that morning by "Alex Hall".

Seconds later, the electrical pulse reached the two pounds of Semtex inlaid between the panels of the door. Luke Ames never felt what happened next.

He never felt anything ever again…

11:31 A.M.
The safehouse
Culpeper, Virginia

As he'd told Carol, CIA field officers were trained to prepare for every contingency. That didn't mean you actually expected the day to come.

Harry placed the third long gun case under the false floor of the massive Ford Excursion, the one containing his Heckler & Koch UMP-45 submachine gun. It was a duplicate of the gun he had carried into Jerusalem, the gun that had mortally wounded Hamid Zakiri.

It was also illegal for private ownership, but that hadn't stopped him yet. The same with the eight "flash-bang" stun grenades in the mesh bag nestled beside the gun case containing his Mossberg 500.

He stood there for a long moment, mentally reviewing the list of supplies, a list he had memorized so many times. The day was here.

Finally satisfied, Harry replaced the false floor and walked back into the house. The bedroom door was closed, and he was starting to turn away when he heard low voices.

"Carol?" he asked, a sudden alarm filling his heart. Nothing.

One hand on the door and the other on his Colt, he tested the knob. Unlocked.

"Carol?" Still nothing. Just the voices. The Colt slid from the polished leather of its paddle holster and he turned the knob, throwing open the door and entering with the gun leveled.

Carol was sitting on the bed, her knees pulled up to her chin, her eyes focused on the TV screen across the room. "…correspondent Roger Ginsburg and we're here in front of the CIA's Langley campus, where initial reports indicate a bomb went off just over ten minutes ago. Emergency vehicles have flooded the scene and there are reports of fatalities—but we've not been able to obtain details from the Agency…"

Harry holstered his weapon and walked to Carol's side, his hand brushing gently against her shoulder. Her eyes were glistening with tears.

"You're going to be okay," he said, gently kneading her shoulder with his hand as he sat down on the bed beside her. "It's going to be okay."

She looked up at him and then back at the TV and he could sense that she was on the verge of breaking. "Why is all this happening? Dear God, they said people are dead at Langley."

"We'll know," Harry whispered, drawing her towards him as her body convulsed in dry sobs, holding her close to his chest as the tears fell. "We'll know soon enough."

8:31 A.M. Pacific Time
Law Offices of Snell & Kilmer
Las Vegas, Nevada

Work never seemed to stop at Snell & Kilmer, the young man thought, at least not when you were an attorney still trying to make a name for yourself. And that was hard to do when your current focus was tax law. It hadn't been his dream when he'd moved from Pakistan five long years before…but here he was.

And yet the mood was different this morning as he walked onto their floor of the Hughes Center—his co-workers clustered around a small television. "What's going on?" he asked, setting down his latte on his desk, right beside the small brass plate bearing the words *Samir Khan, Attorney at Law*.

No one seemed to hear him, except for his friend Cathy, standing at the edge of the group, her thumbs moving anxiously over the keyboard of her phone. "They're saying that there's been a pair of bombings in Virginia. And Dave isn't answering his phone."

He glanced from the black woman's eyes to the screen, feeling his breathing quicken as he heard the anchor speak. Could it—could *this* be the beginning? "*Ya Allah,*" he breathed, barely even realizing he had spoken aloud—the Arabic coming easily to his lips. Oh, God.

"What did you say?" Cathy asked, her head coming up from her phone.

He forced a smile, moving back toward his desk. "Nothing, Cathy…it is just such a shock. I pray you can reach your husband."

Powering on his computer, he leaned back in his office chair, staring at his fingernails. It had been so many years…so long that he had almost lost faith. *I seek forgiveness from God…*

Yet there was nothing in the Drafts folder of his e-mail when he opened it, no matter how many times he refreshed the account. As if their time had not yet come.

And as he looked around at his co-workers, as his gaze shifted back to the screen, he found himself wondering if he would be ready when it did. *Insh'allah.*

11:42 A.M.
CIA Headquarters
Langley, Virginia

The corner of the parking garage where Chambers' car had been parked had taken on the appearance of a charnel house.

Five dead. Ames, and four members of the Security team. Another four men, including the K-9 handler, had been taken away in ambulances. One was critical.

Flashing lights cast an eerie reflection against the blood-stained concrete as emergency crews worked to repair one of the support beams of the parking garage.

It was nothing he hadn't seen before. Too many times. A mounting fury grew in Kranemeyer's chest as he surveyed the scene and he fought it back, only too aware that he had to retain control.

Michael Shapiro stood a few feet away, a handkerchief over his lips, his face drained of color. "How could this happen?" he asked, shooting a frightened glance over at his DCS.

"Clearly, we underestimated our opponent," Kranemeyer observed, forcing an icy calm into his voice. He had to clear his mind. At that moment, Ron Carter materialized at his side.

"We lost another on the way to the hospital," the analyst announced. "He bled out before they could stabilize him. And that's not all."

"What?"

Carter hesitated. "Our surveillance cameras place Nichols here in the garage less than twenty minutes before he abducted Chambers."

Kranemeyer swore softly. "Where's Parker?"

"Should be at Dulles. He was due there to collect Richards."

"Place a call and tell him I want them both back here. ASAP."

11:57 A.M.
Dulles International Airport
Virginia

Waiting. Intelligence work was often described as long periods of boredom punctuated by brief moments of sheer terror.

For Thomas, waiting in the terminal at Dulles, it was some combination of the two. He was sober now, stone-cold.

Harry dropping off the CIA's radar had sufficed for that. And now, six dead at Langley itself.

The morning had gone from bad to worse. He found his hands trembling and shoved them deep into the pockets of his coat. Last thing he needed was TSA agents escorting him from the building.

Waiting. Thomas found himself wishing for a smoke. He'd been a cigar man, himself, back in his days on Wall Street, but he'd finally kicked the habit. Didn't really have any choice, not after he had tried and failed to pass the physicals his first time at the Farm.

Still, the craving was there, every now and again. He drew in a deep breath, forcing himself to turn away. As he did, he saw a tall figure walking across the terminal toward him. "Everything ready?"

"Thought you were never going to get here," Thomas said in exasperation.

The Texan's expression never changed. "Word of the attacks is snarling air traffic. We spent forty-five minutes waiting for clearance to land."

"I thought government flights had priority."

"They do," Tex replied, casting a sharp glance in the direction of his old teammate. "The sky's swarming with feds."

"Yeah, well, the ground's not any different."

"Figures. Let's get moving," the big man admonished, "the sooner we get to the safehouse, the better."

"No dice—we've been ordered back to Langley, right away."

"Why?" Tex asked, turning to look Thomas in the eye.

"Forty minutes ago, a bomb went off in the parking garage at Langley. Six fatalities. Kranemeyer wants you on-site."

The Texan reached out and put a hand on his arm. "Harry's going to go blacker than black, you know that as well as I do. Intercepting him at the safehouse is our best, maybe even our only, chance."

"I know."

12:04 P.M.
The safehouse
Culpeper, Virginia

There was an address book in the middle drawer of the bedroom's dresser. Inside, on the third page, there was a list of numbers. No names, just numbers. It didn't matter—he had committed the names to memory long ago.

Harry palmed a prepaid cellphone and started entering the fourth number from the bottom. The phone had only been activated within the last five minutes, but it would be best to keep the call short all the same.

He pressed SEND and listened as it began to ring. Once, then twice. He cast a glance toward the closed bathroom door behind him. Carol was dressing.

They needed to move. On the fourth ring, it was answered, a woman's voice, her tones rich with a Jamaican accent. "Hello?"

Harry allowed himself a faint smile. "You're as cautious as ever, Rhoda. Haven't forgotten a thing, have you?"

"Why are you calling?" the woman asked, punctuating her words with a French oath. "Your name's out to law enforcement—they're already throwing out a net over northern Virginia."

"If you know that, then you know why I'm calling."

A long pause. "I'm good at what I do, but I can't work magic, Harry. Not really. All the voodoo in the world couldn't save your butt now—what did you do to get this reaction?"

"Not over the phone. You know that," Harry responded, clearing his throat. "You've forgotten Kingston?"

Another pause, and then the woman sighed. A long, heavy sigh of resignation. "No, I haven't. What time should I expect you?"

"We'll be on your doorstep within the hour," Harry replied, closing the phone. The old Hollywood myth of the lone spy was just that—a myth. Nobody out in the cold survived without a network. It was just a matter of doing whatever it took to activate it. Sometimes that meant calling in favors and stepping on more than a few toes.

11:32 A.M. Central Time
Dearborn, Michigan

It was perhaps one of the greatest ironies of Dearborn that in this city, once home to so many of America's autoworkers, most of the residents now relied upon public transportation subsidized by the federal government.

But it did help ease traffic problems. The black man let out a snort of disgust as he glanced into the rear-view mirror, checking for any signs of the police. *How have the mighty fallen.*

Now, the state and federal governments subsidized well nigh the entire police force of Dearborn. The only choice, really—for it was a safe bet that half the city's population didn't make enough to pay taxes, and the other half had no interest in a police force.

Abdul Aziz Omar fit squarely in the second category, particularly on a day like today.

He glanced into his rear-view again, catching a glimpse of his passengers. Names? He didn't know theirs—but the man in the middle, the young man with the faraway, almost ethereal gaze, he knew simply as the Shaikh.

What he was doing here in Dearborn was also a mystery.

All of which would be revealed in due time, the black man mused, reaching for his thermos of tea in the center console. *Insh'allah.*

12:34 P.M. Eastern Time
U.S. Route 211
Virginia

He'd had the feeling once before—chasing a serial killer across five states, back in the days before he'd joined the Bureau's Counterterrorism Division. A sickening feeling of being just one step behind, always too late.

Vic Caruso rounded the end of the SUV to find Marika Altmann standing there, holding a clear plastic baggie up to the sunlight.

"Any luck finding the casing?" he asked, zipping up his coat against the wind.

Altmann replied with a shake of her head, placing the baggie containing the deformed .45-caliber slug back in the evidence tray on the floor of the vehicle. "If he's Agency, he probably picked up his brass. My guess is this guy is good."

"He is," Caruso responded quietly. His partner shot him a sharp, piercing glance.

"You know him?"

"After a fashion," he replied, turning to look her in the eye. "In mid-September, I was assigned to head up an investigation into a CIA leak. He was one of the targets."

"And?" Marika pressed, a shrewd look in her eyes.

"And that's a long story." Long story indeed, Caruso thought, looking out across the highway to where the bodies had lain. He'd looked down the barrel of that 1911 Colt .45.

The investigation had been blown when Nichols had come back and found Caruso in his home searching through computer files. He'd seen death in Nichols' eyes, and lived. The two out on the highway hadn't been so fortunate.

"What do you think of this Russian immigrant—the guy our briefing ID'd as the bomber?"

The woman didn't answer for a moment, her face strangely unreadable as she stared out across the snowy countryside. A wisp of silver-gold hair escaped her ball cap and she tucked it back over her ear.

"I think we're being played for mushrooms," she said finally, her voice cold as the wind that whipped around the SUV. "Kept in the dark and fed horse crap."

Chapter 4

He was never more frightening than when he was silent. Carol regarded her companion for another long moment, then turned her attention back out the window of the SUV, to the dirt-brown piles of snow shoved brusquely against the side of the roadway.

He hadn't spoken five sentences since they had left the safehouse. She could still see the expression on his face when he had executed the Russian—a look devoid of emotion. Calculating. Ruthless.

The same look he wore now. The man who had held her close and comforted her as they sat on the bed of the safehouse was gone, replaced by...*this*. "What makes you so sure this woman will help us?" she asked finally, glancing over at him. His leather jacket was unzipped, gaping open to expose the bulge of the Colt holstered to his side. A weapon, just like the man himself.

"Because she doesn't have any other choice," came the cryptic response. "Spend enough time out in the field and you learn that people will do things out of fear that they'd never do for love."

Blackmail. Carol had worked long enough at the Agency that it didn't surprise her. Still, she found the reality unsettling, out from behind the protective walls of Langley.

"How did you end up at the Agency?" she asked, watching the countryside speed past.

He looked over at her, surprise glinting in those steel-blue eyes. "Why?"

"No reason, really," Carol replied, taken off-guard herself by the intensity of his response.

Silence fell once again between the two of them as Harry turned the SUV onto a side road. When he spoke again, his voice was heavy with irony. "Sometimes you have to lay down your dreams and pick up a gun...just because it's the right thing to do and there's no one else to do it. Not much point in looking back." He pointed up the road at an off-white double-wide trailer nestled in a grove of leafless trees. "We're here. Do me a favor."

She hesitated for a moment, then nodded. "What?"

"Let me do the talking."

11:57 A.M.
The mosque
Dearborn, Michigan

Words of purity. Words of truth. The words of God, *subhanahu wa ta'ala*. The most glorified, the most high. Tarik Abdul Muhammad's fingers traced over the flowing Arabic calligraphy, reading the sacred words of the Qur'an. *Who doth more wrong than he who inventeth a lie against God...*

"*Salaam alaikum*, my brother," a familiar voice greeted, interrupting his thoughts. Blessing and peace be upon you.

A smile crossed Tarik's face as he turned, looking into the eyes of the mosque's imam, a grey-bearded man in his late fifties. He was dressed in Western clothing, as were they all. There was no point in drawing attention to themselves.

"*Alaikum salaam*," he replied, placing both of his hands on the shoulders of the older man and drawing him close as they kissed on both cheeks in the traditional Arab greeting. "Is everything prepared for my brothers?"

"Arrangements have been made," Imam Abu Kareem al-Fileestini replied, turning and giving a warm smile to Tarik's four companions. "They will be provided for, *inshallah*."

"And the scientist?"

"At hand," was the imam's response. Abu Kareem turned and beckoned to a swarthy young man standing in the doorway, a can of Mountain Dew clutched in his hand.

About five or six years younger than himself, Tarik thought, taking the measure of the man in one sweeping glance as the imam kept talking. "Our brother from Lebanon, Jamal al-Khalidi, an honor student at U of M."

Tarik smiled, reaching out to enfold the young man's hand in both of his own. "Wolverines..."

1:19 P.M. Eastern Time
Graves Mill, Virginia

As the camera's shutter clicked crisply, taking picture after picture, they all showed basically the same thing: a smiling, happy couple—family snapshots—a doting husband, an adoring wife.

Who said pictures never lie?

"I've got enough," Rhoda Stevens announced at length, laying down her camera and retreating behind her laptop. In her mid-fifties, she still moved with the grace of the runner she was.

Carol reached up and firmly removed Harry's hand from her shoulder as she stood and stretched.

She walked over to where the Jamaican woman sat, now diligently working away in a photo-editing program. The green screen that had served as their background had now disappeared from view, replaced by a glorious vista of the Blue Ridge Mountains.

Smoke curled upward from the cigarette clutched tightly in the woman's ebony hand, wispy tendrils filling the air with the pungent smell of marijuana.

"You've done this before, haven't you?"

Rhoda chuckled, a rich, throaty sound. "Thirty years, both sides of the law. Wish I could do the same thing in real life—wouldn't look so old."

Out of the corner of her eye, Carol saw Harry cross the room, cautiously glancing out the window. "How soon can you have the documents ready, Rhoda?"

"Forty minutes, give or take." Another long drag on the joint. "When did you get so nervous, Harry? I don't remember that from before."

The look Harry shot back across the room could have frozen stone. "Just do it as quickly as you can. They're going to throw the net wider with every passing hour."

The black woman was unfazed, her gaze never leaving the screen of her laptop. "Then wait in the next room, will you? Nerves can be contagious."

12:23 P.M. Central Time
Dearborn, Michigan

One of the benefits of Dearborn's crime rate was that there was no difficulty disposing of an unwanted car. Leave it unattended long enough, and it would disappear. No muss, no fuss.

Abdul Aziz Omar reached back into the car one last time, wiping the steering wheel with a cloth. There was no sense in leaving his prints—having spent eight of his thirty-one years behind bars in the state penitentiary meant that the cops had them on file.

He closed the car door and shoved his hands deep into his pockets, fingers closing around the curved grip of a Smith & Wesson Model 27 revolver. It wasn't safe to walk these streets unarmed, the tall black man thought, looking cautiously both ways as he exited the alley where he'd left the car.

The gang-bangers and crackheads preferred semiautomatics when they could get them, which was far too often these days. After all, they were the guns you saw on TV and in music videos.

Omar's choice of the .357 Magnum was more prosaic, based on a simple bit of advice from a fellow inmate. The man had been an unrepentant infidel, serving a life sentence for rape and murder, but his advice had been sound.

Revolvers don't eject their shell casings. Keep your shots few and effective and you can walk off the crime scene with half the evidence the cops usually depend on.

It made sense. His eyes continued to rove the desolate street as he made his way back toward the mosque several blocks away. A paradise of tranquility in the middle of hell.

The same could not be said of the bar to his right as he moved down the street, his long legs covering the ground in smooth, powerful strides. Right now it appeared innocent, almost harmless in the bright rays of daylight, but he knew different.

Another five, six hours and it would be transformed into a noisy, raucous den of iniquity.

He should know, for that had once been his trade. He closed his eyes in remembrance and could once again feel the discs spinning beneath his deft fingers. DD Cool, they'd called him in those days, those heady, sinful days of drugs, sex and music.

The *Cool* was self-explanatory. As for the double *D*, well he'd had his own proclivities back in the day.

Before…he took a deep breath of ice-cold air, shamed that even now his body stirred at the memory. Before he had found the peace of Allah, *subhanahu wa ta'ala.*

In the afterglow of peace, in the dark enclosure of that prison, he had been given a new name. Abdul Aziz, the servant of the Magnificent, one of the hundred names of God.

His steps quickened as he neared the mosque. That's all he was now, a humble servant. A servant on a mission from God…

1:56 P.M. Eastern Time
Graves Mill, Virginia

Nerves. Rhoda's perception had been accurate, as usual—she'd been in the business a long time, longer than him, and not much got past her.

The nerves. When had they started? Harry didn't even need to ask the question, he knew.

Hamid Zakiri. All roads led there, to that devastating moment of betrayal there in Jerusalem. Because, in the end, it didn't matter that Zakiri had eluded detection from everyone else at Langley.

All that mattered was that *he* had failed to see it, and people were dead because of it. One man in particular: Davood Sarami.

His man. One of the team.

With an instinct born of training, Harry pulled himself from his thoughts to cast another cautious glance out the front window of the trailer. A car sped by, its wheels spinning up icy slush.

Too fast for a surveillance team. He felt eyes on his back and turned his head to see Carol staring at him.

At his glance, she looked away, the silence hanging awkwardly between them. "I'm sorry…" she began slowly, her hands shoved deep into the pockets of her jacket.

Carol still wasn't looking at him, but he could see her chewing hesitantly at her lower lip as she considered her next words. He had to build her confidence, prepare her for what lay ahead. Whatever it took, whatever he had to say. Whatever she needed to hear.

"For what?"

"For breaking down—earlier. You don't need that, not now." There was anger flashing in those blue eyes now, anger shining through fresh tears. "I just feel so helpless…so *weak*. I'm ashamed of myself."

Harry crossed the room to stand before her, looking down into her eyes. She started to speak, but he put a finger to her lips. "There's nothin' for you to be ashamed of, nothing in this world. No one does well their first time out in the field—and there's no way to do well at losing someone you've loved."

No way. And as he held her gently against him, even as tears rolled down her face, a part of him was shocked to realize that he actually meant it.

1:59 P.M.
NCS Operations Center
Langley, Virginia

"Any progress on Harry's known associates in the greater D.C.area?" Carter asked, arriving back in the op-center.

Lasker looked over the top of his cubicle and shook his head in the negative. "Most of the people Nichols has worked with over the years are overseas contacts—and they're not the type of people who get handed a green card."

Carter rubbed his forehead. "Is there *anyone* that looks like a possible? Someone he might turn to at this time?"

"There was one."

"Does he live within the current projected search quadrants?"

Lasker cleared his throat. "It's a *she*, and she's dead." He hit a couple buttons and an image came across the screen of his workstation. "Rhoda Stevens, a private 'contractor' for the Agency in the late '90s and early 2000s. Skilled forger, twice arrested for identity theft and falsifying passports, involved with some of the drug traffic in and out of Jamaica. We used her for much the same work, just more…legitimately."

"So, what happened?"

The young CLANDOPS comm chief tapped his screen. "In addition to her more illicit 'talents', Ms. Stevens was a marathoner of no mean stature. She was in the final two miles of the 2012 Boston Marathon when she collapsed. Paramedics responding to the 911 call pronounced her dead of a massive heart attack."

Carter eyed the picture thoughtfully. "Anything else?"

"Matter of fact, yes," Lasker replied, grabbing a print-out off the stack in front of him and handing it back to the analyst. "This from the boys at Ft. Meade. They've spent the last few hours running a fine-toothed comb through the hundreds of cell calls made from the area of the bombing this morning, back-tracing a couple hours before the blast."

"And?"

"A call was placed just five minutes after the bomb went off—the conversation was short, and scrambled, but they finally managed to reconstruct part of it. The caller, a Caucasian male, used the word *Eaglefire*."

Carter's eyebrows went up. "Any idea what that's supposed to mean?"

"It's why the NSA flagged the call—it's one of our codes, or used to be, at least. I remember them phasing it out shortly after I took over Comms last year. It's a call for back-up."

"There seems to be a rash of those lately," Carter mused, his eyes scanning over the sheet. "I'll need to kick this up the chain—any idea where the boss is?"

"Last word had him on the seventh floor with Shapiro—got pulled in for a meeting of the minds."

The analyst snorted. "No wonder they needed Kranemeyer..."

2:01 P.M.
Graves Mill, Virginia

The driver's license and passport were authentic—at least they looked that way. The same with the vacation photos that now filled Carol's new wallet.

Harry snapped the wallet shut and handed it over to Carol. "I think that should do it," he announced, looking over to where Rhoda Stevens still sat behind her laptop. "You've been a friend."

Another raspy chuckle. The black woman stubbed out her cigarette in the engraved pewter ashtray on her desk and rose. "Well, you've still got the feds and half the law enforcement in the state breathing down your neck. Where you headed from here?"

There was something unnatural in her voice, a forced casualness. Alarm bells sounded in Harry's mind as he turned toward her. "Can't say, Rhoda— any idea what the weather forecast is for North Carolina?"

She laughed, looking over to where Carol stood by the door. "No, I don't, but I hear it's beautiful this time of year."

Eyes were on them as they walked out to the SUV. Harry could feel them on his back and the Colt seemed to stir beneath his jacket at the sense of peril. Carol paused as they got to the vehicle. "I wouldn't have told her where we were going," she said, more than a hint of reproof in her voice.

He looked down into her eyes. "You felt it, too."

She nodded as he pulled open the door of the SUV for her. "There's something she wasn't telling us."

Harry walked around the front of the Excursion and levered himself up into the driver's seat. It was only then that he looked over at her. "Then you'll be delighted to know that I lied."

Rhoda watched them go, watched as the SUV pulled out of her driveway and sped off down the road, heading south. It was only when they were safely out of sight that she stepped back from the window and made her way down the hallway, stopping by the bedroom door.

Silence. She knocked lightly, then pushed open the door without waiting for a response.

"I still think you should have told them," she announced, shooting a look of frustration at the big man who lay on her bed, his body wrapped in bandages.

David Lay shook his head wearily, wincing in pain at the effort. "There's no point to it, Rhoda—the knowledge of my presence would only endanger them further. She'll be safe with him."

A moment's pause, and a look of pain not unmingled with despair flickered across the face of the wounded man. "She has to be."

Chapter 5

1:31 P.M. Central Time
Fargo, North Dakota

It took quite a snowstorm to shut Fargo schools, but that was just what they'd had. Twenty-eight inches of the white stuff blanketing the Northern Plains.

Which meant there was no school for her to teach. There had been a day when she would have welcomed the break, but not today. Not since the passing of her sister, less than a month before.

Mary—tall and pretty, long chestnut curls. The cute little sister, four years her junior. Family members had joked that their personalities couldn't have been more different—Mary cheerful and buoyant, not a care in the world. And her own demeanor, reserved, intense. Analytical. They were the skills that had her teaching algebra in one of Fargo's many high schools.

Unmarried, she had never attracted men in the same way as her younger sister. It wasn't that she was without appeal in the looks department, but her personality tended to intimidate men. She wasn't the type to hang out at a singles bar on Friday night.

Alicia Workman looked down at the picture of her sister on her computer desk and felt the tears well up in her eyes. Mary's romanticism, her ability to attract men and fall head over heels into love, had been her undoing.

They'd found Mary dead in her apartment in D.C., dead of an overdose of prescription painkillers. The suicide note was disjointed and rambling. None of it made sense—not unless you had all the pieces.

75

Her hand moved from the picture to the letter lying beneath it. A print-out of her sister's last e-mail, five days before her suicide. All of her hopes and dreams, laid out in stark 12-pt Times New Roman.

Her love for a man.

A married man.

Alicia stole a glance out her apartment's window, at the still-swirling snow. The pieces of a field-stripped Bersa Storm lay beside Mary's letter, taken down for cleaning.

It was a little thing, a pocket semiautomatic chambered in .380 ACP. Having grown up around guns on her grandfather's ranch, Alicia knew all too well the capabilities and limitations of the pistol.

Her gaze flickered to the newspaper clippings and computer print-outs that decorated one wall of the apartment. The smiling face of a man loved by so many.

Only one question remained: would it be enough?

8:35 P.M. Local Time
Bonn, Germany

"Mr. President, can we have a statement?"

"Do you have a statement on the possible dissolution of the EU, Mr. President?"

"Statement?"

"Mr. President! Is there going to be an agree—"

The limousine door closed with a satisfying *click*, the noise outside fading away into a low roar.

"Quite a morning."

President Roger Hancock looked up into the eyes of his Chief of Staff. "That's the understatement of the year, Ian."

The economic troubles that had plagued the European Union ever since the Greek debt crisis had finally come to a head. Spain and Portugal had quickly followed Greece into the dangerous realms of default, sending shock waves across the continent.

With country after country going down the tubes, Germany and France—arguably still the strongest economies in Europe—had come to the decision that remaining in the EU was no longer in their best interests.

And that's why he was here. To use up his remaining political capital trying to convince them otherwise.

At fifty-three, the President of the United States was still a young man, but four years in office had taken its toll upon his once-boyish good looks. Brown hair was now heavily streaked with silver, something his aides had said gave him "gravitas".

Devil take gravitas.

"Any more news out of D.C.?"

Ian Cahill shook his head. The Irishman had been with Hancock for ten years, ever since the Wisconsin native's first run for U.S. Senate. First as campaign manager, then Chief of Staff. Born and raised in Chicago, the sixty-two-year-old Cahill had earned his reputation as a street fighter in the notoriously nasty world of Illinois politics.

It was a reputation that had served him well in Hancock's administration.

"The Bureau's locking down Virginia tighter than a drum, got agents swarming all over the place," Cahill replied, looking down at the screen of his smartphone. "So far...nothing. That goes for both Langley's rogue and the DCIA himself."

Hancock murmured an oath, staring out tinted windows at the signs waved by protesters down the long street. Then the motorcade picked up speed, leaving the shouts and screams of the rioters to fade away in the distance.

If only all problems could be dealt with so easily.

4:11 P.M. Eastern Time
NCS Op-Center
Langley, Virginia

Thomas looked up over the screen of his workstation as Tex Richards entered the small, windowless cubicle.

"Got your text," the Texan announced simply. "Were you able to get access to the satellite feed?"

"Negative," Thomas replied with a shake of his head. "Those are all tied up this morning and heavily restricted—I don't have access, certainly not from this terminal. No, I went around the backdoor and began checking on utilities."

Tex crossed the room to look at the screen, at the continually updating graphs of colored lines zig-zagging across it. "And?"

"Right here—around 1100 hours, water and electric usage spiked at the safehouse. Not a great deal, but if McNab's at work..."

"Is he?" Richards asked, an unusual intensity creeping into his voice as he referenced the retired Air Force pilot who served as the caretaker of the safe house.

Thomas nodded. "He is. I checked with his employers—been at work all morning. Usage levels subsided to their normal levels shortly after noon."

That only left them with one option, and both men knew it.

"He's come and gone," Tex whispered, gazing at the screen. "Harry, what are you trying to do?"

5:02 P.M. Eastern Time
New Market, Virginia

There was no sign that they were being followed. On a good day, the drive from Graves Mill to the antebellum town of New Market took about an hour and a half.

This wasn't a good day, and driving a surveillance detection route, or an SDR, meant that Harry wasn't taking the most direct roads.

"Mind if I ask where we're going?" Carol asked, clearing her throat from the passenger seat beside him. She didn't mince words, a refreshing change from a lot of the women he had known. And it was probably time to tell her.

Harry took his eyes off the road long enough to glance over at her. "Does the name Samuel Han mean anything to you?"

A long moment of silence, then, "He was one of your men, wasn't he?"

That she even knew the name took Harry by surprise. He hadn't expected...

"Yeah. He was," Harry replied, staring out the windshield at the passing forests of Appalachia, denuded of leaves and covered in a fresh coat of snow. Flakes of white drifted down past the speeding Excursion as dusk fell.

What to say? How to sum up a man's life in the space of a moment?

Harry had always been good with words—good at using them to persuade, to manipulate.

To deceive...but now, as a flood tide of emotion came swirling back with the memories, words failed him.

Han had been one of the best the Agency had ever seen. The son of a Nung mercenary who had fought alongside the U.S. in Vietnam—Samuel, or Sammy as the men of Alpha Team had called him, had come to the CIA's Special Activities Division direct from Little Creek, Virginia, the home of SEAL Team Two.

A big man, the direct contradiction of the stereotypical Asian, Sammy had been a gentle giant, probably the kindest man Harry had run across in fifteen years of running clandestine operations.

Lethal on the battlefield, at home he was a loving husband and father of two small boys. Of course, that had all been before the fall.

"Yeah," Harry repeated, almost more to himself than her. "Sammy was a friend."

5:12 P.M.
CIA Headquarters
Langley, Virginia

On any other day, Michael Shapiro would have already left for home, punctual to the dot of five. Particularly this month, with Christmas shopping to be done.

The twins had deposited their wish lists in his cereal bowl this very morning, a whimsical touch to start off a day that had quickly gone sideways.

Nothing this day had gone according to plan. If it had...well, as it was, the morning had provided fresh proof that sometimes cleaning up one problem only created another. Even when you went to the best.

"One final thing," he said, raising a finger. Bernard Kranemeyer stood in the doorway of Shapiro's office, preparing to leave.

"Yes?"

Shapiro took a deep breath. He had never been comfortable around the DCS. The former Delta Force sergeant just didn't *fit* into the Beltway culture. And someone that didn't fit—you just couldn't trust them to react predictably—to shut up and do what they were told when the situation required it.

"I need you to sideline Alpha Team."

Raised eyebrows. "Why?"

Shapiro swore silently. Delta Force, or the Unit, as insiders sometimes called it, was made up almost entirely of non-commissioned officers—no one lower. And with that reality, the D-boys weren't used to taking orders without question. Unit briefings had been known to turn into shouting matches.

"They're too close to the developing situation."

"Bull," Kranemeyer replied, light flashing in those eyes. "The Bureau is handling the 'situation'. I need every man I've got on stand-by for the extraction operations we've initiated. *Every* man—Richards and Parker are two of my best."

The DD(I) took another deep breath. He wasn't used to confrontation. "In October, Alpha Team's second-in-command, Hamid Zakiri, was found to be a sleeper agent, working for the ayatollahs. This very morning, their Team Lead took a hostage from *this* building and is currently the subject of a manhunt. My order stands, Kranemeyer. Put them on leave, get them out of the circle before it's too late."

"Done," the DCS assented, nodding his head. "Will there be anything else?"

"No, no, that's all," Shapiro replied, at once relieved and taken off-guard by Kranemeyer's sudden capitulation. It wasn't natural.

And then Kranemeyer was gone, but the vague sense of disquiet remained. Shapiro stared down at the screen of his computer, at the phone number displayed there. Something wasn't right…

5:34 P.M.
Cypress Manor
Cypress, Virginia

Darkness had fallen, but the lights set up by the dozen or so FBI agents swarming over the old antebellum mansion lit up the yard and lane, casting monstrous shadows in the form of the boxwoods lining the walk.

It had been dark here, completely dark on his last visit to Nichols' home. A visit just as unprofitable as this one.

Vic looked up from searching the credenza to see Marika Altmann descending the mahogany staircase. Her hands were buried in the pockets of her windbreaker, the look on her face anything but reassuring.

"What's the good word? Manage to crack Nichols' safe?"

The glare told him just about everything he needed to know. "Yes. And no. He had a self-destruct code programmed into the mechanism."

"And?"

She swore under her breath. "And all the documents inside were charred to ashes, Vic."

Caruso closed the drawer of the credenza with a gloved hand and nodded. "Coming up dry here too. Nothing in the least bit damning."

"I've worked some paranoid suspects before, but…" The older woman looked over at him. "This one takes the cake."

5:41 P.M.
Staples
New Market, Virginia

The snow was falling faster as Harry closed the door of the SUV and looked over at a woman loading bags of groceries into the trunk of her sedan.

The plaza of the shopping mall was full of cars, no doubt due to the snow. It would never fail to amaze him, but every time it was the same—no one was ever prepared ahead of time.

But he wasn't here for the groceries. He took a look ahead, taking in his target—the Staples store—then back across the parking lot to the two Virginia State Police patrol cars parked at the Dunkin' Donuts.

With any luck, they were cold, hungry, and tired of looking for a phantom. No use in depending on luck.

He checked his watch. Five minutes.

A snowflake stung his cheek and he pulled up the collar of his leather jacket against his face, striding into the warmth of the store.

Harry had barely gotten through the door when a clerk approached, asking if he needed help.

"Not tonight," he heard himself say. *Blasted customer service. Four minutes.*

The laptops were displayed at one end of the store, lined up in a nice row with placards proclaiming their speed, hard drive size, etc. He knew it was his age talking, but he could remember when disk space had been measured in megabytes.

The good thing about Staples was that their laptops were connected to the Internet. After a brief pretense of looking over the various models, Harry clicked on the Internet Explorer icon and went on-line.

It didn't take long to find what he was looking for—not far outside town, either.

He took a pen from an inside pocket and scrawled the address on the palm of his hand.

Three minutes. The Mapquest page loaded and he typed both his current address and the destination into the search box.

Got it.

6:03 P.M.
CIA Headquarters
Langley, Virginia

The pungent aroma of cigarette smoke struck Thomas's nostrils as he pushed open the door to Kranemeyer's office. As a federal building, smoking was officially prohibited, but the DCS had never been known for following the rules.

He closed the door behind him and advanced into the room, only then catching sight of Richards, already seated in front of Kranemeyer's desk.

"Have a seat, Thomas," Kranemeyer gestured with a flick of his hand. The offending cigarette lay a couple inches in front of him, still smoldering in the ashtray.

"What's going on?" Thomas asked, still standing. Something was wrong. It was only when the DCS waved his hand once more that he sat down.

"Was waiting till you got here." Kranemeyer looked down at his desk, then back at the two men. "Orders have come down from the top. The two of you are to be sidelined until Nichols is apprehended and this investigation is over."

Thomas started to speak, but the DCS cut him off. "I've already appealed the decision, but it stands, and will continue to do so as long as Shapiro is acting director."

"Then we're being placed under arrest?" This from Tex, his coal-black eyes expressionless. Only the set of his chin revealed the tension there.

"Not exactly," Kranemeyer responded, letting out a heavy sigh. "Shapiro just wants you as far out of the loop as possible. Got a few days of deer season left, I'd make the most of it."

Thomas blinked as though he hadn't heard correctly. The DCIA was missing and presumed dead or taken hostage, their colleagues had been blown up in the bowels of the Headquarters building itself, and their Team Lead was the subject of a manhunt. Take a vacation?

Then Kranemeyer picked up the laptop from off his desk and swiveled the screen toward the two paramilitaries.

Across the screen, a simple message read: MEET ME AT THE BLACK ROOSTER. 2100 HOURS.

The former Delta Force sergeant smiled briefly and pressed Backspace. Another moment, and the message had disappeared.

"Any questions?" Kranemeyer asked, clearly not referring to the message.

There were none.

6:21 P.M.
A warehouse
Manassas, Virginia

The warehouse was a poor staging area, but it would have to do. Sergei Korsakov had seen worse.

The Russian Army had always been short on money, even after the fall of the Soviet Union, and even in the "elite" *Spetsnaz* units.

So, you learned to improvise—make do with what you had. The hackneyed old cliché of necessity being the mother of invention came to mind.

"Anything yet, Viktor?" Korsakov asked, rubbing his hands together for warmth.

The gaunt young man looked up from the Toshiba laptop he had perched precariously on top of a fifty-gallon oil drum. "*Nyet.*"

At twenty-one, the Bulgarian-born Viktor was the youngest member of the team and the only one with no prior military experience. A scraggly black beard masked the lower half of a death-pale face and the Glock 19 looked ludicrously out of place in its holster on his skinny hip. But what he lacked in physique, he made up for in technical expertise.

They'd been a team for six years, ever since Korsakov had rescued him from the Black Sea brothel where he'd been enslaved.

Six years, and yet the boy still cowered whenever a stranger came near him. His body still bore the scars.

Most of his quickness with a computer he owed to the fact that he had been forced to upload videos from the brothel to the servers of a pornographic website.

That he had received most of the scars from being nearly beaten to death after he had infected those video files with a homemade computer virus only proved to Korsakov that the boy still had spirit.

"Are you sure the American's not playing games with us, Viktor?" Korsakov asked softly, laying a hand on his protégé's shoulder. He felt the boy quiver at his touch and murmured a silent curse. The owners of the brothel were dead, killed by his own hand, but nothing could undo the damage they had wrought.

The boy thought for a moment. "It's hard to know if he's restricted my access when I don't know everything that's supposed to be there. But I'm on the FBI's servers, this much I know. Look, I'll show you their patrol grid."

His hands danced over the keyboard, bringing up a map overlay of the tri-state area. "Red dots, FBI-DHS. From the memos I've seen—their Department of Homeland Security is trying to take over the search."

Another couple clicks, and yellow dots scattered across the screen, adding to the growing web. "Police of the state of Virginia."

Blue dots. "The locals—sheriffs' deputies, so forth."

Korsakov swore under his breath. They were everywhere. Had his own mission not been so critical, it might have been awe-inspiring—the full might of the American federal government thrown out after one man. But now...

"Keep a close eye on things, Viktor. If they find Nichols and Chambers, we'll have to be ready to intercept."

"*Da, tovarisch.*"

The assassin had already turned away when it occurred to him. "Viktor?"

"*Da?*"

"How long until the second tracker goes live?"

The boy glanced at the computer screen, then consulted his watch as though there might be a contradiction. When he looked up into Korsakov's face, his eyes held the expectation of a rebuke. "Sixteen hours."

6:29 P.M.
Outside New Market
Virginia

Snow was still falling when Harry climbed back into the driver's seat of the SUV. "Looks like everything's clear."

He saw her face in the brief moment before the dome light went back off, plunging them both into darkness. She looked weary, rumpled, her face shadowed by the grief of the day. The Kahr .45 was still in her lap, clutched tightly in both hands, the way it had been ever since he'd left her alone.

Harry moved the torn packaging of a consumed MRE off the center console and put the vehicle into gear, moving slowly down the lane, past the realtor sign that had become ever more common in the years since the financial crisis of 2008: *Foreclosed.*

The abandoned split-level was off the main road, tucked into what Harry's grandfather would have called a "hollow." Perfect for their purposes.

Harry's lockpick gun got them through both the deadbolt and front door lock in under a minute. As he had always said, locks were for honest people.

Gripping a tactical light between his teeth and his 1911 in both hands, Harry led the way into the deserted house, clearing it room by room.

The former homeowners had left a bed and a moth-eaten recliner in a downstairs bedroom, a room decorated on one wall with a mural of a unicorn. A little girl's room.

Once upon a time, it might have been beautiful, but now the fading image loomed threateningly in the glare of Harry's tactical light. A relic from more prosperous times.

He gave the recliner a suspicious prod with his foot, as though wondering if it would crumble into pieces.

It didn't. His light swept the room once again, a final check before he turned to face her. "The bed's yours."

He couldn't see her face, but he could hear the hesitancy in her reply. "Thanks, I guess. Are you going to be able to sleep in that recliner?"

Harry pulled back his jacket, sliding the big Colt into its leather holster. "I won't be doing much in the way of sleeping."

8:53 P.M.
The Black Rooster Pub
Washington, D.C.

Thomas had never been to the Black Rooster, had never even heard of it before doing a Google search for the words on Kranemeyer's screen.

Arriving on-site, it wasn't hard to understand why. The bar occupied the corner of an office building on L Street, its brick exterior about the only thing distinguishing it from the rest of the buildings.

Warm air and the sound of '70s music hit him in the face as he entered. He brushed a melting snowflake off the sleeve of his jacket, looking around him.

Tex was already there, his long legs wrapped around a barstool in front of the massive wooden bar. Even from across the pub, Thomas could see the big man's eyes—watching the mirrors that hung behind the bar. Nearly the perfect setup.

"What you having, buddy?" the bartender asked, a weary smile on his face as Thomas took the stool beside Tex.

"All depends—what's my friend having?" he asked, eyeing the clear liquid in Tex's glass.

The smile was replaced by a crooked smirk. "Water."

Of course. Thomas shook his head. What a day...he knew Tex didn't drink. He went to the same church as Harry—of course he didn't drink. How could it have slipped his mind?

"What would you recommend?"

"Maybe a Dark and Stormy?" the bartender asked speculatively, looking up from the shot glass he was wiping. "Jamaican rum and ginger beer."

"Sounds like a plan."

"He's here," Tex announced beneath his breath, waiting until the bartender had turned to fill the order. Thomas looked up into the mirrors, seeing the form of the DCS, a shadowy presence in the door of the bar.

Nine o'clock on the dot. 2100 hours. Punctual as ever.

The Dark Lord crossed the barroom and put his hand on Thomas's shoulder. "Glad to see you could make it, boys."

And then he was gone, moving toward an empty booth at the back of the pub. Thomas put out a hand toward his glass, tilting it back with a sudden, brusque motion. The rum slid down his throat, warming him against the coldness within.

It wasn't going to be enough. He drained the glass and set it back down on the bar, following after Kranemeyer.

Party's over.

9:05 P.M.
The foreclosed house
New Market, Virginia

She wasn't sleeping. Harry knew it from the moment he walked into the room, but he closed the door with all the care he would have shown if she'd been sound asleep.

He shifted the AK-47 to his right hand and sat down quietly in the recliner. The rifle had been chosen from the weapons in the vehicle after a moment's careful consideration. The motorcyclists had been wearing body armor.

He could barely make out Carol's form in the darkness, laying there on the bed, wrapped up in the sleeping bag they'd brought from the safehouse.

Laying there awake. He could tell by her breathing—he'd had a lifetime of listening to people sleep. Not all of them had woken back up.

Harry leaned back in the recliner, letting the assault rifle rest across his lap. It was cold in the house, bitterly cold, but there was no way around it, with the utilities cut to the house. The bi-level, like so many houses built in the mid-90s, had been built with no thought of any heat source aside from electric. It hadn't been until near the end of the Obama administration, when utility rates had skyrocketed, that people had started to reconsider.

Cold. Yeah, that's where he was. Out in the cold. He'd known it from the moment he had seen his picture splashed across Rhoda Stevens' TV screen along with the Bureau's APB. A bad picture, blurry even…but that life was forever over. His days on the run were only beginning.

Harry rose to his feet, a slightly sardonic smile tugging at the corners of his mouth. He ran a gloved hand over the receiver of the Kalashnikov, feeling cold gunmetal through the neoprene fabric. Perhaps he'd always known that it would come to this.

9:15 P.M.
The Black Rooster
Washington, D.C.

One thing that inevitably resulted in social awkwardness among spies was a universal desire to sit facing the door. It was a mark of their respect for the older man that Thomas and Tex gave Bernard Kranemeyer that seat.

Respect, and to the extent that such men gave it, their trust. He'd been through enough hell to earn it.

At length, Jamal walked back to the couch, standing behind him hesitantly. "Forgive me, brother…family should not argue like this. What's happened to me? I have found a faith that I once thought I'd lost," he whispered, a reverent intensity in his voice, along with a shadow of the brother he once had been. "And it has given me purpose in this life of ours. That's all I want for you."

He reached down, squeezing Nasir's shoulder. "That's all our father would have wanted."

And then he was gone, leaving Nasir sitting alone in the cramped, now-darkened living room of the small apartment.

Family. That meant everything—their only lifeline back to the world they had once known. No matter their differences, he couldn't betray that…which was why Jamal's name had never appeared in the reports he left in weekly dead drops in exchange for his freedom.

And yet he knew, much as he had tried to deny it—had tried to lie to himself.

It has given me purpose…

His brother was involved.

9:32 P.M. Eastern Time
The Black Rooster
Washington, D.C.

"…we knew we couldn't go after Yusuf without the Israelis' help, and the last thing Bill Clinton wanted to do was offend Arafat in the very twilight of his presidency." Kranemeyer snorted. "For all I know, he might have even thought of pardoning the dirtbag, but someone convinced him that we could make the snatch. Grab him in the West Bank, throw a bag over his head and fly him out to Egypt. Let Mubarak's boys give him a going over."

"Extraordinary rendition," Tex remarked quietly. It seemed strange to refer to Mubarak now, years after his fall from power, but he had once been the face of Egypt.

A nod from the DCS. "Exactly, but things didn't go as planned."

"Does it ever?" Thomas asked, a caustic edge to his voice. He glanced down at the glass of brandy in his hand, his third drink of the night. The liquor was starting to affect him, he knew that—but hang it all, what a day!

"On the day of the operation, Nichols went into Ramallah before dawn, carrying a Kalashnikov and dressed as a Palestinian *fellah*. We didn't hear from him for hours. I suited up with Avi ben Shoham and an assault team from the Sayeret Matkal. We were going to head into Ramallah in the back of a pick-up truck, black balaclavas over our heads and flying the green flag of Hamas. Any luck, the PLO and Hamas would blame each other, not us."

The DCS paused to take a sip of his drink. "With twenty minutes to go, Nichols made contact. *Free fall.* That particular emergency code had been designated as the signal for mission abort. Turns out we'd been walking straight into a trap. At first we thought our informant had sold us down the river, but five days later, the man's body was dropped off in front of the embassy gates in Tel Aviv, his genitals cut off and stuffed in his mouth."

That was the Middle East for you, Thomas thought, glancing around the bar in hopes of catching the eye of a waitress to refill his drink. They played hardball. "What happened to Yusuf?"

"Six weeks after the abort of RUMBLEWAY, Yusuf stepped into his car and it blew up, killing him, his bodyguard, and his fourteen-year-old son. Our best intel was that it was a Mossad hit." The DCS shook his head. "Moral of the story? Don't mess with the Jews."

Tex cleared his throat. "What's all that got to do with today?"

Thomas smiled to himself, turning his glass between his fingers. Right to the point, as always. No beating around the bush. That was Tex.

"Just to be honest with you, I don't know," Kranemeyer replied. "But it was the only operation that Lay, Nichols, and I were all involved in—before I became DCS."

"A signal?" Thomas asked.

The older man nodded. "Ten minutes after the attack on Lay's SUV, a call was placed from an encrypted satellite phone in the area. From what Fort Meade has been able to decrypt, the caller used the phrase *Eaglefire*. That was also a RUMBLEWAY code." He leaned across the table. The music was changing in the bar, a hard beat replacing the slower vibe of happy hour. The voice of Bruce Springsteen belting out "Born in the U.S.A" served to further obscure Kranemeyer's words.

"I'm not going to ask either of you if you know where Nichols went," the DCS began. Neither of them looked at each other. "But I know how these things go. Everyone in this business has a fall-back plan. We did back in my Delta Force days, I still do. The FBI catches up with Harry, they're going to toss him in a cell and throw away the key. And if my suspicions are correct, if he's acting on orders from David Lay, we need to talk to him first."

"And you want us to find him for you?" Tex asked, his eyes a dark void as he stared across at their boss.

"Officially," Kranemeyer replied, closing the netbook and returning it to the satchel at his side, "no. Everyone knows the CIA can't operate on U.S. soil."

His eyes hardened, a look of determination passing over his features. "Unofficially…don't come back without him." Kranemeyer rose, pulling on his overcoat. "And if it turns out he *is* part of the problem, well, you know what to do. Good huntin', boys."

And he was gone…

Chapter 6

She could feel him, there in the darkness. Could feel his eyes, watching her. What time was it?

A hand pressed gently down on her shoulder. "Time to leave."

Harry's voice. Carol rolled onto her back, stretching wearily as she looked up at him. She could barely make out his face against the darkness.

"Get any sleep?"

Her only reply was a shake of the head. She unzipped the sleeping bag and swung her legs out over the side of the bed. "You?"

"Not so's you'd notice it." A mirthless chuckle punctuated his words. "Got six inches of snow last night, still coming down."

His voice had changed, she noticed. "Is that going to be a problem?"

"Could be," he responded, looking at her as he rolled up the sleeping bag. "Might be a blessing—the snow is going to ground their choppers, but they'll fling out a wider dragnet today all the same."

She reached for the Kahr and slipped it inside her jacket, close to her body. "Do you have a plan?"

"Might call it that."

4:23 A.M.
The Virginia-West Virginia Border
Near Orkney

The morning was cold—cold and dark, falling snow highlighted against blue and red flashing lights. The metal barrel of the Mossberg 500 in the hands of Sheriff's Deputy Ricardo Sanchez was colder still.

Murmuring an oath under his breath, the twenty-seven-year-old Sanchez laid the shotgun across the hood of the Shenandoah County Sheriff's car and reached for a thermos of coffee.

Four hours. Three to go. Man, it was raw. The form of his partner materialized from the other side of the two-car roadblock on the Virginia side of the mountain bridge.

"What's the news?" Sanchez asked, spotting the cellphone.

"Nada, Rick," Deputy Matthew Wilkes responded, slinging his department-issued AR-15 over his shoulder. "That was the wife. Wondering when I'd be back. She's cold."

Sanchez laughed at that. He just had to. "Married three months, right? How'd she stay warm before she ran into the likes of you?"

"Never asked," Wilkes responded with a wry chuckle. "Not sure I want to know."

"Smart man. It's what, ten minutes till check-in?"

"Five. They upped the frequency—this Nichols fellow has somebody's shorts in a bind for some reason."

"You see the info dump on FOX News at eleven?" Sanchez asked, shooting a look of disbelief over at his partner. "Afghanistan, Iraq—this guy's been everywhere, and that's just the stuff they're willing to talk about."

"So?"

Sanchez shook his head. Wilkes had always been one to talk tough—usually he could back it up. But tonight? "So...we're dealing with Jason Bourne and you'd better be taking it seriously, *compadre.*"

4:31 A.M.
The safehouse
Culpeper, Virginia

"Listen, I'm sorry, fellas." It was probably the sixth time those words had come from Steve McNab's lips in five hours, the words of a man who didn't know what else to say

"Nothing to be sorry for," Thomas responded, looking over his shoulder at the retired F-16 pilot who'd been the safehouse's caretaker. "You followed protocol. Protocol said if the chalk was up, you were to stay away. So you stayed away until you got our call."

"Sometimes protocol bites you in the butt," came Tex's succinct comment. He was kneeling at the door of the open gun safe, a notepad in his hands.

"Give us a few, Steve," Thomas asked, motioning for the pilot to leave the room. He waited until McNab had disappeared behind the closing door and opened the screen of his laptop. "Harry's driving a 2004 Ford Excursion, NY plates, license number Alpha Delta niner Romeo two seven. The vehicle is registered under the name Robert L. Stephenson, so that's likely his alias."

Tex looked up from his notes. "Any credit cards under that name?"

"Likely—I'm looking into it now."

"Harry always preferred American Express, if that helps any."

"Figures," Thomas said, clicking rapidly through the on-screen database. "Don't leave home without it. Got it—expiration date 2/18, registered in the name of Robert Lewis Stephenson. Well, he's not lost his sense of humor."

"Gonna be able to do anything with it?"

Thomas's eyes narrowed as he scrolled down to the bottom of the screen. "Think so. The trouble is going to be doing it without Langley's firepower. There's a backdoor into the AmEx network—Carol showed me how to get in during the Caracas op two years ago."

"Caracas?" Tex asked, getting up and coming over to the laptop. "That was right after she came to Langley—how'd she have the clearance to know about a backdoor like that?"

An amused smile crossed Thomas's face. "The way I understood the story, it's *her* backdoor. Nobody asked too many questions. If I can get in, the minute Harry makes a purchase—we've got him."

"That might be awhile."

Thomas looked up at Tex, his friend's face shifting in and out of focus. He blinked, fighting against fatigue and the alcohol still coursing through his bloodstream. "Why?"

"He cleared out all his cash."

"Great," Thomas whispered, burying his head in his hands. He should have realized…

"How much?"

"Judging by the size of the security box—by the likely denomination—I'd say 10k. Minimum. He's not going to get within ten klicks of an airport, and that's about the only place he'd use plastic."

Time to go to Plan B. The only question: what was *that*?

5:02 A.M.
The SUV

"So, what are we doing?"

Brushing her hair back out of her eyes, Carol looked up from the maps she had been studying under the glow of the dome light. "We're near Orkney Springs. Another ten miles and we'll be in West Virginia." She looked out at the darkness surrounding the vehicle and switched the light off. "When were you going to tell me the plan?"

When? He shifted the Excursion into gear and got back on the road.

"I believe I mentioned Samuel Han."

"You did."

Harry cleared his throat, focusing briefly on the task at hand. The back roads hadn't been treated—the state of Virginia, like just about every state in the union, had been running short of money for years. Anymore, it took a blizzard to get any salt spread on the highways before Christmas.

Back roads? Forget about it.

"Sammy was one of the best operators I ever worked with," he said after a moment. "Rock-solid. He'd married a girl by the name of Sherri from Virginia Beach, had a couple kids—twin boys. They'd gotten married when he was still at Little Creek, so she knew the score. Or thought she did."

He could feel her eyes on him as he paused. "He was different...well, to be blunt—no one wears their wedding band on an op. A lot of guys use that as an excuse to sleep around when they're overseas. Not Sammy—theirs was a love story. American dream."

"Was?" Harry could feel the pain in her question. A survivor's pain.

"Yeah. There's always a *was*. Sherri was used to him going off in the middle of the night—but she never got used to the accelerated op tempo of the Special Activities Division. Sammy was gone more than he was home. A lot of women would have turned around and left right then, but she stuck it out."

The Excursion's tires fishtailed slightly in wet, slushy snow and Harry turned his attention back to the road. "We're coming up to a fork—right or left?"

"Left," she responded, consulting the map in her hand.

"Sammy was deployed when it happened," Harry continued, swinging the SUV onto the left fork of the road. "His son Lee was playing ball in the street near their house in Norfolk when he was struck by a car. Turned out to be an old fellow in his mid-eighties, got confused—hit the gas instead of the brakes.

We were in the Yemeni desert when I got the call. Had to make the choice of whether to tell him."

"You didn't, did you?" she asked when he hesitated.

"A distracted operator is a dead operator," Harry replied calmly. "We'd been deep black for three weeks—I had two choices: tell Sammy and abort the mission—or see it through."

"Three," Carol interjected, an icy chill to her voice.

"What?"

"You had a third option—tell Han and *trust* him to keep his mind on the mission."

Harry looked out the SUV's window, white snow drifting down against the darkness of the Appalachian night. Pine trees heavy with snow flashed past in the glare of the headlights.

"That wasn't on the table," he said finally. "People speak of trust as if were some sort of virtue. It's not—it's probably the greatest—the most seductive, of all vices. Trust kills."

5:17 A.M.
The West Virginia border

Boredom. That was the worst part of the job. Deputy Sanchez hefted the twelve-gauge shotgun in his hand and moved to the front of the patrol car.

He'd joined the Shenandoah County Sheriff's Department three years before, on a whim. At the time, he'd been laid off from his construction job—and the government was about the only entity hiring. It had to be more exciting than driving a bulldozer.

Cradling the Mossberg under the crook of his arm, he blew steam on his hands and chuckled to himself. Exciting.

Yeah, right. He'd fired his department-issued Glock in the line of duty twice in three years. Didn't even take it to the range that much anymore.

A vehicle materialized out of the snowy night without warning, the lights of a big Ford Excursion spotlighting the deputy.

The fourth vehicle of a largely uneventful night. Sanchez walked out into the middle of the night, Wilkes moving into position behind him as he waved the SUV to a halt.

The driver's side window rolled down as Sanchez approached.

"Deputy Sanchez, Shenandoah County Sheriffs' Department. License and registration, sir," the deputy requested, addressing the only occupant of the Excursion, a man who looked to be in his mid-forties.

The profile of his face... Sanchez looked down at the crumpled print-out in his hand. The picture of Nichols hadn't been that good to begin with, but now the falling snow had blurred the photocopy. They weren't allowed to print in color anymore, not with the budget cuts.

"Sure thing," the SUV's driver responded, reaching slowly into the glove compartment. "Out looking for the spy?"

Sanchez stiffened. "Why?"

The driver chuckled, handing out his paperwork through the window. "Else this is one heavily armed sobriety checkpoint. I watched the whole thing on CNN last night, some crazy stuff goin' on, right?"

"Sure is," the deputy responded, looking carefully at the photo on the driver's license. *Robert Stephenson.*

"You're from New York?"

"At the moment," Harry replied, looking the Hispanic deputy in the eye. "My wife moved down for her work a month back—I'll be here as soon as I can find a job."

The deputy handed back his license and papers with a snort. "This is a bad time to be finding one of those. What's your wife do?"

It seemed like a casual question, but Harry could see the glint there. Not bad. "She's a private nurse. Her patient—used to be a big shot with Apple—was recommended to get out of the city—smog, pollution, all that. So he moved down here."

A nod. "And what brings you out on the roads at this time of night, Mr. Stephenson?"

"Haven't seen her in twenty-eight days, bro," Harry spread his hands. "No sense stopping for the night when she's right over the mountain. I've been lonely."

"And frustrated," came the deputy's comment, along with a sideways grin.

Harry laughed. "Yeah, that too."

The grin vanished as quickly as it had come. "I'd like you to step out of the vehicle, Mr. Stephenson. Keep your hands where I can see them."

There was no time to wonder what had triggered the command. Harry reached low and unbuckled his seat belt, pushing open the door of the Excursion. It was a two-man roadblock, the second deputy hustling toward them now, an AR-15 clutched in his gloved hands.

The way he held the carbine told Harry everything he needed to know. The deputy didn't know how to use it. Might be good, might be bad.

"Keep him covered, Wilkes."

His gaze swept south, taking in his surroundings in a single glance just before the first deputy turned him around against the hood of the SUV and began frisking him.

There were lights there to the south, the lights of a house shining through the snow. Probably not a hundred yards off the road. Close enough to hear if shots were fired.

Harry felt the deputy's hands run up his body, underneath his jacket, and he smiled, thankful he had given the 1911 to Carol. Now if she'd just remember what he'd told her—stay away...

"He's clean," he heard the deputy announce, taking a step back. "If you'll give us your keys, I'll take a look in the back, Mr. Stephenson."

So many years, so many times in the field, but Harry could feel his body tense at the question. The point where the lies broke down. The guns—well, the guns were securely hidden away in the compartment custom-built into the false floor of the Excursion. But the MREs, the other supplies—would raise too many questions. Now or never.

"Keys are in the ignition," he gestured, taking the opportunity for one last fix of the men's positions. The man called Sanchez was about four feet to his left, near the open door of the SUV—he would be the one to go for the keys.

The second deputy was about three feet behind him, carelessly close, the AR-15 held loosely in both hands. If he was following his training, the safety was still on.

Men like him knew nothing but their training.

Lowering the shotgun, Sanchez leaned his upper body into the Excursion, his fingers groping the ignition area for the missing keys. It was at that moment that Harry struck, throwing his body weight against the open door.

The driver's side door of the Excursion had been armored to withstand the impact of 7.62mm rifle rounds. What resulted was a heavy door swinging shut across Sanchez's lower legs, pinning him. A scream of pain and surprise rent the night.

Harry pivoted in the snow, his hand coming up as the second deputy took a step backward, his fingers fumbling with the safety of the AR-15.

Harry's hand connected with Wilkes' throat, a brutal edge-of-hand blow that sent him reeling.

The deputy collapsed into the snow, clutching at his crushed vocal cords. Dropping to one knee beside him, Harry jerked the Glock 19 from Wilkes' retention holster, bringing it up and pulling back the slide to chamber a round.

Movement out of the corner of his eye and Harry pressed the Glock's barrel against the temple of the prone, gasping deputy. He looked up to see Sanchez limping toward him, the Mossberg leveled. The muzzle of the twelve-gauge gaped large as the mouth of a cannon, a yawning hole dark as the night.

"Another step and I put a bullet through his brain," Harry announced calmly, looking up at Sanchez. The deputy stopped stock-still, the shotgun wavering in his hands. He was breathing heavily, great gasps of steam escaping his lips and drifting off into the darkness. The red and blue lights of the patrol cars continued to flash across the snow, adding a surreal aspect to the scene.

"You—you wouldn't," he said finally, his voice trembling. "You wouldn't kill a cop."

Harry's eyes never changed, his lips forming into a cold, hard smile. "Believe that if you want to—you can even tell his widow the same thing. I've spent fifteen years of my life killing…what's one more body?"

"You're never gonna make it out of here alive," Sanchez insisted, raising the shotgun to his shoulder once again. Harry could see his hands shaking, could see the uncertainty written across his face. The emotional anguish of a man who didn't know if he could pull the trigger.

"This isn't a movie, son," Harry said, extending his left hand. "So, don't try to be a hero. Nobody needs to die here. Just lay down the gun—everyone goes home."

A long moment passed, the deputy caught in torturous indecision. Finally Sanchez shifted the Mossberg into his left hand and threw it into the snow. "You win."

Harry rose, the Glock in his hand now aimed at Sanchez's heart. "Turn around."

4:28 A.M. Central Time
An apartment
Dearborn, Michigan

Tarik rose before the dawn, before the call to *fajr*, morning prayer, had rung out over the city.

A recording, yes—but a beautiful sound, and one increasingly common in this land.

A quiet smile crossed the Pakistani's face, a light flickering for a brief moment in those dreaming eyes. Such was the will of Allah. He walked over to the window and opened the venetian blinds, looking out over the city, lights sparkling in the darkness. *Dar el Harb.*

The house of war.

His laptop was open on the small table beside his bed, a website he had visited the previous night still on-screen.

The face of a woman stared back at him, boldly, without shame—a woman in her fifties, her naked face framed by brown hair. *United States Representative Laura Gilpin, Texas*, read the caption beneath her picture.

He remembered the face. He would always remember it, distorted in anger behind a bank of microphones. She had led the opposition against his release from Guantanamo, a self-proclaimed crusader. So typical of the Americans, using words without beginning to comprehend their meaning.

Tarik smiled and reached for the mouse, double-clicking on the Events button on her webpage and scrolling down until he reached the bottom. December 25th—eleven days away. Only eleven days. The Pakistani leaned back in his chair, falling into meditation as the words of the *sura* flowed through his mind.

Do they feel secure from the coming against them? Of the covering veil. The wrath of God. Or of the coming against them—of the Hour. Suddenly while they perceive it not?

5:31 A.M. Eastern Time
Crooked Run RD
The Virginia-West Virginia border

Harry had just finished loading the unconscious and zip-cuffed bodies of the deputies into the back seat of the patrol car when he sensed movement, a sound in the snow behind him.

He unceremoniously dropped the body of Deputy Sanchez onto the backseat, the Glock coming up level in both hands as he turned, aimed toward the threat.

Carol. He lowered the gun, taking his finger off the trigger. "I thought I told you to circle through the trees and wait for me down the road."

She brushed a falling snowflake off her sleeve, never taking her eyes off his face as she moved closer. "You were also going to lie your way through. What went wrong?"

"They asked too many questions." He closed the rear door of the patrol car. "We need to get out of here—this place is going to be swarming with Bureau types once they fail to report back in. And they're going to have our license number."

Carol looked at him. "Not necessarily."

Harry shook his head, returning the Glock to the inside of his jacket. "They run the tags, their search is logged by the database. It's SOP."

Her lips parted in the first real smile he had seen from her since the beginning of the nightmare. "It *is* standard operating procedure—that doesn't mean the database can't be hacked. If I can switch the numbers before the search is flagged..."

It was tempting—almost too tempting. "We don't have the time to run a hack," he said finally. "Sorry."

She took a step closer, her eyes burning into him with a formidable intensity. "I can do this. Five minutes."

A long moment passed before he responded, an answering smile passing across his face. He reached out, putting a hand on her arm as he moved on past, to take up an overlook position down the road. "Knock yourself out."

6:42 A.M.
NCS Operations Center
Langley, Virginia

The op-center was buzzing when Danny Lasker came through the door, tucking his keycard back into the pocket of his shirt.

It wasn't like the place ever slept—the Clandestine Service maintained a skeleton crew of comm specialists and analysts 24/7—but this morning was different.

"Mornin', Ron," Lasker greeted as he passed the analyst's cubicle. A grunt served as his reply. He dropped his coat over the back of his own desk chair before throwing a second glance at Carter.

Blue dress shirt, stained with sweat. Black pants that weren't on speaking terms with a crease. The same tie, loosened at the neck, red and green Christmas ornaments dancing down its length.

His gaze swept over Carter's workstation. A large thermos of coffee sat beside the LCD monitor on one side—a decimated box of bagels on the other. "You didn't go home last night, did you?"

A shake of the head. "Take a look at this."

Lasker gave himself a push, sending his desk chair rolling across the floor to Carter's side. "What's going on?"

The analyst opened a browser window, bringing a picture of Harry Nichols onto the screen. An old picture, surveillance-camera quality. "This is what went out to the Bureau and local law enforcement yesterday. It's been altered."

"Are you sure?"

Carter let out an exasperated sigh. "I'm a photoanalyst—of course I'm sure. Someone deliberately tampered with the picture before it was sent out."

"Who had access?"

"That's what I can't tell—they clearly wanted to make the Bureau's job tougher." Carter's face hardened, anger creeping into his bloodshot eyes. "That's not the only thing. Somebody's messin' with us, Danny."

A couple clicks and another picture came onto the screen. "What do you make of this?"

The image was clearly of the underside of a man's arm. A dead man's arm.

"A friend of mine at the Bureau sent these over last night. Morgue snapshots of the two Russian KIAs from the highway yesterday." As Lasker watched, Ron used his mouse to draw a red circle around a small white patch of scar tissue.

"Looks like someone tried to have laser tattoo removal," Danny observed, leaning back in his chair. "Old girlfriend of mine had a dragon taken off her lower back—looked just like that."

Another time, Carter might have made a joke about it, might have given him a hard time. Not this morning. "Do you know what this is—it's Cyrillic."

"So? The Bureau said they were Russkies."

An exasperated curse escaped Carter's lips. "That's not the point—these are the Cyrillic letters for AB. The other man has an O on the underside of his arm."

"Their blood type," Lasker breathed. It was like a light had been turned on. "*Spetsnaz.*"

"Exactly. Odds on, Korsakov's men. And the Bureau's acting like these are ODCs." Ordinary decent criminals.

"That doesn't make any sense. Why would they do it?"

"Don't know. But hanged if I won't find out." Carter looked over at him, his dark face twisting into a grimace of sorrow. "I sent Luke to his death, Danny. I'm gonna know why."

8:29 A.M.
The warehouse
Manassas, Virginia

On-screen, figures in blue jackets with FBI emblazoned across the back deployed in the suburban Virginia development, moving from cover to cover. Their target, seen through the helmet-mounted camera of one of the agents: a white split-level at the end of the cul-de-sac, a gray Ford Excursion parked in the driveway.

As the agents moved forward, moving in a tactical formation, AR-15s at the ready—a gray-haired man emerged from the garage door of the split-level, still dressed in his housecoat.

Guns came up. "On the ground! Put your hands where I can see them! FBI!"

A quiet smile crossed Korsakov's face as he switched off the video feed. "How long ago did this raid take place?"

"Twenty minutes."

"Well, your instincts were correct, Viktor. As usual."

The boy grinned. "*Da*. They were good," he admitted grudgingly, "but sloppy. Maybe they work fast? A couple fragments of code left from the pre-hack entry in the database."

"Is it enough to reconstruct the authentic license number?"

Viktor thought for a moment, running his fingers through the scruff of his beard as he stared at the computer. "*Nyet*," he said finally. "They did a good job, but none of that matters."

Right. "How long till Chambers' tracker goes live?"

"Ninety minutes."

9:33 A.M.
West Virginia

"How long do you think we have?"

They were deep in the mountains now—had passed a couple snowplows a few miles back. The only vehicles they'd seen in thirty minutes. Harry tapped the brakes of the Excursion, slowing slightly to negotiate the curve of the mountain road. Snow softened the profile of the sheer drop-off to the one side of the road, but it was still there.

"Hard to tell," he replied. "It's been a while since I had the Bureau looking for me."

The look on her face was worth the price of admission. "A while? This has happened before?"

Harry shook his head. "Not exactly. Summer of '05, extended re-training at the Farm. They turned six of us loose in D.C. with sealed orders—and two hours head start on the G-men."

"You've been hanging around Carter for too long," she observed. "How'd you do?"

"Two of us survived the forty-eight hours—saw the mission through. Turned out Kranemeyer had placed a thousand-dollar wager with the head of the FBI's Counterterrorism Division. He collected."

"So you made it through—who was the other lucky guy?"

His eyes darkened at the memory, the gray steel of gunmetal mixing with the blue.

"Sammy Han."

9:38 A.M.
The Allegheny Mountains, near Bickle Knob
West Virginia

The forest was deathly silent, the heavy snow of the early morning covering everything like a shroud.

Snow crunched beneath snowshoes as a large man glided from between the trees, moving with practiced ease over the surface of the snow. His pants and parka were winter digital camouflage, US Army issue of a few years before. From a few yards out he effectively disappeared into the background.

He stood there for a moment, surveying the scene before him. Movement from down the mountainside caught his attention and he removed his Raybans, revealing a narrow face, sharply-chiseled Asian features. He couldn't have been much more than forty-one, forty-three at most, but his face—his *eyes* were older. The eyes of a man who'd seen too much of life. Too much of death.

The .308 FNH SCAR battle rifle in his hands came up, aiming down the vale toward the movement. There—the head of a deer came into focus through the SCAR's scope and a shudder rippled through Samuel Han's body.

He lowered the rifle and wiped his forehead with a gloved hand. Fifteen degrees Fahrenheit—five below with the wind chill—and he'd been sweating.

It was time to head back, he realized. A person could only take so much. Couldn't let himself go where he'd gone last time. Too many memories.

Han put the SCAR's safety back on and turned west. Toward home. A compass rested in the breast pocket of his parka, but he didn't bother consulting it. Two and a half years patrolling these woods—he knew them almost as well as he'd once known the desert.

So many memories…

9:41 A.M.
West Virginia

"What happened?"

Harry took a look into his rearview. There was a car back there now—last few minutes. Four-door Nissan. Something to keep an eye on. "Happened to whom?"

"Han. With his marriage." There was an odd tone to her voice, curious but hesitant.

"By the time Sammy got back from Yemen, his kid had spent two weeks in ICU. Life support," Harry replied, taking a deep breath. "He did eventually pull through—you know what they say about little kids—you keep all the pieces in the same room and they'll recover, but it was six months before he came home. He never walked again. Sammy took it hard, started spending more time at Langley."

Behind them, the Nissan turned off onto a side road. False alarm. "It was like it hurt him to be around his family—so he threw himself into his work. The cure was worse than the disease. I stopped by the house one day, had a long talk with Sherri. She wanted to keep things together, but the strain of being a mother, nurse, and wife to an absent husband was grinding her down. Talking with Sammy was like talkin' to a wall and neither her nor I could get through."

"And she left?" Carol asked quietly. He nodded. A low, mirthless chuckle escaped her lips.

"What's funny?"

"Nothing," she replied, looking back at him. "You're just the first man I've ever heard that didn't try to blame a divorce on the woman."

He shrugged, focusing his attention back on the road. Black ice had formed underneath the shadow of an evergreen and he guided the SUV around it. The armored Excursion didn't handle like your average vehicle. "When a relationship goes to hell, there's generally enough blame to go all the way around. In the end, it didn't matter. After the divorce went through Sammy petitioned Kranemeyer to get back out in the field. It took us a couple weeks to decide, but we finally approved his request."

"And?"

"And the next mission was Azerbaijan," Harry responded. Out of the corner of his eye, he caught her wince. It had taken place before she joined the Agency, but the Azeri mission was legendary at Langley. For all the wrong reasons.

Ten men parachuted into the Azeri winter. Two full strike teams—Alpha and Charlie. Their target: a Russian convoy believed to be transporting nuclear weapons to Iran.

With forty-eight hours to wheels-up, the Charlie team leader had come down with pneumonia. And Sammy volunteered to take his place.

At the time, it had seemed like a good idea. Despite his subordinate position in Alpha Team, the Asian had leadership experience from his years in the SEALs.

Harry cleared his throat. "Yeah. Azerbaijan. Ten men in—only five men came back out. Two men got caught up in the mountain cross-winds and never even survived the landing. Sammy was the only survivor of Charlie—it was the final straw."

"What does he have to do with us being in West Virginia?"

"Everything," Harry replied. "Two days after returning from the Azeri mission, he handed in his resignation. Sold his apartment and most of what he owned and moved off-grid, to these mountains. It's a secluded spot, cut off from most of the surrounding world. Just the way Sammy wanted it."

"And he's going to be happy to see you?"

It was a long time before Harry answered, debating what he should say—how much honesty was appropriate at this time. But none of that really made a difference, she'd know soon enough.

"No," he replied finally. "No, he's not going to be happy at all."

Chapter 7

One minute. Fifty-nine seconds. Fifty-eight. Viktor's eyes never left the Toshiba's screen, his breathing shallow as the counter ticked down. It was cold in the warehouse, but the boy rubbed sweaty palms against his ski pants. It was this adrenaline rush that had sustained him through those dark nights in the brothel. The thrill of what he could do, despite his physical limitations. *Power.*

"Do we have their location yet?" It was Korsakov, coming back into the warehouse alone. Everyone else was already loaded up in the three Suburbans.

Viktor held up one finger, watching as the locator icon came flashing on-screen. "*Da, da*, we do." His fingers danced over the keyboard, bringing up a Google Maps overlay. "They're in the state of West Virginia, right *here*. Moving west, maybe fifty-five, sixty kilometers an hour."

Korsakov slapped him on the shoulder. "*Spasiba*, Viktor, excellent! Take the laptop with you and load up."

The ex-*Spetsnaz* assassin took a long look around the now-empty warehouse. Everything was clean.

Turning to leave, Korsakov zipped up his heavy winter jacket, covering the Type III ballistic vest he wore beneath. It was time to strike.

10:41 A.M.
Crooked Run RD
Virginia

The snow was turning to slush as the sun rose higher in the sky, beating down on the backs of the two men.

"If you were Harry, what would be your next move?"

Tex lowered the high-powered binoculars and handed them over. "Hard to say."

Thomas clicked a button on the side of the binoculars to turn on thermal imaging and aimed them through the trees down the hill toward the section of road cordoned off by crime scene tape.

"Are we certain Harry was even involved in this incident?"

"His fingerprints are all over it," Tex replied, raising himself up on his elbows. "Certain? No."

"Not having proper intel is a pain in the butt," Thomas observed. There were still three FBI agents down there, having fun with their forensics equipment. Playing in the snow. That was the Bureau for you.

A nod this time. "Welcome to life in the cold."

Cold. Yeah, that was true. Thomas grimaced as he rose to a crouch. Water from the melting slush had seeped through the outer layer of his parka.

"Where do we go from here?"

"Harry's always been partial to mountains," came Tex's laconic observation as he gazed westward, into West Virginia.

Their eyes met and something clicked inside Thomas. "Are you thinking what I'm thinking?"

"Probably. Do we have a location?"

"Negative. But I know how we can get one..."

11:13 A.M.
The Alleghenies
West Virginia

Having one's face plastered across every TV in three hundred miles made even getting gas awkward. Fortunately, the mountain wind was cold enough to make the black and red checkered scarf wrapped around the lower half of Harry's face seem perfectly natural.

"Armoring up an SUV is a tree-hugger's nightmare," he said, glancing at the fuel gauge as he climbed back in the Excursion. "Sends your fuel economy plunging right through the floor. My estimate is we'll reach our destination in another thirty, forty minutes."

"And then what?"

Harry looked over at her as he put the Excursion in drive. "What do you mean, then what?"

"I want to find them, Harry."

"Yeah. Well, right now the important thing is that they don't find you first. Sammy's cabin is the safest place for you right now. Those were my orders."

"I don't think you heard me," she retorted, a brittle calm in her voice. "I'm going to find the men who murdered my father. And I'm going to see them die."

"Hand me the maps," Harry instructed quietly. It took him a moment to locate the road he was looking for. His estimate was pretty close. He looked both ways and pulled out onto the road. "I don't think you know what you're talking about."

He could see the bitterness written across her face, the angry retort forming on her lips. He held up a hand.

"Taking a human life...you cross a bridge in your soul. There's no going back, no matter how much you may want to—and trust me, *you will*."

He paused before going on, his voice trembling with emotion. "I was twenty-three when I first killed a man. It's been fifteen years and I can still see his face, the look in his eyes as he died. God knows how I've tried to forget."

She remained silent and Harry glanced over at her. "He may have been the first, but he was far from the last. All of them the same. I'm never alone, Carol. The ghost of every man I've ever killed walks beside me."

11:47 A.M.
CIA Headquarters
Langley, Virginia

"I don't see how I can help you." Ron Carter's windbreaker was zipped tight to his neck, against the cold wind blowing across the CIA campus. He glanced around, toward the nearest security guard fifty yards away across the parking lot, then tucked his legs closer together underneath the bench.

"You do realize this call is being monitored, don't you?" Carter asked in exasperation, turning his attention from his cellphone to the lit cigarette in his left hand. He was supposed to be on his smoke break.

As he watched, the wind extinguished the burning ember. He swore.

"I'll do what I can," he said finally. "Give me five minutes to access my workstation. I'll get back to you from a clean line."

Abnormal and often-missed meal times were about the only reason for his still-trim waistline, Carter thought. At any normal workplace, the office would have been shut down for lunch.

Not the op-center. Still, a few had cleared out—enough to give him some privacy. He accessed his workstation before opening his desk and reached for what he had styled his "emergency" phone. It was a prepaid cell, technically untraceable. That wasn't the same as saying Fort Meade couldn't listen in.

"Listen," he said when Thomas's voice answered the other end of the line. "When Samuel Han left Langley, he became a caretaker of government property."

"A caretaker?"

"Yeah. A decommissioned bunker on a mountaintop in West Virginia, codename CHRYSALIS. Back in the early '50s, it was intended as a shelter for top Pentagon brass. A place from which the lucky chosen could ride out the apocalypse. Helicopters were still in their infancy, but some progressive thinking architect put in a helipad so that they could reach the shelter in a hurry."

"So—what happened?"

Carter let out a sharp laugh. "The H-bomb happened. The bunker had only been designed for bombs the size of the Fat Man, so it was finally decommissioned as an emergency shelter in 1957. Government efficiency being what it is, taxpayers kept footing the bill until 2012."

"And Han is there now—can you get me an address?"

"Just give me a moment," the analyst replied. "That type of stuff will be on the DoD servers."

A few keystrokes and a password request came flashing on-screen. Carter entered his CIA log-in and the database opened.

"Doing a search now," he announced, providing a running commentary as his fingers worked their magic on the keyboard. What on earth? No freakin' way...

"Thomas, we've got a problem."

"I'm listening."

"It looks like the CHRYSALIS file was one of the ones pillaged in the Anonymous attack on the Pentagon. It's gone."

"Don't you guys keep back-ups? Redundancies for just such an emergency?"

"Listen," Carter retorted, an offended look crossing his face. "I am *not* a DoD track toad, so don't give me that 'you guys' crap. If I recall correctly, the dweebs over at the Puzzle Palace moved a bunch of obsolete files to a vulnerable server just a month before a hacker styling himself Legion1337 launched his attack. Anonymous took responsibility, but Legion1337 was never located or identified and with only old Cold War files out in the open, the DoD decided to cut its losses. If there's a back-up for the CHRYSALIS file, I can't find it."

"Then we're back to square one."

"Looks like it...wait a minute." Carter minimized the DoD database and brought up a background window, his eyes running down the screen. "There's something odd going on here. The Pentagon files were published through Wikileaks—all except one. The file on the CHRYSALIS bunker. And that's not all. The cyber attack took place within five weeks of Han's departure from the CIA..."

Thomas let out a low whistle. "What are you trying to tell me?"

"It's what they teach you at the Farm, isn't it?" Carter asked, rubbing a hand over his forehead. "Cover your tracks?"

12:03 P.M.
The Alleghenies
West Virginia

Han was out for nearly five hours every morning—a routine he varied just enough to keep it from being predictable.

It was probably senseless, but the morning patrol of his property was near the only thing keeping him sane.

He shook his head as he made his way up the low rise toward the ridge that overlooked the cabin. Then again, what sane man spends five hours of every day wandering through the woods with a loaded battle rifle?

Han reached the top of the ridge and looked west, his eyes opening wide in surprise.

It was a moment of pure, blinding instinct. He threw himself prone, his hands unslinging the SCAR and bringing it to bear.

There was an SUV sitting in his driveway, a blacked-out Ford Excursion. Low to the ground, probably armored.

The type of vehicle executive protection companies used. The type the *government* used.

He took a deep breath and steadied the gun, glassing the vehicle through the SCAR's scope. Sixty yards. It was an easy shot.

"You think driving right up is a good idea?" Carol asked, looking through the front windshield of the Excursion at the hunting cabin.

They were the first words she had spoken since the gas station. Harry shook his head. "It's not, but trying to sneak up on Sammy is a good way to get killed. That's why I didn't try to get here last night."

"There's something you're not telling me."

He sighed. "Yeah. Sammy's last psych eval before leaving Langley diagnosed him with 'acute workplace stress'."

A mirthless chuckle escaped Harry's lips. "That's what PTSD is for a spy…workplace stress. It's a cute way for the bureaucrats to shrug it off. So let me do the talking, if you will."

He paused long enough to see her nod before he shoved open the door of the Excursion and stepped out into fresh-fallen snow.

The wind was blowing wild and raw through the leafless trees, and Harry reached down to zip up his jacket.

His fingers froze in place. There, dancing over the fabric of his shirt. The luminescent red dot of a laser.

Time itself seemed to slow down. The sound of Carol's door shutting reached his ears, but it seemed distant and faraway. He felt preternaturally aware in this moment, sensing every breath. Every movement. The awareness of death.

His hand came up, moving slowly, deliberately. "Don't move," he ordered, looking back over his shoulder at Carol.

"What's going on?"

"Just stay behind the vehicle and don't move." He took a half-step forward, his eyes scanning the ridgeline. Judging from the angle…

"That you, Sammy?" It sounded lame, but it was as good as anything.

No response. The laser dot remained focused on his chest, unwavering now.

With the same methodical motion, Harry pulled his jacket open, shrugging it off his shoulders. He tossed the jacket on the hood of the Excursion before reaching for his holstered Colt with his left hand.

The gun was of no use to him. Not now. He pulled it out with his fingertips and dropped it in the snow. Backed away.

A voice rang out over the mountaintop, strangely disembodied but familiar, despite the three years that had passed since the last time he'd heard it.

"That's a good start."

11:09 A.M. Central Time
The mosque
Dearborn, Michigan

"We need to know what we will be dealing with on the inside," Tarik announced, spinning the laptop around so that his small audience could see the images on-screen. "Pictures are one thing—but there is so little perspective, so little reality. We need dimensions, a sense of the space. Our timing has to be precise."

Jamal al-Khalidi cleared his throat. "It is possible that I could get you the floor plans. I know a couple architectural students at UofM—they may have access to the blueprints through their program."

The shaikh turned that hypnotic gaze in his direction. "This is possible? Without alerting the authorities as to your interest in the building?"

The college student shrugged, a smile crossing his face. "Hey, this is America, man. Land of the free, home of the brave. And the foolish."

Across the table, al-Fileestini's eyes had never left the laptop. "It is as Jamal says," he acknowledged, apparently deep in thought as he stroked his graying beard. "Certain freedoms of this apostate land work to our benefit, *insh'allah*. However, there may be a shorter way."

"And what would that be, father?" Tarik asked, turning toward the imam.

"As God has willed, one of our number has performed at this very building." Al-Fileestini raised his hand, beckoning to a man standing by the door. "Call for Omar."

Tarik's eyebrows went up. "The negro?"

12:11 P.M. Eastern Time
The CHRYSALIS cabin
West Virginia

He'd felt colder winds. It had been colder in the mountains of the Hindu Kush. Intellectually, he knew that.

Still, he had never run around the Hindu Kush in his boxers. Harry crossed his arms over his bare chest, forcing himself to ignore the cold.

"Turn all the way around," the voice ordered from its still-invisible perch somewhere up on the ridge.

"Satisfied, Sammy?" he asked, performing a less-than-graceful pirouette in the snow. His gaze slid over to where Carol stood a few feet away. Her jacket and the Kahr were laid on the hood of the Excursion, but that was as far as *that* had gone. So much for equal opportunity...

A figure materialized from sixty yards up the snowy ridge, the digital camouflage giving him the appearance of the Abominable Snowman as he stalked forward. He didn't lower the SCAR.

"Better put your clothes back on, Nichols," Han admonished, gesturing with the rifle. "Before you catch a cold."

Harry held his gaze for a moment longer, staring down his old teammate. Then he reached for his pants.

"Nichols, you're gettin' old. Didn't used to be that easy to get the drop on you."

Harry looked up. "That goes double, Sammy. When did you start trusting women?"

"Oh, her?" Han asked with a wave of his hand, still keeping his distance. Five yards now. "Carol Chambers has many talents, but she's not the threat you are."

There was something in his voice. Harry shrugged on his shirt over his shoulders, looking from Sammy to Carol and back again. "I'm missing something here. You two have met?"

Carol started to respond, but Han cut her off. "Not exactly. Chatted a couple times, though. Haven't we, Legion1337?"

12:15 P.M.
A Suburban
Virginia

American roads took some getting used to. Along with the fact that the American state police actually needed a *reason* to stop you.

Still, Korsakov was glad he wasn't the one behind the wheel. Yuri, a short, muscular man from Leningrad—*St. Petersburg*, Korsakov corrected himself subconsciously—was driving.

"They've stopped moving," Viktor announced from the backseat. "We can reach them in three hours. With good roads."

"Assuming they stay there that long," Korsakov mused. "What type of terrain surrounds them, Viktor?"

A pause. "I don't know." The boy sounded puzzled and Korsakov glanced into the rear-view.

"What's wrong?"

Viktor leaned back, running his hand over the stubble of his beard as he glared at the screen of the laptop. "The software is phasing out when I try to pan—no visual on the site. Maybe mountains are doing it. Never seen this before."

Korsakov shook his head. Mountains wouldn't explain the phenomenon. A government installation might...

12:21 P.M.
The CHRYSALIS cabin
West Virginia

"You did *what?*" She could feel his gaze on her, cold and accusative.

"It was a job, Harry," Carol answered, lifting her face to meet his eyes. "I had sources inside the Pentagon—knew when the files were being moved. It was a simple hack. In and out, all evidence of CHRYSALIS erased."

She looked over at Han. In person, the retired SEAL seemed different. Perhaps it was the intervening years—perhaps it was knowing the rest of his story. The big man looked deceptively relaxed as he stood there, the rifle cradled in his hands. "And he paid well."

"You know what's going to happen if they ever figure out who did it?" Harry asked, shaking his head. "You'll go down—and hard."

"Why do you think we implicated Anonymous and WikiLeaks in the attack?"

She could see Harry's response forming on his lips, but Han cut them both off. "You know what, the two of you can have this out later. Right now it doesn't explain what you're both doing here."

Harry looked over at Carol, then back at his old...friend?

"Mind if we talk this over inside?"

"I do," Han replied, steel in his voice. "You're going to answer my question before we go any further. What do you think you're doing here?"

"David Lay is dead, Sammy. A Russian hit team took him out yesterday morning in Virginia." Harry saw Carol flinch at the blunt brutality of the statement. Han's face hadn't changed.

"What does that have to do with me?"

Chapter 8

Most of her time may have been spent with computers, but Carol hadn't forgotten how to read body language. And Han's was anything but good.

They were standing in the kitchen of the hunting cabin, a glass of ice-cold spring water in her hand.

"What were you thinking, Nichols?" Han asked as Harry finished his story. The SEAL's face was pale in the light of the fireplace. "You know I'm out."

Harry shook his head, determination in his eyes. "Then what are you doing wandering the woods with a battle rifle? Don't kid yourself, Sammy. No one's ever out of the game. You're no diff—"

"It's not a game!" Han swore, taking a step forward. His dark eyes blazed fire, barely controlled anger. "Why do you think I moved out to this godforsaken piece of country? *I didn't want to be found.*"

Yeah, he knew that. Had known it from the beginning. But Sammy had changed.

Harry met the eyes of his friend, his coldness meeting Han's anger. "You know I wouldn't have come if there was any other way, Sammy. You have to know that."

Han passed a hand over his brow, turning away from Harry to stare into the fireplace. Fire burned away at the wood, sparks disappearing up the chimney. Flickering, devouring tongues of fire. A piece of wood broke in the middle and collapsed against the chimney, the sudden noise startling them.

"You know, Harry, you haven't changed a bit," the former SEAL said finally, his tones bitter. When he looked up, the fire had gone from his eyes, replaced by an ineffable sadness. "It's all about the mission, isn't it? Whatever it takes, whoever you have to *destroy* to get the job done."

Harry looked over to where Carol stood, leaning against the wooden island. Emotion warred within him, wanting to deny the accusation, but he couldn't bring himself to do it. It was the truth. And it didn't matter.

"You've been there, Sammy," he replied. "Don't pretend you don't know why. You can't let emotion get in the way of completing the mission. You do, you're dead. Or have you forgotten?"

Han sunk back into one of the kitchen chairs. A sigh, and he buried his head in his hands, running his fingers through the stubble of his buzz-cut black hair. "No, I haven't. Are you sure you weren't followed?"

"I'm sure," Harry replied, watching him closely. The voice had changed, years of past experience coloring the question. And in that moment, he knew that he had won. It was a dirty feeling.

Han rose to his feet, glancing from Harry to Carol and back again. "You can stay. The hunting cabin has a garage—we can get your vehicle under cover, hopefully before the NRO decides to dedicate satellites to this search. Sorenson still running the show over there?"

Harry smiled, pushing away the feeling of guilt with an effort. "Yeah, he is, Sammy. I'll come out and give you a hand."

12:07 P.M. Central Time
The mosque
Dearborn, Michigan

"What type of hardware are we talking about?" Omar asked, cradling the laptop in his dark hands as his eyes roved the screen. Yes, this was familiar. Had he closed his eyes, he could have traveled back to that night, the pinnacle of his career. The screams of the crowd—the bestial look in the eyes of the women who had torn at his clothes as he left the building, surrounded by his security.

Tarik looked momentarily confused. "I do not understand. Hardware?"

"American slang," al-Fileestini interjected, his tone apologetic. "He means guns."

"Ah!" the Pakistani smiled. "We are prepared—Kalashnikovs for every man of the assault team. It should be enough to overwhelm the security."

"You're talking some serious firepower, brother. Mind if I ask where you think you're gettin' them?"

The hynoptic eyes of the shaikh narrowed in suspicion, but al-Fileestini lifted his hand. "You are in the presence of the *ikhwan*, Shaikh." The brothers. "You can speak freely in front of Omar."

Tarik nodded at the older man's reassurance. He took the laptop from Omar's hands and typed in a command, his slender, almost feminine, fingers moving rapidly over the keys. "We will receive the weapons and conventional explosives from the same man who helped us get into the country. This man." He moved the screen so that they all could see. "Valentin Stephanovich Andropov. We meet him in five days."

1:36 P.M. Eastern Time
CIA Headquarters
Langley, Virginia

Bond was not in his blood. Michael Shapiro had known that for years.

Stress gave him migraines, and he'd had the mother of all headaches ever since the bomb blast that had taken David Lay's life the day before.

He popped off the childproof lid of the aspirin bottle in his hand, eyeing the last two pills.

That was the problem, wasn't it? He winced as he leaned forward, shaking both pills out into a sweaty palm. He didn't *know* that Lay was dead. No one knew.

Nothing had gone according to plan. Shapiro's fingers trembled as he reached for the glass of water on his desk. In his mind's eye, he almost half-expected Lay to come walking through the door.

It was supposed to have been a clean kill. The thought made him angry now.

The DD(I) wiped the water away from the edges of his mouth with the back of his hand and reached for his cellphone, scrolling down the screen with a thick finger until Kranemeyer's number came up.

SEND. Shapiro stared across the office at the wall clock as the phone continued to ring. Over twenty-four hours since Nichols had gone rogue, taking Lay's daughter with him. That hadn't gone according to plan either—so far the Bureau was drawing a blank.

Four rings, and the DCS picked up. "Kranemeyer—go."

"Listen, Barney," Shapiro began, forcing calm into his voice. "I was talking with Director Haskell earlier today and he thought it would be helpful for the Bureau to interview Nichols' team members. If you'd handle that, I'd appreciate it—just make sure Richards and Parker stop by the Alexandria field office this evening."

There was a long pause, so long that for a moment the DD(I) thought they'd been disconnected. Then Kranemeyer replied, "I placed both men on indefinite leave late yesterday, Shapiro. I thought you wanted them out of the loop."

"I do—I mean I *did*—surely you have a way to contact them?"

"No," came the flat reply. "It's deer season—Richards' spoke of taking a hunting trip. Knowing him, I'm reasonably sure they wouldn't take their phones."

Shapiro stood, walking over to an oaken credenza by the big window. A crystal decanter of brandy glistened in the chill sunlight. Alcohol and pills, the winning combination. He took a deep breath, rubbing his forehead with the palm of his hand. "Well, do what you can."

4:32 P.M. Central Time
An apartment
Fargo, North Dakota

"...the gunman, later identified as John Warnock Hinckley, Jr." Alicia reached for the remote and hit replay, leaning back against the couch as the footage rolled. The video was raw, grainy, but clear enough. A smiling face, a wave to the crowds. Then gunshots.

It was probably the tenth time she had watched the video. Enough times to know what *wouldn't* work. Enough times to know that she wouldn't be walking away afterward. And there would be no second chance.

Footsteps in the hallway outside her apartment door broke her concentration and she glanced at her watch. It was well past time that she should have been grading the math tests that her students had turned in earlier in the day, but she found it difficult to feel motivated. The principal was only going to raise all the failing scores by ten points. It was part of the legacy of George W. Bush's No Child Left Behind Act. With school districts frightened of losing what little federal money there was to go around, the solution was simple: everyone cheated.

She didn't want to stop and ponder what life lesson that was teaching the kids.

Alicia's gaze shifted back to the TV screen and then to the small semiautomatic on the little coffee table. Didn't really want to think about what lesson they'd learn from her own actions.

In the end, it didn't matter. She'd majored in math, but she knew one thing about history: people always learned the wrong lessons from it.

6:23 P.M. Eastern Time
The CHRYSALIS bunker
West Virginia

Opulence had not been factored into the design plans used by the architects of CHRYSALIS. That much was obvious, even in the flickering, swaying glow of the Coleman lamp in Han's hand. Harry and Carol followed close behind as he led his way down the steps into the bunker.

"From the beginning, CHRYSALIS wasn't designed as a continuity of government installation," the big man stated, lifting the lantern above his head. Light reflected off the stark concrete walls, casting strange shadows around them. "The whole idea was just to keep the military's top brass alive long enough to mount a counterattack. You punch me in the chin, I kick you in the groin. That sort of thing—they never planned to shelter more than one hundred and fifty. Greenbrier came later, once the politicians woke up and realized they'd need a place to ride out nuclear winter. Don't think they ever built bunkers for the civvies. Never have figured out what they thought they'd be governing, what with the rest of the country slagged."

Harry snorted. "That's bureaucrats for you. Cover your own butt institutionalized. Is there any electric down here?"

A shake of the head. "Disconnected. This whole thing was built to run off a huge diesel generator—I could probably get it up in running in a few hours if I needed to. The cabin's power is separate from the bunker."

"Makes sense," Harry nodded, moving into the "living room" of the bunker's upper level. "Do you have a computer?"

Han turned to look at him. "Yeah, I think…I mean it's an old laptop, I don't know—why?"

6:43 P.M.
Elkins, West Virginia

Despite the hour, they were nearly the only diners at the Denny's. Korsakov took another glance around the restaurant, glad he had sent the other half of his team to the McDonald's on the other side of town. Eight men would have attracted too much attention.

"Still nothing?" he asked, looking across the table. Viktor was seated on the opposite side of the booth, his laptop set up. He'd barely touched his burger, intensity written across his face as he stared at the screen.

"*Nyet.* I've run it through every satellite database I can access. No good. My maps show nothing there, just a mountain."

Beside Korsakov, Yuri swallowed the french fry he'd been eating and cleared his throat. "Maybe *you're* the one being blocked."

"What are you trying to say?" Korsakov asked, shooting him a look. With Pavel's death the previous day, Yuri was technically the second-in-command. Second-guesser, more like it. He'd been the loudest voice against accepting the contract on the CIA director. That hadn't changed.

"I'm saying what I've said since the beginning," Yuri replied, struggling to keep his voice to a conversational level. "I don't believe for a minute that he's actually inside the federal servers. We've been played—right from the start."

Korsakov leaned back in the booth, crossing his arms over his broad chest. "You doubt Valentin's word? This is my decision, *da?*"

Yuri met his eyes and for a moment he thought the Leningrad native was going to challenge his authority.

"*Da*, it is your decision," Yuri relented finally, looking away. "It's nothing personal. I've never met Andropov. I don't trust people I don't know."

Korsakov took another sip of his Coca-cola, eyeing the waitress out of the corner of his eye. She was still far enough away. "He's a *tovarisch*, Yuri, from the old days. I've known him longer than I've known you. If he says we have access to the American intranet, I believe him."

"Then what's *your* solution?" Yuri fired back. Korsakov saw Viktor watching them over the top of his screen, his young eyes filled with anxiety—fear. Arguments always brought flashbacks of his time in the brothel.

Korsakov smiled indulgently and clapped his lieutenant on the shoulder. "You and I, Yuri, are going up that mountain. Tonight."

7:01 P.M.
CHRYSALIS bunker
West Virginia

It seemed a bad time to bring it up, but there wasn't going to be a good time. "There's something that's been bothering me," Harry announced, glancing across the small living room at Carol. Sammy hadn't yet returned, but the Coleman sat on the low coffee table in front of her, its glow pushing back at the darkness.

"And that would be?" she asked, looking up at his words. Her golden-brown hair glistened in the lantern light, a dirty blond. Ignore it. *Focus.*

"That video—the director knew why he was being targeted. He knew in advance." He crossed the room to take a seat on the couch opposite her. People were always more liable to talk to someone on their level. Put her at her ease. "Do you have any ideas?"

"No," Carol replied slowly. She didn't look at him, staring straight into the flame of the Coleman. "Dad never talked shop—never talked much at all."

She lifted her head, a defiant knuckle brushing a tear from the corner of her eye. "We'd just started to reestablish a relationship, but he's been different, moody these last couple months. Ever since the Jerusalem op. I thought it was just the discovery of a traitor in the Clandestine Service, but now I don't know."

"We've all changed," Harry acknowledged, filing away the mental note for future reference. "Anything else out of the ordinary?"

She started to shake her head, then paused. "I don't know how to say this…but you probably knew him better than I did. For more years."

Worst thing of it, she was probably right. His eyes narrowed as he stared across the room, watching her closely. If she was lying, he needed to know it. "What of it?"

"What were his political views?" she asked, responding with a question of her own.

So much for seeing that coming. Harry allowed himself a wry smile. "Political views? The director was a political agnostic—registered Independent, but always claimed that he didn't vote. I never heard him speak well of any politician. Why?"

Carol sat across from him in silence for a long moment, biting at her lower lip. "That's what I thought. He'd become obsessed with the presidential election—I'd never seen him so angry as the morning the lower court approved those contested Hancock votes in New Mexico."

It didn't make any sense. Harry opened his mouth, about to ask another question, but footsteps resounded on the concrete of the hallway, signaling Sammy's arrival.

"This is what I got," Han announced, placing a laptop on the table between them. "Battery's good for an hour, maybe two depending on your usage."

Harry acknowledged him with a nod, reaching into the inside pocket of his leather jacket. He saw Sammy tense involuntarily and he withdrew his hand with painful slowness, laying his TACSAT on the table beside the computer. "I loaded the Korsakov files onto my phone before leaving Langley. Everything right here. What's the USB interface on this thing?"

Han propped the computer up and hit the power button. "Don't know— it's an old Dell Inspiron. USB 2.0, I think."

"That's going to be a problem," Carol announced, looking at the men. Harry nodded.

"Why?" Han asked.

Carol spun the laptop around until it was facing her. "From the moment he inserts the SIM card and powers on the phone, we've got thirty seconds until Langley has our general location. Sixty seconds and they'll have us down cold. The antique interface is going to slow the file transfer. Maybe too much."

Harry started to speak, but she cut him off, shooting a look at the ceiling of the bunker.

"Is this the lowest level of the bunker?"

"No—the stairs down that hall lead to the generator and on toward the helipad."

"How many feet below the surface?"

Han chuckled. "What Indian war are you fighting, girl? The generator room is located fifteen *meters* below the cabin."

"It'll be enough to block the signal," was Carol's reply, closing the laptop and tucking it under her arm as she stood. "Let's do this. We've got a long night ahead of us."

Chapter 9

They were going in blind. Korsakov pulled on the winter camouflage parka over his body armor and walked to the back of the Suburban. "Any ideas, Viktor?"

The night was cold, well below freezing, but sweat had beaded on the boy's face. There was a look of desperation in his eyes as he bent over the laptop, typing in commands. "*Nyet, nyet.* It just disappeared."

The assassin let out a sigh. He'd seen Viktor like this before, typically when something was going wrong. Crisis brought out the worst in the boy, a legacy of abuse. It had all started when the tracker had disappeared just over four hours before.

"*Nichevo,*" Korsakov whispered, placing a hand on Viktor's shoulder. It doesn't matter.

"Ready?" Yuri materialized out of the darkness, casting a critical glance at the wooded slope they had to traverse to reach the tracker's last known position. Korsakov pulled a Steyr AUG out of the back of the SUV and slapped a 42-round magazine of 5.56mm NATO into the buttstock of the bullpup rifle.

"*Da.* Let's do this."

9:39 A.M. Local Time
Bonn, Germany

He still tied his own ties. Maybe that would be his footnote in history. Roger Hancock leaned closer to the mirror, fiddling with his collar as he adjusted the Windsor knot of his necktie. The face of the President of the United States stared back at him.

He hadn't slept. There were dark circles under his eyes, but his makeup team would take care of that. They always did. Getting ready for the cameras required him to wear about twice as much makeup as your average streetwalker. An apt comparison, Hancock thought, reaching for his cufflinks.

The G-20 conference was going down the tubes, and the EU along with it. This was to be his legacy. Another four years might have fixed everything, but now that dream seemed to be vanishing too.

Two months ago, with backroom deals and the promise of Iranian oil flooding onto the US market, everything had looked bright. So bright to be extinguished so soon.

The door opened without preamble or ceremony, revealing Cahill's diminutive form in the entrance, flanked by Secret Service agents. "Anna's waiting for you, Mr. President. We're on in fifty."

"I'll be there," Hancock nodded, waiting until the Irishman disappeared and the door closed. He hadn't heard anything from the States—a disturbing silence.

The President reached for his suit jacket and threw it on, glancing at his iPhone on the nightstand of the hotel suite. Traditionally, the Secret Service had controlled all forms of Presidential communication, but Barack Obama's Blackberry had set a precedent that Hancock was only too happy to follow.

Just enough time to place a call.

4:23 A.M. Eastern Time
The CHRYSALIS bunker
West Virginia

The percolator was on the end of the counter, near the refrigerator. Harry made his way into the kitchen through the darkness, not bothering to turn on the lights.

He'd been that way even as a kid. Put him in a room once and he could find his way back through it in the dark. Times it came in handy.

They hadn't found anything worthwhile on Korsakov the previous night. Maybe if they'd had access to Ft. Meade's Crays…

125

Something told him that processing power wouldn't have helped. The ex-*Spetsnaz* hitman had never worked in the Western Hemisphere. Everything was Eastern Europe, with a sole anomaly.

Korsakov had killed a Russian businessman in Sudan in 2008, back before the Sudan became two separate countries. The guy had been an arms dealer—the consensus in the intelligence community was that a rival had ordered the hit.

Carol had pored over the laptop until her eyes were red. Nothing.

Harry tipped the coffee pot back, eyeing the day-old brew dubiously. Well, he'd always liked it black.

He'd told her to go to bed at midnight. Get some sleep.

What disturbed him was that he actually cared. There was something about her…

Caring was dangerous. It had been years since he had pursued a relationship with anyone.

Years since he'd wanted to. Harry let out a heavy sigh and poured the contents of the coffee pot into a mug. Things would be clearer once he'd woken up.

Movement in the doorway. "Early riser, I see." Sammy's voice.

The SEAL was already dressed for the weather—the SCAR in the crook of his arm. Dawn patrol. "Couldn't sleep?"

Harry shook his head. "You?"

"No," Han replied, crossing the kitchen toward the outside door.

"You're really not fond of windows, are you?" It was the first thing Harry had noticed upon arriving the previous afternoon. The beautiful picture window of the hunting cabin had been taken out and replaced by reinforced concrete—as had most of the other windows. Those that remained left the snow outside looking green in the sunlight—heavy, bullet-resistant glass. Too small to crawl through.

Han turned to look back at him.

"What's that verse you used to quote out on an op, Harry? 'For they have loved darkness rather than light'." He laughed. "Nobody survives, not in the end. We're not expected to. What's the operational strength of the Special Activities Division?"

"One hundred and fifty men," Harry replied, looking his old friend in the eye.

"Yeah," Han continued bitterly, "you see what I mean. One hundred and fifty men to fight a war without end. It's like tossin' sand into the teeth of the wind."

Harry started to respond, but Han cut him off, his hand on the door. "Get out of this business, Harry. While you still can. Before you end up like me."

And he was gone.

4:01 A.M. Central Time
Dearborn, Michigan

Allahu akbar. La illaha illa Allah. Muhammad rasul Allah. Allahu akbar. God is great. There is no God but God. Muhammad is His prophet. God is great.

Abdul Aziz Omar rose from the *fajr*, the dawn prayer, his dark hands moving reverently to fold the prayer mat. "*Astaghfirullah*," he whispered, repeating the phrase three times. I ask Allah forgiveness.

When he had approached al-Fileestini the previous year to volunteer for jihad, he had never anticipated this. Never anticipated something that would so test his faith. He hadn't entered a nightclub since he had found the peace of Allah—since he'd been released from prison. Now, with their target revealed, he felt weak. So pitifully weak.

The beads of the *tasbih* rolled between his fingers as he mouthed an earnest prayer. "I seek refuge in Allah from the outcast Satan... "

5:17 A.M. Eastern Time
The CHRYSALIS cabin
West Virginia

Staring at the ceiling got old, if you did it long enough. Carol rolled over on the mattress of the bunk bed, staring into the luminous dial of her watch. Time to get up.

She slipped out from beneath the blanket and got dressed in the darkness. It wasn't hard when there was only one set of clothes to choose.

There was no mirror in the small bedroom of the bunker, but she knew her hair was a mess. That much she could feel.

Harry was sitting at the kitchen table when she arrived, newspapers spread out over the wooden table. His field-stripped 1911 was laid out before him, a cleaning brush held delicately in his long fingers.

"Coffee's perking," came the terse announcement, but he didn't look up. "Orange concentrate is in the fridge. Just add water."

He was different this morning, she realized, pausing with her hand on the refrigerator door. The care she'd seen in his eyes the previous night, the tenderness—it was all gone, like a switch had been thrown.

It left her to wonder which was real and which was the façade. Walls within walls. A *maze...*

"You find anything more on Korsakov?" she asked, forcing herself to focus.

Harry shook his head, his eyes narrowing as he held the Colt's slide up to the light. "Might know someone with the answers."

"Who?" Carol turned to face him, brushing her blond hair back from her eyes.

"His name is Alexei Mikhailovich Vasiliev. Former KGB, transferred over to the FSB." A wry smile crept across Harry's face. "Same job, different letterheads. He's currently their 'chief of security' at the San Francisco consulate. Read: top spy. If there's a player in the Russkie underworld capable of bringing Korsakov into the States, he would know who it is. But it's going to require a face-to-face."

There was something about the way he said it. "Is that going to be a problem?"

"Problem? No, it's just that the last time I saw Alexei Mikhailovich I had a gun on him..."

6:23 A.M.
West Virginia

"What do you mean it's back?" Korsakov asked, the realization sinking in. He pulled the Steyr's sling from around his shoulders, holding the assault rifle loosely in his right hand as he moved around the open back of the Suburban to see the screen of the laptop. It was snowing again, heavy wet flakes falling down out of the night sky, sliding off the sleek metal skin of the SUV.

Viktor ignored the question, his attention focused on his work. "The mountain—what did you find?"

"There's a dacha a few hundred feet below the crest—a small hunting lodge. Nothing remarkable."

"You say a government installation, perhaps?"

Korsakov shook his head. "Doesn't look like it from the outside, but I don't know how to explain the satellites. The tracker is back on-line?"

"*Da.* About an hour. Could there be a basement—a bunker?"

The assassin's eyes lit up. "What are you saying?"

"If the tracker goes ten meters below the surface, we lose the signal. It's the only explanation."

Ten meters. Korsakov exchanged looks with Yuri and the man from Leningrad scowled back. Government.

That presented its own problems. And advantages. Governments were more predictable than a rogue agent.

"Well, they're not going anywhere with this snow," the assassin observed, opening the passenger door of the Suburban. "Yuri, take us back to the rally point. Viktor, I want you to set up a phone call for me."

"Where to?"

Korsakov slipped the Steyr into its carrying case and glanced into the rearview, allowing himself a faint smile. "The Federal Bureau of Investigation."

8:38 A.M.
The FBI Field Office
Alexandria, Virginia

Getting up late never did wonders for Caruso's mood, and his temperament wasn't improved by the sight of Marika Altmann standing in the foyer of the Alexandria field office, tucking up her greying hair under an FBI baseball cap.

Her suit jacket was off, lying over the back of a nearby chair. It had been replaced by a Level II flak vest. As he stood in the door, watching, she threw on a parka with the letters *FBI* across the back, covering up her .40 Glock.

"Going to stand there all day, Vic?" she asked, shooting a sharp glance over at him.

There was no good answer to that question, so Caruso elected to respond with another question. "What's going on?"

"We've got a lead on Nichols," Marika replied, scooping up an AR-15 carbine from the couch beside her and tossing it to him. That earned her a glance of shock and disapproval from the office receptionist, but it didn't seem to faze Altmann.

"Credible?"

The older woman snorted. "Haskel thinks so."

Coming from Altmann, that wasn't saying much. The Bureau chief had cut his law enforcement teeth in the Holder DOJ and his involvement in the ATF's infamous "Fast and Furious" op wasn't the type of record to endear him to his field agents.

"Where is he?" Caruso asked, following the woman back to the armory. Knowing Nichols, body armor was going to be mandatory.

"A hunting lodge in West Virginia. Klaus Jicha's flyin' in from Pittsburgh on a Gulfstream, along with the rest of the HRT. We're meeting him at the airport in twenty."

Haskel had to think it was serious. The Hostage Rescue Team was the FBI's elite. Even the director didn't pull them in on a whim. Caruso looked up from buttoning his jacket. "And you were planning on calling me—when?"

Altmann smiled, standing there with her arms folded across her chest. "You're *my* partner. If you can't keep up, just say the word."

9:19 A.M.
The CHRYSALIS cabin
West Virginia

"You know, this could look like a postcard."

Harry glanced up from the laptop's screen, from the Korsakov dossier he'd been poring over. Carol was standing beside the kitchen window, staring out at the falling snow.

"Stay away from the windows," he said, watching her out of the corner of his eye. Small as they were, hardened as they might be—there was no sense in not taking precautions.

There was no response, and for a moment he wondered if she had even heard his words. She took another long sip of her coffee. "A Christmas postcard."

He rose from his chair and crossed the kitchen to stand behind her. She was right. It did look a lot like a postcard—wet, heavy flakes falling straight down out of a gray sky, coating the mountainside in a heavy blanket. Weighing down the evergreens. "As well it should," he said, placing a hand on her waist, "with Christmas only ten days away. It *is* a beautiful sight."

"It's hard to think of Christmas, with him gone." She looked up into his eyes. "I did love him, Harry. I truly did, despite all the years apart."

She didn't pull away from his hand. "He knew that," Harry whispered, his lips only inches away from her ear. He took a deep breath, trying to ignore the emotions roiling within his heart. This wasn't safe, caring never was. He had to focus on the mission. Say what needed to be said—what she needed to hear. "And he loved you more than life itself."

Minutes passed before she spoke again, a long, ragged sigh escaping her. "When I was three, he came home for Christmas. Home from where, I don't know. All I know is he brought me a *matryoshka*."

A genuine smile touched his lips. "A wooden nesting doll."

"Yes," she replied, watching the steam rise up from the mug of coffee in her hands. "Dolls within dolls, each one smaller than the next. It was the last Christmas present he gave me as a child. The next year, he was just gone."

There was nothing to say, so Harry didn't say anything. Sometimes silence was the only effective tactic.

Tactic. He could have cursed himself for thinking of it that way.

"Half a dozen times I nearly threw it away," Carol continued. "I hated him so much for leaving us. But I could never quite bring myself to it. It was only as I grew older that I realized my father was a lot like the *matryoshka*. Layers within layers, hardness concealing the man beneath. A man I could forgive—a man I could love."

Her voice caught and she stopped talking abruptly. Harry just stood there, wanting to say something, but the words felt empty on his lips. It was the price of having spent a lifetime dealing in manipulation and deceit. Soon, you didn't know how to handle a relationship without manipulation—and you couldn't care for anyone you were playing.

There was nothing he could say to her that he hadn't said a thousand times before, working an angle. Nothing.

He stepped back, suddenly aware of her warmth, of his hand on her waist, of their closeness.

"I'm getting worried about Sammy," he announced, changing the subject as he moved to the window—ignoring his own advice. "He should have been back by now."

"He *is* back," a cold voice announced from the stairs to the bunker. Startled, Harry and Carol turned almost as one.

Samuel Han stood there across the kitchen from them, still dressed in his parka, his snow-encrusted boots dripping onto the wooden floor. His Sig-Sauer was drawn, held loosely to his side. "Do you have any idea what you've done?"

9:30 A.M.
Dulles International Airport
Virginia

On a normal December day, Dulles would have been crowded with holiday travelers. The sight of the lone Gulfstream on the tarmac, surrounded by blacked-out Suburbans, was a reminder that this day was anything but normal.

Following the bombing at Langley, National Terrorism Advisory alerts had gone out across the country, and all civilian air traffic into the District of Columbia had been diverted.

Unfortunately, Vic thought as he pushed open the door of his SUV, the same could not be said for ground traffic. Even with their official status, the trip from Alexandria to Dulles had taken over an hour. With suspects still on the loose, the government had decided to minimize the panic by restricting media access. It was having the opposite effect.

A drug deal gone bad ten blocks from the Capitol earlier in the morning had resulted in three DOAs—and brushfire rumors that it was another terrorist attack.

Klaus Jicha was standing near the stairs of the Gulfstream as Vic and Marika approached.

"Everyone ready?" Jicha asked, looking pointedly at his watch. The HRT leader was a huge man, towering above Vic. A knit cap was pulled down low over his ears to the back of his collar, obscuring what there was of a short, very thick neck. Overall, it gave him the appearance of an immense bulldog.

Altmann nodded, extending a hand. "I'm Agent Altmann, the Special Agent in Charge. We'll be ready as soon as your men can load up."

"You've had my men sitting on their thumbs for the last forty-five minutes, S-A-C." Jicha ignored the proffered hand.

"Unexpectedly heavy traffic, Agent Jicha," she retorted, not backing down an inch. "We're coordinating with local LEOs to clear the route on the way back out. It's still going to be a long ride, so I trust your team has packed MREs."

Vic took a look up at the sky, at the sun beating down on the mounds of dirt-brown snow piled up at the edges of the airport. "Why can't we go in by air? A couple Blackhawks and we could be there by zero-eleven hundred. It'd give us a much better target window."

Altmann and Jicha exchanged glances, then the big man cleared his throat. "It's snowing in West Virginia, Caruso. Nothing's flying in or out. We go in by road, or we don't go in at all. Now, let's get this circus on the road."

9:32 A.M.
The CHRYSALIS cabin
West Virginia

"What are you playing at, Sammy?" Harry demanded, taking a step forward to place himself between Carol and Han.

The Sig-Sauer came up, held rock-steady in the SEAL's hands. It was about the only thing that was steady, fire blazing in Han's eyes. "You said you weren't followed—you *promised* me you weren't."

Harry shook his head, moving another cautious step. "I don't know what you're talking about." It was just a matter of getting close enough to take the gun...

"I'm talking about Russians—Korsakov and his team."

"Here?"

"You've got that straight," Han replied. "I found tracks on the northern ridge—two men. They were watching the cabin last night."

Harry shook his head. "It's deer season, Sammy, hunters all over these mountains—what makes you think it was *Spetsnaz*?"

"I followed them." The pistol was wavering now, perspiration flecking Han's brow. "I tracked them through the snow to the road and found them by their vehicle. They were packing serious heat—automatic weapons. It looked like a command and control vehicle."

Harry exchanged glances with Carol. Something had gone horribly wrong. He made a cautious move toward Han, his hand outstretched. "We can work through this, Sammy. We've done it before. Just give me the gun—don't want anybody getting hurt here."

"That's impossible, Nichols," Han replied, staring at Harry down the barrel of his semiautomatic. "People always get hurt when you come around—like you're some sort of grim reaper. I should never have let you stay."

It took everything in him not to flinch at the words, but he'd been walling up his emotions for years. You learned not to take anything personally. "I got you into this, Sammy," Harry began, watching the eyes of his old compatriot, "and I'll get you out. You have my word."

The former SEAL laughed, a short, sneering bark. "Your *word*? I know exactly what that's worth. Or have you forgotten that I worked with you? That I was like you once? We did what was best for the mission, the devil take everything and everyone else. And you haven't changed. No, Harry, you're not getting me out. You're staying here."

Harry looked from the face of his old friend, out through the window into the driving snow. It wasn't like they had many other options. At length, he nodded. "All right, Sammy. We'll play this your way."

Chapter 10

When the cellphone in his pocket buzzed with an incoming text, Carter was grabbing a double espresso in the CIA's cafeteria. Anything to keep himself awake for the ride home.

Ron placed a ten-dollar bill down on the counter and flipped the phone open as he waited for his change. Inflation being what it was, there wouldn't be much of it.

There were two words printed there on the screen. CALL ME.

It wasn't a request.

Thirty-five cents. The change almost wasn't worth taking, but Ron swept it into his pocket all the same, dialing a number as he headed for the door.

"What's going on?" he asked when the phone was picked up on the second ring.

"That's what I was going to ask you." Tex's voice. "I'd like to know why a full surveillance team has been dedicated to my apartment."

"Word around the office is that they wanted you pulled back in and put on the box. Kranemeyer told the Banker you'd gone hunting. My guess is that someone's checking out his story."

"Anything else?"

Carter cast a long look around as he reached his car. The number of guards overseeing parking had been doubled ever since the bombing that had taken Ames' life.

"Yeah," he said, sliding into the driver's seat of the Hyundai. He fingered the USB flash drive in his pocket as though assuring himself of its presence. A deep breath. "We need to meet."

5:24 P.M.
The CHRYSALIS cabin
West Virginia

There was one fundamental truth about high-capacity magazines, one that every shooter—from the weekend marksman to the clandestine operator—knew.

They took many times longer to fill than they did to empty. Which is why you didn't want to be reloading them in the middle of a firefight.

Harry extended his thumb, pressing a twentieth cartridge between the aluminum lips of the SCAR's magazine. He didn't like being on the defensive, but there wasn't much choice. Prepare for war.

Carol was sitting on the floor, knees drawn up nearly to her chin as she leaned back against the wall of the bedroom. There was an open box of .308 beside her, the long brass cartridges looking strangely out of place in her hands.

She must have felt his eyes on her, because she looked up suddenly, meeting his gaze.

It was a self-conscious moment, for a reason he couldn't quite place his finger on. He cleared his throat, looking away as he placed the loaded magazine beside the SCAR.

"Sammy seems better now," she observed.

Harry nodded. "It's the PTSD. Some guys experience claustrophobia—panic attacks. Sammy—he was never like that. He just got angry. It comes and goes."

There was a long moment before she spoke again, but he could see the question in her eyes. Dreaded it. "What he said—was it true?"

"About me?"

A nod, as though she didn't trust herself to speak. He turned back to his work—unable to look her in the eye. Holding the magazine upright in his hand, he inserted it into the mag well of the SCAR, pulling back on the charging handle. Locked and loaded. "Yeah, it's all true. Every last word of it."

Silence. He reached for an empty magazine and a fresh box of cartridges. "I've done a lot of things in fifteen years. Regret many of them."

"Why?"

"You asked how I ended up at Langley."

No response. It didn't matter. Why he'd decided to tell her he didn't know, but he was certain that it was a bad decision.

"It wasn't a childhood dream." An ironic half-smile touched his face. "Anything but. I was studying at Georgetown in '97—my junior year."

Harry glanced over and could see her mentally calculating the years. He smiled. "My folks were serious over-achievers—I entered college early. The Agency came knocking in the fall of that year. They were recruiting for their Middle Eastern desk, and well, that was my area of studies. Langley was just starting to wake up to their need of people who knew the region, its people, its languages. I'd always loved languages, loved learning them, watching how they related to each other. But the intelligence community wasn't for me. I had other plans for my life. So I turned them down."

He couldn't read the expression on her face, but she had stopped loading. No way to tell if that was bad or good. He slipped another brass cartridge into the SCAR's magazine, testing the tension spring with his thumb. "My best friend didn't. His name was Robert, but everybody called him Rob. As the only two Christians in our class, we'd grown close. Brothers in all but blood, as the saying goes. He signed an agreement with Langley allowing him to finish out his Georgetown classes via e-mail. That wasn't common back in those days. I'll never forget that last day in the dorm room, kneeling together in prayer as he prepared to leave. I didn't realize then that I'd never see him again—alive."

"What happened?" Carol asked, her voice quiet.

He took a deep breath. Hadn't allowed himself to think about it in a long time. *Years.* "As typical of a bureaucracy, Langley had woken up to their need of his skills several years too late. The following August, a man named Mohammed al-'Owhali drove a truck filled with TNT and aluminum nitrate into the American embassy in Kenya. Rob had been assigned to Station Nairobi, as an analyst. He was killed instantly."

"And you joined the Agency?"

"It didn't take the seventh son of a seventh son to see what was coming—all you needed to understand was the theology of fundamentalist Islam, the nature of its people. Most Americans still don't know how much money the *Ikhwan* poured into Stateside universities in the '90s, trying to keep this country blinded. It worked."

He saw her nod at the mention of the Muslim Brothers. She knew.

"And you never looked back?"

It was a long time before he could answer the question, or at least it seemed that way. His vision narrowed, the weak light of the Coleman glittering off the brass in his hand. When he spoke, it took a mighty effort.

"Nothing there," he replied, looking down at his hands. "There's no going back once you've taken the mark of Cain."

6:07 P.M.
The Denny's
Elkins, West Virginia

"What's their ETA?" Korsakov asked, leaning across the booth toward Viktor. It was only the third time he had asked in the past forty minutes.

The boy waved dismissively, focusing in on the laptop. "Ten minutes."

"You've said that before."

"They're updating, *tovarisch*. The weather is a problem."

That was for certain. Monitoring the progress of the FBI's Hostage Rescue Team was maddeningly slow work. "They'll need a couple hours to get in place in this snow. We should have time."

"What are they using for intel support?"

The boy took another sip of his Coca-Cola, glancing at the image of the polar bear on the glass bottle. "A KH-13 spy satellite—equipped with thermal imaging."

Yuri swore, his eyes fixed on Korsakov's face. "They'll see us the moment we go in."

Viktor held up a finger, a smile dancing in his eyes. "Unless..."

"Unless *what*, Viktor?" Korsakov demanded. It was clear that the boy was enjoying himself, but time was critical. No time for games.

"The spy sat will come in range in the next hour. Three hours over target. Then, gone."

Yuri shook his head. "No good. They could launch the assault any time within the window—we have to be on that mountain."

"*Nichevo*," Viktor replied. It was his moment of triumph. "It won't matter if their network is blinded by a worm."

"You can do this?" Korsakov could have laughed.

A smile. "*Da*."

6:21 P.M.
The National Mall
Washington, D.C.

He wasn't cut out for field work. That much Ron Carter knew. If he'd ever held any romantic delusions of the spy business, they were evaporating as the grass of the National Mall crunched beneath his feet.

It was a deuce of a place for a covert meeting. If he had to have guessed, Thomas had picked the spot. The New Yorker had always had a regrettable flair for the dramatic.

On any normal night, the mall would have been filled with tourists, enjoying the sight of D.C. after dark. It was deserted now.

A lone security guard walked past, pushing his bike over the icy grass. He didn't give Carter a second glance.

On a bench near the WWII memorial, Carter found the signal, a vertical line of yellow chalk against the wood. What was this, the Cold War?

He brushed the dusting of snow off the bench and sat down, easing the strap of the laptop case off his shoulder.

The HP booted up quickly and he went to work, preparing.

The sound of footsteps—someone moving off to his left and Ron glanced up, his fingers trembling. Was every moment in the field like this?

It was nothing, just a drunk moving up the pathway—his swaying form backlit by the lights of the Memorial. As Carter watched, the wino tilted a small bottle of vodka back and emptied it in a single draught.

Ron shook his head, turning back to his laptop. He found himself wondering if the drunk would survive the night.

Singing, as the man wavered closer—an off-key rendition of a rap song. He was about to pass the bench when he turned suddenly, placing a hand on Carter's knee. "How's it goin'?"

Thomas's voice. Ron nearly came out of his skin. "Don't do that to me!" he exclaimed, punctuating his words with a curse. A flair for the dramatic. Yeah, right.

Thomas collapsed onto the bench beside him, laughing. "I thought that was one of my better impressions. Had enough practice."

"Could we get down to business?" Tex materialized out of the darkness from the opposite direction.

Carter nodded. It was going to take hours for his heart rate to go back down. He inserted his thumb drive into the USB port of the laptop and brought up a picture. "Can you tell me who this is?"

Tex took a seat. "It looks like Harry sitting there with his back to the camera—the other man's Sammy Han."

"Yeah, I know, those are obvious," Carter replied. "Look at the woman sitting at the *other* table. I had to digitally enhance her face."

He heard Thomas's sharp intake of breath, and knew that he was right. "That's Rhoda Stevens—when was this shot taken?"

"January of 2013. Over eight months after I attended her funeral."

7:19 P.M.
The CHRYSALIS cabin

"With any luck, we should be able to take out roughly half of the assault team at the entry point," Han observed, looking up from his work. He finished taping the last packet of C-4 to the frame of the door and tested the knob. Locked. Reaching up, he unfastened the heavy deadbolt. It was going to stay that way. A strong kick would send the door crashing inward—and detonate the explosives. "Any idea of Korsakov's actual strength?"

Harry shook his head.

"Oh, joy," the SEAL murmured. "At least tell me you have an estimate."

"Judging from his previous ops, I'd say he brought 10-15 men into the country. Two of them are dead. You do the math."

"We can figure on at least three-quarters of them assaulting the house—probably Korsakov himself will hold back to provide command and control—a few snipers in the treeline." Han gestured from the wired door and windows down the long corridor that led to the bunker. "We've got the two Claymores in the corridor—they should take out more of the assaulters if we camouflage them well enough. Any survivors? They'll be caught between you and I when they enter the bunker—enfilading fields of fire. No chance to react. No quarter."

The former SEAL paused as the reality of his own words washed over him. His body shuddered and he leaned against the doorframe. "I don't know if I can do this, Harry. You give two decades of your life to your country and what do you get out of it? A broken marriage—a wife that hangs up every time you call. Two little boys that don't even remember they once called you 'daddy'. Visions of the men you've killed haunting you at night. It doesn't matter how much they deserved to die—you don't remember that when they visit you in your dreams. I don't need any new ghosts."

Harry looked up from wiring the Claymore mines. Linked together, they would spray the passageway with ball bearings, eviscerating anything in their path. "I know, Sammy."

"I know you do—you think I'd bother telling someone who didn't understand?" Han walked over and put his hand on Harry's shoulder. "We were brothers once, you and I—and I would give my life for yours. I'm not going to desert you now. But I *will* remember your role in bringing this day to pass."

There was a quiet threat there in his old friend's eyes, but Harry just nodded. "I can live with that."

"Good," Han replied, turning away after a long moment. "Because I'm not sure I can…"

7:56 P.M.
The Tactical Operations Center
West Virginia

Getting a tight perimeter in place was always a challenge—toss in the darkness, the blinding snow, the vagaries of the West Virginian mountains, and it was turning into a full-fledged nightmare.

Caruso dug a gloved hand from the depths of his pocket and reached out, opening the door of the mobile trailer that served as the HRT's Tactical Operations Center, or TOC, in the community parlance. The trailer was parked crossways on the narrow road, in itself forming an effective roadblock against anyone who sought egress from the mountain.

Marika was already inside, working over the computers with one of the members of the support team.

"Do we have the perimeter in place?"

She looked up. "Take it easy, Vic—just because you're good at groping about in the darkness doesn't mean we all are. We just got satellite support fifteen minutes ago—Petersen nearly went over a cliff before she saw it was there. Thank God for technology."

Leah Petersen was the HRT's lead sniper. "Where's Jicha?"

"In the back with Russ—running over the plan one last time. We send him in within fifteen minutes."

Caruso nodded. William Russell Cole was a living legend among hostage negotiators, a small-framed, gentle man in his early sixties. In thirty-odd years with the Bureau, he'd never worn a gun.

Spend five minutes with him—you'd feel like you had a new best friend. That's why he was so good at what he did.

He found the two men near the back of the trailer. "We'll have two snipers here…and here," Jicha was saying, drawing his finger across the touchscreen of the computer. "They'll be in position to cover you as you walk up to the cabin, but, you know our ROE."

The negotiator smiled, patting Jicha on the arm. "It's not a problem, Klaus. Never has been. If I do my job right, your boys can go home without firing their weapons. Now, if you'll excuse me, I need to suit up."

"Don't underestimate him, Russ," Jicha warned as the negotiator turned away.

"Nichols?" Caruso could see a shadowed look there in Russ's eyes as he asked the question. "Don't worry, Klaus. I won't."

8:12 P.M.
Washington, D.C.

Waiting—that was the biggest part of the spy business. Just waiting. It didn't do wonders for one's blood pressure—or waistline.

Thomas tapped his hand idly against the passenger window of the Malibu, waiting. He needed a drink.

He glanced over at Tex in the driver's seat, wondering if he should wake him. The big man had the seat all the way back, his lanky form stretched out, his hands folded over his chest. He was a Marine, after all. Never stand when you can sit...never sit when you can lie down...never lie down when you can sleep—because you never know when you'll have another chance.

"You think Carter will come through for us?"

Tex's right eye came open, a single black orb staring over at Thomas. The news that the FBI had located Harry had come as a shock to them both. As usual, the Texan was dealing with it better.

"Going back into Langley at this hour is going to raise some eyebrows—but if anyone is known for odd hours, it's Ron." Carter hadn't known anything more than the basics, but he'd promised to get back on Langley's servers and find out where the Bureau was staging.

As if on cue, it was at that moment that Tex's cellphone chose to ring. "Yes? Yeah, I've got a pen—go ahead and give me the coordinates."

Flicking the dome light on, the Texan cradled the phone against his shoulder as he scrawled a series of latitude and longitude coordinates on the back of his hand. He listened for another moment, then tucked the phone back in his pocket.

Thomas waited as Tex put the Malibu into drive, heading south. "Where's the FBI raid going down?"

"West Virginia. Got a long drive ahead of us."

8:15 P.M.
The CHRYSALIS cabin
West Virginia

Harry was in the bedroom when Carol found him, tucking the Colt .45 into a paddle holster at his hip. Preparing for war. His AK-47 was clutched in his left hand, a pair of spare magazines in a pouch on his belt.

He didn't turn around, simply gestured toward a ballistic vest lying there on the bedspread. "I need you to put that on under your shirt."

"Where do you want me?" she asked, peeling off her jacket as she entered the room. She dropped it on the bed and picked up the vest, holding it up against herself.

"You can change in there," he said, indicating the direction of the bathroom with a curt nod. It was almost as if his previous display of emotion had embarrassed him.

The vest had been designed for a woman, Carol realized, tracing the outline of the built-in bra cups. Han's wife?

Closing the door behind her, she stripped out of her blouse and pulled the vest on over her head. It was more than a little loose, but the 6-point strapping system offered enough adjustability to make it work. Just enough.

When she re-opened the door, Harry was still there, checking his weapons one final time. "That's not what I meant," she began, buttoning her blouse over the vest. "Where do you want me when the assault hits?"

"In the bunker. Stay in the back, near the helicopter if you want to. Just keep your head down."

"That's it?" she heard herself ask. "These men killed my father and you just want me to keep my head down?"

He looked up, meeting her gaze for the first time since she'd entered the room. "You're missing the point. If anything happens to you, they succeed." Those ice-blue eyes blazed with a flash of intensity as he added, "And I fail."

Carol took her jacket off the bed and started to push past him toward the door, but his hand closed around her wrist. "I need to hear you say it," he warned, his grip firm but not painful. *Not yet.*

She felt her breath catch as she stared back into his eyes, unyielding. And in that moment, she knew. If it was necessary to save her life, he wouldn't hesitate to snap her wrist like a straw. "Say it…"

Surrender was the only option and she realized it. Didn't make the words come any easier.

"Harry!" Han's shout came from the front of the cabin. "Get your butt out here—we've got company."

Silence. The only sound he could hear was the noise of the wind whipping around the mountainside. The cabin remained silent, no one answering his hail.

Russ fingered the bullhorn in his hands, debating how long he should wait before trying again. Over thirty years, he'd dealt with bank robbers, pyschotic parents, crackheads, and terrorists. He'd seen it all.

Yet the shiver that rippled through his body had nothing to do with the wind. Or the falling snow. Tonight was different.

He'd seen Nichols in action before—they'd worked together when Cole had been deployed to Islamabad as part of the Joint Terrorism Task Force in the fall of 2009.

Unpredictable. That was the CIA officer. Brilliant, ruthless—other adjectives that came immediately to mind. What had caused him to go rogue, Russ had no idea. One thing and only one thing he knew. Nichols would be playing to win.

A figure stood in the middle of the cabin's driveway, ankle-deep in snow, glowing in Harry's night-vision. "What do you make of it?"

Harry looked back at his friend. "I recognize him," he said finally. "It's William Russell Cole. We worked together in Pakistan with the JTTF."

Han's face was drawn and white in the darkness. "What are you trying to tell me?"

"It's not a trick—we're up against the HRT."

7:24 P.M. Central Time
Fargo, North Dakota

It was the night of the school Christmas party. She should have been there, but she didn't feel like partying, particularly with her fellow teachers.

The glass of wine on the coffee table was half-empty, Bing Crosby's voice on the radio in the kitchen crooning, *It's the most wonderful time of the year.*

Yeah, right. She and Mary had gone to the Christmas party together last year, right before she left for Washington. She could still remember the sight of her pretty sister dancing in the arms of Nicholas, the phys-ed teacher. He'd been smitten.

Bing's voice trailed off into the ether as the radio station broke for news. "...the parallel attacks in Virginia on the 13th and the widespread panic which has followed, President Roger Hancock has announced that he is leaving the G-20 summit to return to D.C. White House spokesman Dominic Reyes quoted the President in an exclusive with FOX News. 'A leader's place in time of crisis is in his nation's capital'."

Alicia smiled, reaching for the bottle of pinot noir in front of her. She'd already had two glasses, enough to necessitate coffee in the morning. But he was coming back to the States. That called for a celebration...

8:31 P.M. Eastern Time
The CHRYSALIS cabin

Fifteen minutes since the Bureau man had first appeared outside the cabin. They'd let him cool his heels for long enough.

With a nod to Han, Harry cranked the front window open. His hand grazed the packet of C-4 below the window sill. Disconnected, but it could still be detonated at a moment's notice.

Time to open up a dialogue. "How's it going, Russ?"

It was him. The older man drew his jacket tighter around his body, turning to face the voice. "I've had better nights, Harry, but let's not talk about me. I'm here to listen to you, to find out what you need. I just want everyone to walk out of here—keep everybody safe."

"I know, Russ," the voice replied. "You're a good man. You don't want a tactical assault any more than I want to draw down on agents I've worked with for so many years."

Calm. Nichols' voice was almost dangerously calm. That was another thing he remembered about the CIA man.

"We can resolve this, Harry. Those security officers at Langley—that was reactive, a split-second decision—*and you didn't kill them*. I know you feel alone, I know nerves can fray under pressure, but we can bring closure to this without anyone getting hurt."

There was a laugh from the direction of the cabin. "Correction, Russ. I'm not workin' this one alone. I've got a partner. So you can tell Leah to get her cross-hairs out of my face."

The TOC

"Blast it!" Altmann exclaimed, listening to the exchange through her headphones. "How did he know?"

Vic shook his head. "It's not that hard. He knows our protocols. He knows our people. Leah's been the HRT's top sniper for the better part of a decade."

The woman sighed, looking over at Klaus Jicha. "Get Sgt. Petersen on comm. Tell her to stand by—but do not, repeat, do *not* take the shot."

7:42 P.M. Central Time
The mosque
Dearborn, Michigan

It had taken them five weeks to make the basement of the mosque airtight. Another two to acquire the equipment needed and move it into place.

Jamal al-Khalidi smiled, slipping the gas mask over his head. This wasn't like nukes. Most of the equipment he'd needed he had secured over the Internet. In times like these, eBay was your friend.

A pair of the shaikh's Pakistanis entered the room through the hermetically sealed door, bearing a large container between them.

"Just set it down over there on the table," Jamal instructed in English, switching to Arabic when they failed to comprehend. Didn't everyone understand English these days?

Snapping gloves onto his hands, the University of Michigan chemistry student walked over, typing in the sequence of numbers of the container's keypad. There was a buzz and the locks disengaged, allowing him to push open the lid.

He had known what to expect, but his breath still caught at the sight. Four large conical artillery shells lay within, inscribed in flowing Arabic script. He reached in, hefting one of the unwieldy munitions in both of his hands. Weighing in at eighty-four kilograms, the 180-mm shell had been designed to be fired out of the Soviet S-23 howitzer, exported to Quaddafi's Libya.

And now, with the fall of the tyrant and the rise of the *Ikhwan*, he held it in his hands. Such power.

His fingers traced the script almost reverently, knowing that what filled the shell was not the ordinary mix of high explosive and shrapnel. Rather, what his chemistry professor would have referred to as pinacolyl methylphosphonoflouridate. Soman.

Nerve gas.

8:57 P.M. Eastern Time
The TOC
West Virginia

"We have three signatures—here, here—and here," Klaus Jicha announced, tracing his finger across the thermal image. "It's reasonable to assume that our two subjects are here, probably conferring. The signature here, in the corner, is likely Miss Chambers."

"And if you're wrong, Klaus?" Russ asked, staring at the HRT leader. He didn't like the way this conversation was heading.

"No one is pretending this is an exact science," the big man replied, shooting him a look of annoyance. "We can position entry teams at the side and rear—use shaped charges along the wall. As long as we know where our subjects are, it should go down clean."

"I'd prefer to avoid that as long as possible," the negotiator interjected, standing there in the middle of the trailer with his hands on his hips. It was an unusually aggressive posture for him. "You and I both know that the tactical solution is always the least desirable. You send in the guys with guns, it introduces too many variables. Just give me a few more hours."

Klaus shook his head. "Three more hours—the sat goes out of range and we lose our best intel on placement of the subjects. You want to talk about variables? *That* will be a crap shoot."

An oath exploded from the lips of Marika Altmann and both men turned to see her staring at the bank of screens covering one end of the trailer. "What's going on?"

"We're losing our satellite coverage," Marika responded. "Looks like a software glitch—the whole feed's going down."

"Deliberate?"

The older woman shook her head. "No way to tell—but in a couple minutes we're gonna be blind."

9:00 P.M.
West Virginia

Korsakov found himself holding his breath as Viktor continued to type commands into the Toshiba. The kid upturned his can of Coca-cola, wiping the brown liquid away from his lips. Like most of his generation, he seemed to do his best work while in that caffeine-induced high.

At length, he looked up, a broad smile creeping across his face. "It's done. They are—how they say, blind as bats? As long as the worm remains active and I maintain control of the feed, I can guide you right in."

The assassin slapped him on the back. "Well done, Viktor. *Spasiba.*" Thank you.

With a shove, Korsakov forced open the back doors of the Suburban, leaping out onto the snowy mountain road. Despite the cold, he could feel adrenaline flowing like fire through his veins. It was time to make their move.

9:34 P.M.
The CHRYSALIS cabin

Things had gotten quiet after the hostage negotiator had disappeared back into the darkness. The wind howling around the western end of the cabin was the only thing they could hear.

"What are they doing?" Carol asked at length.

Harry looked back at her, to where she sat on the floor. "Staging for an early morning assault, most likely. Sometime between zero one and zero three hundred—that's when the human body goes through its deepest REM cycles. It's the way I'd do it."

Han cleared his throat. "You going through with this, Harry?"

It was a good question. That didn't change the answer one bit. "Of course. There aren't many other options, are there?"

The SEAL shook his head. "You're talkin' about killing federal agents, Harry. For the love of God, these are *our* people."

The worst of it was, he was right. "If you want to go out and give yourself up, I won't hold it against you," Harry replied, watching his friend's eyes closely. "You've not broken any laws—feel free to say that I took you hostage as well."

"That's not what I'm saying," Han retorted, anger creeping into his voice. Dangerous ground there. "I'm talking about you—running E&E from the feds is one thing. Trading shots with the HRT is a whole new ballgame. We need to get the two of you out of here."

Harry gave him a tight smile. "There's only one way out of here—and that's with that old surplus helo of yours. Listen to the wind, to the snow. The best pilot in the world couldn't exfil from this mountain tonight."

Han seemed to consider his words for a long moment, then he slung the SCAR over his shoulder and turned toward the corridor leading to the bunker.

"Where are you going?"

"Won't hurt to have it fueled up."

9:47 P.M.

There they were—the FBI's sniper team. Directly ahead of him, maybe eight, nine meters. Dressed in winter ghillie suits, he never would have seen them if he'd hadn't known where to look, the satellite feed on his phone guiding him in.

Yuri left the AK-47 on his back and bent down, removing his suppressed Beretta 92 from its ankle holster. Just a matter of waiting.

He glanced at the screen of his phone, watching on the satellite as the rest of the *Spetsnaz* moved into position. The man from Leningrad smiled in the darkness. This was going to be good.

11:59 P.M. Local Time
Air Force One
Over the Atlantic

He was going to miss this, Roger Hancock thought, glancing around at the opulence of the Presidential bedroom. It might have been 35,000 feet in the air, but you would never have known it from looking at the furnishings.

Yes, he was going to miss this, whether he won his bid for reelection or not. At some point, it all had to end. America's living, breathing Constitution still didn't leave enough leeway for him to remain in office indefinitely. A shame, really. Four years, or even eight, just wasn't enough for a man to fulfill his dreams.

A knock came at the door and Hancock levered himself up to a sitting position in bed, adjusting the sheet so that it covered the sleeping form of the intern who lay beside him.

She wasn't as much fun as Mary had been before her overdose, but it had still been an eventful night.

"Come in!" Curt Hawkins, the agent-in-charge of Hancock's detail, pushed the door open and entered without further ceremony.

"We'll be landing within an hour and a half, Mr. President." The Secret Service agent was a heavy-set man of medium height, his suits expertly tailored to conceal the Sig-Sauer P229 he carried underneath his jacket. He still spoke with the slow drawl of his native Mississippi. "Directors Haskel and Shapiro are meeting you at Andrews, as you requested."

That was another thing he was going to miss, Hancock mused, a shadow passing across his face. A presidential "request" carried the weight of an order.

And if those two directors didn't have the answers he was looking for, there'd be the devil to pay…

10:03 P.M. Eastern Time
The CHRYSALIS cabin
West Virginia

The snow seemed to be letting up, Harry thought, staring out the open window through his night-vision goggles.

He had no illusions about how this was going to end. The HRT was good. Even if he succeeded...he'd be killing his own people.

Blue on blue.

Dear Lord, don't let it come to that, he whispered, murmuring a brief prayer. He knew too many of the FBI agents. Knew their families.

Despite the legendary rivalry between Langley and the Bureau, they all played for the same team in the end.

His only hope was to hold off the HRT until the storm passed, until they could make their escape from the mountain. And that was a long shot.

A figure materialized out of the wind-blown snow and Harry brought his rifle to bear before recognizing the hostage negotiator. It had been twenty minutes since last contact—with no phones in the cabin, the negotiation was taking on a highly unorthodox form.

"Do you remember Islamabad, Harry?" Russell asked, moving closer to the cabin. "Do you remember those three months we worked together?"

No answer. "You've had a fine career, fifteen years in the service of your country. Neither one of us wants to see it end here."

A short laugh from the cabin. Nichols' voice. "You and I both know that it's already ended, Russ. It was over the moment my face was splashed across national TV. I've been burned—there's no going back."

"It doesn't have to be that way, not if we can end this now. Nobody's gotten hurt up to this point, and I want to thank you for that. You've shown control. That's going to count for a lot, but you're going to need to meet us half-way by putting down your weapon and coming out."

"He's right, you know," Carol announced from her seat in the corner.

Harry shook his head, forcing himself to remain focused on the world outside. "How so?"

"You kill one of those agents, you won't be able to live with yourself. I know you're just trying to protect me, to follow the orders my father gave you, but I can't let you do it."

"You're not *letting* me—" There was something in her voice, an unusual intensity. He turned. She wasn't sitting any longer—she was standing five feet from the front door, the subcompact Kahr leveled in her hands. Pointed at him.

"What do you think you're doing?"

"I'm going out there, to talk to the negotiator, to *resolve* this."

She meant to do it, Harry realized, reading the determination in her eyes. As impossible as it was, she really meant to do it.

"They're not going to believe you," he replied, casting a sidelong glance toward the corridor. If only he could stall her for long enough. *Come on, Sammy.*

"Russ is trained in dealing with Stockholm. They'll just bundle you back to the TOC and resume their demands for our surrender."

She shook her head. "I'm not going to have good men kill each other for my sake. That's something I'll have to risk. Don't try to stop me."

10:25 P.M.
The TOC

"How much longer?" Marika Altmann demanded, leaning over the shoulder of the young computer tech. What was he—seventeen, eighteen? She could've had grandchildren his age, had any of her marriages lasted long enough for kids.

He jumped as her hand descended on his shoulder—probably the closest contact he'd ever had with a woman, she thought. "Uh—five, maybe ten minutes. Maybe less—it's hard to tell. I've got to clear out the infected packets and restore the firewall before we can safely reconnect with the Key Hole sat."

"Tick-tock, Bishop," she replied, turning away. "The sat moves out of range in thirty. Get it done."

10:29 P.M.

Icy beads of sweat clung to Viktor's forearms as he typed in another series of commands into the Toshiba. Nothing happened. He was losing control.

He threw his arm up over the rear seat of the Suburban, fighting off the panic attack, the urge to curl up in a ball as he had done in those years at the brothel. As the whip had descended upon his naked body.

Struggling to control his voice, he toggled his lip mike to contact the *Spetsnaz*. He was one of them. He was. He was...

From the moment Korsakov heard the boy's voice over the radio, he knew something was wrong. "They're rooting out the worm—don't know how much longer I can stay in control of their sat."

"Give me an estimate, *tovarisch*," the assassin replied, controlling his tones. He'd always known the boy's pysche was delicate. Getting angry with him would accomplish nothing.

"*Da.* Two or three minutes before they can see you."

The realization struck Korsakov with the force of a bullet, and he had all he could do to refrain from swearing. His men were spread out—six with him and another six spread out across the mountain. There was no time to retreat. He turned to the men immediately flanking him, both of them armed with Soviet-era RPG-7s. "One rocket through the western wall of the cabin. One into the FBI trailer. Wait for my signal…"

10:34 P.M.
The TOC

"I've got it, Agent Altmann. We're coming through with the satellite feed."

About time. Klaus and Vic were already staging with the entry teams, preparing to launch their assault in the twenty-minute window they had left. "Put it up on the big screen," was Marika's peremptory command as she crossed the trailer to the computer tech's side.

Another few keystrokes and it was there. A huge image of the entire mountain. It didn't take the older woman but a moment to realize that something was wrong. There were too many thermal signatures on the mountain to be accounted for. Way too many.

A curse on her lips, Marika headed for the door of the trailer, toggling her headset as she did so.

"All teams. All teams…we have hostiles at our six. Prepare to engage."

She hadn't taken more than ten steps away from the trailer before a pair of rocket-propelled grenades flew from the treeline…

The CHRYSALIS cabin

"Don't try to stop me, Harry." Carol shook her head, taking another cautious step toward the front door of the cabin.

This wasn't working. It crossed his mind that arguing with her was a lot like arguing with the DCIA. Didn't get you anywhere.

It was at that moment that he heard it—the low, lethal *whoosh* he had heard so many times, so many places. Basra. Lahore. County Armagh.

There was no time to speak, no time to argue. Harry grabbed her by the shoulders, the Kahr falling from her hands as he shoved her down behind the table. A cry escaped her lips as he landed on top, covering her with his body.

The next moment the room exploded around them…

The blast took William Russell Cole off his feet, falling backward into a snowdrift as the western wall of the cabin vanished in a pall of smoke and fire. Moments later, the chatter of automatic weapons filled the air.

Leah Petersen and her partner died instantly, the FBI sniper team taken off-guard by the man from Leningrad. Across the perimeter, agents went down as Korsakov's men moved in.

Her ears ringing from the explosion, Marika rolled onto her back in the snow, looking back at the TOC. Or rather, what was left of it.

The trailer was in flames, dark, oily tongues of fire licking out at the falling snow. The HRT's nerve center was gone.

She closed her eyes, cursing bitterly. So many lives lost.

None of it made any sense. Where had their assailants come from?

Bullets whistled through the air above her head as Marika rolled to her feet, drawing her service Glock from its holster at her side. This wasn't Hollywood—the pistol was near useless in the firefight that was unfolding, but she snapped off a couple shots at the camouflaged men emerging from the treeline.

Turning, she made a crouched run for Jicha's truck, parked twenty feet beyond the flaming TOC. She put three bullets through the window of the Silverado, shattering the glass—the HRT leader had never invested in bulletresistant glass for his personal vehicle.

Her breathing was quick and shallow by the time she reached the truck, the mountain air stabbing at her lungs with icy daggers. Getting old was no fun. She reached through the broken glass of the window and swung the door open.

There was a rifle case behind the seat and Marika pulled it out, extracting his Colt M-4 and four loaded magazines of 5.56mm. One hundred and twenty rounds. Little enough.

Taking cover behind the engine block of the Silverado, she dug a satellite phone from her pocket. If they didn't get backup, they were all going to die.

10:39 P.M.
The CHRYSALIS cabin

Smoke. Flames. Noise beating like hammers against his head. Harry reached out, feeling soft flesh beneath his hand, warm fluid trickling between his fingers.

Blood. A hand descended on his shoulder and he rolled onto his back, pulling the 1911 halfway out of its holster.

Sammy. It was Sammy. He saw the SEAL's lips move, but he couldn't hear a thing, his ears still ringing from the force of the explosion.

Didn't matter—he could guess. They didn't have much time. He shook his head in an effort to clear it.

Where was Carol? He shouted her name and winced, the words echoing and reverberating within his skull.

Han pointed, and Harry followed the direction of his finger. She was right beside him, laying there facedown on the floor of the cabin. Flames licked at the roof above them, snow melting and dripping down on them in the inferno.

Blood trickled from the back of her right thigh, a thick five-inch wooden splinter protruding from the flesh. A deep wound. Ideally, they wouldn't have moved her. There was nothing ideal about this situation.

"Take her," he bellowed, watching Han's face as he regained his feet. Her safety was all that mattered. Nothing else.

His rifle was gone—somewhere. No time to look for it. The SEAL caught Harry's gestures and unslung his rifle, handing it over as he bent down to scoop Carol up in his arms.

Fighting retreat…

10:42 P.M.

Help was on the way. That was the Bureau's assurance, but Marika knew exactly how empty that assurance was. By the time the Hoover Building could mobilize reinforcements, the issue would be decided.

They'd be there in time to fill the body bags.

She pulled back the charging handle on the carbine, hearing a click as the round slid into the chamber. It was only one gun.

Deep breath—she swung herself up, leaning across the Silverado's hood as she steadied the rifle. Five targets, clustered near the cabin. Eighty, maybe a hundred meters out. A single man, gesturing to the others.

Her finger tightened around the trigger as she centered the red dot of the scope on the white balaclava of the leader. Slow, steady.

The first burst went wild and she swore. In all her years in the Bureau, she'd never engaged targets at this range. Never done anything more than qualify. And now she was paying the price.

But it got their attention.

10:44 P.M.

The bullets fanning the air around his ears were Korsakov's first indication that the FBI agents were starting to regroup, to rally from the ambush. He caught a glimpse of a lone figure firing over the hood of a truck down the slope as he threw himself into the snow.

Focus. Don't let it distract from the mission. There was twenty-five million dollars—just on the other side of the cabin's door. And vengeance for Pavel's death.

It was only one agent. "*Nyet*," he whispered impatiently, putting a restraining hand on Yuri's shoulder. "Two of you stay here, provide covering fire—the rest of you come with me."

Yuri glanced toward the cabin door, blown nearly off its hinges by the blast—toward the inferno consuming the roof. "*Da.* It's now or never."

It was all coming back—gunfire, explosions, the swirling snow. Azerbaijan.

Samuel Han laid Carol down in the passenger cabin of the helicopter, motioning for her to lie still. They would need to remove that splinter before it caused an infection.

Azerbaijan. Han took a step back, feeling the past roll over him like a torrent. He moved toward the helicopter's door, feeling as if the earth itself had opened at his feet. Focus. He had to remain calm. Hold the memories in check.

Passing a hand over his forehead, the SEAL jumped down onto the concrete floor of the bunker's hangar, moving toward the control panel mounted on the far wall.

Aged hydraulics, operating massive blast doors which opened out onto the helipad. The power from the generator was already engaged, running for the last hour.

There was only one question left in his mind: after all these years—would the doors still open? If they didn't—then he'd led them into a death trap. Just like he had that winter so long ago.

He took a deep breath and pulled the lever...

10:47 P.M.

Korsakov wasn't the first man through the door, into the cabin. Or the second. It was protocol—bad American action movies aside, a team leader never took point. It also saved his life.

The first room of the cabin was on fire and littered with debris—splintered wood and shards of glass thrown about as if by a giant's hand. Among the chaos, the destruction, the tripwire stretching across the entrance to the corridor went unnoticed.

Red laser beams cut through the flaming darkness as the *Spetsnaz* picked their way over the wreckage. Almost—the point man stepped into the corridor, the toe of his boot catching on the wire.

Korsakov's team never knew what hit them. The pair of M18A2 Claymores were wired together, to a single trigger. Decimation—three pounds of C-4 explosive between them, fourteen hundred steel balls flying outward in a sixty-degree arc.

The man standing beside Korsakov—in the doorway of the cabin—screamed, an unearthly, haunting cry, as he doubled over, clutching at what remained of his stomach.

Blood stained the white snow.

Nothing like this had ever happened before—never in thirty years with the Bureau. He'd never seen so many agents die.

William Russell Cole raised himself up on his elbows in the snow, beside the corpse of a young HRT assaulter. The kid had been the youngest member of Jicha's assault team—now he lay there, on his side in the snow—a ragged hole in his temple. Sightless eyes staring out into the winter night.

The negotiator whispered a silent prayer, moving the young man's stiffening arms to remove the sling of the Heckler & Koch MP-5 from around his shoulders.

He'd never fired a submachine gun in combat before in his life, but this was turning into a night of evil firsts. Cole rolled onto his side, pulling back the charging handle to chamber a round.

Movement in the darkness. There, beside a tree—only a few feet away. No way he could move fast enough.

"Easy, Russ. It's just me." He looked up into the face of Vic Caruso and nearly collapsed in relief. The FBI agent's right arm hung limply at his side, dark blood staining the sleeve. No one had escaped unscathed...

10:53 P.M.

A cold blast of air smote Harry in the face as he entered the hangar, closing the door behind him and spinning the handles until it locked.

He turned, taking in the aged Sikorsky S-55 helicopter sitting there in the middle of the hangar—his eyes flickering toward the open blast doors.

"How's she doing?" he asked, moving across the concrete floor. Sammy was kneeling at the bulbous nose of the Sikorsky, the clamshell doors peeled back to reveal the engine.

"Still losing blood," the Asian SEAL replied, removing a screwdriver from between his teeth. "I'll do my best to extract the splinter once we're airborne."

Harry cast a critical glance out into the darkness, wind-driven snow sweeping across the exposed helipad. "There something wrong with the engine?"

"Negative," Han replied, reaching briefly inside the engine. He tapped something and pulled the screwdriver back out. "Nothing that I can tell—but the last time this bird flew, Jimmy Carter was President. We've only got one chance at this, Harry."

That went without saying and a part of him didn't appreciate it being voiced. Harry moved back, hoisting himself into the Sikorsky's cockpit. He'd held a pilot's license for eight years—the Agency had trained him to fly most types of small aircraft and helos. Unfortunately, 1950s avionics hadn't been covered in the syllabus. A lot had changed. Maybe too much.

He looked out through the high windows of the Sikorsky, toward the door separating the hangar from the rest of the bunker. Korsakov and his men would be through there soon, once they'd regrouped from the Claymores.

One chance…

11:01 P.M.
Warren County, Virginia

Watching Tex drive was enough to drive a man to drink. Actually being in the car—that was even worse. Thomas waited a moment to make sure he wasn't being watched, then tilted back the hip flask of brandy until the amber liquid spilled down his throat.

"Drinking again?" Tex asked, no emotion showing in his voice.

Crap. There were times when he thought the big man was psychic. "Yeah, and thinkin' again." He was surprised to hear the slur in his own words. He hadn't been drinking *that* much. Or had he? It was so hard to remember…

"Put it away," came the peremptory order. He looked over into the Texan's eyes, obsidian orbs staring back at him. Expressionless. A moment passed, then Tex added, "You're no good to me drunk. No good to anyone."

With a languid flourish, Thomas screwed the cap back on the flask and dropped it into the side pocket of the Malibu's door. "Satisfied, *padre?*"

11:03 P.M.
West Virginia

One thing struck Harry from the moment the Sikorsky's 700-horsepower radial engine roared to life from beneath his feet. The old helo wasn't going to cut him any slack—it hailed from a different era—back in the days before crew comfort was considered, and the term "ergonomics" had yet to be commonly used. Going to need a smooth touch. Very smooth...

The noise was deafening, or would have been, if the explosion hadn't already taken care of his hearing. The main rotor transmission was located inches behind his head, gears meshing and whining with all the delightful harmony of an amped-up Black Sabbath.

In a modern transmission, the gears would have been cut on an angle to ensure a quieter operation. Unfortunately, in 1949, no one had figured out how to do that—or cared, apparently.

A hand on his arm, Han's lips forming the word, *Ready*.

Harry nodded, motioning back toward the cabin. "Look after her."

He couldn't even hear his own words, but the SEAL nodded and disappeared. His gloved hand closed over the collective lever, gently increasing the power as the Sikorsky began to taxi across the floor of the hangar.

Taxi might have been the wrong word—it was more of a drunken stagger. He tapped the tail rotor pedals to steer the Sikorsky toward the open door, trying to keep his feet out of the linkage, a spider's tangle of cables and chains connecting the pedals to the large tail rotor.

A muffled *thump*, as though from an explosion, struck his ears even over the persistent roar of the engine. Harry looked back just in time to see the massive door connecting the hangar and bunker fly inward off its hinges, dust and smoke billowing from the gaping hole.

The flash of red lasersights cutting through the cloud, through the darkness. Korsakov's men. It was well past time to go.

A downdraft buffeted the helicopter as it left the hangar's shelter, the Sikorsky's wheels skidding sideways in the wet snow. He heard a death rattle of bullets striking the fuselage as the *Spetsnaz* opened fire and whispered a prayer, easing the cyclic stick forward.

The helicopter's wheels left the ground, rising into the teeth of the wind. Harry seized the collective with his left hand, coaxing more power out of the aged engine.

He saw him out of the corner of his eye, raising the RPG-7 to his shoulder. *The fool.* A single press of the trigger and the helo would be immolated. "Cease firing!" Korsakov bellowed, his words whipped away by the wind as he raced to Yuri's side, knocking the rocket tube aside just as it fired.

Searing hot air from the backblast of the RPG fanned the assassin's cheek as the grenade arced through the night, striking the side of a mountain hundreds of meters away. "What were you thinking?" Korsakov demanded, his nostrils flaring with anger. "She's no good to us dead—we don't get *paid*!"

For a long moment Yuri met his gaze—hatred flashing in those dark eyes—then the man from Leningrad turned away, apparently accepting the rebuke.

Korsakov nodded, walking to the edge of the helipad, his booted feet leaving tracks in the snow. In the light of the moon, he could still see the helicopter, maybe a thousand meters off now, fighting for altitude.

He raised his right hand to his brow, snapping off a mock salute. *May you survive—until we meet again.*

11:37 P.M.

They found Klaus Jicha where he had fallen, blood staining the snow around his body, a tight grouping of bullet holes in the back of his neck, inches above the armor vest.

Marika felt for a pulse, but the body was already cold and stiffening. "He's dead," she announced.

Vic nodded, standing there with his Colt Delta Elite clutched in his left hand. "Never knew what hit him."

None of them had. The mountain was silent now, but she couldn't escape the feeling that their assailants were still out there.

The Russians, the bogeymen of her life. There was no mistaking that language—the orders she had heard barked out through the storm of gunfire.

She rose from her crouch beside Jicha's body, a bitter curse escaping her lips.

Russ met her gaze, the hostage negotiator looking strangely out of place with the submachine gun in his hands. Uncomfortable.

Marika shook her head. They were both way too old for this crap. Too old and too weary.

A bone-chilling wind howled across the West Virginian mountaintop, but she was past feeling it, hatred burning like fire deep within her soul. "We're going to kill them . ."

11:49 P.M.
Andrews Air Force Base
Washington, D.C.

Low. Fast. A pair of F-15s flashed past overhead as President Hancock descended the stairs from Air Force One, his Secret Service surrounding him like a Macedonian phalanx.

Loud didn't begin to describe the fighter jets—his ears ringing from the noise.

Marine One sat fifty yards off on the tarmac, rotor blades turning. The Marine guard waiting beside it was wearing camouflage BDUs instead of dress blues, and he carried an M-16A4 at the ready.

Something was wrong. "What's going on?" Hancock asked.

Hawkins materialized at his side, taking hold of his shoulder and hustling him into the Marine Whitehawk. "The FBI's Hostage Rescue Team was ambushed in West Virginia," the agent responded, raising his voice to be heard over the roar of the engines. "At least thirty agents are dead—my orders are to get you to safety, Mr. President."

"Shapiro? Haskel? They were supposed to be here—to meet me," Hancock protested.

"The directors will be following in one of the decoy choppers. Now, we need to get you airborne, Mr. President."

Chapter 11

They were out of the mountains now, flying west-southwest on a compass heading of 224 degrees. Out of the mountains, but not out of trouble. Not by any definition.

Harry's gaze swept from right to left across the cockpit, watching the gauges, focusing on keeping the rotor RPM in the safe green arc, between 170 and 245.

He'd flown Sikorskys before—a lot of them had what pilots called a "heavy" collective, meaning that if you didn't hold it up manually, it was going to drop, effectively cutting thrust to the main rotor and taking the chopper down with it. Something you rather wanted to avoid.

His left arm was numb, braced against his side as he grasped the collective—it felt like he was lifting the chopper up with one hand.

Despite the engine noise, the deafening roar of gears behind his head, he felt Han before he saw him, his head poking up from beneath the co-pilot's seat, from the narrow passageway leading down into the passenger cabin.

"How is she?" It felt like he was shouting into a barrel, his voice ringing and reverberating in his own ears.

"Okay," was the shouted reply as the SEAL hoisted himself up till his mouth was only inches from Harry's ear. Han looked tired, his face pale in the control panel lights.

"Where are we?"

Harry shrugged. "Flying southwest, bro. Hanged if I know anything more. Been too busy keeping this heap of junk in the air. Passed over a river about five minutes ago, might have been the Kanawha."

He saw his old friend's eyes drift toward the gauges and Harry nodded. "Switching over to the reserve in ten—we used a lot of fuel getting out of the Alleghenies."

"The reserve isn't going to last long—we're going to have to find a place to set down."

These truths declare themselves to be self-evident. A bright glow appeared on the horizon—probably a city. Something to be avoided—they were pretty near invisible as long as they avoided densely populated areas.

With a sigh, Harry mashed his foot against the right tail rotor pedal, guiding the helo away from the lights and further west. At their current rate of consumption, they had another hour—hour and a half, in the air.

Maybe less.

2:03 A.M.
Pendleton County
West Virginia

It would have taken a drunk not to realize something was wrong as Tex and Thomas pulled into the small Sunoco off US Rt 33. Even the brandy wasn't affecting him *that* much.

There were five patrol cars in front of the convenience store, three state and two bearing the logo of the Pendleton County Sheriff's department. Either they'd had one deuce of an armed robbery, or…

His gaze drifted across the parking lot to the van emblazoned with the FBI shield. This wasn't some hick cash-drawer-and-cigarettes holdup.

"Take a pass?" Thomas asked, glancing over at his companion.

The Texan shook his head, guiding the Malibu toward the only empty gas pump. "Not an option."

The needle *was* dangerously close to "E".

"Stay here," Tex cautioned, removing the holstered Glock from inside the waistband of his jeans and tucking it under the seat. No sense in causing problems.

He swung his door open and stepped out into the chill night air, striding toward the convenience store, his Stetson pulled low over his eyes.

"Hundred and twenty on pump five," he announced, sliding six bills across the counter toward the teenaged attendant. Gas money didn't go very far these days.

The kid seemed to be moving on autopilot, his attention and that of several other patrons focused on the TV mounted in the corner. "What's going on?" he asked, catching a glimpse of a blonde reporter on-screen, backlit by flashing lights. Your typical newsbabe.

"Where you been, dude?" the kid asked, tapping the amount into his register. "You see all the feds? Bunch of them got whacked over in Randolph County, just up the road from here. Something like thirty of 'em dead, they got people comin' in from all over."

He knew it, even before the map came flashing up on the TV screen, a cold feeling gnawing at his insides. The map was only confirmation.

Thirty agents dead.

And Harry was involved. No, he was more than involved. He was at the bottom of it...

2:23 A.M.
West Virginia

The boy hadn't spoken a word since they'd returned to the vehicles. Hadn't even been able to look him in the eye.

His own anger was responsible for it, Korsakov realized, eyeing the boy in the rear-view mirror, Viktor's face illuminated by the pale glow of his laptop. Misplaced anger. If it hadn't been for Viktor's insistence on the tracking chip in the beginning, they would have lost their target long before this.

Things looked dark enough as it was. He had gambled and lost with the FBI—and lost another four men in the process. He swore under his breath, trying to remain focused on the road as they sped south, out of the mountains.

He'd underestimated the CIA agent, underestimated his resourcefulness, his capacity for violence. It wasn't going to happen again.

Inside the pocket of the assassin's shirt, his cellphone began to vibrate, throbbing with an incoming call. Korsakov let out a long, weary sigh—one hand on the wheel as he plucked the phone from his pocket.

The number was blocked, but he didn't need to guess at the identity of the caller. He knew. A long moment passed as he stared at the screen, then he slowly pressed the REJECT button.

The time for talk had passed. This mission was taking on a life of its own.

2:43 A.M.
The Sikorsky
Kentucky

Night landings were something a helicopter pilot tried to avoid. Even with the moon, there were far too many things that could go wrong.

It wasn't like he had a choice. Nearly four hours after departing from CHRYSALIS, they were over northern Kentucky and bingo-fuel. A helo wasn't like a plane—you didn't have a prayer of gliding.

If it hadn't been for Carol…Harry glanced down at the luminescent screen of Han's phone. It was a prepaid Tracfone—Internet capable and equipped with GPS. It was Carol who had figured out how to use it to pinpoint their own position—and located the small private airfield to their west. According to the website, they didn't conduct night operations. It should be deserted.

Harry shut the phone down and pulled his night-vision goggles down low over his eyes, guiding the Sikorsky on a western course. Should be only a couple more minutes.

The landscape shone dark green in the glow of his night-vision, the helo's downwash buffeting the leafless trees below them.

He eased off on the throttle, deliberately bleeding away airspeed as they closed in. They wouldn't have time or fuel for a go-round. The airfield had a single runway, running east-west. Just a couple hundred feet, long enough for a Cessna…or a helicopter.

The cyclic came back in his hand, the Sikorsky rising slightly as they came up over the hill overlooking the airfield. Lights. Glare. Pain. *Blast it!* Harry ripped the night-vision goggles off his eyes, throwing them against the side of the cockpit. The long, slow rotor blades of the Sikorsky began to whip with the sudden movement of the stick and he fought for control of the aircraft, struggling to keep it to a steady airspeed of 55 knots.

The airfield was lit up like New York Harbor on the 4th of July, flares outlining the dirt runway, the headlights of a pickup truck aimed at a Cessna parked near the western end of the strip. Men running back and forth, shadowy forms flickering in and out of the light.

They didn't have another choice. It was this—or crash in the trees. Harry pulled gently back on the cyclic, flaring the S-55 as they came in, tail-low.

Taking his hand off the collective for the fraction of a moment, he rapped hard on the cover of the co-pilot's seat. *Be ready.*

2:59 A.M.
The double-wide
Graves Mill, Virginia

It was his bladder that roused him, but it was the sound of the TV that brought him fully awake.

Reaching for his crutches, David Lay swung himself out of bed, grunting as his feet hit the floor. Losing some weight wasn't a bad idea.

He'd only been out of bed a couple times since Rhoda had brought him to the trailer. She didn't think he was ready.

Ready. He pushed open the doorway of the bedroom and tottered out into the hallway. She'd been sleeping on the couch ever since his arrival. There had been a time when that might have been different, but neither of them had been prepared to commit. Once burned, twice shy, as the saying went.

Rhoda was sitting at the table, her back turned to the hallway, a glass of milk in front of her. The channel changed just as he entered the kitchen. "What are you doing up, David?" There were moments when he could have sworn the woman was psychic.

He eased himself forward, bending down to kiss her dark lips as she turned to face him. That was how he remembered her. The smell of pot filled his nostrils and he grimaced. Yes, another of the reasons the relationship hadn't worked out.

"What were you watching?"

She smiled, gesturing at the TV. "Cooking. Old re-runs of Paula Deen."

Another time he might have found the response humorous, but not now. "Don't lie to me, Rhoda," he retorted, an edge of steel creeping into his voice.

Her gaze faltered and a cold chill seized his heart. Before she could react, the remote was in his hand and he pressed the button for channel return. CNN.

"...the death count is still climbing in West Virginia, with 34 FBI agents now counted among the fatalities. Sources within the administration have confirmed that the ambush of the Hostage Rescue Team was connected with the ongoing search for the rogue CIA agent. If you have information regarding this case, please contact..."

The voice of the anchor seemed to fade away, the room beginning to swirl around him. He felt his fingers grip the edge of the tabletop as he sank back into the chair, burying his face in his hands.

What had he set in motion?

3:01 A.M.
The airfield
Northern Kentucky

The lights of a pick-up truck pierced the cockpit as Harry guided the Sikorsky to a rolling stop, placing the right side of the helo away from the Cessna and the lights. "Ready?"

Han nodded before ducking back down beneath the seat, disappearing. Harry reached into his jacket and extracted his Colt 1911, screwing a long suppressor into the barrel of the weapon. Who they were dealing with, he didn't know—but it wasn't legitimate.

And illegitimate meant people with guns.

He swung his legs out the window of the helicopter and clambered down. The cabin door was already open. Han wasn't wasting any time.

Footsteps as he rounded the bulbous nose of the Sikorsky. Five men, moving across the runway toward him, their figures backlit by the lights. Amateur hour.

"Who the devil are you?" the leader demanded, a Kentucky twang flavoring his words. He was a big man, heavy. Some people might have said he had a beer belly—it looked more like he had swallowed the keg. "What you doing here?"

Harry smiled, taking in the odds. Five men, three white, two Hispanic. Only one visible weapon, a pistol-gripped Mossberg shotgun, but this *was* Kentucky.

"My name doesn't matter," he replied, shrugging. "I'm not a cop. As for what I'm doing here—just passin' through. Ran out of fuel."

The big man took a step closer, running a hand across his beard. At length he shook his head, spewing a viscous stream of tobacco into the dirt. "You sure picked a bad night for it."

Sammy should be almost ready. Harry inclined his head, measuring the distance between them. "I agree—for you."

At his words, a pair of muffled shots rang out from Han's suppressed Sig-Sauer, sounding like hammer blows in the night. The headlights of the pick-up went out almost simultaneously, plunging the airfield into a darkness punctuated only by the eerie orange light of the flares.

The big man swore, reaching inside his jacket, but Harry's Colt was already in his hand. "Don't even think it. Light 'em up, Sammy!"

The SCAR's laser came flickering out of the darkness, centering on the head of the redneck with the Mossberg. For a moment it looked like he might drop the scattergun and flee.

"Tell your men to put their guns on the ground." The leader's hand reached toward his belt, but Harry shook his head. "Left hand. Pull it out with your fingers."

"What do you want, man?" the leader demanded, his words almost a hoarse scream. He was wearing a long-barreled .44 Smith & Wesson—too long for a good draw. It fell to the ground with a dull thud.

"That depends—what you boys smuggling?" Harry asked, moving in closer, his pistol still leveled. "Marijuana? Hillbilly heroin?"

The man looked momentarily frightened. "None of your business, lawman."

Movement out of the corner of his eye and Harry saw a pistol materialize in the hand of one of the Hispanics, a report reverberating out through the night as the bullet sliced through the air past his head.

Time seemed to slow down as the Colt came up in his hand. He fired two shots, both of them going wild in the darkness. Pandemonium. Harry threw himself prone. The big man dove for his discarded revolver.

There could be no hesitation—there wasn't time to second-guess yourself, no matter how much you hated it. Han felt the bile rise in his throat as he lined up the laser sight on the young man's chest. He couldn't have been more than nineteen, twenty at the most. Not even old enough to drink.

No time.

He knew what to do, his finger curling around the SCAR's trigger, taking up the slack. A motion as natural as taking breath as he squeezed—once, twice, three times in rapid succession.

The .308 slugs caught the kid high in the chest, smashing through his lungs. The pistol fell from his fingers and he toppled backward, his arms and legs moving spasmodically.

Dear God...

The leader had been elsewhere the day they passed out the brains. He heard the kid cry out and froze, realizing that he was staring down the barrel of Harry's Colt less than six feet away. He didn't take his hand off the butt of the S&W.

Harry shot him once, in the left knee, and the man pitched forward, groveling in the dirt as he screamed.

And the firefight was over as quickly as it had started, the rest of the drugrunners shocked into submission. Harry walked over to the groaning man. "Nobody needed to get hurt," he said, a quiet menace in his voice. "Now, we're taking your plane."

"No, no, you can't do that," the big man screamed, trying to roll onto his back. Harry kicked the revolver away, out of reach. Remove the temptation. "Manuel'll kill me."

"Doesn't sound like my problem," Harry responded coldly, tapping the suppressor against the man's temple. "All you need to worry about is what *I'll* do if you get in my way."

4:57 A.M.
The White House
Washington, D.C.

It was moments like this when he questioned how much he really wanted the Presidency—questioned all he'd done to retain this power. Power? He'd never felt more powerless. His fifth phone call—nothing. And Shapiro hadn't been able to do anything to help.

"Roger—we need to talk." Hancock slipped the iPhone into his shirt pocket and turned.

His "better half" stood in the doorway of the Residence's bedroom. At forty-six, Nicole Hancock was several years his junior, a tall, elegant brunette. She *looked* like a First Lady.

She might have even carried it off with him, if not for the look of steel in those emerald green eyes. God—if there was a God—knew she was twice the political operative he was.

He let out a bitter sigh. Could this night get any worse?

"I don't suppose this can wait?"

"You're not the only one keeping late hours, Roger. I just got in from a meeting with Trevor Ellison at the Hay Adams."

That got his attention. Ellison was the managing editor of *The Washington Post*. "What did he want?"

She closed the door behind them and gestured to the manila envelope on the Victorian-era writing desk by the bed. *His* bed—she slept elsewhere in the Residence, a fact that the media had yet to latch hold of. They didn't call it the *Secret* Service for nothing.

A premonition seized hold of Hancock as he ripped open the flap. The first picture showed him on-stage at a summit in Cancun the first week of October. Mary Workman was standing at his shoulder, along with the rest of his staff. But her face was circled in red. The second picture, from the same summit, had been taken with a telephoto lens.

Mary, dressed in a black bikini, standing on the balcony of his hotel. She'd been watching the sunset, he remembered. He looked closer at the photo and his breath caught in his throat. A pair of arms were wrapped around her bare waist in a loving embrace, a figure leaning over her shoulder.

The next picture was a duplicate, lightened and digitally enhanced. In it, you could clearly make out the face of her lover. It was him.

He ran a hand over his face and laid the photos down. "I need a drink."

"It gets better, Roger," the First Lady observed, standing there against the door, her arms folded across her chest. "The journalist that approached Trevor with the story has established that Mary had no prior history of drug use. He's speculating that she became an inconvenient paramour. *Your* paramour."

"Is he going to run the story?"

She sniffed. "No. No one prizes their access more than Trevor Ellison—he's not going to give that up just to publish a speculative hit piece."

Hancock let out a long sigh of relief, but she wasn't done yet. "When we were first married, we both knew that our union was nothing more than a political alliance. That's why I agreed that it would be an open marriage. I only had one requirement, Roger. Do you remember what it was?"

He did. All too well. "That my affairs would be discreet."

She threw the balcony picture down on the desk. "Does that look *discreet* to you?"

And she was gone.

6:17 A.M.
The airport
Northern Kentucky

They still had roughly another hour till the sun was up, but the faint glow of the morning sun had started to creep over the trees. Time to leave.

Harry walked back over to where the four surviving drugrunners lay in front of the hangar, their hands zip-tied behind their backs. "I'm sure Manuel will come looking for you sooner or later, so don't worry."

The leader shook his head furiously, but he couldn't speak past the oil-stained rag stuffed in his mouth. Harry took another look at the bandages Han had applied to his shattered knee and nodded. "You won't bleed out, but if I were you, I'd lose a few pounds before I put weight on that knee again. Manuel can find his cocaine over in our helo, so don't worry about him," he added, turning to leave. "Call it a Christmas gift to my favorite drugrunners."

Harry paused as if in afterthought, extracting a small black box from the pocket of his leather jacket. His finger pressed down on the detonator, the Sikorsky exploding in flame, a pillar of fire lighting up the sky.

"Softly as I leave you," he whispered, a dark smile passing across his face.

He turned and walked away into the sunrise...

Chapter 12

12:47 P.M.
FBI Regional Field Office
Richmond, Virginia

Suspended pending further investigation. Part of her knew it was protocol—she *had* been the S-A-C overseeing the worst disaster in FBI history. Another part of her couldn't escape the notion that there was something deeper. That they'd been set up.

Her gut.

Marika Altmann sat there for a few more minutes, staring at the black screen where Director Haskel's face had been only moments earlier.

Time to go. She rose and left the conference room, both hands thrust into her jacket, lost in her thoughts.

"Special Agent Altmann!" She turned to see a young agent walking toward her, his hand outstretched. "I'll need you to turn in your sidearm."

She nodded, pulling her jacket aside to remove the holstered Glock. Out of the corner of her eye, she could see Vic Caruso coming down the corridor toward them, and she handed over the weapon without another word. The Italian's right arm was bandaged and cradled in a sling.

"There's something going on, Marika," Caruso announced quietly, taking her by the shoulder and guiding her into a nearby alcove.

"You'll need to talk to someone else about it." She shrugged off his hand, turning to face him. "I've been suspended."

He nodded. "So have I. Same deal with Russ. See what I mean?"

That *didn't* make any sense. Caruso went on. "Everyone that walked off that mountain has been sidelined. And they're saying that the Russians were working with Nichols."

"Did they already take your statement?" Marika asked, glancing around to make sure their conversation was private. Another nod. "There's no way to draw that conclusion—what do they think, that we killed those four Russians in the cabin?"

She reached up, brushing a strand of silver hair back from her forehead. "Last time I checked, land mines weren't Bureau issue."

"There's something going on, something we've not been briefed on—a larger picture." An agent walked by and Vic stopped talking.

Their conversation had gone on long enough. Marika reached out, touching him lightly on the arm. "Go home and get some rest, Vic."

"What about you?"

A distant look came into her eyes. "It's time to call in a marker…"

12:23 P.M. Central Time
A gun range
Fargo, North Dakota

"Once you pick out your targets, just go through the door to the left there. I'll ring you up on your way out." The boy smiled. "And for pete's sake put on your ear protection before going in."

Alicia Workman nodded, lost in her own thoughts. A variety of targets hung on the wall—from standard round bulls-eyes to mil-spec silhouettes. There were even a few targets emblazoned with the portrait of Osama bin Laden, despite the years he had been in the ground. Or the sea, depending on which version of the story you believed.

There were none with the President's face, and asking didn't seem like a smart policy.

The crowd was sparse on an early Sunday afternoon, just an elderly man at the other end of the range, what looked like a Belgian-made FN-FAL in his hands. A long, snow-white ponytail hung out the back of his baseball cap as his fingers moved over the rifle with military efficiency.

Likely a Vietnam vet, judging by his age.

She attached her target to the overhead carriage and ran it out to fifteen yards, removing her pistol from its carrying case. The Bersa was a perfect fit—she'd always had small hands.

She brought the semiautomatic up in both hands, standing there, feet slightly spread. The face of the silhouette came into view through her gunsights.

Focus.

The first shot startled her, even though she was expecting it. Something to remember, she realized, emptying the magazine downrange. Three shots had pierced the head of the target. The other four weren't even on paper.

Her lips formed a curse that would have shocked her students. She was going to have to do better...

1:03 P.M.
A mall
Dearborn, Michigan

The mall wasn't their target, but he found himself analyzing it as though it was.

Tarik Abdul Muhammad's eyes roved around the center of the mall as he listened to the sales clerk explain the wonders of the new Bluetooth headsets.

Only one security guard within sight—"armed" with a radio and riot baton. That might have worked in Hollywood's licentious movies, but he'd be gunned down within minutes in real life.

The ultimate soft target. Tarik rubbed his chin, the bare skin feeling strange in place of the beard he'd worn for so many years. All of America was soft, a ripe fruit waiting to fall into the hand of the believer.

At length, he cut the clerk short. "I'll take ten."

A look of surprise came over the boy's pimpled face, the reddish splotches contrasting oddly with his pale skin. Tarik smiled. "Extended family— Bluetooth seems to be the gift of choice this Christmas."

He paid for the headsets and left the store, the clerk's parting "happy holidays" ringing in his ears.

The negro was waiting for him by the central fountain, watching children toss pennies into the sparkling water.

"Ready to go?"

The Pakistani nodded, a mesmerizing look coming into his eyes. "Look around us, my brother, at how Americans are spending their Sunday."

"Yes?"

"This is why we will win," Tarik announced, gesturing with his hand. "These Americans—they are no longer people of the Book..."

2:45 P.M. Eastern Time
Ashland Regional Airport
Kentucky

Americans were amusing. At times. "I have nothing to do with your stupid Manuel," Korsakov repeated, staring the drugrunner in the face.

The big man seemed to pale under his gaze. "Do you know their range?"

"Why?"

Without warning, Korsakov backhanded him across the face. "None of your concern. Just answer the question."

"Easy, dude—just take it easy." The American spat, a mixture of saliva and blood from his broken lip. "It's a Skylane—maybe a thousand-mile range."

"Is that all?"

A shake of the head. "No—we'd installed a couple of extra tanks—extends it by a hundred, maybe hundred and fifty miles. It's a trade-off, but heroin don't weigh that much, ya know?"

That explained the positioning of the tracker. They'd gotten quite a head start. "Are there any other planes here at the airport?" the assassin asked, glancing over at the smoldering remains of the Sikorsky.

Another shake of the head. The man didn't seem to trust himself to speak.

Korsakov let out a snort of disgust, turning back toward the Suburbans. He reached inside the pocket of his jacket and extracted his phone. Six missed calls. Six voicemails.

He pressed SEND to retrieve his messages, listening to the voicemail, each of them sounding progressively more panicked. Americans had no backbone. How had they *ever* won the Cold War?

Then the last message. "We have to talk, Sergei. There are people inside the Bureau—they're starting to get suspicious. We have to tie up loose ends—it may require you sending a couple of your people back to D.C. I know this will require more money, but I swear to God, if you don't follow through on this, I'll see you brought down. Call me."

A sigh. Korsakov stared down at his phone. Sometimes there was little choice but to play the game. He looked back to where Yuri stood over the four drugrunners. "*Ubei,*" he ordered, his voice ringing clearly through the chill air. "*Ubei ih vsekh.*" Kill them. Kill them all.

He caught a glimpse of it in the rear-view mirror as he climbed into the Suburban, lifeless bodies sprawled on the tarmac. Drug dealers. The scum of the earth…

1:53 P.M. Central Time
A small airport
Rural Kansas

"I'm surprised there was no one here," Carol observed, coming up behind Harry at the equipment shed. He looked up from the padlock in his hand.

"I'm not," he responded. "This is Kansas…around here a lot of people still go to church on Sunday. Honest folk—it's why there's no perimeter fence here. No security cameras."

The tumblers moved beneath the pressure of his lockpick and the padlock sprung open, falling easily into his hand.

There was something about the way he'd said it. "You sound envious."

He looked back to where she stood, favoring her injured right leg. "I am," he said slowly. "Always wished I could retire to the Midwest. Always wanted to believe that the world could actually be this simple. No guile, no deception— just take life on its face, live it the way it was meant to be lived."

"How long do you think you'd last?" she asked, inclining her head to one side. Her blond hair fell across her face, and she brushed it back, revealing a look of skepticism in those blue eyes.

It wasn't so much the frankness of her question that took him by surprise, but the readiness with which the answer formed in his mind. *Not two weeks.*

He didn't respond, swinging open the door to reveal the fifty-gallon drums of aviation fuel stacked inside. "Go find Sammy—I'm going to need his help moving these over to the plane."

2:38 P.M. Eastern Time
Church of the Holy Trinity
Washington, D.C.

"*In nomine Patri, et Fili, et Spiritus Sanctum.*" In the name of the Father, the Son, and the Holy Ghost.

Michael Shapiro made the sign of the cross over his chest, bowing his head in prayer. It wasn't often that he made Mass these days, but today was special, with his little son Marc serving as altar boy.

He felt Marc's twin sister stir restlessly in the pew beside him and a guilty smile crossed the deputy director's face. She took after him.

His phone began to buzz within the pocket of his Armani suit and he rose from the pew, catching the look of disapproval on his wife's face as he left the church.

"Yes?" he asked, answering the phone as he strode toward the doors.

"I hope I'm not disturbing you, Michael." That voice.

Shapiro stepped outside, a cold, snow-laden breeze cutting through the thin fabric of his dress pants. He was sweating. "What do you want?"

"Complications have arisen. I need you to go back to Langley and remove a sniper rifle from the equipment lockers in the Clandestine Service ready room. A Barrett would be preferable. Make sure you take a couple of magazines of ammunition, as well."

The deputy director stopped stock-still, unable to answer for a long moment.

"Is there a problem, Michael?"

"That depends," Shapiro replied, mustering up what was left of his defiance. "What am I do with it?"

"I will call you again in three hours with further instructions. Have it by then."

A click and he found himself holding a dead phone up to his ear. He stood there for a long moment, listening to the words, the music drifting out of the church behind him. *Then pealed the bells more loud and deep: "God is not dead, nor doth He sleep..."*

That was what scared him.

5:03 P.M.
CIA Headquarters
Langley, Virginia

Three days. That's all it had taken to turn his world upside down. "I'll need some time to run that down," he heard himself saying.

"How much time?" the woman on the other end of the phone asked.

Carter glanced across the op-center to meet the eyes of Danny Lasker and he looked away. Didn't know whom he could trust—not anymore. "Twenty-four hours, Marika. Do you remember how to get to my apartment?"

"Of course, Ron," the FBI agent replied. "How could I forget? Do you still have Maxwell?"

Carter stifled a laugh. Maxwell, named after the lead character of the '60s spy show *Get Smart*, was his cat, a Japanese Bobtail he had brought back from Okinawa when he'd been in Air Force intelligence. "Yeah, Max is getting old, but he's still with me."

"Glad to hear it." Her voice changed, re-focusing. "Twenty-four hours, Ron. Don't let me down."

The analyst closed his phone, returning it to its resting place in his shirt pocket. As he did so, the familiar sound of the op-center doors opening struck his ears and he looked up to see Director Shapiro leaving.

What had the Banker been doing here…on a Sunday?

3:43 P.M. Mountain Time
The Cessna
Over New Mexico

"Alexei Vasiliev," Han repeated thoughtfully. "I remember him."

Harry didn't reply, his eyes focused on the sky before him—concentrating on keeping the Cessna Skylane below 3,000 ASL. "More specifically," the SEAL continued, "I remember him trying to kill you."

A shrug. "You can hardly blame Alexei for that—we *were* trying to take out his principal. He was just doing his job." Harry smiled. "Six months later we were having lunch in the shadow of the Eiffel Tower and debating religion late into the night. I've known worse guys."

"Leave him out of this, Harry," Han admonished, a shadow passing across his face. "He's former KGB—there's no way you can trust him."

The New Mexico desert continued to flash past below them, the sinking sun casting long shadows over the foothills. They were going to have to land before nightfall, or face all sorts of questions as to why they hadn't filed the mandatory IFR flight plan.

"Assuming he's in a cooperative mood, Alexei will be able to give us the information we need," Harry replied, looking over at his old team member. "But I had no intention of trusting him…"

8:35 P.M. Eastern Time
Anacostia
Washington, D.C.

Five minutes late. Yuri shifted his body weight in the front seat of the Escalade, checking his watch. The lights of the SUV were out as they sat there, looking out into the river.

They'd already seen two Coast Guard cutters go by in the chill moonlight. No doubt about it, this city was on a war footing. Which is why they didn't want to stay here any longer than necessary.

"You know," Yuri announced, looking over at his partner, "sitting here in the dark would look much more natural if you were a hot blonde."

His companion, a Latvian Yuri knew only as Kalnins, laughed. "This is true, *tovarisch*. And both of us would be much happier."

Lights crept down the road toward them and Yuri's hand moved to the Beretta at his side. He could feel Kalnins tensing in the darkness. A police car was the last thing they needed.

He'd had a bad feeling about this contract from the beginning—not that his opinion had mattered to Korsakov. Success...success had the ability to make men arrogant.

The sedan slowed to a stop across from them and briefly flashed its lights. Yuri returned the signal and left the headlights of the Escalade on as a short man in a trench coat exited the sedan, a suitcase in his right hand. The Russian consulted the picture filling the screen of his smartphone. It was him: *Michael Shapiro, Deputy Director(Intelligence)...*

9:35 P.M. Mountain Time
Motel 6
Cedar Springs, Arizona

Carol was sitting cross-legged on the bed when Harry came back into the motel room, her Dell only inches from her bare feet. "Internet?" he asked. It certainly hadn't come with the room.

She arched an eyebrow. "The network password is... 'password'."

"Welcome to the twenty-first century," he observed, a wry smile on his face as he placed the briefcase containing the UMP-45 on the top of the dresser.

"Do you think they suspected anything at the airport?"

Harry thought for a moment. They had landed at the small airport outside Cedar Springs just before dusk and left the plane in the keeping of the airport's two employees, one of whom had driven them into town.

He shook his head. "No. Doesn't really matter if they did—this is the Navajo Nation."

A glance into the mirror told him that she hadn't understood the comment. "I had a friend at college—a schoolteacher coming back for his master's. Said the Nation was the best place in the States to get your foot in the door of the education system. *If* you lived long enough. Folks around here have never warmed to the thought of calling in the feds."

There was a long silence between them, then Carol looked up over the screen of her laptop. "You should know that I agree with Han—bringing an outside party into this is only going to complicate matters. You and I both believe that my father knew who was behind the assassination—it's just a matter of figuring out what he knew."

"And how do you propose to do that?" Harry asked, staring across the room at her. It was a rhetorical question—they'd been over this ground before. "Even if there *was* a way, it would leave us exposed."

He paused and she could see the uncertainty in his eyes. As if realizing his vulnerability, he turned away from her and unlocked the briefcase, withdrawing the submachine gun and extending its folding stock. "West Virginia was as secure as it gets—and Korsakov tracked us down there. I still don't know how."

"All the more reason to leave Vasiliev out of this."

"Alexei has connections, connections we need," he repeated, looking back over his shoulder. "All you need to know is that wherever I need to go, whatever I need to do—I will protect you."

Whatever I need to do. There was no bravado there, no pretense—just a simple statement of fact. It sent a chill through her body. Carol ran a hand through her hair, her eyes running down the webpage before her. The CIA dossier on Alexei Mikhailovich Vasiliev.

Date: 2003. An SVR agent in Chechnya taken hostage in the mountains by Muslim guerillas. Vladimir Putin had dispatched Vasiliev to negotiate his release.

His method of "negotiation" had been effective, if reminiscent of Capone's Chicago in its brutal simplicity. For every body part sent to Grozny, he'd executed two members of the rebel leader's family, starting with his wife. It hadn't saved the agent, but it was the last time the Chechens messed with the SVR. "Is this true?" she asked, turning the laptop's screen toward Harry.

It was a moment before he responded, his face veiled in the shadows of the motel room. She couldn't see his eyes, and she found herself glad of it. "There's no Boy Scouts in this business, Carol…"

Chapter 13

One of the benefits of never calling in sick was that when you actually did it, no one questioned your integrity.

Carter leaned back in his desk chair, interlacing his long fingers behind his head. It had taken him nine hours to access the FBI's servers. Using his own log-in, it would have taken all of three minutes, but that was like leaving your business card at the scene of a crime.

As it was, when the Bureau eventually realized their list of users had been hacked, the trail would run cold in a maze of Bulgarian servers and IP addresses.

A *meow*, and Maxwell the cat launched himself up onto the desk, pale yellow eyes staring him down.

"Easy, Max," Carter whispered, a weary smile crossing his face as he swept the bobtailed cat away from the computer keyboard. He'd never forget how Maxwell had knocked over a cup of coffee on his laptop one day, frying the hard drive. Never forget the half-sheepish look on the cat's face, as though he was emulating his namesake.

Catastrophe averted, the analyst went back to his work, filtering through another layer of security on the Bureau server. Marika had been sure that someone had hacked into their network and compromised the West Virginia op. If she was right, the hacker should have left some sort of a trail...

10:01 A.M.
The safehouse
Culpeper, Virginia

"We've got a hit." Those quietly spoken words were enough to bring Tex Richards instantly awake.

Thomas shook his head. He'd never known the big man to truly be asleep—maybe it was the Apache blood running through his veins. "Where?"

"Arizona," Thomas replied, tapping the screen of his laptop. "His American Express card was used to rent a Ford Expedition at an agency in Flagstaff—fifteen minutes ago."

"He's crossed the continent in less than thirty hours," the Texan observed. "Somewhere—somehow, he got on a plane."

"Let's face it. Our boy's brilliant."

Tex's lips compressed into a thin, bloodless line. "We'll see about that. Run back over the last twenty-four hours—see if you can track down any incidents at general aviation airfields this side of the Mississippi. Anything abnormal."

"How soon do we leave?"

"We don't," came the terse answer.

Thomas looked up in surprise. "What do you mean?"

"A stern chase is a long chase—something our corpsman used to say in A-stan. We don't follow Harry, we find someone who knows where he's going."

Thomas looked back to see his partner holding up a print-out of the surveillance photo Carter had provided. "Rhoda Stevens…"

9:43 A.M. Mountain Time
I-40 west of Ash Fork
Arizona

There was dead silence in the SUV as he dialed the number, and it wasn't out of courtesy. Harry knew that much. More like disapproval. And he knew why.

Three rings, then four. Five before it was answered. "Hello?"

"*Kak dela,* Alexei?" How are you?

There was a moment's pause, then Vasiliev chuckled. "With half your nation's hounds out after you, I hardly expected to hear your voice."

The Russian was good. He hadn't used his name, nothing for the SIGINT boys at Fort Meade to grab hold of.

"I suppose it would be pointless to ask how you got my private cell number?"

"Hey, you're a public figure, whether you like it or not." Harry smiled. "A celebrity."

A laugh. "So, tell me, *tovarisch*, what is so important that you must rouse me from bed with my wife?"

"Indeed? Please accept my congratulations. I was unaware that you were married again."

"She's a beautiful girl, my friend," Vasiliev replied. "The love of my life."

Well, he'd heard that line before. Regarding Mrs. Vasiliev #1 and #2. "We need to meet, Alexei. As soon as possible."

"Why?" the Russian asked, a note of suspicion creeping into his voice. Perhaps he was remembering their *last* meeting.

"You have a security problem. One of your countrymen has brought in—specialists...I need your advice."

"The same specialists responsible for the Dominion fireworks show?" The bombing in Virginia. Yeah, Vasiliev didn't miss a beat.

"*Da*, Alexei. The same."

"Then, if what you say is true...I agree with you, *tovarisch*. We *do* need to meet—perhaps at the bistro on Baker Street for lunch tomorrow? Ten hundred hours?"

Harry looked over at Han before responding. The Asian SEAL inclined his head, then nodded almost imperceptibly.

"Sounds like a plan."

"Then I will see you there—one more thing."

"Yes?"

He could hear Vasiliev clearing his throat. "Put a gun to my head again and I *will* kill you. And this time I won't miss..."

2:52 P.M. Eastern Time
An abandoned apartment complex
Clarksville, MD

The apartment complex had been a casualty of the 2008 collapse of the housing market. Half-completed, it had remained empty ever since. The owners hadn't been able to raise the money to finance completion—and with Maryland's real estate plunging through the floor, they hadn't been able to unload the property either.

It had become a virtual no-man's land, the habitat of drug addicts and the homeless.

"Target reacquired," Yuri announced, closing one eye to focus down the scope of the Barrett M98B. Careful.

Slow, shallow breaths. The firing reticle centered on the black man's temple, holding steady.

A couple hundred meters—just across the street, really. No crosswind. An easy shot.

The sniper rifle was set up well back of the window, resting on a pair of packing crates and stabilized by sandbags. As rock-solid as it got.

He saw the target's hand move downward, beside his computer, to a phone on the desk. "Ready?"

Kalnins nodded, moving closer to the window on his hands and knees. Bracing himself, the Latvian aimed the laser microphone across the street, focusing on the window of their target's apartment.

A couple moments' delay and then the vibrations on the glass of the window came filtering back through the software on Yuri's laptop, broadcasting once again as human voice.

"This is Carter. Yeah, I've been in the system for about seven hours, going over their user profiles. A lot of anomalies. This is going deep, Marika. A lot deeper than either of us thought."

4:06 P.M. Central Time
The mosque
Dearborn, Michigan

There was a thrill to being only inches away from one of the deadliest nerve agents known to man. A nervous, queasy thrill. Jamal al-Khalidi felt the beads of sweat trickling down his face and wished for a moment that he could wipe them away. The hazardous materials suit shrouding his body made that difficult.

Getting the HAZMAT suit hadn't been much more difficult than any of the other equipment—with emergency services across the U.S. downsizing from lack of funding, he'd been able to pick one up online, the ad describing it as "gently used". Americans and their semantics.

He picked up the rotary saw and consulted the schematics strewn over his lab tables one last time. The shell had been disarmed, the explosives rendered inert. The next step was to cut open the casing and extract the paper-thin metal container holding the powdered soman.

Jamal took a deep breath and moved to the table where the huge artillery shell lay, held in position by a pair of clamps.

What was it one of his classmates called it? The moment of truth. He took one final look around, assuring himself that everything was in place.

La illaha illa Allah, he breathed, whispering the essence of his creed. It might be the last time he said it in this life, before he repeated the words of praise and homage to Mounkir and Nakir. *Muhammad rasul Allah…*

A noise broke upon his reverie and his eyes flew open. Tarik Abdul Muhammad stood just within the formerly airtight door of the lab, arms folded easily across his chest. He was dressed in his street clothes.

"Ignore me," he announced. "I am only here to observe."

"B-but, shaikh," Jamal stammered, "there is only one suit—if the saw pierces the metal containing the soman…it will be your death."

The eyes of a prophet stared back at him. Calm, mesmerizing. Unrelenting. "Allah will guide your hands…"

6:13 P.M.
St. Louis, Missouri

The Mississippi. The Father of Waters, as it had once been called. It was a magnificent river. Korsakov dialed the number from memory, standing by the side of the Suburban.

"Are you sure?" he asked, turning back to Viktor. The boy nodded. They'd pulled off the road after his discovery, and now they stood in an alley overlooking the river.

Four rings and the phone picked up. "Yes?" a voice asked in clear, if accented, English.

"We have a problem," Korsakov announced without greeting or preamble. They didn't have time.

"I could tell that much from CNN." There was sarcasm in the tones. "I brought you into this country because I trusted you to do the job, Sergei. Was my trust misplaced?"

The assassin took a deep breath. "*Nyet*. The contract will be finished as we agreed, but there is something you need to know."

"And that would be?"

"As we speak, the target is within thirty miles of you. It is only safe to assume that the CIA officer is still with her. You may be in danger."

A curse. "What do they know?"

Neither of them had the answer to that question. "Where are you now?"

Korsakov glanced over at Viktor. He could be signing their death warrant. "We're in the city of St. Louis."

"I will send my Gulfstream for you—be at the airport in five hours."

"*Spasiba bolshoi, tovarisch.*" Thank you very much.

And it was done.

It was the first target. He was sure of it. Short, stocky, his deep tan hinting at his Mediterranean background. There was a military bearing to his gait as he walked across the street in the pale glow of the streetlights.

Yuri adjusted the magnification ring, enhancing the zoom as his reticule centered on the man's face, watching him exhale, steam billowing into the cold night.

Caruso paused at the door of the apartment complex, unsure whether to go on in or not. Marika's contact was Agency. His favorite people.

As it turned out, he didn't have long to wait. Altmann materialized out of the twilight, a heavy jacket shrouding her lithe figure, a Ravens baseball cap pulled low over her eyes. "What are you waiting for, Vic? An engraved invitation?"

"They're inside. Are you in position?"

"Almost," the man called Kalnins whispered, pulling himself onto the top of the concrete wall that ran around the back of the apartment complex. He dropped down on the other side, unslinging the Uzi from around his neck.

From his position he could cover the maintenance exit from the building, as well as the fire escape. With a smooth practiced motion, the Latvian extended the weapon's folding sheetmetal stock, bracing it against his shoulder.

"Ready."

Four flights of stairs—the two FBI agents took them quickly, with Marika in the lead.

"I feel naked without my sidearm," she grumbled, turning for the final flight. Caruso suppressed a smile. That was the way it was when you'd been in the field as long as Altmann. Things like wearing a gun...a badge—they were more than second nature. They were a part of you.

It had been six years since her feet had last touched these steps. Not that long in the great scheme of things, but it felt like an eternity.

She'd needed his help back then as well, maybe one of the reasons nothing had ever happened between them. She didn't like *needing* people.

At the door, Marika paused before knocking, as if checking the apartment number. She knew it by heart.

Footsteps at the knock, a moment's pause and then the bolt slid back, the door opening by little more than a crack.

Carter's face. "Come in, come in." The analyst beckoned nervously and they both followed him into the apartment.

It was cleaner than she remembered—perhaps men actually learned something as they grew older. The thick venetian blinds were drawn, shutting out the night. "What are we looking at, Ron?"

"The Bureau has been compromised, Marika. At a very high level." The quality of the laser mic's audio was impressive, that much Yuri had to admit.

They needed to know how much had been uncovered. There were three targets in the apartment now—each of them glowing bright in the Barrett's thermal imaging, piercing through the closed blinds. Three targets...and a cat.

"You were right," the black man went on, his voice strained with tension. "The NRO spy sat *was* commandeered—by a legitimate FBI user account. Username: SunDancer1350. The account was created from scratch two weeks ago and given full access."

"Full access?" It was the woman this time. "What are you saying?"

"I'm saying this joker knew the brand of Haskel's briefs. Everything. There wasn't a place on the Bureau's network that he couldn't go."

"Who could have set up an account like that?"

He'd heard everything he needed to know. Yuri's finger curled around the Barrett's match trigger, applying pressure...

In cold air, sound travels at an average rate of 1,085 feet per second. The 300-grain slug spat from the Barrett's muzzle at almost three times that speed. It's a truism: you never hear the shot that kills you.

Marika would never remember Carter's answer to her question. She would never forget what happened next. Her first inkling of danger was when something warm and wet sprayed against the back of her neck.

She turned to see Caruso fall, a strangled cry escaping his lips, blood spraying from a ragged hole in his chest. Time itself seemed to slow down, the thunderous report of the shot striking their ears as her partner collapsed, his legs flailing against the faded linoleum of the kitchenette.

"Vic!" She screamed, pushing Carter down and out of the way as a second bullet ripped through the apartment. They fell together by the stove, flattening themselves against the floor.

A third shot came crashing through the window, spraying fragments of glass everywhere. She started to move, but the analyst caught her by the arm. "Stay down!"

None of that mattered. Not now. She shook off his hand, crawling on her hands and knees across the bloodstained linoleum to where Vic lay. He was bleeding profusely, fading in and out of consciousness.

"Come on, Vic," she whispered, cursing underneath her breath as she ripped off her jacket, pressing it against the wound in an attempt to staunch the flow. It was a futile gesture. "Stay with me, you coward."

Taunting him, swearing, trying to provoke an angry response. *Any* response.

Nothing. His head lolled to one side, unseeing eyes staring across the floor. She bent over his lifeless form, his blood soaking her jeans, a helpless anger flowing through her body. "Vic!"

5:02 P.M. Pacific Time
Los Angeles, California

"You think he'll come alone?" It seemed an innocent enough question, but Harry shook his head.

"Alexei? No, he'll have back-up—minimum of two, maybe three—the bistro is only a quarter-mile from the consulate. He didn't pick it for the view."

Sammy absorbed the information quietly, glancing out the windows of the hotel room. Out to where the sun was setting over the city of angels. A crimson-red orb disappearing into the sea, bathing the waters in blood. "And you trust me enough to back your play?"

"Of course," Harry replied, shooting a look of surprise at his old friend. It was a lie, but it came easily to his lips.

What made it worse was that Han knew it. The SEAL turned away, examining the fruit basket that had been delivered by the hotel.

Silence, and then the sound of water from the bathroom, a showerhead being turned on. Carol. Unfortunately their operations didn't allow for a great deal of privacy. The room didn't even have two beds, but a bedroll on the floor would do. "There in Kentucky, I killed a man for you, Harry. Not even a man, really. A *kid*. A kid with a gun. So don't lie to me. You don't trust me now any more than you did in Yemen. You're not capable of it…"

8:06 P.M. Eastern Time
The abandoned apartments
Clarksville, MD

This wasn't going according to plan. Yuri lifted his eyes from the scope, only too aware that only one of his targets was dead. They were running out of time, he realized, listening to the police chatter coming across the scanner on the table. People were streaming into the street as though the building was on fire and he could see several on their cell phones. He toggled his lip mike. "I can provide covering fire, Kalnins. Finish this."

"We can't stay here." It was an obvious observation as yet another heavy rifle slug ripped through the apartment, but she made it anyway. "Do you own a gun?"

Carter put his head up long enough to look at her. "Blast it, Marika, I'm an analyst, not a freakin' field officer. What do *you* think?"

It had been worth asking. She brushed a silver strand of hair out of her eyes, forcing herself to think, to concentrate. She was getting too old for this.

Vic! They'd both had their service weapons impounded after West Virginia, but Vic...

She crawled to where he lay on the floor, rolling him over on his stomach. His head struck the linoleum with a sickening thud and Marika cringed at the sound. There it was, a "baby Glock" tucked in a holster in the small of his back, a subcompact 10mm Glock 29.

She jerked it from its holster, laying on her back as she racked the slide to chamber a round.

"Do you have a plan?" This from Carter.

A shake of the head in the negative. "The shots should bring the local LEOs running, maybe even SWAT, if we get lucky."

The thought hit her suddenly, fear seizing hold. "Ron, when they get here—your computer, it's gonna be evidence."

It took a moment for her words to strike home, but then the analyst's face blanched. All the records, every last electronic vestige of his hack into the Bureau's servers. Evidence...

Kalnins had been in the *Spetsnaz* for thirteen years before leaving Russia's special forces for the more lucrative trade of the mercenary. One choice he'd never regretted. The Latvian took the stairs two at a time, the Uzi's folding stock pressed into his shoulder as he bounded upward.

He half expected someone to come out of one of the apartments to stop him, perhaps one of America's infamous private gun owners, but it didn't happen. Everyone was either already in the street or hiding under their beds.

Home of the brave? A smile crossed the mercenary's face as he reached the fourth floor, pausing outside his target's door. Time to do this.

"How much longer?" Marika asked from her position behind the overturned kitchen table.

In the semi-darkness of the apartment, she could barely see Carter holding up three fingers as he lay underneath the computer desk. "Data corruption has already begun, but the electromagnet's gonna need a few more minutes. Then we'll—"

Whatever the analyst had been about to say was lost as the apartment's door came flying inward, a burst of machine-gun fire tearing through the night. Bullets puncturing the drywall. Suppressive fire.

In the end, Maxwell saved their lives. As the shooter came through the door, the bobtailed cat leaped from the bookshelf where he had been cowering ever since the shooting started.

Kalnins turned reflexively at the movement, firing a burst into the empty shelf. It was a fatal distraction.

He saw the muzzle flash, down low, near the floor—heard the slug embed itself in the wall beside his head. Another flash, two blasts coming almost as one, and he recoiled backward, gasping in pain. His Level II tactical vest stopped both rounds, but it was like being hit in the ribs with a sledgehammer. The breath driven from his body.

He swayed, reaching back for the doorframe to support himself as he raised the Uzi in one hand, firing a wild burst. No targets.

The Latvian swore, gritting his teeth against the pain as he moved deeper into the apartment, the submachine gun against his shoulder. Every instinct of his mind screamed caution, but police sirens sounded in the distance.

He was running out of time. "Hold fire," he ordered, keying his lip mike. The last thing he needed was to be shot by his own team.

Caution to the wind. He stepped into the kitchen, the barrel of the Uzi leading the way.

"Don't shoot!" A man's voice and Kalnins turned on heel, seeing the black man on his knees near the computer desk. His hands locked behind his head.

Perfect target...his brain never had time to finish processing the thought. Something cold and hard struck him in the back of the neck and he felt himself falling, the Uzi slipping from his fingers. Then everything went black.

Never leave your partner. It had been her life, the mantra of her training. Second nature.

A life that had now been turned upside down. Old rules now. There was no help for it. Marika pulled her gaze away from Vic's corpse, looking over to where Carter knelt crouched by the desk.

Pull yourself together. Let the dead bury their dead.

She hit the Glock's magazine release and slid the double-stack magazine out into her hand. Seven rounds left.

"On my signal—head for the door. Don't stop till you reach the landing. Keep your head down."

A nod. She took a deep breath, visualizing her target. Replaying the mental image of the muzzle flashes, the open window. *Now!*

"Go, go, *go!*"

She fell forward on one knee, the subcompact coming up in both hands. There. The window across the street—just as she had envisioned it. The Glock recoiled into her hand, the slide cycling. One, two shots.

Cover fire.

Next moment she was up and on her feet, moving toward the apartment door. She caught up with Carter on the landing.

No time to stop, no time for words. Her hand came down on the analyst's shoulder, pushing him forward. On into the night...

No shot, no clear angle. Yuri swore, slamming his gloved hand against the sandbagged firing rest. Just like that, his targets were gone.

Sirens jarred him from his trance. *Focus.* Think. He took a final look down the Barrett's scope, picking out the heat signature of his partner, laying on the apartment's floor.

He wasn't dead.

The assassin made his decision in a trice. Forget loyalty. Forget honor— there was no such thing in this business. It was simply the practicality of the matter. You didn't leave someone behind, someone who could talk. Be identified.

And his mission had changed. Recover Kalnins.

Chapter 14

12:03 A.M. Eastern Time, December 18th
Clarksville, Maryland

A chill breeze tugged at the flap of Kranemeyer's trench coat as he pushed open the door of the Agency Suburban, stepping into the street.

Flying blind. He didn't like that. Never had. Never would. Blind left you crippled—as he knew all too well. Approaching the line of police tape, he held up his CIA identification, transfixing the young Bureau agent there with a hard stare.

A moment, and then she waved him through. "Director's in the building—top floor."

It was Carter's building, he knew that much. Didn't explain getting a call in the middle of the night from the director of the FBI.

As it turned out, the FBI director was coming down as he made his way up. "What's going on, Haskel?"

They weren't on a first-name basis, at least as far as Kranemeyer was concerned.

"What isn't, Barney?" The forty-four-year-old Haskel possessed all the easy familiarity of a skilled lawyer. Which he was. "Do you know a Ronald Jefferson Carter?"

The DCS never blinked. "Name sounds familiar. Is he in the movies?"

"Don't give me that need-to-know crap, Barney," Haskel exclaimed impatiently. The oiled façade slipping. "We know he works for the Agency, we know he works for you."

190

"Then why waste my time with rhetorical questions?" He didn't like being played with. "Get to the point."

"The point is I've got an agent DOA upstairs and your man Carter is nowhere to be found." The FBI head cleared his throat, continuing on down the stairs. Kranemeyer fell in step beside him. "Shell casings all over the apartment, at least two weapons—9mm and 10mm. Sniper in the abandoned complex across the street. Care to know what we found over there?"

No response was necessary, and Haskel didn't wait for one. "A Barrett M98B—it's an Agency weapon, Barney."

Kranemeyer shook his head. "What have you been smoking, Haskel? No way that's possible."

Haskel ran three fingers through his sandy hair, the gesture causing his coat to fall open. *A suit and tie?* At midnight?

Even Haskel wasn't that sartorial. Not on short notice. "I don't know what to tell you, Barney. Give me another working option. We've spent the last two hours running the rifle's serial through our database—finally lost it in a maze of near untraceable JSOC procurements. You know what that means."

Agency. Kranemeyer hit the door with the flat of his hand, leading the way back onto the street. "Mind telling me what your man was doing here in the first place? You want to talk to my people—you come through *me.*"

The FBI director put up both hands, a defensive posture. "He wasn't on official business, that much I can tell you. Trust me, no one wants to know the answer to that question more than I."

Trust me. Never trust a man that asks for it, Kranemeyer mused, staring into the darkness of the December night. Movement out of the corner of his eye caught his attention, agents converging on the perimeter.

"Weapon on the ground! Get down—hands behind your head. *Now!*"

A thin black man stumbled into the bright beams of FBI flashlights, a small Glock held loosely in his right hand.

Carter. Kranemeyer watched as his analyst fell to his knees on the cold pavement, dropping the pistol. The Bureau was all over him in seconds, cuffing his hands behind his back.

The DCS turned to see Haskel standing there, open-mouthed and strangely pale. It was probably the closest the former DOJ lawyer had ever been to the scene of an actual arrest.

"I want him," Kranemeyer announced suddenly, sizing up his opponent.

The FBI director looked up, startled—as if he hadn't heard the question. "What?"

"I want Carter transferred to my custody."

A disbelieving look crossed Haskel's face. "That flies in the face of every procedure in the book. No way. Not happening."

"Think about it," Kranemeyer said, taking a step toward Haskel—moving in close, into the man's comfort zone. "Just think about it, Haskel. This nation's been under attack for the last five days. You've lost more agents than any prior director. Let me take responsibility for Carter's protection—we'll use an Agency safehouse."

"Two of my agents go with you?" The FBI director's acquiescence seemed sudden, unnatural. Kranemeyer's eyes narrowed. *What are you playing at?*

There was nothing to do—nothing except play it through, to the end. "Of course."

5:21 A.M. Pacific Time
Van Nuys Airport
Los Angeles, California

Try as you might, you never really slept on a plane. Not really. Then again, he hadn't *really* slept in years.

Korsakov roused himself as the Gulfstream's landing gear touched down, striking the tarmac with a barely discernible *thump*. This pilot was good—a lot better than the underpaid, underfed Federation pilots that had flown he and his comrades into Chechnya.

The fall of communism had brought no freedom to Russia—they had but traded one set of shackles for another. Party had been replaced by capital, the ruble by the petrodollar. But the end was the same. The few controlled everything.

A few—the oligarchs. Like Valentin Stephanovich Andropov. Those who had succeeded where he'd failed.

In the end, it was curious how little resentment he felt, Korsakov mused, drawing back the curtain of the luxury jet's windows to gaze out at the airport lights—the convoy of vehicles awaiting him, the nose of Andropov's Sikorsky executive helicopter peeking out of a nearby hangar. Perhaps, in his younger years, he would have. Now? Now he was only concerned with parlaying his talents to the highest bidder—grateful that there still were high bidders like Andropov.

Perhaps he too was a capitalist. Perhaps. As the Gulfstream taxied to a stop, the assassin rose from his seat, touching Viktor on the arm as he moved toward the door. "It is time to be going."

5:41 A.M.
The hotel

Keep her safe. Those were his orders. She was his responsibility. That was all.

Or was it? He looked back toward the bed to where Carol lay, her form outlined beneath the sheets. He couldn't describe how he felt, except that he had started to *care* and it bothered him.

Out in the field, you learned to fear your emotions. Isolate. Compartmentalize. Don't let anything break down those barriers. *Never* become emotionally attached to your principal. All those cardinal rules—so easy to recite, so hard to keep.

He clipped the holstered Colt into the waistband of his pants, padding softly across the carpeted room. Day was coming, all too soon.

Her hair was splayed out against the pillow, a tousled mess of gold in the dim glow of the nightlight. Beautiful.

Focus. It had been years since he'd felt this...this reluctant *stirring* within. Years since he'd permitted himself to care—about anyone.

Perhaps, after all this was over...

Don't go there. She stirred in her sleep, and he turned away, turning his back on her, and those emotions.

It would do nothing...except get them both killed.

9:03 A.M. Central Time
The mosque
Dearborn, Michigan

"It is a beautiful weapon," Tarik announced, sliding a hand across the polished receiver of the Kalashnikov, fingers brushing the folding polymer stock, an aftermarket American addition. "Have any of you ever fired one?"

Jamal looked over to see al-Fileestini and Omar shaking their heads. The shaikh's eyes drifted across the room to rest on him. "Have you, my brother?"

"No."

A smile of amusement crossed the face of Tarik Abdul Muhammad. "Now this will never suit our purposes. How many of you have fired a weapon before—any weapon?"

Omar inclined his head. "A few pistols back in my days on the street, nothing more. Guns were for intimidation, for show."

"I was a young man during the First Intifada," al-Fileestini said at last, clearing his throat. "I did what I could, but it has been many years."

The shaikh paused for a moment, seemingly lost in thought. "Your prowess does not concern me, father. Allah has not ordained that you accompany us on this holy mission. As for the others—they will need to become accustomed to the feel of the weapon in their hands. You have ammunition?"

"Indeed." Al-Fileestini spoke briefly to Omar, and the negro disappeared into a back room. "But any shots here in the city...the Dearborn police are corrupt and inadequate, but not so much so as to ignore automatic weapons fire."

"Allah will provide," Tarik replied with a dismissive wave of the hand. "Did you not say that we have a brother several hours north along the peninsula? You spoke of a ...cabin, I believe. Secluded?"

The imam nodded, reaching into the pocket of his trousers. "I will make a few calls."

10:17 A.M. Eastern Time
The apartments
Clarksville, MD

As crime scenes went, this one was messy. Or so he'd been told. Bullets and brass everywhere. He watched a crime scene investigator emerge from behind the apartment building, a small plastic evidence bag in his hand. They'd been digging spent rounds out of the building *behind* the apartments. Apparently, one didn't mess with a .338 Lapua Magnum. Haskel took another step away from his agents, listening carefully to the voice on the other end of the phone.

"You're certain she was here last night? You're *sure*?"

"Of course I am," the voice replied, no longer calm. That in itself was disturbing.

They'd met back during Haskel's days as an attorney with the Holder DOJ, exchanging their dreams over lunch on K Street. The world needed a leader, a man of unimaginable vision and tenacity. The ability to remake the world and the ruthless determination to see it through.

Over the years he had never known the man to lose his cool. Until now. With the stakes higher than ever.

"I didn't want her killed," the FBI director hissed, taking another look around him. "What are you trying to accomplish?"

"Wrapping up loose ends, Eric. They were close. Very close. The threat we buried with David Lay...we can't risk its reemergence."

"How much does she know?" Haskel asked, passing a hand over his forehead. He didn't really want to know. He'd never dreamed that it would come to this, but one thing led to another.

He listened for another few minutes, then nodded. "Don't do *anything* else unless you talk to me first. I can sideline her easily enough—have her working something else. As for the CIA angle…that's covered."

10:42 A.M.
A CIA safehouse
Georgetown, Maryland

The safehouse was nothing special, just your standard split-level. Nondescript was the order of the day. Reinforced locks, bulletproof windows, and a sophisticated security system were the only real additions. And the alarm alerted Langley, not the local PD.

Kranemeyer pulled back the drapes of the top-floor window, taking a look down the quiet street. The FBI wasn't happy with security arrangements, which suited him just fine. They'd nearly parked a pair of black Suburbans with government tags out front, announcing their presence to the world.

Subtlety wasn't Haskel's strong suit. Never had been, but the Bureau chief wasn't himself. Could be the recent wave of terrorist attacks. Could be something more.

Kranemeyer dropped his jacket on the back of the chair and pulled it away from the folding table. The Heckler & Koch USP .45 rode prominently on his hip, a reminder that the Delta Force operator was never far from the surface. "Shall we begin with what this Victor Caruso was doing at your apartment. What did he want?"

Silence. The DCS traded glances with the pair of FBI agents assigned to provide 'oversight'.

"Give me something I can work with, Ron. I've gone through your file— you had no prior contact with Agent Caruso. Your only connection to him was during the aftermath of TALON in September. And the two of you never met. What's with the late-night social call?"

Carter squirmed uncomfortably, eyeing Haskel's men. He wasn't trained for field work, and it was showing. His eyes revealed too much. "Can we go for a walk—alone?"

7:05 A.M. Pacific Time
Beverly Hills, California

It was obvious why Americans loved California, even to a foreigner like Korsakov. Loved it in spite of themselves. A monument to hedonism, to the excesses of their beloved capitalism.

The Mercedes M Class slowed as it turned onto the access road. Two hours of surveillance detection runs had finally convinced Andropov's driver that they were safe.

The driver reached into the center console, pulling out a small remote and entering his access code. He aimed it at the sculptured iron gates, a smile of satisfaction crossing his face as they swung open.

Opening outward. Another security measure, Korsakov noted. It would make them less vulnerable to a ramming attack. He glanced at the cameras evenly spaced along the perimeter wall as the SUV rolled into the compound. Paranoia? Not really—after all, Andropov had made his millions selling Kalashnikovs, not toothpaste. His rise from *Spetsnaz* colonel to *mafiya* arms dealer had been a bloody one.

Even the paranoid have enemies.

Korsakov slid his satphone surreptitiously from his jacket, consulting the screen. Nothing. He should have received confirmation from Yuri or Kalnins, something by now. Unless something had gone wrong.

As if on cue, the phone began to pulse. With a look toward the driver and the sleeping Viktor, Korsakov raised it to his ear. "*Da?*"

"Thirty-three percent," came the announcement. Yuri, strain showing in his voice.

Korsakov swore softly. *Thirty-three percent.* One out of three targets taken out. A failure, by his standards. More importantly, by Andropov's. "Where are you now?"

"Baltimore."

"Kalnins?"

"With me, injured. A concussion, I would say."

The assassin swore beneath his breath. "We need to regroup—ditch your equipment and get on a plane."

"The contract is unfinished." The hostility was still there in Yuri's voice, ever simmering just beneath the surface.

Korsakov glanced out the tinted windows of the Mercedes, toward the portico of the mansion, palm trees shading the sidewalk. "To the devil with the contract."

11:24 A.M. Eastern Time
Georgetown, MD

The Bureau had thrown the expected hissy fit at the very thought of Carter's proposed walk. Even now, they weren't truly alone—not if you counted the pair of Bureau sniper teams that were supposed to be providing overwatch.

As alone as they were going to be. Kranemeyer paused with one foot on the embankment, looking out across the murky waters of the Sassafras River. "Mind telling me what's going on?"

Carter took a final glance toward their minders, then turned his face away. He might lack field training, but he wasn't dumb. The Bureau was known to employ lip-readers.

"The fiasco in West Virginia didn't just happen," he said finally, letting out the breath he had been holding, steam expelled into the chill morning air. "And it had nothing to do with Nichols."

Kranemeyer glanced over at his analyst. "You've been on my payroll for, what, three years—give or take?"

A nod. "Moved over permanently from the Intelligence Directorate the year following NIGHTSHADE."

"Then you know you have my confidence, Ron. But believe me when I say that this had better not be one of your hunches."

"It's not." Carter took another look around him. Georgetown was a sleepy river town, particularly in the off-season. Almost no one on the nearby streets.

Just the FBI's watchers.

"Someone inside the government is working with the terrorists, and they're trying to make it look like Nichols is behind it. They had real-time intel in West Virginia."

"What type of intel?"

"They were controlling the NRO satellite tasked to the Bureau's mission. They were in command of the feed."

"How is that even possible?" Kranemeyer almost turned to face Carter, then thought better of it. *Watchers.*

"It was a legit user account, set up a few days before the bombings in Virginia. Sundancer1350. No idea who is behind it, but they didn't hack their way in. They were *given* access."

"By who?"

A long pause, the silence falling heavy between the two men. "I don't know...but they had the run of the place."

The DCS swore. "You do know what you're saying, Ron?"

"That's what Marika asked," Carter replied, a thin, humorless smile turning up his lips. He felt Kranemeyer's hand descend on his arm and the color drained from his face.

"Would you mind telling me who *that* is?"

The analyst closed his eyes, cursing himself for the admission. Such a Freudian slip.

Kranemeyer's hand fell away and Carter looked up to see the DCS fishing in the pocket of his jacket for his phone. "Yes?"

As hard as he might try, it was impossible to hear the other side of the conversation. The DCS said little, his face gradually distorting with anger as he listened.

At length, "Thanks, Danny."

Kranemeyer thrust the phone back in his pocket and took Carter by the shoulder, propelling him back toward the road.

"What's going on?"

The look on Kranemeyer's face was frightening, dark coals of fire flashing in his eyes. The face of death incarnate. "Nichols was only the beginning—they're taking the Service apart, Ron. One by one. *My* people…"

11:57 A.M.
Norfolk, Virginia

Finding a person who was supposed to be dead was about as hard as one might expect. Them having relatives helped. Being on a close timetable didn't.

"How long will we have?" Thomas asked, glancing at his watch.

Tex shrugged. "I can give you five minutes to clone the SIM. In and out."

Thomas looked out the tinted windows of the Malibu, across the street to the windowed storefront of the beauty salon. The proprietor was Rhoda Stevens' sister, and he could make out the form of their target within the interior. "Her assistant goes on lunch break in fifteen. I can do this."

"You sober?" The words contained no inflection, no accusation. Just a question, and yet he felt a flash of anger.

"Stone cold."

The Texan nodded, but there was a reluctance there, a skepticism.

Didn't anyone trust him anymore? Thomas's phone rang suddenly, before he could utter the angry words rising to his lips. He palmed it off the dashboard, scanning the screen. *Kranemeyer.*

"Hello," he answered, putting the phone on speaker.

"The two of you need to go to ground," the DCS announced, his words clipped, tension filling his voice. "And stay there."

"What's going on?"

"You'll see it on the news soon enough." Explanations weren't Kranemeyer's specialty. "Someone's turning us inside out—an FBI agent was murdered last night and the murder weapon was…an Agency Barrett."

"That's crazy."

"Like usual, the truth doesn't really matter. I struck a deal with Haskel to throttle things back—keep your faces off the television for the moment…but the FBI's Counterterrorism Division has expressed an interest in your whereabouts all the same. They'll be looking for you within the hour, rattling the bushes to see what flies out. Go to ground, get out of sight."

And then he was gone, breaking contact without so much as a farewell. The two men exchanged glances, absorbing the news.

After a long moment, Thomas inclined his head toward the salon. "We're already here. Shall we?"

A nod.

9:48 A.M. Pacific Time
Baker Street Bistro
San Francisco, California

When it came right down to it, it didn't much matter if you were in San Francisco or Istanbul. Clandestine meetings were dicey business. You could never be sure what your "ally" might do.

Harry's eyes scanned the bistro as the waiter led them to their table, outside on the veranda. This might have been America, but with the Consulate mere blocks to the west, it was Vasiliev's turf. He counted at least two Russians near the front of the bistro, one more outside at one of the open-air tables. Might be security personnel from the Consulate, might be immigrants. Frisco *was* a melting pot.

Part of his mind insisted that Alexei would never attempt a snatch in public place, an American city—but he knew better, knew the danger of the course he had chosen. If America had made one mistake consistently through the last fifty years, it was what the intel community called "mirror imaging". The belief that everyone made decisions the same way you did. That their rationale, their very *definition* of logic was the same. September 11th had proven otherwise, but not everyone had gotten the memo.

He ushered Carol into the chair closest to the garden wall and took his own seat, the Colt trembling beneath his light jacket. From where he sat, he could watch the front door of the bistro.

Meeting with Alexei wasn't a choice. It was a necessity. Unavoidable.

The tension was palpable, Carol thought, giving her menu a disinterested glance. She could sense it in his body language. This meeting was a bad idea, and he knew it.

Her gaze lifted from the table, scanning the surrounding rooftops. Nothing.

Not to say that no one was there. She saw Han enter the bistro, making his way to a table near the front door. Moments later, his voice came over her earbud: "In position."

"Copy that," Harry breathed beside her, acknowledging his receipt of the message.

Without warning, a shadow fell over their table and she looked up, feeling Harry tense. Vasiliev stood there across from them, one hand clasping the back of the chair, the other held in front of him, index finger extended from a clenched fist.

A smile played across the Russian's weathered face, the breeze rippling through his silver hair. "Bang, you're dead."

9:53 A.M.
The mansion
Beverly Hills, California

It was a Nicholas Poussin, or so the head of Andropov's security had said. Whatever that was supposed to mean.

Korsakov stood there for a moment, taking a speculative sip from the wine glass as he stared at the painting over the fireplace. *King Midas at the Source of the Pactole River.*

It was an ironic choice. Andropov had always been that way. Like the fabled king, everything he touched had turned to gold. And this…this mansion—the gilded fixtures, the Renaissance artwork, these were the fruits of it.

Korsakov turned, feeling Viktor's eyes on him. "What do you think, *tovarisch?*" he asked, raising his glass as if in a toast. The boy didn't drink—it brought back flashbacks. Memories of being drugged and raped.

Viktor hesitated, as if rendered speechless by the grandeur of the sitting room. The assassin smiled. "My old comrade has done well for himself, has he not? The *Midas* touch."

The smile vanished from Korsakov's face as quickly as it had come. Andropov *had* done well, which was why he was still in bed with his mistress while the two of them cooled their heels on the first floor.

The privileges of wealth. He threw back his head, draining the wine glass in a single, angry swallow. These cursed capitalists…

9:54 A.M.
The Baker Street Bistro
San Francisco, California

The Russian looked older than the fifty-eight years his CIA dossier indicated. Much older. He had once been a handsome man, that much was obvious, but his once-lean frame had now begun to carry the weight of middle age. Blue eyes stared out from a face worn and lined by the decades, his thinning silver hair swept back rakishly from the brow.

"I appreciate you coming, Alexei," Harry began, motioning for his old adversary to take a seat. "I know it is not without its risks for you."

Vasiliev sat down, gesturing for their waiter. "There was a time, *tovarisch*. There was a time when I would have had to write up a five-page contact report after this meeting."

"And now?"

"And now…I am the *head* of security. I am, how would you say? Ah yes—a law unto myself." His hands moving in quick efficient motions, Vasiliev spread the napkin across his lap, smiling as if very pleased with himself. "And who is your sexy lady friend?" he asked, switching into Russian.

"Someone who doesn't make a practice of meeting with KGB thugs," Carol replied in the same language, an icy calm in her voice.

The Russian looked startled for a brief moment, then his body shook with laughter. "Perhaps you should have warned me, Harry."

"I didn't know myself," he replied, shooting her a sharp look. The message was clear in his eyes: *watch your step*. There was too much at stake.

"What did you find, Alexei?" Harry asked, leaning forward. "Do you have a name for me?"

"I do," Vasiliev replied, scanning his menu as the waiter arrived. "May I recommend the *Steak à Cheval?*"

Harry responded with an impatient nod and Vasiliev passed their menus to the waiter, adding, "A steak for the gentleman at the table by the door as well. Just add it to my tab."

They both followed the direction of his gaze: Samuel Han. Vasiliev smiled. "You thought I wouldn't notice, *tovarisch*? I may be growing old, but I never forget a face. It was February of 2004. Qatar."

Harry nodded in remembrance. Han *had* been there then, on "loan" to the CIA from the Teams. "Zelimkhan Yandarbiyev. You were in Doha to kill him. It was the first time I ever worked with the FSB."

"The Chechen president?" Carol asked.

Harry acknowledged her comment with a nod. "And a driving force behind the Islamization of the conflict. We were all well rid of him."

The waiter arrived with their drinks, handing a bottle of spring water to Harry and placing an empty glass in front of Vasiliev.

"You are learning, my friend," the Russian observed with a smile.

Harry twisted off the cap, breaking the seal. "I was well taught, by one of your countrywomen. Never drink from anything but a sealed bottle in a public place."

Seeing Vasiliev's look of interest, he continued. "She was a journalist. Dead now."

Vasiliev shrugged, pulling a flask from an inner pocket of his coat. "Journalism is a profession not without its...hazards. Particularly in Mother Russia."

He held up the flask of vodka to the light, eyeing it critically before pouring a shot into the glass before him. "My own solution to that problem—bring your own beer, I believe you Americans call it. Or vodka, as the case may be."

There was something quixotic, even faintly mocking, in the Russian's posture as he sat there, glass poised delicately between long, slender fingers. "To the future."

12:23 P.M. Central Time
Dearborn, Michigan

Prices had gone up at the supermarket. Again. If he'd been able to afford the gas, Nasir al-Khalidi thought—he would have loved to have driven around, just to see if prices were the same everywhere, or whether the American government was artificially inflating the prices in Muslim neighborhoods. It wasn't outside the realm of possibility. He set the bags on the floor and pulled open the door of the apartment's small refrigerator. The government *he* worked for.

It hadn't been his choice. Just one of those things that had befallen him. Fate.

Footsteps on the stairs outside, the rattling of a key in the lock. Jamal came hustling into the apartment, stopping short as he saw his brother.

"What are you doing home?"

Nasir balanced the milk on top of the eggs. His brother was growing more absent-minded these days. As if some great concern was occupying his thoughts. "This is my day off," he explained patiently, casting a weary glance in Jamal's direction. "What do you need?"

It wasn't like Jamal to be at a loss for words, but he stammered a moment. "I forgot my student ID. With the attacks in Virginia…the campus is taking their security seriously."

Didn't make any sense. At noon? He waited until his brother had disappeared in the bedroom, then put his fingers carefully between the dusty venetian blinds, peering down at the street, at the unfamiliar car that had brought his brother back from campus. A white Chrysler Sebring.

Something was wrong. Deciding quickly, he grabbed a pen off the card table that formed the centerpiece of their kitchen. The tip pressed into tender flesh as he scribbled the license number into the palm of his hand. *Kilo 8 7 November Tango.*

Omar was waiting in the Sebring when Jamal returned. "What took so long?"

He threw the packet of earplugs on the console between himself and the Negro. "My brother was home."

The black man closed his eyes. *So much must be sacrificed for the jihad. At times even families must be separated.* "Will that be a problem?"

"Of course not. My brother…" Jamal hesitated. "My brother finds the decadence of America alluring, but he would never betray us. Not after what happened in our homeland, not after our father was killed, American weapons in the hands of the Jew."

Omar considered that for a moment, then put the Sebring in drive. "*Insh'allah.*"

10:32 A.M. Pacific Time
Baker Street Bistro
San Francisco, California

"The name of the man you are looking for," Vasiliev began, dabbing his thin, bloodless lips with a napkin, "is Valentin Stephanovich Andropov. Former *Spetsnaz* colonel, weapons dealer, and current expatriate oligarch. He made his millions selling weapons to Sudan, Somalia, a hundred other godforsaken backwaters. He's the man who brought Korsakov's team into the US."

"You can prove this?" Harry asked, taking another careful glance around them.

The Russian regarded him with a look of disbelief. "Since when have you and I concerned ourselves with proof, Harry?"

Vasiliev shook his head. " 'Innocent till proven guilty' isn't even in our lexicon. Andropov has the money, the power, the access with the *mafiya*. If anyone could bring a spec-ops team into this country, it would be him. And he and Korsakov served together in the first Chechen War."

Guilt by association. Harry had seen it kill men before. Sometimes, in the ever-shifting war on terror, association was all you had to go on. Leads vanishing into the mist.

"Where is he?" he heard himself ask.

Vasiliev snorted. "Living peacefully in Beverly Hills, with his bodyguards, his son, and his current mistress, typically one of your blonde starlets, much better endowed physically than mentally."

"If all you say is true," Carol put in, the skepticism clearly visible in her eyes. "then why isn't Andropov on our watch lists? Why is he living free here in the United States?"

Vasiliev let out a tired sigh, reaching for his phone. He ran a calloused thumb across the screen, scrolling through a series of photos. Finally he turned the screen to face them. "He's re-cast himself as a benefactor of the common good—a philanthropist. Here you see him, during the 2008 Republican primary, at a dinner with Senator John McCain. And here—five months later—standing at the side of Barack Obama in Los Angeles. When Roger Hancock ran, a PAC bankrolled by Andropov was one of his biggest supporters." The Russian leaned back in his chair, pocketing the phone. "Let's face it, he's played your country's political system."

"Like a Stradivarius," Harry mused. "So you're saying he's untouchable."

Vasiliev toyed with his knife, gazing intently across the table. "No man is untouchable, *tovarisch*. For some, though…you need asbestos gloves."

"What are you suggesting?"

A smile. "I suggest *nothing*. I ask nothing, save one simple question: how far are you willing to go?"

10:42 A.M.
The mansion
Beverly Hills, California

Andropov's mistress was awake at the very least, already stretched out facedown on a blanket by the heart-shaped pool. Nothing mattered more than a tan in California, Korsakov thought, eyeing her critically.

About the only point in her favor was her youth. Twenty-one, twenty-three at most. No doubt hoping that sharing the oligarch's bed would further her career.

Bleached blonde, burnt flesh, and undeniably spoiled—there was a time when his old friend had possessed better taste in women. Times had changed.

"Sergei!" a familiar voice exclaimed, the door opening behind the assassin. He turned on heel just in time to see one of the bodyguards usher Andropov into the room.

Times *had* changed. The former colonel had aged in the ten years since they had last met face to face. Andropov had never been a small man, but his frame now carried the bulk that went along with fine dining and a sedentary lifestyle.

"You look well, comrade," he whispered, embracing Korsakov and kissing him on both cheeks in the traditional Russian greeting.

"As do you," the assassin lied, forcing a smile to his face as Andropov guided him to a seat on the sofa.

The oligarch nodded his head toward Viktor. "I have heard much about you from Sergei—you are a genius with computers, yes?"

The boy flushed, looking down at his feet. The traumas of his childhood had left him socially awkward, but he seemed particularly so in these opulent surroundings.

"My son Pyotr is about your age," Andropov continued, "a junior at UCLA."

Small talk. Korsakov remembered it well, the colonel's way of putting people at ease…before moving in for the kill.

"He should be getting a fine education, wouldn't one think?" The oligarch didn't wait for an answer—he had clearly mastered the art of the one-sided conversation. He threw up his hands in a dramatic flourish. "He might be if he actually bothered to study, instead of partying away his nights in some bar, an American whore sitting on his lap."

Korsakov gazed idly out the window at the sunbathing form of Andropov's mistress. One had to wonder where the son had developed *those* proclivities.

"Competence," the oligarch sighed. "It is such a rare trait these days, my old comrade. It is all the more reason that I have been glad of your aid. Someone I can trust."

With those words, his voice shed every last vestige of pleasantry. His eyes bored into Korsakov's face. "What *is* the status of the contract, Sergei?"

11:01 A.M.
Baker Street Bistro
San Francisco, California

"Does the FSB keep these type of files on every Russian citizen?" Carol asked, looking up from her laptop. The waiter had cleared the plates away, and left them alone after Vasiliev had pressed a fifty-dollar bill into his hand.

The Russian chuckled. "Only those we deem likely to cause trouble. In a word...yes."

Harry looked over at the screen, watching as the file transfer approached 100%. He could feel Carol's irritation with Alexei—there *was* nothing remotely humorous about Russia's treatment of its citizens, of its journalists.

Reforms? They had been little more than window dressing. The shackles of slavery freshly adorned with the garland of freedom. Men like Vasiliev had moved from the old world into the new and scarce noticed the difference. "We appreciate your help, Alexei," he replied, his voice neutral as he pulled the thumb drive out of the laptop and handed it back to the Russian. "This should give us all the information we need. As far as I'm concerned, this meeting never took place. You were never involved."

Vasiliev tucked the drive in his shirt pocket, a strange look on his face as he regarded Harry. "Would that life were so simple, *tovarisch*."

"What do you mean?" Harry asked. His hand moved beneath the table, coming to rest on his thigh, only inches away from the Colt.

"You still need me." The Russian reached for his glass, tossing back another shot of vodka. He looked over at Carol, a smile on his face. "Our friend Nichols is a strict teetotaler, and yet he has never once lectured me on my drinking. I admire his reserve."

Harry transfixed him with a cold stare. "Perhaps I simply believe the world would be a better place were you to die of cirrhosis."

"Well said," Vasiliev laughed, nearly choking on his drink. "Well said, but I fear that my demise is in no way imminent. I have been thinking...how was Korsakov able to find you in West Virginia?"

The million-dollar question. The one Harry had asked himself a thousand times. No good answers, and from the look on Alexei's face, he knew as much.

Vasiliev went on without waiting for a response. "I won't patronize you by asking if you swept her for a tracker, Harry," the Russian said, inclining his head in Carol's direction. "I know you would have. And you probably found at least one. Am I right?"

"Two."

A raise of the eyebrows. "Redundancy. We Russians are thorough. What I'm more interested in is what you were *unable* to find."

Vasiliev reached into his shirt pocket, laying a small plastic capsule about the size and color of a grain of rice on the tablecloth. "Ever seen one of these before?"

"It's a GPS tracker," Carol replied. "The US did pioneer the technology, after all."

The Russian's only immediate reply was a nod. He stared across the table at them for a long moment, as if deliberating on his next words. "You may have been the pioneers, but you have been eclipsed. By China, now the world's leading developer of the technology. It is only due to the industrial espionage of my partners in the SVR that Moscow has access to this little gem. A self-contained unit, with over three months of battery life."

"Exactly why do you think this would have escaped my scanner?" Harry asked, his eyes locked on Vasiliev's face. Looking for the faintest trace of duplicity. Of guile.

Nothing.

"Because that's what it is designed to do," came the quiet reply. "I am an old dog, Harry, and the technical details escape me, but this tracker is programmed to detect the activation of a scanner and go into passive mode for the duration of the scan."

Harry's skepticism must have showed on his face, for Vasiliev added, "It's complicated. Or so the children in our tech department blithely assure me."

Another time Harry might have smiled at the disdainful comment, but not now. If what the Russian said was true...then all their attempts to evade Korsakov had been fruitless. And it explained everything.

"If this tracker as sophisticated as you claim, then how can it ever be detected?"

"Hospital-grade medical equipment," Vasiliev replied. "An X-ray can detect it—they're often installed in a tooth of the person being tracked."

Harry glanced over at Carol, seeing his own fear reflected in her eyes. The noise of the restaurant had faded into the background, the silence falling over them like a heavy cloud. Oppression.

He reached out and took her hand in his, an empty reassurance. "The last few months...had any dental work done?"

A nod, as though she could scarcely trust her voice. "November 21st, I believe, if I remember correctly. One of the molars—needed a crown."

Vasiliev spread his hands in a gesture of *What did I tell you?* "May I make a suggestion?"

Harry shot him a dark look. "You may."

The Russian tilted his flask forward, watching the clear liquor spill into the small glass. When he spoke again, it was as if the thought had just occurred to him. "The clinic at the consulate...we have the necessary equipment."

"No."

3:27 P.M. Central Time
Northeastern Michigan

It wasn't hard to see why al-Fileestini had thought it was a safe place to train with the Kalashnikov. The area surrounding the cabin was one of the most desolate places Jamal had ever seen, the pine forest covered in a fresh blanket of snow.

The college student rubbed his hands together vigorously, glancing back toward the warmth of the vehicles. With the Pakistanis along, they'd needed to bring two, with he and Omar being the "designated drivers".

Fortunately, the cold air dissipated their smell. It had been somewhat disillusioning to realize that the *mujahideen* he had so admired as a child knew nothing of the basics of personal hygiene. Driving up the peninsula with the windows rolled up had been a challenge.

But the *mujahideen* knew their weapons, he had to admit. He bent down on one knee in the snow, examining the open can of ammunition that the owner of the cabin had brought out to them. The markings on the can read "US Army M-2 .50 cal" but it was filled with little black boxes labeled *Tulammo*. Jamal slid one of the boxes open, extracting a long, gray, missile-shaped round. Seven-point-six-two-millimeter.

May Allah guide its flight, he breathed, rolling the cartridge between his fingers.

He heard his name being called and looked up to see Tarik's lieutenant, a man named Walid, waving him over.

"It is time," Walid announced without preamble, handing him the rifle. The cold gunmetal felt like fire against the bare flesh of his hands as he lifted the heavy assault rifle to his shoulder, struggling to focus on the *mujahid*'s instructions.

Fire selector all the way down. Full automatic. He pressed his cheek against the stock, his finger curling around the trigger.

Now! Fire rippled from the barrel as he squeezed the trigger, a thrill flooding through his body. *Power*.

He lowered the weapon, gazing out to forty yards where the Pakistanis had placed a bucket of ice.

Shattered now, water pouring onto the snow. Jamal threw a fist into the air, his excitement overwhelming him. *Yes, yes! Death to the unbelievers.*

4:35 P.M. Eastern Time
The J. Edgar Hoover Building
Washington, D.C.

There were days when normalcy was unsettling. Days when nothing added up. Marika Altmann leaned back in her desk chair, staring at the report that had just come across her screen.

She nearly hadn't come into work, nearly convinced herself that she should run. But she knew the power of what she was attempting to evade.

She had, after all, spent most of her adult life using the resources of the Bureau to track down people on the run. Her safety, if there was any to be found, was in keeping things routine. Staying under the radar, as unlikely as it was that she would be able to do so. Yet there had been nothing.

Two unfamiliar faces stared back at her from the screen. Both identified as CIA personnel. Both implicated in the previous night's shooting.

Her own name was nowhere to be seen. Marika reached for the cup of coffee sitting on the desk of her cubicle and, finding it empty, threw it in the trash. Something was wrong, she could feel it.

She closed her eyes and suddenly all she could see was Caruso's body, lying there in a congealing pool of his own blood.

Very wrong...

5:01 P.M. Eastern Time
CIA Headquarters
Langley, Virginia

When the phone rang, Kranemeyer knew who it was, and exactly why they were calling.

"Do you know what the penalty is for obstructing a federal investigation, Kranemeyer?" Shapiro's voice, injected with a little more testosterone than usual.

"Am I to assume that you have the statute in front of you?" the DCS asked. Baiting the deputy director was a dangerous game, but this was one game *he* hadn't started.

"A copy of the information we provided to the FBI just crossed my desk. *Incomplete* information," Shapiro added, his voice trembling as he continued. "And you went over my head to demand that Haskel restrict access to this information to a select task force from his counterterrorism division. Why? Why would you do something like this?"

"Are you quite done?" Kranemeyer asked, an icy calm pervading his tones. "We withheld from the Bureau nothing that would impede their investigation."

"What are you trying to say? I saw the report, all of the redactions from the dossier for Richards and Parker—page after page completely blacked out. I *saw* it!"

It was hard to resist the urge to laugh, the irony of using the bureaucrats' system against them was so rich. *Hoist by their own petard.* "I took what steps were necessary to protect on-going Agency operations, steps that you should have had the forethought to take. We gave the Bureau everything they need to pursue their investigation, and you may have just outed two of my best officers. If you're wrong about this—any of this, there will be hell to pay."

"Is that supposed to be a threat?" Bluster now, classic Shapiro—but it was no longer amusing.

Kranemeyer waited perhaps thirty seconds before responding. "I don't deal in threats, Shapiro, you should know that by now. I was just telling your fortune. Take it however you wish."

He ended the call without warning, replacing the phone in its cradle on his desk. The DCS sat there for a moment, staring at the opposite wall.

Loyalty meant nothing in the Beltway...to the point that the politicos didn't even understand how to cope when they encountered it.

He reached into his shirt pocket and extracted a small, old-style pager. A single line of red text scrolling across the screen at the top. THE PACKAGE IS READY FOR PICKUP.

Without further hesitation, Kranemeyer rose, balancing himself against the desk as he found his feet. There was always that one moment of uncertainty with the prosthesis.

No, the power players of Washington didn't begin to understand that loyalty, the bond forged between men who had faced battle together. Didn't know what to make of it. It would be their undoing.

He would see to that.

Chapter 15

2:34 P.M. Pacific Time
The Russian Consulate
San Francisco, California

The "clinic," if one wanted to dignify it by that name, was a small, windowless set of rooms on the third floor of the consulate, a building distinguished from the rest of the neighborhood by its brick façade on three sides.

"This was our effort at self-sufficiency during the Cold War," Vasiliev explained, following Harry into the room. "We couldn't risk our people visiting an American doctor, so we stretched the budget for whatever equipment and personnel we could accommodate. Even so, most of our personnel went into the city for the superior medical care of a hospital. Still do, actually. Our staff doesn't see many patients."

"You're not exactly filling me with confidence here, Alexei." Harry's eyes swept the clinic, taking everything in. Just the one exit, an essentially bare room except for the dentist's chair and his supplies on a table near the far wall. A pane of one-way glass filled one half of the western wall, presumably another room and begging the question of what else the room might be used for.

It was as close to a controllable environment as he was going to get.

The Russian spread his hands. "What did you expect, *tovarisch*, Johns Hopkins? We make the best of what we have…what is that expression—any port in a storm?"

Harry turned to Carol as Vasiliev left the room, putting his hand lightly on her shoulder. "Are you sure you can go through with this?"

She managed a half-smile, determination creeping into her features. "I don't really have any other choice, do I? If they are able to keep tracking us…"

Her voice trailed off, but it didn't matter. She was right.

Vasiliev reappeared with a younger Russian in tow. "Dr. Petrov, our dentist-in-residence. He's the son of our naval attache and went to dental school here in the States, if that's any comfort to you."

The dentist flushed, responding with a somewhat shame-faced greeting. His English was very good, with just a trace of accent. "We will need to use a sedative, ma'am. Our goal is to remove the tracker without rendering it inoperative. It will require a delicate touch."

"Do what you have to do," Carol replied, looking him in the eye.

"Then let's leave him alone, shall we?" Vasiliev suggested. "We can observe from the other side of that window."

Harry turned to the former KGB officer. "And if there's a problem?"

"We can be in here within twenty-five seconds."

2:49 P.M.
The mansion
Beverly Hills, California

"They're at the consulate?" Andropov demanded, sweeping into the room with his bodyguards flanking him. He'd been gone for most of the afternoon, out of contact. But he had obviously received Korsakov's voicemail.

Viktor looked up from the computer perched precariously in his lap. "*Da.* They arrived…thirty minutes ago, yes?" He looked to Korsakov for confirmation.

A nod.

The oligarch removed his gloves, moving behind Viktor's chair so that he could see the screen for himself. A curse escaped his lips. "What are they doing there?"

"It doesn't matter," Korsakov interjected. "Give me twenty minutes to assemble my team and I can be on the road. Chambers will be dead before nightfall, along with this Nichols."

Andropov seemed to consider the suggestion for a long moment. Then he shook his head.

"You and your men have made two attempts already. You've failed both times and each time your *targets* come closer to me. I fear this CIA officer is more dangerous than you give him credit for."

Korsakov started to speak, but the oligarch held up a hand. "You have served me well in years past, Sergei, and I have not forgotten it. But our third chance will also be our last, and we must make it count. What is the update on your absent team members?"

The assassin took a deep breath, trying to master his emotions. His old comrade had lost none of his teeth.

He gestured toward Viktor's screen. "They are en route to Philadelphia International. It's the nearest large airport that isn't under complete lockdown. Their flight has a scheduled layover in Chicago—they should land in LAX tomorrow evening."

"Then we wait," Andropov admonished. "And move with our full strength when *we* are ready. You are old enough of a warrior to know this, Sergei. Never allow your opponent to dictate your moves."

"Well done," he continued, patting Viktor on the shoulder as he moved away. One of his bodyguards handed him a cellphone. "I have contacts in the consulate. One of them should know why they are there."

3:02 P.M.
The Russian Consulate
San Francisco, California

It was something they taught at the Agency. *Maintain control of your circumstances.*

The manual was somewhat fuzzier on what to do when you couldn't. Harry glanced at his watch, then back through the glass to where Carol lay sedated in the dentist's chair.

He had always resorted to prayer in those moments, as awkward as it felt to enter the presence of God with blood on his hands.

And so he prayed, standing there with his eyes open, watching for any signs of danger. Prayed for her safety, most of all.

"The security footage of our entrance into the consulate—"

"Has been erased," Alexei interrupted. A smile crept across his aging face. "As I said, I am very much a law unto myself. The reward of decades of loyal service."

Harry acknowledged the information with a nod. He had to protect her, that was all that mattered.

And it had nothing to do with his orders, he realized with shocking clarity. He actually *cared* for her, in a way he hadn't cared about anyone in a very long time. It was an alien feeling.

Out there on the edge, he had learned *not* to care. You couldn't manipulate someone you cared for. You couldn't care for someone you had manipulated—

they were only to be despised. And in a world where manipulation kept you alive, you quickly made the decision of what you could live without.

May God forgive me.

The lights of the office dimmed once, then twice, casting an eerie shadow over the double-headed eagle on the far wall, the old symbol of Russia.

Danger. The hairs on the back of Harry's neck prickled, his hand flickering toward his hip, toward the now-empty holster. It was a movement born of instinct—he had left his Colt with Vasiliev's security personnel at the rear entrance.

Overload the power grid, shut down the building's security systems—then move in for the kill. It's what he would have done. It's what he *had* done, he thought, his mind flashing back across the years to a long-ago night on an airport tarmac in Paraguay.

"Give me your sidearm," he hissed, staring across at the Russian.

A peculiar smile on his face, Vasiliev opened his jacket. He wasn't wearing a weapon.

The lights surged back to full power and the smile grew wider. "This *is* California, Harry. Out here, we've gotten used to 'rolling blackouts', as your media likes to call them."

False alarm. Harry closed his eyes, willing his body to relax. "You don't carry a weapon?"

"Rarely. I entered the service of my country at the height of the Cold War, and firearms training was not the priority of the First Directorate." Vasiliev's eyes grew reflective. "Those were the days, Harry, back before everyone strapped it on like James Bond. There were rules to this game—back before these religious fanatics came bursting upon the scene with their *fatwas* and wild-eyed clerics, Visigoths come to ravage Rome. Yes, those were the days."

"When you tortured men and women in the basement of the Lubyanka," Harry replied flatly. There were no rose-colored pictures of the past.

Vasiliev spread his hands. "I said there were rules, not that we agreed on all of them."

His cellphone rang and he stepped away from Harry to answer it, a grim expression coming over his face as he listened.

The call didn't last more than ninety seconds—Harry timed it, keeping an eye on his watch as Alexei carried on a conversation in rapid-fire Russian.

"We have a problem," Vasiliev announced, tucking his phone back into his pocket. "Someone is making inquiries about the identities of our American visitors. Someone powerful."

5:23 P.M. Central Time
The mosque
Dearborn, Michigan

This is the Hell of which ye were repeatedly warned. Embrace ye the Fire this day, for that ye persistently rejected Truth. Tarik Abdul Muhammad closed his Qur'an and laid it aside, a strange feeling of disquiet settling over his body. Something was wrong.

It was a gift from Allah, the ability to sense danger. He knew enough not to ignore it. It had saved his life twice in the years since the American government had released him from Guantanamo. Since they had come to realize their mistake in so doing.

But what was it now, as he moved so close to fulfilling the will of God? Brushing a speck of lint off his slacks, Tarik rose and moved toward the window of the imam's living quarters. Nothing out of the ordinary in the street outside.

A loud vibrating buzz rose from his cellphone and he palmed it off the desk. *Jamal.*

"Yes?"

The torrent of words that poured forth from the young man was more than even Tarik could process. "Stop," he said finally, his eyes growing dark. "Start again, slowly this time. And remember, this is an open line."

5:31 P.M.
Northern Michigan

Slowly. Of course. Jamal took another look out the window of the parked Sebring, forcing himself to calm down. He felt as if he was hyperventilating. Flashing lights filled the highway scarce a hundred meters away from where he sat, illuminating the gathering dusk. Red, white, blue.

"*Ya Allah*, it happened so fast. There was just no time." He heard more sirens, an ambulance closing in fast from the south.

"No time? What are you talking about?"

The college student closed his eyes, reliving the horror. It had all started an hour before, as they'd field-stripped the Kalashnikov, placing it back in the Honda's trunk, underneath a basket of dirty laundry.

That was when the trouble began. Emboldened by an afternoon with his familiar weaponry, Walid had insisted on driving, on proving his manhood on the open road.

"You weren't here," Jamal stammered, wavering between anger and a holy awe. Surely if the Shaikh had only been present...

He and Omar had stood together, but their combined powers of persuasion had not been enough. The Pakistanis had piled into the Honda and torn away from the cabin, setting such a breakneck pace that even the negro had been hard-pressed to keep up.

"*Ya Allah*," he breathed again, still almost incapable of coherent thought. Thirty miles—that's how long they'd lasted.

The driver's door was still wedged shut from the impact, Lieutenant Nick Dubroznik observed, playing his flashlight over the wreckage. The EMTs had been forced to extract the dead body of the driver out through the passenger side door. His neck had been snapped on impact. Five years in the Michigan State Police, and he'd never seen the like. Another corpse in the back seat, driver's side.

According to eyewitnesses, the driver of the Honda had tried to pass the car ahead of him, a risky high-speed pass that hadn't paid off.

Fishtailing on a patch of black ice, the Honda had spun into the path of an oncoming semi.

A fully-loaded semi truck needs roughly a hundred yards to slow from highway speeds to a complete stop. It'd had only thirty. In the end, it was the mathematics that had killed them.

Witnesses had reported two, possibly three more passengers fleeing from the vehicle. A miracle that anyone had walked away, but it wasn't surprising that they had fled. Neither of the victims had been carrying ID, probably illegals from the looks of them. Drugs, maybe?

He'd seen it a hundred times before. Marijuana, heroin, crack. Over the last few years the use of *khat*, an amphetamine native to the Arabian peninsula, had become steadily prevalent in the Islamic community. It wasn't considered highly addictive, but enough so to get the DEA's shorts in a bind.

The two men *might* have been Arabs, Dubroznik reflected. He took one look at the buckled trunk lid of the Honda and walked back to his patrol car, retrieving a short-handled crowbar.

Time to apply a little leverage. He slid one end of the bar under the lid and applied pressure, his breath billowing away from his lips in great clouds of steam.

The trunk popped open on the second try and the lieutenant let the crowbar fall to the ground, taking the flashlight from between his teeth.

Something glinted in the beam, and Dubroznik's breath caught in his throat. He'd been prepared for neatly-wrapped packets of drugs—maybe a suitcase of money. Nothing like this.

The trunk was awash in rifle cartridges spilling out from two ruptured cardboard boxes, light reflecting off the steel casings. And then he saw it, half-hidden beneath a pile of men's shorts. A disassembled assault rifle, what was that they called it...an AK?

His fingers trembled, and it had nothing to do with the cold. They were going to have to bring the Bureau into this.

5:49 P.M.
The mosque
Dearborn, Michigan

Astagfirullah, Tarik whispered, staring at the cellphone now laying there on the desk, now silent, an inanimate piece of plastic. I ask Allah forgiveness.

Where had he failed? Two of his men were dead, another missing. Trained *mujahideen,* his friends. His brothers. The *Ikhwan* was more than just a name. They had fought and bled together in the mountains of his homeland. To die here.

A part of him wanted to rage against the injustice of it all, but he could not. There was no doubting the will of Allah, the most glorified, the most high. There was still a path, there had to be.

Show it to me, God.

It was a long moment before he rose, closing his laptop computer and sliding it into his satchel. As much as he had found respite among the faithful, Dearborn would no longer be safe. Not after this...

3:52 P.M.
The Russian Consulate
San Francisco, California

"How high can they take this, Alexei?" Harry asked, following the Russian into his office. He glanced at his watch. It had been thirty minutes since Petrov had finished the delicate task of extracting the still-functioning tracker, but Carol still hadn't even begun to come out from under the anesthesia. If Andropov had continued to make inquiries...

Vasiliev looked up. "It's already as high as it's going to go, Harry. You need not worry about that."

"You're not concerned that Andropov might have purchased himself influence with the consul?"

An eyebrow went up. "Vournikov? Right now he's probably laying out on the beach down at Baker with his boyfriend. It's where he spends most of his days while I run the consulate. Even on the cold days."

Harry shook his head. Every time you thought you were to the point that nothing would surprise you...

And then Vasiliev reached into his desk, retrieving a holstered pistol. An MP-443 *Grach*, from the looks of it. Standard-issue to the Russian military, the semiautomatic was chambered in 9mm Luger. Seventeen-round magazine.

"I thought you didn't carry a weapon."

The former KGB officer slid the paddle holster onto his belt and handed Harry his Colt. "What's that old saying of yours? 'To every thing there is a season and a time to every purpose under the heaven'...where's that from, if I may ask?"

"The Bible," Harry replied, pulling back the Colt's slide to chamber a round. Cocked and locked. "Ecclesiastes, the wisdom of Solomon."

An odd grin crossed Vasiliev's face, and he clapped Harry on the shoulder as he moved toward the door. "Small wonder I had never heard of it."

9:23 P.M. Eastern Time
Bethesda, Maryland

One look at Lasker's residence was enough to dispel any notions of the spy business being lucrative. The small, faded brick townhouse was itself split into two apartments.

Kranemeyer mounted the steps of the porch, kicking the snow from his boots. He took another long look into the dark, sleet-filled night, then scanned the letterboxes for Lasker's name. The apartment on the left.

He didn't bother with the doorbell, bringing up his left hand and rapping on the metal of the door. A hard, peremptory knock.

Two minutes. Then three. Finally, he heard movement from within and the porch light flicked on, nearly blinding him. Kranemeyer swore under his breath, taking a step back.

He had just been exposed to the full view of anyone watching. *Even the paranoid have enemies.*

The deadbolt slid back and the door opened a crack, a young brunette looking out at him. She couldn't have been much more than twenty-one, maybe twenty-two. Lasker *had* always liked to hook up with coeds. "What do you want?"

"My name's Kranemeyer. I've come to see Daniel."

The girl regarded him for another long moment, shifting her gum from one corner of her mouth to the other. At length she nodded. "He's mentioned you. Come on in."

The DCS stepped in out of the cold, closing the door behind him. Lasker's apartment was what he might have expected of the CLANDOPS comm chief, displaying the same sort of mad genius disorganization he brought to the workplace.

The brunette led the way, running a hand through her stringy hair as she padded barefoot across the shag carpet. "Danny!"

Kranemeyer heard the sound of a door opening and closing from the back of the apartment and then Lasker appeared, a towel wrapped around his mid-section.

His face flushed. "What's going on, sir? I wasn't expecting to see you tonight."

"That's apparent," was Kranemeyer's dry reply. The kid would never learn to stop calling him *sir*. He cast a sideways glance at the brunette, standing there in her pajama bottoms and tank top. "Can you give us a moment?"

She gave Lasker an impatient look, then disappeared into the bedroom with a toss of her head.

"Where *do* you find them?" Kranemeyer asked, slightly bemused.

"What?" Lasker seemed preoccupied with his towel. "Oh, her? A junior at Georgetown, majoring in international relations."

The DCS raised an eyebrow and Lasker went on, "Was there something I can do for you, sir?"

Kranemeyer nodded, taking another look down the hallway to make sure the girl was nowhere in sight. He reached into his pocket, extracting the phone SIM card that Thomas Parker had cloned earlier in the day.

"Where did you get this?" Lasker asked, taking it from him.

"This is for me, Danny. And you don't have need-to-know." He held the young comm chief's gaze, willing him not to ask too many questions. If Lasker knew under what circumstances it had been obtained...

"What exactly are we looking for?"

"I want a list of the most commonly called numbers, along with names and usual call zones. Anything that can help us pin down their location. If any of the numbers belong to pre-paid cells, I want that noted. Make this a priority, and give me a call the minute you have something."

"Will do." Kranemeyer turned to leave, his hand on the door, when Lasker spoke again.

"Sir? You want me to keep this on the down low?"

Another night, another time the choice of words might have brought a smile to Kranemeyer's face. As it was, he simply nodded. "That would be best."

And then he was gone.

9:34 P.M.
Altmann's apartment
Alexandria, Virginia

There were no answers. She'd arrived at that conclusion after a hot shower, a "supper" of stale crackers and a half-empty can of Corona. No reason why the Bureau hadn't already placed her at the scene of Vic's murder.

A tired face, lined with age, looked back at Marika Altmann when she glanced in the mirror. She really should retire. A traitor at the highest levels of the Bureau? What was this, the Stasi?

It was time to give it up, the fight that she'd waged ever since coming to this land of the free. It just didn't matter anymore.

It was as if the rules had changed, passing her by as if she'd been standing still. Were there still rules? Or was it just the alcohol talking?

She walked into her small bedroom, taking in the sight of the loaded Glock on her nightstand. She hadn't always lived this way, in fear.

Her phone began to vibrate without warning, buzzing against the wood of the nightstand. The display told her it was the Bureau. "Altmann here," she answered, trying to focus her thoughts.

The next words accomplished that for her. "Pack your bags. We've got a situation developing on the Michigan peninsula."

6:09 P.M.
A safehouse
San Francisco, California

Numb. That was the best way to describe it. Her tongue felt dry, as if her mouth had been stuffed with cotton. A dull, throbbing pain in her mouth.

Carol's eyes flickered open, staring up at the dull, off-white paint of the ceiling. *Where?*

Voices. She tried to sit up, grabbing the edge of the bed's headboard as another wave of dizziness washed over her.

Her vision cleared for a moment and she could glimpse another room through the partially-closed bedroom door. *Kitchen?*

Vasiliev was in her line of sight, his back to her as he leaned forward, both of his hands on the kitchen table. She could hear Han's voice—then Harry's, louder now.

"We're going to need a panel van—tinted windows would be a plus."

"Rent or buy?" Han moved into view, his face impassive.

"Buy—we'll be ditching it when we're done." Harry's voice seemed to be closer than it had been before and she looked up to see a blurred figure standing in the doorway.

The room began to spin, and Carol put out a hand to steady herself.

An arm wrapped itself gently around her waist, providing support. "Take it easy, there."

Harry.

A glass pressed against her lips, cool water trickling down her throat. The repeated assurance, "Easy, there."

She leaned back against the pillows, surrendering to the darkness. So tired…

Harry closed the door softly behind him, returning the empty glass to the sink. "How's she doing?" Han asked, looking up from his wallet.

"Out cold," Harry responded. "More than I'd expect from a normal anesthetic."

His head came up, staring at Vasiliev. "What *did* your dentist give her?"

Vasiliev shrugged. "To remove a microchip without damaging the tracking mechanism…is an operation of great delicacy. It is imperative that the patient be motionless."

"What did he give her?" Harry repeated, an edge of steel creeping into his voice.

"I didn't ask," the former KGB officer responded. "I relied upon his professionalism in doing the job we required of him. He did say that it would probably be tomorrow morning before she is completely over the effects."

Great.

Vasiliev moved to the table, looking at the maps Han had printed off the safehouse's desktop computer. "At first glance, there are not many good ways to approach the Andropov estate. High walls on three sides, he's built himself a well-nigh impregnable fortress."

Harry shook his head, motioning for Han to go secure their van. "Nothing is impregnable. Man never built a fortress that man couldn't take."

Chapter 16

The night is darkest just before the dawn, or so the writers say. At the very least, the early hours of morning are when the human body experiences its deepest sleep.

Noise. The sound of a door being slammed, somewhere distant, penetrating through a cobweb of dreams. On the street, maybe—a car door?

Nasir al-Khalidi came awake slowly, realizing that it wasn't street noise. And it wasn't one of their neighbors, paper-thin though the walls of the tenement were. It was in the very room with him.

He threw off the thin blanket, reaching under the pillow for the switchblade he kept with him as he slept. Ten times he had asked the Americans to give him a gun, ten times they had denied him, saying it was too "dangerous."

Dangerous. As if what he was doing for *them* wasn't? He had been in Lebanon, had seen what the jihadis could do. There had been a time...he had even believed in their cause.

His bare feet touched the carpet, the shag cold between his toes. The heat must have shut off at some point in the night. Typical.

A drawer slid open, wood squeaking against wood and his breath caught in his throat. Light. He needed light.

The knife turned in his hand until he found the button, the rusty five-inch blade flipping open with a faint *snick*. It was little enough in the face of an intruder.

222

The drawer shut with a thud. Nasir thrust his hand out along the wall, finding the light switch and flicking it up.

The single compact fluorescent bulb in the ceiling came slowly to life, casting a faint glow over the room, the intruder on his knees in front of the faded wood dresser. The man looked up, his face ghostly white, the picture of terror.

"Jamal!" Nasir nearly dropped the knife. "What are you doing?"

In recent years, his older brother had always possessed confidence enough for the both of them, a surety of purpose. A faith, as if he believed his very steps were guided from Allah, *subhanahu wa ta'ala.*

None of that was visible now. He was shaking. And then Nasir saw what his brother had been searching for in the dresser drawer. A small, snub-nosed revolver laying there on the carpet, worn blue steel gleaming in the pale light. *No...*

"What is going on, Jamal?" he asked, palming the switchblade and laying it on the bed. "If something is wrong...if you are in trouble, I will do whatever I can."

He expected a cocky dismissal, but none was forthcoming. His brother was too shaken, too afraid. A cold fear gripped Nasir's heart. For his brother to be this frightened...

"It wasn't supposed to happen like this," Jamal stammered. He paced over to the window, running his fingers through his short hair. "They weren't supposed to die, not here—not in this way. Their work wasn't done. I saw the police there...it's only a matter of time."

"*What* happened?" He felt like shaking his brother, but took him by the shoulder instead, guiding him to a seat on the bed.

It would take two hours to get the full story—and even then Nasir wondered if his pious brother had been drinking. Nerve gas? Here?

After all that they had seen in Lebanon, how could he...

"I will go with you," he said finally, his mind struggling to absorb all that he had been told.

This wasn't betrayal, he told himself. He would never betray his brother, his faith. It wasn't *that.*

The lie didn't even sound convincing to his ears. He dropped the revolver into a pocket of his cargo pants, along with the small box of .38 Special cartridges that Jamal had secreted in the drawer. Then together—his arm wrapped around his older brother's shoulders—they left the apartment, melting into the darkness of the Dearborn night.

The door had scarce closed behind him before the cellphone stuffed under his threadbare mattress began to buzz insistently. Unheard and forgotten, the cellphone's screen read NUMBER WITHHELD…

3:36 A.M.
A Gulfstream IV
Inbound to Detroit Metro Airport

"He's not answering his phone." Altmann swore softly under her breath, gazing off into space. She closed her phone, tucking it back into a pocket of her vest.

"Maybe to do so would compromise himself." She looked up at the words, into the eyes of William Russell Cole. She'd drafted him to accompany her to Michigan—there was no telling when you might need a good hostage negotiator. Particularly when there were terrorists involved. And he had worked in Pakistan with the JTTF, knew the Islamic culture better than she did.

"Maybe." Altmann stared out the window of the Gulfstream, into the night. "Maybe his cover has already been blown. Could be dead."

"We'll cross that bridge when we come to it, Marika," the negotiator said calmly. "There's any number of answers—you've run enough CIs to know, it's not like having an actual agent undercover. They don't have the training, and their loyalties are at best divided. For all we know Nasir abu Rashid may have done a runner on us."

Altmann shot him a glare. "Isn't that a comforting thought, Russ?"

"Never said it was supposed to be. Simply a possibility we must consider." He paused. "Are you sure you're ready for this?"

"Why?" The question didn't come out the way she'd meant it to, an icy chill to her voice.

The negotiator never seemed to notice. "You lost your partner, Marika. There's been no time for you to grieve."

"There's never time, Russ. Vic wasn't the first agent I've lost through the years—nothing to do but keep moving, keep fighting. No time for grief."

There was a long pause as he held her gaze, seeming to stare into her very soul. "And that…that is the most dangerous thing of all."

4:02 A.M. Pacific Time
The safehouse
San Francisco, California

The sound of running water brought her awake slowly, the aftereffects of the anesthesia still dulling her senses.

Carol opened her eyes, blinking back sleep. A narrow shaft of light pierced the darkness, streaming from the half-open door of the adjoining bathroom.

It took a moment for her to place where she was, what had happened. Then it all came flooding back.

Her vision cleared and her eyes focused in on the light. She could see Harry standing in front of the sink, stripped to the waist, running water over his hands.

She'd seen pictures of torture. They'd been part of her training at Camp Peary. But nothing had prepared her for this.

His back and shoulders were a mass of old scars, purplish and discolored in the pale light—crisscrossing and overlapping each other as if he had been beaten to within an inch of his life.

He had. She could remember reading the after-action report in his dossier, the story of his capture by the Taliban in 2008. They'd nearly killed him. That he had ever been able to go back out into the field at all was testament to a sheer force of will.

Carol pushed back the blankets, reaching for the robe folded neatly on the nightstand. She didn't remember undressing the previous night and a flush spread across her face as she realized that *she* hadn't.

Water dripped down Harry's face, droplets catching in the rough black stubble of his beard as he ran the steaming cloth over his shoulders, feeling the warmth seep into his skin. *Scars.*

There was no pain, not anymore, but the scars were never going away.

The cloth moved lower, pausing briefly near a scar on his upper right chest, a pockmarked, discolored indentation in his flesh. The relic of a dark night in Basra, 2005.

They'd been meeting with an informant—been ambushed by Shiite militants loyal to Muqtada al-Sadr. He'd been shot with an AK-47, the jacketed 7.62mm round passing straight through, missing his lung by inches. It would have been enough to qualify him for the Purple Heart if he'd been military—but he wasn't and it didn't.

He didn't exist.

Harry felt her standing there before he saw her, half-hidden by shadows. "Hideous, isn't it?" he asked, a wry smile crossing his face as he looked back to catch her eye.

He'd grown accustomed to the stares—but the look on her face was something different.

Pain—his pain—was reflected in those blue eyes, pain not unmixed with sympathy. It was the first time he had ever seen her with her defenses down, stripped of that look of determination that reminded him so much of her father.

"It was Afghanistan, wasn't it?" she asked, her voice low and tender.

Harry nodded, feeling suddenly vulnerable. It wasn't something he was used to. He laid down the washcloth and reached for his shirt, drawing it on over his arms. "Ancient history."

He started to leave the bathroom, moving past her, but she put out a hand, catching him by the arm. "Thank you," she whispered.

"For what?" he asked, pausing there in the doorway. She was so beautiful, standing there in the half-light, hair still askew from a night's sleep. Close enough to take her into his arms, but something held him back.

There were so many things he could have said, but he'd said them all before, to others through the years. *Lies.*

And he couldn't say the words now, even though he meant them with all his heart. Even though they were true.

Carol didn't look at him. "You've risked your life to protect me. Sacrificed your career. Why?"

He hadn't been expecting that question.

What is truth? That he cared for her? That she had roused feelings he'd long thought dead?

"Your father was my friend, but the *why* doesn't matter—not in the end," he said finally, his fingers smoothing back a lock of golden hair, touching her cheek lightly. "Just know that I'm here for you—we've come this far together. Not going to leave you now."

She nodded, glancing up into his eyes. "I know."

So beautiful, he thought, the voice within whispering, *Don't get involved.*

"Han got in around three," he announced, more for his benefit than hers, his hand falling away from her shoulder. Reminding himself that they weren't alone, strength to his resolve. "He was able to find a van."

The moment passed and he left her standing there in the doorway as he moved into the bedroom, buttoning his shirt. "When all this is over—what will you do?"

Something he hadn't given much thought. "Don't really know," he replied, reaching for his 1911.

He flashed her a grim smile. "Sufficient to the day is the evil thereof."

7:46 A.M. Eastern Time
CIA Headquarters
Langley, Virginia

The call log had confirmed his worst fears. Lasker rubbed the bridge of his nose, his eyes scanning the op-center. What Kranemeyer had asked him to do...well, "illegal" didn't even begin to cover it.

Rumor had it that Carter had overstepped the boundaries of the Agency's charter, and now he was under house arrest, in joint CIA/FBI custody. He had no desire to follow him down.

An uneaten bagel still sat in its box beside Lasker's keyboard. His appetite was long gone.

Six calls over the course of three weeks, none of them lasting longer than four minutes. All of them made within CONUS, likely by an American citizen. Illegal territory without a FISA warrant, and he was operating without any written authorization at all. *Quicksand.*

The SIM card didn't belong to your average Joe Sixpack. The owner was a player—all six calls had been made to the same number. No one did that.

The target number was...another prepaid cellphone, purchased in Manassas around the same time and activated by an *A. Smith.*

Lasker sniffed. Why people couldn't show some imagination with their aliases...

A shadow loomed over his workstation and he nearly came out of his skin, tapping his mouse to minimize the open window. He looked up into the coal-black eyes of Bernard Kranemeyer.

"Any results, Danny?"

5:30 A.M. Pacific Time
The safehouse
San Francisco, California

When all this is over—what will you do? Carol's words came streaming back through his mind, the one question he didn't want to face.

Harry pushed his chair back from the table, walking over to the refrigerator. Barring a miracle, there was no going back to the Agency. He'd been burned.

The reality hadn't really sunk in yet, he hadn't *permitted* himself to consider it. Out of a job, out in the cold.

He'd spent every last year of his adult life hunting men. Hunting them down and killing them. As cold as it sounded, those were his skillsets.

As he buttered a piece of toast he glanced into the safehouse's living room to where Han sat, poring over the laptop. Perhaps it was time to hang it up, while he still had a life, a future. Before he was broken.

A future. It was something he had never really considered before. Before what…*Carol?*

As if on cue, she appeared in the doorway of the kitchen. "Toast will be ready in a few minutes," he announced as she came up behind him. "Alexei will be here by nine to go over his plan."

"He has a plan?"

"Yeah." Harry nodded, turning to face her. "And I doubt you're going to like it."

8:57 A.M. Central Time
Dearborn Police Station
Dearborn, Michigan

"The call came in four hours ago—and you have yet to send anyone to the scene?" Marika Altmann leaned back against the door, folding her arms across her chest.

The police chief got up from his chair and came around the front of his desk. He was just tall enough to look her in the eye, white hair swept back from a receding hairline. His face spoke of a man who had seen it all.

In five years as Dearborn's chief of police, he probably had.

He shook his head, gesturing out the window toward Michigan Avenue. "We can't do what we once did, Special Agent Altmann. I've got three bureaus: Detective, Traffic, and Juvenile. Less than thirty officers in each one. Just over eighty police in a city of ninety-nine thousand."

Taking in her look of surprise, he continued. "Budget cuts. We've all seen our salaries slashed—can't even keep the streetlights on at night. This city's in bad shape. I've had seven homicides in the last twenty-four hours. The fire department didn't find any bodies in the ruins of the apartment building, so it's been low on the priorities list. If we'd known that an FBI confidential informant was living in the building…"

No way that would have happened, Marika thought, her mind already moving on to the next question. Too much risk of a leak when you brought in the local LEOs. "So, when did the fire department receive the call about abu Rashid's apartment being ablaze?"

The chief let out a weary sigh. "Five-thirty this morning. Well over an hour after they believe it started. A cleaning crew working at Parklane Towers spotted the blaze on the horizon and called it in. By the time the fire department was able to mobilize, the building had burned to the ground."

Nothing he said was making sense. She shot a look over at Russell, who was nodding—as if he understood. "So you're telling me that, what...fifty or more people evacuated a burning building and no one thought to dial 911?"

He shook his head. "Oh, they thought it, ma'am. They thought it. But no one acted on the thought."

"Why?"

"The estimates vary, but I'd say 45-50% of them are illegals. Many of them don't even speak English. You go into their communities, and it's like visiting a foreign country. It is, really. They only come out for work, if that, and we don't go in."

"What you're saying is that you don't patrol?"

"That's exactly what I'm saying. These people have no loyalty except to themselves. If a crime happens, they mention it to their imam and it's handled in-house. Should we happen to find out about it, everyone develops a sudden case of 'see no evil'."

"Then—our CI...what are you telling me?"

His eyes narrowed as he stared across the room at her. "The only way you're ever going to find him is if he wants to make contact. If he *can* make contact. As for any investigation of your own, he might as well be on the far side of the moon."

9:14 A.M.
The mosque
Dearborn, Michigan

The silence was unnerving. Nasir blew gently across the surface of his tea, feeling the black man's eyes on his back. His brother had been gone for the better part of two hours.

He willed his fingers not to tremble as the negro paced back and forth, like a huge African cat.

The last time he'd been this frightened...he'd been hiding under a fire-gutted Hyundai in Beirut, Jewish bombs raining down. Each one closer than the one before it. The bombs that had killed his father.

His mortality had been inescapable in that moment. The helplessness. It was the same feeling now.

Though we know death is certain, we have not prepared ourselves for it.

Words of truth. He was in the hands of Allah now.

The door to the small basement room opened, admitting Jamal and another man, so tall that he had to duck to enter the room.

"*Salaam alaikum,* Nasir," the tall man began, a holy light shining from his blue eyes. He went on without waiting for the greeting to be returned. "Your brother informs me that you took up arms alongside our brethren in Lebanon against the Zionist aggressor. And yet, since you have come to America...you have ceased to pursue the holy jihad. Why?"

"*Astagfirullah,*" Nasir whispered, his eyes downcast in reverence. *I ask forgiveness of Allah.* "I have lacked opportunity."

The tall man smiled, apparently satisfied by the answer. "Then may you have no more lack, my brother. *Insh'allah.*"

8:32 A.M. Pacific Time
Andropov's residence
Beverly Hills, California

"There has been a...complication," Viktor announced, taking his seat across from Korsakov at the kitchen table. His face was distorted with the anguish of being a bearer of bad news.

"What is it?" the assassin asked gently, reaching across to touch the boy's fingertips. His breakfast was forgotten for the moment.

"This—from Yuri." Viktor pushed the phone across the table, stroking his beard nervously. A text message was displayed on the touchscreen. FLIGHT GROUNDED IN CHICAGO. SNOWSTORM. ETA UNKNOWN.

Korsakov stifled an angry curse. Andropov was *waiting* on them. A snowstorm...it was what an insurance company might have called an "act of God," but he didn't believe in such superstition.

Neither did Andropov.

He looked up to see that Viktor was no longer paying attention to him. His face drained of color, he was looking off to the right, over Korsakov's shoulder into the kitchen.

Danger.

The assassin's head whipped around, but the only thing he saw was the slender form of Andropov's young mistress maybe fifteen feet away, standing near the kitchen's massive island. She was peeling an apple.

"I heard them," Viktor murmured insistently, speaking Russian. "Heard him strike her, heard his voice raised—angry. Just like before."

And then he saw it. Her left eye was swollen shut, a puffy, purplish bruise adorning her cheekbone.

Brutality had been part of Korsakov's work for so long that he had ceased to even take note of it. When the girl had made her appearance moments before, his eyes had never made it as far north as her face.

Violence was quite simply a fact of life. As natural an act as the breaking of the eggs that formed his breakfast. But not for his young companion.

Just like before. "What did you say?" he demanded, turning back to face Viktor.

But the boy was gone. *Gone…*

9:07 A.M.
The safehouse
San Francisco, California

Orange marmalade. On a generous slab of lightly toasted white bread.

Harry watched as Vasiliev shoved one end of the bread in his mouth, chewing with infuriating slowness. It was a tactic for the Russian, just one of his bag of tricks to keep his opponent off-balance. Opponent? Alexei viewed everyone as an opponent.

He shot a glance over at Han before addressing his question to Vasiliev. "I believe you said you had a plan?"

"Indeed." Clenching the toast between his teeth, Vasiliev reached into his leather messenger bag and extracted a thin folder, tossing it across the table to Harry.

From the letterhead, the Cyrillic script across the top—it looked like an official FSB dossier. But all it contained was a single 8x10 surveillance photo, blown up and digitally enhanced. The face of an arrogantly handsome young man stared back from the print, no more than twenty, twenty-one at the most, his features undeniably Slavic.

"Nineteen," the Russian announced, supplying the answer to Harry's unasked question.

"His name is Pyotr, but he reportedly prefers the anglicized *Peter*." Vasiliev sniffed audibly. "This generation, they have no appreciation for their heritage."

"The point, Alexei?"

The older man reached for a napkin, wiping a smudge of marmalade from his lip. "You're right—his first name is unimportant. His last name…is Andropov. Valentin's son."

And in that moment, Vasiliev's "plan" became painfully clear, in all of its brutal simplicity. Characteristic of the Russian.

"No," Carol interjected, her head coming up sharply. "No way."

Vasiliev threw up his hands. "Americans—they always want results, but they rarely wish to dirty their hands in obtaining them. You want an omelet? You have to break some eggs. You want to find the man behind your father's murder? This is the most linear path."

Anger flashed from her blue eyes. "He's also *nineteen*! He's guilty of nothing."

"Guilty?" He gave her an indulgent smile. "What do I look like—a judge? There are none innocent in this world. All due respect, Miss Chambers, but this is not your operation. Harry knows the truth of what I say."

No. She looked over at Harry, silently begging him to deny it, to bring a stop to this.

One glimpse of his face and that hope died within her. He was nodding, the life—the *love*—she had seen earlier gone from his eyes. Replaced by...nothing.

"Alexei's right."

9:12 A.M.
Beverly Hills, California

Darkness. Heat. Flesh against flesh, sweaty hands against his body. The whip coming down against his naked back.

Pain.

He was too exposed—had to find a place to hide. Couldn't keep running. Had to keep running. The breeze fanned Viktor's hair as he ran, his feet pounding against the the concrete of the sidewalk.

Darkness.

He reached into the pocket of his windbreaker, pulling out his cellphone. He ripped off the back panel and tore out both the battery and the SIM card, shoving them into the pocket of his jeans.

They would never find him now. They *could* never find him. His breath was coming fast, panic consuming him.

That voice. The harsh laugh.

He choked back a sob, all the memories flooding back. The dank smell of the basement, the harsh glare of the lights. Her *screams*. The crack of a bullwhip, blood spraying into the air.

He could still remember the wounded, pleading look in her eyes, laying there bleeding to death against the cold concrete.

Never again. A car was coming up on his right and he cast a panicked look over his shoulder.

No. It wasn't his pursuers. Just a young man his own age, driving slowly down the street, the stereo of his sports car turned all the way up. Enjoying his day in the sun.

Viktor's hand slid inside his unzipped jacket, fingers closing on the smooth polymer of his Glock, the gun that Korsakov had given him.

Korsakov. The only man he had ever trusted.

Fresh tears streamed down his cheeks, tears of grief and anger. He turned, running out into the road in front of the sports car, the gun coming free in his hand—a scream on his lips. "Out of the car! Out! *Out!*"

10:31 A.M. Pacific Time
The safehouse
San Francisco, California

"Are you sure this is a bridge you want to cross?" Han closed the dossier, placing it on the table between them. The Russian had left thirty minutes before, to attend to his consulate duties. Apparently, being a law unto oneself was not limitless. His dark eyes lifted to meet Harry's. "Kidnapping is serious business."

"We've done it before," Harry responded evenly. "It never bothered you then."

"Different times and a different place—it was our *mission.*"

Harry shot a glance toward the closed bedroom door, lowering his voice so that she wouldn't overhear. "The director was assassinated, Sammy. We both know that. It's still our mission."

"Pyotr Andropov's mother was a Hollywood starlet in the days before she met Valentin. Before she died in a car accident over eighteen years ago—shortly after his birth," the former SEAL replied, tapping the dossier with a long index finger. "He holds dual citizenship in the United States and Russia. There's no road back from this."

He was right. Harry knew that. Knew he had to offer a way out. He rose from his seat at the table. "I've been accused of complicity in Lay's death, Sammy. My *face* is on the television. That's already the case for me. But you don't need to go down with me."

He laid a hand on Han's shoulder. "You don't owe me this. If you're not here when I return, I'll understand."

"Where are you going?"

Harry inclined his head toward the bedroom. "Wish me luck."

Her back was turned to him when he entered the room. Her laptop was open on the bed, her fingers flying over the keyboard.

"Carol, I—"

She held up a hand to silence him. "One moment…here, I have it."

"Have what?" he asked, stopping in the center of the room. She turned the laptop to face him, revealing a maze of code and what looked like schematics onscreen.

"Your way in."

He took a seat on the bed beside her. "What am I looking at?"

"The power grid that services Beverly Hills and the western half of Los Angeles County. I can take it down."

She was good.

"NIGHTSHADE," he whispered, grasping her intent in a trice. He could still remember the night of that operation in Paraguay, the smell of gunpowder and burning fuel in his nostrils. Carter had overloaded the Ciudad del Este power grid, giving him the diversion he needed to escape. This would give them a way in.

"The blackout will take Andropov's security systems off-line, and should give you enough time to breach the perimeter." She smiled. "And we don't need to kidnap his son."

If only things could be that simple, Harry thought, his lips pressing together into a single, bloodless line. She had solved one of their problems, but only one. And getting inside had never been his uppermost concern.

He reached out, his fingers touching her arm lightly. "Once inside, we will need leverage. Andropov was *Spetsnaz,* and although he may have grown soft over his years in the West, I doubt he's forgotten his training. He was trained to resist interrogation…as I was."

She looked up and he could see the pain in her eyes. "He's just a college kid."

"Then perhaps it's time he realized how his old man made his billions."

There was a long silence before she spoke again, and he let it hang. Most people talked too much. It was enough to plant the seed—one never tried to force the decision.

At length, she closed the laptop, glancing into his eyes. "Promise me that you won't hurt him."

He nodded. "I promise."

Her blue eyes burned with a fierce intensity. "Swear it…"

Nothing was ever certain in a field op. She'd been Agency long enough to know that. It was the nature of the business. But he wasn't going to get this done without her cooperation.

"He won't be harmed," he whispered, holding her gaze. "I swear before God."

3:02 P.M. Central Time
The mosque
Dearborn, Michigan

Her face stared back at him from his computer, the face of a bold woman. Defiant. Brazen. Unbowed.

Tarik Abdul Muhammad placed his fingertips together, staring pensively at the screen, at the image of Congresswoman Laura Gilpin. So close, yet so far away. One mistake, and years of planning could be all for nothing. All those years behind barbed wire, staring out at the sea. Knowing that his destiny was out *there*. Vengeance…

Just one mistake, like the one Walid had made on an icy highway. Fate. Yet how could this be anything but the will of Allah?

He scrolled down the open itinerary there on her website, searching for any possible alternate targets. Another way to accomplish his holy mission.

There were none. They had to strike at the appointed time. No other choice.

He looked up to see al-Fileestini standing in the open doorway, a sober look on the imam's face.

"My mind has been made up," al-Fileestini announced. "I will accompany you to Nevada."

The Pakistani clicked his mouse to minimize the browser, gesturing for the older man to take a seat across from him.

"I thought we had already discussed this," he began carefully. The imam was too influential to risk offending. "None of us will be returning, *insh'allah*. You, father, are too vital to our cause in this country to die the death of a *shahid*, worthy as that is."

The imam turned away to cough, a violent, hacking sound. "I am not asking your permission, Tarik. I have supported your operation and this is what I require in return. As to where I am most useful, do not presume to instruct Allah, *subhanahu wa ta'ala*."

"I would not dream of such blasphemy, father," Tarik responded, his blue eyes narrowing as he gazed across the desk at al-Fileestini. Something was present here, some motive he couldn't discern.

"Then it is settled." The imam smiled, fishing a cellphone out of his suit jacket, laying it on the desk between them. A text message was displayed on the screen, consisting of a series of GPS coordinates and the brief message: EARLY DELIVERY APPROVED. MORNING OF THE 21st.

"Andropov has come through for us, just as I said he would. We leave before nightfall."

Tarik nodded. "*Inshallah.*"

2:59 P.M. Pacific Time
Andropov's mansion
Beverly Hills, California

It had happened once before. The memory was still fresh in Korsakov's mind. Three months after he had rescued Viktor from the brothel, the boy had run away. They'd been in Budapest at the time and the teenager had seen a face in the crowd. Or thought he had, his frayed nerves making it impossible to ever know the truth.

It had been three days before Korsakov had found him, huddled under a bridge on the banks of the Danube, living out of a cardboard box and reeking of urine and human waste.

He murmured a curse under his breath, scanning the map of the location where they'd lost Viktor's cellphone signal. Andropov wasn't going to give him three days. Not with their contract already at a critical phase.

The assassin ran a hand through his hair. Looking back he still couldn't remember why he had decided to rescue the boy. One of those moments when a man acted, not from logic or reason—simply because a voice inside him said that he *must*.

A long-dormant conscience? God? The question brought a faint smile to Korsakov's face. It begged the question of why God would bother speaking to a man who had never believed in His existence...

He felt movement behind him, a presence entering the room. The assassin turned to find Andropov standing there.

"Any progress?"

Korsakov shook his head. "Viktor—Viktor is not like other young men. Years of trauma have left him...delicate. Prone to snapping."

The oligarch took off his gloves, a baffled look on his face. "Prone? This has happened before?"

"Several times," Korsakov replied, turning back to the laptop. "He suffers from flashbacks—the line between reality and memory blurs."

He looked up to find Andropov regarding him with a look of disbelief. "Then why haven't you rid yourself of him before this?"

Why? An impossible question, really. "I'm the only thing he has left in the world," the assassin responded, looking his old comrade in the face. How the years had changed them.

Andropov sniffed. "When did you go soft on me, Sergei? He's jeopardized our mission and *your* contract. Remember that. With him gone, we will need to move rapidly. Go ahead and pull up the tracking device—there is no time to wait on the rest of your team."

"*Da.*" Korsakov took a deep breath, reminding himself of the Golden Rule as he typed an authentication code into the laptop. *He who has the gold makes the rules.*

If he didn't give Andropov what he wanted, the oligarch would find someone who would. That was the life of the mercenary.

With the authentication code entered, the tracking software booted up, a whirring sound coming from the computer. And then...a second authentication screen.

The assassin's brow furrowed in bewilderment. A *second* authentication? He only knew one code.

After a brief pause, he began again, hesitant fingers dancing over the keyboard—entering the same code once more. He tapped *enter*, and almost instantly his ears were assaulted with an insistent *beep*, the log-in menu fading away only to be replaced by a blue screen. SYSTEM LOCKDOWN INITIATING...

A curse exploded from his lips as the laptop began to enter shutdown mode. They were flying blind...

4:52 P.M.
The safehouse
San Francisco, California

"Satellite photos aren't going to be enough," Han observed, placing his glass of water on the counter and walking over to stand beside Harry.

The two of them had papered an entire wall of the safehouse with satellite imagery, showing every available detail of the Andropov estate. They were all open-source images, supplemented by Google Street View—Carol's laptop didn't begin to give her the firepower needed to hack into the NRO.

Han's comment always held true. As good as PHOTINT was, it was no substitute for an actual reconnaissance. Nothing like being there.

"The van's going to attract attention in that neighborhood. Can't just go rolling around unnoticed," the former SEAL added, as if reading Harry's mind. Perhaps he was…they had worked together for years.

Harry's eyes focused in on one of the Street View images, on the house in the image. Across the street, two down from their target. There was something about it, a certain feel…

"We may not have to," he whispered, removing the picture from the wall and turning away from his friend. He stalked back across the room to where Carol sat, working on her laptop. A wireless printer was propped up on a cardboard box at her feet, sheets of paper print-outs strewn over the floor seemingly at random. "What do you have?"

"There aren't many public security cameras in the area," she responded. "Most of them are on private networks, protected by the best encryption money can buy."

"No use in giving the paparazzi a leg up," Harry mused, handing her the picture. "What can you find on this?"

He watched as she entered the address into the computer, page after page of search results filling the screen within seconds.

It was as he'd hoped. The top results were real estate listings.

"The house has been on the market since 2011," Carol announced. "Ten million dollars. No takers."

"Big surprise there," Han observed, turning to face them.

A smile touched the corner of Harry's mouth. "Always have loved an empty house."

11:03 P.M. Central Time
The Dearborn Police Station
Dearborn, Michigan

"According to his reports, Nasir abu Rashid was rooming with another Lebanese immigrant, a student at University of Michigan named Jamal al-Khalidi."

Marika looked up from the computer in front of her. "Was there any connection between the two men? Any prior history?"

Russell shook his head. "If there was, he never mentioned it in his reports. Beyond both men being native to Lebanon…nothing."

"Could he have been hiding something?" It was a rhetorical question, and they both knew it. Informants were *always* hiding something. "The file mentions his contact with a local imam, Abu Kareem al-Fileestini." Marika lifted her eyes, glancing across the room to where the police chief stood beside the coffee percolator. "What can you tell me about him?"

There was a long pause before the chief turned to face her, a steaming cup of coffee in his hand. "Al-Fileestini? Not very much, I'm afraid."

"Have you met him?"

"Yes." A guarded edge had crept into his voice, a hesitation Marika hadn't heard before. There was something he wasn't saying.

"And? What is your opinion of the imam?"

The chief took a long sip of his coffee. "I don't have one. Doesn't pay."

"Bull," Marika shot back. She rose to her feet, taking full advantage of her height. "I'm asking you for a straight answer and I've no intention of asking again."

A look of resignation passed across the police chief's face. He reached into the top drawer of his desk and extracted two photos, handing her the top photo. "I don't *want* to have an opinion, because there's no margin in it. It's a career-ender. This is your man, Dearborn's most influential imam. He's heavily tied in with the Muslim Brotherhood and chairman of the IICSO, the Islamic Inter-Collegiate Students' Organization. You don't get crossways of al-Fileestini's influence and hold office in this town."

Local politics. That was always an obstacle. Marika sighed, glancing over at Russell. "I couldn't care less. I work for the feds, not the town of Dearborn."

He didn't respond directly, just handed her the second photograph. It was as he did so that she realized his fingers were trembling. "This is al-Fileestini last fall, at the FBI training center in Quantico. Under the Hancock administration, he's become heavily instrumental in making sure that new agents are trained to be sensitive to issues of Middle Eastern culture and Islamic law. He's been a guest at the White House four times. If you think you're going to launch an investigation involving him, think again. He's politically connected—untouchable."

She looked up from the picture into his face, her eyes narrowing. "Do *you* think there's any chance that he's involved in this? Off the record."

The police chief held her gaze for a moment, then reached out, taking both photos back in a quick, brusque motion. "I have nothing to say."

Marika let a sigh escape her lips. Fear. It was always the worst obstruction any investigation faced. But this was the *chief of police*! She turned back toward Russell. "Abu Rashid's original handler is...where?"

"Maternity leave," Russell replied, his focus still on the police chief.

She ran a hand over her forehead. "Get her on the phone."

"Now?"

"Of course, Russell. *Now*. If she's got a screaming infant, she'll be up."

11:16 P.M. Pacific Time
Beverly Hills, California

The night was cool, a slight breeze rustling in the trees over their head. Harry shifted his weight from one leg to another, the Colt heavy in his gloved hands. "Any progress?"

Carol looked up, her face lit by the screen glow of the PDA in her hands. Wires stretched from the back of the small computer to the security keypad. "Patience...you do realize that your KGB friend couldn't pick out decent electronics to save his life."

Harry chuckled in spite of himself. "When Alexei got into this business, computers took up entire rooms. Technology isn't exactly his thing."

A beeping noise came from the PDA, the screen lighting up. "The password is 071289," Carol announced. "The date of the realtor's anniversary."

"Do I want to ask how you know that?"

A faint smile played around her lips as she punched the number into the keypad with a gloved finger. "Probably not. If people had the faintest idea how much of their personal information was available on the Internet..."

An LED light began blinking to one side of the pad, a message scrolling across the top. ALARMS DISABLED.

She gestured for him to take the lead and his fingers reached out, touching the doorknob. The door swung open and Harry brought the Colt up in both hands, stepping into the four-car garage.

Empty. He marked the position of the door switches, then lifted the shortwave radio to his lips. "We're in, Sammy. Come on home."

Chapter 17

Darkness. The room was spinning around him, blood trickling from between his fingers, wet and viscous. So weak. Polished wood —the nightstand—beneath his outstretched fingers, but he couldn't begin to pull himself up. Dying...

Hancock came awake with a start, his breath coming fast and heavy, his mind racing. He raised his hands, staring at them in the darkness as if he expected them to be drenched in blood.

He pushed back the sheets, realizing slowly that his clothing was soaked in sweat. Something was happening. Somehow—he had never been a man given to dreams. Or nightmares.

It's just a dream. Of course. He flicked on the switch, letting out a sigh as the room filled with light. He was alone—Nicole had gone to Camp David, beginning her Christmas vacation. Against the "recommendations" of the Secret Service, but that was Nicole. The traditional, retiring role of First Lady had never been for her.

It was nerves, yes, that was it. He'd been working too hard. Needed a rest. Needed a woman. That was all it was. There was one of Cahill's aides...what was her name?

Just a dream. He'd never dreamed of his own death. Hancock looked down at his fingers, realizing that they were still trembling. So real...

6:19 A.M. Central Time
Dearborn, Michigan

It hadn't been the first night in her life that she had stayed up till three in the morning trying to connect nonexistent dots, but it had been a while. And she'd been younger.

The ring of her cellphone on the nightstand of the Holiday Inn jarred her from a sound sleep, her hand flailing out from beneath the covers.

"Altmann here."

"Special Agent Altmann?" The voice was young, she realized, trying to clear the fog from her brain. Young and slightly accented.

Middle Eastern.

That brought her fully awake. "Who is this?"

"Please, listen to me," the voice continued. "I am Nasir. Nasir abu Rashid. I have been working for your FBI."

"I know," Marika responded, reaching for her pants at the foot of the bed. "How did you get this number?"

"My handler. I only have a few minutes. They may be back at any moment."

"They? What is going on, Nasir—who are you involved with?" So many questions flooding her mind. So little time. They'd suspected that his disappearance was linked to the Michigan State Police's discovery of that fully-automatic Kalashnikov, but there had been no direct ties. Silence. "Is an attack imminent?"

A moment passed, then he came back on, his voice even lower than before. "I don't know—we're leaving the city tonight."

"We? I need names, Nasir." There was no time to establish a relationship with this informant—no time for anything.

"I don't have them," the informant stammered. "You have to believe me, I knew of none of this before this morning. My brother had said nothing to me, absolutely nothing...the leader—they call him the 'Shaikh.' A tall man, with eyes the color of the sea."

"Your brother?"

"My brother—no, *one* of the brothers, I mean." She could hear the fear in his tones. The uncertainty. The *deception*. He had lied to her, but what about? Did he have family involved...

He went on before she could respond, announcing abruptly. "I will call you again."

The phone's screen went black, eliciting a curse from Marika. She dropped the phone back into the front pocket of her jeans, pulling on a sweater over her head.

The holstered Glock in her hand, she padded across the hotel room to knock on Russell's door. "We've got a situation."

5:45 A.M. Pacific Time
The empty mansion
Beverly Hills, California

Despite being empty for several years, the house had lost none of its grandeur. The bathroom appeared massive in the morning light, the sunrise streaming in through double french doors leading out onto a balcony.

Good sniper post, Harry observed, mentally calculating the range. Open the doors, and a man lying prone on the tiles of the bathroom floor would have a clear shot at anyone coming out of Valentin Andropov's front door. *Over* the protective wall. In the absence of a dedicated sniper rifle, the FN SCAR had the range to do it.

By the time he'd made his way out to the kitchen, Carol was already sitting there. A solitary barstool was about the only piece of furniture left in the place, and she had commandeered it, her laptop resting securely on the granite countertop.

"How's the battery back-up working out?" Han had run more errands, this time for the electronics they needed to set up shop.

She brushed her hair out of her eyes, looking up at him. "They're not top-of-the-line, but they'll serve our purposes. With just the laptop and the cameras, we should have well over forty-eight hours of battery power."

Might be enough. Might not. It was impossible to say when the target window would open.

Harry walked over to the windows, eyeing the placement of the cameras. Mounting them under the eaves of the mansion had been tricky, but they were in position.

The more "eyes" you could have on a surveillance mission, the better.

"Have you done anything with the laser mic?" he asked, glancing back to where she sat.

A nod. "It's not going to work—he's utilizing vibration maskers on all the windows facing the street."

"Privacy freak," Harry observed. "I hate people like that."

Carol looked up from her laptop. "Fortunately, his son Pyotr isn't nearly as obsessed. He's got an electronic footprint the size of Silicon Valley."

"Can you exploit it?"

A smile. "Already have," she replied, tapping the screen with a finger.

Harry looked where she was pointing. The e-mail link was headlined with an "alluring" photo of a European girl, with the caption, "Hot women in live action—FREE!"

"Let me guess—he clicked?"

"Of course. Have to hand it to him, though…it took him five minutes to decide. The average is two minutes…or so Carter used to say."

He shook his head. That would be Carter. "So, what happened after our boy clicked on the link?"

"He went on and enjoyed his cam show, of course," Carol replied. "While the Trojan opened a gateway into his system. I have his passwords and account information for every site he's ever accessed—Facebook, Twitter, e-mail, everything."

Social media. It had never failed to amaze him how much people willingly posted about themselves on-line. An intelligence officer's gold mine, all of it…just there for the taking. "Seen anything actionable?"

"Of course. He updates his Twitter from his phone roughly every half hour—on a slow day. Talks about what he's doing, where he's going. And each tweet is embedded with his geo-tracking information."

"Like painting a bulls-eye on his own backside," Harry said. The naivete was darkly amusing.

When he looked back, the humor had left her eyes. "What's wrong?"

"We're really doing this, aren't we?" she whispered, holding up a hand before her face. Her fingers were trembling, ever so slightly. "It's different…being this close to it."

"It is."

"I keep trying to think of him as a target, but it's not working." She waved at the screen. "Not when he comes through as a kid in every post. Just a rich, stupid, oversexed kid."

"Then don't look. Not any more than you have to."

Carol looked up into his eyes, incredulous. "Close your eyes—that's your solution? Doesn't it ever bother you?"

He sighed. "I told you the story of how I got into the CIA, but I never told you what I had *intended* to do when I left Georgetown, did I?"

"No."

"I…believed that God had called me to be a missionary. There was a team in Beirut, working to translate Gospel tracts into Arabic. They needed another translator, and I'd met with their team leader twice stateside. Had it all sorted. Or so I thought. When I finally ended up in the Middle East I was carrying a

Kalashnikov instead of a Bible." A grim smile passed across his face. "Sounds ironic, doesn't it?"

She didn't say anything for a long moment, silence filling the room. "Do you ever regret your choice?"

Harry shrugged. "Youth mistakes many things for the will of God. In the end, it's always hard to say. I was in Iraq in 2004 when I received word—the leader of that translation team had been killed. He'd stepped onboard a bus in Beersheba moments before a suicide bomber triggered their vest. He was killed instantly, along with his wife and his two-month-old son. It's true what they say. Only the good die young."

"I'm sorry."

"Don't be." He moved behind her, his hands resting gently on her shoulders. "You ask if it ever bothers me? The answer is no—not when it's compared with the alternative."

8:59 A.M. Eastern Time
The White House
Washington, D.C.

His tie was straight. Of course it was. Haskel tugged at it anyway, casting one final look into the mirror. He was nervous, and the Secret Service took a dim view of visibly nervous people meeting with the President of the United States.

Delivering the daily briefing wasn't his job, he thought, as he made his way down the hallway toward the Oval Office, flanked by agents. That came within the purview of the Director of National Intelligence, Lawrence Bell—but after the bombings he had been whisked away to an "undisclosed location."

He and Hancock had been friends once, but there was too much water underneath that particular bridge. Too many unfulfilled promises on the path to power. Now they were just allies.

Cahill was at the end of the hallway, what passed for a smile on his face. It seemed impossible that someone could work in D.C. for such a long time and remain an unknown quantity, but that was Cahill. The President's chief of staff was a black hole.

"It's good to see you again, Eric," he murmured smoothly, escorting him into the Oval Office. The President was nowhere to be seen.

"He'll be here in five minutes," Cahill announced, in answer to an unasked question. "Have a seat."

Haskel took a deep breath. "I need you to look at this."

The chief of staff looked down at the folder in Haskel's hand as if it was poisoned. "What is it?"

"We got a FISA warrant request from a field agent of ours in Michigan a few hours ago."

"So?"

"So it's someone we know," Haskel retorted, gesturing for Cahill to open the folder. "Abu Kareem al-Fileestini."

A curse escaped Cahill's lips. "You're kidding me, right, Eric? Al-Fileestini was here a few months ago. He and the President *sat together* at the Ramadan dinner."

"I know, I know," the FBI director replied, holding up a hand. "That's why I brought it to you first."

Cahill's eyes scanned down the page, his face purpling as he continued to read. "Listen, Eric, I lost a cousin when the World Trade Center collapsed. He was a firefighter—went back into that smoky hell to find somebody else to save. Never came back out."

"I didn't know that."

"Doesn't matter—let me finish. I'm just sayin', I *get it*. I understand the fears that still permeate this country...but for the love of all that's holy, what type of people do you have working for you? This reads like some sort of Islamophobic hate rag—the type of stuff I'd expect to hear off talk radio, not coming from a federal agent."

"Then you wouldn't advise bringing it to the President's attention?" Haskel asked. He leaned back in his chair, glancing at his watch.

The chief of staff snorted. "I'm wondering why you even brought it to *my* attention, Eric. If it weren't for the help of moderates like al-Fileestini, we would have lost this blasted war on terror a long time ago. I don't want to see him harassed by a glory hound."

"I concur," Haskel said, reaching out to take back the FISA request. "I met Abu Kareem myself when he spoke at Quantico—a finer man I've never had the pleasure of knowing."

"Then we're all playing off the same sheet music here?"

"Absolutely."

8:45 A.M.
Beverly Hills, California

The hardest part of survival was finding the will to do it. It was one of two primary lessons Viktor remembered from his childhood, from his years as a sex slave. The other one was, *trust no one.*

Korsakov. He pulled his knees tight up against his chin, curled up into a tight ball on top of the green trash dumpster. After all the years of abuse, he had idolized his rescuer.

All men were the same, in the end. They all wanted more than you were prepared to give—whether your body or your loyalty. He stared down through a haze of tears at the SIM card in his hand.

Call him.

The impulse was there, never so strong. *Resist it.* The leering face of the oligarch rose up before him. Just the way he remembered him.

The way he remembered everything. That feeling of helplessness. He fingered the SIM card aimlessly, replacing it at last in the pocket of his jacket.

He had to. But not yet…

10:32 A.M. Central Time
I-80
Northern Illinois

He wasn't used to driving without music. American rap, turned all the way up.

Not this unbearable quiet, just the sound of wheels against the road, the hum of a powerful engine.

"Where are we headed?" Nasir asked, glancing across the cab of the tractor-trailer at the negro.

Omar looked up from his pocket copy of the Qur'an, dark fingers paging through the flowing script. "That's not for me to say. The shaikh will answer your questions—or not, as Allah guides him."

Nasir shook his head, trying to keep his nerves in check, the fear that he'd felt while talking with the FBI woman threatening to overwhelm him. "And yet you expect me to drive the truck?"

"Just keep driving till we reach Joliet. We'll stop for lunch there." Omar inclined his head. "You're an illegal, right?"

The question was so unexpected—it was impossible not to react. "What?"

The negro laughed, flashing a smile full of white teeth. "Easy there, bro. No need to take it like that—I give props to anyone that finds a way to beat the system." A pause. "Speaking of beatin' the system—how does an illegal get a CDL?"

Nasir's knuckles whitened around the big steering wheel, a silent prayer racing through his mind. The Americans had helped him get his commercial driver's license, in exchange for the information he had supplied to them. In exchange for his treachery. It was to have been only the beginning.

"There are ways," he responded, struggling to keep his voice under control. "Long story."

"Ways? Tell me about them, brother," came the reply, an edge creeping into the black man's voice. "We have all day."

12:38 P.M. Eastern Time
Arlington National Cemetery
Virginia

He would always remember the first time he had come to Arlington, as a small child. A young Marine, a friend of the family, killed half-way around the world in the bombing of the Marine barracks in Beirut. Taken too young.

The snowy grass crunched beneath Thomas's feet as he moved up the hill, past row after row of markers. He had come alone, for the sake of safety.

There was nothing unusual about a lone mourner, particularly not at this time of year.

A cold wind whipped through the denuded branches of the maple trees near the top of the hill, tousling his brown hair. It was a lonely place, as all cemeteries.

He knelt by the headstone of Robert L. Krag, running his fingers reverently over the inscription. The lieutenant commander had perished with the crew of the ill-fated *U.S.S. Thresher*, back in '63. Before his time.

A tragic footnote to history. Thomas pulled off his gloves, groping in the fresh-fallen snow. A moment later, he found what he was looking for—a small, waterproof tube.

Straightening, he broke the seal, unfolding the small scrap of paper inside, printed letters against the yellow back-ground of a post-it note. An address, in Graves Mills, Virginia. And a note: VOICEPRINT CONFIRMED 87%. IT'S HER.

A smile of satisfaction crossed his lips, the same feeling he'd always had when a target entered his cross-hairs.

Rhoda Stevens was still in circulation. And he had her dead to rights.

10:14 A.M. Pacific Time
The empty mansion
Beverly Hills, California

Surveilling a target was nowhere near as exciting as Hollywood made it out to be. It was roughly as exhilarating as babysitting, with the caveat that you couldn't watch TV.

You could eat. And the average stakeout consumed more snacks than a frat house's Super Bowl party.

"This is just like Berlin back in '87," Vasiliev groused, reaching for a handful of Doritos. "Two weeks watching a suspected Stasi defector—I gained eight pounds."

The faintest hint of a smile crossed Harry's face. "And you still lost the war."

"You're certain of that, *tovarisch?*" the former KGB field officer chuckled, arching an eyebrow. "When I was first assigned to the San Francisco consulate in February of 2009, I fly into LAX and what is the first thing I see upon disembarking? A magazine cover proclaiming, *'We are all socialists now'.*"

The man had a point.

Before he could come up with a suitable rejoinder, Harry's two-way radio sitting on the card table before him crackled with static. Han. "EAGLE SIX, we have movement. Looks like they're coming out."

Vasiliev swore in Russian, brushing crumbs off his shirt as he rose, his eyes focusing on the slowly opening gates of the oligarch's estate. They had been prepared for this, but so was Andropov.

Three vehicles. A pair of gleaming Mercedes M Class SUVs took point and rearguard positions in the convoy, providing security for a sleek black Maybach Landaulet. All three of them were riding low—the limousine most of all—undoubtedly heavily armored.

"So, this is the way a billionaire travels," Harry breathed, training his binoculars on the limo in an effort to penetrate the tinted windows. No dice.

The Russian smiled. "Who said the wages of sin were all bad?"

There was no time for deliberation—not with their target on the move. "We'll need to tail them."

Vasiliev shook his head. "What are you thinking, *tovarisch?* Three security teams, you're looking at 10-12 men. On the move, they'll be at the highest alert possible."

"I know how executive protection works, Alexei. I also know he could be leaving the country." Harry laid down the binoculars and picked up his leather jacket, drawing it on over his tall frame. "Carol, can you get us into the CalTrans camera network?"

"Anything's possible—I just need time and processing power. I've been working all morning on building a bot-net to supply extra juice, but it will be a couple hours."

"Then stay here with Sammy," he instructed, his fingers lightly brushing over her shoulder. It didn't feel right, to leave her. It was the only choice.

There were so many things he wanted to say in that moment, but he found it impossible to voice them.

Kiss them goodbye, a voice from the past whispered, the words echoing within his mind. It took him a moment to place the speaker, and then he remembered.

Samuel Han, standing on the sidewalk outside his suburban Virginia home. Twin boys under his powerful arms, squealing and kicking in the spring breeze. Innocence.

The American dream.

And then they had left, together, for Yemen. And all that followed. *Always kiss them good-bye.*

"Stay safe," he whispered, scarce trusting himself to speak. As if his very voice might reveal more than he dared. "We're going to have to do this the old-fashioned way. Alexei, you're with me."

And they were gone.

10:37 A.M.
The Andropov estate

Patience. It had always been Korsakov's watchword, the only reason he had remained alive. He waited a full thirty minutes after Andropov's departure to make his way upstairs, toward the quarters of the young American woman.

Just like before. Whatever had triggered Viktor's panic, his disappearance, the answer seemed to lay with her. Whether she knew what it was or not was another question.

Korsakov surmounted the carved staircase and made his way down the hall, his movements quick, purposeful.

The house exuded opulence, an interior decorator's ecstasy—the hallway lit by electric lights in golden sconces. Real gold? He wouldn't have doubted it for a minute.

His old friend had changed. Whether he had lost his edge completely remained to be seen.

He hadn't. There were two bodyguards stationed outside the girl's door and Korsakov passed right by them, careful not to break stride. He turned farther down the hallway, down yet another corridor of the massive house. Two men? To guard a woman?

It seemed excessive, even given Andropov's legendary jealousy. The assassin allowed himself a momentary flash of humor at the thought that the men might be eunuchs.

In the end, it didn't really matter. Asking to speak to the girl was only going to get him trouble for his pains. Trouble he didn't need.

His phone vibrated in the pocket of his shirt, an incoming text. Undoubtedly the weather-bound Yuri, Korsakov thought, flipping it open. Andropov's injunction that he not move until the rest of his team arrived from Chicago was chafing at him.

It wasn't Yuri. The sender was blocked and the message contained only an address, followed by the admonition: *Meet me now. Alone. Unarmed.* Мapт *17.*

Viktor. *Мapt* 17, the seventeenth of March, the day he had rescued him from the brothel. There was no use in sending a reply—the boy would already be powering down the phone, removing the SIM card. The way Korsakov had taught him.

Taught him well.

Unarmed. He contemplated going back to his room, retrieving his pistol at the very least. The idea of going out without it…

12:09 P.M.
San Fernando Valley
California

If Harry had harbored any doubts about Vasiliev's "other" roles at the consulate, they'd been answered when he first saw the Russian's car. It was a dingy gray Ford Taurus, a bit of rust near the tailpipe—the paint faded and chipped. It also had a V-8 engine.

It might as well have been built for the job they were asking it to do.

"Any ideas, *tovarisch?*"

Harry looked up from his maps and shook his head. They'd spent an hour and a half tailing Andropov's convoy around the Valley as his drivers went through surveillance detection route after surveillance detection route, or SDRs, as they were called.

It was dangerous to stay behind a target this long—ideally they would have had multiple cars, at least four teams, more likely five. Dangerous if your quarry knew what he was doing or had hired people who did. Taking the oligarch's money into account, Harry had no doubt he'd have hired the best.

But that wasn't the uppermost thing on his mind. Harry cleared his throat. "Won't they be missing you back at the office, Alexei?"

"I cleared my schedule," the Russian replied, his eyes on the road ahead. He tapped the gas, accelerating powerfully into the passing lane. "Anything for a friend—and as I've said, I am a law unto myself."

"Yeah...you've mentioned that a time or two." A pause. "But that's one load of bullcrap I'm not buying."

"What?" Vasiliev demanded, feigning surprise. He glanced over, then down at the Colt held in Harry's lap. Pointed straight at him. And this time the surprise was real. "What are you playing at, my old friend?"

"Just keep driving," Harry ordered. "You've got an angle in all this—care to fill me in?"

The older man smiled. "An angle? I took your call when you had no one else to turn to. If that gives me an agenda...distrust is one thing, Harry. Paranoia is another."

It was there, in his eyes. Nothing more than a flicker in their dark depths. He was lying.

"That wasn't a request, Alexei." Harry thumbed off the Colt's safety, the pad of his finger caressing the trigger.

"If I thought you'd really pull that trigger, I would have crashed this car by now," the Russian observed coolly. Distract. Divert.

No profit in backing down. Not now. "If you think I won't, you're getting too old for this business. A straight answer, Alexei. That's all I'm asking."

Vasiliev looked over again, seeming to consider his options. At length, he nodded.

"You're right, *tovarisch*. I am getting too old for this." He let out a heavy sigh. "And I have my reasons for helping you."

"Using me, you mean," Harry interjected, his face hardening with anger.

The Russian shrugged, easing back on the gas to maintain a safe following distance from their quarry. "*Using* is such a harsh word. It would imply that you got nothing from the arrangement."

"I don't have time for semantics."

"As you wish. Valentin Andropov *is* the man you are looking for—if anyone in the *mafiya* could bring the *Spetsnaz* into your country, it would be him."

Harry glanced forward, toward the convoy several cars ahead of them. "Your point?"

"Putin wants him dead. That's the reason for the heavy security, the reason he moved to the US in the first place."

The irony of it all. That a man who had made his billions selling weapons to terrorists would find refuge in the land of the free. He watched Vasiliev's eyes, careful for any signs of further deception. "What did he do?"

"No idea. In Russia, when you hear that Vladimir wants a man dead—you do not ask why, only how."

Harry shook his head. "The more things change...I suppose you want my help killing him?"

A smile. "I had assumed that was part of *your* plan. You would get what you want—and I would get a promotion from Moscow. Maybe even retirement."

It was clever—and typical of the Russian. It was why Han had advised against contacting him. Always had an angle, a pawn to sacrifice in order to advance his own agenda.

"All I want is information," Harry said finally. "Who paid him to assassinate David Lay. Once I have that information, he's yours."

The smile never left Vasiliev's face. "See? There was no reason for us to disagree."

"No reason for you to deceive me, either," Harry retorted, lowering the Colt. There was a *click* as he put the safety back on, letting the gun rest in his lap.

"True." Vasiliev inclined his head. "I always find myself forgetting how different you are from your countrymen. Their emotionalism is difficult to work with—but you, you are different. Almost Russian."

Coming from Alexei, that was the ultimate compliment. Almost as if he was leading up to something.

Ahead, their target was slowing, the convoy heading for the freeway exit and Vasiliev slid into the right-hand lane, moving into position two cars behind them.

"There *is* one other thing." The Russian paused, as if choosing his words very carefully. "Pyotr is part of the contract."

2:31 P.M. Central Time
The mosque
Dearborn, Michigan

"I'm fairly certain that Haskel didn't intend for you to interpret his orders this way."

And she hadn't wanted to do it this way. Marika unbuckled her seatbelt, looking across the street from where they had parked toward the mosque. Her hand on the door, she looked back across at him. "If you'd rather sit in the car, Russell, have at it. In the mean time, I'll see if Abu Kareem can spare a few moments for a woman."

She hadn't taken five steps across the street before she heard the car door open and close behind her. A tight smile.

Russell had never been known to balk at bending a few rules in order to achieve his ends. The difference between the two of them was that he had always been able to "negotiate" his way out of the resulting trouble.

She hadn't.

Her orders had been clear, but even the clearest orders left room for creative interpretation. The FISA request was denied. She was not to continue "harassing" Abu Kareem al-Fileestini. They hadn't said anything about not interviewing him...

There was something wrong about this, she realized halfway across the street, her boots crunching against the thin layer of ice. There was a vacant feeling to the building, just looking at it. Couldn't quite place it. She glanced up at the overcast, snow-laden sky, then back at the mosque.

No interior lights.

There was a shoulder-high iron fence around the exterior of the building—iron bars covering the windows. That wasn't uncommon, this was Dearborn, after all, and even religious institutions had to protect themselves against vandals—copper thieves in particular.

The front gate was secured with a chain and heavy padlock, and she hefted both in her gloved hand, staring through the gate at the imposing building. "Look at this, Russell."

The padlock was encased in ice. Thick ice.

The negotiator shook his head, looking up and down the street. "There's no one inside."

1:05 P.M. Pacific Time
Los Angeles, California

The address he had been given was for an abandoned industrial park about fifteen minutes off the 405. Of course that was going by the directions Korsakov had printed off the Internet. Given the legendary LA traffic, it was more like thirty.

The main gate no longer existed, rusty sections of chainlink pushed down all along the perimeter. The buildings were faded and weather-worn, windows shattered by vagrants—weeds growing in the cracks of the asphalt. The picture of desolation. A billboard atop the office building near the gate supplied the ultimate irony. *GreenTek Energies: The Jobs of the Future."*

Korsakov swore under his breath, casting a wary eye to his surroundings as he drove deeper into the industrial park. He should have brought a gun.

His phone buzzed and he slowed the Suburban to a crawl, digging it out of his jacket. GET OUT OF THE CAR.

Okay. That meant line of sight. Meant Viktor was watching him. The assassin paused with his hand on the door, gazing out from behind the SUV's tinted windows. Scanning for threats.

Nothing. But a hundred places to hide. And Viktor was treating him like the enemy.

No use delaying the inevitable. Korsakov pushed the door open and stepped forth, keeping his hands in the open. Keeping them raised.

Silence. A solitary gull hopped across the broken pavement, the only movement as far as the eye could see. Had he been played?

And then he felt it. Eyes on his back, his neck hairs prickling with danger.

Hands still raised, the assassin turned. Ever so slowly. Viktor was standing there, not five meters away—a Glock clutched in his outstretched hands. Aimed straight at his head.

His hands were shaking, tears running down his cheeks—his breath coming in ragged sobs.

"Please…just talk to me, Vitya," Korsakov whispered, using the diminutive of the boy's name as he cautiously extended a hand toward him. "What is it?"

The pistol wavered, fear and indecision playing across the young face, salty tears clinging to the scraggly black hair of his beard.

"You're safe, Vitya," the assassin continued, his tones gentle. "You're safe. You have my word, no one is going to do you harm. The people who abused you…they are dead."

The Glock came back up, a light flaring in the boy's eyes. He swore hoarsely, choking out the oath. "Not—another—word."

1:28 P.M.
I-15
California

"She doesn't have to see it," Vasiliev commented, taking his eyes off the road long enough to glance over at Harry. "None of you do. What is that great American expression…'out of sight, out of mind'?"

Harry looked up from his map, his eyes flashing with anger. "I gave her my word that Pyotr would not be harmed."

The idea was clearly the source of some amusement for the Russian. "Your *word*? I know you better than that, *tovarisch*—you know how to handle a situation like this. You tell her what she needs to hear, then do what *you* need to do."

It was true. Harry closed his eyes, the memories flooding over him. Another day, another time—it's exactly what he would have done. *For the greater good.* Or just out of sheer pragmatism, he hardly knew the difference anymore.

"We're not having this conversation, Alexei," he returned coldly, focusing his attention back to the maps. They had what Carol optimistically called "limited" access to the CalTrans camera system. While the situation wasn't ideal, it was enough to let them drop about ten cars back of Andropov's convoy.

Breathing room. But if they stayed on I-15 for much longer, they were going to cross into Nevada—and lose their coverage.

"You love her, don't you?" The question came out of nowhere, taking Harry off-balance. Of all things he might have expected the Russian to say...

"What makes you ask that?"

"I've never been to Langley—is that something they teach you there? To answer every question with another question?" A long pause. "I've seen the way you look at her."

Harry took a deep breath, his mind racing. Never give someone anything that could be used against you. Never expose a weakness. "Of course I've looked. She's a beautiful woman. That's all."

The lie felt hollow even as it left his lips, and it drew a laugh from Vasiliev. "Is it? You should never be ashamed of your heart, *tovarisch*. Never."

It was Harry's turn to laugh. "That's good, coming from you. You've been married what—three times, Alexei? Were you ashamed of your heart or did you just weary of their bodies?"

The Russian kept driving, but the look on his face was that of a man that had been physically struck. At length he cleared his throat. "You know me well, Harry. Perhaps even a little too well. And it is as you say. They were young, they were desperate, and I represented everything they lacked. If I hadn't been there—where might they have ended up? In a brothel? Beaten and raped on the Internet for the viewing pleasure of teenage boys here? It doesn't change the fact that *I* used them. I am not without my regrets."

The former KGB field officer dug into the pocket of his shirt and retrieved a small wallet-sized photograph. "My wife, Anya."

Harry took the photo from him and turned it over casually, knowing what he would find. Vasiliev's first two wives had both been blondes, breathtakingly beautiful—and young enough to be his daughters, indeed barely out of their teens.

The face staring back at him from the photograph was not what he had expected to see. A plain, unremarkable face lined and worn with age, the face of a woman in her mid-sixties. She was standing with her back against the rail of a ship, the sea breeze playing with her graying hair.

It was the eyes. The way they gazed into the camera. Confident. Full of love.

She was beautiful.

"It's not what you were expecting...is it, *tovarisch*?" Vasiliev asked quietly. He went on without waiting for a response, an unusual earnestness filling his voice. "Love—true love—only comes to a man once in his life, and often he does not recognize the form it takes when it comes. I never knew what love was until I met her."

Harry stared out the window of the car at the traffic, processing the Russian's words. Afraid that he was right.

"You grow old," the Russian continued, hesitating. "You grow old and realize one day that you are alone. All that you have done for your country, all that you have sacrificed—and you are left with nothing. A fistful of sand, your life slipping through your fingers."

He felt a chill pass over his body as the older man kept speaking. A premonition of evil.

"You've been trained to distrust your heart, *tovarisch*, and there was reason for it, but do not let this stand in your way now. If you truly love this woman...never let her go."

4:09 P.M. Central Time
The mosque
Dearborn, Michigan

"And what are you going to do if you trigger an alarm?" There was a quiet amusement in the negotiator's voice as he stood above her, in the slush of the alley.

"Run like the devil," Marika retorted, slipping on a pair of gloves and removing a set of lockpicks from an inner pocket of her coat. The back door of the mosque was protected by a heavy iron grate, secured with another padlock.

Any other partner she'd ever had would have been back at the vehicle by now, reporting her actions to D.C. That Russell wasn't said more about his concern than his common sense.

Failing in their initial visit to the mosque, they had driven out to Abu Kareem's house, a small bungalow in a housing development out in the suburbs. A suitably modest residence for a man of God.

There was no car in the garage, unmarked snow covering his driveway. He hadn't been home since the previous night.

He was gone. It coincided uncannily with the timing of Nasir's call.

Given Haskel's reaction to the FISA warrant earlier in the day, a search warrant for the mosque was out of the question. Which was why she found herself kneeling in the slushy snow, a lockpick in her hands.

The alley reeked of the stench of garbage and human waste. Even the below-freezing temps couldn't cover the smell. She knelt close to the grate, her hand holding the padlock firmly as she listened, ever alert for that *click*.

There. The lock sprung open in her hands, and she pulled it away, swinging back the grate.

She found her hands trembling as she went to work on the door itself, her ear pressed close to the lock. It wasn't about the cold.

"It's open," she announced moments later, testing the knob with a gloved hand.

"You're sure about this?" the negotiator asked, pulling a tactical flashlight from his pocket. Even after West Virginia, he had balked at the idea of carrying a gun.

She hesitated, for one long moment in time. To cross the line between law enforcer and law breaker. Or perhaps she had already crossed that line, concealing her presence at the site of Vic's murder.

Nothing was black and white. *Not anymore.* She drew her Glock, motioning toward the door.

"Follow me in."

2:27 P.M. Pacific Time
The industrial park
Los Angeles

"Dear God," Korsakov whispered, running a hand through his close-cropped hair. It was a particularly odd expression coming from his lips, but it *all* seemed unreal, even after hearing Viktor's story for the second time.

It was not that the assassin was unaccustomed to brutality. It was a means to achieve an end. But this...

He wrapped an arm around the boy's trembling shoulders, drawing him close as they sat together on a stack of pallets near the Suburban. The Glock lay discarded a few feet away. *No longer a threat.*

"Why did you not come to me, Vitya? All of this, this misunderstanding—it could have been avoided."

And yet what would he have done differently, Korsakov asked himself. He did not choose his contracts based on the "morality" of his employer, and at his very core, the story did not surprise him. Andropov had always been a turbulent man. The idea that he could have whipped a teenage prostitute to death after repeatedly violating her body...it was not at all unbelievable. Yet, as he viewed it through Viktor's eyes, the story filled him with horror. Revulsion.

It didn't change what he had to do.

Tears rolled unchecked down the boy's cheeks as he slipped in and out of a near-catatonic state. He needed sleep, reassurance, comfort. Everything that Korsakov was unable to provide.

Not now.

With gentle fingers, he brushed the matted hair back from Viktor's forehead. Feeling the boy's grief. "This can all be over, Vitya—we can leave this all behind us and be back in Russia within the week. But first you must unlock the laptop…"

4:31 P.M. Central Time
The mosque
Dearborn, Michigan

Marika held the Glock in both hands, the tactical light below the barrel switched on as she led the way down a long hallway. The light cast strange shadows against the cheap wood paneling, keeping her on edge.

The floor sloped beneath her feet, leading them down—it was more of a ramp, than anything, she realized. Freshly poured, by the looks of the concrete.

The ground floor of the mosque had been deserted, just as she had suspected. If it hadn't been…well, there was no use thinking about that now.

"Don't like the looks of this," Russell observed as they reached the door at the bottom of the ramp. The short man stepped around her, his flashlight clenched between his teeth as he reached up, fingering the seal. "Airtight."

"Why do you need an airtight room in a mosque?" It was a rhetorical question, and they both knew it.

You didn't.

He tried the knob. It was unlocked. Just waiting to be entered.

Russell cleared his throat. "I think this is the point where we bring in the rest of the Bureau."

"And tell them what?" Marika asked, shaking her head. "That we found a strange door while executing a warrantless search?"

Without waiting for a reply, she stepped forward, the Glock in her right hand as she pulled the door open. There was a rush of air as the seals opened, cold air striking her in the face.

She moved into the darkness, feeling the chill pierce through her clothing. The beams of their tactical lights swept the room, a rare curse escaping from Russell's lips as he spotted a piece of equipment near the far wall.

"You wanted something to report?" he whispered. "Report this: we're standing in some kind of weapons lab."

5:23 P.M. Mountain Time
Grand Junction, Colorado

A burger and fries. Salty, the way Americans liked their food. Nasir shook the last of the fries out onto his tray, looking at the golden arches-emblazoned red carton for a moment before crumpling the flimsy cardboard in his fist.

The manager had gone out of his way to assure them that the food was kosher. It was as close as they were going to come to *halal* in the Rocky Mountains. Nasir shook his head. Even here, the reach of the Jew was undiminished.

He glanced across the table into the eyes of Abu Kareem al-Fileestini. The imam picked a chicken nugget off his tray with two fingers and popped it into his mouth, a faint smile crossing his lips. "Noori would have frowned upon this meal. Too fattening, she would have said. She was a good woman—knew her place—but that didn't stop her from watching out for my weight."

"Was?"

Sadness crept into the eyes of the imam. "My wife has been dead for five years. You didn't know that, did you?"

Nasir shook his head.

"No matter," Abu Kareem replied dismissively. "There was no way you could have known. I always regretted that your work did not permit you to attend prayers at the masjid with your brother. We could have gotten to know one another."

The tips of Nasir's fingers began to tremble, almost imperceptibly. Fear seizing hold. The imam was a man of subtlety, not one given to idle words.

He swallowed hard, feeling the salt of the fries dry and rough against his tongue.

"Everything you told Omar—about you acquiring the commercial driver's license..." Abu Kareem's voice trailed off for a long moment as his eyes met Nasir's. "It checked out. All of it."

Relief flooded his body and he struggled to keep it out of his eyes, out of his voice. Anything that might betray him now, in his moment of safety.

"You doubted it?"

The imam shrugged. "Ever since I entered the *Dar el Harb*, thirty long years ago, I doubt all things—save the will of Allah."

"Fair enough," Nasir replied, forcing a smile to his face. "May His name be glorified."

He watched as the older man took a small bottle from his coat pocket, shaking two round capsules into his palm.

"Pain medication," Abu Kareem said, answering the unasked question. "The doctors tell me that I have only a few months left to live. Cancer."

"There's no treatment?"

"None that could save my life—by the time they found it, it had spread all through my lungs."

He looked up, visibly hesitating. "I do not wish Tarik to know of this—I am trusting you to keep this secret, my son. It is the last wish of my life that I die as I have lived, in the service of God."

6:19 P.M. Pacific Time
The empty mansion
Beverly Hills, California

The Suburban that had left earlier in the day was returning, the remotely-controlled gates of the Andropov mansion swinging open wide to admit it.

Han raised the camera, adjusting the telephoto lens as he snapped picture after picture. It was a fruitless exercise, given the blacked-out windows and the fact that he already had the license number. *Alpha-one-five-Bravo-Papa-Delta.*

But it was training, old reflexes taking back over. Being in special ops was like riding a bicycle. Some things, you never forgot.

No matter how hard you tried.

He was laying prone on a dirty mattress, the stock of a sniper rifle pressed against his shoulder. Watching a street full of people through the scope, each of them only a hair's-breadth away from death. Ciudad del Este. Paraguay.

One target.

His hands trembled at the unbidden memory, and he lowered the camera, realizing suddenly that he was sweating, a thin sheen of perspiration covering his forearms.

Get a grip.

He passed a hand over his face, walking back through the empty rooms of the house until he arrived at the kitchen.

"The Suburban is back," the former SEAL announced, glancing over toward where Carol sat. "Couldn't get an ID on the driver."

She acknowledged his words with a nod. "Harry called—they had just crossed the city limits of Las Vegas. Still shadowing Andropov."

"And they've not been detected?" Han pursed his lips together. "That's impressive."

"I hope so," she murmured. "If they've been able to stay behind them this long—Vasiliev must be good at what he does."

"Vasiliev...is the best," Han replied, laying the camera on the granite of the kitchen's island. "He made it through the hell of Afghanistan in the eighties, stayed alive in the middle of the power struggles that followed the dissolution of the USSR. He's a survivor. I've never met anyone like him."

"I wish Harry hadn't gone with him," Carol observed, her voice suddenly brittle. "It's not safe."

He looked at her for a long moment, sadness growing in his eyes. He knew that tone. *Sherri.*

All those years, and he could still hear the pain in his wife's voice, still feel the tension as they spent their last night together before deployment. Before Yemen.

He remembered her body shuddering as she lay in his arms, tears falling from her eyes. It was as though she had *known.* Their souls inextricably linked.

"You care for him, don't you?" The words came out more abruptly than he intended, but there was no reaction. Not for a painfully long moment.

"There are moments..." She hesitated as if searching for the right words, still not looking at him. "Moments when I see another side of him...and in those moments I tell myself that this is a man I could love."

The SEAL stared down at his hands, big fingers splayed against the granite. Memories.

"Don't do this to yourself."

She turned toward him, disbelief and anger playing across her features. "What do you mean?"

He fell silent for a moment. "Harry is one of the few men I truly respect—there was a time in my life when I would have crossed hell in a rubber raft had he given the order. It doesn't change one simple reality: he's going to end up just like me."

There was no response. He could see her fingers trembling, whether from anger or fear, he couldn't tell. When the phone rang a moment later, she didn't move to answer it.

He picked the cellphone off the countertop, answering it with a simple, "Hello."

It was Harry.

The SEAL listened without commenting for a couple minutes, then responded, "We'll keep you updated from our end."

He closed the phone, turning back to Carol. "They've lost Andropov."

9:59 P.M. Eastern Time
Graves Mill, Virginia

Open ground. The sniper in him hated it. Thomas moved out from cover, the stubble of a snow-frosted corn field jabbing through his skin. The briars in the hedgerow of multiflora behind him had already pulled and tugged at his makeshift ghillie suit, but he preferred it to the nakedness of the open field.

You never got to choose your tactical environment. Or your conditions. There were some forms of cover you couldn't *see* from. He lifted a small pair of binoculars to his eyes, staring across the mounded snow, toward the mobile home nestled beneath a copse of trees at the edge of the field. A single vehicle in the driveway. A light in a rear window, presumably a bedroom by the placement.

"What's your sitrep, LONGBOW?" Tex's voice, crackling through the static on his earpiece.

"I'm in position." Thomas glanced at his watch, marking the time. *Twenty-two hundred hours.* "Watch and wait."

Chapter 18

The security camera was smashed in the parking garage where Vasiliev parked the Taurus. An old act of vandalism, judging by the weathering of the cracked plastic housing. As if it had been broken the previous year and no one had possessed the time or money needed to replace it.

"Leave your pistol in the car," Vasiliev instructed as Harry opened the door.

Harry looked at him. Just because he knew why didn't mean he had to like it. "It's only five blocks to the club, and you can't get inside with it." A smile crossed the Russian's face. "Just because the place is run by the *mafiya*, don't think that we're completely lawless."

He opened the center console and pulled out a pair of Bluetooth earpieces. "We'll use these to stay in contact if we need to separate. The miracle of technology, *tovarisch*. Twenty years ago, sitting at a bar with a wire protruding from your ear—you might as well tattoo *spy* on your forehead. But now…"

It also made identifying your opponents a lot harder, Harry thought, briefly testing the device to make sure it worked. For every technology, there was a downside. And a countermeasure.

"I assume it's occurred to you that someone may recognize you, Alexei. You are the consulate's head of security, after all."

Vasiliev came around the end of the car, taking in Harry's worn leather jacket and faded jeans at a glance. "It has. In point of fact, I am counting on it. Your fashion sense certainly isn't going to get us past the bouncer."

11:04 P.M. Central Time
The mosque
Dearborn, Michigan

If there was one thing Marika had learned about the Bureau over her years of service, it was that subtlety wasn't their strong suit. In the hours following Russell's call, they had descended on the mosque in force—forty agents at last count.

Snow crunched beneath her feet as she ducked under the crime scene tape, heading for her car. Behind her the mosque was bathed in floodlights, ahead the Dearborn PD had officers stationed, keeping the crowd back. At least fifteen officers, a sizable percentage of their entire force.

Russell was already in the passenger seat of the sedan, his thermos raised to his lips. "Find out anything?"

The response from Washington had been impressive, but it didn't mean Haskel was pleased with their efforts. They'd both been sidelined, for the second time in a week. She shook her head. "They don't know anything to tell. The place is sterile—and Abu Kareem's lawyer arrived five minutes ago."

The negotiator nodded patiently. "Any idea where his employer is?"

"Negative. Not likely to find out either, not for days. All that, and all we have is a hermetically sealed room. No trace of any toxins, nothing." A wry smile turned up her lips. "I think we did ourselves in this time, Russ. Sorry to take you down with me."

He shrugged. "I'll be fine. Spend some time with my grandkids. They're growing up fast. Go on that deep-sea fishing trip my brother is always talking about."

My brother.

"Hand me my laptop," Marika instructed suddenly, pulling off her gloves and turning the car's heater all the way up.

"What are you thinking?"

"Something our CI said." She balanced the laptop on her knees, opening the FBI database. Her access codes still worked, though it was hard to tell for how much longer. "Nasir's roommate—the university student—what was his name?"

"Jamal al-Khalidi," Russell said, after a moment's thought. The negotiator never forgot a name.

"What was his major?"

"We didn't check."

Marika scrolled down the screen. "I'm thinking that was a mistake. According to this...he was a chemist, enrolled in their postgraduate program. Going for his Master's."

"Are you sayin'..."

"Worse," she replied, pulling up two photos side by side on the screen. "Look at this."

An expression of surprise crossed the negotiator's face. "They're brothers."

"Our CI lied to us."

9:23 P.M. Pacific Time
The club
Las Vegas, Nevada

The world over, gentlemen's clubs were all built around one central theme. The casual observer might have said that it was sex, but the truth was far more elemental.

Power.

Being above the law was its own aphrodisiac, as men like Andropov knew so well.

The music was still slow this early in the evening, the tension just starting to build. Piano music, supplied by a grey-haired man up there stage left, his thin fingers dancing over the ivory keys.

"Any sign of Andropov?" Harry asked, nursing his club soda as his eyes moved around the club.

"Negative, *tovarisch*. But I am certain this is where he would come. The man's...how would you say? A security freak. Here among the *mafiya*, he is safe."

"And this safety extends to you as well?" Harry leaned back in his chair, hands resting easily on the tabletop. Only inches away from his gun, had he worn it. After all these years, the posture came naturally.

Vasiliev shrugged. "In Russia, the government is the *mafiya* and the *mafiya* is the government. Doesn't pay to piss either party off. We have what I would call a...'working relationship'."

"You come here often?"

"Often enough," the Russian replied, turning his shot glass between his fingers. "If I have an asset in need of cultivation. It's the atmosphere, I think. The liquor. The women. Men talk under such circumstances...and even more later on, when they fear the danger of their wife seeing the pictures."

It was the way the game was played. The way it had always been played.

"I'll be glad to be out," he said, more to himself than Vasiliev. "Put this life behind me."

His gaze drifted toward the bar, momentarily catching the eye of a young prostitute working the johns there. She looked Eastern European, dark-haired and artificially tanned. Maybe eighteen or nineteen at the most.

Prostitution was officially illegal in Vegas, but such regulations were subject to such nuance and parsing as to be effectively useless. It didn't protect girls like her.

"Tell me we're not wasting our time sitting here."

"We're not," Vasiliev retorted evenly, reaching into his shirt pocket. Gold glinted between his fingers as he slid a coin across the table toward Harry.

"What's this?" It was a ten-ruble coin from 1911, the face of Tsar Nicholas II decorating the obverse. Pure gold, evident from its heft.

"It is a key, *tovarisch*." A smile. "And oh, the doors that it will open."

He flipped it between his fingers, staring at the double-headed eagle of imperial Russia. "Cut to the chase, Alexei."

"When doing business with the *mafiya*, it is always good to have an edge...cards under the table, if you will. Take the piano player for instance—his stage name is Mike Carroll. His real name is Mikhail..."

The Russian lifted the shot glass to his lips, grimacing as the vodka slid down his throat. He smiled. "If Andropov has been through these doors tonight, Mike will know. Go talk to him. I have your back."

The chords of "Some Enchanted Evening" rose from the piano as Harry rose from the table, the man's fingers conveying a vibrant touch.

Harry paused as the pianist began to sing, a mellow voice rising above the low murmur of the club noise. It was an incongruous song for the surroundings, a throwback to a simpler day.

A song of hope. Of love. Never in his life had he been able to carry a tune, but he found himself humming along, despite himself.

A dream—of another life. No more deception. No more pain.

He glanced over to find the young prostitute staring at him, her face bringing him back to reality. He had a mission to perform.

The pianist glanced up at him as he stepped onto the stage, a gentle smile crossing the old man's face. It wasn't the face of an operator...or was it?

Harry's hands came out of his jacket, the coin in one palm, the photo of Andropov in the other. "Have you seen this man?" he asked in perfect Russian.

"Who are you?" the man asked, his voice low. The smile was still plastered to his face, but he had paled—fingers trembling as he spoke.

"My name doesn't matter, *tovarisch*. You know who sent me."

The pianist cast a long glance out into the darkness of the club. "I do," he replied slowly, turning toward Harry. "The man you are looking for…arrived an hour ago. He and his bodyguards are in the VIP."

"Is there anyone in there with them?"

A shake of the head. "No. They're waiting…"

9:58 P.M. Pacific Time
A warehouse, North Las Vegas
Nevada

The taillights of the tractor-trailer glowed red against the sheet metal of the warehouse as Nasir tapped the brakes, holding his breath as the big truck eased back, passing within inches of the doorframe as it rolled under cover.

He looked over into the smiling eyes of the negro. "Hey, bro, you survived."

Yeah. The irony of the words did not escape him. They were all on a suicide mission. All to be welcomed to paradise soon enough, if paradise indeed awaited the evil-doer. Nasir shoved open the truck door, feeling the chill night air envelop his tired limbs. It had been a long drive.

Tarik Abdul Muhammad was standing in the middle of the warehouse floor, flanked by the remnants of his Pakistani contingent. A round metal barrel was before them, flames leaping from its depths—casting strange shadows against the shaikh's face.

"We are entering the final stages of the project, my brothers. Tonight we take delivery of the weapons that will enable us to strike a blow against the *khafir*, a blow for the freedom of our people."

Freedom? The jihadis, and he among them, had brought down the wrath of the Jews upon the whole of Lebanon, leaving the once-beautiful Beirut in ruins. Was that freedom—an end to be desired?

"Most of you disposed of your cellphones and personal electronics before even starting this journey. If you did not, do so now. We cannot have the Americans listening in at this critical hour. Not with what has happened."

"What's going on?" It was Abu Kareem, standing just within the shadows. If he had been kept out of the loop…

"I have heard from one of our brothers in Michigan," Tarik replied, slowly turning his head to face the imam. "The *masjid* was raided within hours of our departure."

A gasp went up from the assembled jihadis, and Nasir felt himself joining in, even if there were different reasons for his fear.

"Even now the American FBI may be looking for us," the shaikh announced, his eyes darting back and forth. Searching the faces before him.

Abu Kareem cleared his throat. "Do we need to move up the timing of the attack?"

"The attack will proceed as planned, *insh'allah.*" Tarik looked away for a moment, his voice taking on a new intensity. "It *must.* And they will be powerless to stop us. This is the moment that we disappear from the Americans' eyes—from their mighty technology. For surely it was spoken by the Prophet, peace be upon him, 'It is God's Law that He brings down whatever rises high in the world'. Now...your phones."

To Nasir's left, Omar moved forward, removing his cellphone from his shirt pocket and tossing it into the flames.

He looked up to see the shaikh staring directly at him, his eyes seeming to glow in the light of the fire. As if he knew.

Making a desperate effort to ignore the fear clawing at his heart, Nasir took a step toward the fire, reaching into his back pocket to retrieve his phone. His last connection to the FBI.

His lifeline.

He watched as it fell into the flames, watched until the battery exploded in the heat of the inferno. Until it was consumed.

Now he was in the hands of Allah. As ever...

10:32 P.M.
The club
Las Vegas, Nevada

There were four guards within sight, not including anyone that might be guarding the entrance to the VIP—each of them wearing a Sig Sauer P226 in a prominent hip holster.

The fact that they were—to a man—focused on the stripper that had just walked on-stage belied whatever aura of professionalism their choice of weaponry might have given them.

Harry leaned back in his chair, tuning out the music and flashing strobes as he calculated the distance between himself and the nearest guard. Seven meters. If he needed a gun, taking one would not be difficult.

He and Alexei had separated, with the Russian taking up a position closer to the lounge. They didn't have a line of sight, though. And there was no way to get one without becoming conspicuous.

"I can fill your drink, sir," a soft voice announced from above him. He looked up into the eyes of the prostitute from the bar.

Ice mingled with the remnants of the soda at the bottom of his glass. "I'm fine," he replied.

She smiled, slipping smoothly into Alexei's seat—scooting closer to him. Too close, her hand touching his knee. "You look lonely. Are you sure there's nothing else you might need?"

There was urgency there in her voice, a raw fear behind the thin veneer of the seductress. Desperation.

Up close, he found himself revising his estimate of her age. Seventeen? Young enough to have been his daughter, had he been blessed with a normal life.

She was Romanian by the accent, a mane of dark hair falling over her shoulders. Once upon a time, Harry thought, his hand sliding down to capture her roving fingers—once upon a time she had been a beauty. Now she walked the ragged edge between slender and anorexic, her exposed stomach gaunt beneath the black lace of the crop top.

"No," he whispered firmly, regarding her with sadness. "I'm fine."

Her bare arm bore the marks of a needle—drug addiction, always the favored ploy of a pimp. That—and beatings, as evidenced by the purplish bruise near her shoulder. He doubted that any of her clients were sober enough to notice. Or that they would care if they did. The tragic reality lurking just behind the façade of their fantasy world.

And yet...she was still living. When others had died. And he could find in himself no condemnation for how she had done it. The choices offered by life were often just that simple. Life...death—no choice at all, really.

He could see the reluctance in her eyes as she rose to leave. The fear. He'd seen it before. So many times.

His hand reached out, gently brushing against her fingers. He hesitated for a long moment, then unbuttoned his shirt pocket, pressing a hundred-dollar bill into her thin palm.

Surprise lit up those dark, tired eyes. It was a futile gesture, and they both knew it. She wouldn't be able to keep the money. But it might keep her from a beating. *Maybe.*

"*Mulțumesc mult,*" she whispered, tucking the bill into her top. *Thank you.*

And then she was gone, disappearing into the darkness of the club. A ghost in the night.

Harry let out a long, heavy sigh, swishing the last of the drink together in his glass.

You couldn't save everyone—that was a lesson he had learned years ago. You had to make choices, decide who to save...as much as that felt like playing God.

Knowing the reality had never helped him sleep at night. He tossed the glass back—an angry gesture—the icy, carbonated water hitting the back of his throat.

There was no purpose to dwelling on it. He reached up, switching on his Bluetooth. "Any signs of life, Alexei?"

1:48 A.M. Eastern Time, December 21st
The White House
Washington, D.C.

"I have to ask, Ian," the President demanded, still buttoning his shirt as a pair of Secret Service agents ushered him into the Treaty Room. "What in the name of heaven could be important enough that it couldn't wait six hours?"

"This," a grim-faced Cahill replied, handing over a folder. Hancock took it and retreated to the other side of the large Renaissance revival-style table, his detail still flanking him.

If not for the gravity of the situation, the chief of staff might have been amused. He had *made* Hancock, and yet the Secret Service didn't trust him enough to be left in the same room with the POTUS.

Paranoia.

He leaned back in his chair, waiting until he heard an oath escape the President's lips.

"How could they do this?" Hancock asked, looking up in disbelief. "Raid a mosque—doesn't Haskel understand that I'm fighting for my life with this election in the hands of the Court? The last thing I need is for the American people to see CAIR protesting in the streets."

"Keep reading," Cahill advised coolly. "It gets worse. Haskel really had no choice."

The color drained from the President's face as he leafed through the folder. "What do we do now?" he asked finally, closing it and pushing back his armchair.

"I would make sure all our resources are focused on finding and *stopping* Abu Kareem."

"That's not what I'm talking about." Hancock closed his eyes, his hands clenching and unclenching as if he was trying to regain his composure. He shot a glare toward his detail. "Give us the room."

"Mr. President—"

"Hawkins, what part of 'give us the room' do you fail to grasp?"

It was a credit to the agent's professionalism that he didn't react. He simply inclined his head to one side, nodding, "As you wish, Mr. President. We'll be outside."

The President waited until the door had closed behind them, then turned back to his chief of staff. "Haskel can focus on finding Abu Kareem—the DHS can give him whatever help he requires. Right now, *our* biggest problem is how to spin this, if Abu Kareem can truly be tied to an impending terrorist attack. This man sat beside me in this very room not four months ago—how do I survive something like that, Ian?"

Cahill stared at him for a long moment in disbelief, before beginning to chuckle. "You're a cold sonuvagun, aren't you, Roger?"

11:03 P.M. Pacific Time
The nightclub
Las Vegas, Nevada

It was one of those feelings. Call it instinct. Call it intuition—spend enough time out on the edge, you learned not to disregard it. It would save your life.

The four men were together. It didn't matter that they had come through the doors of the nightclub separately—or that they weren't standing together. Their behavior marked them as clearly as if they had been standing in a line-up. It was hard to see their faces distinctly in the dim light, but their features were Middle Eastern—three of them. And an African with them.

"We've got company," Harry announced, keying his mike. "Look alive."

"*Da.*"

A fifth man came through the doors of the club at that moment, tall and well-dressed, his bearing that of a leader. He wasn't from the Mediterranean like the other men—his face bore none of the features of the Levant. It was something more like what Harry remembered from those long months in the Hindu Kush. Pakistani—Pashtun, perhaps?

A barely imperceptible nod as he took off his Raybans and his men began to converge, falling into formation behind him.

Harry rose from the table, his phone in his hand. He needed a photo. Something for Carol to run.

A faint smile crossed his face—the tactical environment couldn't have been more perfect. All around him, there were men doing the same thing, their phones aimed at the girl on-stage, body arched back as she spun around the pole, her hair flying.

There was no one to notice one more photographer as the men crossed the club, making their way toward the VIP lounge.

Click. Click. Click.

11:08 P.M.
The abandoned mansion
Beverly Hills, California

Do what you can to ID remotely, the text message read. *The leader looks familiar.*

Carol pulled a new USB cord from the shopping bag on the kitchen counter, stripping away the packaging as she plugged one end into her laptop and the other into the phone. If there was one thing Harry did not do well, it was texting—it was the first typed-out message she had seen in five years.

He's going to end up just like me. Han's words, replaying themselves back through her mind.

"No," she whispered, her fingers gripping the edge of the granite counter. It wasn't true. It couldn't be. The way he had held her after the murder of her father. She had seen another side of him in those moments—a man wounded by all that he had sacrificed for his country. Yet still gentle. Still capable of love.

Not the way Han had described him. Not *that* man.

A *whirring* sound brought her attention back to the laptop as the connection was completed, the picture coming up on-screen automatically.

Her eyes locked in on the image, a gasp escaping her lips. "This isn't good..."

"What is it?" Han demanded, hurrying in from the abandoned living room.

"He's back," she announced. "Tarik Abdul Muhammad..."

11:10 P.M.
The club
Las Vegas, Nevada

The music in the VIP lounge was softer, less insistent than that out in the main area of the club—but still loud enough to disrupt any listening devices. Nasir raised his arms and allowed himself to be patted down by the Russians at the door, his eyes adjusting to the dim light as he went inside.

The man who rose from the leather couches to greet them still possessed the bearing of a soldier, despite his age. He took a step away from his bodyguards and toward Tarik, extending a fleshy hand. "I was delighted to hear of your safe arrival, *tovarisch*. Welcome to Las Vegas."

"No more delighted than I was to arrive, Mr. Andropov," the Pakistani replied. Nasir could see his lips turn up in the barest hint of a smile. "Is everything in readiness?"

"*Da.*" Andropov nodded. "Everything you asked for—including the reaction times of the LVMPD SWAT and their travel routes. You can take delivery of the weapons in the morning."

"The weapons," he heard Tarik begin. "You were able to get what I requested?"

"As I explained to you in our prior communiques, your requests were not easy to fulfill." The Russian beckoned to a blonde girl curled up on the couch behind him and she rose, wordlessly handing him his wine glass. Her eyes were glazed—lifeless, Nasir noted, feeling a chill pass over him. It was like watching an automaton.

Andropov took a sip of the rosé, favoring the girl with a smile before she retreated. "Not easy at all, but that *is* why you contacted me, is it not?"

Tarik waved a hand toward Abu Karim. "My sources assured me that you possessed the network to not only acquire the weaponry, but smuggle it across the American border."

"You were not misinformed," the arms dealer replied. "In the world of heavy arms, I acknowledge no equal. SA-24s are not common—a few years ago, your request would have been impossible—but the fall of Muammar al-Quaddafi resulted in their dissemination across the Arab world. Ironic, is it not? The late colonel had no use for your jihad, and yet, without his weapons…"

Another smile. "I was able to secure a single SA-24 man-portable surface-to-air missile—the most advanced *Igla* deployed to the Russian Army."

"I requested two." Nasir could see Tarik exchange glances with the imam. What manner of attack were they contemplating?

The Russian's smile never wavered. "I was, how should I say…outbid. By the Revolutionary Guards. There are times when you cannot obtain *everything* you wish."

"*Insh'allah,*" Tarik murmured, nodding—a grudging acquiescence. "It is as you say."

"Always."

11:21 P.M.

His breath smelled of whiskey, his shirtfront damp from where the amber fluid had splashed over him. At least Harry thought it was whiskey—he'd scarfed the abandoned drink off a nearby table and it was hard to be particular when you were in a hurry.

He staggered, putting out a hand as if to steady himself. Carrying out the act.

"Where do you think you're going?" The man's English was heavily accented—Russian, by the sound of it. Andropov apparently relied upon homegrown talent, rather than bringing in a Western security firm, as had many of his peers

"Well, well," he slurred, glancing down the long hallway toward the closed entrance of the VIP. He shook a finger toward the nearest guard. "Aren't you the one with the questions?"

The man reached out with surprising speed for a man of his bulk, seizing Harry's wrist with an iron grip.

Don't react.

He could have broken the man's arm in a trice, but violence would have gained nothing. Instead, he allowed astonishment to spread across his face, fear breaking through the supposed inebriation. "This is the way to the crapper, ain't it? I gotta take a leak."

"No, it isn't," the bodyguard snarled, giving him a shove. "Get lost."

A laugh escaped Harry's lips as he reeled against the wall. "No need to hate." He reached down, fumbling with his zipper. "You'd rather I do it right here?"

The man shook his head in disgust, apparently thoroughly convinced by the act. "That way."

Harry made a half-bow, then stumbled toward the exit. He collapsed into the nearest chair, keying his mike.

"His security is airtight, and they're pros. We're not going to bluff our way inside. Does anyone have any more brilliant ideas?"

11:29 P.M.
The abandoned mansion
Beverly Hills, California

"Yes," Carol responded, almost before she could stop herself. The very thought of it still sickened her, but this was different, somehow. This went beyond revenge. The line between white and black—right and wrong—had been irreparably blurred. She felt as if she was looking out over an abyss.

"I have eyes on Andropov's son," she blurted. "We can make the grab and use Pyotr as a bargaining chip."

Harry's voice again. "What do you mean you have 'eyes' on him?"

"Exactly what it sounds like," Carol replied, her gaze drifting over to the computer screen, the figures draped over a couch in a dimly lit room. "Using

Pyotr's Twitter account and cellphone data, we tracked him to an off-campus DKE frat house on the south side of LA. The HDTV in the main room of the frat house is equipped with an internally wired camera and microphones, all of which are tied into the building's wireless network."

She heard Vasiliev murmur a curse, then start laughing. "Are *all* Americans this stupid?"

"Can you be sure it's Pyotr?"

On-screen, the figures continued to move together, a rhythm as old as time. "Affirmative."

A moment, then Harry responded. "We can't make that play, not here. Too many wild cards in a public venue like this. There's no back-up plan in place if this should fail."

Was this the way it happened? One thing led to another and by the time you woke up, you could scarcely recognize the face in the mirror. She was advocating for a kidnapping. She glanced over at Han, her face pale. "We have to do *something*...Tarik Abdul Muhammad didn't come to Vegas for the roulette."

"At the risk of sounding ignorant," Vasiliev interjected calmly, "who is this man and why is he important?"

Carol cleared her throat. "In 2004, Tarik was captured fighting against American soldiers in A-stan and sent to Gitmo. At the time of his detention, he was sixteen."

That elicited a snort from the Russian. "And you call me brutal...I thought your facilities at Guantanamo were reserved for high-value detainees. What was special about a teenager?"

"He had spent time with Ayman al-Zawahiri in Pakistan—his father was believed to be a close associate of the doctor. We always took information regarding al-Qaeda's No. 2 seriously."

"*If* this is all true, how did he end up here?"

She started to reply, but Harry cut her off. "This is ancient history, people. We need an action plan, and we need it now."

Nothing. Han shot a look in her direction, as if waiting for orders. Then the Russian's voice broke the silence. "If you want eyes inside the VIP, *tovarisch*, I *can* make it happen..."

2:34 A.M. Eastern Time
Graves Mills, Virginia

The flask was empty. Had been for several hours, and he found himself missing its fiery warmth. Thomas shifted position, brushing snow off the sleeve of his jacket. Surveillance was always a pain—doing it in "inclement" weather only made matters worse.

His radio crackled with static. "Sitrep, LONGBOW?"

It took a moment for him to respond, primarily because he hadn't been paying attention—boredom setting in after so many long hours.

"I have movement near the back of the trailer—in a bathroom, I guess?" He found himself cursing his own inattention. This was the stuff that got you killed.

"Are you sure?"

"No, lights come on by themselves and shadows move in front of windows without anyone there." It might have been the fatigue—might have been the liquor talking. Either way, he felt on edge. "Why?"

"I have someone at this end of the house—picking up a human signature." Tex had their thermal imager. It might not have been the most recent generation of hardware—but on a night like tonight...

"Everything we found on Stevens," Tex went on, "she doesn't have children, does she?"

"No record of it."

The Texan fell silent for several minutes. "One car in the drive—two people in the house? Something's wrong here."

There was milk in the refrigerator. A half-carton, a few days away from its expiration date. David Lay leaned heavily against the counter as he poured himself a glass.

He was still weak. Too weak.

It took him a moment to realize that he wasn't the only one awake—light coming from another part of the house.

The DCIA limped out of the kitchen, grasping hold of a chair to keep his balance. The smell of cannabis filled his nostrils, mixing with the taste of the milk in his mouth, and he fought the urge to retch.

Rhoda Stevens was in the living room of the double-wide, curtains drawn—a smoldering joint in the ashtray beside her laptop.

"What are you doing up at this hour?" he asked, leaning against the wall.

She didn't even look up. "I could ask the same question, David. I doubt you'd have any better answer. Look at this."

The Jamaican woman was gesturing to something on her screen. "What is it?" Lay asked, pain shooting through his body as he moved into the room, circling behind her.

"My insurance policy," she retorted. "A backdoor into the intel community's networks. A favor from a friend of a friend of a friend. They started running my name through their databases a few days ago—a request originating with the Clandestine Service."

"Why are you just now learning about this?"

"It's the malware—several years old and buggy. Not like we can go in and install updates. It only functions 45-50% of the time. Not much of an early warning system, but it's the best I can do."

His eyes scanned down the screen, a cold fear seizing hold. "They're making the connection between us…if they haven't made it already."

"Running searches is a long way from actually finding us, David," she replied, her brow furrowing as she brought up another window. "If you recall, we're both supposed to be dead. They're still searching for my real name, not the one I'm using now."

It wasn't that simple. "You think," he countered, unable to suppress the agitation building inside him. A sixth sense. "You said the malware wasn't reliable."

Rhoda looked up from the computer and he could see it in her eyes. She felt it too. He lowered his voice as if afraid that someone could be listening.

"Do you own a gun?"

11:39 P.M. Pacific Time
The club
Las Vegas, Nevada

That moment when you put someone else's life on the line…it was a feeling that you could never get used to. A dirty feeling.

"You don't have to go through with this," Harry whispered, his hand sliding across the girl's shoulder and down her bare arm. As if he was one of her clients—all just part of the charade. As with so much of his life. "I'm not going to lie to you. If they suspect that you're spying on them—they'll kill you. And there will be nothing we can do."

"I know…it's always that way with Alexei."

"How long?"

The young prostitute looked down at her hands, a finger tracing along the needle marks dotting her forearm. "Over a year. He's the only reason I'm still alive. They think that I'm his…favorite. He's connected within the *mafiya*, warned them that if anything happened to me—he would bring them down."

If anything happened. It was painfully obvious that "anything" didn't include rape or drug addiction.

"Be careful," he whispered, starting to rise.

She reached out, her hand brushing his cheek—the faintest hint of life, of warmth in those dark, vacant eyes. "You're a good man."

"Good?" A bitter smile crossed his lips at the thought. "How would you know?"

She slid down off the barstool, adjusting her skirt as she did so. "When your life depends on knowing whether a man will thank you or beat you when he finishes...you know."

And she was gone, moving away from his side. Harry set his glass down on the bar and rose, keying his headset. "She's going in. Do you trust her, Alexei?"

"More than I do you, *tovarisch*."

It would have to be enough.

11:46 P.M.

It had been years since he had been in Vegas—long enough that he had forgotten the effect it had on him. Omar leaned back against the leather of the sofa, trying not to stare at the Russian's companion across from him. A temptation of the flesh, calling the words of the *hadith* to his mind. *After me I have not left any temptation more harmful to men than women.*

Words of truth. How much could he be exposed to without losing his soul? Once again...

The sight of Andropov standing to his feet brought Omar's attention back to the matter at hand. "I believe that concludes our business of the night, *da?*"

The shaikh nodded. "The money will be transferred to your account once we've taken delivery of the weapons tomorrow morning."

"You are a cautious man, Tarik," Andropov replied, a smile crossing the oligarch's face. "I respect that. Still, it has been a very profitable deal for us both, has it not? I think it calls for a celebration, some entertainment at the end of a long day."

What was going on? Omar leaned forward in his seat, his jacket falling open—exposing the Smith & Wesson holstered at his waist. The Russian depressed a small button on the endtable, the same smile still plastered across his face.

They were outnumbered—the black man realized that. If this was a trap, they would stand no chance. But if this was the time of Allah's choosing...they would sell their lives dearly. Did the place of death matter to a *shahid?*

The door opened, the din of the club momentarily breaking the tense silence. One of the Russians stepped inside, holding the door open as six young women filed in—the foremost, a redhead bearing a bottle of champagne on a silver platter.

None of them out of their teens. *Whores.*

Images flooded his mind, perverse, sinful memories. Endless nights of his past. Omar buried his head in his hands, striving to block them from his mind.

No use. A tightness seized hold of his chest, and it felt as if he could hardly breathe, the voices around him fading into the background. He saw Tarik take a seat on the couch, watched as the shaikh splashed champagne into a tall flute—a wide smile on his face as he beckoned to one of the young girls.

He felt himself rise, the urge to escape filling his mind. He heard a voice call after him through the haze, felt a Russian hand descend on his arm.

The black man shook it off with an angry gesture, brushing past the bodyguards and out of the VIP, his steps hastening as he moved down the corridor. Walking as if in a dream.

"Omar!"

A shout, barely audible over the techno beat pounding the club. Harry's eyes came up, staring toward the VIP. It couldn't be—not so soon after they had sent her in. She couldn't be in danger.

The black man he had seen before came into the open, hustling, his powerful form carrying him across the club floor in long stride. His head down, brow furrowed as if in pain.

And then behind him, maybe fifteen feet back—the oldest of the quartet that had accompanied Tarik Abdul Muhammad, hurrying as if to catch up. He seemed as if he might call after his companion, then thought better of it.

"Alexei," Harry whispered, "I have eyes on two subjects. Heading for the exit."

"*Da.* I have them. Do you want me to follow them?"

It was a choice not without its temptations. "Negative. Our primary targets remain Andropov and Tarik. Stay in position."

The cold night air struck Omar like a blow to the face, biting into his cheeks. He staggered to one side on the sidewalk, hands on his knees as the taste of bile filled his mouth—his stomach heaving.

A hand touched him on the shoulder and he looked up into the eyes of Abu Kareem. "Are you okay, my son?"

Coming from the man who had brought him into the light…it was an ironic question.

"How, father," Omar began, his face distorted in anguish, "how can we expect the blessings of God on our mission? How, when we spit upon the teachings of the Prophet?"

He looked into the imam's face, expecting to find an answer there and finding only turmoil. "You must understand, Omar...this is war. A war against the enemies of Allah. And to this war a strong man may offer his courage, the strength of his arms, and it is blessed by Allah—even if the man himself is immoral and licentious."

A couple passed on the sidewalk and Abu Kareem waited for them to disappear into the darkness before continuing. "For a man to be moral is praiseworthy, but his morality...benefits no one but himself. Do not allow doubt to fill your heart toward Tarik and the others. Allah has a mighty use for their strength."

He turned as if to go back into the club, but Omar reached out, catching him by the arm. "Call me weak, if you will, but I cannot go back in. *Never*."

Abu Kareem paused. "What are you saying?"

"On the appointed day...give me another task." The black man's eyes brightened. "Give me the missile, my father. I can still do my part for the jihad—I can bring the Americans down from the sky..."

2:28 A.M. Central Time
Police Headquarters
Dearborn, Michigan

"You could really use some sleep." Marika looked up from her desk—or rather the desk she had commandeered—into the eyes of the negotiator.

She snorted. "Now look who's talking, Russ."

He leaned forward, resting both hands against the desk. "And you know that I'm right. Particularly when you're not even supposed to still be on this case."

"That's a matter of perspective." She shoved the stack of printouts to one side, picking up her cellphone. "As long as Nasir abu Rashid—or whatever his name is—remains our only lead, I'm indispensable. This is the only contact number he has, and there's no way D.C. wants to spook him by having a stranger pick up the phone."

There was that. And it was the only card she held.

"You can only stall for so long, Marika." The negotiator's voice was soft, as always. "And we both know it—particularly as sketchy as this CI's info is."

But it was a lifeline—back to the career that she had spent her life pursuing. Back to the career that she had, for all intents and purposes, ended the moment she broke into the mosque. "Look at this," she announced, tapping the screen of the laptop. "Nasir's CDL—the one we secured for him—was used to rent a tractor-trailer on the 18th. Right before they skipped town."

Russell's eyes lit up. "Does the company use GPS to keep tabs on their fleet?"

"Can't tell," Marika responded, reaching for her phone. "Do me a favor and get the S-A-C in here. He's going to want to see this."

1:30 A.M. Pacific Time
San Francisco, California

It wasn't a tactical environment he was comfortable in. He preferred to control the situation—staging an assault took time.

Korsakov lowered the binoculars, staring through the tinted windows of the Suburban at the front of the townhouse across the street.

Their target, dimly lit in the faint, cold glow of a streetlight. The door and windows were reinforced with iron grates, ruling out just about anything except an explosive entry. Beside him, their driver took picture after picture, the soft *click* of the camera shutter the only sound breaking the silence.

The Russian ran a hand over his day-old beard. "Are you sure it's that building?"

"*Da,*" Viktor replied from the back seat of the SUV, looking up from his laptop. "Our target is…maybe eight feet from the—the outer wall."

It was a two-story building, a garage underneath the living area. The front door was on the second level, ten concrete steps to the top.

They couldn't linger for the extended surveillance Korsakov would have preferred. Not in this neighborhood.

He glanced in the rear-view, spotting a young Latino leaning against a car about a hundred meters back—saggy pants nearly down to his knees, the glow of a lit cigarette between his fingers. And he was giving them the eye.

"Let's drive, Misha," Korsakov announced softly, tapping his driver on the arm. "Our friends are due into San Francisco International within the hour. I need to get Valentin on the phone."

1:39 A.M.
The abandoned mansion
Beverly Hills, California

"You don't know how much I regret those years…" Her father's face, drifting before her eyes. Old before his time. So different from her dim memories. *"All the time we lost."*

Lost…

Somewhere a door closed, a draft of cool air billowing into the kitchen. Carol jerked awake, struggling for a moment to place her surroundings. The dream had seemed so real. As if he was still alive.

But it was only a dream. A mirage of what could have been.

She raised her head from the granite countertop, instinctively checking the surveillance feeds open on the laptop. Nothing. Everything looked right.

But the door hadn't been part of the dream.

Where's Han? Movement in the shadows of the living room—her hand flew outward, fingers closing around the butt of the Kahr.

"Hold it, hold it." Han stood in the doorway, his hands out. Open. "Easy."

Of course, she remembered, all of it coming back. He had gone out. "Find anything?"

He shook his head, tossing his jacket on the island. "They're having a party five houses down. You can hear the music from here, if you're outside. Andropov has a few lights on. No movement. Any word from Harry?"

"Nothing."

The former SEAL swore under his breath. "This feels just like the old days. All of it. Except we never worked in the US."

She saw his fist clench as he stared off into the darkness, his jaw moving, but no words coming out. "And you know the sick part? I enjoyed it. Despite all the deployments. Despite all the times I left in the middle of the night. Despite all the time I spent away from Michelle and kids. I loved every minute of it." He paused, as if uncertain whether he dared continue. "I was living my dream—never realized how I was hurting her until it was too late to do anything about it. Not a day's passed since that I haven't regretted the time we lost."

Lost...

2:07 A.M.
The club
Las Vegas, Nevada

The girl stirred beneath his arm, her thin fingers running down over his chest.

She had been good, Nasir thought, opening his eyes. Almost good enough to make him forget his peril.

Almost.

He reached out a hand, stroking her dark hair. She was gaunt, her ribs showing as she lay there on her side.

In the semi-darkness, he could see his brother's form sprawled over the white leather sofa near the other end of the lounge. The champagne bottle had been emptied in the course of the night. And replaced. And emptied again.

Nasir shook his head, attempting to clear away the fog. His eyes picked out the figure of the shaikh, his body almost concealed by cushions. He was still moving.

The Russian's bodyguards still flanked the door, undistracted by the bacchanalian scene around them. He had to find a way...

He lay back, forcing back the wave of panic that washed over him. Willing his breathing to slow.

Calm down. He had to contact the American FBI. Somehow.

He stared down at the prostitute in his arms, as if his solution lay with her. Maybe...

Her name? His brow furrowed as he tried to remember. The women had been paraded before them, like prize heifers in the market, the Russian calling out their names as they passed.

"Ileana," he whispered, a finger passing along her cheek. She raised her head from his chest, fear and surprise visible in those dark eyes.

He couldn't trust her, couldn't trust anyone. But he had no other choice. His left hand went out, groping around in the darkness for his discarded shirt. He pulled a fifty-dollar bill out of the pocket, extending it toward her.

"I need...a phone."

2:15 A.M.

"We have a problem, *tovarisch.*" Harry perked up at the sound of Alexei's voice in his headset.

"Just when I thought things were getting boring."

"I received a text from my man at the safehouse. Korsakov made a surveillance run through the neighborhood."

"Your man, Alexei? I thought you were just the consulate's head of security. The personnel at a safehouse...they would fall within the purview of the FSB, wouldn't they?"

The Russian swore in exasperation. "You know who I am, Harry. You've always known. But I'm not risking the lives of *my* people for your op. I'm going to order him to evacuate the safehouse before Korsakov returns."

"You knew the risks when we began playing—and you have more to gain from this than I do. If the tracker stops moving, Korsakov will know he's being conned," Harry retorted, his tone cold as ice.

"If I have to start shipping FSB officers back to Moscow in black body bags…" Alexei growled. "There's no, how would you say it, 'upside,' to that."

There would be no budging him, that much was clear from the sound of the Russian's voice. "I think there's another way to accomplish our ends."

"And that would be?"

Harry was about to reply when he looked over the railing, down to the club floor below him. Ileana had just emerged from the VIP, standing there in the midst of the crowd, buttoning her blouse.

Their eyes met through the flashing strobes and she put her head down, working her way through the boisterous crowd.

"I'm about to make contact, Alexei," Harry intoned, watching her ascend the stairs. "How did she escape your notice?"

"I was texting."

Harry stifled a laugh. "Heaven help us, you sound like my nephew. Eyes on the prize, *tovarisch*."

The young prostitute's eyes were downcast as she moved toward his table, steps furtive. Her pale skin was covered with a thin sheen of sweat, her hands trembling as she took a seat across from him.

"I did…as you asked," she began hesitantly. "But I learned only a little. They did not want to talk in front of us, I think."

It had been a long shot—a hope that the men would neglect operational security in the presence of the women and the liquor, as so many men had done, throughout the history of mankind.

Apparently not this time.

She cleared her throat. "The man who took me asked me to come out here, to bring him something. And I don't know how to get it."

"What is it?" Harry asked, leaning forward, taking in the look on her face.

"A phone."

5:30 A.M. Eastern Time
Graves Mill, Virginia

The sound of a door opening and shutting reached Thomas's ears through the cold morning air, an alien sound in the stillness. His head came up, scanning the ground through his binoculars.

Nothing.

"LONGBOW, I have movement." The Texan paused. "Someone's starting the car."

The information was so unexpected that it took Thomas a moment to react. They hadn't planned for this. Not now.

But it wasn't his decision to make, and Richards never hesitated. "Move in, move in. Prepare to execute on my signal."

Thomas pushed himself up, the loose folds of the ghillie suit flowing around him—a white ghost arising from the stubble of the snowy cornfield.

The dark muzzle of the Beretta led the way as he moved forward, clutching the pistol in both hands.

The moment when a surveillance mission went hot...

"The car started, David," Rhoda announced, the screen door of the double-wide slamming shut as she reentered the trailer. "No severed wires, no flat tires. No bombs."

Her voice betrayed her skepticism. He looked up from where he sat at the kitchen, an open box of .38 Special cartridges in front of him. The Ruger GP-141 in his hands was well-worn, the bluing almost entirely gone.

It had been years since he had held a gun, and his fingers trembled as he slipped a final cartridge into the chamber.

"I know you think I'm paranoid," he acknowledged, pulling himself to his feet. He swayed slightly and reached out for her hand to steady himself. "But I can't afford to underestimate him. Not again."

The Jamaican woman smiled finally, wrapping his left arm around her shoulders. His right hand hung down by his side, holding the Ruger. "Remember, David, the world's thought me dead for a long time. I know these fears. They're natural. Now, if we're going to go..."

Click-click. Nothing more over the radio, but it was enough to tell Thomas that Richards was in position, out there in the darkness. He found himself holding his breath, his body pressed against the siding of the trailer, the Beretta held low in front of him.

Safety off.

The light inside the double-wide went off, the parking lights of the Honda Accord the only illumination remaining.

Click-click. Get ready.

A pair of figures emerged from the door to his left, a woman and a heavyset man leaning on her shoulder. *Stevens?*

They had just reached the bottom step when the laser aimpoint of Tex's Glock came out of nowhere, centering on the man's chest. "Stop right there— let me see your hands!"

The Texan's shout didn't have the desired effect. The figures separated, the man standing there silhouetted for a moment against the faint glow of the parking lights. His hand coming up.

Gun.

The realization had barely entered Thomas's mind before the pistol spat fire, the report shattering the stillness of the cold Virginia night.

Instinct took over, the nightsights of the Beretta centering on target. His finger squeezing the trigger.

The 9mm slug caught the man high in the chest, sending him reeling backward. Thomas fired a second time and he collapsed onto the snowy ground, the gun falling from his fingers.

Threat eliminated.

Thomas moved forward to the side of the fallen man, kicking the revolver to the side. Out of the way. The woman was sitting back against the rear wheel of the Honda, seemingly in shock. "Keep your hands where I can see them."

He switched on his flashlight, looking down into the man's pale face, and his heart nearly stopped.

As if through a dream, he heard Tex's voice calling out, *"I'm coming in"*—heard himself acknowledge the warning. It seemed surreal.

The director…

He dropped to one knee in the bloody snow, his fingers closing around Lay's wrist—feeling for a pulse. Ever so faint. They were going to need the one thing they didn't have. A medevac…

2:39 A.M. Pacific Time
The club
Las Vegas, Nevada

Voices. The young whore and one of the Russian's bodyguards—at the door of the VIP. Fear flowed through Nasir's veins, and he fought against the urge to open his eyes.

He had tried to go to sleep after she left, but it was impossible, his body rigid with tension. The Americans could reason it away however it pleased them, but it was *his* life at stake here.

If she betrayed him…

Nasir felt the leather cushions of the couch shift as she straddled his body, bending forward to kiss him on the forehead. A small hand holding a phone slipped into the pocket of his jeans, and his heart began to beat again.

His eyes flickered open to see her smile. *Beautiful,* Nasir thought, relief flooding over him. He reached up, his hand finding the back of her head, his lips capturing hers.

Life itself was a beautiful thing.

2:45 A.M.
The abandoned mansion
Beverly Hills, California

"Do you have it on your screens?"

Carol paused, Harry's question still ringing in her ears—a strange feeling of disquiet seizing hold. A premonition of evil.

It had nothing to do with what they were doing. It was a feeling far more primal than that.

Her mind flickered back to the day her mother had lost her battle with cancer. She had known, before the call even reached her at work.

It was the same feeling.

"Are you there, Carol? Do you have a fix on the phone we gave the subject?"

"Y-yes," she stammered, shaken. She glanced over to find Han regarding her strangely. *Focus.* "Yes, I have his positioning data on my screen. Working on getting audio from the phone now."

Smartphones, she thought, trying to banish the misgivings from her heart. The average owner had little to no idea of the power of the device he held in his hand. It was a microphone, a camera, a tracking device, and—when compared to the technology that had existed when she had done her first hack—a supercomputer.

A few keystrokes and she was in, activating the phone's microphone with a single click of the mouse. Another moment, and the audio went streaming out live over her network, to both Harry and Vasiliev.

It took her a second to recognize the sounds, and then a flush spread across her face.

Vasiliev was the first to react. "Well, at least *someone* gets to enjoy their evening."

6:17 A.M. Eastern Time
Graves Mill, Virginia

He heard it long before he saw it, standing there in the darkness—a pair of chemlights in his outstretched arms.

The unmarked UH-60 Blackhawk came swirling out of the darkness, descending into the snowy cornfield. Its downwash threw up snow and stubble, buffeting Thomas in the face. He never even flinched.

Numb. He felt numb, as if he was living a dream. Two figures slid from the open door of the helicopter, the foremost man limping across the uneven ground toward him.

"Is he still alive?" Kranemeyer demanded. The DCS made a foreboding figure in the night, leaning heavily on his good leg. His black eyes seemed to take on a demonic aspect in the red glow of the chemlights.

Thomas nodded. "We've got him on a table in the trailer—Tex is with him, but it's not looking good."

"Have you dressed the wound?" This from the man behind Kranemeyer. It took a moment for Thomas to place his voice, and then he remembered—a surgeon on the staff of the Special Activities Division.

He nodded, turning to lead the way back across the cornfield. "The bullet—my bullet," he added, as if realizing it for the first time himself, "collapsed his right lung. The occlusive dressing sealed the wound, but the cavity hasn't expanded yet—not completely."

The surgeon shook his head. "There's only going to be so much I can do—we'll need to prep him for immediate transport to a Level One Trauma Center."

"That's not happening." Both men turned to look at Kranemeyer.

The surgeon took a step forward, his mouth opening in protest. "We're talking about the life of the DCIA."

"As am I," Kranemeyer replied, cold resolution in his voice. "He's been targeted for assassination—he was driven underground, and he preferred to let people think he was dead or taken hostage rather than face the alternative. And *my* people have risked their lives extracting assets from hostile countries because of it. He'd better have a good reason…or I'll kill him myself."

3:49 A.M. Pacific Time
The club
Las Vegas, Nevada

"They're moving." Carol's voice, over his earpiece. Harry's gaze flickered across the club, toward the VIP.

"Do you have eyes on our subjects, Alexei?"

"Negative."

A burst of static interference over the connection, and they heard a Russian voice. Clearly himself on the phone. "…don't care. Find Pyotr and don't take any of his crap. I want to know where he is every second of the day until this whole thing is over. Stay on him."

Vasiliev murmured a curse. "That's Andropov—I recognize his voice."

"And Pyotr…" Carol left the thought unfinished, but everyone knew what she was thinking.

Harry closed his eyes. Your only safety out in the night was in being able to stay one step ahead of a disintegrating situation. Manipulating it to your will.

Adapt. That was what made the spy. "Do you still have a visual?"

A moment's pause, then Carol replied, "Yes."

"You and Han need to make the snatch." He could hear her sharp intake of breath, hear the hesitation in her voice when she spoke again.

"I-I don't know if I can…"

"It isn't a question of *if.* Alexei and I won't be able to make it back to California in time. The two of you are going to have to grab him. Right away."

Silence. Then, "Have you seen Andropov and the Arabs yet?"

"No. You, Alexei?"

"*Nyet.*"

"The tracker is fifty meters away from your position and moving west," Carol announced. "I'm picking up street noise…there must be another exit from the VIP."

Harry pushed back his chair, nearly knocking into a dancing couple behind him. A blue strobe hit him full in the face and he ducked his head down, moving down the stairs onto the club floor. "Stay on them—we can't afford to lose track of them. Alexei, meet me on the street ASAP."

The rear doors of the dirty gray van opened and Nasir vaulted inside, taking his seat on the bench along the side of the vehicle. It was a work van, used to transport migrant workers around the city, and his nose wrinkled at the smell.

His hand slid into the pocket of his rumpled jeans, feeling for the cellphone. *There.*

Jamal slid in beside him, still chuckling. "Good, wasn't it, brother?"

Nasir felt himself nod, his sweaty fingers closing around the phone, running along the plastic case as he tried to pry off the back. He closed his eyes as more of the martyrs climbed into the van, forcing himself to focus.

The back of the phone came off with what seemed like an unnaturally loud *snap*, and Nasir's eyes darted around the darkened interior of the van, certain that someone must have heard it.

Nothing. They were laughing among themselves, backslapping over their prowess of the night.

He felt the exposed battery beneath his fingers, ever so close. Almost there…

The cold night air struck Harry in the face as he burst through the door of the club, descending the steps onto the street. Vasiliev was just a moment behind him, his silver hair glistening in the glow of the streetlight. "Where now, *tovarisch*?"

"He's northwest of you now—in a vehicle from the sound of it," Carol interjected. "Two hundred meters and building."

There was no time for indecision. "Never going to catch them on foot," he announced, turning to the Russian. "We'll need your car. I'll take up pursuit from here."

"On what?"

"I'll find something," Harry shot back, eyeing a blue and silver Harley parked near the curb. "Carol, can you overlay the GPS map with a street grid and send it to my phone?"

She didn't respond, and for a moment he thought their connection had been broken. "Do you copy?"

When she spoke again, she sounded surprised, uncertain. "He's gone, Harry."

Chapter 19

Two minutes. The figure on-screen hadn't moved. Carol's gaze shifted from the laptop down to the phone in her hand.

"Think he'll take the bait?" Han asked, rubbing his hands together. It was cold in the back of the panel van, but they couldn't leave it running.

"Our boy's a player," she responded. "I had to work back through his chat and SMS history to figure out which of his four girlfriends was the one you see on-screen."

Actually, all they could currently see of her was an ankle poking out from beneath the blankets, but that was beside the point.

"And?"

"None of the above." Carol rolled her eyes. "He's not just getting it on the side, he's getting it on the side of the side."

The former SEAL chuckled. "Had a guy like that in the Teams, a 'geographic bachelor', if you will. Never did figure out how he pulled it off."

"Envious?"

"No, more worried whether his pillow talk would violate opsec. Never did, that I knew. What did you send him?"

"A 'picture' from girlfriend #3. They had a fight last week and haven't made up yet. Which is why she wants to meet."

When she looked over, Han's face was serious once more. Pensive, even. As if he was remembering.

Carol looked down at her hands, unsure what to say. There were no words that could ease the hurt of those memories.

Movement on-screen and their target emerged from the tangle of blankets, the cellphone in his fist.

He ran a hand through his hair, a satisfied smile on his face as he apparently looked for his pants.

"You were right, he's coming out," Han observed. He reached into his jacket and pulled out a piece of dark cloth. "Put this on."

"What is it?"

"It's called a balaclava—they're worn by skiers," he replied, pulling one on over his own head. His eyes shone out from the black mask, a face suddenly stripped of its humanity.

Skiers were hardly the most notable end users, Carol thought, sweeping her blond hair up under the stretchy fabric. The world had yet to forget the image of the ski-masked Palestinian terrorist on the Munich balcony in 1973.

The former SEAL bent to one knee by the back door of the van, a riot baton clutched in his gloved right hand. "Give me the signal."

Her fingers moved across the laptop's trackpad, switching screens to the small webcam mounted on the mirror of the utility van. It was nothing fancy, a low-quality camera they'd picked up at Walmart. The image was grainy, but as she watched, the form of Pyotr Andropov entered the range of its lens, walking down the sidewalk toward his car.

Toward them. Perhaps it was the alcohol dulling his senses, but he seemed unperturbed by the darkness—never even noticed that the streetlight above his head had been smashed.

"Almost," she whispered. "One...two..."

It seemed dark, darker somehow than when he had gone in. Of course it was, Pyotr thought, attempting to shake the fog from his brain. The sun had barely been setting when he entered the frat house. That was it.

He reached into the pocket of his jeans, fumbling for his car keys as he moved toward the royal blue Lamborghini Aventador parked at the curb. He'd had the car for just over six months—a birthday gift from his father.

Footsteps behind him, he started to turn. Something hard struck him in the small of the back, excruciating pain rippling through his body as a metal bar connected with his kidneys.

A hand wrapped itself around his throat, gloved fingers closing over his mouth before the scream forming on his lips could even be uttered.

His head slammed against the hood of his car, his mind still struggling to process the situation as the hand on his throat tightened, slowly choking off the oxygen supply to his brain.

Zip ties bit into the flesh of his wrists as his arms were pinioned behind him. He heard a woman speaking in the background as things began to grow dark, her voice hushed as if she was speaking into a phone. "We have the package. On our way now."

And darkness closed around him...

7:03 A.M.
A convention center
Las Vegas, Nevada

The building had once been a popular convention center, but now it was nothing but empty space, the mammoth room feeling like a cavern. The first glow of the early morning sun trickled down from the skylights high above, giving an eerie aspect to the scene.

The recession had hurt everyone in Vegas—but most of the major players had managed to weather the storm, even if the price of survival for some of them had been getting in bed with the Russian *mafiya*. For convention centers like this one, they hadn't stood a chance.

Nasir could feel the hair on the back of his neck prickle as he surveyed the weapons laid out on the tables in the center of the room. His gaze flickered over the row of Kalashnikov rifles, their magazines stacked beside them. Seven magazines to a gun—each man of the assault team would be carrying over two hundred rounds into battle with him.

A frightening amount of firepower. To assault *what*?

He glanced over toward Tarik Abdul Muhammad as if hoping to find his answer there. As if he were trusted enough to be told.

The tall Pakistani was standing there in conversation with Andropov, beside a pair of rocket-propelled grenade launchers—maybe fifteen meters off. The Russian seemed to be doing most of the talking.

"...they're not going to deploy with everything they have. Not at first. But it will be enough. You can intercept their reaction force...*here*. Hit them with RPGs and automatic weapons. Pin them down. Overwhelm the system."

"I have set up an ambush before, Valentin," Tarik interjected, lifting his eyes to meet Nasir's. As if he had *felt* his gaze. Their stare only lasted a moment before Nasir looked away, but it left him trembling as if in the grip of a fever.

He fingered the dismantled cellphone in the pocket of his jeans. If he was found out...

There was no time to think of that. Not now. It would only paralyze him. Render him incapable of acting. He had to place the call.

Movement behind him, and he turned to find his older brother standing there, a smile on his unshaven face. "I can't tell you what this means to me, Nasir, that you are here with us. With *me*."

Jamal reached out, warmth in his dark eyes, drawing him close into his embrace. "You don't know how it frightened me—that I might have lost my brother to this apostate land. But this...this is how it should be, brothers together at the end. In the cause of God."

And he felt as if a knife was being stabbed into his own heart—the reality of the betrayal that must come.

"*Insh'allah.*"

10:22 A.M. Eastern Time
Graves Mill, Virginia

The CIA surgeon looked exhausted as he came out of the bedroom. He stripped off his surgical gloves and threw them in the trash, not even looking at Kranemeyer or Thomas.

With a heavy sigh, he turned on the kitchen faucet full blast, splashing cold water over his face before turning to face them.

"What's your verdict?"

A shrug. "I've inserted an endotracheal tube—he's breathing, though still with difficulty. He's lucid, you can go talk to him if you want, but I don't want you to tire him. Things are still very delicate." He cast a pointed look at Thomas. "We're very lucky that the second bullet smashed his collarbone instead of going into the lung along with the first. I don't think I could have patched two holes."

Kranemeyer rose, pushing back his chair. "I'll go speak to him."

"One moment, Director. How soon can we talk about moving him to a real hospital?"

"I don't know," the DCS replied. "Why?"

"I can only leave the ET tube in for a few days, at the outside. Longer than that, there's a high chance for infection. For pneumonia. Or both. Given his weakness, the wounds he apparently sustained in the assassination attempt, his body won't be able to fight it off."

Those dark eyes flashed. "I fully realize what's at stake here."

"No," the surgeon shot back, his gaze unwavering. "I don't think you do, so let me make it abundantly clear. If Director Lay contracts pneumonia, he will die. It's no more complicated than that."

The DCIA was a wreck, bloody bandages swathing his upper chest. "You look worse than the devil, David."

Lay coughed, managing the faintest of smiles. "That...must be an improvement," he whispered, motioning Kranemeyer closer to the bed. "Nichols?"

Kranemeyer hesitated, casting a glance toward the open door of the bedroom. "He has your daughter, David. Took her out of Langley at gunpoint the morning you were—well, the morning we all *thought* you died. The Bureau believes he was involved."

The director closed his eyes, a look of pain crossing his features as he shook his head. "No...orders. *My* orders."

"Who did this?" Kranemeyer demanded, easing himself into a chair by the bed. Stress brought on the pain from his leg, and it was throbbing now—a memory of a limb that no longer existed. "Who is targeting you, David?"

Fear. It took him a moment to place the emotion on Lay's face, but it was fear—and Kranemeyer found that more frightening than anything else. The DCIA had been running ops since the Cold War. If he was afraid...

He reached out a feeble hand, seizing Kranemeyer's wrist. "Ask Rhoda to come in."

Reluctantly, Kranemeyer moved toward the door, calling out for Stevens. The Jamaican woman appeared almost at once, slipping past him to stand beside the bed.

Rhoda Stevens. Kranemeyer could still remember standing there beside her casket, embracing her sister. Their grief that day. Had she known then—that it was all a charade?

"The key," Lay motioned. "Give him the key."

He could feel her eyes on him, eyes full of skepticism. Distrust. "Are you sure, David?"

A nod. Without another word, Rhoda turned to leave the room, beckoning for Kranemeyer to follow her across the narrow hall of the mobile home.

"It's been a long time, Barney," she observed, pushing open the door to her bedroom.

"Not my fault, Rhoda." He stood in the doorway, watching as she opened one of the drawers of her dresser, sorting through folded running shorts. "I attended your funeral."

"My sister told me." She seemed amused by the thought, and he found that it nettled him.

"Why?"

"Circumstances…at the time it was best for me to simply disappear. Just like it is for David now. It's something I learned a long time ago—people's search for you ends at the grave. But you're not going to let him do that, are you?"

"He's the DCIA," Kranemeyer responded. "This goes with the territory. Do you have something for me?"

She straightened, laying a small key on the top of the dresser. "This."

The metal face of the key was stamped *Alibek-376A5*. As he reached out to take it, her eyes flashed a warning. "This is only the beginning."

8:28 A.M. Pacific Time
Andropov estate
Beverly Hills, California

Korsakov was quite sure the pool table in the billiard room of Andropov's mansion had never been put to such unorthodox use.

Pool balls cleared away, Yuri had a rude wooden frame laid out on the table and was affixing plastic explosives around the outside edge to form a breaching charge.

"It's good to have you back with us, *tovarisch*," Korsakov said as he entered the room, Viktor at his side. It was only half a lie. He might have difficulty getting along with his second-in-command, but having him at the other end of the country was a headache he was glad to have over and done with. "How soon will your charges be ready?"

"Thirty minutes," was the reply. "What's the plan?"

Korsakov motioned for Viktor to hand him the laptop, and he opened it up on the pool table in front of Yuri.

"You and Kalnins will enter the building behind the target structure and make your way to the roof to provide overwatch and cut off any escape. I will accompany the entry team into the house, using your breaching charge on the front door."

The ex-*Spetsnaz* sergeant gave him a grudging nod. "It should work, but I was there in West Virginia. Let's not underestimate this man again. We'll go in under the cover of darkness, I assume?"

"No," Korsakov replied. So often the answer to the complex problem was to do the unthinkable. Take your opponent off-guard. "We strike at noon."

8:35 A.M.
The abandoned mansion

From Han's account, it seemed that the kidnapping had gone as well as possible, Harry thought. Those ops were always dicey—the target turned out to be accompanied, there were witnesses—any one of a hundred things.

Pyotr sat in the chair opposite him, bound hand and foot to the legs of the chair. Hooded.

Claustrophobia. Most people were susceptible to it, particularly when it was brought on by sensory deprivation. In training at Camp Peary, Harry had seen trainees panic within moments of the hood going on.

He had nearly done so himself, the first time. The fear was so overwhelming. It was one of the most effective methods of torture on an untrained subject—and, like all good methods, never required physical violence. The human mind would supply all the violence necessary.

And two hours without sight had worked its effect on Pyotr, as the stench proved. He had soiled himself, urine soaking the leg of his pants.

Harry glanced over at Vasiliev, a masked, silent figure there by the door. The two of them had been back from Nevada a scant twenty minutes.

Time enough. He stood, dragging his chair loudly over the marble tile of the bathroom. The young man flinched as if he had been struck, beginning to whimper again.

"What do you want? I can pay you—my dad has money, lots of money. You can be rich men, all of you, but you have to let me go!"

Harry pulled the ski mask down over his face till only his eyes, his lips, were visible. They couldn't risk him being able to identify any of them.

"What do you think, *tovarisch*?" Vasiliev asked, a smile playing at the corners of his mouth.

"I think," Harry responded, ripping the hood off Pyotr's head without warning, "that there is nothing we *have* to do. Do you understand me?"

The boy sat there, blinking like an owl caught in the daylight—eyes wide and trembling with fear. Harry circled around to his front, Pyotr's wallet open in his hands. "Money? Do you think we're after your father's money?"

Hope flickered in those eyes. "Everyone wants money."

"They do?" With a sudden gesture, Harry pulled a handful of hundred-dollar bills from the wallet, holding them up before the boy's eyes. A Bic lighter appeared in his right hand, flame spurting from the tip. "Are you sure?"

He could see the hope turn to uncertainty, then fear—the flame reflected in their captive's eyes. Another inch and the flame leaped from the lighter to the paper, igniting first one bill, and then the next. And the next.

Harry held on until the heat licked at his fingers, then threw the flaming mass onto the marble floor between Pyotr's bare feet, eliciting a scream.

He stepped in close until his lips nearly touched the boy's ear, his voice no higher than a whisper. "Do you think I care about your money?"

A vigorous shake of the head. The arrogant confidence of the college frat boy was long gone, tears sliding down his cheeks.

"Then you'd better start thinking of what you might have that I could want," Harry observed, pulling the hood back over the boy's head as he thrashed against the chair.

"Think fast. You're on the clock."

9:01 A.M.
Las Vegas, Nevada

"No, no, you listen to me, Sergei." Andropov swore under his breath, glancing over at his bodyguard. "I don't care what you were planning—I'm paying you and *this* is now what I expect you to do. I want you to find out where he's gone."

A pause as he listened to Korsakov on the other end of the phone. "No, he's not with one of his girlfriends. How? Because he drives them everywhere in his car. And we've found it—and the girl that he was sleeping with last time anyone saw him. This is important to me, Sergei. I have a business deal going down in the next few days and I don't want him running around loose."

He listened for another long moment, his face growing more pained by the moment. "You still have the tracker beacon, *da*? Then here's what you will do. Find Pyotr. If you can't find him by nightfall, finish the contract."

The oligarch shut his phone with a vicious gesture, a curse exploding from his lips. A cold wind swept over the Vegas parking lot, tugging at the edge of his coat. "Do you have a son, Maxim?" he asked, turning to the head of his security detail. The man was former MVD, Russia's infamous Ministry of Internal Affairs, and had won the right to wear the much-coveted maroon beret during his time in the service. Short, heavily-built, and in his late forties, he worked through punishing exercise routines on a daily basis, hammering his body into shape.

He never stopped scanning the surrounding cars for threats, but his lip curled up in what passed for a smile. "Not that I know of."

Andropov actually laughed, clapping his security chief on the shoulder. "Come, let us go. I have a—how do the Americans say it? A prodigal son to find…"

12:39 P.M. Eastern Time
Outside Alexandria, Virginia

There was a paper trail associated with renting a storage container, but it was relatively minimal compared with other means of storage. Nothing Lay wouldn't have been able to fake, particularly if he'd had the help of Rhoda Stevens.

Kranemeyer stared through the heavily tinted windows of his Suburban toward the Alibek E-Z-Store storage facility across the street, taking in the single dome security camera near the gate.

That was the risk. If the NSA were wired into the camera's feed—and these days it was never safe to assume that they weren't—his appearance would raise red flags. Cause them to take a look at the facility.

He stared down at the key in his hand. He'd come this far. Might as well play it through to the end.

Reaching for the Washington Senators baseball cap on the passenger seat, Kranemeyer pulled it low over his forehead, wrapping a long black scarf around his neck and lower face.

Time to roll.

Bluffing his way past the rent-a-cop at the front gate hadn't been hard, Kranemeyer thought twenty minutes later, moving on foot down a long row of self-storage containers. It had been painfully obvious that the man had never seen a security threat greater than a rowdy group of teenagers bent on vandalism.

Which was to his advantage. The container matching the number on the key was nearly all the way to the western end of the facility and Kranemeyer paused, glancing toward the security fence. No passerby in the parking lot outside. No further cameras that he could detect.

The door came open with a heavy, grating noise—metal against metal. He cringed, his eyes adjusting to the darkness as he peered inside.

Nothing. The storage container was, to all appearances, empty.

Dropping to his good knee, Kranemeyer ran his fingers along the concrete edge of the container, feeling for a tripwire, a pressure mat, anything. He was being paranoid.

At length, he straightened, stepping cautiously into the interior of the steel box.

He hadn't been sent out here to find an empty box, that much he knew. The fear in Rhoda Stevens' eyes had told him that.

There was something here…unless someone had traced this container back to David Lay and already removed it. If they had managed to make the connection, getting in wouldn't have been hard, as he had proved.

Nothing to do but cover every inch.

10:05 A.M. Pacific Time
The Bellagio Hotel & Casino
Las Vegas, Nevada

"Ah, Ms. Morgan, it's good to finally meet you." Brooke Morgan looked up to see the Bellagio's events manager striding across the ballroom toward her.

The young woman smiled, reaching out her hand. "Likewise—we've talked on the phone so many times. I love what you've done with the room."

The "room" might have been an overly casual way to refer to the Bellagio's 38,000-square-foot Tower Ballroom, but the events manager didn't seem to take offense.

"I certainly hope it meets your expectations."

"It surpasses them," she replied, flashing him another dazzling smile as her gaze took in the room—the red, white, and blue bunting-bedecked stage, a color scheme that spilled over onto the hundreds of round banquet tables. "You've made all the arrangements for the evening's entertainment?"

"Of course. The evening for your guests will begin here, with the banquet and speakers, then transition into the Cirque du Soleil for a special evening performance of 'O'. A delightful way to spend Christmas Eve, I should say."

"And Congresswoman Gilpin wished me to convey her most sincere thanks for the way your hotel has gone out of their way to accommodate our requests. The Cirque du Soleil is indescribably magnificent."

"It is truly our pleasure. As you know, our owner was one of the congresswoman's most enthusiastic backers. He couldn't be more happy to play host to this celebration of her victory."

Brooke nodded, an almost wistful smile crossing her face. "It's been a hard-fought campaign. I finally got home last week to see my kids. First weekend I had spent at home since September."

"Then, may I say, that this celebration is most well-deserved. There's no place to party like Las Vegas, and no one knows how to party like we do here at the Bellagio…"

1:23 P.M. Eastern Time
Outside the Alibek E-Z-Store Storage Facility
Alexandria, Virginia

It had taken Kranemeyer three searches of the storage container before he'd finally found what he had been looking for. A small USB thumb drive tucked beneath a lip of metal near the back of the container and secured with duct tape.

He swung his leg up into the Suburban and closed the door, holding the drive up to the light. If it was password-protected, he was going to be in difficulties. With Carter still in CIA protective custody and sequestered down at Camp Peary, he could hardly turn to him for aid...

Opening his laptop, he plugged the drive into the USB port on the side, waiting as the computer booted up.

His eyes drifted out the window, locking in on a passing vehicle. It was nothing...probably, but he hadn't seen a great deal of traffic. He reached inside his overcoat, pulling the H&K USP semiautomatic pistol from its shoulder holster and laying it on the center console, within easy reach.

A Welcome screen appeared, and Kranemeyer entered his password, swearing as his fingers played clumsily with the trackpad. Computers were a necessary evil of life in the 21st century. Didn't mean he had to be happy about it.

The USB drive opened automatically, revealing several scanned documents and a folder full of .jpegs. He turned to the pictures first and clicked to open one. It had clearly been taken from a distance, probably with a high-powered telephoto lens.

Agency surveillance?

Two men, standing beside a park bench, a briefcase in the taller man's hand. But it was his companion that caught Kranemeyer's attention—the silhouette. So familiar.

He clicked to advance to the next picture, and his breath caught in his throat. The man had turned ever so slightly, his face standing out in full relief.

Yes. It was him. And they were in more trouble than he could have imagined.

Kranemeyer dug his cellphone out, dialing a number from memory. Two, three rings.

"Roy, we need to meet." No pleasantries. No time for such things—he was too shaken.

He remained silent as the man on the other end of the phone responded, barely listening. Rhoda Stevens' words still ringing in his ears.

"This is only the beginning."

2:09 P.M.
The White House
Washington, D.C.

Cahill's arrival in the Oval Office was as unceremonious as it was unannounced. He was ushered in through the protective ring of Secret Service by Curt Hawkins himself and shown in to see the President with only the briefest of delays.

Hancock looked up from the Resolute desk as his chief of staff entered. "Tell me you have some good news, Ian."

The faintest hint of a smile passed across Cahill's face as he collapsed into a chair. The Irishman was typically rumpled, his tie loose around his neck—his sweat-stained collar unbuttoned. "You might call it that. You'll be sitting behind that desk for another four years."

The President fairly beamed. "I take it Senator Coftey was able to bring the Justice around?"

"As I had told you he would," Cahill replied. "I've known the man for years—he didn't become a Chief Justice by being a risk taker. Given a hard decision...and the right inducements, of course, he'll make the safe choice."

"And they say the Court is apolitical," Hancock mused, getting up from his chair. There was a decanter on the endtable and he poured three fingers of brandy into a crystal snifter, handing it to Cahill.

"How soon will they make their announcement?"

"On the first of the new year, in a 5-4 decision. You'll be sworn in on the 20th, right on schedule. We owe Coftey...his willingness to run with the ball on this has been invaluable."

"I always pay my debts." The President raised his glass. "To success—and the damnation of our enemies."

"As ever."

11:54 A.M. Pacific Time
The abandoned mansion

"How are things coming along?" Harry asked, coming back through the kitchen.

Carol didn't look up. "Fine. I nearly have the botnet formed, just need to exploit a couple dozen more computers before I can run a test."

"A botnet?" The term seemed familiar, but he couldn't place it.

"This one laptop doesn't give me nearly enough firepower to bring down the grid. LA has used DHS dollars to harden their defenses over the last few years. I've been working since last night to build a network of a couple hundred infected computers. With their combined power, I can brute-force the system and bring it down—at least for a few minutes. Long enough for you and Han to get in. That's the good news."

"And the bad news?"

"From the energy outputs I'm seeing, it looks like Andropov's security system is hooked to his back-up generator, located in the poolhouse...here," she said, tapping the satellite photo with her index finger.

"How long does that give us?"

She shrugged. "Some of the modern generators...ten, fifteen seconds."

Yeah, that didn't give them much time. Not much time at all. He cast a glance toward the door of the bathroom where Pyotr was imprisoned, his mind working through the possibilities. But she wasn't done talking. "You might be able to get over the wall and to the door of the house in that time, but then..."

"There's a security keypad on that side patio door, isn't there?"

"Yeah." She finally glanced up to meet his eyes. "What are you thinking?"

"I'm thinking that Pyotr is going to give us those codes."

A look of pain spread across her countenance. "Harry..."

"What's wrong?" It seemed an inane question, but it was the one he asked. A human impulse.

"I don't know." Carol looked away, as if unwilling to face him. "He's just a kid—a big, stupid kid. The panic on his face when Han ambushed him..."

She was silent for a long moment. "How do you deal with it—living life this way?"

He yearned to reach out, to hold her in his arms...to tell her that everything was going to be okay. But it wasn't, and the walls he had built around his heart were too high, no matter what he might have wished.

"The same way you deal with anything in life," he responded coldly. "Just keep putting one foot in front of another. Keep moving forward. Do what you have to do."

"The end justifies the means?" she asked—a bitter echo of himself, years earlier. A lifetime ago, or so it seemed.

He shook his head. "No...no it doesn't. It's just a matter of deciding which set of consequences you can live with. That's all it is, in the end. Nothing more complicated."

Chapter 20

There'd been a six-pack of Coors in Stevens' refrigerator. Past tense. There were only two left, including the half-empty one in Thomas's hand as he leaned against the counter.

Nothing from Kranemeyer. He'd been gone for hours now, leaving them to guard the DCIA. Yeah...

He felt someone's eyes on him and looked up to see Tex standing there in the doorway.

"How's it going, bro?" he asked, registering somewhere in a dark recess of his mind that he was slurring the words. He hadn't had *that* much to drink.

Tex crossed the kitchen, a strange look on his face. *Darkness.* "Just look at you."

Before Thomas could react, the Texan reached out, ripping the beer can from his grasp and crushing it in one of his big hands.

"What are you doing?" Froth bubbled over the Texan's fingers as he threw the demolished can into the sink.

"*You* are on duty, soldier," he replied, taking a step into Thomas's zone—a dark light shining from his eyes. It was the closest Thomas had seen the big man come to displaying emotion, but he ignored the warning sign.

"I...can handle my liquor," he replied, putting up a hand. "You know that."

"Handle it?" Tex demanded. "You *shot* the Director of the CIA. My op, my responsibility—you pulled the trigger."

"It was dark, okay? He fired first."

"And you'd been drinking." It wasn't a question, but a simple, cold accusation, hanging there between them. "I know Harry had been covering for you with Kranemeyer, before all this started. He never said anything, but he had to be."

The Texan paused, as if choosing his next words carefully. "I won't."

4:09 P.M.
1806 I Street
Washington, D.C.

"Convivial men the world over find pleasure and recreation in the association of others so minded." So began the 1884 charter of the Alibi Club, but its founders had faced a far different world.

As for Kranemeyer, he was in anything but a convivial mood as he approached the 19th-century Italianate brick townhouse that housed D.C.'s premiere men's social club. On foot, he carried the laptop in a carrying case slung over one shoulder.

The building itself was nondescript, the DCS thought, waiting on the doorstep. So unremarkable that the National Register of Historic Places didn't even list the name of its architect. Which was as it should be—perfect for men who valued their privacy.

The Alibi Club had never numbered more than fifty, but they had counted among their ranks Washington's most powerful in their day, including Allen Dulles—the director of the CIA during the '50s.

He left his coat with the doorkeeper, retaining the H&K under his suit jacket as a young blonde woman ushered him up a flight of stairs and into a second-floor den, its walls decorated with over a century's worth of memorabilia. The room exuded warmth, flames crackling in the fireplace to Kranemeyer's right. Age. *Power.*

"Barney," a familiar voice greeted him, a silver-haired figure rising from a leather chair on the far side of the den. "It's been far too long."

"Likewise, Roy," Kranemeyer responded, managing what passed for a smile as he reached out to shake the senator's hand. Currently on his sixth term as a U.S. Senator from Oklahoma, Roy Coftey was the chairman of the powerful Senate Select Committee On Intelligence. And, in another life...a Special Forces lieutenant. "You had enough of the Democrats yet?"

The older man laughed, a throaty rumble rising from deep within his belly. "They were good enough for my daddy, and his father before him. I reckon that means they're good enough for me."

Kranemeyer shook his head. "Give me that old time religion..."

"That's right, Barney. Melody, will you bring us something to drink?" His attention turned from the blonde back to Kranemeyer. "You still take your bourbon neat?"

"Yes."

"Then just bring us up a bottle." The senator watched her sashay out of the room, an appreciative smile on his face.

"That girl's got a great future ahead of her," he observed, giving Kranemeyer a crooked grin that left little doubt as to who controlled that future or what she might be doing to obtain it.

She was hardly the first.

"Be careful, Roy." The DCS paused. "A man in your position...can be vulnerable to blackmail."

Coftey inclined his head to one side. "The only folks in this town who lose sleep over blackmailers are the people pretending to be saints. Everyone knows I'm an old goat."

"If you say so."

Before they could say anything further, the blonde returned, bearing a bottle of Maker's Mark and a pair of shot glasses on a silver tray.

"So, tell me, Barney," the senator began, splashing the amber liquid into both glasses. He passed one over to Kranemeyer. "What's on your mind?"

Kranemeyer took a sip of his bourbon—waiting until the woman left the room, closing the door behind her. "Something's come up and I need your advice, Roy...no, forget that. I *know* what has to be done. I just need air support."

Coftey straightened in his chair, a glint entering his eyes. He was still a warrior, Kranemeyer thought, regarding his old friend carefully.

Still the same man that, in the early months of '67, had led his Special Forces team across the border into Cambodia as part of Operation *Daniel Boone*. He knew what it was like to be out there, on the edge of the world. Knew what it felt like to have politicians trying to push you off.

"Go on," the senator urged, gesturing with his glass. "What's this all about?"

"The assassination of David Lay," Kranemeyer said quietly, opening up his laptop case. "I believe that I know why he was killed—and who was behind the hit."

"Then why are you here? You should be talking to the FBI."

The DCS rose and placed the laptop on the edge of the desk. "That's not an option. Not yet. Look at this." He clicked through the first couple of photos.

Coftey's brow furrowed as he stared at the screen. "That's the Deputy Director, isn't it?"

"It is." Kranemeyer took a deep breath. "The photos and accompanying documents provide conclusive proof that Michael Shapiro has been passing CIA secrets to the Iranians over the last few months, at least as far back as Operation TALON."

"The hostage rescue, correct?" Coftey asked, staring intently at the screen.

"Yes."

"Who took these, Barney?"

"David Lay, to the best of my knowledge. Of several meets between Shapiro and members of the Iranian delegation to the UN. The man in the picture here is head of security for UN Ambassador Nasrollah Najafi. The PDF files are scanned pages of CIA documents with notes in Farsi scribbled over them. Apparently print-outs of the documents Shapiro passed to him."

The senator shook his head. "How would we—or Lay—
have access to *those*?"

"I have no idea. Unless David went behind my back and commissioned members of the Intelligence Support Activity for an off-books mission…"

"But you're certain that all of this is genuine?"

"Yes. And I believe that it caused Lay's death."

For a moment, the senator sat there in silence, clicking through the photos. At length his face hardened. "If what you say is true, then we have a decision to make."

We. That was promising. "And that is?"

"You know that none of this would be admissible in court. We can't play this that way. Which is why you came to me." Coftey paused, ice-cold fire dancing in his eyes. "Which begs the question: how far are you willing to go?"

1:57 P.M. Pacific Time
The abandoned mansion
Beverly Hills, California

"Andropov is back," Han observed, lowering the binoculars from his eyes. "And maybe eight men with him. Only one of the Mercedes came back."

"Probably out looking for Pyotr." Harry joined him at the window, staying a careful distance back from the glass. Far enough that the sun glare off the window would mask him from the eyes of anyone looking across the road. "You figured what—four in the house?"

"Five. And the pair of guard dogs."

Another complication that Han had observed patrolling the grounds the preceding afternoon. A pair of massive Central Asian Shepherds, or *Volkodavs*, as they were commonly known. Roughly translated from the Russian, the name meant "Wolf Crusher".

"Thirteen. An unlucky number." Long odds, thirteen men against their three. He glanced at his watch. "As for the dogs…Vasiliev will be here in thirty minutes."

"You think you can trust him?"

A hard question. Harry looked away, remembering the look in the Russian's eyes. *Pyotr is part of the contract.*

"No," he acknowledged. "But he's brought us this far. Might as well go all the way."

"Just like old times." A sad smile crept across the SEAL's face. "You know, I never thought I'd kill again, Harry. Funny thing—you never forget how. No matter how many years or how hard you try."

"I'm sorry. If there had been another way—"

Han cut him off, an edge to his voice. "You would have taken it, just so long as the mission was accomplished in the end. You haven't changed."

It was hard to tell whether that was praise or condemnation. Likely a mixture of both. "If you want out…"

Silence. Finally Han shook his head. "Like you say—come this far, we might as well go all the way. You think the van will give us enough height to get over the wall?"

"Close enough."

3:09 P.M.
Los Angeles, California

It was the little things that killed you. Always the little things. The dead leaves that concealed a sniper. The figure loitering on a corner near a parked car.

The shards of shattered plexiglass beneath a freshly broken streetlight.

Korsakov dropped down to one knee on the sidewalk, turning one of the rough shards between his fingers. The edge was sharp,

He heard the sound of footsteps behind him and turned to see Yuri approaching. "They smashed the streetlight before they took him," Korsakov announced. "Would have made sure the street was dark—plenty of shadows to hide in."

"They?"

"Hard to say. A man like Valentin…many enemies."

Yuri's face took on a dour expression. "As if *we* need any more of them."

Korsakov ignored his lieutenant's displeasure, his eyes roving the street for nearby security cameras. "The liquor store there on the corner. Take Viktor with you and persuade the proprietor to let you look through his surveillance tapes from last night."

"Viktor?"

"*Da*, and make it quick." The assassin cast a glance toward the west, the setting sun. "We're running short on time."

5:15 P.M. Central Time
Police Headquarters
Dearborn, Michigan

One had to love modern technology...when it worked. And right now, the GPS locator on the tractor-trailer Nasir abu Rashid had been driving wasn't.

Marika swore angrily, giving the computer screen in front of her a murderous look. Too much caffeine had her on edge. It had taken all day to convince the company to turn over their GPS records to the Bureau, only to have the signal trail die in central Colorado.

The alert had already gone out to the Denver field office and they were mobilizing half of the FBI team in Dearborn to fly into the region.

She took another look at the screen. The Rockies—the most forboding mountain range in the continental United States. And somewhere in those mountains, the trail of a terrorist sleeper cell had run cold.

Russell came bustling into the room at that moment, a small bag over his shoulder. "We're going," he announced without ceremony. "The S-A-C has given his approval."

That was, in itself, a surprise. Maybe her career wasn't over...just yet. "How soon do we leave?"

"Ten minutes. They've got a 737 on the runway at Detroit Metropolitan."

6:27 P.M. Eastern Time
Washington, D.C.

It was dark when Kranemeyer left the Alibi Club, night enfolding the city like a heavy garment. Rain was falling, mingled with sleet—slippery beneath his dress shoes. On the way back to his Suburban, he passed a panhandler on the street, the sign in his hands reading "Homeless Vet."

Was he? It was hard to say—for every veteran the government had left abandoned on the streets, there were two more using the claim of service as a meal ticket. More deceit, in a city full of it.

There's no going back, Barney. Not once you've started down this road.

Kranemeyer pushed the senator's words away as he levered himself up into the SUV, forcing himself to focus on the task ahead.

One thing and only one thing mattered. It wasn't justice, there was none to be had in this world. Right and wrong...those were issues to be decided at a later date.

They did this to my men in Cambodia, Coftey had said, gazing into the open flames of the fireplace. *Sent us out into the night and abandoned us. Never again.*

The DCS sat there for a long moment, in the darkness of the vehicle, sleet tapping against the windshield like a ghostly finger.

It was a personal failure. He was the spymaster, and he had never even suspected Shapiro, much as he might have disliked him. God only knew how many lives had been lost because of it.

Reaching inside his unbuttoned jacket, he retrieved the H&K USP from its holster, his movements slow and methodical as he screwed a suppressor into the muzzle. Practiced.

He caught a glimpse of his own face in the overhead mirror, hellishly illuminated in the red taillights of a passing car. An implacable Ares.

Do whatever you need to do, Barney—know that I have your back, all the way. Just don't let him walk.

The slide of the semiautomatic slid forward with a metallic *click*, chambering a cartridge.

Kranemeyer laid the weapon on the passenger seat beside him and shifted the Suburban into drive.

No one was walking away from this...

4:02 P.M. Pacific Time
Los Angeles, California

"*Nyet.* Nothing." Korsakov shook his head in disgust, speaking into the phone. The store surveillance feeds had been effectively useless. "Two people made the snatch."

He paused, listening to Andropov on the other end of the line. "They knew what they were doing—beyond that I cannot say. The license plate of the van wasn't visible from the angle of the camera. *Da,* I do have some idea of how many gray panel vans there are in LA...we passed eight of them on the way here."

It was maddening, the assassin thought, placing a hand against the hood of the SUV as he leaned forward. Finding Andropov's son was not part of his contract. Capturing Chambers was…which was why he had already dispatched Yuri and the rest of his team back to San Francisco to stage for the assault.

"*Da*, I think it's a very good possibility that they could be involved." Whether they were or not wasn't Korsakov's affair. It would put him one step closer to completing his primary mission. He listened for another long moment, his frustration building.

Viktor appeared at his side, laptop in hand, gesturing for his attention. "What is it?"

His eyes focused in on the documents displayed on-screen, and in that moment, everything changed. A maze of deeds and lease agreements, seeming dead ends leading back to one indisputable conclusion.

"Yes, yes, I'm still here," Korsakov stammered, in response to Andropov's query. "I have received new intelligence…the house in the Tenderloin—it belongs to the Russian consulate. It is an FSB safehouse."

Taking on the Americans was one thing. He had been on their radar for years—some of the best contracts available required that he work at "cross purposes" to them. But this…

His employer was still talking. And making less sense. His years of wealth and power seemed to have inured him to reality.

"That's all very well for you to say," Korsakov retorted, punctuating his words with an oath, "but *I* don't have the luxury of retiring to Tahiti in the arms of a brainless and buxom American. When all of this is over, I still need to work in Eastern Europe and I can't do that if the FSB is hunting me down. No, it *is* my concern."

Korsakov motioned to the boy to get back in the car, lowering his voice as he interrupted Andropov one final time. "Listen to me, Valentin. You have six hours. Find a way to remove the FSB protection from Chambers and the CIA officer—or find a new contractor."

5:04 P.M.
Las Vegas, Nevada

Nerves. Omar reached out to grasp the metal of the railing as he moved onto the last flight of stairs, only too aware that his fingers were slick with sweat. Even as the moment approached, Satan seemed determined to test his faith.

He glanced up the stairs into the eyes of the shaikh, trying to push past the doubts. *To this war a strong man may offer his courage…*

That the shaikh was strong was not in question—but still. The black man shook his head, attempting to banish from his mind the image of their leader there in the club, alcohol in his hand and a prostitute at his feet.

Haram. Forbidden since the days of the Prophet. Were they all to be damned in the end?

A low rumble passed overhead, the railing vibrating under Omar's hand as the building shook around him. Putting his doubts aside, he charged up the final few steps, reaching the side of the shaikh just as he pushed open the roof access door.

Cold air struck Omar in the face as he stepped out onto the flat roof, gravel crunching beneath his feet. The roar of jet engines buffeted his ears and he looked up to see the receding landing lights of a huge jumbo jet—that unmistakable symbol of American power—heading in for final approach to McCarran. It was close enough to see the landing gear extending from its massive belly.

He looked over to see the shaikh smiling there in the darkness. "Abu Kareem told me of your…reservations regarding our operation," the Pakistani said softly, reaching out to place a hand on Omar's shoulder. "I respect a man who knows his limitations—and understands how best he can serve the will of Allah."

He hoped that his doubt did not show in his eyes. Following the teachings of the Prophet was a *limitation*?

The shaikh turned abruptly, his eyes darting fire as he strode to the edge of the roof, looking out over the City of Sin. "You will have only one shot—and you must not miss. Can you do this?"

"*Insh'allah.*"

"And then there will be one final task for you."

6:03 P.M.
The abandoned mansion
Beverly Hills, California

"…you'll be the second person over the wall. The dogs will be your concern."

Alexei chuckled, squinting down the bull barrel of the Ruger Mark II semiautomatic in his hands. "If I should miss, *tovarisch*…they will be your concern soon enough."

"Then don't miss," Harry retorted, giving the Russian a baleful glare.

Han cleared his throat. "Are you sure you don't need me on the assault team?"

313

A nod from Harry. "Korsakov is still out there—hasn't done anything more than feint toward our bait at the safehouse. If he comes back…"

He lowered his voice, glancing toward the kitchen, where Carol sat with her back to them. Pulling together the last remnants of the botnet. "Her safety is of the utmost importance. If everything goes sideways, take her and run."

It was a strategic decision, but the accompanying risks…

"Body armor?" Vasiliev asked, shrugging as he screwed a suppressor into the threaded end of the Ruger's long barrel.

"Depends on how much time they have to react—more than likely by the time we're done."

The Russian smiled, tapping his forehead as if to indicate the aimpoint. "Then we'll plan accordingly."

7:21 P.M.
A spa
San Francisco, California

Find a way. Perhaps Andropov had taken that too literally, Korsakov thought, doubt surging back to the fore. The same doubts that had been plaguing him ever since he and Viktor had boarded the oligarch's private Sikorsky S-76 in Los Angeles for the helicopter flight to San Francisco. He forced a smile to his face as he made his way down the corridor toward the spa's sauna room, toward the man standing at the door.

Standing guard.

"Good evening."

"You can't go in there," came the brusque rejoinder, a hand reaching out to grab Korsakov's arm as he brushed by.

First mistake.

His fingers closed around the guard's arm like the teeth of a vise, catching him off-balance and pulling him forward till his head smashed into the drywall.

The man reeled backward, an arm up to defend his face as he fumbled inside his jacket. Korsakov glimpsed the leather straps of a shoulder holster— light glinting on the blued steel of a gunbarrel and he lashed out, his booted foot connecting with the man's groin.

A strangled cry of agony echoed off the walls, the half-drawn pistol clattering to the tile.

Last mistake, Korsakov thought—pivoting as the edge of his hand came down on the man's neck, hard against the bone.

The guard crumpled, sagging into Korsakov's arms as the assassin lowered him to the floor. The "fight", if one wanted to call it that, had lasted a scant forty-five seconds. Someone needed better security.

Retrieving the pistol with a gloved hand, Korsakov pushed open the door to the sauna, steam billowing in his face as he entered.

Droplets of water condensed on his face as he moved forward, making out the figure of a middle-aged man reclining on a wooden bench near the far corner of the room, arms folded across his naked chest. The target.

Alone.

If the rich and powerful had a weakness, it was that they valued their privacy. Solitude. Aside from the obvious benefits, it made Korsakov's job much easier.

"Who are you?" the man demanded, reaching for his towel as the assassin approached.

Too late. Much too late. Korsakov was on him as he rose to his feet, one hand closing around the man's throat—forcing him against the wall of the sauna.

"Dmitri Vournikov, I presume?" Korsakov sneered, staring down into the Russian consul's bulging eyes.

A frightened nod, but the older man made no attempt to resist. Surrender, survival, those were the watchwords of the bureaucrat. "What do you want with me?"

The words came out as a squeak.

Korsakov stared into the man's eyes for an eternity of a moment, watching him begin to gasp for breath—the awareness of his own impending death spreading across his face.

"Valentin sends his regards," he announced, allowing Vournikov to fall back against the bench, massaging his bruised vocal chords.

Korsakov stalked back to the center of the small room, drawing the bodyguard's SR-1 Gyurza from his pocket and ejecting the magazine. Fully loaded. "You know Valentin Andropov, do you not?"

Another nod.

"Good. Then you have some idea what I am capable of—and what I will do if you lie to me."

"*Da, da.*"

"Who is really in charge at *your* consulate?"

10:19 P.M. Eastern Time
"The Farm"
Camp Peary, Virginia

No Internet. No cellphone. No PDA. It had been a couple of decades since Carter had been so disconnected. He'd been given a computer when he first arrived in isolation at Camp Peary, an aging Dell loaded with a copy of *Fallout 3*. That had lasted all of two days—until his FBI wardens realized that he had reconfigured it to access the Internet through a vulnerability in the Farm's secure network…

And that was the end of his computer. In its place, someone with a bad sense of humor had supplied a few issues of *Dog Fancy*.

He wasn't a dog person. Never had been.

Maxwell…Carter shook his head, staring at the featureless wall of his "room". Prison, more like it. No one had been able to tell him whether his cat had survived the carnage at his apartment. The FBI wasn't particularly communicative.

The door opened and one of the CIA personnel entered. A tall, lanky man with a full head of silver hair, Carter knew him only as "Frank". He looked about as old as time itself, unsmiling mud-brown eyes shining out from a leathery face.

"You have a call," he announced, dispensing with the pleasantries and handing a small disposable cellphone to Carter without another word of explanation.

"This is Carter. Hello?"

"Listen to me carefully, Ron." Kranemeyer's voice, full of all the usual intensity. And something else. "I need you to do something for me."

Carter cast a glance toward the CIA man standing there by the door, arms folded across his chest. "We're not secure, boss."

"Frank? You can trust him. In fact, you're going to have to. I need you on-line and Frank is going to get you secure access."

"What about the FBI?"

Silence. Then, "We don't have another alternative. You'll just have to work around them."

Yeah. That sounded easy.

8:24 P.M. Pacific Time
The abandoned mansion
Beverly Hills, California

"She'll be there," Vasiliev observed, sliding a loaded magazine into the butt of his Grach. "You're prepared for that, aren't you?"

Harry finished securing the clasps of his body armor, pulling his shirt on over it. It wasn't heavy enough to stop a rifle bullet, but he'd have to make the most of it. Speed vs. armor, a trade-off as old as war itself. "Who do you mean?"

"Andropov's mistress," the Russian replied, glancing toward the kitchen. The fluorescent glare of a tripod-mounted construction light illuminated the scene, casting strange shadows against the bare white walls. "If we allow our assault to be slowed…"

His implication was clear. And he was right. There were only the two of them—they had to maintain the element of surprise if they were to remain alive.

Yet she was an innocent. Harry pulled back the charging handle of the UMP-45, chambering a round. He raised the submachine gun to his shoulder, making sure the sling was adjusted properly.

"No."

Vasiliev arched an eyebrow. "These lines you draw, *tovarisch*—they are pointless, aren't they? And who will know of your lofty principles when you're dead?"

"I will," came the quiet response. Harry turned without another word, leading the way into the kitchen. His stun grenades lay on the counter near Carol's laptop—their only edge once surprise was lost.

"Don't use these until I give the signal," he cautioned, handing one of them to Vasiliev.

"I *have* been to this dance a time or two," the Russian chuckled. "I think I can promise not to embarrass…"

His voice trailed off and Harry looked back to see Vasiliev's phone in his hand, a strange look on his face. He put up a hand for quiet. "I have to take this."

"Who?"

"Vournikov," Alexei replied, opening the phone. "*Da*? This is Vasiliev."

He listened for a long moment, a frown spreading across his face. "Where am I? I'm in a hotel at the moment—the Best Western out on the 405. No, no I'm not alone. Would you like to speak to her?"

The Russian winced, gesturing with his phone toward Carol.

She froze, slowly realizing his intentions. And the part she was being asked to play. Her throat felt dry as she reached out for the phone, bringing it up to her ear. "Who are you?" came the first question, a heavily accented Slavic voice ringing in her ears.

"Maria," Carol responded, her voice trembling ever so slightly. As many times as she had seen this done...

"And you're in a hotel with Alexei?"

She hesitated a moment before responding, making up the script as she went.

"*Si.* If that is his name?" She stammered. "*Por favor, senor,* only little English."

It was the final straw, and the other end of the line exploded in curses, punctuated by the gravelly command, "Put him back on, whore."

A smile crossed her lips as she extended the phone to Vasiliev, watching as he took it. His brow furrowed as he continued listening to the consul. "*Nyet,* I've been here most of the evening. I can contact my men at the safehouses to confirm, but if this has been done, it has been without my knowledge."

An emphatic shake of the head. "We have no men at that location—haven't for several weeks. Perhaps a break-in? *Da,* I can check. Just give me a couple of hours to look into it."

Vasiliev closed the phone and turned without warning, smashing it against the granite countertop.

"What's going on?" This from Han, entering the room behind the Russian.

"Someone got to him," Vasiliev replied, his eyes locking with Harry's. "Someone is putting pressure on Vournikov to find you—and they know for certain you were at the consulate."

The Russian's air of self-assurance was gone, completely gone. "He said all this?" Harry demanded.

"No," Vasiliev replied, reaching for his jacket. "It's what he *didn't* say. He doesn't trust me."

"Imagine that," Han murmured. Harry shot him a dark look, but if the ex-KGB officer had heard the remark, he took no notice of it.

"Do they have your location?"

"*Nyet.*" Vasiliev gestured to the destroyed phone. "This phone was set up to receive calls forwarded from my consulate-supplied Blackberry. It *is* in a motel on the 405. And that is the GPS signal they'll be tracking, if they get that far."

Someone had taught the old dog all the new tricks. But it would buy them precious little time. Harry turned toward Carol. "Is everything in place?"

A brief nod was her only reply, her long fingers dancing over the keyboard as she entered the final commands.

He looked down at the luminous dial of his watch, noting the time. "Let's do this, gentlemen."

8:49 P.M.
The Andropov Estate

Whenever possible, Valentin Andropov surrounded himself with people he knew. People he could trust, as far as that went. It was why he had hired Sergei Korsakov. And now he was wondering if that had been a mistake.

"*Da*, everything is cleared to proceed, Sergei," he replied over the phone, rolling his eyes at the head of his security detail. "Vournikov confirms that there are no consulate personnel on site."

His old comrade had changed over the years, despite his many successful contracts. Grown more cautious, hesitant even. And it was testing his patience. "Stop acting like an old woman, Sergei," Andropov snarled, biting sarcasm in his tones. "Just get in there and complete your contract. Call me when you have the girl."

He placed the phone on the desk in front of him, shaking his head as he glared across the room at his chief of security. "It appears that I may have overestimated Korsakov's usefulness. Sergei and his team...they won't be leaving the country."

The former MVD colonel nodded his understanding.

"Betraying a comrade is not something I would do lightly," Andropov said, using a guillotine cutter to trim the end of the hand-rolled cigar in his hand. "You understand this, Maxim. Sergei was an old friend—we fought together in the war. But I can no longer trust him implicitly. And that is something I require."

The oligarch fished a lighter out of his pocket, holding the open flame to the tip of his cigar. "I can count on you in this, *da?*"

There was no time for a response—the next moment, the room was plunged into darkness, the only illumination coming from the flickering ember at the end of Andropov's cigar.

"All the taxes I pay to this state," Andropov swore, "and still these blackouts."

8:51 P.M.

Impact. Harry landed in a bed of Serbian bellflowers, throwing out a hand to catch himself as he pitched forward. He heard movement behind him, Vasiliev surmounting the wall, but he paid it no heed.

The door. Propelling himself upright, he hurtled forward, feet pounding across the turf toward the patio, his eyes focused in on the keypad.

He was half-way there when he heard the dogs begin to bark.

Vasiliev heard them too, from his position in the shadow of the wall. He dropped to one knee, the suppressed Ruger Mark II clutched in both hands, a rock-steady grip.

Back in the van, the SEAL had called the weapon a "hush puppy", exhibiting a dark sense of humor that Alexei hadn't seen from him before. Time to see if it lived up to its name.

Volkodav. Wolf crusher. The dogs came around the corner of the house at full gallop, great slavering beasts. In Chechnya, they had accompanied he and his men into the mountains, but they seemed larger than he remembered. Perhaps it was all a matter of perspective.

Nichols was at the door, his dark form obscuring the keypad—but the dogs had him spotted now. Moving too fast...

No time.

Raising his voice just loud enough for the dogs to hear, Vasiliev spat out a command in Russian, one of several he remembered from that long Chechen winter.

They slowed, hesitating at the sound of the familiar command. The foremost dog let out a howl of frustration, turning his massive head toward Vasiliev.

Sight picture. The Russian's finger closed around the Mark II's trigger, squeezing ever so gently.

A whisper of death spat from the long, dark barrel, barely audible even to Vasiliev. The subsonic .22-caliber round slammed into the dog's nose from fifteen feet away, smashing through bone and tissue until it reached the brain.

The dog swayed sideways, sprawling across the grass. His companion turned, a snarl escaping his lips as he recognized the new threat in Vasiliev.

The Russian's first shot caught the dog in the flank, a splotch of red appearing against the fur as he sprung toward him.

Not enough.

320

Vasiliev rose as the dog charged, firing the Ruger offhand, emptying the magazine as his right hand stole toward the Grach at his hip, jerking it from its holster.

Last resort.

Eight rounds and the dog's body crashed against his legs, quivering in its death throes as the Ruger's slide locked back on an empty magazine.

It was only then, as Vasiliev stared down at the blood staining his pants, that he realized he'd been holding his breath ever since the dog charged.

He inserted a fresh magazine, putting one final round through the *Volkodav*'s head before looking up to find Harry waving him in.

This night had only begun.

8:53 P.M.

Overhead, the lights glowed once again, browning tremulously as the electricity surged back on, the massive generator straining to provide every last ounce of power consumed by the mansion. With a nod to Maxim, Andropov walked to the window, staring out at his neighbors.

Most of them were still in the dark, or operating under only partial power. Wealth had its privileges. Even his dogs had ceased their barking—whatever had startled them apparently having passed.

"Go check on Stacy, will you?" the oligarch said idly, tobacco smoke drifting from between his lips as he gestured to his security chief. "Tell her to put on something nice and be ready for me later."

8:54 P.M.
The abandoned mansion

"Are they in?" Han took his eyes off the SCAR's scope, looking back to where Carol stood.

He shook his head. "Impossible to say. The lights are back on—there's no sign of an alarm being raised. No way to check in with them, either."

Using the equipment Vasiliev had provided, Carol had been able to jam the cellphone network and shut down radio comms for a mile radius. A must for an assault of this sort, but it came with a downside: the equipment wasn't sophisticated enough to allow their own channel to get through without bringing everything back on-line. If Andropov was deaf and dumb, so were they.

The former SEAL lowered his cheek to the buttstock of the rifle, Harry's words running unbidden through his mind. A memory of an operation in the Egyptian desert. Years before.

"There's times when prayer is the only commlink that stays up."

"What did you say?" Carol asked from behind her computer, startling him with the realization that he had spoken aloud.

He hesitated…it had been so long. *Years.* "I said, 'Pray'."

Andropov's estate

Darkness. A low noise, voices—maybe from a TV, maybe not. The kitchen leading off the patio had been empty.

Vasiliev at his shoulder, Harry led the way forward down the hallway toward the light streaming from an open door. The plush carpet muffled their footfalls.

The voices were coming from a huge plasma TV mounted on the far wall as Harry came around the edge of the door. It was a soccer game, the excited voice of the sports announcer coming clearly through the speakers. A single man on the sofa, his face turned away from them as he watched the players. Alone.

There was a large bowl of potato chips on the endtable, right beside a Glock.

Threat. The UMP-45 came up in Harry's hands, iron sights centering on the man's temple. He felt a hand on his shoulder and looked back to see Vasiliev shaking his head, a finger pressed to his lips.

The Russian took a step around him—into the room—his eyes betraying no hint of emotion as he squeezed the trigger of the suppressed Ruger. A small ragged hole appeared just back of the target's ear and he swayed, his outstretched hand striking the table as he went down.

"Never make a sound you don't have to," Vasiliev announced, looking for all the world like a hunter surveying his kill as he stood over the corpse. The Ruger *was* far quieter than even Harry's submachine gun, but it had been a risk. "Room clear."

Harry glanced down at the red stain spreading over the fabric of sofa and nodded.

No time to second-guess the decision—even as he stood there, a voice called from out in the hall. "Sasha?"

Vasiliev swore under his breath, dropping to one knee by the corpse, his pistol aimed at the doorway. Waiting.

The man that appeared in the doorway was dressed simply, jeans and a t-shirt. There was a gun on his hip and with the knife in his hand he was peeling an apple.

He saw Vasiliev—saw the gun, his mouth opening in a perfect "O" of surprise. And those were the last things he ever saw.

9:00 P.M.

No signal. The oligarch stared at his phone in a mixture of astonishment and disgust. The blackout couldn't possibly have taken down the entire cellphone network, could it?

Maybe it was just *his* phone. Maxim could try to reach Vegas. He picked up the encrypted radio handset on his desk, keying the mike.

Static. Nothing but static. They had never failed him before. A sudden feeling of dread clutched at his throat, punctuated by a muted thud from outside the room.

A body falling.

He pulled open the center drawer of his desk, his gaze falling on the small Walther stashed there.

"Don't even think it." Andropov's head came up, his fingers trembling as his eyes focused in on the masked figure standing in the door of his study. Ice-cold blue eyes staring forth from the holes in a balaclava ski mask, lips curled upward in an inhuman smile.

The Heckler & Koch submachine gun in his hands was aimed at Andropov's head.

Stall. Buy time. The oligarch glanced at the dead radio, his foot creeping toward the silent alarm switch. "W-what do you want?"

"Many things," Harry replied in fluent Russian, centering the iron sights of his UMP-45 between the Russian's eyes. "Mostly answers."

Behind him, Vasiliev entered the room, weapon drawn. Five of Andropov' bodyguards were dead—eight more remained somewhere around the estate.

If their estimate was correct.

"Who paid you to facilitate the assassination of David Lay?" Harry demanded, circling Andropov like a predatory cat.

"I have no idea what you are talking about." The oligarch's voice was too confident—too sure of himself. As if he knew something they didn't. "You'll never leave here alive," he continued. "You know that, don't you?"

"I rather think we will." Holding the buttstock of the UMP-45 tight against his shoulder, Harry pulled his phone out of his pocket with his left hand, thrusting it toward Andropov. A picture of a bound and wide-eyed Pyotr filled up the screen. "We have your son."

To his surprise, Andropov began to chuckle, his shoulders shaking in a paroxysm of laughter. "That bastard."

Harry exchanged glances with Vasiliev. Somehow, somewhere along the way, they'd made a misstep. And they were losing control of the situation. Andropov took in their look and laughed. "Oh, I'm not disparaging Pyotr—I meant that in the *purest* sense of the word."

"What are you saying?"

"Pyotr…is not my son." The oligarch smiled. "A bastard, as I say. His mother…well, she was unfaithful to me. Perhaps you even know how it feels to receive such knowledge? As it happened, Pyotr was two months old when she was killed in a car accident. Brakes failed."

He was stalling. Harry felt the hairs along the back of his neck prickle with danger. "Get to the point."

Andropov shrugged. "My point? You don't have my son—you have a teenager with a penchant for spending my money. I had high hopes for him in those days, and he has done nothing but disappoint. Like his mother."

A dismissive wave of the hand. "Put a bullet through his head if it pleases you. It is no concern of mine."

He wasn't bluffing. Harry could tell that, reading the man's eyes. All the risks they had undergone—all for nothing. A grave miscalculation. *Fatal?*

Before he could even finish the thought, the doors of the study flew open, revealing the man they had identified as Andropov's security chief and two bodyguards standing there in the opening, SR-2 *Veresk* submachine guns trained on he and Vasiliev.

Checkmate.

9:05 P.M.
San Francisco, California

Everything was quiet, Korsakov thought, watching as two members of his assault team affixed a breaching charge to the door of the safehouse.

Too quiet. He didn't like the tactical environment—they'd had to dismount from the vehicles two blocks away and move in on foot. Too many things could go wrong, and they'd have no backup. "Do you still have a fix on the tracker?" he asked quietly, keying his earpiece.

"*Da*," Viktor responded from the SUV. "They're near the back of the apartment—moving into a room on the far left. Maybe a bedroom?"

Another few moments, and it wouldn't matter. Everyone in the house would either be dead or in their hands. "Are you in position, Yuri?"

A burst of static, and his second-in-command came on. "We have a clear line of sight on the back door."

Korsakov caught the signal from the man by the door and moved back, turning his face away from the blast and covering his ear with one hand.

Two outstretched fingers. One…

The shaped charges exploded, their concussive roar shattering the stillness of the night. The door flew inward, dissolved into flying bits of metal and plastic.

Korsakov was on his feet before the noise had even died away, following his team through the breach, weapon drawn. The clock was ticking.

9:05 P.M.
Andropov estate

"This little game is over," Andropov announced. "Put your weapons on the floor."

"Not from my perspective," Harry replied, his voice level. Conversational, even. The UMP-45 in his hands remained aimed at Andropov's head. "I still hold the trump card."

"What do you mean?" Came the demand from behind him, the security chief speaking for the first time.

"You can kill me, no doubt about it." His words were like ice, a cold, unemotional analysis of the situation at hand. "But know this: if you pull that trigger, I will kill Valentin before I die."

He could feel the man's gaze flicker from himself to Andropov and back again. Uncertainty. "You're mad."

That inhuman smile appeared once more on Harry's face, stretching at the fabric of the balaclava. "You really want to roll the dice on my mental state? If I kill your boss, you not only lose a job…you lose his protection. How do you think the US government will react once they realize that you helped terrorists enter this country?"

Fear. He could feel the indecision in the security chief. Time to end this, before reinforcements arrived to bolster his courage. His finger caressed the H&K's trigger, taking up the slack. "Ready to take that chance? Put your guns on the ground…or I put a bullet through your boss's head. Your choice."

"*Nyet,* Maxim," the oligarch exclaimed, his face contorted in fury. "Don't listen to him, you fool."

"*Now,*" Harry prompted gently. "Before I lose my patience."

The man threw his submachine gun on the floor, metal clattering against the wood as he motioned angrily for his companions to do the same. Harry nodded, circling until he stood behind Andropov, his weapon covering both the oligarch and his disarmed security team.

Alexei favored him with an incredulous smile. "Remind me never to play poker with you, *tovarisch*."

"I wasn't bluffing." He knew what had to be done, but it never got any easier. To take a man's life in cold blood. . .

He might have prayed for forgiveness, but that would have been a sacrilege against a God he had offended more than enough. He might have hesitated, but there was no time for that. The UMP-45 came up, its fire selector flipped to full-automatic.

A look of shock crossed the security chief's face, his empty hands coming up, as if the gesture would save him.

Harry squeezed the trigger.

9:07 P.M.
San Francisco

Nothing. Korsakov stepped into the opening of the apartment's main bedroom, the barrel of his Steyr AUG bullpup sweeping the empty space.

"Room clear," he announced softly, shooting his partner a puzzled look. "Give me an update, Viktor."

"The tracker hasn't moved. The back room on the far left from the entry point."

"That's where I am. And the room's clear."

The boy's voice began to tremble nervously. "It has to be there. I can pin it down within a five-foot radius, and that's where it is. I wouldn't lie to you, you know that."

"I know," Korsakov responded, taking a cautious step into the bedroom, his eyes roving for hiding places. The closet?

Motioning for his partner to cover him, he moved in. If it had been an American movie, he might have riddled the doors of the closet with his assault rifle, but his orders were to take Chambers alive.

If at all possible.

A faint metallic *whirring* noise smote Korsakov's ears—something moving, at his very feet. He jumped back, depressing the AUG's trigger almost instinctively.

Automatic rifle fire ripped through the air, sending the small object careening toward the wall of the bedroom.

There was no explosion, no return fire. Nothing. Willing his heart rate to return to normal, Korsakov lowered his weapon. *What was that?*

"*Tovarisch*—are you there?" Viktor's voice, hushed and nervous.

"*Da, da.* False alarm. What is it?"

"The tracker—it disappeared off my screens, just after you opened fire."

He took a step forward, examining the twisted metal and plastic that had once been a small vacuum cleaning robot. A hail of bullets had torn apart the brand name—*Roomba?*

Korsakov shook his head. *It couldn't be.* And yet it was—this was how the tracker had kept moving all over an empty apartment.

They had been played.

9:08 P.M.
Andropov's estate
Beverly Hills

The room smelled of blood—blood and brimstone, the sulphurous smell of gunpowder burning Harry's nostrils as he checked the zip-ties around Andropov's hands and feet. He wasn't going anywhere. Rising to his feet, Harry moved to the door of the study, motioning to Vasiliev.

On my mark. The security chief's lifeless eyes stared accusingly up into his face as he dropped to one knee beside the body, listening.

Voices, low and hushed. Very close. The rest of Andropov's security team? Hard to tell, but they were odds worth gambling on. A Hollywood superhero might have poked his head around the door and taken a look down the hall, but in the real world that was a fast way to get that head blown off.

Ready? He signaled, glancing at the former KGB officer. A nod.

Time to roll the dice. Harry pulled a flashbang from the front of his assault vest, pulling the pin and softly tossing the cylinder out onto the plush carpet of the hallway.

One. Two...

The blinding light of the stun grenade reflected off the study's windows, an ear-shattering wave of sound rolling through the house. There were few things on earth so disorienting, if you weren't prepared for it.

Now! Harry sprang to his feet, the UMP-45 coming up to his shoulder as he entered the hallway, Vasiliev at his right hand. Four men in tactical gear, dazed and disoriented. Blinded by the blast.

The fifth had remained back near the staircase, keeping watch.

No hesitation, no time for mercy. The submachine gun spat fire, the suppressed reports sounding like hammer blows in the narrow confines of the hall, along with the louder crack of Vasiliev's Grach. The young man by the staircase was the first to die, his weapon clattering to the wood as he crashed through the bannister, falling to the marble floor below.

Three of the assaulters went down, the fourth ran for the stairs as the H&K's magazine emptied, returning fire as he went.

Firing wildly.

Bullets tore into the wood paneling around Harry's head as he ejected the empty magazine and replaced it mere seconds later, pulling the charging handle to chamber a round.

A crystal chandelier over Vasiliev's head shattered in a shower of glass, bringing a curse from the Russian as he ducked for cover. Too late. A wild bullet caught him in the left arm, staining his sleeve crimson.

Calm. Focus. Harry raised his weapon, the red dot of a laser beam appearing on the man's forehead. *Squeeze.*

His head snapped back as if he had been struck with a mallet, his nerveless body crumpling to the carpet.

Dead silence.

"You okay, Alexei?" Harry demanded, shooting a glance across the hallway at his partner.

The Russian grunted, pushing himself to his feet. "Of course, *tovarisch*. But the idiot ruined my best shirt."

Harry couldn't help but chuckle. The response was so typically Alexei. His eyes scanned the carnage of the hallway, his heart still racing with the adrenaline of combat. They had been lucky. Very lucky.

And then a woman screamed…

9:12 P.M.
San Francisco

Something was going wrong. Very wrong. He could feel it, an old operational instinct. Korsakov looked down at his phone, verifying the number once again before pressing SEND. He and Andropov had been communicating through a series of "burner" phones, rotating every twenty-four hours.

It was the right number.

Korsakov looked up as his driver accelerated into the passing lane, narrowly inserting the SUV into a hole in the traffic. It wasn't just that Andropov wasn't answering—the call wasn't even connecting.

"I'm not getting through to Valentin. Give me the contact number for Maxim."

He could see the boy tense, his eyes visible in the luminescent glow of the laptop. Fear flickering in their depths. "I don't want to see them again."

"You won't have to," the assassin promised, his mind racing. "Just give me the number."

He listened, punching in the ten-digit number as Viktor read it off. *Send.* It didn't even ring, just a persistent beep informing him that the call could not be completed. Exactly as it had with Andropov.

Korsakov closed the phone, staring out the SUV's tinted windows at the passing traffic—the lights of San Francisco. He could still see the destroyed vacuum laying there in the safehouse. All of it misdirection…

He had a choice to make. Fight or flight, neither of them good options. Every ounce of his common sense screamed *warning*, but walking away wasn't as easy as it might have sounded.

Giving up the contract…if there had been a mistake, he would have to face the wrath of Andropov. Face the havoc that such an enemy could wreak among his business in Eastern Europe. Perhaps Yuri had been right, but there was no time for such recriminations. Not in the face of such danger.

He looked in his mirror, eyes meeting with Viktor's. "Get Andropov's pilot on the phone. Tell him nothing, give him no warning, but divert him to meet up with Yuri at the Commodore Heliport."

The boy looked confused. "That's a private-access helipad. Permission is required before landing."

"Then get permission."

9:13 P.M.
Andropov's estate
Beverly Hills, California

She was barely out of her teens, Harry realized, gazing down from the broken bannister. Blonde, impossibly tanned.

Her nightgown matched the pool of blood at her bare feet—blood still trickling from the broken body of the dying bodyguard.

Too young to be involved in all of this.

He felt movement beside his head, looked up to see Vasiliev's hand outstretched, his finger tightening around the Grach's trigger.

Let him do it, a voice urged, a dark whisper curling around Harry's thoughts. No witnesses. It made sense.

It was just one more life. The face of Andropov's security chief flashed before his eyes, the look of disbelief changing to horror.

Who will know of your lofty principles when you're dead?

Harry thrust his left hand upward, striking Vasiliev's arm just as he pulled the trigger. The bullet buried itself in the wall across the massive foyer. The girl looked up into their eyes, mouth opening as if she would scream, but no sound came out.

For a moment they stood there, a frozen tableau. The living among the dead.

Panic. Tears flowing down her face, she turned to run, bare feet against the tile. "Fool!"

He had been, Harry thought—throwing his H&K aside as he charged down the staircase. If she got away...everything they had done was for nothing, everything they had sacrificed so much to gain.

Ahead of him, a fleeing shape through the darkness of the kitchen. A flash of red lace in the glow of a lamp.

He could hear the girl's sobbing as she fumbled with the patio door, fear slowing her actions even as he closed.

The door opened and she slipped out into the night just as he grabbed her wrist, fingers closing in an iron grip.

She screamed something incoherent, her voice ringing out through the clear, cool air. If someone was passing by on the street...

Her hand came back as if she intended to hit him, and then her eyes settled on the Colt in his hand, the mouth of the long, black suppressor only inches away from her chest.

"Settle down and stay quiet," he stated, his eyes flashing a warning from behind the mask. "No one else needs to die."

9:30 P.M.
Las Vegas, Nevada

"You live proud in your cities, boastful and entrenched in your selfishness." Jamal glanced furtively down at the sheet of notepaper in his hand, then back up at the steady red light of the camera. "You deny to others the gifts of Allah's spacious earth and think it as nothing. I came to this country three years ago, a student, never dreaming that I would have this opportunity to strike a blow for my faith, that I would be chosen to die a *shahid* alongside my brothers."

He caught the approving eye of the shaikh and continued, steadying his voice. "Listen to my words, America, and tremble, for surely you must be extinguished, as was the fate of the Ad and the Thamud, the apostates of Arabia in the days of the Prophet, peace be upon him. How swiftly were they wiped out! As if they had never been?"

Jamal's voice began to swell with excitement as he remembered the words of the *sura*. It seemed impossible that only a few short days had passed since he had left behind his classes at the University of Michigan. "But wrong can *never* stand! *Allahu akbar!*"

The rifle trembled in his hands, his face distorted in passion as he chanted the words of praise into the lens of the camera, imagining the terror that would seize hold of the viewers. The Pakistanis joined in the chorus, their voices ringing across the floor of the convention center, echoing off the concrete walls. This was the moment they had lived their lives for, the fulfillment of destiny. "*Allahu akbar! Allahu akbar!*"

Long live death...

9:35 P.M.
Andropov's estate
Beverly Hills, California

"It was a brilliant plan, really," Harry announced, circling the bound Andropov. "Some people would have kept it simple—just brought in a bombmaker, but you anticipated every eventuality, didn't you?"

The oligarch remained silent. His confidence had evaporated after the execution-style slaying of his bodyguards, replaced by a sullen defiance.

"Sergei Korsakov is expensive enough..." Harry paused, watching the man's eyes for any sign of recognition. Just a momentary flash, almost gone before he caught it. "But you hired his entire team, ex-*Spetsnaz* all. That tells me that money was no object—that your cut was large enough that you could afford to hire the best. Overkill even, but that always was what you Soviets were best known for."

Out of the corner of his eye, he saw Vasiliev smile. His glance flickered to the opposite side of the room, where Andropov's mistress sat, gagged and bound to a chair. If the incident with her had meant anything, it had only confirmed that he couldn't trust the Russian.

Fortunately, trust was something he could work without. "Are we ready?"

A nod from Vasiliev. Harry walked over to Andropov's desk, unfolding one of the thick, plush hand towels they had taken from the master bathroom. He dropped to one knee, plunging the towel elbow-deep into one of the five-gallon buckets of water he had carried up to the study. Alexei had tried to help, but with his arm...

"You know what I'm going to do, don't you?" Harry asked, walking back around to the front of the oligarch, sparkling drops of water dripping all over the carpet.

"*Da*," Andropov admitted grudgingly. "Do you think it will work?"

Harry smiled, pushing the oligarch's chair until it tilted back against the desk, Andropov's feet in the air. "I think we'll both find out, now won't we?"

He reached behind the man's head, tying the towel tight back of the ears and arranging it over the forehead and eyes.

"Time to boogie, Valentin. Unless you'd rather save me the trouble?"

Drip. Drip. Drip. He felt the water splash against his bare cheeks, cold water, his brain registering the chill. The towel began to moisten, growing heavier as it hugged his face.

Drip. Drip. A calloused hand running over the bottom of his face, up his cheek until it met the edge of the towel, tugging the wet cloth down over his nose, then mouth. *Drip, drip, drip.*

The water was coming faster now, the soaked, heavy fabric sealing off his air.

Andropov closed his eyes against the blackness, forcing himself to focus. To remain calm.

Droplets trickled down his throat as he struggled to breathe, his oxygen-starved lungs inhaling the water instead. A burning sensation overwhelmed him, pain searing through his body.

Drowning, one of man's most primal fears. He gagged violently, thrashing uncontrollably against the restraints that bound him to the chair.

He felt the metallic taste of blood in his mouth and realized through the near-unconscious haze that he had bitten his own tongue.

The darkness seemed to reach out, enfolding him, drawing him into its bosom. Almost gone—the cloth was ripped back suddenly, leaving him to gasp in huge mouthfuls of air.

The masked face appeared over him, hazy, almost as if he were hallucinating—seeing double. "You know what they all say about waterboarding, that it's 'unreliable'—makes people lie, tell their interrogator whatever he wants to hear? Well that leaves you in a bit of a bind, Valentin...because you have no idea what I want to hear, and I *will* know if you lie to me."

Before he could even think of a response, the towel descended again, plunging him back into the depths of hell.

10:02 P.M.
The abandoned mansion

They had been inside well over an hour, Carol thought, glancing down at the clock in the lower right-hand corner of her computer screen. A pre-arranged signal of shades opening and closing in an upper window was their only assurance that Harry and Vasiliev had been successful.

Successful? She wondered for a moment what was going on across the street, then decided it was probably better that she didn't know.

In her desire to get to the bottom of her father's murder, she had unleashed the forces of destruction. And there was as much hope of capturing the wind as reining them in now.

A beeping sound emitted from the computer, a program that she had set up as an early warning system monitoring the online police bandwidth.

We have a possible four-one-five, neighbor reporting a domestic disturbance. The address was for the Andropov estate.

Raising a hand, she waved Han over to where she sat. "We've got a new problem."

Andropov's estate

"I really don't enjoy doing this, Valentin," Harry announced, pulling the wet, blood-flecked towel away from the Russian's nose and mouth. "But then it doesn't matter what I enjoy, does it? Because this is business—and I can keep it up all night unless you give me what I want."

Andropov shook his head, his eyes still defiant against the ghostly pallor of his face. "No, you can't."

"Care to tell me who is going to stop me, Valentin Stephanovich?"

The oligarch coughed, spitting bloody phlegm onto the carpet of the study. "You are."

Harry inclined his head to one side, regarding him incredulously. "Is that a fact?"

"*Da.*" Andropov managed a weak, yet contemptuous smile. "I have been trained to resist torture, but the human body can only take so much. We both know that."

His chest heaved in another fit of coughing, his face distorted in pain as he endeavored to continue. "Keep this up much longer, no matter how careful you are, and I will begin to suffer brain damage. You're not prepared to risk that, are you? To take the chance that the information you need so desperately could be gone forever?"

The worst of it was that Andropov was dead right, pinpointing the one thing they could not afford to place in jeopardy. Their weakness. Harry and Vasiliev exchanged glances. *How far?*

At that moment, Harry's earpiece crackled with static. Carol's voice. "Harry, you have a police cruiser inbound. Apparently someone contacted them regarding a domestic disturbance."

"How did that get out?" he demanded softly, walking to the far side of the study so that Andropov couldn't hear him. "I thought you had everything locked down."

"I did. I don't know how it happened, but you both need to get out of there now."

His face hardened. "That's not an option. How much time do I have?"

10:11 P.M.
Beverly Hills, California

Being a cop in Beverly Hills sounded a lot more glamorous than it was, Deputy Joshua Lambert thought, guiding his Crown Victoria up the darkened street.

Drug laws were broken on a daily basis in these neighborhoods—the four-one-five that had been reported was probably nothing more than a wife screaming at her movie star husband about a just-discovered affair. Or, better yet, that the blackout made it impossible to do her hair!

The young police officer pulled his car off to the side of the road at the front of the Andropov estate, blocking the driveway.

He cast an envious glance up at the mansion, through the massive steel gates. Now that was what one called living. The way a man could live if he were lucky in life.

He'd never been lucky, he thought, shaking his head as he climbed out of the car. And paying child support every month took most of his paycheck.

Might as well deal with this "crisis." Another day, another dollar.

"Are you sure you want to do this, *tovarisch?*" Vasiliev asked, glancing cautiously out the window. Down the driveway toward the front gate, through the fronds of the palm trees lining the asphalt, they could see the flashing lights of the patrol car. "You know your face has been on the television."

Harry shook his head, unslinging his H&K and carefully laying it down on the step. "You're not going to do it," he said, gesturing toward the Russian's bandaged arm. "That leaves me."

He pulled the balaclava off his head and stuffed it in his pocket, running a hand through his tousled black hair. "Don't kill anyone till I get back, okay, Alexei?"

There were lights on within the mansion, Deputy Lambert thought, speaking once more into the call box mounted on the gatepost. "This is Deputy Lambert of the Los Angeles County Sheriffs' Department. We received a report of a domestic disturbance."

Nothing.

He felt a chill wash over his body. His lieutenant had warned him to tread carefully around the politically-connected Andropov. No way he was going into the estate under his own authority.

A tall figure in black materialized out of the night on the other side of gate, the red flashers of the Crown Victoria reflected from ice-cold blue eyes above the scruffy black beard that covered the lower half of his face. "Can I help you?" he asked, his expression unconcerned, almost that of boredom, as he stared at the cop. There was something familiar about him, something he couldn't place—but he found it unsettling.

"Who are you?"

The man's identification appeared in his hand almost before Lambert had even realized the hand was moving. "Maxim Fedorenko," he replied, allowing him a brief glimpse of the name on the driver's license. "I'm Mr. Andropov's head of security. Do we have a problem?"

"We had a report of a domestic disturbance," Lambert replied nervously.

"Well, it wasn't here. I've had men on the grounds all night with the blackout in the neighborhood. If something like that had happened, we would have heard it."

"Do you mind if I come in and speak to your boss?"

He made no effort to open the gate, instead favoring Lambert with something that was more sneer than smile. "I do mind. Mr. Andropov has retired to bed, leaving strict orders that he was not to be disturbed."

Lambert took a deep breath. "I'd prefer to have your cooperation, Mr. Fedorenko, but if I need to come back with a warrant, I will."

The man seemed to find the suggestion amusing. "Be my guest. Deputy Lambert, you said?"

"Yes," the deputy replied, feeling a chill run through him.

"I'll make a note of that to your superiors. Have a good night, deputy."

"Everything okay?" Andropov asked pleasantly as Harry reentered the room. Even in the momentary respite, the man had recovered his confidence.

Harry stripped off his gloves, throwing them on the desk. "You and Sergei Korsakov...you served together in Chechnya, didn't you?"

The oligarch seemed to consider the question from all angles, puzzled at the sudden change in tactics. "*Da*, we did. He was one of the best there was, but I have not seen him in many years."

Harry nodded, his eyes narrowing as he gazed into Andropov's pale countenance. "Tell me," he began, "what does Korsakov think of your alliance with al-Qaeda?"

The shadow of fear passed across the Russian's face, leaving him rattled. "What nonsense are you talking about now?"

Harry paced across the room to the window. "You fought together against the *mujahideen* in the midst of the Chechen winter. As jihad spread across the Caucasus, you watched your men bleed and die. I wonder if Sergei knows the prostitute you've become? Selling your services to the highest bidder."

He reached into his pocket, pulling out the cellphone he had taken from Andropov's desk. It was nothing more than a simple flipphone, prepaid. Two incoming calls on the SIM, both of them missed. "Shall we tell him?"

"Go ahead," Andropov scoffed contemptuously, pulling himself together with an effort. "You know nothing to tell."

"Nothing? Is that what you would call your meeting with Tarik Abdul Muhammad?" Harry asked, turning to watch the effect of his words.

Devastation. Surprise washed across the Russian's features, surprise coupled with fear.

"Be sure your sins will find you out, Valentin," Harry laughed, moving in closer—the phone still in his hand. He lowered his voice, his lips only inches from Andropov's ear. "Now you have a choice...you can give me the information I want, and everything of your life can go back to the way it was. Or I can call Korsakov, and give him the whole story. You can use your own imagination as to how *that* ends."

Andropov was sweating, his body trembling with rage and fear. "I will destroy you, I swear to God, you will die for this."

Harry glanced over to where Vasiliev stood, a masked figure by the door. "I've heard that song before. Tick-tock..."

The oligarch swore, a desperate oath escaping his lips. "You really have no idea who you're up against, do you?" He took a deep breath. "I can give you the name of the man who placed the hit on David Lay. Just give me your word that this will be the end of it."

"Go on."

"Roger Hancock financed the operation to take out Lay. That's right," Andropov nodded, taking in the look in Harry's eyes, the moment of confusion. "The American president contracted the hit."

Nothing of the hell of the previous eight days had prepared him for that. It felt as if he had been struck. His eyes searched Andropov's face, searching for any guile, any deceit.

Nothing.

Take her, Harry, take her and run—far and fast. Go dark. Trust no one. Lay's words, coming back to him with new immediacy.

"Why?" he demanded, his voice barely above a whisper.

Andropov shrugged against his restraints. "I don't ask such questions of a client—it was enough that he was well prepared to pay to finance such a risky operation and to provide sufficient cover to enable Korsakov to elude American law enforcement. It was clearly implied that Lay knew more than was good for him."

It was insane, pure madness. And yet...

"He was the only target?" He saw a hesitation in Andropov's eyes and cautioned, "Think carefully, Valentin. You don't want to lie to me."

1:35 A.M. Eastern Time, December 22nd
FBI Headquarters
Washington, D.C.

"By daylight, we're going to have agents all over those mountains. We *will* find them, sir."

Director Haskel rubbed his brow with his thumb and forefinger. "And what if you don't—what then?"

There was a long pause before the voice on the other end of the phone replied. Then, "We're working with HHS on casualty projections, sir. There are over thirteen major population centers within the potential target radius, with Denver and Colorado Springs being two of the closest. If they have a chemical or biological weapon, the result of an attack would be devastating."

He had missed his chance to stop it, Haskel thought, realizing in one bleak moment what a fool he had been. The Altmann woman had sent in her request for a search warrant hours before she had violated procedure and gone in on her own authority.

There had to be a way to get ahead of this, to recover from the damage this threatened to do to him. If only his conversation with Cahill had been on the record.

"Get it done," he whispered, leaning close to the speaker. "Pull surveillance footage, traffic cameras, everything. I don't care what you have to do. Just *find them.*"

10:42 P.M. Pacific Time
The Andropov estate
Beverly Hills, California

"There's something wrong with your story," Harry announced at last, rising from his seat in front of Andropov. "You speak with certainty that Hancock was your client—did he take no precautions to conceal his identity? A man of his stature risks much by a venture of this sort..."

"He was cautious, at first," the oligarch replied, looking him straight in the eye. "And I would have none of it. A contract this dangerous...I needed to be sure that he could provide the umbrella that he was promising."

Harry shook his head, reaching for the prepaid phone once again. "I don't believe you. Shall we see what Sergei has to say about this whole sordid affair?"

Andropov swore in frustration. "I have proof."

Harry and Vasiliev traded glances. The phone went back on the desk. "Let's hear it, Valentin."

"We met in a hangar at Dulles, a campaign donor meeting with the man he helped put in office. Nothing overtly conspiratorial, I'm afraid. At least his detail didn't think so."

"And this proof of yours?"

Andropov inclined his head toward the bookshelf. "Take out the vellum-bound copy of the *Rubaiyat* on the third shelf. You'll find the files on a thumb drive concealed within its pages."

10:56 P.M.
The abandoned mansion

It's just a matter of deciding which set of consequences you can live with. He was right, Carol thought, standing in the door of the mansion's master bathroom, her eyes resting on the bound and blindfolded form of Pyotr Andropov. That's all it was.

And what could you live with?

She took a step into the room, their hostage backlit by the Coleman lantern on the edge of the sunken tub. He was shivering uncontrollably, though the room itself was warm.

He recoiled at her hand on his shoulder, his body tensing. "Here, drink this," she whispered, pressing her water bottle against his parched lips.

Water spilled from the corner of his mouth as he tried to drink, his Adam's apple bobbing up and down as the liquid gurgled down his throat. "Please...just let me go. Whatever those men are paying you—I can double it. My father is very wealthy."

"I know who your father is," Carol replied, emotions warring within her. His cheeks were stained with the salt of long-dried tears, the blindfold damp from sobbing.

A part of her wanted to release him right then and there—before Harry and Vasiliev returned. Before any more destruction could be wrought.

He won't be harmed. I swear before God...

At least not any more than he already *had* been. She closed her eyes, willing herself to continue down the road she had chosen. No matter where it led.

Her fingers trailed over his shoulder as she turned to leave. "Everything's going to be okay, Pyotr. It won't be much longer now."

11:03 P.M.
The Andropov estate

It was true. All of it, as surreal as it was. Andropov's men were good, judging by the photos they had succeeded in taking of the POTUS.

Or had been, Harry reflected, staring at the broken bodies laying only scant yards away.

"Satisfied?" Andropov demanded, glancing down at the restraints that still bound his hands and feet.

"No. That might have been good enough an hour ago, Valentin," Harry replied, pulling himself together—forcing himself to focus on the task at hand. "But now you're bargaining against the certainty of a painful death—and you can do better than this. I want to know what Tarik Abdul Muhammad is planning."

"You must understand—I am a facilitator, nothing more." The oligarch met his eyes with an unwavering gaze. "I was paid to bring the Pakistanis across the border, paid to provide them with weapons. Nothing more."

"How many men did you smuggle into the United States?"

"Five."

"What's their target?"

Andropov shook his head. "I don't know."

Something there in his eyes, the shadow of a falsehood. He was lying. And Americans were going to die because of his deceit.

Harry's eyes flashed with anger. "I gave you a warning," he whispered, opening the phone and beginning to type in the number. "I told you what would happen if you lied to me."

"Wait."

"Why should I?" Harry demanded, turning his head to spit on the carpet. "Give me a reason, Valentin. One good reason, because I'm running out of patience and you're running out of time."

"They're going to strike Las Vegas," Andropov replied desperately. "They paid me to supply them with intelligence on the operational capabilities of the LVMPD. On Christmas Day."

"Vegas is a big place. What was their target? What was the means of their attack?"

"I don't have that information. I truly don't. You have to believe me."

Harry laughed. "No, Valentin. I don't. You see, that's the problem with lying to someone. Once you've been caught, they never trust you again. That leaves you with a choice: never lie...or never get caught. Unfortunately, that choice is now in your rear-view mirror. What weapons did you supply to the Pakistanis?"

The Russian's face was soaked with sweat, fear filling his eyes. "Body armor, fully-automatic Kalashnikovs, fifty pounds of C-4. And that is all I know, I swear it."

Was it the truth? Hard to say—and only one way left to find out. Harry punched SEND, raising the phone to his ear...

11:14 P.M.
Southbound I-5
California

Traffic was heavy on the I-5 as the pair of Suburbans rolled south, with Korsakov in the lead vehicle. His decision had been made—*alea iacta est*, as Caesar would have put it.

The face of Pavel Nevaschin rose before his eyes, a reminder of the friends this contract had cost him. And he would see it through to the end, no matter what he found at Andropov's estate. For they had been played, of that he was sure.

The phone in his pocket vibrated suddenly, startling him from his thoughts. *Andropov?!*

"Yes?" he answered cautiously. "I've been trying to reach you for several hours."

"Then you're going to have to wait a while longer," an unfamiliar voice replied. "Valentin asked me to give you a message—he's terminating your contract. Shutting the operation down. Time to go home, Sergei."

"Who is this?" Korsakov demanded, his face hardening at the audacity of the man's words.

"You know my name."

And he did. The assassin closed his eyes, struggling to control his voice. "Then know this, Mr. Nichols. You killed a friend of mine in Virginia, a man who saved my life in Chechnya."

"Fortunes of war, Sergei. Don't ask me to regret his death."

"Wouldn't dream of it. But if you think that taking Andropov hostage is going to make me stand down, that's a decision you need to rethink."

"Hostage?" the voice on the other end of the phone demanded incredulously. "He's not a hostage. Question is...do you know the type of traitor you've been working for?"

"I don't understand," Korsakov retorted, motioning with his free hand for Viktor to hand him the laptop. There—on the screen, the message from Yuri. *Twenty minutes out.*

"Your buddy Andropov—he's been doing deals with the hajjis. An alliance with The Base to launch an attack against this country."

The base. Al-Qaeda. The ex-*Spetsnaz* assassin swore, his mind racing as he struggled to process the information. If it were true...

"None of that changes what is between us," he said finally. "I will deal with Andropov when I see him."

"I don't think you will," the voice replied, a cold certainty in its tone. He could hear the slide of a pistol being racked back. "See you on the other side, Sergei."

And the phone went dead.

11:20 P.M.
The Andropov estate
Beverly Hills,
California

Harry dropped the phone to the bloodstained carpet of the study, smashing the screen beneath a booted foot.

During the entire conversation, the oligarch had remained stone-faced, silent. Nothing left to bargain with.

Of no further value.

Holding the Colt in one hand, he reached forward, using his combat knife to slice through the restraints holding Andropov against the chair. "Get up."

As he took a step back, the oligarch struggled to his feet, rubbing his wrists to restore circulation. "Well, you've done it now, haven't you?" Andropov asked, a bitter smile playing at his lips.

"Welcome to the end of the road, Valentin." The Colt came up in Harry's hand—the long black suppressor aimed straight at Andropov's head. "On your knees."

"*Nyet*," Andropov replied, seeming to summon up some measure of defiance from deep within himself. "If I'm going to die, I'll die on my feet. And if you're going to kill me, you'll have to look me in the eye."

Harry traded glances with Vasiliev, shrugging. "Have it your way."

His finger took up the slack, the big Colt recoiling back into his hand. Blood and fire...

Chapter 21

11:32 P.M.
The abandoned mansion

"It's done," Harry announced, sweeping back into the kitchen with Vasiliev at his heels. He deposited the thumb drive beside Carol's computer. "We have our evidence."

She didn't respond, her eyes focused intently on the screen in front of her.

"Andropov?" He looked up at the sound of Han's voice to see the former SEAL enter the room from the other side, the SCAR slung over his shoulder.

"Dead," Harry replied. "What's going on?"

Carol entered a few rapid keystrokes, her eyes widening as a window opened on-screen. "We have a problem. You were ID'd."

He looked at the alert indicated by her cursor. It was an all points bulletin—for him—giving the address of the Andropov estate.

Who are you? Had it been surprise he had seen in the deputy's eyes...or recognition? Had he seen it and chosen to ignore it, knowing the alternative was the unthinkable? Killing a cop...

No time to find answers to those questions. Not now. "What's their ETA?"

"The nearest car? Eight minutes out."

"Pack everything up," Harry ordered, his words clipped. "We have to be out of here before they seal off the block. Sammy, help Carol move things out to the van. Alexei and I will get our guest ready for transport."

He turned, motioning for Vasiliev to follow him as he moved down the long hallway toward the master bathroom, their footsteps thudding against the bare, stripped floor.

The Coleman was flickering, the flame sending long shadows glancing off the tiled walls as it ran low of fuel. An eerie sight.

Pyotr's head came up at the sound of their entrance, his blindfolded eyes endeavoring in vain to seek them out.

Harry pulled his combat knife from its sheath, slashing through the zip ties that pinned the boy's legs to the chair.

"What are you planning to do with him?" Carol's voice. He looked up to see her standing in the doorway, a haunted look in her eyes.

"We'll take him with us—drop him once we're out of the state. It will take them hours to find him. Now, get ready."

"I'll do it, *tovarisch*," Vasiliev interjected. "I can drive around for a few hours and throw the hounds off the scent. It's past time we were parting company."

Harry hesitated for a long moment, glancing from Carol to the Russian. His mind screaming danger. He knew what Vasiliev was planning, knew it as certainly as if the words had been spoken.

Pyotr is part of the contract.

Do it, a voice admonished from the dark shadows of his mind. *She'll never be the wiser.*

He didn't *know*. Not really. That was what plausible deniability was all about, the ability to redefine the line between truth and deceit.

To make "truth" what you wanted it to be.

"No," he said finally, his throat dry as he spoke the words, staring Vasiliev full in the face. "No, you won't."

The knife still in his hand, he turned his back on the Russian, bending down to cut through the ties securing Pyotr's wrists to the chair.

He heard Carol scream a warning, the thunderous report of a pistol battering his eardrums. Warm, viscous liquid spattered against his face and clothing.

Death walked among them, he realized, thinking for a moment that it was his own. *Not this time.*

His ears ringing, Harry rose from behind Pyotr's corpse, his movements slow—as if in a dream. His eyes fell upon Vasiliev across the room, the pistol still leveled in the Russian's hand. A faint whisp of hot white smoke curling from the barrel of the Grach.

"I'm sorry, Harry," Vasiliev said, a smile crossing his face. "But the Kremlin was insistent. Father *and* son."

Something snapped. Harry launched himself across the blood-drenched tile floor, the Colt coming out of its holster as he did so. He saw Vasiliev's finger tighten around the trigger, expected him to fire. Expected Death to come for him as well.

He hit the Russian at a full run, slamming the older man against the wall of the bathroom— knocking the wind from his body. The Grach clattered to the tiles.

"He was off-limits," he hissed, his fingers entwined in Vasiliev's collar. "He was *innocent.*"

"Innocent?" The Russian laughed. "And who decides that? Men. Men just like you and I, Harry…the men who send *us* out to play God. We're both of us the same."

No. That wasn't true. He grimaced as if in pain, shoving the muzzle of the Colt into the soft flesh beneath Vasiliev's chin. "This ends now, Alexei. All the men you've killed over the years—no more. It ends tonight."

There was a look of resignation in the Russian's eyes. The weary look of a man at the end of a long journey. No more laughter.

"Tell Anya that I loved her. You'll do that, won't you?" he asked, struggling to breathe, the gun restricting his airflow.

Anya. The face from the photograph flickered back through Harry's mind. Vasiliev's wife, her eyes haunting him. Those eyes full of love. *Love* for the man before him.

He paled, taking a step back from Vasiliev, breathing heavily. His voice trembled as he spoke.

"Leave, Alexei," he warned, gesturing with the barrel of his pistol. "Leave before I kill you."

Vasiliev leaned there against the wall for a long moment, massaging his sore throat, regarding Harry soberly. "Of course, *tovarisch.* As you wish."

Kill him. The impulse came suddenly, without warning and without reason—a premonition of danger entering his soul. Kill him and have done with it.

It was as if the shroud of the future had been pulled back for but a scant moment. *Kill him.*

And yet he found himself incapable of pulling the trigger. He watched the Russian go as if in a haze, smelling the stench of death pervading the room— the presence of a tangible evil.

The straight-eight sights of his Colt centered on the back of Alexei's head as he reached the door—the perfect target for a scant moment of time.

And then he was gone. Harry stood there staring at the empty doorway for a long moment, a strange sense of regret washing over him. A regret that had nothing to do with the murder of Pyotr.

Pyotr. He turned to see Carol on her knees beside the boy's broken body, his blood staining her shirt. "You knew," she whispered, shaking her head as tears rolled down her cheeks. "You *knew.*"

It felt as if a knife had gone through his body. A thousand excuses rose to his lips, but they all rang hollow.

He had made his deal with the devil he knew, and Pyotr had paid the price. It was that simple.

And none of it mattered in this moment. "We have to go," he said, reaching down for her wrist.

She shook off his hand, her fingers stroking Pyotr's lifeless arm. "You swore that he would come to no harm."

Yes. He had. Her hand came up to brush away her tears in an angry gesture, leaving a streak of blood in its wake. "Does this look like 'no harm' to you?"

Sirens in the distance. The rhythmic *thwap-thwap-thwap* of an inbound helicopter. They had to be gone, moments of freedom slipping away the longer they lingered. He slipped the Colt back into its holster, reaching down to grasp her shoulder, pulling her roughly to her feet.

Run...

11:40 P.M.
Beverly Hills, California

Night flying was something that had never appealed to Yuri. Too many memories of operations gone wrong—missions sabotaged by insufficient intelligence or indecisive superiors. He sat just back of the pilot in the Sikorsky S-76 as the helicopter swept over Beverly Hills toward Andropov's estate, one thousand feet over the housetops.

Lifeless. It was the first word that came to his mind as the mansion entered his view through the side windows of the executive helicopter. Everything was dark, no flicker of light from the windows. Nothing.

"Take us around for another pass over the neighborhood," the man from Leningrad instructed. "Lower this time."

The pilot, a young—almost boyish—Russian with an unrecognizable American accent, shook his head. "Can't do that—FAA regs. A thousand feet over residential neighborhoods. Andropov's neighbors...well, they all got nearly as much money as he does and a propensity for complaining to go with it."

Yuri shook his head at his comrades, leaning forward until his face was only inches away from the pilot's. "Do I look like a man who cares about your 'regs' or *his* neighbors?"

He drew back the slide of his Glock deliberately, his eyes never leaving the pilot's face as the young man's eyes widened. "Take us down."

The pilot nodded wordlessly, easing the helicopter's nose forward and circling around for another pass, this time at four hundred feet. It was then that Yuri saw it, a faint movement in the faint glow of a streetlight below. A gray panel van...

He slid his phone open, fingers moving clumsily over the small buttons. *Contact made.*

12:03 P.M.
Beverly Hills, California

The taillights of a minivan glowed red in front of him and Harry shifted into the right lane, accelerating. He was going too fast—he knew that. Running from something he couldn't escape.

Himself.

One who would fight with monsters must take care that he does not become one. What *had* he become?

The answer to that question was a luxury he couldn't afford. Not now. Innocents died in war, had ever since the dawn of time. Pyotr was collateral damage—nothing more, he thought, his face hardening.

They had the intel they had sought. And no way to act on it. They needed support, as risky as that was going to be.

No doubt the bodies of Valentin Andropov and his bodyguards had already been discovered. His son's would take the police a few more hours, but find him they would.

And once more the dragnet would be thrown out. "Do you hear that?" Han asked quietly from the van's front passenger seat.

He didn't have to clarify his question. Harry knew exactly what he was talking about. Had known ever since they had left the neighborhood of Andropov's estate.

A helicopter. He glanced out the window of the panel van, endeavoring to catch a glimpse of it against the night sky. Waiting for the finger of a police searchlight to reach down, pinpointing them in the midst of the traffic. For red-and-blue lights to appear in his rear-view mirror, sirens wailing.

Nothing. And that brought with it a no less troubling conclusion.

Korsakov?

His eyes returned to the road, watching the signs carefully. Two miles. Only a few minutes till he could merge onto the I-10. Lose themselves in the interstate.

Only a few more minutes…

12:47 P.M.
The I-5
Burbank, California

A stern chase is a long chase, Korsakov thought, calling back to mind the words of his father, a sailor in the Red Navy. And this one was going to be very long. The speedometer needle of the Suburban held steady at ninety-five miles per hour as the SUV flew down the interstate. They weren't going to intercept in time.

"Can you give me any satellite coverage?" he asked, glancing in the overhead mirror.

He could see Viktor biting his lip, a rough shock of hair fallen over the boy's face as he worked at the laptop. "I'm working on it—may have to be a commercial sat."

That would provide the bare minimum of coverage in the best of times—and provide no help at all at this hour of the night.

Korsakov looked down at his phone, at the latest message from Yuri, trying to conceal his frustration. The helicopter was running out of fuel, only fifteen minutes away from breaking off the chase.

He glanced at the GPS read-out again, a plan forming in his mind. It was a desperate shot, but for all his personal differences with Yuri, the man was good.

The assassin's thumbs moved over the small keyboard of the phone, hesitating for a moment before finally pressing SEND.

They had no back-up plan.

12:51 A.M.
The helicopter

"Look, I was told not to ask you any questions, but we're nearly bingo-fuel here. This is a ten-million dollar chopper and it belongs to Mr. Andropov, not you."

Yuri shook his head, ignoring the pilot's protest as he glanced down at the glowing screen of the phone in his hand. Had Korsakov gone mad?

He read the message a second time. His employer was tossing caution completely to the wind—and it stood a good chance of killing *him* in the process. Still…

"Valentin Andropov is dead," he announced coolly, bringing his Glock to bear on the pilot. "And you're going to set us down on that highway."

12:59 A.M.
CA-210 East
California

Silence. Harry checked his mirrors, easing into the far left lane of the freeway. He caught Carol's eyes in the rear-view mirror, moments before she looked away.

She hadn't spoken to him since leaving Pyotr's body behind in the mansion, the image of the teenager slumped over dead in the chair still haunting his memories.

A sudden roar assaulted his ears, the sound of a helicopter coming in low and fast. The *helicopter*. They hadn't heard it for nearly a half hour, long enough to dismiss its earlier presence as a fluke.

He looked out the driver's side window of the panel van just in time to see a large civilian Sikorsky sweep by overhead, its rotor wash shaking the van from side to side. Some fluke.

Chaos. The sound of automobile horns filled the night, a night suddenly glowing red with the glare of brake lights.

Harry swerved, watching as an SUV collided with a small family sedan ahead of him, crumpling the side of the car as if it was made of tin and sending it spinning into the path of another vehicle.

The Sikorsky descending from the sky like a ravenous bird of prey.

He saw the side doors open, armed men materializing in the opening and saw in that moment Korsakov's gambit. And a ruthless, desperate gambit it was.

Desperate enough that it just might work.

He caught a glance of Han's face in the glow of the lights and read his expression clear. More innocents were going to die on this night.

Motioning for one of his men to cover the pilot, Yuri leaped from the open door of the hovering executive helicopter to the hard asphalt of the freeway just below him, followed by the two remaining members of his team.

Dropping to one knee, he extended the folding stock of his AK against his shoulder, his weapon a part of himself as he took cover behind a wrecked Mustang. Scanning for the gray van.

Nichols was out there—with nowhere to go in the midst of the massive traffic pile-up, nowhere to hide. A wolf brought to bay. Never more dangerous.

Kill Nichols. Kill everyone with him. Korsakov's new rules of engagement. Chambers was worth nothing to them now.

He could feel someone's eyes on him, a sixth sense warning him of danger. Turning, the Kalashnikov extended in front of him, he saw a woman not five feet away, pinned against the seat of her Toyota by voluminous airbags.

A sacrificial lamb, to bring the wolf out into the open. The mercenary never hesitated, watching as the fear on her face turned to outright panic. His finger squeezed the trigger, a burst of fire ripping open the night.

Chaos. Death.

Despite being walled in by the Dodge in front of them, the sound of automatic weapons fire from their front gave an unmistakable indication of what was going on. And the screams.

Harry glanced in his mirrors, gauging the distance between himself and the surrounding cars. Very little room—the freeway had been transformed in moments into a seething, panicked mass of humanity and crashed vehicles. A man ran past his door, fleeing for his life.

"I'm not going to sit here and listen to this," Carol announced suddenly. He looked back to see her pull the Kahr from its holster inside her jacket, reaching for the side door of the van.

He twisted in his seat, seizing her arm. "There's nothing you can do except get yourself killed. And it is *my* responsibility to protect you."

Defiance shone from her eyes, the ghost of her father. "That's all you've been doing, isn't it? And look at the people that have died because of it."

Another burst of gunfire from their front. There was no time to have this argument. "Get down," he whispered, turning the steering wheel all the way to the left. Aiming it toward a four-foot gap between an abandoned Grand Cherokee and a Chevy Impala.

He looked over at Han, who was busy checking the magazine of Harry's UMP-45. "Hold on tight."

His foot hit the accelerator pedal, jamming it all the way to the floor, tires squealing against the asphalt as the van turned hard, gaining momentum. It slammed into the front bumper of the Impala like a battering ram, tearing it away as though it was made of paper.

Hard right and he broke out into what had been the far left lane of the interstate, the Sikorsky dead ahead, hovering only five, maybe six feet off the roadway.

The death rattle of Kalashnikovs on full-automatic resounded through the night, the windshield disintegrating into a million shards of glass as Harry slid down onto the floor of the van, his arms locking the steering wheel in place.

He felt the van shudder from the impact of high-velocity rounds and looked over to see Han curled up across from him, the submachine gun across his chest.

Braced for impact.

Yuri watched in disbelief as the van raced forward, on a collision course with the Sikorsky. Watched as if in slow-motion as his team members emptied their magazines into the van, its tires exploding, sparks flying from the bare metal.

He shouted a warning, starting to run toward his men, his voice drowned out by the gunfire.

He'd barely taken ten steps when the top of the van connected with the tail boom of the Sikorsky.

The agonizing shriek of metal on metal, audible even over the thunderous roar of the helicopter. The van shuddered from the impact, already decelerating from the friction of rolling on blown tires.

From his position on the floor, near the pedals, Harry heard the whine of the helicopter's rotors as they flailed the air in a futile attempt to stay aloft.

The night exploded in fire.

Heat and flame washed through the shattered windows of the van, igniting the upholstery. Harry drew himself up, hand searching for the door handle. "Out! *Out!* Everyone out."

Han tossed him the SCAR and one of their backpacks as he jumped from the van, pulling open Carol's door. "Let's move it!"

He looked back toward the flaming wreckage of the S-76 as they ran down the highway, taking in with a pitiless glance the sight of one of the mercenaries writhing in the fire.

Fortunes of war.

1:28 A.M.
East of Los Angeles
California

Korsakov checked his phone for what must have been the thirtieth time in as many minutes, each time greeted with the response, *No New Messages.*

Where was Yuri? He should have sent a text by now. A text announcing Nichols' death. That was all that mattered now, revenge for the men he had lost.

Dig two graves, he thought, remembering the old proverb of the vengeful, but his decision had already been made.

"Do you have that satellite yet?" he demanded, glancing into the darkened backseat of the SUV as they continued to speed down the freeway.

"*Da*," the boy replied. "Just coming on-line now. Another moment or two."

For all of its advances, technology could seem painfully slow. "Is it true that Valentin is dead?" Viktor asked, looking over his laptop. His voice seemed to tremble even as he spoke the name.

"It is, Vitya," the assassin responded, letting out a heavy sigh. His employer, the man who had launched them on this godforsaken mission, was dead. With him died any chance of receiving their final payment, a full half of Korsakov's contract price. And yet he could not help but feel a strange sense of relief.

"I am glad," the boy intoned solemnly, and Korsakov found himself in agreement. His old friend had fallen far— to have become the molester of children, the whore of the jihadists. The world was better off with him dead.

He heard a sharp intake of breath from Viktor and he twisted around in his seat, motioning for Misha to keep driving. "What's going on?"

The boy handed him the laptop, pointing wordlessly to the screen, the image live from a Google satellite miles above Yuri's last known position. Flames bloomed across the image, leaping skyward. A pillar of fire by night.

Devastation.

"Can we see what happened?"

The boy leaned forward, his dark eyes shining as his fingers worked their magic on the keyboard, back-timing the satellite footage almost thirty minutes before beginning to play it forward once again

Korsakov watched in morbid fascination as the scene unfolded, leaving no doubt in his mind what had happened. No doubt that his men had failed. Perhaps irredeemably this time.

He watched the helicopter go down, exploding as its rotors hit the target and tore themselves apart. Watched as the fireball engulfed the men he had sent with Yuri.

Movement. His finger tapped the edge of the screen, a vehicle moving away from the inferno.

A sedan. Away from the others, from the chaos of the stampeded herd.

"That's him," he whispered, old instincts taking over. "Can we get the license plate?"

The boy brushed his hair back out of his eyes, excitement written once more on his face. "I can try."

6:38 A.M. Eastern Time
The White House
Washington, D.C.

"...live this morning in Los Angeles, where this story is still developing. I'm standing here in front of the estate of Russian billionaire Valentin Andropov. As you can see, the police are keeping us back, but we're hearing that Mr. Andropov is dead, and unconfirmed reports suggest that he was not the only fatality in what appears to be a mass murder overnight in Beverly Hills."

What? Roger Hancock set down his spoon, resting it on the pink flesh of the grapefruit in the bowl before him as he reached for the remote.

Surely he hadn't heard that right.

He turned the volume up all the way, fear gripping his very soul as the camera panned over the house, the mansion he knew so well. A mansion now lit with police floodlights.

The brunette onscreen continued her report, but she had nothing further to say, nothing that interested the President.

Valentin was dead? He could have rationalized it, could have convinced himself that it was nothing. Andropov had made enemies over the years, powerful enemies even within the *mafiya.*

But it rang hollow within his own heart. The man he had hired to make his problems go away...was now himself dead.

The door opened, and Agent Hawkins entered. "Ian Cahill to see you, Mr. President."

Hancock looked down at his untouched plate, making a mighty effort to compose himself. To stop shaking. Despite the years of their alliance—their friendship, if one wanted to call it that, this was one problem he couldn't trust Cahill to solve.

Not when he had gone this far.

7:59 A.M.
An apartment
Washington, D.C.

There were few things worse than a night without sleep. Kranemeyer wheeled himself over to the window, adjusting the shades to allow the light of the morning sun to come streaming into the apartment.

He'd never had such problems as a young man, he thought, spinning his wheelchair back around toward the apartment's kitchen.

But he was no longer young. Things were no longer so simple. No longer so clear-cut. Black and white had faded to a gray the color of soot—and just as defiling.

He plucked a small, unmarked vial off the counter, holding it up to the light. It might as well have been filled with water, by the look of it, but it was nothing so harmless.

Carter had masked his entrance and exit from the labs of Langley's Directorate of Science & Technology, or "Q Branch" as some of the local wags called it.

Covered his theft electronically, Kranemeyer thought, a sad smile on his face. The analyst was still in the dark concerning what he had actually helped accomplish, and it was safest that way. For both of them.

Coftey's promise of air support only went so far. And he intended to push it to its breaking point.

He replaced the vial with a sigh and rolled back to the window, looking out upon the city. A city which took men's souls and fed them into the meatgrinder of others' ambition. Democrat, Republican, none of that mattered. Perhaps it never had.

How far are you willing to go? The senator's question, still ringing in his ears. Kranemeyer glanced at the vial of poison sitting there in the kitchen, reflecting on his own answer, an answer he was as certain of now as when he had uttered it.

As far as it takes.

6:58 A.M. Pacific Time
An oil field
Tehachapi, California

Day was coming, the first faint rays of sunlight breaking across a cloud-streaked horizon. Abandoned derricks littered the oil field, standing silhouetted against the dawn like the skeletons of creatures from a time gone by.

Carol adjusted the cracked venetian blinds to let in the sun, moving back toward the center of the room. She'd set her laptop on the cheap metal desk that had once been the centerpiece of the office and she moved to boot it up, checking to see how much battery power she had left. Enough to send their signal for help.

Death and taxes—the two things of which every man was assured...and taxes had *brought* death to California's oil industry. A slow, painful death as the state continued to grasp for more and more revenue to stave off its own slide into the abyss. Keynesian economics in their finest hour.

The oil field that had once employed hundreds now sat desolate, everything worth hauling off long since taken by metal scavengers and other thieves.

No more running, Harry had said when they had arrived, and she'd found his grim certainty frightening. Perhaps this oil field would bear witness to their own demise.

Listening to the computer *whirr*, she moved back to the window, catching sight of him out near the car, his tall form moving swiftly through the semi-darkness. Assessing his tactical environment. He hadn't spoken a word to her since they had arrived, hadn't spoken a word beyond necessity since the death of Pyotr.

You swore that he would come to no harm—does this look like 'no harm' to you? She would never forget the way his face had looked in that moment—pale, drawn...as if she had struck him. In a way, she had.

And then that man had disappeared—replaced by the man who had dragged her out of that house and placed her forcibly in the panel van as the police closed in. The man who had driven into a hail of gunfire to protect her, and the lives of others on the freeway.

The man outside.

In the end, was he truly responsible for the murder or Pyotr...or was she?

Who had set them on that course?

You want to find the man behind your father's murder? This is the most linear path. She could still see the look on Vasiliev's face as he had uttered those damning words.

The door to the office trailer opened and he was there, his blue eyes fixed on her face. The way she was standing, he had to know she had been watching him.

"I have the connection established," Carol said finally, breaking the awkward silence between them. "You can upload your message any time you're ready."

She drew the jacket tighter around her body as she moved toward the desk, covering up the bloodstains on her blouse. Pyotr's blood.

She could feel him behind her, his hands coming up to rest tentatively on her shoulders. "How are you holding up?"

"I'll be fine." She was lying, and they both knew it. His hand slipped down, encircling her waist—drawing her close. A comforting presence, despite everything that had gone before.

"No one is ever fine," he whispered. "Not after seeing that. And I deserve every bit of the blame."

"*No.*" She found the words came out more sharply than she had intended, anger and remorse warring within her heart. "I do."

The images of Pyotr's shattered corpse flickered back across her mind and she buried her face in his chest, guilt washing over her, her body wracked with silent sobs. *I do…*

1:04 P.M. Eastern Time
The trailer
Graves Mill, Virginia

The sound of a car engine roused Thomas from his seat at the table, taking his Beretta 92 with him as he moved toward the front of the double-wide.

"It's your boss," Rhoda Stevens announced, giving him a disapproving glance at the sight of his sidearm. What the relationship between her and Lay was—or had been, he would probably never know. But she was taking the DCIA's condition personally. And his role in the affair.

"Gotcha," he retorted, peering through the blinds to see Kranemeyer emerging from the black Suburban, his trench coat flapping in the breeze as he advanced on the house.

The Dark Lord.

Thomas moved to the door, throwing back the bolt just as the DCS reached it.

"Have you established any contact with Nichols?" his boss demanded, not bothering with a greeting. The look on Kranemeyer's face told him something was wrong.

A shake of the head. "I checked the sites this morning, all of them. No signal. What's happened?"

"He's popped back up on the radar," came the terse reply. "A local LEO placed him at that mass shooting in California."

"That Russian?" No way. He'd seen the reports on the morning news. A veritable bloodbath. Someone had gone after a key player of the *mafiya*, eliminating his entire security team and executing him with a bullet to the head. The media had reported the story with their typical glee, mingling blood and gore with their viewers' raisin bran. Harry?

"Yes," Kranemeyer responded, pushing past him into the trailer. "That's the way it's being reported. He's running out of room to run, out of places to hide. Run the sites again."

Thomas led the way back into the living room, firing up his Macbook on the table. "How's David?" Kranemeyer asked as the webpage loaded, regarding Thomas with hooded eyes.

"Doctor says he's stabilizing. A full recovery is weeks away, if ever."

Silence. Thomas loaded the web forums, checking briefly through the new threads. Looking for the code, the signal that would indicate Harry had been there.

Nothing. The second site was the same. Two down, three to go.

He scrolled up to Favorites, selecting Ebay and running a search. And there it was…a new listing, only two hours old. A first edition copy of Ayn Rand's massive tome *Atlas Shrugged*, its cover a blood-red sun glaring down tracks of glistening steel.

Rearden steel.

Despite the gravity of the moment, Thomas found himself smiling. It was Harry who had given him his copy, the outgrowth of a long ago conversation. And the inspiration behind this code.

"It's here," he breathed, mousing over the description until he found it, down near the bottom. A list of pages torn or missing from the book.

As Kranemeyer watched, he grabbed a sheet of notepaper and began jotting down the numbers in sequence.

"It's GPS coordinates," Thomas announced, realizing the import of his statement almost as soon as the words were out of his mouth.

Harry *was* in California, after all.

"And this is a call for help."

1:39 P.M.
The Russell Office Building
Washington, D.C.

"You said you would call me when it was done." Roy Coftey frowned as he descended the marble staircase into the rotunda of what had been known as the Old Senate Office Building. He switched the phone to his right hand, checking his watch.

"Something's come up," the voice on the other end of the phone announced. "I need the use of your plane. A brief flight out to LAX. Two passengers out. Indeterminate on the return trip."

The senator shook his head, making an effort not to use the man's name. Not over the phone. "Do we need to meet?"

"Negative. This is unconnected to our other business. Your Lear *is* on the ground at Dulles, right?"

"Yes, but…everything's grounded." Coftey stopped short, lowering his voice as one of his staffers came hustling down the stairs after him. "I told you I would have your back, but there's only so far anyone can protect you. And if I'm going to get that jet off the ground, I will need an airtight cover story."

"You'll have it. I want my people wheels-up by 1600."

11:02 A.M. Pacific Time
The oil field
California

And his message had not gone unseen. A smile touched Harry's lips for a fleeting moment as his eyes fell upon the top bid: $1186. The number of pages in the first edition of Rand's magnum opus.

The countersign.

"Everything ready?" Han asked, entering the office trailer from the back. He was buttoning his faded black windbreaker over the tactical vest beneath it, the SCAR cradled in the crook of his arm.

Harry checked the file protocols Carol had set up one last time. Everything was in place. If a password wasn't entered every twelve hours, what little information they had on Tarik Abdul Muhammad and his Christmas Day terror attack would go streaming out through cyberspace to the FBI, CIA, DHS, and a round dozen of the other members of the alphabet soup that was D.C. bureaucracy.

"Time to hang out our shingle," he nodded, grabbing up his UMP-45. They were running low on ammunition, almost too low for what was to come.

If waiting had been an option, he would have waited. The cavalry was coming.

But Korsakov had to be taken out of the equation *now*. And the only way to lure the wolf into the trap was to bait it…with themselves.

Chapter 22

Airborne. Kranemeyer read the text message off the screen of his phone, marveling at the brevity. The Texan was as taciturn as ever.

He leaned back against the seat of the Suburban, gazing out the window at the setting sun, rays of light flickering out from behind snow-laden clouds the color of slate.

Valentin Andropov's nineteen-year-old son had been found dead in a house across the street from his estate. Executed with a single bullet to the head—just like his father.

According to the early reports Kranemeyer had seen, the murder weapon had differed between the two, but that didn't really matter. Nor did it matter that Nichols was supposed to be acting under Lay's orders, sketchy as they had been.

They might have swept anything else under the rug—made it go away—but this...this was more difficult.

The son had been an American citizen. And Nichols was now well beyond redemption.

Something to consider when he reflected on his own plans. Kranemeyer flipped open the folder beside him, the printed sheet therein containing Shapiro's evening itinerary.

The Church of the Holy Trinity.

He'd never been a very pious man himself—the morality of what he was about to do gave him no pause.

It wasn't his decision…not really. It was his target's—a decision that had been made when Shapiro *decided* to betray his country.

Send a message, Barney, the senator had said, his eyes glistening with a simmering wrath, the flames of the Alibi Club's fireplace reflected in their depths. *If the fools in this town want to dance, they're going to have to pay the piper.*

1:39 P.M. Pacific Time
California

It had all been a mistake, Korsakov thought, staring murderously at his cellphone as Viktor used his still-active FBI access to read off a list of roadblocks.

The California State Police were sealing off every major artery. And Nichols was gone.

He cast a glance into the back seat of the SUV to where Yuri sat, chewing on a sandwich of deli meat. His lieutenant looked like death itself, his face seared with the heat of the explosion, the hair singed off his forearms.

Four men. That was all he had left—and that was if you counted in both Viktor and himself.

Even as he looked at it, the phone in his hand began to vibrate with an incoming call. His heart almost stopped.

No one had this number. No one living.

"Yes?" he asked, motioning to Viktor to attempt a trace as he answered the call.

"It's time this was ended, Sergei." Nichols' voice. The tone of a man on the edge, barely in control of himself. Trembling with anger.

An encouraging development.

Korsakov listened in silence as the American continued. "Innocent people died last night…for what? You're not going to get paid for this."

The assassin cleared his throat. "I told you. This isn't about the money—this is about the men you have killed. *My* men. And I don't care who has to die, so long as you join them in the end."

Out of the corner of his eye, he saw Viktor hold up four fingers. "You were clever last night, Mr. Nichols. Audacious, even. What is that Latin phrase they teach in your military colleges? Fortune favors the audacious? And even more of my men died."

Three.

"I gave you the chance to walk away last night," Nichols responded. "Leave it all behind—make your way out of the country as best you could. That was before the freeway. No one else had to die…but now you do."

Two. He could see the smile grow on the boy's face. Keep stalling. Keep him on the phone.

"So now you intend to kill me?"

A *click* was all that answered his question, and he shot an anxious glance in Viktor's direction.

Do we have it?

The look of intense concentration on the boy's face was unbroken for a long moment, then he began to nod.

1:44 P.M.
The oil field

"Did he have time?" Harry asked, looking over to where Carol sat in front of her laptop.

It had been so close.

"All depends on how good his tech support is. It's a reasonable hope." She ran a hand over her forehead. "You couldn't stay on the phone any longer—he would have gotten suspicious."

"Do you still have your gun?"

She looked up as though startled by the sudden question, then nodded.

"Keep it handy," he advised, catching Han's eye from across the room. "Time to take up our positions."

2:39 P.M.
The Bellagio Hotel & Casino
Las Vegas, Nevada

Dominoes.

Samir Khan watched, mesmerized, as the dealer shuffled a set of dominoes with slim, agile hands, dealing them out to the players surrounding the table.

Nothing could have prepared him for the luxury, the decadence.

"A drink, sir?" He turned to find a cocktail waitress at his elbow, a tray of drinks in her hand.

"No, not right now," the lawyer responded, finding himself flustered by her smile. All the years he had lived in Vegas, practicing law, he had never entered one of the casinos—and now he understood why. Their allure was irresistible…*seductive*. "What is this that they're playing?"

"Pai gow?" she asked, touching him lightly on the arm. "It's a Chinese game, one of the most popular in the casinos of Macau. Do you want to take a hand?"

Samir shook his head, looking her up and down appreciatively before moving off into the crowd. He had a *purpose* for being here, he thought, forcing himself to focus.

Five years he had lived in this country, ever since leaving his native Pakistan with his men. For five long years they had labored in the house of war, waiting for this moment. For the word of the shaikh.

He thought back to that morning, a week ago—when the message had finally been left in the Drafts folder of his inbox. And he had known in that moment.

Their time had come...

7:39 P.M. Eastern Time
The Church of the Holy Trinity
Washington, D.C.

"God rest ye, merry gentlemen, let nothing you dismay..." Childish voices, lifted in praise to the heavens.

Michael Shapiro leaned back in the pew, smiling as he regarded the form of his son in the choir, shifting awkwardly in his robes.

This was the life worth living. Away from his job, away from all the stresses of the day. Here with his kids, he almost felt at peace.

Almost.

A shadow fell across the pew and he looked up, half-expecting to see his wife. She was supposed to join them later, in time for mass.

"Good evening, Shapiro." The form of Bernard Kranemeyer settled into the pew beside him, awaiting no invitation to sit down.

A puzzled smile flickered across the face of the deputy director. "And to you, Barney. Didn't expect to see you here."

Kranemeyer nodded, his arm stretching out easily along the back of the pew as he gazed up at the choir of children toward the front of the dimly lit sanctuary.

"Didn't imagine you would. Never had much use for church. Or for pious people, for that matter," he added after a pause. "Most of them are frauds, in my experience. People living a lie."

The strange look in the eyes of the DCS grew reflective as Shapiro watched. "Nichols was the only Christian I ever truly respected...and we both know how that's panned out."

"Yeah," Shapiro assented, still puzzled by his appearance.

Those coal-black eyes turned upon him, contempt radiating suddenly from their depths. The deputy director felt a chill wash over his body.

Kranemeyer shook his head, reaching inside his trench coat and pulling forth a handful of photographs. He held one of them up, eyeing it critically in the flickering light of the nearby candles.

"What have you been playing at, Shapiro?" the DCS spat, throwing the photograph into Shapiro's lap.

His fingers beginning to tremble as if in the grip of a fever, he reached for the photo, turning it over.

And there it was. The proof of his betrayal.

Shapiro looked up to see death in the eyes of his colleague—cold, implacable death. His gaze darted wildly around the sanctuary, toward the mute, silent icons along the walls.

No salvation to be found there.

"I—I…this wasn't what it looks like."

The DCS laughed softly. "You can do better than that, Mike. You might be the deputy director, but you're a second-rate liar. I don't have to guess what it 'looks like'. I know what it is…you passing intel to the Iranians. You sold out my men. All I want to know is this: was it worth it?"

He looked over at Shapiro, watching contemptuously as the man trembled, his face ashen.

"These are surveillance photos— taken here in D.C," the deputy director stammered, a drowning man clutching desperately at a straw. "You've violated the CIA's charter—this will never stand up in court."

Kranemeyer closed his eyes, the H&K under his coat seeming to quiver with anger. "Who said anything about court, Mike? Did Davood Sarami get a judge? A jury? God only knows what other assets you compromised."

Silence. He could still remember standing there at Dover, the fall wind rippling through his hair as uniformed Marines carried Davood's body out of the back of a C-5.

"You'll get what you gave, Mike. That's justice, isn't it? Or maybe it's just retribution—I couldn't give a flying crap either way."

"You don't understand, Barney. It's not like that. I didn't have a *choice*."

A bitter smile crossed Kranemeyer's face. "That's an old refrain. And false as it is old. We all make choices. What did the Iranians have on you?"

The deputy director seemed to shrink into his seat, his voice growing soft. "It wasn't the Iranians."

"Indeed?"

Shapiro shook his head desperately, licking his lips with the very tip of his tongue. "You have no idea who you're dealing with, do you?"

"No one who's powerful enough to save you from me, I know that much. But why don't you enlighten me?"

"I can—but I want this all to go away. All of it, the photographs... everything."

It was amazing, Kranemeyer thought—the deputy director was still playing politician. Making deals.

"You don't have anything I want that badly," he retorted, staring up at the rows of white-robed children, their faces smiling down like a heavenly choir of angels. The last innocents left in this city. "And if you get a deal, it will be on *my* terms."

Shapiro ran a hand along the collar of his shirt, his fingers coming away damp with sweat. "Anything. What do you want?"

"Tell me everything you know—I want details, names of everyone involved. *Everything.*"

"And what do I get in return?"

"You get to take the honorable way out. And your family—your kids— never have to know the type of man their father was."

"You mean..." Shapiro's voice trailed off, trembling querulously.

"I do," came the remorseless reply. "Or, so help me, I will destroy them as well."

5:06 P.M. Pacific Time
The oil field
California

"Are you sure they're here?" Korsakov lowered the binoculars from his eyes, glancing back to where Viktor sat in the back seat.

The boy hesitated. "They *were* here. Less than four hours ago. That's all I know."

Korsakov glanced toward the oil field once again, the ghostly spires of the derricks looming out of the gathering twilight. It would have to be good enough.

He pushed open the passenger door of the SUV, moving around to the back to retrieve his Steyr AUG. Korsakov's night-vision goggles were the only pair they had left—everything else having been lost at Andropov's mansion.

They would have to move cautiously, the three of them.

Viktor came around the corner of the vehicle at that moment, his youthful eyes shining above the scraggly black beard that cloaked the lower half of his face. The Glock Korsakov had given him was in his hand, his fingers fumbling with the slide.

"I'm ready."

Korsakov shook his head, stepping forward to put both hands on the boy's thin shoulders. "*Nyet, tovarisch.* I need you here in the car, monitoring communications."

It was a lie, and he could see in the boy's eyes that they both knew it. The assassin hesitated for a long moment, emotions warring within him, then he drew the boy into a fierce embrace.

Guided as if by a premonition, his hand slipped into the pocket of his assault vest, drawing forth a small password-protected thumb drive and pressing it into Viktor's palm. "I'll be back soon, Vitya. *Ne volnuysia.*"

Don't worry.

Another lie, but he would see this through to the end.

There were some things a man simply could not walk away from, the death of his brothers being one. That none of his men were related to him mattered not at all—the bonds of battle were far stronger than those of blood.

Korsakov turned away, motioning for Yuri and Misha to follow him. Spread out, they moved down the side of the road toward the abandoned oil field, flitting from cover to cover like wraiths in the dusk.

Fifty meters and the assassin paused, pulling back the charging bolt of the Steyr to chamber a round. The weapon felt cold in his hands, cold as the certainty of what was to come.

8:11 P.M. Eastern Time
The Church of the Holy Trinity
Washington, D.C.

"And that's *all* you know?" Kranemeyer asked quietly, staring into the eyes of the deputy director. He ignored the singing with an effort, still struggling to process what he had just been told.

"And in despair, I bowed my head. 'There is no peace on earth', I said." The children knew not the gravity of which they sang. Nothing of the evil that lurked around them.

Shapiro swallowed hard, nodding. "Haskel's not in it alone, but he never trusted me."

The DCS snorted. "I wonder why."

"There's someone up higher, I always knew there was. Haskel's too cocky—has to have someone covering his back. Someone powerful. They ordered Lay's murder. I didn't want to be a part of it, you know that, don't you?"

"Go," Kranemeyer whispered, his voice devoid of mercy. Of pity. He had heard enough. He thought for a moment of asking *why*—then decided against it. It could be any one of a dozen things: threats, blackmail, money—to name but a few. Or perhaps most likely, a simple lust for power.

"For hate is strong, and mocks the song of peace on earth, good-will to men!"

He saw the plea in Shapiro's eyes and his face hardened. "*Go.*"

"How do you know that I won't run once I leave this building? That I won't call the police?"

Kranemeyer nodded toward the white-robed boy in the front of the choir, his cherubic face smiling down upon the darkened sanctuary. "Because you know what will become of him if you do. Do you want him to live his life the son of a traitor? Do you want him to remember you that way?"

Indecision. He saw the father glance up toward his son, agony on his countenance. Then a nod. Shapiro rose, pulling his jacket close around his body as if to shut out the cold. "I'm sorry."

There was no suitable response, and Kranemeyer made no attempt to offer one.

He remained in his seat, arm over the back of the pew, as Shapiro made his way to the aisle, hurrying toward the vestibule. And still the children sang. "*Then pealed the bells more loud and deep: God is not dead, nor doth He sleep; The Wrong shall fail, The Right prevail, With peace on earth, good-will to men.*"

Wrong? Right?

There were times when he could scarce tell the difference. He listened as the strains of the final stanza died away, watched as the priest dismissed the children. Watched as a little boy scampered down from the platform, his eyes searching the darkness for a father that was no longer there.

A father that would never return again.

Rising from the pew, Kranemeyer walked forward, taking a candle from the tray and mounting it. Pulling his Bic from his pocket he touched fire to wick, watching as it blossomed into full flame, casting dark shadows across his face as it flickered.

He glanced up toward the crucifix, his voice rich with irony as he whispered, "Forgive me, Father—for I have sinned…"

8:24 P.M.
The Francis Scott Key Bridge
Washington, D.C.

How many times? How many times had he driven over this very bridge? Shapiro glanced from the sidewalk into the six lanes of traffic spanning the width of the bridge. Traffic unabated even at this hour of the night.

Mute witnesses to his impending death.

He shuddered, the wind tugging at the hem of his coat. Where had he gone wrong?

Wrong? He had dismissed the very idea as irrelevant during his days in college. All that mattered was *der Wille zur Macht*, as Nietzsche put it. The will to power. Moral absolutes? Archaic rubbish from a bygone era.

God is not dead, nor doth He sleep.

He forged on, out toward the central arch, a solitary plodding figure in the glare of the oncoming lights. He thought with regret of the twins, a tear leaving its icy trail down his cheek.

No good-byes. Perhaps it was better that way—they deserved better than the man he had become.

He paused at the edge of the parapet, his body trembling uncontrollably, the wind cutting straight through his thin coat, chilling him to the bone.

Tears running down his face, Shapiro mounted the parapet, feeling a sudden attack of vertigo overcoming him as he stared down into the choppy, ice-cold waters of the Potomac, nearly a hundred feet below. He swayed, the fingers of his left hand digging into the concrete in desperation.

Suicide. It was an unpardonable sin, yet how could it be any more damning than all that he had already done?

The deputy director paused, torn by fear and indecision. He could see the traffic from where he had come, but no one noticed. Or no one cared. It could have been either.

His right hand came up, making the sign of the cross over his chest. *In the name of the Father...and of the Son...and of the Holy Ghost.*

Closing his eyes, he released his grip on the parapet, his dress shoes slipping from the ice-slick concrete, a scream of panic escaping his lips. Falling into the darkness below.

The abyss.

5:35 P.M. Pacific Time
The oilfield
California

He had given consideration to climbing one of the derricks to get a better view of the surrounding territory, but rejected that idea rather quickly.

Beyond height, a derrick offered none of the other necessities that a sniper required—most importantly, the ability to move readily after firing a single shot. It might have worked well in the movies...but not in real life.

Harry moved into position behind a deserted forklift, its yellow paint chipped and rusting. He and Sammy had traded weapons, leaving him with the SCAR.

He raised the weapon to his shoulder, adjusting his eye to the night-vision scope and using it to scan the surrounding terrain. The oilfield's perimeter fence was down in any number of places—pushed down by vagrants in the years since the field's abandonment.

Too many avenues of attack. And they had scarcely eighty rounds of ammunition among the three of them—everything else having been abandoned in the van the preceding night, rounds left to cook off as the vehicle went up in flames.

He swung the SCAR's barrel in a slow one-hundred-eighty degree arc, scoping out the perimeter. Back and forth.

Just a few yards away from his position, the aging metal of a pumpjack groaned in the breeze—the giant "horse head" box gently nodding.

There. Movement...or was it his imagination? He stopped, aiming the rifle toward the base of a derrick near the remains of the fence to the southwest.

Nothing immediately apparent. He took a deep breath to steady the gun, inhaling the grease he had smeared across his face and neck to darken his skin against the night.

A man's head appeared cautiously, almost furtively, around the corner of the derrick.

Target sighted. Harry reached up, toggling his mike once, then twice. Alerting Han.

A body followed the head, moving forward in a crouch. A weapon held at the ready.

Harry watched as the figure sprinted from his cover toward the next derrick. Waiting, his cross-hairs still trained on the spot from which the man had emerged.

A second head appeared, and it all became perfectly clear. Bound and overwatch. One man providing cover as the other one advanced.

And there could be more. Watch and wait.

Arrogance. That summed up the expression, the look on Roger Hancock's face in the pictures taken by Andropov's team. The man who had ordered her father's murder.

All of this, only to find that their perpetrator was beyond reach. The realization was bitter.

Carol clicked to advance to the next picture, glancing toward the door that led into the outer office of the trailer. The Kahr lay at her fingertips.

Wait for us, he had said. *Don't come out until I come for you.*

Neither one of them had dared to speak of the other possibility. That he might never come.

It was just the two of them. The foremost man had an earpiece, but there was no indication that either of them were using comms.

Time to end this. The cross-hairs centered on the second man's chest just as he began to move. The big rifle recoiled into Harry's shoulder as he fired, the report echoing across the oilfield.

He fired three shots, pulling the trigger as fast as he could reacquire his sight picture. The man reeled backward, his broken body crumpling into the short grass.

And then the night erupted in fire, incoming rounds hammering the forklift. From the wrong direction.

He'd been played.

5:41 P.M.

It was…everything. Viktor shook his head, tracing his fingers over the numbers displayed on-screen. The encryption on the thumb drive had been somewhat less than formidable.

He would have to talk to Korsakov about that when he returned, the boy thought absently.

The series of figures added up to 2.3 million dollars in US currency, deposited in over ten separate offshore accounts. It didn't represent even half the buying power that it would have three years before…but it was still an overwhelming fortune.

Why? The boy thought, staring at the screen of his laptop. Why had Korsakov given him this?

It was access to everything in the assassin's accounts—all of it. He could withdraw at will, have the money wired anywhere in the world. All by himself, without Korsakov.

Without Korsakov. A cold fear began to gnaw at the boy's heart, his hands trembling. And he knew. His friend wasn't coming back. His breath began to come shallow and fast, the all-too familiar onset of a panic attack.

Gunshots off to the north penetrated the haze surrounding him, and he fought against the urge to hide. With trembling fingers, he jerked the Glock from its holster at his waist, feeling its reassuring bulk in his hand.

More gunfire. He forced his breathing to slow, blinking back tears. All the money in the world meant nothing—not without a friend. Not without the man who had saved his life.

Viktor reached for the door, stumbling out into the darkness of the night. He had to reach him.

8:44 P.M. Eastern Time
Georgetown, Washington D.C.

Christmas lights, flashing through the tinted windows of the SUV. Even with the alert levels raised and the threat of another terror attack hanging over the East Coast, people had carried on with their holiday decorations.

Years before, Kranemeyer would have attributed it to the American spirit, defiant in the face of intimidation.

Now it struck him more as the ambivalent apathy of those still asleep.

Someone inside the government is working with the terrorists, and they're trying to make it look like Nichols is behind it.

Haskel. It made sense now, Kranemeyer thought, remembering Carter's words. He should have seen it, even then.

They were given access.

Was this the secret that had so nearly cost Lay his life? If so, why? What was Haskel's angle...what did he stand to gain?

Questions without answers. The throwaway phone in Kranemeyer's breast pocket buzzed with an incoming text and he pulled it out with a gloved hand, reading the message off the screen. Thomas.

Approx forty minutes out from last known location. Will apprise when we have the package.

Two of his best, closing in on their former team leader. A man who had kidnapped and murdered an American teenager.

An innocent, no matter what his father might have done.

Where did you go wrong, Nichols? Kranemeyer mused, pondering the irony of the question. Where, indeed?

He tucked the phone back inside his pocket and pushed the door of the SUV open, stepping out onto an ice-slick sidewalk. Deniable vehicle or no, it was safest to approach his target on foot.

The alarm would be raised within the hour—people would start looking for Shapiro.

What thou doest, do thou quickly.

5:45 P.M. Pacific Time
The oilfield
Tehachapi, California

They had night-vision. At least one of them did. And he didn't have the ammunition necessary for a prolonged firefight.

Harry spat out sand as bullets chewed up the dirt near him, lifting himself up just far enough to return fire. One, two shots.

"I could use some help over here, Sammy," he hissed into his mike, rolling over on the ground till he was staring up at the looming pumpjack.

No response. As there hadn't been before. If they had outflanked him so successfully, perhaps Han was already dead.

Laying in the shadow of the pump, he hit the SCAR's magazine release, checking his remaining ammunition.

Four .308 cartridges left. A couple magazines for his Colt, but a pistol was near useless against a trained marksman with a rifle.

Rounds continued to strike around him, caroming off the solid steel of the pump.

He closed his eyes, forcing himself to focus, to concentrate. Listening as the fire from the southwest faded away for a moment. There would be no second chances.

He rolled to one knee, acquiring a sight picture as his rifle came up. A man charging toward the pump, out in the open, his weapon weaving from side to side as he ran.

Harry pulled the trigger, the scope's cross-hairs centering on the man's chest. Once, twice.

The mercenary fell, throwing out a bloody hand as he hit the gravel. He tried to pull himself up, the expression of agony on his face clear even through the greenish glow of the night-vision scope.

A pair of shots came out of the night without warning, striking Harry in the side, sledgehammer blows to the ribs. *A double-tap.*

The SCAR dropped from his hands as he swayed, catching himself against the side of the pumpjack—his mind struggling to process what had just happened.

He looked up to see Korsakov standing there, barely five feet away, a semiautomatic pistol in his outstretched hands. "Almost good enough, Mr. Nichols. *Almost.*"

The vest, Harry thought, attempting to get his breath back. His assault vest must have stopped the slugs, leaving his ribs hammered from the blunt impact of the rounds. Not that it mattered, he thought, staring into the muzzle of Korsakov's Skyph.

"Turn around."

Harry shook his head, a bitter smile crossing his face. It hurt even to speak, but he found himself chuckling.

"You first." *Keep him off-balance.*

"They were good men—the men you killed," Korsakov whispered, a note of sadness in the assassin's voice. He took a step closer, placing himself between Harry and the pumpjack. "My brothers."

"Cry me a river."

Korsakov's eyes narrowed, his finger tightening around the trigger. "It's time to say good-bye, Mr. Nichols."

Footsteps on the gravel, and Harry turned his head to see Han standing there, the UMP-45 leveled in his hands. And he knew that he was in the SEAL's line of fire.

The assassin gestured with the barrel of his pistol. "Back away or I kill him."

"Take the shot, Sammy," Harry ordered. He could feel the presence of Death, as if it stood beside him—could sense his friend's hesitation. It was a hard shot, perhaps too hard in the darkness.

And death for him might as easily come from Han's weapon as Korsakov's. Little matter. "Don't let him leave here alive—just take the *shot.*"

There was no time, he could see that in Korsakov's eyes. One of them was going to die.

He pitched sideways, throwing out a hand to catch himself—fire blossoming from the muzzle of the Russian's pistol. Blinding pain tore through his body from his injured ribs as he went down into the gravel, his right hand clawing for the butt of his Colt.

Faraway, as if in a dream, he heard the staccato of Han's H&K. Felt drops of something warm spray over his face.

Ignoring the pain shooting through his ribs, Harry rolled onto his back, aiming the Colt skyward.

Korsakov swayed above him, clutching at what remained of his throat. His legs gave out from under him and he crumpled to the gravel.

Breathing heavily, Harry pushed himself up on one knee, struggling to stand. He found his feet after a moment, standing there above the dying Russian, his cocked pistol in his hand.

The man was struggling to breathe, a bloody froth escaping his lips. Yet the defiance was still there in his eyes, visible even through the agony distorting his face. Unbowed, even in death.

Harry raised the pistol, seeing Korsakov's face through his gunsights. "This one's for you, David."

The thunder of the Colt reverberated across the oilfield, and then all was silent. The silence of the grave.

8:51 P.M. Eastern Time
Georgetown, Washington, D.C.

"You're the last person I expected to see tonight, Barney." Haskel closed the door, ushering Kranemeyer in out of the sleet. The DCS brushed the icy crystals off his trench coat, eyeing the house critically. Stairs led to a second floor and presumably bedrooms.

"We have a situation," he announced. The best lies were the ones that clung most closely to the truth. "The Agency has been compromised."

Surprise showed in Haskel's eyes. "Indeed?"

A nod. "You know I wouldn't be here if I thought I had anywhere else to turn," Kranemeyer acknowledged bluntly. "Is your wife home?"

The FBI director shook his head. "She left this morning, took the kids with her. Driving to South Carolina to be with the grandparents for Christmas. Why don't we go into the den?"

Haskel led the way down the hall, past a Thomas Kinkade landscape flanked by ornamental sconces.

"What's the nature of this crisis, Barney?" he asked, opening the door to reveal a small library, leather-bound books adorning oaken shelves and several plush armchairs completing the set. A small wet bar stood at one end, a pair of stools in front and several bottles of whisky on the smooth granite of the bartop.

"We have a mole inside our government, inside the Agency," Kranemeyer replied. "Tied to the hit on David. And I need your help exposing him."

"Of course. Anything. Who is it?"

There was a false note of concern, almost of eagerness, in Haskel's voice, Kranemeyer thought, confirming everything that Shapiro had told him. "Long story," he said, inclining his head toward the bar. "And I could use a stiff drink."

Haskel waved his hand. "Be my guest."

5:59 P.M. Pacific Time
The oilfield
Tehachapi, California

Pain. Harry closed his eyes as Carol probed his side with her fingers. "I don't think the ribs are broken," she observed, her tone studiously neutral. "But the flesh is already starting to purple. You're going to have a painful bruise."

"No kidding," he whispered, looking over to where his tactical vest hung over the back of the chair. Both bullets were visible, the slugs nearly buried in the plating.

He reached out for her as he stood, wrapping an arm around her shoulders. "You're going to get through this," he breathed, ignoring the pain with an effort. "This is all going to be over soon. All of the killing, all the deception. All of it past. I want to start anew, leave all of it behind."

"Can you?" came the quiet, piercing question, sadness in her voice. He stood there as she pulled away, the words on his very lips.

If you come with me, I can. The one thing he found himself wanting more than anything in the world. A *normal* life—the American dream. The strength of the desire frightened him.

And the words remained unspoken. He watched her move to the far side of the desk, cursing himself bitterly beneath his breath. He knew what to say—knew exactly what to say, but after all of the lies…

He reached for his shirt, buttoning it over his bare chest. A vague sense of misgiving entered his heart and he shrugged on the tactical vest over his head before reaching for his Colt. *Han should have returned by now.*

Five minutes, Harry thought, glancing at his watch. The SEAL had only gone out to the car, the sedan they had stolen from the freeway the night before. "Everything okay, Sammy?" he asked, keying his mike.

Nothing. Something was wrong, very wrong.

"Stay here," he ordered, shooting her a look. "And keep your head down. I'll be back."

He reached for the door, bringing the Colt up as he exited the office trailer. Stepping into the night.

Nothing. Everything was still, barely a whisper of wind stirring through the bones of long-deserted industry. "Sammy?"

Gooseflesh rose along the skin of his arms as he sprinted across the gravel toward the nearest cover. A fear that perhaps he was too late.

Voices. He could hear someone speaking. Rising from his crouch, he moved among the pallets of abandoned equipment until he could see the pumpjack where Korsakov had died.

Threat. It was that, and yet something more. Han stared into the muzzle of a Glock, watching tears run down the face of the boy holding it. Tears of anger and grief.

"You don't want to die," Han warned, keeping his hands well away from his sides. From his own gun. "Not like this."

The boy seemed to waver, the Glock's barrel trembling as he extended it in one hand. Indecision.

It was good, Han thought. He could talk him down, could talk him into lowering the gun. He wouldn't need to kill him—no one else needed to die.

What was life, without a friend? Viktor glanced down at Korsakov's broken body, at the once-kind eyes now lifeless. He scarcely even heard the man's lies.

Lies, the story of his short life. Everyone had lied to him, everyone except Korsakov. They had lied to him when his parents had died, leaving him an orphan at ten. *Come along, there's a nice home waiting.*

He could still remember the first time, the drugged stupor—a man's hands sliding along his young body. A demon's voice at his ear and again, the lies. *This won't hurt.*

Countless lies. He choked on a sob, remembering his friend's last words. *"I'll be back soon, Vitya. Don't worry."*

Had even that been a lie? No, no, it couldn't have been. He stared down the barrel of his Glock at Korsakov's killer, watching his face, his lips moving. "Just give me the gun—no one needs to get hurt."

More lies. A scream of impotent fury escaped his lips, his left hand coming up to support the Glock, his mind consumed with a single purpose. *Kill.*

Dimly, as if through the haze of a dream, he heard an explosion to his left, felt a pair of bullets rip into him.

Falling. He hit the ground hard, his hand reaching out in an attempt to pull himself up. His side felt suddenly warm, his movements sluggish. Ever weaker.

Then darkness closed over him and he never felt anything...ever again.

"He wasn't going to give me the gun...was he?" Han asked as Harry emerged from the shadows.

"No—no he wasn't, Sammy," came his friend's reply. Without a word, Harry stooped down, prying the Glock from the boy's lifeless hand.

He had *known* it, the SEAL thought, forcing his breathing to slow—the knowledge frightening him even more than how close he had come to death. In the face of everything that he knew, all of his old training, he had wanted to believe that he could talk the boy down. Emotion overruling the cold realization of what he had to do.

You've been out of the field too long.

And sooner or later, it was going to kill him, he thought—looking over to where Harry stood, a dark, forboding form in the pale moonlight. Him...or someone else.

9:00 P.M. Eastern Time
Georgetown, Washington, D.C.

"To the confusion of America's enemies," Haskel said with a smile, taking the tumbler of whisky from Kranemeyer's hand.

The irony. The DCS favored him with a dispassionate smile, raising his own glass in salute. "I'll drink to that."

He took a slow sip, watching as the FBI director drained his glass. "You know, Eric—I've heard it said that the ritual of touching glasses in a toast came about so that, as liquor splashed from one to another, both parties could be assured that the drink wasn't poisoned. Or that could just be an old wives' tale, of course."

Haskel chuckled. "I suppose it's nice to know that paranoia isn't a product of our modern age." A puzzled frown furrowed his brow as he glanced over, taking in Kranemeyer's coat, gloves. "Feel free to make yourself comfortable, Barney."

"They say that even the paranoid have enemies, Eric," Kranemeyer announced, setting his glass on the endtable with a gloved hand. His eyes locked with Haskel's. "Why did you do it?"

The blood drained from Haskel's face as he grasped the import of the question. Of what had preceded it.

His gaze flickered down to the tumbler in his hand, the small pool of amber liquid still remaining in the bottom. There was fear in his eyes, the shadow of an unspeakable question.

Kranemeyer nodded.

"What are you going to do if I call the police?" Haskel demanded. It was a hollow attempt at bravado.

"You would never make it to the door," the DCS replied calmly, allowing his trench coat to fall open, revealing the holstered H&K.

"You wouldn't dare." The FBI director's words came out in a hoarse rasp.

Kranemeyer inclined his head to one side, regarding his counterpart with a look of contempt. "Shapiro is dead, Eric—took a header off the Key Bridge less than an hour ago. But he gave you up."

He went on without pausing, his voice level, remorseless. "As the poison works its way into your bloodstream, your muscles will weaken until you can't even hold yourself upright in your chair. Within two hours, you'll be dead."

Reaching into a pocket of his trench coat, Kranemeyer extracted a small, clear vial, placing it beside his tumbler of whisky. "The antidote. Once administered, you should make a full recovery within twenty-four hours. And it's yours if you'll give me the information I need. I want to know who you've been working with...who ordered the murder of David Lay. All of it."

Create a world of despair, then become the subject's beacon of hope. It was Interrogation 101.

"C'mon, Barney," Haskel retorted, his voice trembling. "The DCIA makes a lot of enemies. We both know that."

"And I know that you're involved." A pause. "One other thing...if the antidote is going to be effective, I have to give it to you within the next forty-five minutes. Beyond that..."

Silence.

6:11 P.M. Pacific Time
Tehachapi, California

Two miles out. Thomas reached down into the messenger bag at his feet for probably the tenth time in the last fifteen minutes, checking for his Beretta. It was loaded, just as it had been when he'd last checked.

The drive up from LAX had taken longer than normal, working their way around the police roadblocks set up in the wake of the previous night's murders. Every last weapon in the trunk of their rental sedan was illegal in California, and they couldn't afford being stopped.

"What do you think?" he asked, breaking the silence for the first time in miles.

The Texan never took his eyes off the road. "Of what?"

Thomas digested the question for a long moment, choosing his words carefully. "Of Harry. Do you think he killed that boy?"

"I don't think at all," came the stolid reply. "My orders were clear—bring him in. Nothing was said about being his judge."

"But don't you—"

"No," Tex cut him off. "We secure him, we secure Carol. Kranemeyer will get everything else sorted."

Nothing is personal, Thomas thought, the unspoken subtext within the big man's words.

After all the years. It was surreal.

The car crested the rise and they could see what remained of the perimeter fence below them in the pale beams of the sedan's headlights.

"Get ready."

Thomas nodded reluctantly, reaching into his bag to retrieve his pistol, the rasping sound of metal on metal as he pulled back the slide.

"Ready."

Only the good die young. Perhaps that was true, Harry thought, running his hand over the boy's bearded face, up to where the open eyes stared hauntingly up into the night sky. Impossible to say—he had seen it in the boy's eyes in those final moments before he pulled the trigger. The wild look of someone whose mind had broken long before their body.

His fingers reached up, gently closing the eyelids, a final service for the dead. *Last rites.*

There was a small USB drive in his jeans, and Harry tucked it into his shirt pocket—perhaps it would reveal something. There was nothing else, no wallet, no identification. Just a nameless kid, dead and gone.

Harry grasped the boy's shoulder, wincing with the effort as he rolled him over onto his stomach, his cheek pressed against the cold black tarpaulin. "Ready?" he asked, looking up into the SEAL's eyes.

It was the last body, yet he could sense the reluctance in Han's body language. Always the ones you couldn't save.

He heard the engine of an approaching car at that moment, his hand slipping underneath his jacket to close around the butt of the Colt.

"Follow me."

The car's lights were off by the time they approached it, a man emerging from the driver's side door and another man already standing in front of the car.

His gun was up, the Colt's hammer back, a round in the chamber. An easy shot. Yet there was something familiar in the profile of the target, in his movements as he closed the car door.

Something he had seen a hundred times before.

"Tex!" he called out, recognizing the form of Thomas near the front of the car as the men turned toward him. A tired smile broke across his face. The cavalry had arrived.

"Harry," the Texan replied simply, extending his hand. The bonds forged in battle.

Harry reached out to clasp it, drawing the big man into an embrace. "Glad you could make it to the dance, my friend," he whispered, making a feeble attempt at humor. "I'm afraid we had to start without—"

And there was a gun barrel pressed against his stomach, a Glock in the Texan's hand.

He recoiled, searching out his friend's eyes, but there was nothing to be found there—just black, expressionless pools against the crushing darkness of the night. It was like looking into the face of a stranger.

"I'm sorry, Harry," the stranger's lips moved, forming words without emotion. "I need you to cuff yourself."

9:15 P.M. Eastern Time
Georgetown, Washington, D.C.

Somewhere in the big house, a clock struck the quarter hour, its tones resounding through the silence.

Kranemeyer took a sip of his whisky, watching as drool escaped from Haskel's mouth, trailing down the side of his face.

The FBI director was slumped to one side in his chair, slowly losing control over his body. It was a pathetic sight, but Kranemeyer could find in himself no pity. Only a growing sense of impatience.

"Do you hear that, Eric? That's your life...slowly ticking away. What little you have left. *Who* is running your op?"

A desperate anger showed in Haskel's face, struggling to speak, his lips forming an obscenity. "...yourself."

"Impossible, Eric. I lack the flexibility of a politician." He drained the tumbler of whisky and set it back on the end-table. "Tick-tock."

The phone in his breast pocket buzzed and Kranemeyer glanced at it, the message plain on the screen. *The package is secure.*

Simple words, belying tragedy. They had found Nichols. He didn't realize till that moment how much he had hoped they would not.

"Why...you doing this?" Haskel gasped. "What is it to you?"

The anger boiled over. "You politicians don't believe in loyalty to anything, do you?" Kranemeyer spat, rising from his chair. "Nothing higher than your own ambition?"

He paused, tasting the bile on his tongue. "I have no faith. I believe in nothing save the men I lead into battle. Men who deserve better *leaders*. These days? They deserve a better country. And I would rather die than fail them."

A faint laugh escaped Haskel's lips. "Men like...men like Hamid Zakiri?"

Fury. He turned without warning, backhanding Haskel across the face with a gloved hand. The FBI director fell to the floor, his hands unable to support his weight, his cheek pressed against the Persian carpet.

"Within twenty minutes, this whole room will stink of your own excrement, Eric," Kranemeyer hissed, falling to one knee beside the body. "You'll lose all control of your bowels. And then the pain begins. Oh, yes...did I fail to mention the pain? You'll want to scream, but you won't be able to. You'll want to tell me everything you know, but you won't be able to do that either."

Haskel's eyes went wide, struggling to focus—white with terror. "You'll die in agony...and the autopsy will reveal a massive stroke. Our people are so very *good* at what they do. But you'll know that all first-hand. Soon enough."

"*No*," came the desperate whisper, the man's fingers clawing at the carpet. "*God*, no."

"I don't think God is listening to you, Eric. But I am...if you have anything worth hearing."

"The...computer."

6:21 P.M. Pacific Time
Las Vegas, Nevada

"Take this in." The voice intruded upon his thoughts and Nasir looked up as Omar pressed eighty dollars into his palm. He looked up at the lights of the Arco gas station and nodded.

As the day drew near, they were operating on cash only now. Untraceable.

With a brief glance into the backseat at his brother, Nasir pushed open the door of the van, walking hurriedly across the crowded plaza to the convenience store.

Alone. He was alone.

His legs felt as if they were made of rubber, threatening to give way from under him as he pulled open the door, moving toward the attendant by the register.

"Eighty on pump six," he announced, shoving the wad of bills across the counter. He looked across at the dark-skinned attendant. Indian? Or *Pakistani*?

He couldn't tell, and the moments were ticking away. He licked his dry lips, unable to hide his nervousness. "Can I use your restroom?"

The young man hesitated before shrugging. "It's not *supposed* to be public, but you look like you've had a rough night already, man. Right back through there."

"Thanks." His heart pounding, Nasir made his way back along the shelves until he reached the small room, digging the phone out of the pocket of his jeans and reassembling it. The number...what was it again? A wave of panic nearly washed over him, his fingers fumbling with the lock on the flimsy door. He couldn't have forgotten...

He leaned back against the sink trying to remember. *There.* He closed his eyes, the phone trembling as he pressed each button hesitantly.

And then it was ringing. Once. Twice. "*Ya Allah,*" he breathed.

Three rings. *Just pick up.*

7:23 P.M. Mountain Time
FBI Regional Field Office
Denver, Colorado

Meetings. It was what the Bureau did best, Marika thought.

"This isn't going to take long," Greg Buhler announced from the head of the room. The S-A-C of FBI Denver, he couldn't have been older than thirty-five. He smiled. "For the tech-obsessed among us, you'll be reunited with your phones in under ten minutes. But we need to keep security on this one airtight. Understood?"

There wasn't much to understand—their phones were under lock and key in a cabinet outside the soundproofed conference room.

"We've had several developments, most recently an hour ago—when we got a hit on the photo of Abu Kareem that we've been passing around. One of our field agents talked with the manager of a Mickey D's in Grand Junction and he placed Kareem in his restaurant on the 19th. Remembered him because of his inquiry about a kosher meal. Now, this is dated, but we believe..."

Locked away outside, Marika's cellphone began to pulsate. One, twice, three times. A fourth "ring" and it went to voicemail.

The gas station
Las Vegas, Nevada

No. Nasir listened numbly as the voicemail rolled, a woman's voice announcing his own fate. The realization sank in. She wasn't picking up.

Despair closed over him like a wave, a drowning swimmer going under for the last time.

Panic. How long had he been in the restroom? It couldn't have been more than a couple minutes, but it seemed like an hour. Omar was going to be asking questions. Questions he couldn't answer.

He took the phone apart with sweat-slick fingers, cramming it back in his pocket as he tried to calm his heart rate.

His feet carried him out of the convenience store and into the Vegas night. Omar was already back in the van, the hose replaced in its holder.

"Where were you?" the negro asked, glancing at him as he climbed back up in the van.

"Had to take a leak." The words came out of Nasir's mouth almost unbidden, leaving him trembling, afraid to even look at the black man's face.

But the answer seemed to be satisfactory—the next moment the van shifted into gear, rolling forward. Toward the end of his life...

9:26 P.M. Eastern Time
Georgetown, Washington, D.C.

He knew what he was looking at. It was leverage...against the most powerful man in the world. The FBI director had been nothing if not cautious.

Outside the study, sleet tapped against the window. The finger of an insistent Death.

"Dear God, Eric," Kranemeyer breathed, scrolling down the laptop's screen as he waited for the files to copy onto a portable USB drive. "What have you *done?*"

He had seen treachery in his day—thought he had gazed into its foulest depth when Zakiri betrayed his comrades. He hadn't begun to suspect that it was only the beginning, that it could have reached this far.

The President.

"Why?" he asked himself, only realizing after the words were out of his mouth that he had spoken aloud.

A moan seemed to come in response and Kranemeyer looked over to the chair where he had propped the weakened, dying director.

"You...don't understand," Haskel gasped, struggling even to take a breath. "We were on the brink...of a new or-der in the Middle East. An end to all—of it. All the violence."

Even as he slumped there in the chair, Kranemeyer could see the light in his eyes. The excitement. The *lust.*

"Peace in our lifetimes. A permanent end to…the energy crisis for America. It was going to be real—all we had to do was stand back."

"And watch people die."

Haskel coughed, spittle flecking his shirt. "Morality is a limiting thing."

There were no words. A loud *beep* alerted Kranemeyer that the file transfer had been completed, and he removed the thumb drive from the machine, closing the lid of the laptop with a gloved hand. He tucked it within the pocket of his overcoat, picking up both tumblers and the bottle of whisky.

"I believe my work here is done," he announced, glancing at the clock. Half-past nine.

Fear showed suddenly in Haskel's eyes, a panicked desperation. "The…antidote, Barney. I—gave you what you wanted. All of it. I did."

Kranemeyer paused, his hand on the door of the study. "Antidote, Eric? I'm afraid there is no antidote for that poison. Not yet, anyway, although I'm sure the boys in S&T are working on one."

Disbelief.

"But—you promised. You said there was one. And…I gave you everything, I swear it." He reached out in despair, suddenly overbalanced. The DCS watched in silence as Haskel toppled forward, landing on his side on the rug.

His eyes stared wildly up, eyes wet with tears. Pleading for hope. For life.

"I lied," Kranemeyer replied, cold indifference in his voice. "Morality, Eric…is a limiting thing."

And he was gone.

7:34 P.M. Mountain Time
FBI Denver
Denver, Colorado

"Here you go." Marika took her cell from the secretary, shaking her head.

Meetings. It had been a waste of time, she thought, flipping open her phone to check for messages. The Bureau's most recent intel was forty-eight hours cold. Anything but operational.

There was a missed call, a strange number on-screen. She moved down the hallway toward the temporary office she had been assigned, pressing redial as she did so.

Nothing. It didn't even ring. Just a mechanical recording announcing that voicemail was not available.

It might have been a telemarketer. Might have been a wrong number. Marika swore under her breath, cursing Buhler and his meetings. It might have been her CI.

She moved back into the rabbit warren of cubicles, rapping loudly on the partition separating her from the nearest Bureau tech. "I need everything you can get me on this number," she ordered, shoving the phone toward him. "I need to know if it's a cell. I need location history. *Everything*."

"How soon do you need it?" the young man asked, taking a glance at the screen of his own phone.

"Yesterday," came the acid reply.

7:04 P.M. Pacific Time
The oilfield
Tehachapi, California

A warm breeze drifting across the terrace. The shadow of a man falling across her table. A man old before his time, worn by the decades. Made old by sorrow.

An awkward half-smile. "It's been so many years."

Carol closed her eyes, remembering that first time—the first meal she had shared with her father after her arrival at Langley. Lunch there at the Ardeo in Cleveland Park.

That smile.

Alive. It was impossible, as impossible as his *death* had been a few short days earlier. She seemed to move as in a dream, afraid of waking. Afraid that, even yet, his tenuous hold on life might be broken.

"I need to go to him," she whispered, more to herself than anyone else in the room.

Richards shook his head, glancing over at Thomas Parker. "I can't do that. Sorry."

Thomas cleared his throat. "The director needs to remain in complete isolation until either his...injuries have healed to the point where we can move him without risk, or the threat against him has been eliminated."

"My orders," Tex said, walking over to where Harry sat, "are to get you back to Camp Peary. No idea how to do that with the hornets' nest you've stirred up. The roads to LAX are a nightmare."

Harry glanced down at his cuffed hands, the zip ties cutting into the flesh of his wrists.

He had escaped from them before, it wasn't hard. But this wasn't something he could fight his way out of. Not without dropping the hammer on men that had followed him into hell.

Prioritize. "That's the least of your worries," he announced, looking up into his friend's eyes.

The Texan took a cautious step back, wary of guile. Of danger. "Go on."

"Tarik Abdul Muhammad is in-country. In Vegas."

"Is he planning an attack?"

From across the room, Han spoke for the first time. "That's the general impression."

11:26 P.M. Eastern Time
Foxstone Park
Vienna, Virginia

Silence. Kranemeyer exhaled, watching as his breath evaporated into the darkness of the surrounding trees. A brook gurgled beneath the snow-covered footbridge upon which he stood, icy water splashing over the rocks.

He stared off toward the small parking lot, the single light there providing the only illumination to be seen.

Foxstone Park was no stranger to treachery, to deceit.

It had once been a favorite haunt of Soviet FBI mole Robert Hanssen, up until his arrest in 2001. It was also only a scant three miles from Senator Coftey's Washington-area residence.

The sound of a vehicle from the entry road, lights swinging through the trees. Kranemeyer drew his H&K, holding it out to his side as an SUV pulled into the parking lot. Its lights dimmed, then went out completely as a man emerged, his form swathed in a heavy overcoat.

Kranemeyer heard the sound of the driver's side door being closed, watched as the figure strode through the sleet toward him.

"Given the history of this place, I'd compliment your sense of irony, but I thought I made myself clear, Barney. Better for both of us if we give each other a wide berth. No calls, no meetings."

"You did," Kranemeyer replied, looking the senator full in the face. "Shapiro and Haskel are dead."

Coftey blanched. "*Haskel?*"

"As far as it takes, Roy," came the grim rejoinder. "Or were those just words?"

The older man shook his head, his face hardening. "No...it's time people were taught a lesson. Have you covered your tracks?"

"I used three phones over the course of the evening. All of them at the bottom of the Potomac now. Director Haskel was the victim of a stroke and—"

"I don't need details. Why am I here?"

The DCS extracted the thumb drive from the pocket of his trench coat. "This isn't over."

"Who?"

"Roger Hancock."

A string of curses escaped Coftey's lips. "Do you *realize* what you're saying?"

"He was willing to sacrifice a nation on the altar of 'peace,' Roy. He was willing to kill my men to conceal his treason. And he's skating toward a second term. I want him brought down." Kranemeyer paused, letting his words hang there between them. "You…or me?"

The implication couldn't have been more clear, but he could see the hesitation in the senator's eyes. *The President.*

They were standing on the edge of a precipice—long way down.

Coftey reached over, taking the USB drive from his hand with a heavy sigh. "Never been one for idle talk, Barney. Let's burn it down."

Chapter 23

The White House
Washington, D.C.

The room seemed to swirl around him, dragging him down into the abyss. Pain—fire shooting through his body.

Fear. He looked down to see something dark, red, staining the front of his tailored shirt.

A stain pulsating, spreading ever wider with every beat of his heart.

Hancock came awake with the sound of the clock striking midnight, his eyes opening almost convulsively, his heart thudding against his ribs. *Again.*

His eyes darted around the darkened bedroom as he struggled to calm himself, a slick sheen of sweat covering his chest, his fingers entwined in the sheets.

Danger. He swung his legs out until his feet touched the floor, casting a brief glance back at the undisturbed, still-sleeping form of the woman who shared his bed.

Drawing his housecoat around him, the president padded barefoot into the adjoining bathroom, staring at his reflection in the mirror. Hollow eyes gazed back, rimmed with darkness. People were starting to notice, first among them the woman who did his makeup.

His fingers dug into the rim of the countertop as he forced his breathing to slow. He was the safest man in the world. The Secret Service made sure of that.

But if they *knew*…what then?

And Valentin Andropov was dead, butchered by that rogue CIA officer. The one variable no one had seen coming.

Variable? They had all been variables, leading him down this road. To this place. Hancock closed his eyes, swearing softly. What had happened to him?

"I know what you've done." The voice of David Lay, drifting through his mind. That morning in the Oval Office, two weeks after Election Day. *"I don't know why—not yet, but I have the evidence of your treason."*

The words that had sealed his fate.

1:09 A.M. Pacific Time
The oilfield
Tehachapi, California

"Kranemeyer still isn't answering his phone." Tex looked up from the laptop as Thomas re-entered the room, cellphone in hand. "I tried the back-up number as well—no joy."

"Then stop calling," the Texan replied sharply. "You don't want to get flagged by ECHELON."

There was a moment's hesitation as the meaning sank in. "Then it's true."

A nod as he gestured at the computer screen. "Looks that way."

It seemed incomprehensible, the big man thought, rubbing a hand across the dark stubble of his beard. That the betrayals could have continued so far. So high.

First Hamid. Now this—the *President.* Everything he had once trusted, shaken to the very core. Almost everything.

"We can't just sit by and watch a terrorist attack go down," Thomas protested, his gaze flickering from Tex to where Harry sat across the room, his hands tied in front of him.

Harry shook his head, glancing down at his wrists. "No one said anything about sitting by. We can still stop it, but we can't go through regular channels."

"You're not in charge of this op," Tex shot back, his dark eyes flashing. "My orders are to take you in."

Orders. They were the big man's strong suit. Dependable as the sunrise. Always faithful. Ever the Marine.

Semper Fidelis.

Harry's eyes locked with Richards'. "So do your job—take me in...after all of this is over. After we've stopped Tarik."

"You have a plan?" This from Thomas.

Harry nodded, extending his bound wrists. Neither man moved. "How many years," he began, looking from one to the other. Struggling to maintain his own composure. "How many years has it been? We've been through hell together. If you can't believe me...then there is no one on this earth you can believe."

Yet he could see the doubt in their eyes, the detritus of betrayal. And in his own mind he found himself in Jerusalem again, watching as the barrel of Hamid's suppressed Glock swung toward the security camera.

Even in death, he continued to wreak havoc. "I'm not going to run from what I've been forced to do. Never have—I see no reason to start now. All I ask is that you hear me out. I've earned that."

After a long moment, the Texan nodded, moving in close enough to cut Harry's ties with the combat knife in his hand. "What's your plan?"

Harry rubbed his wrists, the red marks where the ties had cut into his tanned flesh. His head came up, eyes meeting Thomas' face. "Do you remember Nicole Powers?"

4:21 A.M. Eastern Time
Kranemeyer's apartment
Washington, D.C.

It had been years. Years since he had taken a life. And those times...had been nothing like this.

Kranemeyer sat alone in his darkened bedroom, staring out the window at the city. Had it destroyed him too?

Impossible to say. His choice had been made for him, somewhere back in the halls of power by men conspiring for "peace." The myth of the greater good, their perpetual justification for evil. Seeking peace, they had launched a war.

A war that he'd just brought crashing down around their ears. No regrets.

A phone rang in the night, the sound of his Agency cell from the bedroom, Jon Bon Jovi's voice breaking the stillness of the apartment. And he knew.

Rising from his chair with reluctance, Kranemeyer walked into the bedroom, grabbing up the phone just before it went to voicemail. "Kranemeyer here."

It was Lasker. "We've got a situation, sir. The DDI left his protective detail behind last night—took his kids to the Church of the Holy Trinity. No one has seen him since, his children were alone when his wife arrived. Metro's canvassing the city and we're monitoring the usual suspects for chatter."

"I'll be right in."

"That would be good, sir."

Kranemeyer pressed the kill button on his phone, staring down at the screen for a long moment.

And so it began...

3:45 A.M. Pacific Time
The convention center
Las Vegas, Nevada

No sleep. He couldn't possibly sleep. Leaving his bedroll, Nasir found himself passing like a ghost through the massive convention center, making his way toward the small room that once again served as their kitchen.

Perhaps he could make the call yet this night.

He had to find a way of escape from this nightmare. Jamal...perhaps even Jamal was not beyond saving. They were brothers, after all—even if there were times when he felt as if he was faced with a stranger.

He flicked on the light, the fluorescents in the ceiling casting a pale glow over the small room. The refrigerator was only a few feet inside the doorway and he pulled out a carton of milk, pouring part of it into a styrofoam cup.

The silence reminded him of Lebanon. Waiting for the Jewish bombs to fall. His hand trembled as milk splashed into the cup. Maybe this would calm him.

Nasir rubbed his palm against the leg of his jeans, feeling the slight bulge of the disassembled phone in his pocket. *Make the call*, a voice whispered within him. *Do it now.*

It was right. He might get no better opportunity. He turned, raising the cup toward his lips.

Abu Kareem stood in front of him, leaning against the doorway. "Having trouble sleeping?"

Nasir nearly choked on the milk in his mouth. "Y-y-yes. Yes I was, my father."

The imam regarded him with a look of kindness. "Is it anything that I could help you with?"

No. The imam was a *threat.* And yet, despite himself, he heard his lips form the opposite response.

Abu Kareem patted him on the shoulder and reached past him for the milk. "Have a seat, Nasir, and tell me what's on your mind. *Insh'allah*, I may be able to help."

He could feel perspiration moistening the palms of his hands as he sat down at the small card table, a nervous terror threatening to overcome him. And yet he yearned to trust. To have an *answer*.

"Are we right? In what we are about to do, I mean."

The imam paused, and Nasir could hear him filling a cup. "Yes, we are. You know the words of the Prophet, peace be upon him. Did he not truly say, 'I have been commanded to fight the people until they testify that there is no deity worthy of worship except Allah, and that Muhammad is the Messenger of Allah'?"

"Yes," the young man replied, staring down into his milk as the imam took a seat opposite him. "Yet…I have heard it preached that this hadith refers only to the pagans of Arabia, that it should not be used to justify the spreading of Islam by violence. Is it not written, 'If the enemy incline towards peace, do thou also incline towards peace, and trust in Allah: for He is the One that heareth and knoweth all things'?" He looked up, his eyes pleading. "What *is* God's truth?"

Abu Kareem took a deep breath, seeming to consider his words with care. "I understand what you are saying, my son. And I understand what you have heard. More importantly, I understand *why* you have heard it. It is a necessity in these days, when the followers of the Prophet are oppressed and afflicted across the world—that we present one truth to the unbelievers and another to the children of God."

"But to lie is a sin before Allah."

"No," the imam said patiently, leaning forward until his elbows rested upon the table. "To lie is a sin *if* you lie for your own benefit. To lie for the benefit of Allah's cause…is another matter entirely. Indeed, it is obligatory to lie to the oppressors of His people. And thus we have done. As the treaty of Hudaybiyyah, which the Prophet made in a time of necessity and dissolved thereafter, so must our peace with the West be."

Nasir felt a shiver run through his body as he gazed into Abu Kareem's eyes. The older man leaned back in his chair,

"Do you understand the point I am making, Nasir?"

"Yes."

4:02 A.M.
The oilfield
Tehachapi, California

The bed was empty. And she was nowhere to be seen.

391

Harry came awake, staring around the small back room of the trailer. She was gone. It couldn't be possible. *No.* He rose from the chair where he had been sleeping, wincing as pain shot through his stiff ribs.

Ignore it. He staggered toward the door, sliding his Colt from the polished leather of its holster.

He thought of calling out, rejected it just as quickly. If there *was* an enemy, he would accomplish nothing more than giving away his own position.

And there she sat, in front of the computer, its luminescent glow reflected in her weary eyes.

"What are you doing?" he asked, the question coming out more brusquely than he had intended.

"Powers," Carol responded, not even looking up. As he moved closer, he could see she had been crying. "I have their address—it's in Summerlin, outside Vegas. I looked at her Facebook."

"And?"

"They're expecting their first child." He could see the pain, the exhaustion in her eyes.

"You need to get some rest," he whispered, placing a hand on her shoulder.

"I can't." She paused, her body shuddering. "I close my eyes, and I see his face."

Harry found himself whispering a prayer, dreading her next question. "Does it...ever go away?" she asked, looking up into his eyes in the semi-darkness.

He didn't ask *what*. Didn't need to. He knew. The stain of blood. The scars left upon the soul by the taking of a life.

It seemed as if it was forever before he responded, a silent figure standing there behind her chair.

"No," came the soft reply, cutting to the very fibers of her being. She could feel his fingers brush at her hair, his hands kneading the taut muscles of her shoulders through the soft fabric of her blouse. "It never leaves you—not really. But you can overcome it. And you will."

"How do you know?"

"I don't. But I believe."

Carol closed her eyes, the image of Pyotr's shattered body once again flickering across her mind. A tear escaped, running down her cheek as she leaned back into his hands. "*Why?*"

She could feel his hesitation, the tension in his fingertips. "Because I need you," he whispered finally, his lips almost touching her ear. "Like nothing else, I *need* you."

By the time she turned around, he was gone.

6:34 A.M. Mountain Time
Denver, Colorado

Head down, the chill morning wind whipped around her ears, stabbing at her lungs as she breathed. Marika ignored the sensations, never breaking her stride as she ran down the side of the road.

Her morning run, a defiant routine against the increasing demands of "getting older."

A routine that was becoming less so. Her phone vibrated against her ribs and she swore in frustration, unbuttoning the light windbreaker she wore. "Altmann," she gasped out, realizing just how out of breath the run had left her.

"Where are you?" Russ.

"Running," she shot back, glancing at the watch on her wrist. "I'll be there by seven."

"You need to get in *now*." There was tension in the negotiator's voice, something rattling his unflappable calm.

Marika sucked in another breath of icy air. "What's going on?"

"Just got a flash from D.C and things have exploded around here. Haskel was found dead in his Georgetown home this morning."

"Murdered?" She cast a glance down the road as a car flashed past. A mile back to her car.

"No idea. No one knows yet. Just get in here. And, Marika..."

"Yes?"

"Your tech buddy got the results of the cell trace back. The phone is off-grid now, but the last time it communicated with a tower was moments after placing the call to you. Near Vegas."

She swore angrily. *It was him.* Had to be.

"I'll be there."

8:32 A.M. Eastern Time
The White House
Washington, D.C.

"No," President Hancock whispered, glaring across the room at Cahill. "It can't be true. I just talked with Eric *yesterday*."

"And the ME's preliminary reports indicate that he suffered a massive stroke shortly before midnight," his chief of staff replied calmly, as if speaking to a child. "I know the two of you were close, Roger. I'm sorry, but he's gone."

Hancock turned away, wiping his mouth with the back of his hand. He couldn't show fear—not in front of Cahill. As ruthless a political player as the Irishman was, he would never sanction the lengths to which the President had gone. Haskel's death was no accident.

"Has Metro uncovered any new developments with Shapiro?"

"Not yet," came the chilling reply. "One of the Jesuits remembers him entering the church with his kids before the rehearsal. Doesn't seem like anyone saw him leave."

First Andropov. Then Haskel. Shapiro?

He was dead, Hancock realized suddenly. Dead or on the run. Dead might, in fact, be preferable—in light of all that had happened.

His fingers shook as he poured himself a drink, a finger of brandy in a crystal snifter. *Blood.* His dream came washing back over him in unsettling clarity. A vision of death.

He hadn't dreamed the danger. He tossed back the brandy, swallowing hard. "Has the media caught wind of any of this?"

"Not yet." It was only a matter of time—they both knew that. D.C. was the city of leaks.

"Keep me in the loop...on everything, Ian. We can't have our intelligence community compromised again. Shapiro has to be found."

6:57 A.M. Pacific Time
The oilfield
Tehachapi, California

"You can trust him," Harry observed, placing his equipment bag in the trunk of the car, underneath a tarpaulin.

Tex straightened, looking him in the eye. The sun was just beginning to stream over the hill overlooking the oil field. "What do you mean?"

"Saw the way you looked at Sammy. I know how you felt when he left the team."

The big man shook his head. "Doesn't matter how I feel. Trusting him again is another story. Not even sure I can trust you."

"Yeah." Harry closed the trunk with one hand, zipping up his leather jacket against the cold. "About that. I never intended to draw you into this."

"I know," came the slow reply. "You were following orders, same as always. But what happened to that boy in Beverly Hills?"

"I didn't kill him."

"I know...that's what Carol told me. Still your op." Tex paused. "We'll roll with your play for Powers. Long drive, longer odds—but it might pay off."

He could feel the tension. Harry let out a deep breath, watching it billow into the chill morning air. "Thank you," he said finally. Didn't seem like much of anything else to say.

"I don't have any other options. Just pray it works."

"As ever." Harry had just started to turn away when the Texan spoke again. "How'd it ever come to this?"

"One betrayal at a time..."

10:04 A.M. Mountain Time
FBI Regional Headquarters
Denver, Colorado

"Look, D.C. is breathing down my neck...the freakin' *director* is dead, and you want me to go hunt down a wrong number?" The look on Greg Buhler's face was one of incredulity.

Marika crossed her legs, wiping a fleck of dirt off her jeans. She hadn't taken the time to change. Hadn't seemed like a priority at the time.

"No. I'm following up on a lead," she replied, favoring the S-A-C with a cold glance. "What do you have to lose? Las Vegas was on your potential targets list. If Russ and I can confirm that...we've just found your needle."

Buhler ran a hand across his forehead. "They warned me that you were a pain in the butt."

Her face never changed. She had heard it all from men at the Bureau over the years, every name in the book and quite a few too obscene to be put in a book. Didn't matter.

At length, he looked up, realizing that his comment had failed to provoke a reaction. "Fine," he relented, a heavy sigh escaping his lips. "But I can't spare a chopper—they're all combing the mountains. You and Russell will have to take the next commercial out to McCarran. If you go off the reservation again...well, it will be Powers' problem, not mine."

"Powers?"

"Trent Powers, the Vegas S-A-C. Give him my best." Buhler smiled. "On second thought, don't mention me as being responsible for sending you. He still owes me drinks."

"I'll keep that in mind," Marika responded, rising from her chair. She knew Buhler's type—politicians all the way. Comfortable so long as nothing threatened their bureaucracy.

"Good hunting."

Indeed.

1:03 P.M. Pacific Time
The warehouse
Las Vegas, Nevada

"We'll approach from the north entrance," Tarik Abdul Muhammad noted, tapping the map with a forefinger. "You have everything in readiness there, don't you?"

"Yes," came the imam's reply. "Your concern will be getting your weapons in."

"That shouldn't take long," Jamal replied, the confidence of the college student asserting itself. He could feel the eyes of the shaikh on him, listening to *his* words. "The entire floor is handicap-accessible—so that wealthy old Americans can gamble away their children's inheritance. Gambling...a work of Satan, as it was written of the Prophet."

"You had a point, Jamal?" Abu Kareem asked, clearing his throat.

Jamal flushed, feeling the unspoken rebuke. "Yes. What I have are the cylinders of the nerve agent rigged with explosives surrounding them—each of them weighing roughly twenty pounds. Hard to handle while fighting our way in, *but* we can roll them quickly across the casino on one of the hotel's luggage carts. Only one man needed for their transportation."

The shaikh smiled. "Well done, Jamal. That will be advantageous. The Americans have security at the door—here, and here. We will need to take them down before advancing on the theatre."

"Time?" Jamal looked behind him to see one of the *mujahideen* speaking. His English was rough, but he was an experienced fighter. Jamal had even heard whispers that he had been involved in the planning stages of *Lashkar-e-Taiba*'s assault on Mumbai.

It was a crucial question.

The shaikh glanced at his watch. "From the moment the first shot is fired...we need to have secured her within two minutes. They will make an effort to lock us out of the theatre—we have to be prepared for that."

"We will be," Abu Kareem interjected, the older man's countenance taking on a look of serenity. "*Insh'allah.*"

4:30 P.M. Eastern Time
Theodore Roosevelt Island
Washington, D.C.

The sun was setting, slipping behind the clouds in the west—a chill wind blowing off the water. Bernard Kranemeyer stood off to one side, his dress shoes half-buried in the silty mud of the beach.

The glare of a crime scene investigator's flashbulb briefly lit the gathering darkness, all eyes focused on the body lying there in the mud. *Michael Shapiro.*

"On the face of it, looks like he washed in with the tide," the DCS observed, speaking to an FBI agent standing nearby.

"That it does."

"Who is going to have jurisdiction of the investigation…the Bureau? Or D.C. Metro?"

"We will," the young man replied without blinking. "National security."

Indeed. "Make sure you keep me in the loop on this one, all right?"

"I'm sure you'll be informed on a need-to-know basis," came the stiff rejoinder.

Kranemeyer took a step into the agent's zone, his dark eyes snapping. "Mike…was a friend. More importantly, his death leaves me the acting director of the CIA, serving at the pleasure of the President. I need to know everything. Am I making myself understood?"

"Loud and clear."

2:17 P.M. Pacific Time
Summerlin, Nevada

"You know what you are supposed to do, right?" Harry asked, glancing in the rear-view mirror above his head.

"Yes," Thomas replied from the backseat of the car. "I do. All too well, matter of fact."

Harry shook his head. "We've been over this, Thomas. It's the only way to establish contact."

"I know."

Carol cleared her throat from the passenger seat beside him, her words clipped. "According to her Facebook wall, she left for the grocery store fifteen minutes ago. I can monitor Foursquare, but that's not gonna give us her location in real-time. You need to get in there."

A nod from Thomas and he stepped out onto the sidewalk as the car slowed.

A roll of the dice. That's all this was, Harry realized, watching in his rear-view as he pulled back out onto the road, heading out of the housing development. Long odds.

"What did you mean?"

He took his attention off the road for a brief moment to glance over at Carol. "About what?"

"You said that you needed me."

He'd known the question was coming, didn't mean that he was prepared to answer it...honestly. It felt as if there was a wall between them, a wall he had erected.

A wall that had to come down.

"Once this is done...I have to get out. Leave all of it in the past. Everything I've fought for—I have to experience it for myself. I want to have a normal life. A family. *Kids.*"

The American dream. He could feel her eyes on him, felt as if he was naked before her. Stripped of the lies.

Suddenly vulnerable.

It was a long moment before she spoke again, and when she did, her voice was soft. Barely above a whisper. "Do you think you can...leave it all in the past, I mean?"

The impossible question, and his heart whispered a lie. *Yes.* The easy answer, what he *wanted* to tell her.

The truth...was never so easy.

His headset crackled with static before he could respond. Han's voice, intruding on his thoughts. Drawing him back to the reality at hand. "We're at the back door. Prepping for entry."

"Roger that," Harry replied, his mission voice returning. "Standing by."

2:31 P.M.
McCarran International Airport
Las Vegas, Nevada

Nothing. Marika ran her calloused thumb over the phone's screen to remove the "No missed calls" message, cursing under her breath.

So much for hope. She looked up to see Russ emerge from the line behind her, a bag over his shoulder. "Flying two days before Christmas...never a good idea."

It hadn't been. Buhler had been forced to pull strings even to get them seats. "No calls."

"I don't know if you should have expected one," the negotiator replied, his voice calm. Gentle, even. "Do you really have a plan, Marika?"

She hesitated for only a moment. No sense in trying to fool Russ. "No, I don't. No plan. Just a gut feeling."

"What kind of feeling?"

Marika looked off into the city, thousands of windows glimmering in the afternoon sun. "That it all happens here."

Chapter 24

Betrayal. It never got old, no matter how many times you had done it before. Using people—getting close to them, *learning* them, using that knowledge against them. Exploiting their mistakes. Their sins.

And there were times even you didn't know what you were doing, or what it would become. Like now.

One night had brought him to this. Just one night. A fling. And now it was their leverage.

Thomas picked up a framed picture off the coffee table, glancing into the eyes of a wife. A loving husband. Soon-to-be parents.

"Her check-in just placed her at a gas station three miles away," the voice in his ear informed him. Carol. "Be ready."

Right.

He knew when she entered the driveway, the chime of an alarm going off within the house. Heard her footsteps on the stairs outside in the garage, fumbling with a key in the door.

Showtime, and just like any good show, it was made of lies.

The fluorescent in the kitchen came flickering on, catching her in its light. The photo...hadn't done her justice. She was more beautiful than he had remembered—radiant in the flush of her pregnancy.

Thomas waited for her to set down her purse on the counter, laying her phone beside it.

"Hello, Nicole," he said, moving from the shadows of the family room. He saw her face go white at the sound of his voice, her voice trembling as she began to speak.

"W-what are you doing here? I told you it was over—it was a *mistake*. I told you never to call me again." The words came tumbling out of her mouth in almost a panicked rush.

"So I didn't call you," Thomas replied calmly, eyeing the distance between her and her cellphone. "I just came. You weren't that hard to find."

She made no move toward it, indecision in her eyes. "What if Trent comes home—finds you here?"

"I'm counting on him doing just that," he replied, a note of sadness in his voice. "In fact, I want you to call him, just to be sure he does."

"*Why?* We've been happy these last few years, I'm expecting his child—and yes, don't look at me like that—it is *his* child," she retorted angrily. "I can't allow you to ruin all of that."

"And I won't," he lied, knowing it was an impossible promise. "You know I work in homeland security. I need to talk to him—can't use normal channels. I just need you to get him to come home."

She stood there, a look of disbelief on her face. "How?"

Thomas took a deep breath. It was Harry's playbook, all the way to the bitter end. "Tell him you're in labor..."

3:56 P.M.
FBI Field Office
Las Vegas, Nevada

"Special Agent Altmann," Marika announced, flashing her badge. "We just flew in from Denver—you should have received a flash from the S-A-C there. We're following up on a lead in the Abu Kareem case."

"We did," the young woman behind the desk responded, barely looking up from her work. "What can I do?"

"I was ordered to liaise with Special Agent Powers. Can you direct me to him?"

"You'll have to speak with me instead." The woman got up from behind her desk, setting aside a stack of papers. "Agent Chase, a pleasure to meet you."

"What's the problem?"

"Powers just went home. His wife is expecting a child." A smile, for the first time. "Apparently she just went into labor. Men...they have no idea what we go through, do they?"

If you say so, Marika thought. "What are you doing concerning the threat?"

"The LVMPD has been brought into the loop as much as we've deemed necessary and the resorts have been notified that Abu Kareem is a person of interest."

"Is that all?"

Agent Chase half-turned, looking into Marika's eyes. "This city deals with terrorist threats several times a year, Agent Altmann. We've even had chatter that suggested *Lashkar-e-Taiba* sympathizers might be operating in the city. That was over a year ago, but we don't let our guard *down*. The resorts—their facial recognition software is more advanced than ours and interfaced with the DMV databases, in addition to ours and Interpol's. If Abu Kareem darkens their door, we'll know within minutes."

7:09 P.M. Eastern Time
Vienna, Virginia

The pale glow of the laptop was the only light illuminating the library, a cold light absorbed in the dark furniture, the towering oaken bookshelves.

Roy Coftey lowered his empty glass to the desk, still tasting the rum on his lips. The way forward was…unclear, to put it mildly.

His hand slid across the smooth mahogany of the desktop, tapping gently on the computer mouse. It was all there—everything, all the evidence of treason. E-mails dating back over the course of nine months, back to the time when Hancock's campaign had first encountered trouble.

Coftey remembered it well. Remembered the late night teleconferences with Ian Cahill. *You have to deliver Oklahoma, Roy.*

With the Sooner State's electoral votes numbering a scant nine, he'd known they were desperate at that point. Known they'd be pulling out all the stops.

He just hadn't known how many stops there were to pull. Voter fraud was one thing—they'd done it for years, no big deal. Just the way the game was played. But this…this was beyond the pale.

His shirt was damp with sweat, the tie loose around his throat. He ran a hand through his greying hair, the memories flickering across his mind's eye.

Waist-deep in a rice paddy, the sun burning down. Even now he could smell the burning, sulphurous stench of gunpowder, hear the sound of slugs splashing into the water around him.

They'd been out in the open that day in Cambodia. On their own. Deniable.

Just like Kranemeyer's team in Israel. Betrayed by their own leaders. *Politicians.*

Coftey shook his head, favoring his empty glass with a weary glance. That was why he'd come to Washington those many years ago, wasn't it?

To be *better* than them. To make a difference. And somewhere along the way...he had become like all the rest.

Thirty-four years was enough to corrupt a saint, and he'd never qualified in that category.

What had he become?

He cast another long glance at the evidence on-screen, his lips curling up in a sneer of disgust. Not *that*.

His hand slipped out, fingers encircling the bottle of rum as he poured himself another glass. Taking Hancock down would require going up against his own party, depriving them of their chance to retake the White House.

In all likelihood, it would be the death of his political career. Of everything he had worked to build over the decades.

He could feel a presence and he looked up to see Melody standing in the doorway of the library, her slender form draped in a robe. "Planning to join me?"

"Yeah," Coftey replied, a slow smile passing across his lips. "Just as soon as I finish my rum."

He watched her go before turning back to the computer—remembering his words to Kranemeyer.

"Let's burn it down."

Indeed, and his own fortunes with it. He shook his head, pulling the USB drive from the side of machine.

Let it burn...

4:17 P.M. Pacific Time
McCarran International Airport
Las Vegas, Nevada

"Welcome to Vegas, Congresswoman. It's a rare pleasure."

Laura Gilpin smiled, taking the proffered hand as she descended the steps of the LearJet onto the tarmac. Fifty-three and unmarried, she was known in D.C. as the "Iron Maiden", as much for the physical discipline of her daily jogging as her heated debates on the floor of the House.

She could have passed for at least five years younger, maybe ten—depending on how prejudiced the eye.

"The pleasure is all mine, Steve, but there was really no need to send your own jet," Gilpin laughed easily, displaying the effortless Texas charm that had swept her into office twice. "We'll let the media play with that ball of yarn for a few days, shall we?"

"So long as you're willing to break the President's embargo of Vegas," Steve Winfield responded, answering her smile with one of his own. The casino owner glanced up the stairs into the darkened interior of the Lear. "Don't you usually travel with your own security, Laura?"

"Never when I'm visiting my friends at the Bellagio, Steve. Gave them Christmas off to be with their families. You'll watch out for me, won't you?"

"Of course." Winfield turned to the short, stocky man at his side as they moved toward the waiting limousine. "Gilad, you'll be personally responsible for the congresswoman's safety from now until she leaves Vegas. Understood?"

"Yes, sir," the man replied, the runway lights reflecting off his shaven head as he extended a hand toward the congresswoman. "My name's Cohen, Gilad Cohen. I'll do my best."

Winfield laughed. "Don't let Gilad fool you—he's the best there is. Former Israeli special forces, the head of my security team ever since I stole him away from Adelson at the Venetian."

The Israeli never even smiled, moving to flank Gilpin as they entered the limo. "Can you update me on your threat profile, congresswoman?"

Gilpin let out a heavy sigh, running a hand through her shoulder-length brown hair. She leaned back into the white leather of the limo. "The usual crazies, you know the drill. I get a couple death threats on Twitter every day, a few people ranting in all caps how they'd like to 'remove me from office,' nothing serious. Nothing like it was a year ago, right after my appearance with Frank Gaffney."

"So, no threats that you would consider credible?"

"None."

4:24 P.M.
Summerlin, Nevada

He could remember it all clearly now, Thomas thought, looking down into his whiskey. A night in D.C., just back from the sandbox—spending the evening in the Atlas Room. A blonde, alone at the bar.

No ring.

"What are you going to say?" Nicole Powers asked, her eyes pleading with him across the kitchen table.

"About what?"

"Us, of course."

Thomas shrugged, tossing back the last of the whiskey she had poured for him. "What's there to say?"

What, indeed. It had only been hours later, back in his room, that she had gotten a call from her husband. Out of the country, in the Sudan to be exact, working with the JTTF.

"He should have been here by now," he observed, glancing at his watch. How many minutes was it since he had entered the house? He didn't remember.

He pushed the glass away from him, silently cursing himself for giving in to the temptation. His weakness.

The sound of footsteps on the stairs outside and the door burst open, revealing the silhouette of her husband. "Honey, I got here as quickly as I could, the traffic was heavy and I…"

His voice trailed off as he saw Thomas sitting there at the table. "Who are you?"

"Have a seat, Trent," Thomas admonished, gesturing to the chair beside Nicole. "We really need to talk."

5:17 P.M.
A grocery store
Las Vegas, Nevada

He had to do it. *Go now,* the voice within warned him. Nasir glanced ahead—they were almost to the check-out counter. Only one customer ahead of them, an overweight American woman with a cart heaped full of snack food, undoubtedly destined for a Christmas Eve party…or perhaps it was all for her. It was hard to tell.

Just enough time. He watched as Omar grabbed a pack of Trident gum off the display, placing it on the counter beside their loaves of bread.

"I gotta take a leak," he whispered, nudging his brother in the side.

"Yeah, yeah," Jamal replied, seeming preoccupied. "We'll see you at the car."

And it was that simple. Nasir felt sweat trickle down his face as he walked away, struggling not to run—not to call attention to himself. He moved up one aisle and turned, heading down another toward the back of the store, scarce daring to breathe. *Freedom.*

A double door marked "Employees Only" stood in his path and he pushed it open, half-expecting an alarm to sound. Nothing.

Nasir found himself standing in the storage room of the small grocery store, shelves filled with toilet tissue and paper towels rising above him toward the ceiling ten or eleven feet above his head. His hands fumbling with the back of the phone, he moved behind a nearby shelf, crouching down.

Redial. His breath caught in his throat as he stared down at the phone's screen, watching as it began to ring.

He murmured a curse in Arabic, his hands trembling. *Pick up.* He nearly dropped the phone when a woman's voice answered, "Yes?"

The woman from the FBI. His handler.

Alhamdulillah. God be praised.

"Please, please—you have to help me. They're moving forward with the attack."

"Details, Nasir. I need the details—what is the target?"

He closed his eyes, shaking his head back and forth. "No, no, no. You come and get me first—then I will tell you everything. Once I am safe. I'm done."

"Where is your brother?" Omar asked, holding the grocery bags easily in his massive hands as he and Jamal left the check-out counter.

"He'll be with us in a couple moments," the college student responded carelessly. "Men's room."

Omar nodded, starting to push open the door of the convenience store. *Good enough.*

All at once, he stopped, his eyes fixed on a little sign hanging just outside, printed in both English and Spanish.

No Public Restrooms.

His heart nearly stopped, the words of the imam that morning flickering through his mind. *Keep an eye on Nasir...I fear his heart is not with us.*

And he knew. They had been betrayed. "Find him," Omar hissed, ignoring Jamal's look of disbelief—his eyes darting around the small store. He patted his jacket with anxious fingers, feeling the bulge of the Smith & Wesson underneath. "Quickly."

A noise, something moving in the store outside—and Nasir looked up, sweat trickling down his face. "I'll meet you at the back of the store," he whispered into the phone. "I can tell you their plans for the attack, everything—just please hurry."

"We'll be there in under ten minutes, Nasir," the woman's voice responded. "Just need to cross town. But you need to give me the information now."

He hesitated, an agonizing moment of indecision—running a hand through his matted, sweat-soaked hair. The rough concrete floor of the storeroom cut into his knee as he leaned against a nearby shelf.

Giving her the information…it meant giving up what leverage he had. All his assurances of safety. "How can I trust you—that you'll still come for me, once I've given you what you want?"

"You have my word. It's for your own safety, Nasir. The more quickly we can get these men in cuffs, the safer you'll be. I'm coming for you."

Faith…in a stranger. He swore in frustration. *No.* "I'll meet you behind the store, and I'll tell what you need to know—"

"Nasir? Nasir?"

He tried to respond, but his mouth wouldn't form the words, his throat suddenly dry. He was staring into a muzzle of blued steel, into Omar's dark eyes behind it. Eyes full of disappointment and rage.

"Give me the phone."

Helpless. Marika could hear a shout, then the line exploded in static. The sound of a phone being destroyed. She knew it well. Knew all that it meant.

She swore, an oath filled with fury, pressing her foot down on the accelerator. The car in front of them refused to budge, continuing to plod along just below the speed limit.

"Get the LVMPD on the phone." She didn't even glance at Russ, her eyes fixed on the road ahead. "And Powers. Have them meet us there."

She paused for a long moment, struggling with the cold reality of what she had heard. She had given him her word—that she would protect him, that his work for the FBI would not be forgotten. All of it…for what?

"We just lost our CI."

5:26 P.M.
Summerlin, Nevada

"Why should I believe that any of this intelligence is reliable…Mr. Todd?"

"Why should you?" Thomas responded, maintaining his composure. Everything in Powers' body language screamed of a man who had yet to be convinced. "Take it with you. Run your own analysis. You'll find the facial recognition is an 83% match with photos of Tarik Abdul Muhammad from his time in Gitmo. We ran it through the Agency systems when our source first flagged it."

"Your source?"

Thomas spread his hands out on the tabletop. "That's need-to-know, I'm afraid. Above both our pay grades."

Powers shook his head, cursing under his breath. "What is the Agency doing running 'sources' on U.S. soil—care to tell me that?"

A smile. "Once again…pay grade. Now, the bigger question, can you afford to take the chance that it might be true?"

The FBI agent's eyes locked with his. "I'll have to take all of this back to the field office, begin to verify it through our databases."

"Understood. And you understand that I will have to accompany you— Agency protocols, this intel doesn't leave my presence."

Powers hesitated for only a moment. "What can I say…you check out. I suppose this request is reasonable."

"It wasn't a request," Thomas replied, maintaining his poker face. This was one of the benefits of using an Agency backstopped legend. He had rolled the dice that the bureaucrats at Langley wouldn't have thought to close it down. Gambled and won.

"Now…I need to know something." The agent paused, as if choosing his words carefully. "How do you know my wife?"

No warning, no indication of what he had sensed. Nothing leading up to it. Just *the question.*

He could see her out of the corner of his eye, in the kitchen. The look of desperation on her face. Thomas smiled easily, as if the question was of no import. "We met once in D.C., years ago. A political event, if I recall correctly. We—"

The phone on the table beside Powers' hand began to vibrate, and the FBI man glanced at it. "I need to take this."

Thomas waved a hand, fighting against the nerves that plagued him. "Of course."

He waited as the agent went into the next room, wishing he could get another drink. Knowing that he couldn't handle one. *Keep control of yourself…*

When Powers reappeared, he was pulling on his coat. "We need to go— right now. You were right. They're here. In Vegas."

Thomas didn't see Nicole as he left the house. Just as well—nothing to say, only the hope that whatever news the phone call had brought, it would be enough to distract her husband from asking too many more questions. Powers popped the remote entry key of his Subaru, moving around the other side of the vehicle.

"Talk to me, Thomas," the voice in his ear interjected. Harry, this time. "What's going on?"

He cast a glance around, making out their car near the end of the block. Powers was inside the SUV now, the engine roaring to life. "When I know, Harry…you'll know."

Something was happening, Harry thought, watching as Thomas entered the vehicle with the FBI agent. He could feel it. And somehow, he feared that they had been too late.

5:58 P.M.
The convention center
Las Vegas, Nevada

The concrete floor came rushing up to meet him, scraping the skin from the side of his face. A booted foot landed in his ribs, and Nasir could hear them crack under the impact.

A scream, almost inhuman in its sound, a pain-soaked fog descending over his eyes. He could taste blood in his mouth, a raw, sickening taste.

He rolled into a ball, head against his knees, trying to shield his damaged ribs—just as another boot smashed into the small of his back. Pain rippled like fire through his body, another scream escaping his lips.

I'm coming for you. The voice of the woman, playing itself through his mind. *Don't be afraid.*

Lies.

Spittle struck him in the face and he looked up, his vision clearing just enough to make out the form of his brother standing over him. "Jamal..." he whispered, blood trickling from the corner of his mouth. "Jamal..."

"Shut *up!*" The image seemed to waver, fading in and out as his head throbbed. But it was his brother. "*How could you*—how could you have betrayed our faith?"

I didn't. His lips tried to form the words, but all that came out was a moan of agony. Then he saw his brother's foot drawn back once more...and he closed his eyes.

6:15 P.M.
The convenience store

"Agent Altmann?" A tall woman in an FBI windbreaker turned as they approached across the parking lot, ducking under the crime scene tape.

"Yes," she responded simply, extending a hand to Powers as Thomas looked on.

"Trent Powers, Vegas S-A-C. What do we have?"

"Not much," the woman replied, glancing in Thomas's direction. "Who's he?"

"Steven Todd." The FBI man waved him forward. "He's Agency. They came into possession of intel on the terrorist cell."

"Indeed? Then maybe they can tell me where to find my CI—because all I have is this," Altmann retorted, bitterness sweeping across her features. She held up a sealed evidence bag containing the smashed phone. It was completely mangled, twisted metal and plastic. "No signs of a struggle in the back room where he placed the call, nothing except the phone. My guess is that he was taken at gunpoint."

"Witnesses?"

"None of the crime. No one paid any attention to them exiting the store. Showed Nasir's photo to the clerk. He was in there with another Arab and a black guy, best they could recall."

Powers nodded, his gaze sweeping the front of the store. "Security footage?"

"Two cameras," came the short reply. "The tapes are already on their way to your field office. We'll have to see what they tell us."

Her eyes came to rest on Thomas, and he felt as if the older woman was looking straight through him. "What is your intel telling you?"

"That Tarik Abdul Muhammad is in-country...and Vegas is his target."

10:04 P.M. Eastern Time
CIA Headquarters
Langley, Virginia

"Sir, I need you to look at this."

Kranemeyer glanced up to see Daniel Lasker standing in the doorway of his office. "What is it, Danny?"

"A flash from the FBI's Las Vegas field office just hit the op-center. They've lost a CI in the Abu Kareem manhunt, with his last transmission from a convenience store in the Vegas metro area. They believe his cover has been blown."

The DCS took a deep breath. "So, we've got a homegrown terror cell in a major American city...potentially in possession of a WMD."

"No." Lasker hesitated for a moment, unusual for the talkative young comm chief. "They don't believe it to be homegrown—they have new intel that seems to indicate that Tarik Abdul Muhammad is in-country and heading up the attack."

"Where did they get *that* intel?" Kranemeyer demanded, cursing underneath his breath. If it were true...

Another long, unnatural pause. "According to the Vegas S-A-C...they're getting it from *us*. More specifically, from an officer named Steven Todd."

"So?" The name meant nothing to Kranemeyer, nothing that he could think of. "Is he one of ours?"

"Steven Todd is an official Agency legend...for Thomas Parker. And I can't find any reason for him being in Vegas. He was supposed to be on vacation—a hunting trip. And the FBI was looking for him."

"I know," the DCS replied significantly, staring Lasker in the eye. "Run with it."

"You mean...?" The comm chief's voice trailed off. "Sir, under the terms of the CIA charter, we *can't* operate on U.S. soil. It's illegal."

Kranemeyer pushed his chair back away from his desk and rose, leaning heavily on his bad leg. "Rules were made to be broken, Danny. And it's on *me*. Not you. Not Parker. We'll deal with those niceties later."

He limped over to the percolator, pouring himself a cup of coffee. "Confirm Parker's intel to the Bureau and kick it upstairs. Make sure the President receives the latest."

8:02 P.M.
A motel
Henderson, Nevada

It hurt to breathe, a stabbing pain in his side. Harry winced, holding the hot, wet cloth against his ribs for a moment longer before pulling it away to reveal a purplish bruise.

"We're missing something here," he announced, buttoning his shirt as he came back out of the bathroom. Things weren't adding up—two plus two equaling five. "Why Vegas?"

Tex was sitting on the edge of the bed, a glass of water in his hand. "It's a symbol of Western decadence?"

It was the most logical explanation, but there was something missing. "Why now?"

"Christmas?" Harry turned to find Han standing in the doorway of the adjoining room. "One of the biggest Christian holidays...the birth of Christ."

"Allah has no son," Harry mused, remembering the words of the Qur'an. It was possible.

"An influx of tourists even with the recession," the SEAL added. "Vegas is a high-value target on a normal week...but Christmas? You do the math."

He had. "Let's go over this again. What do we know about Tarik Abdul Muhammad?" Harry asked, glancing over to where Carol sat.

A shrug. "Not much to know, really. He spent eight years in Gitmo following his capture in 2004. According to soldiers assigned to guard him,

Tarik was considered devout, often spending hours reading the Qur'an. It was said among his fellow prisoners that he was a *hafiz*, having memorized the Islamic scriptures during those years in captivity. In 2012, political pressure from the administration strong-armed a military tribunal into dismissing the most serious charges against him. Against the protests of several prominent members of Congress, he was then returned to Pakistan—sort of an olive branch after the Bin Laden raid."

"Where he cropped up on our radar again within six months." Harry shook his head, running a hand through his dark hair. "You can't argue with the success of soft power."

"Some of the intel we gathered suggested an affiliation with *Lashkar-e-Taiba*, but that was never confirmed. His followers call him 'The Shaikh,' a sign of respect, we believe, for his knowledge of the *Sunnah*. A couple of local attacks on Coalition military in Afghanistan before our withdrawal were tied to him…but he's largely stayed in the shadows. Waiting."

"And now he's back."

9:35 P.M.
The convention center
Las Vegas, Nevada

"I suspected that we had been betrayed," the shaikh began, his normally soft voice trembling ever so slightly with anger. "When the FBI raided our house of worship in Michigan, I suspected it. But I didn't want to believe that one of our brethren—one of Allah's faithful, was apostate."

His hypnotic blue eyes came to rest on Jamal's face. "And where do your loyalties lie? With your brother? Or with your God?"

The college student's fists clenched, tears of anger running afresh down his face. "I have no brother. My life is pledged to the holy struggle, as Allah wills."

Silence. Tarik seemed to consider his words for a moment, looking around at the group assembled in the middle of the convention center. His *mujahideen*. The men he had prayed Allah for every lonely day in Cuba, spreading out his prayer mat overlooking the sea—toward Mecca.

And God had answered his prayers…yet given him this test. They must not fail.

"If that is true, then you must show yourself prepared to deal with those guilty of apostasy. What were the instructions of Allah's Apostle?"

Jamal's eyes were closed, his hands trembling. "To fight and slay the pagans wherever they are found."

The shaikh nodded, motioning for one of the *mujahideen* to bring him a long, thin box from a nearby table. With slow, reverent movements, he opened it, revealing the glistening steel of a Japanese *katana*.

Holding it by blade and hilt, he passed the sword to Jamal. "The cameras are already in place. Do as the Prophet has bidden."

10:03 P.M.
FBI Las Vegas Field Office

He was at the other end of the country, but from the clarity of the video feed, he might as well have been in the next room.

"Tell me you have some good news, Agent...Powers," the President of the United States began, appearing to consult the sheet in front of him for the name.

Marika glanced over at the S-A-C. They had nothing. They'd been over the footage again and again, but it was the same every time. Three cameras—one inside the convenience store, one in the parking lot, another in an ATM across the street.

None of them showed the terrorists' vehicle. Unfortunately, Vegas wasn't NYC, not yet. Once you got off the Strip, cameras were sparse.

"I'm afraid not, Mr. President," Powers responded. "It is my opinion that we need to put Vegas on high alert. Ground all flights in and out of McCarran, lock this city down."

To her surprise, the President shook his head. "That's out of the question, Agent Powers. Our best intelligence is that we're dealing with a terrorist who has access to a chemical weapon."

"Exactly!" Marika spat out, ignoring a warning look from the S-A-C. "We have to use every asset at our disposal, Mr. President, even if it means going public."

"You're not following me, Agent, uh...Altmann," Hancock replied, seeming surprised by her outburst. "If we move openly, publicly, we risk spooking them into launching the attack early. Releasing the weapon on the street."

The President looked off-screen. "Vegas is a city of nearly 600,000 souls. Never mind that holiday tourists have swelled those numbers. There's no way to evacuate this city quickly enough. Even if I ordered an evacuation now, we wouldn't have near enough time."

As if he sensed her temper about to explode, Russ laid a hand on her arm. "He's right. I was in the New Orleans field office during Katrina."

"Do we alert the resorts?" This from Agent Chase.

"No," the President responded. "Not yet. We have to keep this circle small if we're going to avoid a panic. I am told that the facial recognition software they employ is state-of -the-art, and that their databases interface with the Bureau and Interpol. Our only option is to find these criminals and shut them down permanently."

Marika opened her mouth, then closed it again, rethinking her words.

"The CIA's intelligence indicates that the attack will take place the day after tomorrow—Christmas Day. If we are unable to find Abu Kareem's cell…"

Powers hesitated, having voiced everyone's worst fears. "At what point do I have your authorization to shut down McCarran International and move the city to full alert?"

The President once again seemed to consult someone off-screen, a heavy sigh coming through his microphone. "Agent Powers, if you have not apprehended Abu Kareem and his men by 2100 hours tomorrow night—then you have my authorization to take whatever steps you deem necessary. What do we have on your informant's companions?"

"The other Arab is identified by facial recognition as Jamal al-Khalidi," Agent Chase began, staring at her screens. "A student at University of Michigan, and former roommate of the missing CI."

"His brother," Marika interrupted.

"His alleged brother," Chase corrected, still reading off her notes. "The African-American is a 75% positive as Keon Washington. Thirty-one years old, he became famous as a rapper under the handle of DD Cool well over a decade ago, before assault charges landed him in federal penitentiary."

"Assault?"

"A drunken brawl. Washington broke a man's neck, left him paralyzed and on a feeding tube. Was sent up for fifteen years, but the judge commuted it to eight."

That was the way the justice system worked. Marika snorted. "Then how did he wind up here?"

"He converted to Islam several years into his sentence and changed his name to Abdul Aziz Omar. He's been under the wing of Abu Kareem ever since."

Agent Powers glanced over at the interactive map of Las Vegas thrown up on the plasma—lines radiating outward from the convenience store where Nasir abu Rashid had disappeared. He took a step forward, staring directly at the President. "Teams from Denver and Los Angeles will be here by morning to provide support, Mr. President. We'll scour this city from one end to the other. We will *find* them."

1:27 A.M., December 24th
The convention center
Las Vegas, Nevada

The night was cool and clear, the stars of heaven above shining down upon the two men standing in the parking lot of the convention center, just outside the service entrance.

In the distance, the neon of The Strip flashed on, eternally.

"The city will be swarming with the American police by the time the sun rises, Tarik," Abu Kareem began, zipping up his jacket against the chill. "Perhaps it is time to reconsider our plans."

"No," the shaikh whispered, a light in his eyes as he stared toward the city. The eyes of a mystic.

It struck Abu Kareem in that moment as never before just how young he looked. His time in American imprisonment had always made him seem older than he really was.

"But the men whom Allah has given you. The weapons that you have obtained." The imam held up a hand, struggling to know which words to choose. "Do we throw all that away?"

The younger man never even looked at him, gazing on toward the lights of the Strip. "Allah has provided the men. Allah has provided the weapons. And you think that He cannot show us the way...as He has in the past?"

Abu Kareem fell silent, feeling the sting of the rebuke. It was true enough—how many times had the followers of the Prophet faced overwhelming odds?

Faced them, and overcome. He cursed the doubt in his own heart, yet the voice of caution still seemed to speak from within. *Please God,* how?

The eyes of the shaikh were closed, his lips moving—as if in prayer. His face shadowed in the glow of the lights from the nearby highway.

Even as Abu Kareem watched, Tarik's visage seemed to clear. "The way...will require a sacrifice."

"As the path of Allah always does."

"Of you."

2:45 A.M.
The motel
Henderson, Nevada

Years at war had left him a light sleeper. An insomnia that had everything to do with memories.

A sound brought Harry awake, glancing quickly over to the bed where Carol lay.

He could make out her form in the dim ambient light coming through the window from the parking lot outside, sheets twisted and kicked to one side—her body shaking in almost-silent sobs.

The sound he had heard.

And he knew, all too well. The feeling of guilt, the stain it left on the soul. He closed his eyes, murmuring a prayer. That she might be spared.

Moving silently, like a cat, he found himself crossing the motel room to stand by the side of her bed, looking down upon her. Her eyes were closed, still held in the thrall of a dream, tears leaking out from beneath the lids to run down her cheek.

He reached out to her as he sat down on the bed, running a gentle hand down her bare arm. So much he wanted to say, but there were no words. Nothing that could help.

Her hand came up as she awakened, fingers interlacing with his—squeezing gently, as if she took comfort in the touch.

"When does this…end?" came the question, choked out between sobs. The soul-wrenching grief of death—of having *caused* death. Harry closed his eyes, taking her into his arms. The only answer was a lie, a lie he couldn't tell her. Beyond that…*nothing*.

He held her head against his chest, brushing tear-soaked strands of blonde hair back from her face. "I don't know," he whispered finally, telling her the truth. "I only know that I'll still be here when it does."

Chapter 25

Kneeling toward Mecca, Tarik Abdul Muhammad raised his forehead from the prayer mat, hands on his knees as he straightened, performing the *taslim*. He glanced toward his right where Jamal prayed, his eyes meeting those of the college student. "*Assalaamu 'alaykum wa rahmatu-Allah.*"

The peace and blessings of God be upon you.

For a moment, there was something in Jamal's expression—a hesitation—and then he replied, repeating the ancient words of blessing back upon him.

His face turned to the left, catching the eye of the negro. "*Assalaamu 'alaykum wa rahmatu-Allah.*"

He could hear his followers repeat the chant behind him, finishing the *fajr*, the dawn prayer, even as the first faint glow brightened the horizon toward the east.

Tarik rose to his feet, a rare smile touching his lips as he turned to greet his men. "When next we greet the dawn, we will do so in Paradise. And where is Paradise to be found, my brothers?"

"Neath the shade of swords," Jamal responded from beside him, and the room erupted, the cries echoing off the empty walls. "*Allahu akbar! Allahu akbar!*"

417

6:35 A.M.
The motel
Henderson, Nevada

The bed was empty by the time she woke, the warmth of the covers enfolding her, tucked carefully around her body.

Another side of this man, Carol thought, remembering his words of the previous night as if they had been spoken in a dream. *I'll still be here…*

And he had held her close as she cried herself to sleep, his chest a pillow for her head. She could still feel his arms encircling her waist—those rough, deeply calloused hands. Hands that had killed…and wiped away her tears.

Contradictions.

"I have to get out. Leave all of it in the past." She turned her head, looking across the room to the recliner where he slept, studying his face, his chin shrouded in thick black stubble.

But could he? Leave it all behind…

Despite everything that had gone before, she found herself praying that he could. Before it destroyed him.

Carol pushed back the covers, padding barefoot into the bathroom. A glimpse of herself in the mirror and she shook her head, taking in the dark circles under her eyes.

She thought of the FBI in that moment, picking up her watch from beside the sink. They'd heard nothing from Parker—not since Richards and Han had shadowed him to the Bureau's Las Vegas Field Office.

And the attack was only twenty-four hours away…

8:03 A.M. Mountain Time
Billings, Montana

"Who knew a uniform could look so good?"

Paula Gonzalez smiled, glancing back to where her husband still lay in bed.

"You've said that before," she retorted, brushing a speck of lint away from the Delta Airlines logo as she buttoned her shirt.

"So?" He arched an eyebrow. "Just means it's still true."

She laughed, making a face at him in the mirror. After forty years on earth and two pregnancies, she wasn't the girl he had married. Not any longer. But he hadn't seemed to mind.

"You're just feeling guilty that you get to lay in bed while I go to work."

A shrug. "I never said you had to take an extra flight."

"I know," Paula replied, reaching for her pilot's hat. Delta was one of the few airlines that still required their pilots to wear the hat as part of their full uniform. It was a nice touch...even if it did bad things to her hair. "But we can use the extra money."

An understatement. He hadn't had an hour of overtime in months. "Remember what I told you, baby," she continued. "The kids only get one present tonight. The rest...have to wait till tomorrow morning when I get home. Remember?

"Yeah, yeah. What time does your flight get in to Vegas?"

She leaned down to kiss him on the lips. "We've got a brief lay-over in Salt Lake City—should touch down at McCarran a few minutes before eight..."

9:27 A.M. Pacific Time
FBI Field Office
Las Vegas, Nevada

"We're coming up empty, boss," a voice announced from the computer. Marika reached for her cup of coffee, listening to the reports come in from the FBI agents that were now fanning out across Vegas. Watching screens wasn't the same as being out there. In the field.

They had gone to the mosques first, three of them just within a few miles of downtown Vegas. Call it profiling—it was reality. They knew who they were dealing with.

"We just left the Masjid Ibrahim. The imam, Edward Fayed, said that he was familiar with Abu Kareem," the agent's voice continued. "Didn't know him personally, didn't know he was in the Vegas area."

"Do you believe him?" Powers asked. Marika glanced over at him—the S-A-C had come to work in a suit, but the jacket had been discarded hours before, revealing the Glock in his shoulder holster.

"Yes. Remember two years ago, when Fayed alerted us to that wannabe jihadi in his congregation?"

A nod from Powers. "Carry on, then. Initial reports from Masjid al-Noor are also negative."

The door opened just then and Agent Chase burst in, seemingly out of breath. "We just got a flash from the LA Field Office. They've had a sighting of Abu Kareem. Just a few miles from LAX."

A curse erupted from Powers' lips. "Is it a positive ID?"

"Assistant Director Dietz seems to think so. He's already given the callback orders to his teams here in the city."

There were no words. Marika closed her eyes, forcing herself to take a deep breath. "He can't do this—has it *occurred* to Dietz that Abu Kareem's presence in LA could be a diversion?"

The S-A-C shook his head. "He can and he has. We're grasping at straws here—and if they have a lead on Abu Kareem, that's our best shot."

A pause before Powers went on. "You realize...we could have been played. LA could be the target and Nasir abu Rashid's presence here the distraction. If they suspected him, they could have fed him false intel, knowing it would get back to us."

"But the CIA's intel—"

"Has been wrong before," he retorted, cutting her off. "Agent Chase, get me a direct line to LA. I want to talk with Dietz—have him patch us in to everything that goes down there."

10:48 A.M.
The convention center

"I have not spoken of this till now," Tarik began, looking around at his men, "for I feared that we had been betrayed...but Allah has not left us alone in this struggle."

He gestured to the map of Las Vegas spread-out on the table before them. "There has been a cell of *mujahideen* in this city for years, led by a lawyer named Samir. Simply waiting—going about their lives as they were bidden. They will join us in the attack."

"How many?" Omar asked, moving closer to the map.

"A dozen men, all of them veterans of our fight against the imperialists in the mountains of Afghanistan. Half their number will aid you, the other half join us in the main attack."

"*Insh'allah*," the negro murmured, his eyes closing as if in prayer.

"It is time that you left for your appointed post," Tarik advised, turning toward him. "Yours it is to strike the first blow."

He reached out, embracing the black man and kissing him on both cheeks. "Go with Allah's blessing, my brother. We will meet in Paradise."

The emotion of the moment...it felt as if it might overcome him. All those years in prison. The years of his youth.

Vengeance.

11:04 A.M.
The motel
Henderson, Nevada

"I don't like staying here," Carol exclaimed suddenly, looking up from her computer. She was hooked into the motel's wi-fi network, monitoring the news coming out of the city. None of it relevant. "Not being able to know what is happening."

Harry moved away from the window, letting the shades fall back in place. "Thomas will contact us when it is necessary to do so. He's a professional, none better."

"Welcome to field work," Tex observed, looking up from the small desk at one end of the motel room. The big man had his Glock field-stripped and laid out on the newspaper in front of him for cleaning.

It was true, Harry thought, taking the case containing his UMP-45 and opening it on the bed. For all the glamor that the movies showed, most of a spy's life was spent in motel rooms like this one.

Waiting.

The cellphone in his shirt pocket buzzed even as his hands moved over the metal receiver of the submachine gun and he plucked it out of his pocket. *Thomas. Speak of the devil...*

"Hello."

"I only have a moment," his teammate responded. "But I need an answer from you. How credible was your intel on Vegas?"

Harry took a deep breath, ignoring Carol's inquiring gaze. Forcing himself to remember.

He could remember the night, the tension in the room. The sweat beading Andropov's face. Every detail as clear as polished glass in his mind's eye.

"I am a facilitator, nothing more... they're going to strike Las Vegas."

True? Or false? He could still see the fear in the Russian's eyes, hear the slight tremor in his voice. Truth? *Or lies?*

And lives rested in the balance.

"He was telling the truth," he replied finally, breathing a prayer that he was right. "It was solid intel. Vegas *is* Tarik Abdul Muhammad's target."

"Because the Bureau's LA field office is currently following up on a sighting of Abu Kareem a few miles from LAX this morning with another man, possibly a foreign national. They think the disappearance of their CI in Vegas is a diversion."

"No."

12:14 P.M.
Las Vegas, Nevada

Alone. With his thoughts. And his God.

Omar bent forward, his forehead touching the surface of the prayer rug as he whispered the *takbir*. Words of praise.

Twenty-five steps, he thought, distracted for a moment by the sight of his Kalashnikov propped in the corner of the empty room.

Twenty-five steps for him to reach his firing position. Just out the door, up the stairs—onto the roof. That's all it was.

I seek refuge in Allah from the outcast Satan, he breathed, quelling his own fears. He had seen men die, the first when he was nineteen. A drug deal gone wrong.

He could remember that moment as if it were yesterday, the look of fear in the other man's eyes as his gun came out. The surge of power that came from pulling the trigger. The blood flecking the dirty asphalt.

What would it feel like to *be* that man? He raised himself from off the mat, the question caroming around his mind, itself unstoppable.

Soon enough, he would know. As would the Americans…

2:45 P.M.
FBI Field Office

"It's been two hours. No one in or out." Agent Powers stared at the screen in front of him, the images from the helmet-cams of the Los Angeles Field Office's tactical team.

"Did you run down the building's owner, Dietz?" he asked, speaking into his Bluetooth headset.

The screen shifted away from the Canoga Park-area commercial building, revealing the face of LA Assistant Director-in-Charge Anthony Dietz. "Yeah…it's Wells Fargo. The bank took the entire property four years ago—it was part of a chain of pawn shops."

"What is thermal giving you?"

"Two men in a back room. Based on the statements of a witness, we're reasonably certain that it's Abu Kareem and the foreign national. They just seem to be waiting…maybe on the rest of the cell. I've staged my teams out of sight—if anyone shows up, we'll be able to deploy within seconds."

"Any hits on his companion?"

A shake of the head. "Negative, ran him by Interpol and the boys at Langley. Whoever he is, he's not thrown up any red flags prior to this."

"Keep me updated."

"When I know, you'll know." The screen went dark without further comment.

"Where are we at here in the city?" Powers asked, moving back to the task at hand.

Marika watched as Agent Chase picked up the remote, changing the view on the plasma back to the map of Las Vegas. "Nothing, as of yet. We're focusing on properties like the one in Canoga Park, places that are unoccupied. Any buildings rented within the last six months."

It was a lot of territory, Marika thought. And they had scarcely a hundred agents. The reinforcements Buhler had sent from Denver had no sooner landed at McCarran than they had packed back up and headed for LA.

She got up from the conference table, passing the CIA agent on her way out the door. He had to have been in his late thirties, but he looked younger.

"Walk with me," she said as she passed. It wasn't a request.

A nod and he turned to follow her as they moved out into the corridor. "Who are you?"

A faint smile passed across the man's boyish face and he unclipped his visitor badge, passing it to her without a word.

She snorted, glancing down at the name printed there.

"Right. You're not an analyst—not the type of desk jockey Langley generally sends over. What are you in...the SAD?" Marika asked, referencing the Special Activities Division.

"No comment," he replied with an easy shrug. "See no evil, speak no evil?"

"Not until this is over. Then there *will* be an investigation into who authorized an op on American soil."

"I'm sure there will be," came the even response. "In the mean time, we're occupying Ground Zero...but you know that, don't you?"

She nodded, glancing down the corridor. "I know it, you know it...I think even Powers can feel it. But until D.C. knows it—until they give the order to the other field offices, our hands are tied."

4:01 P.M. Mountain Time
Billings Logan International Airport
Billings, Montana

"Delta Flight 94, this is Tower. You are cleared for departure on Runway 2."

Captain Paula Gonzalez acknowledged the order, glancing over at her co-pilot as they began rolling down the runway, the huge Pratt & Whitney turbofans roaring into life on either side of the fuselage.

"Christmas Eve in Vegas? It could be worse—right?"

She laughed. "Right. Then back to see Andrew and Julie unwrap their presents. If Keith can keep them in bed that long."

"Relax," he replied as the Delta Airlines 757 rose into the sky, carrying two hundred and thirty-three souls.

"It'll be a milk run."

6:17 P.M. Eastern Time
The White House
Washington, D.C.

"The President will join you momentarily," the Secret Service agent announced, ushering Kranemeyer into the Treaty Room.

The President. Kranemeyer's eyes flickered around the room, coming to rest on the old Theobald Chartran painting on the wall across from him, of the signing of peace protocols between the United States and Spain in 1898.

Men coming together for peace. Back in a day when wars had been fought between nation-states—and a treaty had meant something.

A simpler time.

Voices at the door, and the DCS turned as President Hancock entered the room, flanked by his detail.

"Thank you for coming, director," Hancock said, his voice smooth as silk as he gripped Kranemeyer's hand. "I wish we could have met under better circumstances, but this is our lot in life, isn't it?"

Kranemeyer nodded his acknowledgment, Haskel's face flickering across his mind's eye. The way he had looked, groveling on the carpet. Dying.

"Peace in our lifetimes. A permanent end to…the energy crisis for America. It was going to be real—all we had to do was stand back."

Politicians, Kranemeyer thought, maintaining a studiously neutral expression.

"I'm due for some good news, director. I trust you've come to give it to me." The President looked tired, fatigue betraying the smooth veneer.

"I'm afraid not." Kranemeyer passed an open folder across the table to the President. "If anything, our assets on the West Coast are being spread thin, misdirected."

His words seemed to rattle Hancock. "What are you saying?"

"Every piece of intel we've been able to gather indicates that the attack is against Las Vegas. The pictures we have are of both Abu Kareem al-Fileestini and Tarik Abdul Muhammad together in a Vegas strip club just a few days ago. There was nothing on LA until this morning, when Abu Kareem showed up there." He was going out on a limb, trusting the intel Parker had provided him. *Trust your men.*

Could he still do that...after Hamid?

"But he *is* there," Hancock responded, tapping the folder nervously. "And the FBI has him pinned down. They're just waiting for the rest of the cell to show up."

Kranemeyer inclined his head to one side. "And what if they don't show up, Mr. President?"

"What do you mean?"

"I mean...what if our intelligence is, in fact, correct? What if Abu Kareem is a decoy?"

"But that would mean that we have *nothing*." Hancock leaned forward. "And your intel could be wrong. I have to go with what we have, director. Terrorists have brought a weapon of mass destruction onto our soil...and I have to follow our best chance of stopping it. I can't let a terrorist attack of this scale be the legacy of my presidency."

"Then you won't countermand the orders coming out of the Bureau's regional field offices?"

Silence. Kranemeyer could see the indecision written on the President's countenance. Torturous uncertainty.

"No. I can't."

4:49 P.M. Pacific Time
FBI Field Office
Las Vegas, Nevada

The moment Agent Chase reentered the conference room, Marika knew something was wrong.

The younger woman's face was pale, the pasty look of someone who had just vomited. "There's something I need to show you," she stammered, glancing from Marika to the S-A-C. "It was forwarded to us from Fort Meade—they picked it up less than fifteen minutes ago as it was being uploaded."

"Throw it up on the plasma."

She hesitated at Powers' instruction. "It's graphic."

And Marika knew. She heard the S-A-C repeat his order as if in a haze, then turned toward the screen as a video began to play.

It was low-resolution, not much better than webcam quality. But she knew the face. *Nasir abu Rashid.* Or al-Khalidi—or whatever his name had been, really.

Her CI. Kneeling in what appeared to be a large, darkened room…facing the camera.

The wall behind him was covered with the flag of jihad, bearing the *shahada* in flowing Arabic, white script on a hell-black background. *There is no god but God—and Muhammad is his Prophet.*

She watched as the man standing at his side began speaking in rapid-fire, nervous Arabic, his face shrouded by a black balaclava, clearly pronouncing a death sentence.

Nasir's lips were moving, but the microphone couldn't pick up his final plea for mercy.

Don't worry, Nasir. I'm coming for you. A promise she hadn't kept, Marika thought…watching as the executioner took a step back, drawing a glistening steel katana from its sheath. *You'll be safe.*

She remained watching, stone-faced as the sword fell with a cry of *"Allahu akbar!"*

Blood sprayed into the air, a strangled scream reaching the microphone—a wet blade pulled back to strike again and again until the head fell to the floor, completely severed. The decapitated torso remained kneeling for another half-second before it toppled to one side.

Marika looked over to see Agent Chase covering her eyes. "Look!" she hissed from between clenched teeth, seizing the younger woman by the wrist. "*We* sent him out there, we failed him—we let him get killed getting intel we needed…don't you *dare* hide your eyes."

She rose from the table, her body trembling with anger. "Take that video apart—I want to see every frame over and over until we find out where it was filmed. Let's *get* them."

5:23 P.M.
Canoga Park, California

"Still out there?" Abu Kareem asked in Arabic as the Pakistani fighter re-entered the room.

The man nodded, responding in the same language. "Two snipers that I can see out the front."

It didn't matter, he thought, his fingertips lightly caressing the butt of the Sig-Sauer P226 holstered under his light windbreaker…just beneath the edge of the explosive vest he was wearing. They had no intentions of leaving here alive.

The imam ran a hand over his beard, glancing at the bare white interior walls of the shop. This wasn't the way he had envisioned himself dying, but that was not for a man to choose. It was enough for his life to be given in a holy cause.

He glanced at his watch, smiling as the hands moved on inexorably toward their destination. Two and a half hours…

Chapter 26

5:38 P.M.
FBI Field Office
Las Vegas, Nevada

"By judging the light—the shadows, we can get approximate dimensions for the room." Agent Chase brushed her hair back from her eyes, attracting Thomas' attention. "I'd say we're looking at a room maybe 20' x 23'…maybe a little larger. We've also run the audio—we're not getting the type of feedback that you would expect if the walls were solid."

"What then?" he asked, moving closer to where she sat. Chase glanced between him and Powers.

"I'd say we're looking at glass walls on at least three sides…taken together with the room dimension, perhaps a conference room?"

It was such a narrow thread. He walked over to the plasma as the tape began to roll again, advancing forward frame-by-frame. There was something…ninety seconds in he held up a hand. "Roll that back."

And there it was again. He pointed toward an edge of the jihadists' banner—something on the wall just behind it, barely revealed by a fold of the cloth. Letters, and something else. "Can we enhance the image?"

She made a face. "We're dealing with poor source-quality…I can try."

"Do it." Thomas looked back at the sound of Agent Altmann's voice. The look of cold resolution on her face hadn't wavered since the video first played.

"It will be up in a few seconds."

And there it was, on the big screen. Barely visible—the logo probably wasn't more than six inches. Five black letters, surmounted by a swirl of red. *H-I-L-D-R.*

"It's a company logo," Marika announced from his elbow, startling him. He hadn't heard her approach.

"Then we need to find the company," Thomas announced, turning back toward the table. "You find the company—you find their properties or the last time they *rented* property in the region. Narrow it down to buildings that are no longer occupied. We work from there."

6:03 P.M.
The Bellagio Hotel & Casino
Las Vegas, Nevada

"…and it is with pleasure that I welcome Congresswoman Laura Gilpin to the Bellagio tonight."

Steve Winfield moved back from the microphone, extending a hand as Gilpin mounted the stage. "Thank you, Steve," she whispered, squeezing his arm. "You've outdone yourself."

Applause erupted from the room as she came to the podium, looking out over the bunting-bedecked tables, the faces looking back at her through the darkness.

All of the years. All of the fighting. To get here. Politics was intoxicating in these moments, she thought—these rare moments of adulation. It was these moments that people inside the Beltway *lived* all their lives for, every waking moment. This feeling of power.

"I'd like to thank my dear friend Steve Winfield and the staff of the Bellagio for their hospitality tonight. And my aide Brooke Morgan for managing the logistics of the evening—making it all come together. And to all of you for your support through a long and tiring campaign. After all the hours of campaigning, after all the shoe leather worn bare, after all the phone calls we placed together…this is *your* night. We work hard, and we *play* hard. This, my friends," she finished with a smile, "is your night to play."

9:31 P.M. Eastern Time
The White House
Washington, D.C.

"We've caught a break," Ian Cahill announced, sweeping back into the Oval Office. "The Bureau's field office in Las Vegas believes that they have a location on the rest of the terror cell."

"Where?" Relief broke across Hancock's features, the look of a man just released from prison.

"An abandoned convention center on the outskirts of Vegas. It has lain empty for two years, but someone purchased it nine months ago. The Bureau is still following the money trail, but it looks like the fingerprints of the House of Saud are all over this one. Perhaps it goes no farther than financing...but they're involved."

Hancock looked down at his hands. "What is the plan, exactly?"

"They're going to take down both locations simultaneously, the one in Vegas and the building in Canoga Park." Cahill paused. "If you want, you can monitor everything in real-time from the Situation Room."

The President hesitated for only a moment before rising from his seat. "Let's go."

7:29 P.M. Pacific Time
Las Vegas, Nevada

"Stay out of sight until I give the go-order—then close with the target," the S-A-C announced, speaking into his headset, as he looked out the tinted windows of the unmarked SUV at the target building.. "We'll breach the building from three sides, with another tac team covering the rear."

"Copy that."

He glanced over at Thomas. "We've jammed all communications coming in and out of the building to prevent the terrorists from using a remote detonator, leaving only a single frequency open for our use. But no cellphones are going to work, nothing else."

A grim smile. "The moment of truth."

"Yeah," Powers replied, suddenly seeming distant. He listened to the chatter on the team radio for a long moment. "I need to know...was it you?"

Startled by the question, Thomas managed a blank look. "What are you talking about?"

The FBI agent shook his head, his lips pursed into a thin line. "I know my wife cheated on me those years ago—I've known it for a long time, and it really...doesn't matter. I love her, and I love the child she carries. But I saw the way she looked at you in our kitchen last night. And I want the truth—did you sleep with her?"

"Yes," Thomas replied, an unaccustomed feeling rolling over him...was it shame? "It was late—we both were drunk. Too drunk to think things through."

Powers snorted. "So it's true what they say about you boys at the Agency, after all? James freakin' Bond..."

He shook his head in disgust, the look on his face belying his earlier words. *Anger.*

"You'll stay on the perimeter," he added, pushing open the door of the SUV. "I don't need *you* on the entry team. We breach in five."

It was going down, Marika thought, eyeing her wristwatch. *7:38.* All the anxiety she had felt for Nasir was gone, replaced by a cold fury.

Powers' teams were marked on the computer display in front of her, each position marked out. She could see his men from where she sat, staging for entry on the side door. Thermal wasn't giving them anything—if there was anyone inside, they were deep within the building.

Ninety seconds...

The passenger door of her Suburban opened and the CIA man hoisted himself up into the seat. "Ready?"

She nodded. They'd had to make a choice—go in with NBC gear to protect against the possibility of the nerve agent being released and sacrifice situational awareness and speed of movement in the enveloping suits. Or take their chances and go in unprotected.

Powers had chosen the latter option. It made sound tactical sense...she could only pray that he was right.

She saw the lead man move back, his rifle covering the door as his partner knelt down to mirror the door, checking for any wires that would indicate a booby-trap.

Hand signals flashing between the men as the battering ram slammed into the side door of the convention center with a mighty thud, the hinges ripping away as the door fell into the corridor beyond.

Inside.

7:40 P.M. Pacific Time
Canoga Park, California

He could hear them coming—American boots on the stairs outside. Abu Kareem closed his eyes, whispering the *shahada* beneath his breath. The creed of his life.

Living among these people. *That* had always been his jihad, to subvert from within even as others struck from without.

There was something soul-cleansing about this final act of sacrifice, the imam thought, his hand closing around the detonator of his suicide vest. As if it wiped away all the lies.

He glanced over to where the Pakistani fighter sat at the other side of the room, his jacket gaping open to reveal a similar vest. The man's lips were moving, as if in a final prayer—his eyes fixed on the small cylinder sitting in the center of the room, maybe twice the size of an ordinary aerosol can. Jamal's creation, from back in the lab in Dearborn. Filled with the nerve agent.

The door came flying open as if hit by a ram, the clang of metal on concrete as a stun grenade was hurled in.

A shockwave of noise hammered Abu Kareem's ears, a blinding light filling the room.

And he pressed the button...

10:41 P.M. Eastern Time
The Situation Room of the White House
Washington, D.C.

"Why can't we hear anything?" Hancock exclaimed, his fraying patience showing through.

Ian Cahill looked away from the real-time satellite imagery up on the massive screens of the Situation Room, back to where the President sat. "They're jamming all transmissions in and out of the target locations. That includes their own. We'll receive a transmission when they've secured the sites and the nerve agent."

"*If* they secure the nerve agent," Hancock murmured, daubing his face with a handkerchief. "I wish Haskel could be on this one."

"They will, Mr. President," Cahill responded, using his title in the presence of the personnel manning the Situation Room. "The FBI has their best people on this, and they will—"

He stopped as the blood suddenly seemed to drain from the President's face, his eyes staring toward the screens as if transfixed.

Cahill turned on heel, his own mouth falling open. A fiery bloom of flames and debris had burst from the target building, seeming to spread outward for a split-second before it was sucked back into the maw of the explosion.

"Dear God…"

7:42 P.M. Pacific Time
The convention center
Las Vegas, Nevada

Thomas heard the warning come over the team radio, but there was no time to respond, no time even to react as the explosion followed a fraction of a second later.

The fireball seemed to expand out the upper windows of the convention center, angry flames licking at the supporting beams. Debris rained down on the street separating them from the target building, a half-broken concrete block smashing into the hood of a parked car."

He looked over into Marika's face, seeing his shock mirrored in her eyes.

It only seemed to last for a moment before she shoved open the driver's side door, her gun hand coming out with a Glock. "Powers?" she demanded, speaking into her radio. "Carlson? Rodriguez? Boehm?"

Static.

Thomas stepped out onto the asphalt, slipping his Beretta from underneath his jacket, gazing across the debris-strewn pavement to the flaming shell of the building the FBI tactical teams had entered only minutes before.

They'd been led into a trap.

Marika's radio crackled as she came around the front of the Suburban. "…don't. It's not—"

She stopped stock-still. "Did not copy your last—we're coming for you. Just hold on."

More white noise and then the voice was back. Loud enough for Thomas to hear him. "—no." The agent on the other end coughed loudly, a rough, hacking sound. "…the nerve gas…released."

7:44 P.M.
Delta Flight 94

"Flight 94, please continue in holding pattern at 9,000 MSL."

The lights of the Vegas Strip shone thousands of feet below as Pamela Gonzalez acknowledged the order, guiding the massive Boeing into the inbound leg of the pattern.

"If they'd known we were going to run into this delay, they'd have held us back at SLC," her flight officer observed, referencing their lay-over in Salt Lake City.

He was right. It was standard operating procedure—even with their airspeed held down to just over two hundred knots, every moment in air cost Delta big-time in fuel.

"We'll be down in a few minutes," she responded. "Plans?"

"I always visit the Venetian—always lose. We'll see if tonight I can break even."

"Maybe you'll get lucky."

He grinned. "That too."

The radio came alive again. "Flight 94, this is Tower. You are cleared to land, runway three."

7:45 P.M.

Omar rose from his kneeling position on the flat, gravel-covered roof, staring up into the night sky. "There is no god but God," he whispered, stilling his trembling hands.

He could hear the whine of jet turbines coming toward him as he raised the SA-24 to his shoulder, gripping the missile firmly with both hands. His fingers closed around the pistol grip, flicking the selector into automatic mode.

And there it was, descending toward him—a winged beast out of the night. It must have still been a mile off, but the jet loomed large in the *Igla's* night-vision scope. *And Muhammad is His Prophet...*

His finger curled around the trigger, pulling back firmly as the Boeing 757 filled his sight picture.

The *Igla* recoiled in his hands, an intensely physical release—all of the tension leaving his body in that moment, as the missile's flaming backblast curled into the night behind him.

Screaming into the sky, the SA-24 *Igla* flew toward Delta Airlines Flight 94, closing the distance at nearly six hundred meters a second, homing in on the heat signature of the Boeing's engines.

Moments later, it impacted just inches from the 757's starboard engine, igniting the fuel stored there in the wing.

Captain Gonzalez felt the aircraft shudder beneath her as if it had run into an invisible wall. The Boeing pitched right, veering off the approach to McCarran.

Altitude: 6,000 MSL and falling fast. Too fast now, a sick feeling of dropping from the sky.

She reached forward, taking the yoke in her own hands as she switched off the autopilot.

"We just lost the starboard engine," her flight officer announced, an edge of panic to his voice.

Fighting back her own fear, Pamela glanced out the cockpit—only to see the starboard engine engulfed in flames, tongues of firing licking up and down the entire surface of the wing.

There was no time to react…nothing that could have been done in any case. The next moment, Delta Flight 94 exploded, disintegrating in mid-air, fiery debris raining down upon Las Vegas.

Omar shielded his eyes from the explosion, realizing only then, as a ball of fire lit up the sky, that he'd been holding his breath ever since the missile left his shoulder.

It seemed surreal, as if a dream. He screamed, barely even recognizing his own voice in the heat of the moment. "*Allahu akbar!*"

To strike a blow for God.

7:48 P.M.
The motel
Henderson, Nevada

"Harry, you need to see this." There was an unmistakable note of urgency in Carol's voice.

He crossed the room to stand at her side. "What is it?"

"I know why Tarik Abdul Muhammad is in Vegas. Look at this."

She scrolled across the local news station's webpage, double-clicking on a woman's picture. "Congresswoman Laura Gilpin. I didn't see this till just now."

"So? How does she fit into this picture?"

"She spearheaded the Congressional effort to block his release from Gitmo. Nearly succeeded too, only needed ten more votes." She glanced up into his eyes. "She's here in Vegas tonight, giving a dinner at the Bellagio for the supporters of her successful reelection bid. *She's* the target."

And it all became clear. "Wait…you said the dinner is tonight?"

"Yes."

Without another word, Harry walked to the door of the adjoining motel room, throwing it open without knocking. "Boots and saddles, people—it's going down now. We've been played."

He shot a finger toward Carol. "Get everything packed up. I'll get Thomas on the phone, he can alert the Bureau."

As if on cue, the phone in his hand vibrated with an incoming call. *Thomas.* "Yes?"

"It's already begun…"

7:50 P.M.
The Bellagio
Las Vegas, Nevada

There was no spectacle on earth like the Cirque. No place to experience it like the "O".

A smile crossed Laura Gilpin's lips as she glanced over at Steve Winfield's face in the half-darkness of the theatre. They'd known each other since college, and he was in his element on a night like tonight. Surrounded by his friends and playing host.

Heralded by swelling music, a steel-framed ship flew out over the flooded stage, its crew of acrobats swinging from one end of the ship to the other.

The Bateau, she thought, remembering a previous performance as she spotted the muscular Barrel Organ Grinder near the prow. It was magnificent.

She heard voices behind her and looked back to see the Bellagio's head of security leaning over Steve's shoulder, whispering something. "…we have a situation…a plane just blew up on approach to McCarran."

The casino owner's response was unintelligible, but she reached over to grasp his hand as the Israeli walked away. "What's going on, Steve?"

There was a look she had never seen before in his eyes as he responded, "I don't know."

The SUVs pulled into the north valet entrance, one right behind the other. Pulling the black balaclava mask over his face, Jamal looked out the tinted windows of the Suburban to see the Bellagio crest over the ornate entrance.

This was the moment. All of the months, waiting for *this*…

The Pakistani beside him threw open the door, his Kalashnikov leading the way as he jumped out on the pavement.

Jamal heard a shout of surprise, followed almost instantly by a burst of rifle fire.

He saw a uniformed guard fall back into the shattered glass doors of the Bellagio, staining the stone with his blood as the *mujahideen* fanned out from the vehicles.

It took the sound of yet another full-automatic burst to break Jamal's focus on the body of fallen guard, reminding him of the job he had been chosen to do.

Stumbling out of the vehicle, Jamal seized hold of the nearest luggage cart. Out of the corner of his eye, he saw two of the Pakistanis enter the casino, saw the muzzle flashes from within. *Death.*

His hands trembled as he manhandled the two bombs containing the nerve agent onto the luggage cart. Weighing nearly twenty pounds each, they contained the rest of the soman, far more than they had left at the convention center...or sent with Abu Kareem.

He found himself sweating, afraid to drop the bombs in his haste. *Two minutes*, he thought, recalling the words of the shaikh. *"From the moment the first shot is fired..."*

The Bellagio, like most of the resorts on the Strip, was a surveillance state in microcosm, with cameras covering every table, every dealer, every entrance.

And the men manning the resort's security center watched in dumbfounded shock as the *mujahideen* swept from the atrium of the Bellagio into the casino itself, firing as they came.

One of them reached for the phone—the casino's landline—dialing 911.

Busy...

Gilad Cohen had nearly reached the Bellagio's poker room when he heard the shots, the unmistakable sound of automatic weapons fire drowning out the silken voice of Sinatra coming through the casino's sound system.

Pulling his jacket open, he jerked his Jericho 941 from its shoulder holster, falling back toward the "O" theatre. The Israeli switched on his earbud mike, connecting him to the Bellagio's security network. "This is Cohen, report in. What is our status?"

"At least a dozen shooters," an anxious voice responded. "They'll be on top of your position in thirty seconds. We've got dead and injured all over the place."

"Roberts and the QRF?" Cohen demanded, raising the Jericho in both hands as one of the terrorists appeared from the poker room. He squeezed off two rounds, the 9mm slugs going wild among the machines.

"Two minutes." The quick reaction force wasn't going to be quick enough to save them, Cohen thought, collapsing behind a pillar as a hail of fire came his way. He saw one of the guards from the "O" doors fall, his body pierced by bullets.

"I'm going in—they're going to be taken." There was a moment's silence on the other end of the radio as his man digested his words.

"What are you saying?"

"We're going to need someone on the inside."

7:57 P.M.
The motel
Henderson, Nevada

Had Andropov lied? Or had he himself been deceived? None of that really mattered now. Harry thrust aside the questions angrily, doing one last sweep through the motel room to ensure that they were leaving no trace of their presence behind.

The door to the outside opened, a cold rush of night air following Samuel Han into the room. "Got a flash from Thomas—the Bellagio was just stormed by masked gunmen."

"They didn't get the warning in time?" Harry glanced over at Carol as she asked the question, taking in the mixture of anger and grief on her face.

The response was a shake of the head.

Harry shrugged on his leather jacket over the holstered Colt on his hip. "Do they have a twenty on Congresswoman Gilpin?"

"No one has a twenty on anyone, Harry," the former SEAL replied. "Vegas is in chaos and 911 is overwhelmed with calls. My guess is that we're either looking at a hostage situation or she's already dead."

Harry closed his eyes, fighting against the anger that rose within him. The feeling of helplessness. "How long before the LVMPD SWAT has their teams on-scene?"

"Thomas didn't know. No one seems to. But he's en-route to the Bellagio, wants you to join him and the remnants of the Bureau team there. Provide tactical support for a possible rescue."

For a moment, Harry didn't respond, emotions warring within him. He knew what he wanted to do, knew the right thing to do. "It won't do anyone any good—I'll be arrested the moment I set foot on the Strip."

"He says he can get you in."

Run, his mind warned him, screaming of danger. He had spent his career breaking the law, but this had been different. Prison was the best thing lying at the end of this road. Yet it wasn't in him to turn away.

"Tell him we'll be there," he said, feeling as if the earth had opened at his feet, a yawning chasm threatening to engulf him whole.

The door closed behind Han, leaving the two of them alone once more. "You're doing the right thing," he heard her offer. *Was it?* He couldn't bring himself to reply, unable to shake the feeling deep within him...that this was the end of it all.

There was so much he wanted to say in that moment, but honest words had never come easily to him.

She reached for the doorknob and Harry found himself putting out a hand to hold it closed. *Now or never.*

He leaned down, capturing her lips with his own, his hands around her waist as he drew her close, her back pressed against the door.

The salt of tears was on her lips as he kissed her fiercely, as if it was their last moment on earth. Her fingers came up to caress his cheek, running gently over the stubble of his beard, the warmth of her body pressing against him.

"You have to promise me," he breathed, holding her close. "After all of this is over, after the last shots are fired...that this won't be the end."

He paused, almost afraid to go on. "That there will be a future—for *us.* Beyond all the fighting. All of the war." The words slipped from his lips with painful uncertainty and he found himself incapable of looking into her eyes. "*Promise me.*"

It seemed an eternity before she responded, and when she did, it was in a voice filled with tears. "*Yes.*"

8:03 P.M.
The Bellagio
Las Vegas, Nevada

It seemed a nightmare—blood and fire.

A scene from hell, the god of chaos unleashed. Laura could hear the screams ringing in her ears, still see the blood staining the waters of the "O", dead bodies slumped over the crimson seats of the theatre.

"In here," Cohen hissed, taking her by the shoulder and thrusting her into a darkened room backstage. She caught a glimpse of the pistol in his hand just before he closed the door upon them.

"Where's Steve?" she asked, her breath coming in quick, short gasps as she leaned back against a nearby table.

"I don't know," came the Israeli's voice in the half-darkness. "Two of my men were with him—*you* were my responsibility."

"Who are they?"

"I don't know," he replied. "We'd received a flash from Metro just before the assault—an airliner was shot down over the city."

"Dear God," she whispered. She could still remember the morning of 9/11, watching the smoke rise into the autumn sky from a wounded Pentagon. And she'd known that day that it would happen again. Only a matter of time.

"There were at least a dozen gunmen," the bodyguard continued. "Armed with Kalashnikovs—fully-automatic too. God only knows where they got them."

Cohen caught himself. "But you don't need to think about all that. You'll be safe here."

"Those are *my* people," she retorted, anger flaring within her. She put a hand back on the table, realizing suddenly that she was touching a costume-bedecked mannequin. "I can't stay here and let them die."

"My orders are to ensure your safety." The Israeli put a hand on her shoulder, a firm grasp that brooked no disagreement. "You won't do them any good dead."

10:08 P.M. Central Time
Fargo, North Dakota

"...we're on the phone with our affiliate, KSNV MyNews 3, in Las Vegas, Nevada, where things are in chaos and it appears that a terrorist attack has taken place. What can you tell us, Jason?"

Alicia Workman watched in disbelief, raw cellphone footage playing on-screen as the disembodied voice of the reporter began to speak. A fireball fading away into the night sky over the city.

"...an air traffic controller at McCarran, speaking off-the-record, has said that the downed flight was Southwest Flight 295 out of St. Louis, Missouri, but we have been unable to confirm that information. We honestly haven't been able to confirm anything, Vai. There are reports of automatic weapons fire from north of the Strip and the cellphone network here in Las Vegas just went down moments ago—no one seems to know whether that is also part of the attack, or whether it was simply overloaded with calls."

The female anchor looked up into the camera, visibly shaken. "And I'd like to thank Jason Cameron for updating us, live from a city under siege. Stay safe, Jason."

It seemed impossible, she thought, clutching her arms to herself as she sat there on the sofa. But it wasn't. It was happening again. America was being attacked...

8:13 P.M. Pacific Time
Las Vegas, Nevada

Driving in Vegas could be challenging at the best of times, but it was pandemonium on this night. There'd already been accidents, causing traffic heading out of the city to bottleneck,

"I'm not reaching Thomas," she heard Han announce from the front seat of the sedan. Another moment and he added, "No signal."

Harry nodded. "Goin' in blind. Good times."

He was the professional once again, all business. As if a switch had been flipped, somewhere within him.

She could still taste his kiss on her lips, feel the fire of his touch. *"Promise me."*

There had been no artifice in that moment, she thought, replaying the moment through her mind. No lies.

No walls—armor cast aside to reveal the man beneath, his vulnerability. His humanity.

A man who had cast everything aside to protect her. A man she had begun to love.

She looked out the window at the city moving past, wrestling with the emotions within her. Whatever came of the next few hours, they would see it through. *Whatever came...*

8:15 P.M.
The Bellagio

Footsteps outside, a door opening somewhere down the corridor. It might have been a fellow fugitive, but the steps were too measured, too purposeful.

A searcher.

"Get down," Cohen whispered, pushing her down behind one of the tables. She could sense him moving toward the door, his form barely lit in the red glow of the EXIT sign.

Toward the danger.

And the footsteps returned, closer now, a hand testing the door. Gilpin found herself holding her breath, fear and anger roiling within her as the door came open, light spilling into the room from the corridor without.

Another step, and a figure entered the room, preceded by a rifle barrel. *Where was Cohen?*

Movement from the shadows as the Israeli attacked, his elbow lashing out, connecting with the terrorist's throat. The man reeled, Cohen following him back. She could see the blur of his hands , closing around his target's neck.

The room erupted suddenly in gunfire, the muzzle flash of an AK-47 lighting up the darkness. The mannequin on the table beside her seemed to dissolve, styrofoam showering her face as bullets whined through the air over head, the reports sounding like cannon fire in the small room...

Over twenty minutes, and their primary target was still missing. They were falling behind schedule.

Gunshots. His head came up, glancing first up toward where the college student and one of his Pakistanis were mounting explosive charges on the main doors of the theatre, then toward the hostages, separated into two groups of thirty there above the first tier of seats.

Backstage. An eerie silence followed the gunfire, an oath escaping his lips. "Status report?" he demanded in Arabic, speaking into his radio headset.

One by one the four men he had dispatched to search for Congresswoman Gilpin checked in.

And then another voice came on the network, a man's voice growling a foul Arab obscenity. It had to be a bodyguard—to have been able to kill his man. The leader swore, his face flushing with anger. *Time to end this.*

He advanced on the nearest group of hostages, feeling them shrink away from him as he approached. *Power.*

Roving across the group, his eyes fell on a young woman in the front row, a brunette—not more than thirty, the hem of her dress riding just above her knees as she knelt there. She reminded him of someone...perhaps one of the American girls that he had known back in those early years when he had first come to this land. Before he had rediscovered his faith.

Without warning, he reached down, grabbing a fistful of her long, dark hair. She pitched forward, screaming as he dragged her out into the open on the blood-stained blue carpet of the theatre, throwing her down on her back.

"What is your name?" He bent forward, his knee pressing into her chest, the muzzle of his Glock only inches away from her frightened eyes. She seemed unable to speak and he was forced to repeat the question, louder this time—his eyes boring into hers.

"B-Brooke," she stammered, wincing in pain. "Please..."

"I know you can hear me, Congresswoman Gilpin," he announced, toggling his radio mike. "I want you to know this. I will see you here before me in five minutes. When the time is up, I will put a bullet through Brooke's right kneecap and let you hear her screams. Ten minutes, the left kneecap. And I will work my way upward…it will take her a long time to die."

"Think carefully." Cohen listened, his face impassive, as the terrorist finished speaking. It was nothing new to the Israeli. A decade of violence in his own country…he'd seen all the barbarism mankind had to offer.

He looked over into the congresswoman's pale face, seeing the fear, the determination written in her eyes. "I have to go out there."

"He'll kill her anyway," he replied bluntly. Diplomacy was of no use to them now.

She didn't flinch, surprising him with her mettle. "I know…but I can't hide here while it happens."

He glanced from the Kalashnikov in his hands down to the dead body before him, the terrorist's neck skewed sideways at an obscene angle. *Once she's made up her mind, all hell couldn't stop her*, he thought, recalling one of Winfield's comments the previous day. All that was left was to protect her as best as he could.

Without another word, he dropped the rifle onto the corpse, beckoning for her to follow him out into the corridor.

They had made it halfway back to the theatre when the first shot rang out…

8:23 P.M.

Red. White. Blue. Harry glanced toward the Bellagio as the lights of surrounding police cars continued to wash across his face. Christmas trees filled the gardens of the resort, bedecked with the glories of the season and twinkling brightly in the darkness. A strange counterpoint to the death and destruction within.

The perimeter was loose, disordered—chaotic, to be perfectly blunt. If Tarik Abdul Muhammad had a martyr on the outside waiting to perform a double-tap on the first responders, they were all dead. The Metro cop who had met him at the *Do Not Cross* tape had only glanced briefly at his government ID before hurrying off to find Parker at his request.

"Thomas!" he called out, watching his friend come toward him. Harry ducked under the tape, grasping Thomas's hand. "We couldn't reach you on your cell—what's our sitrep?"

"The cellphone network is down."

"Overload or part of the attack?"

"Your guess is as good as mine," Thomas replied, waving the rest of Harry's team in from the darkness. "No one knows anything for sure. There's been more gunfire from inside the theatre within the last ten minutes. What's left of the Bellagio's security team is evacuating the rest of the casino—providing cover for the paramedics."

"Who's heading up the team?"

"Their chief of security's a retired Israeli paratrooper—named Gilad Cohen, but he went into the theatre and they haven't been able to raise him on their comms since."

"Any demands?"

"Not yet."

That wasn't a good thing. Harry's eyes swept the ground ahead of them, between the road and the entrance of the Bellagio, taking in the uniforms clustered here and there. "What's the ETA on the SWAT teams?"

It was a moment before Thomas responded, a strange look passing across his face. "There isn't one, Harry. Metro's Zebra units responded to the reported launch position of the missile that took down Delta 94. A full roll-out, everyone that was on duty. They were ambushed turning off 589 into Winchester, a car bomb taking out part of their convoy before they were hit from both sides with RPGs and automatic weapons."

He could hear Han behind him, cursing under his breath. "So, who is taking point on the hostage rescue?"

"You are."

8:25 P.M.
St. Joan of Arc Catholic Church
North Las Vegas

A police car passed him as he crossed the street, running behind schedule. In the chaos that they had created, it had taken fifteen minutes longer to reach his destination than he had planned. Precious time.

Even as Omar's footsteps carried him across the road, he could hear the sound of gunfire from the south, borne on the wind.

It felt like an act of cowardice not to rush to the aid of his brothers, but they all had their own parts to play. As Allah had ordained.

He glanced up at the church in the darkness, a mural of Isa nailed to the cross covering the space over the door, the dying eyes of the prophet staring down upon him.

The door was unexpectedly locked, refusing to move under his grasp, and he lifted his hand to knock. "Please...I beg of you, let me in."

A moment passed, sirens wailing in the distance of the night. Then he heard the sound of a bolt being slid back, a face peering out at him. "I need shelter."

The priest hesitated only for a moment before opening the door wide enough for him to step through. "Come in—quickly, my friend. There is evil out there tonight, attacking our city."

Omar followed him into the sanctuary, gazing around at the worshipers, no doubt gathered for the Christmas Eve mass.

"My brother-in-law is a lieutenant in the Metro police," the priest continued, clearly nervous. "I called him from the landline in the office—asked his advice. He suggested that we all stay here until they can get the situation under control."

Civilians, Omar thought, barely hearing the priest's words as he looked about him. And the Qur'an forbad their murder.

Innocents…or were they? He closed his eyes, remembering those months following his conversion in prison, the teachings of Abu Kareem. *They vote…*

"Won't you join us?" the priest asked. "As we pray for our city, we remember that on this night God sent forth His Son."

Omar's face tightened, his eyes darting around the sanctuary, up at the stained glass windows—saints keeping watch. *Idolatry.* Much as it had been in Mecca in the days of the Prophet.

His hand came out of the pocket of his jacket in one final moment of decision, detonator clenched between his fingers.

"God has no son…"

8:27 P.M.
The theatre

"Lie still," Gilpin whispered, cradling her aide's head in her lap. She looked down into the wounded eyes of the young woman, thinking of all the times they had spent together in the course of the campaign. Of the two little children awaiting her at home.

Steve Winfield lay a few feet away, apparently unconscious, bleeding from a gash across his forehead.

"You're going to make it through this, you hear me," she continued, struggling to force a smile to her face as her gaze flickered across Brooke's shattered knee, blood seeping out from underneath a rude tourniquet fashioned from her jacket. "Rachel and Danny…you're going to see them tomorrow. God will protect us."

She looked up into the eyes of the terrorists' leader, inhuman eyes shining out from beneath the balaclava.

"Enough talking," came the hiss from beneath the mask. Gilpin met his gaze with hers, a stare of unyielding defiance. These people had given so much of themselves for her...she had to be strong for all of them now.

The muscles around his eyes tensed, the only warning she would receive as he lashed out, backhanding her across the cheek.

She heard Brooke scream, caught herself from falling with an outstretched hand. *Pain.* Her cheek burned from the impact, taking her breath away.

Reeling, she brought her head up, her eyes locking once again with his, proud—unyielding. For a moment, she thought he might strike her again, but he turned away, barking an order to one of his men.

And then she saw the video camera...

8:30 P.M.

"No." Marika shook her head, unable to believe that she was even entertaining the idea. "Do you have any ideas how many laws we would be breaking—an Agency team...conducting an operation on American soil?

She turned on heel, a long finger jabbing out toward Nichols. "Particularly one led by the target of a federal manhunt. I should put you in cuffs now."

"If that's your decision," the tall man responded quietly, the lights of the computer screens in the back of the LVMPD command vehicle casting a glow across his face. "I don't want to be here anymore than you want me here. If you have other options, I strongly suggest that you employ them."

His tone made her think of Russ, now inside the Bellagio attempting to establish communications with the terrorists. Cool, dispassionate. Reasoned.

She shot a glare toward both of the CIA officers, focusing in on the one she knew as "Steven Todd." The man Nichols had called "Thomas."

More deception from the Agency, lies within lies. The fact that D.C. had validated *his* credentials barely mitigated her concerns.

"The FBI's tactical teams were shredded in the explosion at the convention center," Marika admitted bitterly. "Metro's HAZMAT units are deployed to the scene, trying to contain the nerve gas. The city's in chaos."

"Have they identified the gas?"

She nodded. "Yes, it's soman. Dissipates more quickly than VX, but for the time being...a horrible way to die. We lost good people."

"How about help from the outside?" Thomas asked.

"Nothing can get in by air, not after the shootdown of an airliner—we have no way of knowing what else is out there. LA is two hours out and dealing with their own release of the nerve agent from the Canoga Park site."

"Denver?"

She shook her head in the negative. "With multiple attack scenarios already in progress, Buhler's locking the city down. We're on our own, at least for the next few hours."

An eternity of time. Marika looked over to find Nichols glancing along the row of screens on one side of the vehicle, focused on a map of the LVMPD deployments.

"If you assemble a team that has no experience handling these situations," he announced slowly. "It's going to be a bloodbath. If the tangos are even half-way competent, you'll lose every last hostage—probably your entry team as well."

It was the truth, and she knew it. "But how can I trust *you?*"

Nichols straightened, looking her in the eye. "You can't...and I wouldn't."

Vic had believed that he was innocent, she thought, calling to mind the image of her partner, lying in a pool of his own blood.

Before she could even reply, one of the LVMPD sergeants called to her from the far end of the vehicle. "This just hit the Internet, going out live."

The image was shaking slightly, as if perhaps the video camera was hand-held. But it was clear enough, showing the red seats of the "O" theatre in the background. Congresswoman Laura Gilpin was on her knees in front of the camera, staring defiantly into the lens, seeming to disregard the Glock aimed at her head, the masked figure standing behind her.

"...speak to America, and the President of the United States. We have proved our ability to strike at the heart of your cities. To bring you down from the skies. Did you think that you could defy God for so long, that your sins would not reach even to Paradise?"

"What do you want?" Altmann murmured, as if expecting an answer from the screen.

"Within ninety minutes, a plane will touch down at the American military base in Guantanamo Bay, the prison where I was tortured for so many years. In return for the lives of Congresswoman Gilpin and the rest of the hostages, you will trade us Khaled Sheikh Mohammed, ending his unjust captivity by your imperialist forces. If he is not on the plane two hours from now, leaving freely—every hostage will pay the blood price."

"Do you have an open comm with D.C. yet?" she asked, glancing over at the sergeant.

"Still working on it."

The camera panned as the masked figure abandoned Gilpin, walking over to the group of hostages. "To assure you that I will not fail to keep my promise if our demands are not met, I will execute one hostage every twenty minutes until the plane departs from Guantanamo with the warrior of Allah aboard. Starting now."

There was no warning, nothing. Just his gun hand coming up, the Glock moving to cover a middle-aged woman in the front row.

There was nothing anyone could have done. Marika watched in cold fury as the muzzle of his pistol exploded in fire, the camera recording every gruesome detail for the world to see. *Death.*

The screams of the yet-living.

"You have your authorization," she began, turning to Nichols. "On my authority and mine alone."

A nod. He knew exactly what she meant. "We'll all twist in the wind together."

Chapter 27

11:40 P.M. Eastern Time
The Situation Room
Washington, D.C.

"I want it taken down…now."

"They're working on it, Roger," Cahill answered, placing a bottle of water on the table in front of the President. "It's being streamed through someplace in the Middle East…DHS has already shut off stateside service providers from being able to access it."

Hancock looked up at the clocks on the wall of the Situation Room. "What is our status with the Joint Chiefs, Ian?"

Cahill shook his head. "It's Christmas Eve. General Nealen is on his way in from the Commandant's residence, but he's the only one in town—the rest of the JCS is scattered. We're trying to establish a satellite uplink with General Rosenberg in St. Thomas. I'll be frank. We can't wait on them to help make a decision. The situation demands swift action on your part."

"Don't patronize me! I know what I need to do." The President ran a hand across his face. "We have to get ahead of this, Ian. This is the largest attack since 9/11 and it's happening on *my* watch."

An aide entered before Cahill could respond. "We have Las Vegas for you, Mr. President."

"Put them up on the screen." Hancock watched as the large plasma came to life, revealing a middle-aged woman standing in what appeared to be a darkened vehicle—perhaps a mobile command center. She was wearing an FBI windbreaker, her hair tucked up under a ball cap. She looked familiar.

"Mr. President."

"Special Agent...uh—"

"Altmann, Mr. President. Marika Altmann. After the death of S-A-C Powers, I became the ranking agent on-scene."

"A tragic loss," Hancock murmured. "What is the situation at present, Agent Altmann? We're hearing everything and nothing at the same time."

"The Bellagio's security, working with LVMPD officers, has successfully contained the terrorist threat there to the "O" theatre. We're still in the process of evacuating the rest of the resort. Reports are spotty from north of the Strip, but I understand that Metro SWAT is still in a firefight there."

"And the crash site of Delta 94?"

"Emergency personnel were dispatched, sir. I've heard nothing—we're still dealing with the active scenarios. I've been attempting unsuccessfully to establish contact with the Southern Nevada Counterterrorism Center...perhaps you would have more success."

"Understood. Do you anticipate being able to launch an assault to free the hostages before their deadline runs out?"

She looked off-screen for a moment before replying. "I don't know the timeframe, Mr. President. Our tactical team just arrived on-scene. We've begun to prep assault options."

Hancock opened his mouth to say something, hesitating as if thinking better of it. "I want to know...before you go in, Agent Altmann. If an assault proves to be too risky, we may want to consider our—other options."

8:42 P.M. Pacific Time
The Bellagio
Las Vegas, Nevada

"Does anyone know how many people are still inside—how many hostages we're potentially looking at here?" Harry asked, walking through the bullet-shattered doors of the Bellagio's side entrance, into the atrium.

It was like stepping into a charnel house, the tiles smeared with still-wet blood where bodies had been dragged away by the first responders.

Altmann shook her head in the negative, barely a half-step behind him. "We've lost all audio-visual inside the theatre. The stories from those who escaped are all over the place. I'd say the reality is probably between fifty and eighty. *Living* hostages."

"He can keep this up all night." Harry's lips pressed together into a thin, bloodless line, his eyes flickering across the casino floor. The wounded had been evacuated to a makeshift triage being set-up deeper in the hotel, but some of the dead still lay where they fell, one man's lifeless body draped over a video poker machine. "Where are we at on the guest list?"

"Still working on it, in between evacuating the resort," Altmann replied. "It was apparently a special showing of Cirque, so only Gilpin's entourage was in the theatre at the time of the attack."

"He knew that." Harry paused, glancing along the narrow corridor back to the "O". "Knew that all of his targets would be in one place—to themselves. This was well-planned, and he's not leaving anything to chance. Anticipating our tactics."

"What do you mean?"

"Think about it—we'd be trying to delay him, trying to stall when the aircraft lands at Gitmo. Anything to keep them on the ground without rousing their suspicions. But he's taken all that away from us. He's going to execute a hostage every twenty minutes no matter what we do. Every twenty minutes until KSM is safely airborne."

"They're going to give him up, if it comes to that."

Harry snorted. "Then everyone dies. We don't negotiate with terrorists. Never have—even Hancock knows better than to start now."

The look in Altmann's eyes told him something different.

"What do you know?"

The older agent didn't back down an inch, favoring him with a look made of steel. "You are still operating under *my* authorization, Nichols. Giving you authority to lead the assault on the theatre didn't serve to extend your jurisdiction over the entire operation."

He ran a hand over the stubble of his beard, his gaze darting around the casino—taking in the perimeter the LVMPD had established near the entrance to the theatre itself, officers with patrol rifles leveled holding the line. "And since I'm going to be leading the assault...if D.C. has another agenda in all this, I need to know about it."

Altmann hesitated for a long moment before responding. "I could see it in the President's eyes when he spoke of 'other options.' If time runs out, they will release Khaled Sheikh Mohammed."

"Fools..." Harry murmured bitterly. Insulated in their own petty little world of bribery, blackmail, and backroom deals, the politicians couldn't begin to comprehend an enemy who couldn't be negotiated with. An enemy for whom the martyr's death was the ultimate victory. "I want the LVMPD to seal down that perimeter out there, make it airtight. Get their snipers into the high ground—on the roofs of the surrounding resorts. Keep anyone else from slipping in under the wire."

"Already in progress."

He paused. "And if we're dealing with soman...we need a way to treat it. The Agency trains with military-grade equipment, auto-injectors designed for the purpose."

"What are you thinking?"

"The flyboys at Nellis might have a supply on-hand. They'd be the closest."

"I'll get a man out there. And in the meantime?"

"We get eyes and ears back in the theatre."

11:46 P.M. Eastern Time
The Situation Room
Washington, D.C.

"Where could this plane be coming from, general?" Hancock looked up over the rim of his glasses, staring up at the screen on the wall of the Situation Room. The figure of the Chairman of the Joint Chiefs filled the screen, a trim white-haired man in his early sixties. His floral Hawaiian shirt was an incongruous touch, the most informal Hancock had ever seen him in all of his years in office. A well-deserved vacation interrupted.

There was a slight satellite delay before General Neil Rosenberg responded. "Almost anywhere in the Western Hemisphere, Mr. President. Perhaps even someplace as far away as Cape Verde or the Canaries, depending on the airframe. The terrorists have apparently demanded that we refuel the plane while it's on the ground at Guantanamo, so..."

"It could mean they don't have the range for a round trip," the Marine Corps commandant added from his seat just down the table from the President.

"I concur, General Nealen—that is the most likely interpretation. Or it could simply be a ruse."

Hancock cleared his throat, making an exasperated gesture. "So...what are your recommendations, gentlemen?"

On-screen, the figure of General Rosenberg could be seen to shake his head. "We don't negotiate with terrorists, Mr. President—that's been the policy of the United States for decades."

The President snarled an obscenity. "We've never faced this situation before, and everyone here knows it. They've brought down an airliner over an American city—if they did it once, they can probably do it again. And the carnage if a rescue attempt goes wrong...I have to decide whether I can even afford to take that risk."

"What are you saying, Mr. President?" Cahill asked from across the conference table, using his title once again in the presence of the generals.

"I'm saying that freeing Khaled Sheikh Mohammed in exchange for the lives of the hostages not only *is* on the table—it may be the most viable option available to us."

8:55 P.M. Pacific Time
The Bellagio
Las Vegas, Nevada

"Yea, though I walk through the valley of the shadow of death," Gilpin murmured, the words calming her. She cradled her aide's body in her arms, brushing the young woman's hair back from her ashen face.

"Shut up!" one of the terrorists snapped, speaking in clear, almost unaccented English—young eyes glaring out from behind his mask.

"I will fear no evil," she continued, staring him in the eye. "Thy rod and Thy staff, they—"

His rifle butt slammed into her collarbone with a sickening *crunch*, numbing pain shooting through her.

She bit her tongue, the metallic taste of blood pervading her mouth as she struggled not to cry out. Dimly, as if through a fog, she heard someone cry out, a familiar voice, sobbing in terror. Pleading for his life.

"Please, please...no."

Gilpin opened her eyes to see the figure of a young man kneeling in front of the terrorists. Lucas...was it? She could have cursed herself in that moment for forgetting his name. Still in college, he had manned the phone banks for her through the final weeks of the campaign, putting in twelve-hour days. *Don't thank me. This is our country...*

Gilad Cohen could see it all from where he knelt, across the platform—among the second group of hostages. They had separated he and Gilpin when they emerged from the backstage, throwing her down beside her wounded aide and kicking the congresswoman in the stomach as she lay there.

Protect her. But how? His weapon was gone, along with the headset he had used to communicate with the remnants of his security team.

He glanced up the steps of the theatre—seeing one of his men laying dead there perhaps fifteen feet up, his body still draped over one of the seats. Where he had fallen.

His suit jacket was stained with his own blood and gaping open, revealing the butt of his sidearm tucked just within.

Fifteen feet. Cohen took another look at the terrorists as they moved back and forth. He'd be dead before he could reach it...and even if he could—even if he got off a shot, to what end? He couldn't tell whether they were wearing suicide vests, but the bombs between his group and Gilpin's were proof enough of what would happen if he acted in haste.

A quick death. Perhaps it would be more merciful that way, than one by one, begging for their lives.

"Until the meddling of the Zionists is at an end, until America's imperialism has been defeated," he heard the terrorists' leader declaim, looking into the lens of the camera, "...your people will continue to die."

The gun came up...

8:56 P.M.

"Do you have daylight yet?" It was a whisper, nothing more—Thomas's voice coming over his earpiece.

"Negative," Harry replied, watching the small screen in his hands. Placing the camera would be the tricky part, keeping it out of sight of the terrorists while securing a good view of their positions.

The Bellagio's security team had assured them that the maze of lighting in the theatre's ceiling would be more than enough to keep it hidden.

"Harry, I'm picking up on some transmissions coming from the theatre." Carol's voice, from the Bellagio's underground security center where he had dispatched her. "It sounds as if Tarik Abdul Muhammad is using two-way radio to communicate with his team. I'm going to see if we can intercept the transmissions and figure out what he's saying. Fort Meade is monitoring for outbound calls, with Langley in the loop on that."

"Good work. Do it." It took everything in him not to say something more to her...but it was an open channel. And the mission was all that mattered in this moment.

Still nothing worthwhile on the screen, just jostling in the dark, the image shaking. "Audio's coming through loud and clear," he observed, glancing up the ladder to where Thomas had disappeared, a maintenance access.

"Isn't that just peachy?" came the voice again.

A single gunshot echoed from deep within the theatre and Harry felt his breath catch, waiting for the one to be followed by more.

Nothing. Relief washed over him, followed by guilt at the very thought of it. Another of the hostages was dead...but only one.

It was math, he told himself—just that simple. That clear-cut. That *cold.* Don't think of the lives, just the numbers.

Keep it all locked away.

"EAGLE SIX, we have a problem." Harry turned back from the ladder at the sound of Tex's voice, keying his mike.

"Go for it. What are we looking at?" He'd dispatched the former Marine explosives expert to the main entrance of the theatre, along with Han—scoping out their tactical options.

"The doors are wired to blow," came the reply. "Same deal with the balcony entrance, up the escalator."

That effectively ruled out a frontal assault. "Any way to disarm the bombs?"

"No." He'd known the answer, but he had to hear it. "What's thermal giving you?" The LVMPD had managed to scrounge up more than a bit of gear for them. And ammunition.

"No one close to the main entrance doors," Han's voice interjected. "Judging from the blurred image I'm getting, I'd say they're grouped together well inside."

That wasn't going to be enough. "We're going to need those blueprints," Harry said. Agent Altmann was supposed to be getting them. The main door backstage was no doubt guarded as well by now, but there had to be dozens of access points for maintenance. It was just finding the right one—getting inside without being observed.

"Eyes up, EAGLE SIX." He glanced down at the screen in his hand, the picture swaying slightly as Thomas fixed the cam more securely in position.

Tapping in a command on the small keypad, he watched as the wireless camera panned right, swinging across the seats of the theatre until the first group of hostages...and their guards.

It wasn't a perfect image, but it gave them something to work with. Enough to pick out faces. "Come on back—we've got a twenty on the subjects. Looks like Cohen is still alive."

A look at his watch reminded him of the grim reality. *Sixteen minutes—* another would die.

It wasn't going to be enough.

"Altmann," he barked into his radio, "are the Metro snipers in position yet?"

9:06 P.M.
Caesar's Palace

"The service elevator will take you directly to the top floor of the Augustus Tower, sergeant," the concierge said, leading the way down a back hallway. "The roof access is behind the door with the *Employees Only* sign."

"Locked?" Sergeant Wayne Zimmerman asked, extending his left hand to the concierge.

A nod as the man reached into his pocket. "Keycard. Here, take it. And, sergeant..."

Zimmerman paused at the door of the elevator, the hard polymer case containing his sniper rifle clutched in his right hand. "Yes?"

"Thank you."

The sergeant acknowledged the thanks with a silent nod, turning into the elevator. Building materials were piled on top of a stack of pallets in one corner of the service elevator, detritus from one of the Palace's renovation projects. He remembered seeing an article about it in the *Review-Journal*, two weeks before.

It had only been scant hours ago that he'd left home, heading out for another day at the "office". Seemed like a lifetime.

"I'll be home for Christmas," he'd told his wife with a laugh, as they had moved the stash of presents for a fifth(and final) time. And then he had gone out the door.

The LVMPD trained for terrorism. But this...he felt the rage build within him. Too many of his brothers in the Zebra units were already dead—fourteen at the last report coming from Winchester. As many incapacitated.

It felt surreal, almost numbing.

Zimmerman looked up, only then noticing that the wire running from the security camera in one corner of the elevator had been torn away from the wall.

Movement behind him, searing pain as a curved *janbiya* stabbed into his side, just below the edge of his tactical vest. A hand clamping down over his mouth.

He tried to scream, tried to turn—his hand clawing at the butt of his Smith & Wesson 659, but the retention holster held it in place, even as the dagger plunged into his body again and again.

Darkness...

9:14 P.M.
The Bellagio

It was the same for all of them—going to their deaths, begging for mercy. As had his brother.

Jamal walked along the platform, his fingers slick against the hard plastic grip of the Kalashnikov, watching as their leader pulled another hostage from the crowd...a young woman this time, early twenties, no older. She reminded him of a blonde girl in his class at University of Michigan, a fellow chemistry major. Her smile. Her laugh—the way she dressed on a spring morning. *Seductive.*

He had nearly slipped once, he thought, anger building within him at the memory of his weakness.

Allah had kept his feet from falling, but the woman had never paid the price of her indiscretions. He saw her in the girl on her knees before their leader, the fear in her eyes.

Motivated by a sudden impulse, he moved closer to their leader—extending his hand for the Glock. "Let me."

A moment of hesitation...and the pistol was placed in his outstretched hand, butt-first, the polymer cool beneath his fingers.

The girl's slender body shook with sobs, tears streaking down her face as his fingers curled around the Glock's grip—his breath coming faster at the power of it.

A heady feeling. Life and death...in *his* hands. "Who is your Lord?" he murmured, beginning to circle the girl as he recited the words of the Questioners. "Who is His Prophet?"

9:17 P.M.

"We can use the service door there—work our way down the hallway backstage and out...here, onto the balcony."

Tex shook his head at Thomas, drawing a thick finger across the floor plans. "No go, I mirrored the door. They've got it rigged with grenades. Even assuming we could detonate them remotely with a breaching charge of our own, there's too much ground to cover—at least fifty feet before you'd have a clear shot. No time to set up, your aim would be off from the run."

He was right, Harry realized, looking back at the images taken from their covert camera. "Most of them would be dead before we arrived."

Another shot rang out from the theatre, this time accompanied by a muffled scream. Harry's hand stole toward the Colt on his hip...but there was nothing after it. Just silence. The knowledge of death.

He could see it in the eyes of his men.

Reaching out, Han tapped one of the images with his index finger. "They're still wearing their coats...do these guys have s-vests?"

Harry nodded. "We'll have to operate on that assumption, unless one of the people who escaped the theatre might have seen."

He looked toward the door to see Altmann standing there. She nodded. "I'll pass the word to the officers debriefing them."

The female agent tossed a folder onto the table in front of Harry. "The guest list."

He flipped it open, shaking his head as he scanned down the list of names. "This is like a who's who of the Republican Party...do the networks have this?"

"Not yet." The emphasis was clear in her voice. "The cellphone network just came back up five minutes ago."

"And now all hell's gonna break loose in the media."

12:29 A.M. Eastern Time, December 25th
The Situation Room
Washington, D.C.

"Mr. President," General Nealen began, sweeping back into the Situation Room, "we have another option on the table."

Hancock looked back from the scattered sheets of paper in front of him, glaring across at his speechwriter. "This doesn't even sound like *me*, Joyce," he exclaimed, cursing in exasperation. "I need you on your game tonight of all nights."

"I'm sorry, Mr. President," the young woman replied, seemingly cowed by his show of temper.

"Give us the room," Hancock ordered, turning toward the Marine commandant as his speechwriter gathered up her papers and tablet computer. "I'm listening."

"I just got off the phone with CINCLANTFLT, sir. Admiral Price informs me that the USS *Harry S. Truman* is on its way back from deployment in the Med, passing tonight within three hundred miles of Cuba."

"So?" the President demanded, ignoring a warning glance from Cahill.

"You spoke of following through on Tarik Abdul Muhammad's demands, Mr. President. I'm offering a way to do that without the risk of letting one of the most notorious terrorists on earth go free."

"Go on," Hancock replied, waving his hand when Nealen paused.

"We have thirty minutes before the plane touches down at Gitmo—the *Truman's* CO can have a pair of F-18s on the cats ready to launch the moment it takes off with KSM aboard."

"And?"

"Once the hostages in Vegas are safe, the *Truman's* fighters intercept and either force the plane to return to Gitmo...or blow it out of the sky with a Sidewinder."

The President considered the proposal for a long moment, glancing over at his chief of staff. "Ian?"

"It's your call, Mr. President. It's a better alternative than anything we had thirty minutes ago."

Hancock looked down at his hands, realizing that they were trembling. Nothing in the prior four years had prepared him for this moment. "Get Vegas on the phone."

9:32 P.M. Pacific Time
The Bellagio
Las Vegas, Nevada

The face of an angel, flaxen hair splayed out against a rude pillow made of a jacket. The eyes of a child staring up at him, eyes that never should have seen what they had witnessed this night.

"They told me your name was Ashlynn," Harry whispered, stroking a lock of hair back from her cheek. She couldn't have been more than nine. The daughter he'd never had.

She managed a timid nod, seeming to shrink away from his touch. Still in shock from the bullet that had pierced her arm as terrorists stormed the theatre. "It's a pretty name," he continued. "My name is Harry."

The girl seemed to brighten for a moment. "My little brother's name is Harry. He stayed home."

He smiled, squeezing her small hand gently in his. "We're going to get you home to see him, sweetheart. Soon."

"And mommy too?" she asked, transfixing him with trusting, guileless eyes.

He nodded slowly, knowing it was a promise not his to make—holding onto her hand as if his very soul might be lost if he let go. "Yes, of course...mommy too."

And he prayed that it wasn't a lie. "Tell me what you told the lady who was just here...what did you see underneath the jacket of the man who shot you?"

Her face scrunched up as if trying to remember. "It was black...I think. Like that," she said, pointing at his borrowed FBI tactical vest. "Black, with all sorts of wires hanging out. Like Harry's truck when he tore out the battery."

Harry smiled at her analogy, struggling to conceal the fear within him. "Take it easy, sweetheart," he whispered, gripping her hand one final time before rising to his feet.

"Are you going to go find mommy?" That look of trust—it had been so long since he had seen it.

"Yes," he replied, knowing that he was saying what she needed to hear. *Dear Lord, let this be true.* Show *me the way.*

He waited until he was out of range of her ears before keying his mike. "All teams, we have confirmation. The gunmen *are* wearing suicide vests. The bombs at the center of the platform may be loaded with soman, but at this point, that's extraneous. Let just one of those guys get the split-second needed to trigger his vest…ruins our whole day."

There had been something there, Harry thought, hurrying back across the casino floor toward the makeshift command post they had set up near the north entrance of the Bellagio. It wasn't as good as the security center, but it was closer.

Something in the floor plans. *Backstage.* A way in?

He was half-way back when he saw a TV screen lit up, a CNN reporter silhouetted against a flaming building.

"…one of the oldest churches of the Diocese of Las Vegas was the target of a bombing tonight as terror continues to seize hold of the city. Initial reports indicate over twenty people dead, with dozens more injured. Father Ralph Mulholland, the rector of Joan of Arc's, has been confirmed to be among the dead."

Another bombing. He felt like he had been punched in the groin, anger surging through his body. So many already dead…and all because of *his* intel. He saw tears in the eyes of more than one LEO standing nearby. The knowledge of personal loss.

Sometimes, no matter how hard you tried…your best wasn't good enough. And innocents paid the price of your sins.

"Are you going to go find mommy?"

He walked into the room they had cleared for their own use, finding his team watching the same news reports.

"They're dead," he announced flatly, shuffling through the blueprints spread out on the table. He could feel their eyes on him, but he didn't look up. "Nothing we can do about it. All that is left to us…is to save every last person that we *can* inside that theatre. That's all that matters now—that's where I want everyone's focus."

There. What he'd been looking for. In plain sight. He glanced up, his eyes glinting. Blued steel. "Read me?"

"Loud and clear, boss," Thomas replied. Tex merely nodded his assent, leaving Han standing there looking at him.

"Here's how we get in," Harry announced, drawing his finger across the blueprints. "From underwater, with the rebreathers used by the cast of the 'O' and stored backstage. We traverse across the catwalk here, thirty feet above the backstage and fast-rope down—"

He looked up to see Marika Altmann standing in the doorway. "I need a word."

"Can it wait?"

No. The look on her face gave him his answer and he gestured for his team to give them the room. "What's going on?"

"We've been given the order to stand down. The assault has been called off."

For a moment, he couldn't believe what she was saying. "*Why?*"

"Orders from D.C, direct from the POTUS. He's giving them Khaled Sheikh Mohammed in exchange for the hostages. Once the hostages are safe, a pair of Hornets will intercept and force the plane back down."

It didn't make any sense. He looked outside, to where his team awaited. Together they had pursued terrorists around the world…only to find their own nation under attack. This might be the end for him—for all of them. But not like this.

"All the hostages will be murdered the moment Tarik thinks KSM is safe. Every last one of them."

"I know that," Altmann said, setting her thermos of coffee down on the table. "You know that. The politicians don't know that. So here we wait."

Harry reached across the blueprints for his H&K, adjusting the submachine gun's sling around his shoulders.

"No…we don't. Not a chance."

12:42 A.M. Eastern Time
The Situation Room
Washington, D.C.

"Mr. President, Guantanamo's radar is reporting a four-engine turboprop just appeared on their screens. Bearing from the southeast, still over a hundred and seventy kilometers out."

"Our plane?" Cahill asked.

"No way of knowing for sure," the aide replied, seeming nervous in the presence of the President. "If it stays on its current heading and speed, it will be over Guantanamo in twenty minutes."

"Right on schedule." General Nealen tapped his finger against the table. "Do you wish me to alert the *Truman*'s captain, sir? Have him move the F-18s onto the catapults?"

Cahill leaned forward until both his elbows were resting upon the wood of the conference table—his pale eyes fixed on Hancock's face. "Are you sure this is what you want to do, Mr. President?"

Hancock stared at the water bottle in front of him for a long moment, feeling his face flush with anger. It really wasn't fair...after the last four years, after all that he had done, that this—*this* would be his legacy.

"No," he snapped, wishing the bottle held something stronger than water. "Of course I'm not *sure*, Ian. How could I be? I'm going to take the fall for this no matter which way it goes."

The aide came back in. "We've got an incoming call from FBI Las Vegas. Special Agent Altmann for you, Mr. President."

"My last orders were clear. What does she want?"

"She didn't say. Just requested that she be put through to you."

9:46 P.M. Pacific Time
The Bellagio
Las Vegas, Nevada

It had seemed like an eternity as they waited for Hancock to come on the line. Time they didn't have. Couldn't afford to spend.

Tex would be reporting back from his reconnaissance of the catwalk within moments.

"Mr. President." Altmann shot a look in his direction as she heard the President's voice. "I have you on speaker...we're here with the leader of our tactical team."

"I'm assuming that there is a point to this call, Agent Altmann?" A cold voice, hundreds of miles away. The voice of the man who had signed David Lay's death warrant, Harry thought.

A man who had betrayed his oath of office long before this day.

"There is, Mr. President. I called to ask for your authorization to proceed with the assault on the Bellagio's theatre."

Hesitation. "We can't *risk* that, Special Agent, as I made perfectly clear in our last phone call. Not as long as we can still negotiate an end to this situation without even more lives being lost."

"We have an assault plan, Mr. President," she replied, giving Harry a look. "A way into the theatre without being observed by Tarik Abdul Muhammad. Once in place, we can take out he and the rest of the terrorists and free the hostages."

"Look, this isn't complex," Hancock retorted, clearly nettled by her persistence. "We give them KSM, they give us the hostages. Once Congresswoman Gilpin and the rest are safe, we can dispatch the *Truman's* pilots after the plane and either force it down or shoot it out of the sky. In this decision, I'm acting on the best counsel of my advisors, including General

Nealen, here with me on this call now. I really don't care which they have to do—but I will *not* risk a bloodbath storming into that theatre."

"And a bloodbath is exactly what you'll have," Harry stated, leaning in toward the phone on the table. "All due respect to you and the general, Mr. President—but neither of you have ever actually *fought* this enemy. I have. And if I know nothing else...I know this. You can't negotiate with those who only respect force."

"It's not your place to tell me what I can and can't do."

Something wasn't adding up...all of this had been too well-planned. Harry took a deep breath, struggling to keep his composure. "Tarik wouldn't ask for the release of KSM if he didn't have an endgame in all of this. It's too simple—there's no way he's gullible enough to believe that we'll actually turn him over. I can tell you how this ends, Mr. President. It ends with Tarik and his men doing exactly what they came here to do...martyring themselves for their faith—taking as many *kaffir* with them as possible."

There was doubt in the President's voice when he responded, but not enough. "Having already considered all the options on the table, I've made my decision."

So have I. The reply was on his lips, but he bit it back. Now was not the time for truth, for honesty. "Very well, Mr. President. My men and I will be standing by as the situation develops."

Without another word, Harry reached across, tapping the phone's END button, terminating the call.

He looked up into the eyes of Marika Altmann, standing there with her arms folded across her chest. She looked tired, defeated almost. Not quite. "What now?"

"We proceed with the assault, of course," he replied coolly, moving back to the blueprints of the Bellagio.

"But you just said—"

He shook his head. "I said what needed to be said."

"You're talking about deceiving the President of the United States," Altmann hissed, leaning across the table toward him.

"Your point?" Harry asked. "I've deceived many a better man than Roger Hancock. There's something at play here—something we haven't yet grasped. Some reason Tarik Abdul Muhammad is playing the fool."

He didn't wait for her reply. It didn't matter, not really. Defying a presidential order...he knew what lay at the end of that road.

What had he told Carol? *"It's just a matter of deciding which set of consequences you can live with. That's all it is, in the end."*

The hard truth.

"EAGLE SIX to GUNHAND, give me a sitrep," he demanded, keying his mike.

It was a moment before Tex came on the network. Harry could feel Altmann standing behind him, her eyes on the back of his head.

There might have even been a gun in her hand, for all he knew. He didn't turn around. "We have a tango patrolling near the catwalk, EAGLE SIX. Not going to be able to go around him."

"Then we go through him."

There was a crackle of static and Carol's voice came over his headset from the Bellagio's security center. "It's not going to be that simple, Harry. I was finally able to lock in on Tarik's radio comms. He's checking in with his sentries every three minutes."

It wasn't going to be enough time.

"What do you need?" he heard Altmann ask from the other side of the table.

Harry turned to face her. *No gun.* "We could use a miracle...what time does the next one leave?"

Time was running out for the hostages, grains of sand slipping away—there had to be an answer.

"There might be a way to do this," Carol said slowly. He could hear her tapping on a keyboard. "I've been recording the audio of the transmissions...if I can get physical access to one of their radios, I can use the recording to 'reply' to Tarik."

Physical access. He knew what she was saying, knew the danger it could place her in.

But the mission...it was all that mattered. "Meet us in five," he whispered. "I'll find a way to get the radio back up to you."

12:54 A.M. Eastern Time
NCS Op-Center
Langley, Virginia

"They're saying it's an Antonov An-12," Lasker said, looking up from his screens.

Kranemeyer swore. "That's an old Russian job—hundreds of them in existence, all over the world. And enough range to fly KSM anywhere in this hemisphere...maybe even across the Atlantic if they play their cards right."

"They'll have a visual within five minutes," the CLANDOPS comm chief replied. "Maybe we'll get lucky and it will have a tail number?"

"We should be so blessed," Kranemeyer murmured. This wasn't going to end well—he could feel it in his bones. Releasing a terrorist...even for a little while. There were too many variables, too many things that could go wrong. Negotiating with terrorists.

He felt the burner phone vibrate in his inner pocket—the last number he had activated and given to Thomas.

"I'll be right back." He moved past the rows of cubicles in the op-center, bank after bank of plasma screens, monitoring a night that seemed to be exploding around them.

"Yes?"

"Good evening, director," a familiar voice greeted him. The last voice he had expected to hear on this night.

Nichols. "Evening," he replied, careful not to use names. "As you'll see from your television, I'm having a busy night. What's this about?"

"I'm here, director. In Vegas. Preparing to launch an assault on the Bellagio's theatre as we speak."

What? Kranemeyer glanced back to the workstation where Lasker was coordinating the situation, struggling to process what he had just been told. "How?"

"Long story. There's something wrong here with this demand for the release of KSM—something I don't think we're even looking at."

They were both feeling the same thing, instincts born of years out in the night. "What's your gut telling you?"

"That Tarik didn't come all this way for one man. That he's after something much bigger than the long-shot release of an aging terrorist—only a fool would believe that was his endgame."

He was right. "You know what they say about fools and politicians...I don't have the authority to overrule the President in this."

"I know that...but assuming that the release of KSM is *not* the goal—why Gitmo?"

"He spent a lot of years there..." Kranemeyer responded, suddenly realizing where Nichols was headed. "You're saying that this is personal."

"Targeting Gilpin was." Harry paused. "We don't have much time, director. I need you to keep that plane from landing for at least another ten minutes."

"And what then?"

"By then...the hostages will be safe."

12:56 A.M.
The Antonov An-12
Over the Caribbean

The man in the pilot's seat of the Antonov couldn't have been much more than twenty-two years of age—slender fingers dancing over the big plane's instrument panel, a thin, dark beard shrouding the lower half of his face. Eyes ringed with darkness, the look of a man on the point of exhaustion, yet those orbs glistened with a weary excitement. The eyes of the desert from whence he came.

He was alone, had been ever since leaving the military airfield on the outskirts of Maracaibo over three hours earlier. One man, to pilot an aircraft designed for five.

Insh'allah.

He twisted half-way in his seat, glancing back into the Antonov's cavernous cargo hold. A hold packed with drums of aviation fuel, lined with high explosives.

The dark shadow of the Cuban coast stretched in front of him, the lights of the American military base twinkling in the dark.

The moment for which he had been training so long—all the long days in flight school, all the hours he had logged. For *this*.

9:57 P.M. Pacific Time
The Bellagio
Las Vegas

"EAGLE SIX...I have the solution." A whisper, nothing more—a ghost in the night that surrounded him like a cloak.

Harry glanced down from the catwalk into the darkness below him, shadows mingling in odd shades of green in the view of his night-vision. "Roger that, LONGBOW," he replied, acknowledging the transmission.

Thomas was in position. Providing overwatch from a maintenance platform high above the theatre itself, his perch shrouded amidst the scaffolding, the lights.

Their insurance policy.

Stillness. Harry held his breath, listening for any movement, any sign of life from below.

Nothing. Motioning for Tex to hand him the thick nylon rope, he clipped it to one of supports of the catwalk, looping it around the railing and tying it fast. There was no more time for guilt, for recriminations over those they hadn't been able to save.

Time to do this.

Wrapping his hands around the rope, Harry climbed over the railing to stand on the edge—feet pushing away.

And he was falling, the rope burning between his fingers as he descended. The floor rushing up to meet him.

His boots came together on the rope, serving as rude brakes. *Not enough.*

He hit harder than he'd intended, nearly doubling over as pain shot through his bruised ribs, his feet connecting with the floor in an all-too-audible *thud.*

Stabbing pain. He found himself gasping for breath, gritting his teeth to keep from crying out. Letting go of the rope, he left it to dangle, unslinging his H&K from his back.

"He just transmitted, Harry." Carol's voice through his earpiece, from back on the catwalk.

The three minutes started now. "The FLIR has him about ten meters ahead of you…moving your way."

He'd heard the sound. No time for the pain, not now. He stumbled forward, the UMP-45's stock pressed against his shoulder, as he came around a pile of stage equipment.

There. A luminescent figure in his night-vision, not even a man—not really. A target.

The H&K's iron sights centered on the terrorist's forehead as Harry squeezed the trigger—a figure crumpling back into the darkness. Dead before the scream on his lips could even be uttered.

Vengeance. For all that had already fallen this night.

Harry limped over to the body, kicking the Kalashnikov assault rifle away from its lifeless hands. "Tango down."

1:00 A.M. Eastern Time
The Situation Room
Washington, D.C.

"Inform the director that the plane will land at Guantanamo as scheduled," President Hancock replied. He shot a tired look at Cahill. "Bernard Kranemeyer may be the acting DCIA, but I'm the president, and I'm not having the blood of more innocent Americans on my hands just because we decided to push the envelope. What is he thinking?"

His chief of staff shrugged as if it was an impossible question to answer, glancing at his watch. "The Antonov should be landing in moments, Mr. President."

Hancock nodded his acknowledgement, glancing over at one of his aides. "Get a message to CINCLANTFLT...have the *Truman*'s CO ready his fighters."

General Nealen walked back into the Situation Room at that moment, tension showing on his face.

"We have a problem, Mr. President," he announced, handing a clipboard to Hancock. "Just received this CRITIC from Fort Meade."

The President removed the cover sheet and glanced down the message, feeling a strange fear creep over him. "How can this be?" he asked, looking up at the general.

"What is it, Roger?" Cahill demanded, forgetting himself for a moment.

"Voice-print analysis from the NSA," Hancock replied slowly, as if not quite believing his own words. "The man in the theatre—the man we've been negotiating with...is not Tarik Abdul Muhammad."

1:01 A.M.
The NCS Op-Center
Langley, Virginia

Kranemeyer swore an oath as he replaced the phone in its cradle. "They're going to let it land," he announced, glancing across the workstation at Lasker. Something was wrong about this, so very wrong.

The comm chief's eyes lit up suddenly. "We're getting this streamed to us live from ECHELON...the pilot of the Antonov is getting a call—from Vegas."

"Turn it up," Kranemeyer ordered, hearing the voice of a man in Arabic coming over the speakers.

It had been years since Iraq, but he could still remember the language, ingrained upon his memory. He could feel the blood drain from his face, the haunting realization of their mistake.

"He's saying good-bye..."

1:02 A.M.
The Antonov An-12

He could hear the voice of the tower's controller in his ear as the Antonov came in hot, low over the Leeward Point Airfield—less than a hundred feet off the deck—the four massive turboprop engines churning the night air, flaps raised.

"There is no god but God," he whispered, tears streaming down his face as he remembered the words of the shaikh. The indescribable feeling of honor…that he had been chosen to play a role in this holy struggle.

And there was water beneath him once more as the transport swept out over the Bay of Guantanamo. Lights glistening off the waves.

His hands were sweaty as he gripped the controls, aiming the plane toward the large white building standing on the windward shore of the bay.

The Naval Hospital.

There was no time for anyone on the military base to react. No time to counter the sudden threat.

The Soviet-built cargo plane slammed into the western wall of the hospital just above the second floor and burst into flames—the explosives lining the cargo hold going off in a sympathetic detonation mere moments later, an explosion that shook the entire base with the force of an earthquake, sending one of the Antonov's engines spinning through the floor to fall into a dining area below.

Death. Chaos. *Fire…*

10:03 P.M. Pacific Time
The Bellagio
Las Vegas, Nevada

Samir closed the phone, whispering a prayer. The charade was over—the show they had performed for the Americans. Time to ring down the curtain.

The lawyer drew his Glock from its holster on the belt of his jeans as he approached the group of hostages once more, slamming a fresh magazine into the butt of the pistol. No more games, no more deception. Five years living in this land, going to work every day, living among them—living a lie. *No more.*

"When do I see your face, coward?" His head came around at the sound of the woman's voice, eyes falling on Laura Gilpin's face. A purplish bruise was discoloring the flesh around her right cheekbone, from where he had struck her before. It did nothing to mask the look of defiance in her eyes.

"What type of *man* hides behind a mask and a gun?"

Marika Altmann moved toward the screen in the security center, the congresswoman's voice coming through the speakers. "What does she think she's doing?"

Russ shook his head, a look of pain coming into his eyes. This wasn't the way it was supposed to happen. As a hostage, you wanted to blend in—become the gray man...the one your captors didn't even notice. Gilpin was doing the opposite.

Carol came through the door in that moment, returning from the catwalk. She had the radio in her hands.

"It's guilt," the negotiator whispered, glancing up at the screen as he watched the terrorist close in on the congresswoman, shoving his pistol into her face. "She's blaming herself—trying to focus their attention on her. Away from her supporters."

"And it's going to get her killed," Marika observed grimly. "Nichols, I need your sitrep."

Nothing but silence greeted her query. The moments to death ticking down. "LONGBOW," she began, addressing the Agency sniper, "you are weapons-free."

10:04 P.M.

He felt exposed, light filtering down through the fifteen feet of water above him. Harry reached out a foot, kicking away from the underwater portal at the back of the O's tank. Twisting in the water, he gazed upward at the massive machinery of the underwater set, gears intertwining, winches aiding in the raising and lowering of platforms. The bottom of the aquarium was painted black, helping to mask his movements from anyone looking down.

Behind him, a pair of swimmers emerged from the lock, legs kicking against the water. *Richards and Han.*

Harry sucked in a breath of oxygen from the tank on his back, holding his H&K close to his body as he motioned upward. Toward the light. *The surface.*

"Shut up, whore," Samir snarled, realizing suddenly that she was baiting him into focusing on her. *Distraction.*

He drew back his arm, slamming the butt of the Glock into Gilpin's cheek, drawing blood. *She dies last*, the cell leader thought, remembering the instructions of the shaikh.

Turning away, he keyed his radio, in that moment aware that he had missed his schedule of communication by several minutes. "Patrol One, report in."

"All clear."

"Patrol Two?"

"Clear, my brother."

Samir nearly went on, but something seemed to grab hold of him, pulling him back. They were the exact same words from before.

He swore in a mixture of fear and anger, toggling the radio's mike once more. "Patrol Two, are you okay?"

Gilad saw the leader turn, his angry curse attracting the attention of his men. *Now or never.* Waiting would only secure their deaths.

He sprang to his feet, hurling himself up the stairs toward the corpse of his team member. A shout behind him, his foot slipping on the blood-dampened carpet.

He went down, yanking the Sig-Sauer out of the man's holster. A burst of slugs slammed into his leg, splintering bone and ripping through flesh. Fiery pain filled his veins, the sound of a Kalashnikov on full-automatic resounding through the theatre.

The Sig recoiled into his hand as he squeezed off two shots and he saw one of the terrorists stagger, then go down as if pole-axed—the air split with the report of a heavy rifle.

10:06 P.M.

Harry could hear the shots as he kicked his way to the surface, reverberating like summer thunder through the water.

Punctuated by the lightning crack of Thomas's Remington.

It hadn't been supposed to end this way. With the death of more innocents.

He burst from the water, reaching out a hand against the side of the aquarium to steady himself as he brought the submachine gun up.

Pandemonium. Screams filled his ears as the red laser flicked out from the foreend of his H&K, searching for a target.

Terrorist. Civilian. *Shoot. No-shoot.* Hundreds of hours, every year, training for just this. He could see the shoot house now, tires pocked with bullets, mannequins once again arranged as so many times in the past.

Nothing ever truly prepared you for the chaos of battle. He saw one of the terrorists turn toward the stage, fumbling inside his jacket. *Detonator.*

Harry depressed the trigger, getting off a ragged burst—water and brass streaming from the H&K's ejection port as he fired.

Time itself seemed to slow down. It was as if he could see the bullets striking the terrorist, slugs smashing through the man's balaclava and on into his throat, sending him collapsing back against the seats.

He heard the death rattle of Han's weapon, saw another man fall.

Reaching out a hand, Harry pulled himself up onto the edge of the stage, struggling to ignore the pain shooting through his side.

Slugs fanned the air past his ear and he glanced up to see one of the gunmen aiming a Kalashnikov down at him from among the seats, its barrel spurting flame.

Too close. He threw himself to one side, rolling onto his back as he brought the UMP-45 up, his finger applying pressure to the trigger.

No. A woman ran between him and his target in that moment, obscuring his sight picture. He didn't have a clear shot as the terrorist grabbed her by the wrist, jerking her back against his body.

Human shield. He could see the terror in her eyes, the tears running down her face as he rose to his feet, the stock of the H&K extended against his bare shoulder.

"Are you going to go find mommy?"

It might have been her, might not. Might have been someone else's mother.

Take the shot, he thought, the vision of the child filling his mind. Innocence. Hope. *Trust.*

He heard gunshots exploding around him, dimly saw men fall. His vision narrowed, focusing on the woman—her captor. His finger flicked out, switching the selector to single-shot.

A singular eye near the woman's ear, half of a masked head—nothing more. Time itself seemed to slow down.

His breathing became shallow, his left hand closing around the foreend of the H&K in a rock-solid grip. The red dot of the laser stopped dancing, centering on the terrorist's forehead, just above and to the right of the eyehole in the mask.

The trigger broke under the gentle caress of his finger, a single .45-caliber slug exploding from the muzzle—striking the terrorist in the center of the forehead.

He saw the woman's lips open in a silent scream as the gunman's grip on her wrist was suddenly loosed, a fine mist of blood flecking her silk blouse. She fell to her knees, eyes wide with horror, her screams finally finding voice.

Target eliminated.

He glanced across to see Han inserting a fresh magazine into the mag well of his MP-5, practiced hands moving over the action—pulling back the charging handle.

You never forget. No matter how hard you try.

A pall of silence seemed to fall over the theatre as the three of them moved forward, muzzles sweeping over the seats—over the bodies of the slain. The terrorists.

The hostages they had arrived too late to save.

The sulphurous, hellish scent of gunpowder hung in the air, mingling with the smell of blood. *Death.*

No shots greeted them from the balconies overlooking the stage, no explosions as suicide vests were triggered in once last act of defiance.

He could feel the hostages shrink away from him as he approached, water dripping from his body onto the bloodstained carpet of the "O". Just another man with a gun...that's all he was to them in this moment.

"Room clear," Tex announced from his right, moving up the stairs barely a half-step behind him.

Han heard Tex's voice, struggling to control his breathing against the onset of panic as he swept his weapon across the left side of the theatre. The *gunshots*, the sound of a sniper's rifle—bringing all the memories flooding back.

And then it was over, just like that, leaving him trembling. "Room clear."

Harry lowered his weapon, stepping across the body of a dead terrorist to where the congresswoman lay, leaning back against one of the seats. He bent down, his face only inches from hers, his hand reaching down to touch her arm. She met his gaze, eyes that had stared into the face of death now staring into his. Still unbowed.

"You're safe now, ma'am. We've come to take you home."

He hadn't envisioned his own death like this...slowly bleeding to death on the carpet, his destroyed vocal chords making it impossible for him to even call for help. *Failure.*

"Stay calm," he could hear one of the Americans announce. "We're going to get all of you out of here, soon enough."

There was no glory in having failed, in having fallen so short of the will of God. It seemed impossible, even yet...but he could feel himself growing weaker.

Jamal closed his eyes, fighting against the pain, the nausea that threatened to overwhelm him. He reached out, numb fingers groping for the detonator in the pocket of his jacket.

There was still a chance. He could still see the eyes of the shaikh, hear his words replaying themselves through his mind. *"And where is Paradise to be found, my brothers?"*

His own once-confident reply, chanting the *takbir*. *"Neath the shade of swords."*

Yet it seemed death was all that was to be found. The death he had dealt to his brother. He could taste his own blood on his lips as his fingers touched the detonator, struggling to wrap themselves around it.

It felt as if his fingers were made of wood, clumsy—no longer responding to the dictates of his brain. The detonator fell from his pocket, rolling to the carpet.

Almost out of reach, the former college student thought, clawing desperately at the wire that connected it to his suicide vest.

Without warning, a heavy foot descended on his wrist, pinning it to the floor. He glanced up into cold eyes the color of gunmetal, a pistol extending from the American's hand.

The eyes of an angel of death. The avenger of blood.

It entered his mind to beg for mercy, here at the end of his life, but there was no time. And no mercy to be found.

The gun came up, a long suppressor extending from its muzzle—the man's finger tightening around the trigger.

The pistol coughed, a strange deathly sound. And Jamal's world went dark. Forever...

Harry bent down, his fingers closing around the edge of the terrorist's blood-drenched balaclava—pulling it upward with a quick, forceful motion.

The lifeless eyes of a young man stared back at him, matted hair clinging to his forehead. But it wasn't Tarik Abdul Muhammad.

His eyes darted around the stage, at the unmasked bodies of the other terrorists. *Nowhere.*

Something was wrong. He pulled the sealed pouch containing his earbud radio out of his water-logged trousers, inserting it into his ear and tuning it to the Bureau channel.

"Altmann, do you read me?"

"Loud and clear, EAGLE SIX," the FBI agent replied. "My screens are showing you in the room with the hostages—sitrep?"

Harry glanced toward Samuel Han, kneeling over a young woman in the front row off the platform. "We have casualties, but yes...the hostages are secured. We'll evacuate as soon as possible—there's something else. Tarik Abdul Muhammad is MIA. The man on camera...wasn't him."

When she responded, he could hear the hesitation in her voice. "I know—Fort Meade's voiceprint analysis confirmed that moments before you went in. Nichols...there's something else you should be aware of."

"Yes?"

"You were right about Guantanamo...the Antonov was on a suicide mission. Its crew deliberately overshot the Leeward Point Airfield and flew it into the top floor of the naval hospital across the bay."

He closed his eyes, feeling the anger burn within him. The indescribable sense of guilt. *You were right.* But not soon enough.

Cassandra on the walls of Priam's Troy.

"Casualties?" he asked, scarcely daring to hear the answer.

"At least thirty dead, scores of injured. We're just getting the reports."

1:09 A.M. Eastern Time
The Situation Room
Washington, D.C.

"We're getting scattered reports out of Vegas, Mr. President," Cahill announced, entering the small conference room. "It's being said that the FBI assault team went ahead and stormed the theatre."

Hancock seemed stunned as he gazed at the images on-screen, video of the burning hospital in Guantanamo. Wounded men staggering out of the carnage. He seemed to process his chief of staff's words slowly, almost as if in numbed disbelief.

"And?"

"No one knows—yet. There is a report that says the hostages have been secured, but it is unsubtantiated."

"Dear God," the President whispered, shaking his head. "Is there any chance...that they caused *this*?"

He gestured toward the chaos at the hospital.

"What do you mean, Mr. President?"

"If the FBI defied my orders...if they broke the terms of our negotiation, then the strike against Guantanamo could have been retaliation." Hancock paused, his voice trembling. "Inform me the moment they're out of the theatre—the moment you've confirmed that Representative Gilpin is safe...I want to know who ordered this assault. I want their *resignation* on my desk by the time the sun comes up."

10:11 P.M. Pacific Time
The Bellagio
Las Vegas, Nevada

He was dying, Harry could see that—and there was no help for it—his body riddled with bullets.

"Should have waited," he whispered, bending down on knee beside the Israeli.

A wry smile crossed the bodyguard's face, a trickle of blood oozing from the corner of his mouth. "All part of the...job. You never lose your principal—give your life for theirs, if it comes to that."

"And it hasn't," Harry lied, reaching out to examine his wounds. "We're going to get the EMTs in here to help you...just as soon as it is safe."

"Don't bother," Cohen whispered, suddenly overcome by a fit of coughing. "There's others that need you more—I'm done."

He closed his eyes, leaning awkwardly back against one of the seats. As if going to sleep.

Harry could feel someone move up behind him, and he looked back to see Tex standing there.

"We've got a problem," the big man announced, lowering his voice as if to ensure that those nearby wouldn't hear what he was about to say. "The bombs on the platform with the nerve gas ...they weren't set up for command detonation."

"Timed?"

A nod. The look on Richards' face told Harry the answer to his second question: no visible timer.

That was Hollywood—not the real world. No bombmaker worth his salt made it that easy. The explosion would vaporize the soman, spreading the nerve gas throughout every corner of the theatre. And even outside.

"Can you disarm them?" he asked, rising to walk back toward the platform.

"One, maybe...it'd take probably half an hour—maybe more. Whoever built them was a real pro, I'd spend half my time figuring out which of the wires were real and which were decoys."

Too many *maybes*.

"One bomb disarmed and the other one goes..." Harry breathed, squatting down next to the nearest IED. "Still enough soman to kill every last one of us. And we don't have thirty minutes."

The Texan looked over at him. "Based on what?"

"Think about it. Even if they expected us to hold off until the Antonov was supposed to land...they had to know that the moment they flew it into the naval hospital, all bets were off. Which means they would have set this up to go off shortly thereafter."

Tex seemed to consider his words for a moment. "Ten minutes?"

"Tops."

Their options were limited, and they both knew it. The way they had come...there was no possibility of evacuating the injured that way. Too slow—

too many people would die. *Math.* "Focus on disarming the IEDs on the main doors," Harry responded. "That's our only way out of this."

He stepped away from Richards, away from the people they had rescued, keying his mike.

"What's our status on the auto-injectors from Nellis?"

"Only came up with about twenty of them—my agent is on his way back now. Metro finally has Winchester under control, with all the gunmen either dead or in custody." Marika's voice. "Why?"

"The nerve agent is rigged to blow and the doors of the theatre are still sealed with explosives."

"Dear God…" she whispered. "What can I do from here?"

"Start evacuating the resort. All your people, all the first responders—everyone in the triage."

"Understood."

"That means you too, Thomas," Harry added for Parker's benefit. "Get outta here. And know this…if Tarik is still out there, this could be another piece of his plan. He's been one step ahead of us thus far."

"Everyone is on the highest alert. I'll pass the word to the Metro snipers, have them provide cover for the evacuation."

"Do it, and do it quickly. We're livin' on borrowed time."

10:15 P.M.
The roof of Caesar's Palace

"Metro, be advised, we may still have an active subject. Snipers, be prepared to provide cover for the evacuation of the Bellagio. Copy?"

"Roger that," Tarik Abdul Muhammad whispered over the radio headset, the butt of the Accuracy International AE MkIII sniper rifle cradled against his cheek as he lay there on the roof, aiming down and across the street at the north entrance of the Bellagio.

He had hardly expected them to succeed, but it still smote him to the heart to think of all his brethren dead, failed in their mission. As for himself…he had never intended to die this night, *insh'allah.*

I take refuge with my Lord, he thought, remembering the words of the Holy Qur'an, *from every proud one who does not believe in the Day of Reckoning.*

Such a day had been brought to America this night—a day for the sins of men to be weighed in the balances. And many had been found wanting, as the police sergeant he had stabbed to death in the resort's freight elevator.

The shaikh reached forward, pulling back the rifle's bolt to chamber a .308 Winchester cartridge.

The final reckoning was yet to come...

10:19 P.M.
The Bellagio

Five minutes. Half the time Harry had specified...elapsed. And still no one emerged from the theatre.

Carol stood at the edge of the casino floor, not far from a bullet riddled roulette wheel, glimpsing one of the sculptures of Richard McDonald as she gazed back toward the doors of the "O".

Stretchers passed her by on their way out, the bloodied victims of the initial assault.

Marika emerged from the security elevator, spying the young woman standing there—as if waiting for something. *Someone.*

"Chambers," she began, raising her voice slightly. "All of our people are already out, hardening the perimeter. Time to go."

The young woman glanced back over her shoulder, meeting her eyes—and she could see the determination of youth.

"I'll leave with them."

"No purpose in it," Marika replied, moving closer to her—brushing a strand of silver hair up under her FBI ball cap. "Nothing anyone can do at this point."

Run. It's what she had done with Vic—left him lying there facedown in his own blood.

"Pray," came the whisper, so soft that she almost missed it.

"There's that." The older woman shrugged. "God might be able to hear you better outside."

"*No*," Carol replied, shaking her head. The anguish was clearly visible in her eyes, resolution not unmixed with pain. "I'm staying. Right here."

And she could see it.

"You love him, don't you?" Marika asked, her characteristic bluntness coming to the fore. She'd seen the look before...even felt it herself once, in a long-ago time.

It seemed a long time before the young woman replied—and when she did, it was as a single defiant tear fell from her eye, rolling unheeded down her cheek. "Yes..."

"What are we looking at?" Harry asked, dropping down beside Richards at the entrance doors.

The big man shook his head, not even looking up. "Spent most of my time getting the trip wires clamped so I could cut them," he responded, gesturing to the two long wires that had extended out from either side of the IED, spanning the breadth of the entrance. "Then had to get the cover of the housing off before I could even get at the mechanism."

"Trembler switch?"

"None that I've *found*," came the grim response, a small screwdriver clenched between the Texan's teeth. "God knows he's got everything else…a mercury tilt switch over here in this corner of the housing—and from the looks of these wires leading to the encased battery, he set up a collapsing circuit."

Good times, Harry thought. Cut just one wire—didn't matter which one—and the whole thing exploded. Another thing Hollywood wasn't too keen on telling people. "All that matters is getting it off the door—after that…they can throw it in Lake Mead for all I care. Focus on the tilt switch."

"Already on it, boss," Tex replied, taking the screwdriver out of his mouth.

Harry glanced down at the hostages in the seats below them, sensing the raw tension—nerves worn threadbare by the trauma of the night. The delay had them on the brink of panic. If they only knew the half of it…

"And hurry it up if you can. The natives are getting restless."

1:21 A.M. Eastern Time
The Situation Room
Washington, D.C.

"We just received an update from Las Vegas, Mr. President."

Hancock allowed himself a weary smile, glancing across at Cahill before turning his attention back to the aide. "And Congresswoman Gilpin is safe?"

The young man shook his head. "Not yet, sir. The hostages and the rescue team are still trapped inside the Bellagio's theatre trying to disarm the explosives on the main door. Mr. President, the presence of the nerve agent has been confirmed. It's contained in a pair of bombs within the theatre. They were set up for timed detonation."

Hancock's eyes widened, realizing the import of the words. "Then you mean…"

"The terrorists were on a suicide mission." The aide paused, seeming to hesitate before going on. "All the negotiations…were a fraud, just a ruse to receive access into our restricted airspace over Guantanamo."

"Out," the President whispered, anger and fear distorting his features. The look of a man who had been outplayed and knew it. "Just get *out!*"

10:21 P.M. Pacific Time
The Bellagio
Las Vegas, Nevada

"What's he dealing with?" Han asked, glancing up as Harry walked back to him. The SEAL looked exhausted, his expression devoid of emotion.

Harry knelt down beside Gilpin's wounded campaign manager, watching the young woman's eyes. She was in shock, biting down on a pen to keep from screaming as the SEAL bandaged her shattered knee, preparing her to be moved.

"A mercury switch," he replied, keeping his voice low. "If he moves the bomb or even jostles it—game over. He's…making progress."

Neither one of the men needed to look at their watches to know the truth. Time had almost run out.

Any moment now.

"Thank you." Words seemed so…insufficient in this moment, and yet, to leave them unsaid?

"No more," Han whispered, glancing down at the blood covering his hands, his face tightening into a grimace of pain. "After this, Harry, after all of this is done…I never want to see your face again. Where you go, Death follows—and I just can't be a part of it any longer."

Perhaps that was justice, even, Harry thought—unable to bring himself to answer the accusation. Knowing there was no defense.

He glanced over to where Laura Gilpin sat, bruised and battered. Her hand was clutching her side from the beating she had received, the faintest hint of fear showing in her eyes.

"Just a few minutes more," he whispered, taking both of her hands in his. "And everyone will be safe. But I need your help."

"Yes…of course," the congresswoman replied, seeming to summon up whatever last reserves of strength she had within her.

"When those doors open, my partners will help your campaign manager and Mr. Winfield out—and I'll be at your side. But we can't have this turning into a stampede. If it does, more people are going to die. Your bravery's kept these people alive so far this night. I need you to be their leader once more."

She nodded her understanding. "Where's Gilad?"

"Dead," he responded, glancing up the aisle to where the bodyguard lay, the Sig-Sauer still resting beside his lifeless body. "He gave his life for yours—now let's not have that be in vain."

Harry looked up to see Tex standing there at the head of the steps. "The doors are clear."

A nod and he reached down to help Gilpin up, wrapping an arm around her waist. She staggered against him, a moan of pain escaping her lips.

"Now hear this," he called, his voice echoing off the distant wall of the theatre.

Knowing it was time for one final lie.

"The way out is clear—the danger is past. Let's move out calmly, we all get to go home tonight."

He saw several people glance at Gilpin, saw the look of reassurance she gave them.

"Go on," she said, looking over the faces of her supporters. "I'll be the last to leave."

Trust.

10:23 P.M.

She had never imagined that she could feel this way…but she found her breath caught in her throat as she scanned the crowd for his face, watching the people emerging in safety from the Bellagio's theatre.

The people he had saved.

And then she saw him, his ballistic vest cinched over his bare chest, black jeans soaked from their immersion in the tank—supporting the congresswoman as they limped out of the theatre. The last to emerge.

"Thank God you're safe," Carol exclaimed, pushing her way through the crowd to him. It seemed like an eternity since he had disappeared into the darkness, preparing for the assault.

Harry looked up at the sound of her voice, his face changing suddenly. "Why—what are you doing still here? We've got still got two bombs, timed to go off any minute."

He could feel the congresswoman stiffen beneath his arm, but he paid her no heed, staring into Carol's eyes.

Feeling her father staring back.

"And you thought I was going to leave you?" she demanded, and despite himself, despite the horror of the night—he found himself smiling.

"Come on, let's get out of here," he whispered, gesturing for her to take Gilpin's other arm.

They had made it five steps when the theatre behind them exploded, the air suddenly filled with flying debris, the glass doors around them shattering from the force of the shockwave.

Harry felt a shard of something—perhaps glass, stab into the back of his thigh, his knee buckling. He threw out a hand to stabilize himself, catching at the wall.

But he didn't go down. People were running now, running once more in terror—screams filling the resort. And he could smell the faint scent of camphor in the air now surrounding them.

Soman.

"Let's go, let's go!"

10:24 P.M.
The roof of Caesar's Palace

He felt the roof shudder beneath him, the explosion more powerful than even he had expected.

Perhaps it had killed her, the shaikh thought. Perhaps she was lying dead in the ruins of the theatre, choking on the nerve gas.

Perhaps...

He adjusted his eyes again to the Accuracy International's scope, focusing it on the crowd of people running from the resort. Adjusting the zoom until he could see their faces.

There. Emerging from under the shadow of the carport—just within view of his perch. It seemed impossible that Gilpin could still be living, but there she was. He hugged the sniper rifle to his shoulder, centering the reticle on the congresswoman's chest.

His finger curling around the match trigger, a gentle caress...

10:25 P.M.

The flashing lights of emergency vehicles lit up the night—red and blue light washing over them as they ran from the Bellagio, helping the congresswoman along. Harry could hear her cough, prayed that her exposure had not been severe.

"Altmann," he demanded, keying his mike as they ran. "We're going to need those injectors. Our principal was exposed to the nerve agent in the explosion."

It was barely a moment before the FBI agent responded. "Roger that—where are you?"

"Near the ambulances at the south end of the resort. We—"

A supersonic *crack* split the air and he heard the congresswoman groan in sudden pain, felt her twist away from him as if struck by an invisible force.

The sound of a rifle shot smote his ears barely a half-second later—the bullet traveling faster than the speed of sound. And he saw the crimson stain begin to spread across Gilpin's blouse. The stain of death.

And she was falling—still exposed to the marksman.

In his mind's ear, he could hear a rifle bolt being snapped back, ejecting the shell casing—slammed forward, carrying another cartridge into the breech.

The work of a second.

He bent down, covering Gilpin with his own body as he tried to lift her—to carry her into the cover of a nearby ambulance. *"You never lose your principal— give your life for theirs, if it comes to that."*

Cohen's words, ringing through his ears.

He could feel Carol at his side, her hands supporting the congresswoman's head as they lifted, stumbling toward shelter. Gilpin was breathing heavily, her eyes flickering in and out of focus. Most likely shot through a lung.

Out of the corner of his eye, he could see Metro cops running toward them. *Not soon enough*, he thought as they lowered Gilpin to the ground. Not nearly soon enough.

And then he heard it, the sickening sound of a slug smashing into flesh— glanced up to see Carol staring at him, eyes wide.

God, no.

He saw her body sway, her legs seeming to give out from under her. She collapsed into his arms, her head against his chest as they both fell, into the shadow of the ambulance.

His hands came away from her back, fingers wet and sticky with blood. *Her blood*, he realized, feeling as if he moved in a dream. The rifle bullet had slammed into her back, penetrating through layers of ballistic vest and into her body.

No exit wound. He could have staunched the bleeding from her back and it would have done nothing—the internal damage had been done.

He heard a voice on the radio, a raw, inhuman voice—screaming for the paramedics. His own.

"Stay with me, Carol," he breathed, his hand leaving a bloody smear as he caressed her cheek. "Dear *God*, please stay with me."

Nothing else in the world mattered in that moment, all the noise…the shouts fading away into the distance. Only them.

"I'm…sorry." She opened her mouth, struggling to continue, but he shook his head, tears rolling down his face as he held her body close to his…knowing that she was dying—his heart rejecting the truth.

"Don't give up," he whispered, his voice hoarse with desperation. "Don't you dare give up—*please*, don't give up on me now."

"...there will be a future—for us. Beyond all the fighting. All of the war."

All the hopes, all of the dreams—dreams worth more than life itself. All of them gone.

No future, nothing beyond this moment. He could feel her growing weaker, struggling to breathe. Those eyes that had once shone with defiance now fading...becoming glassy.

He bent down, kissing her softly, her lips still warm but no longer responsive to his touch. *Always kiss them goodbye.*

Even this last of all goodbyes.

He looked up to see Han kneeling there in the shelter of a vehicle not ten feet away, a look of reproach in his eyes. *Where you go, Death follows...*

Gunshots in the distance, he felt movement around him as the paramedics moved in, taking Carol's body from his arms.

He heard their voices as if through a haze clouding his mind, tears of anger and grief cascading down his cheeks as he watched, clinging to her hand as to life itself. Heard the barked orders, words of detached professionalism as they endeavored to perform a miracle—to bring her back from the grave.

But all to no avail. Miracles? There were none to be had...not on this Christmas Eve.

"She's gone," he heard one of the paramedics announce. Felt the man's eyes on his face. *No.*

He struggled to his feet, letting go of her hand with painful reluctance. She looked beautiful laying there, golden hair splayed out over someone's jacket. Asleep.

Dead.

Brushing the tears from his cheek with an angry gesture, he strode out into the open road, the sirens ringing in his ears, the nighttime breeze rippling through his hair.

Red lights illuminating the face of death.

He might have been exposed to the sniper—might have been in his very cross-hairs, but he paid it no heed, walking as if lost in a nightmare.

None of that mattered. *Not now.* Not with her dead.

The end of all dreams...

Chapter 28

11:32 A.M., December 31ˢᵗ
NCS Op-Center
Langley, Virginia

"It's good to have you back, Ron."

Yeah, Carter thought, glancing around at the familiar cubicles, the screens lit up with intel streaming in from around the world. "Good to be back, Danny."

It was, wasn't it?

All of this...and they had failed.

Over three hundred of their fellow Americans dead...two hundred and thirty-three of them aboard the doomed Delta flight. Souls flying into the night. To their deaths.

Perhaps *he* had failed.

All of this—and they had managed to completely lose the man responsible for all of it. The man whose praises the keyboard jihadis had been singing for the last six days.

The shaikh.

"Tarik Abdul Muhammad...how did we let him get clear?" Carter asked quietly, glancing away from the screens and back to Lasker.

"Based on what intel we have, I'd say that no one was looking for someone in a police uni." Lasker's face darkened. "We still haven't even confirmed that he was actually the shooter. No prints beyond Sergeant Zimmerman's on the gun. Nothing on surveillance."

"How does that happen?" Carter ran a hand through his hair, quietly cursing. *Helpless.*

It was a sick feeling, coming from deep within. Reminding him of the night Caruso had died in his apartment, bullets churning the air. "Forget *Ocean's Eleven*—these resorts have the best video surveillance in the world. How does a man get in...*and* out, without his face ever appearing on tape?"

"Yet another question we don't have an answer to."

Wrong answer.

Hands trembling with anger, Carter stalked out into the open area of op-center, in front of the big screens—his sudden movement drawing the attention of the rest of his analysts. His team.

"Listen to me," he began, tears streaming down his cheeks as he turned back to face them. "I don't want to hear any more excuses—any more of what we don't know. We are going to find the...people who did *this* to our country. And we are going to see them burn."

6:37 P.M.
The apartment
Manassas, Virginia

Returning home after a mission was always difficult. The innocent cheer in the eyes of those you met on the street, the realization that everyone had gone about their lives without you.

Unmissed. And unmourned.

This time was different, Thomas thought, closing the door of his apartment behind him. He slid the deadbolt into place, placing the case of vodka in his hand on the kitchen counter as he shrugged off his coat.

This time the *people* were different, haunted even—by their awakening to reality. The malls were deserted, signs for post-Christmas sales hanging forlorn in the windows.

Because they had failed. The night had come to their shores, and they had failed to stop it.

With Congresswoman Gilpin still in the ICU, clinging to life, it was hard to say exactly what they *had* accomplished.

He unsealed the first of the small bottles of vodka, feeling the fiery liquid sear his throat. It was cheap stuff, not much better than lighter fluid—but it was good enough for its purpose.

To make him forget.

That's all he wanted—really all he had wanted since Jerusalem. When all of the betrayals had begun.

One bottle down. Eleven to go before morning. Or before he passed out—whichever came first.

He sat down on the couch, his tired muscles settling against the smooth leather as he reached for the TV remote.

"...of the intelligence community in the wake of the Christmas Eve attacks. Senator, you are on the record stating that these attacks could have easily been prevented. What do you believe should have been done differently?"

Easily prevented. The camera panned to the pasty-white face of a politician, eyes full of righteous indignation. Eyes that had never seen the darkness—never looked into the face of the enemy.

He began talking, but Thomas couldn't focus on his words, sipping slowly on the second bottle of vodka. Watching as the screen changed, to cell-phone video of Delta Flight 94 going down...exploding in the skies over Las Vegas. The same images, over and over again. Over and over.

He buried his face in his hands, feeling suddenly nauseous—struggling to clear the image from his mind. *The people you couldn't save...*

Thomas walked into the bedroom, into the adjacent bath, turning the faucet on hot. Bloodshot eyes stared back at him in the mirror as he ran his hands through the stream, as if striving to scrub them clean.

His cellphone was on the dresser in the bedroom as he walked back out. His personal cellphone, the one he always left behind when he went into the field.

"Your voicemail has two new messages," a computerized voice informed him as he walked back into the main room of the apartment, glancing at the now-darkened TV.

The first one was a woman's voice, rather loud, shrill even—the woman who'd spent the night with him just hours before all of this had begun.

Before David Lay had been the target of assassins. Before Nichols had disappeared.

Michelle? Marisa? Monica? Her name had started with an "M," that much he could recall, and nothing more. He tilted the bottle of vodka back as he hit the button to erase her message. Not worth remembering.

"Thomas, you don't know me—but our friend Harry gave me your number."

Harry. He hadn't said a word on the military flight back to the East Coast, eyes empty of emotion, staring down at his hands. The Air Force C-130 had run into turbulence and Nichols hadn't even flinched.

As if he simply didn't care.

"You can call me Walter...I'm his pastor. You probably don't want to hear what I have to say, but I was where you are once. And it cost me everything I valued in life. I think I can help you—or more importantly, that I know the One who can."

There was an earnestness in the pastor's voice...a strangely compelling honesty.

Thomas glanced from the phone to the bottle of vodka in his hand. As nearly empty as the void within him.

His finger slid clumsily across the touchscreen, selecting the "Call Back" button. And he listened as it began to ring...

8:31 A.M. Eastern Time, December 30th
Camp David
Frederick County, Maryland

"Pull!"

An orange disc flew from the low house with a *whirring* sound, cutting through the clear, cold morning air.

Senator Roy Coftey snapped the Krieghoff K-80 over-and-under to his shoulder, leading the clay as it spun through the air.

The thunder of a shotgun blast rent the dawn air, the clay disintegrating into a thousand pieces as the shot hit it square.

"I see you're still smokin' them, Roy."

Coftey lowered his shotgun, popping the empty shells out of the breech as he turned to face the newcomer.

"As ever, Ian—can't lose my touch. I'm assuming that you got my message?"

The President's chief of staff nodded, rubbing his gloved hands together. "Pretty cryptic, if you ask me. You've been hanging out with the spooks for way too long, Roy. Starting to act like them."

"I do what's necessary," the senator replied coolly, slipping another pair of 12-gauge shells into the Krieghoff before pulling the break-action closed. He ran a finger along the engraved receiver—silver with accents of gold, the scene a covey of pheasants rising from the brush. "You've always known that."

Cahill nodded, eyeing him carefully. "Yes, you have. And it's that character trait that has rendered you invaluable to your President—to your party. What's this all about?"

President. Party. Coftey glanced up the rising ground toward the helipad, Marine One glistening there in the early morning sun.

What were any of those worth...really? A man's soul?

"Hancock is through, Ian," he responded, choosing his words carefully. "His time as president of this country is over."

Cahill's face was the picture of surprise. He took a step toward Coftey, his voice lowering despite the fact that they were alone. "I thought you told me everything was settled with the Chief Justice—that you'd spoken with him?"

"I did," came the even reply. "And then I spoke with him again. Made it clear that he will cast the tie-breaking vote *against* Hancock. Told him why."

The chief of staff swore, cutting loose with a string of obscenities. "*Why?* Are you out of your ever-loving mind, Roy?"

Shifting the shotgun to his left hand, Coftey reached into the pocket of his sporting jacket—handing over a USB thumb drive.

"Earlier this year, Roger Hancock made a deal with the devil. Iranian oil was to flow into the United States markets at discounted prices—enough to make everyone involved look the other way. Enough to not only ease the 'pain at the pump', but to provide the economy with a shot in the arm and propel Hancock back into office."

He looked Cahill in the face, a cold, menacing glance. "Any of this sound familiar, Ian?"

The mask of the street-tough Chicago politician was slipping ever so slightly, something that looked distantly like fear entering Cahill's eyes. "No, nothing...go on, Roy."

"In exchange, Hancock promised that when Iran struck at Israel, the United States would stay out of it. Not interfere. And when a CIA spec-ops team got in the way, he sold them out. Operation TALON."

"Dear God," the chief of staff breathed, shaking his head. "That can't be...I mean—"

"Is it all coming back to you?" Coftey demanded, taking a step closer. There was fire in the old soldier's eyes as he glared at Cahill.

"No...that is, all through the campaign, Hancock acted like he had an ace up his sleeve. All the way up till October, and then it all seemed to fall apart. You remember how it was then, Roy." He'd never heard the chief of staff like this before—almost plaintive. "But I didn't know what it was."

The senator shook his head. "Come on, Ian—don't give me this 'I didn't know' bullcrap. You're only the President's chief of staff...Hancock doesn't take a dump without you knowing about it. You think I'm new to this town or something?"

Cahill started to say something, then seemed to think better of it, looking up the slope toward Marine One. "You and I both know I'd do a lot of things to win an election, Roy. Lie, cheat, steal—it's the name of the game and no one plays it better than I do. But I lost a cousin when the towers came down on 9/11. I'd burn in those fires myself before I'd join forces with *them*..."

Truth? It was hard to say. The strange mixture of cunning and "open" arrogance that was Cahill.

The senator shook his head. "You're his closest adviser, Ian...or we all thought you were. Are you going to ask me to believe that even as his plans fell apart around him, even as he was in danger of being exposed—he didn't turn to you?"

"What do you mean?" Cahill demanded, shoving his hands deep into the pockets of his coat.

"Hancock got careless—someone uncovered his role in betraying TALON. And that someone was David Lay."

The chief of staff sucked in a breath of ice-cold air, shooting him a look. "You're not suggesting..."

The senator just nodded. "I am. And now Hancock has a choice. He can concede the election and retire to private life. Or I can burn his life down around his ears."

"The evidence you have here," Cahill began, looking at the USB drive in his hand. "Will it hold up in court?"

Coftey shook his head. "You and I know it doesn't have to. Once a politician has been tried and found guilty in the kangaroo court of public opinion...he's radioactive. You want to wait around for the fallout, Ian?"

There was no response for a long moment as Cahill looked down at the drive, a canny look returning to his eyes as he rolled it between his fingers. "Do me a favor, Roy. Hold off on this—until Hancock takes the oath again. After that...it will be a simple matter for him to step aside and allow the Vice President to finish out his term. And the party holds the White House."

The Faustian bargain...so tempting. As if sensing his hesitation, Cahill took a step closer. "I'll see that you don't regret it, Roy. Do it for the party."

He'd made hundreds of such deals over his decades in Washington, trading away little pieces of his soul—what was one more?

Coftey lifted his head, staring the president's chief of staff in the eye. "The devil take the party."

11:51 A.M., January 20th
CIA Headquarters
Langley, Virginia

So familiar. He could remember the last time he had walked these halls. Could remember a time when he had never expected to return.

The elevator doors opened in front of Harry, a bureaucrat emerging from within. They might have been the same age, but he looked much, much younger.

He looked up from the folder in his hands, into Harry's eyes—looking away almost as quickly. As if frightened by something he had seen in their depths.

Harry moved into the now-empty elevator as if in a trance, leaning back against the side of the elevator as he pressed the button for the seventh floor. The Agency's inner sanctum.

David Lay hadn't returned to the CIA...at least not yet. Word had it that the President-elect had asked him to stay on—that he would be back as soon as his wounds had healed.

Wounds. He had seen the director two weeks earlier...at Carol's funeral. Felt Lay's eyes on his face as he approached her open casket—the look of reproach more painful than an open accusation.

The feeling that his own heart was being ripped open. The knowledge that he had failed—and lost so much that was dear in the failure. So much of his dreams. She had looked so...*perfect* lying there. Almost as if she might awaken at any moment.

That wasn't happening. He'd stood there after everyone had left, the cold Virginia wind whipping at his coat—watching as her casket was lowered into the ground. Watching in silence as they began to fill the grave, each shovelful of earth driving a spike deeper into his heart.

Avenging her death was all that was left to him. He had no idea what he would do after that, no idea where he would go—except back into the field. Back out into the night.

The DCIA's secretary was behind her desk as he approached. She didn't smile. It seemed as if no one had smiled since the Christmas Eve attacks.

"The director has been expecting you. Go on in."

The director? *Of course*, Harry thought, feeling himself react at the words.

He opened the door and stepped inside, unsurprised to see Kranemeyer's form behind the desk. His boss had been tapped as the acting DCIA until Lay's return.

The TV was on in the office, tuned to CNN and broadcasting the presidential inauguration. "I, Richard Norton, do solemnly swear..."

He found his eyes straying to the screen as the oath of office was repeated. "...to protect and defend the Constitution of the United States against all enemies, foreign and domestic."

Kranemeyer snorted, reaching for his remote and the "mute." "They all say that...politicians and their words. We'll see if this one means it."

"I've heard intel to indicate that we've located Tarik Abdul Muhammad," Harry interjected, watching as a strange look passed across Kranemeyer's face. "Is this credible?"

A long pause. "It is…we've confirmed both his arrival in London a week ago and his current presence in Leicester. The Security Services have not been able to account for *how* he arrived in-country—nor have we been able to confirm how he got out of the States."

"How soon do we launch?"

"Have a seat, Harry," Kranemeyer sighed, gesturing with his hand. "The short version is that we don't. The Brits won't sign off on a rendition."

That didn't make sense. Harry could feel the anger rising within him, his hand beginning to tremble. "*Why?*"

"We have no evidence, they say. Nothing that definitively places Tarik at the scene of the terrorist attacks. Nothing that would stand up in court."

"When have they ever demanded that level of proof? We're allies—and we were attacked."

Kranemeyer got up from behind his desk, limping around the front as if his prosthesis was paining him. "The 'special relationship' is a thing of the past, Harry. A different time…perhaps more importantly, a different England. In 2010, there were eight Muslim MPs in the House of Commons. Now? There's twenty-seven, and they've become increasingly Islamist in their ideology. A Gitmo detainee like Tarik Abdul Muhammad is a hero to their constituents, and if 10 Downing Street ordered him taken, there would be blood spilled in Trafalgar Square."

In the battle between fanaticism and apathy, the fanatics were winning. As ever. It was a sickening feeling. "So what are you telling me?"

"We wait…and watch. Our request to dispatch an Agency team to liaison with the Security Services in establishing surveillance on Tarik has been approved."

"How soon do I leave?"

Kranemeyer's eyes locked with his and he could see a note of sadness written there. "You don't, Harry. I don't know the best way to say this…but you're on your way out."

No. Not like this—not with all he had yet to do. "You're firing me?"

"I'd prefer not to. Which is why I'm asking for your resignation instead."

He felt frozen in place…caught in the middle of a nightmare. Wanting to ask why, but fearing the answer too much to speak.

"It has nothing to do with your photo being released to the public," Kranemeyer went on. "The image we used was old and grainy—deliberately so. And it has nothing to do with the murder of Pyotr Andropov…it took work, but we were able to bring down the veil of 'national security' over that investigation. Easy enough to do in light of his connections to the Vegas attacks."

"Then what?"

The DCS paused. "Do you really want to go down this road, Harry? I think we both know where it leads."

It felt like it was all slipping from between his fingers, but he found he couldn't stop himself. *Losing control.* "Just give me one good reason why you're doing this?"

"One?" Fire flashed in Kranemeyer's coal-black eyes. "I could give half a dozen, all of them equally valid. You've been out in the field too long, Harry—and the strain is starting to show. I have video of you executing a downed suicide bomber in the Bellagio. Point-blank, single round to the forehead. A man we could have interrogated if your emotions hadn't gotten the best of you."

He closed his eyes against the accusation, remembering that moment. The feeling of justice as he'd brought the Colt up, iron sights framing his target's face. The fear, the desperation in the young jihadist's eyes. "It was justified."

"It wasn't, and we both know it," Kranemeyer retorted, not giving him an inch. "We walk on the edge of a knife out here—a razor-thin line between light and darkness. And you've crossed that line. Emotion has no place in our business."

The worst of it was knowing he was right. And not being able to do anything about it.

"I have to get out. Leave all of it in the past. All the death. All the killing."

But that had been *before*...before his dreams had found themselves in ashes.

"Please, just let me take the team to Britain. Let me be there when they finally take down Tarik Abdul Muhammad. Then I'm done, my resignation will be on your desk." He'd never begged for anything before in his life, but nothing had ever seemed this important. The anger crept back into his voice, a dangerous presence. "I've served my country for fifteen years, fifteen long years out there in the night—for God's sake, you *owe* me this, Barney!"

The fire was gone from Kranemeyer's eyes, replaced by an unmeasurable sadness. "I'm sorry, Harry, but I can't. And I think you understand why. Parker will go to Britain to liaise with Five. As for you...I need your resignation by the end of the week. Clean out your desk—turn over your access cards. And then leave. Put all of this behind you."

It felt like he was falling off a cliff—sliding into the abyss beneath. *No way back.*

Kranemeyer looked over into Harry's face as he rose from the chair, the emotion seeming to leave him as he did. "You've been one of our best, Harry. It's been an honor to serve with you these years…I only regret that it had to end this way."

"The regrets…are mine." There was something there in those steel-blue eyes. Something dangerous.

"Of course, you understand what it's like to leave the Agency. You're no longer an employee of the federal government, but that doesn't mean they lose interest in you. Any overseas travel in the next thirteen years…will have to be approved by this office, with a full copy of your itinerary submitted for review."

"I understand."

"Then good luck," Kranemeyer said, extending his hand. Harry looked at him for a long moment, then turned away without accepting it.

Another moment, and he was gone.

The DCS limped back to his desk, sighing heavily as he sank down into the chair. It couldn't have been helped.

And the war went on.

A thin line between light and darkness, Kranemeyer thought. A line he himself had crossed, the image of Haskel's face floating before his mind. *Justified?*

"Carter," he asked, picking up the phone. "Has our intel on the Antonov An-12 been verified?"

"As far as we can—from tracking down what parts could be identified and cross-referencing it against available databases and sat imagery, we believe the purchaser to have been Prince Yusuf ibn Talib al-Harbi, a member of the Saudi royal family."

The Saudi royal family, Kranemeyer thought. It wasn't as significant as it sounded…there were literally thousands of princes in the House of Saud, all of them living fat off oil money. American oil money.

Driving their fast cars, enjoying their whores—and atoning to Allah for their sins by waging jihad on the West. "What do we have on him?"

"He's twenty-eight, still single, a graduate of Harvard with a master's degree in law. As far as terrorism goes…Avi ben Shoham has confirmed that he's been on Mossad's radar for several years."

"Work it up," Kranemeyer ordered, glancing back at the TV. At the continuing inauguration. "And get it to my desk. I'll be asking that President Norton issue a finding."

War without end…

11:35 A.M. Central Time
An elementary school
Fargo, North Dakota

She had called off from school, claiming that she was coming down with the flu. She found her hands trembling as she watched the television, and wondered if it might not have been the truth.

Alicia Workman watched as the new President of the United States rolled down Pennsylvania Avenue in his armored limousine. Previous presidents had always walked—at least part of the way, but the Secret Service had overruled, citing security reasons in light of the Vegas attacks.

Would he be any better? Any more honorable than the last man to occupy the office?

Somehow she doubted it, but it didn't really matter. She wouldn't be around to see it.

She glanced up, her eyes flickering around the living room of her small apartment. Each wall festooned with computer print-outs, newspaper clippings. Photos. Tracking Roger Hancock's every movement, recording it—as if for posterity.

And in the midst of the chaotic disorder, a single picture held to the wall by a red thumbtack. A face smiling back at her, as though enshrined.

The face of her beautiful sister.

She bit her lip, staring into those eyes—the tears beginning to fall. As they always did.

I haven't forgotten you, Mary, Alicia found herself whispering. Nor had she forgotten the promise she made.

He was vulnerable now.

7:49 P.M. Eastern Time
Washington, D.C.

There weren't many payphones in the city anymore. Fewer still that hadn't been stripped by vandals. That still worked. Everyone had a cellphone these days…and yet a few still remained, relics of a time gone by.

Harry reached up, the cold air biting into his bare cheeks as he fed quarters into the phone.

He felt nothing—ignoring the wind, the snow falling from the sky above him.

One more quarter, and the phone began to ring. One, two, three…four rings, until he found himself fearing that it wouldn't be answered.

It was on the fifth ring that a familiar voice came on the line. The voice of a woman.

"Rhoda," he began slowly, hesitantly even. There was no road back from this. "I need your help."

Epilogue

9:07 P.M. Pacific Time, March 11th
The Roosevelt Hotel
Hollywood, California

"Did you see it coming, Mr. President?" The use of his title was welcome, even if the question was not.

Roger Hancock glanced around at the opulence of the famous Blossom Ballroom, home of the original Academy Awards—taking a sip of his brandy before replying to the *New York Times* reporter. His first appearance in public society since leaving office…and these were the questions he received?

"No," he replied, honestly enough. Of course he hadn't seen Coftey's betrayal coming—or the reversal from the Chief Justice. "Now get lost."

You didn't tell a member of the press to get lost—he knew that from his years in office. But it felt good, the brandy in his hand doing his talking for him. And he no longer really cared.

He spied a young woman through the mingling crowd, auburn hair cascading over her bare shoulders, above the border of her blue gown. Late twenties, maybe? It looked as if she were alone, a glass of punch in her hand as she surveyed the crowd.

Worth cultivating, Hancock thought, beginning to move toward her…his Secret Service detail following him through the crowd—on the alert. All two of them, he thought…the loss of stature befitting an "ex"-President. Young agents.

Alicia Workman could feel his gaze on her even before she turned, his eyes crawling over her skin. Was this the way he had looked at Mary? Her sister had always been aware of the effect she had on men—had been comfortable with it.

Bold and beautiful.

Even getting into this event had been difficult, had taken most of what she had in savings. Didn't matter. She wouldn't need it again—not after tonight.

She felt her hands moisten with sweat, lifting the cocktail glass to her lips as she turned to face him.

A handsome face greeted her, a smooth, cruel smile tugging at his lips. The smile of a man who didn't know what it was to be denied. "I hate to see such a beautiful woman standing alone."

She returned his smile and he put a gentle hand on her waist as the music began to play above them. "May I have this dance?"

"Of course," she responded, setting her empty glass on the table behind them, smiling up into his eyes as he led her out onto the floor, moving against him.

Knowing even as she did so that it was their last evening on earth. For both of them.

11:09 P.M.

"We can't let you do this, sir," the lead agent announced, stepping between Hancock and the door of the hotel room.

"You really should see the view from the window of my room." His intentions had been obvious, the intoxication visible in his eyes as he had twirled her around on the dance floor of the Roosevelt.

And it had led them up to the penthouse, until finally his Secret Service agents had stopped them.

He lowered his voice as if to spare them both embarrassment, but Alicia heard every word. "Going into a hotel room with a woman you just met...it's too big of a security risk. At least let us search her."

The hunting knife taped to her inner thigh felt suddenly cold against her skin, sending a chill through her body. Perhaps she had been a fool for thinking that she could avenge her sister's death. Perhaps this was where it would all end.

Hancock swore, shooting her a warning look as he moved between her and his detail. "Go on inside, Alicia—and wait for me," he smiled, handing her his keycard.

"I'm not having this again," she heard him exclaim as the door closed behind her. "Two women this month you've scared off trying to feel them up. *Enough*. You cleared all the guests, didn't you?"

"Yes, sir, but—"

"There is no *but*. I'm going to enjoy this evening—and you're going to stand outside this door. Or I will see that you go back to Chicago or wherever you came from and spend your days ticketing double-parked cars."

Alicia took a deep breath, struggling to keep her hands from trembling as the conversation continued without. Only moments left now.

She turned on the soft light beside the bed, settling gently on the sheets as she tugged at the hem of her dress. She still didn't know exactly why she had chosen to leave the Bersa at home—was it some fancy that she would be escaping from this? Or was it just that a knife was so much more personal...for a vengeance that couldn't have been more so.

The thought struck her that it might be safer to remove the knife—to shove it under the satin pillow at the head of the bed...but before she could move, the door opened, Hancock's form framed in the doorway.

"Everything's taken care of, darling," the former president smiled, hanging his jacket on the back of the doorknob. He moved closer, bending down to kiss her as he unbuttoned his shirt.

His breath smelled of alcohol, his hands working clumsily with the buttons. Had Mary seen him like this...or had she been blinded? Falling headlong in love with a man who cared nothing for her. A man who had *caused* her death.

He leaned back, easing his arms out of the shirt—a look of arrogance on his face as he gazed down at her. The look of a man who had always gotten what he wanted. Every vote, every deal. Every woman in his bed.

No.

No more. Something snapped within her, something long ago dead. Something that had gone to the grave with her sister. *Pain*. A blind, unseeing rage. Her hand flickered under the edge of her dress, ripping the tape away from her thigh—the knife coming away. Naked steel glittering in her hand.

The arrogant look in Hancock's eyes fled, replaced by sudden fear—struggling suddenly to free his arms from the sleeves of his dress shirt.

Too late. A wild, unearthly cry escaped her lips as she stabbed forward, the blade burying itself in his chest, blood blossoming around the hilt.

Pain. Fire. This wasn't happening. No. Hancock looked down at the knife hilt protruding from his chest, the room seeming to swirl around him as she jerked it free, a bloody blade flickering before his eyes before she plunged it into him again. *Fury.*

He looked down to see a dark red stain spreading across the front of his undershirt...a stain spreading ever wider with every beat of his heart. *No.*

He fell to his hands and knees, hearing himself scream, the blood trickling from between his fingers. Dimly, as if in a nightmare, he heard the locked door crash open—heard the shouts of his detail. He reached out, the polished wood of the nightstand beneath his hand, but he no longer possessed the strength to pull himself up.

As it had been in his dreams...

Dying. Gunshots resounded through his fast-fading mind as he collapsed onto the carpet, on his side.

Gunshots. One, two, three—another two almost together. He felt something fall beside him and opened his eyes to see the young woman lying there. His murderer.

Her eyes were open, glazing with pain and the coming of Death...but her lips were creased in a smile.

Strangely at peace. Strangely, irrationally, he found himself wanting more than anything else to ask *why*, but he lacked even the strength to form the words. Dying to know.

6:27 P.M., Greenwich Time, March 12th
A pub
Ramsgate, Great Britain

It was still early, the pub barely beginning to fill with its evening traffic.

Just a few couples enjoying their meals—a trio of college students watching a rugby game on the television above the bar.

And a man sitting by himself in the very back of the pub, facing the door. His sandwich sat untouched on his plate, an unopened bottle of spring water before him.

As if waiting for someone—but his face betrayed that assumption...empty blue eyes staring out from a worn, tired face. The face of a man who wasn't waiting for anyone...anymore.

There were no surveillance cameras in the pub—he had made certain of that before entering. Just a place to get a quiet meal before moving on.

Alone and unarmed. It was an unusual feeling, Harry thought, looking down at the sandwich on his plate. *Out in the cold.*

The television changed suddenly, the voice of an announcer coming over the speakers.

"Reporting live from Los Angeles, California—we regret to inform our viewers that Roger Hancock, the former President of the United States, has succumbed to wounds received in a stabbing last night. Here with us is the mayor of Los Angeles to comment on the savage attack..."

The news brought him no satisfaction, but there seemed an irony in it all—perhaps even a *justice*, if there was any of that to be found in this fallen world.

He pulled a wallet from an inner pocket of his leather jacket, unfolding it on the table as he brushed his meal to the side.

The pictures. A sad smile creased his lips as his eyes fell on the images of the two of them.

Together.

The ones Rhoda had taken of them that morning—it seemed so very long ago—a sprawling vista of the Blue Ridge Mountains stretched out behind them in one shot.

Places they had never been. Things they had never done. *Lies*…just like so much else in his life.

Perhaps the love he'd known for her was the only truth in it all.

Flame sprang from the tip of his lighter to the edge of the photographs, the paper curling away from the heat. Curling, blackening, ashes falling unbidden into the tray on the table below—fire searing the tips of his fingers as he held on, hardly daring to let go.

Her eyes staring back at him from the midst of the flames, burning themselves into his memory.

Haunting.

A tear ran down his cheek, and he let it fall, unheeding. Uncaring. Watching as the last traces of those precious memories were consumed.

The mobile phone beneath his hand pulsed with an incoming text and he slid it open, revealing a single word on the screen. *Yes.*

He knew where this road ended—a casket on a flight back across the Atlantic…if he was that lucky. Time to dance with the devil.

He didn't send a reply, replacing the phone within his jacket as he rose—leaving his meal abandoned beside a tray of smoldering embers as he walked from the pub.

The ashes of his past.

A mist was rolling in off the cold North Sea, obscuring the masts of the fishing vessels moored in the Royal Harbour, an icy rain lashing at his body as he walked on…into the night.

No turning back.

The End

Coming Soon. . .A New Novel From Stephen England

He crossed an ocean to avenge the death of the woman he
loved,
Only to find a new evil rising...

Now, cut off from his own government and hunted by the
Security Services,
Harry Nichols must re-ignite past friendships, call in old
debts.

And as the world descends into chaos,
As terrorists take deadly aim at Britain's royal family,

*All that will stand in their way is an alliance forged in the bowels
of hell.*

Embrace the fire...

Look for *Embrace the Fire*, the third full-length volume of the Shadow
Warriors series from bestselling author Stephen England, coming soon.
For news and release information, visit www.stephenwrites.com and sign up
for the mailing list.

*An author lives by word-of-mouth recommendations. If you enjoyed this story,
please consider leaving a customer review (even if only a few lines) on Amazon.
It would be greatly helpful and much appreciated. If you would like to contact
me personally, please drop me a line at stephen@stephenwrites.com*

Author's Note

As I finish *Day of Reckoning*, I find myself amazed at how far this series has come since the launch of *Pandora's Grave* in the summer of 2011—and how far it has yet to go.

When I started work on this series years ago, in the wake of 9/11, I wanted to do more than write a fast-paced action thriller. I wanted to tell the story of a man out there in the shadows, fighting for his country. An intensely personal story of heroism and duty, of tragedy and loss. The story of the psychological, emotional, and even spiritual struggles known by those who would take up arms to defend our freedoms—by whatever means necessary.

That's the story of Harry Nichols, and it is a story that is far from over. If you come away from these "thrillers" with a deeper appreciation of those who have left it all on the field in the service of our country—of those who came home from the wars with scars not easily seen—then I have accomplished my purpose.

To those who have helped make this journey possible, I can only extend my most heartfelt gratitude, and my sincere regret that what follows is only a partial list.

To my parents for their love and support over the years, for encouraging me when there was no one else.

To my cover designer, Louis Vaney—an absolute genius of an artist and the best in the business. As always, you pulled off a masterpiece.

To Janis Zunda Kalnins, the brilliant talent behind the *Day of Reckoning* video trailer. For your perseverance as we pulled everything together on a tight schedule.

To the members of the *Day of Reckoning* beta-reading team: Jan Traeg, Mary Thompson, Tommy Lowther, Barry Taylor, and John Curry. Your diligence in sorting through hundreds of pages looking for typos was much appreciated.

To *NYT* bestselling novelist Brad Thor, with thanks for his support and encouragement with the first novel of this series—and a salute for his willingness to stand in the courage of his convictions, even when those stands came with a cost.

To my fellow novelist Gerard de Marigny, a denizen of Las Vegas whose input on the city was invaluable in constructing the narrative.

And the small group of top-flight independent thriller writers who have become my friends through this process. Robert Bidinotto, Ian Graham, Robert McDermott, and Ian Kharitonov(who provided indispensable advice on the Russian dialogue in *Day of Reckoning*). It's been a pleasure getting to know all of you and I wish you nothing but the best in your own careers.

To a pair of retired pilots who helped me get the "feel" for flying a Korean War-era helicopter.

And to the countless members of America's military, law enforcement, and intelligence communities(both active duty and retired), who provided input on the technical aspects of the book. Any mistakes are my responsibility and mine alone—their assistance was invaluable. Space(and their own need for anonymity) will only permit me to thank just a few by name.

To David Sherer for taking of his time to give me a crash course in bomb disposal.

And Shawn Hinck for his help in keeping my snipers on-target.

And to my friend Dr. Shawn Greener, the CEO of Executive Protection Team, LLC (www.executiveprotectionteam.com), for his advice on vehicles used in the business.

And perhaps most all, my thanks go out to my readers, for being an endless source of support and inspiration over the last few years. Your enthusiasm for Nichols and the rest of the shadow warriors have kept me moving through the times of writer's block, and I thank God for you all.

May God bless America, and those who defend her.

Made in the USA
San Bernardino, CA
26 February 2018